SURVIVING THE FALL

The Complete Series

MIKE KRAUS

Surviving the Fall

The Complete
Surviving the Fall Series
Books 1-12

By

Mike Kraus

© 2017-2019 Mike Kraus

www.MikeKrausBooks.com
hello@mikeKrausBooks.com
www.facebook.com/MikeKrausBooks

Contents

Book 1 - Surviving the Fall

Book 2 - The Gathering Storm

Book 3 - The Shattered Earth

Book 4 - Death of Innocence

Book 5 - The Burning Fields

Book 6 - The Long Road

Book 7 - The Darkest Night

Book 8 - The Edge of the Knife

Book 9 - The Tipping Point

Book 10 - The Trade of Kings

Book 11 - To Steal a March

Book 12 - A New Dawn

Stay Updated

Stay updated on Mike's books by signing up for the Mike Kraus Reading List.

Just visit www.MikeKrausBooks.com and click on the big red button on the home page.

You'll be added to my reading list and I'll also send you a copy of some of my other books to say thank you!

(I hate spam with the burning passion of a thousand suns, and promise that I'll never spam you.)

Special Thanks

This book wouldn't be possible without the help and support of my amazing beta reading team. Thank you for your advice, help and support during the creation of this series.

Book 1 - Surviving the Fall

Before You Read – An Important Note from the Author

This omnibus collection of Surviving the Fall contains the complete series, from stem to stern. This means that it includes the "last time" summaries of the previous books and author's notes for each book. When originally published, each book in this series came out approximately once per month, necessitating a "last time, on Surviving the Fall..." summary which, while not needed in this format, is still a part of the books and is therefore included.

Preface

"...and welcome to Los Angeles!"

The announcer's voice over the loudspeaker was far too cheerful for the day that Rick Waters was having. After several delays across three separate airports he had finally arrived at his destination. Instead of having a night to rest before his big presentation, the flight delays had cost him his entire night's sleep. It was now only a few hours before his meeting was scheduled to start and he would be lucky if he managed to get there on time.

"Come on already..." Rick grumbled as he trudged through the crowd of people around him. Although the air conditioning system in the Los Angeles airport was running full blast, the direct sunlight through the large glass windows of the terminal made him feel like he was about to combust from the heat.

As Rick walked along, he had the sudden feeling of knowing exactly what it was like to be a chicken inside a roasting rack in a grocery store. After a half hour of walking and waiting, the crowd finally thinned out enough that he could start running to try and make up for lost time. His dress shoes ticked against the hard floor and he winced at the blisters he could feel building up on the backs of his feet and his toes.

Born in the rural area in southern Virginia, Rick grew up on a farm where learning how to care for chickens and tend to crops came as naturally as learning how to read and write. By the time he graduated high school, though, he had been overcome with a rebellious streak and set out for Virginia Tech to learn all he could about computers. To his young mind the prospect of working in an air-conditioned office for the rest of his life sounded far more appealing than toiling outdoors.

A few years of partying combined with above-average grades led to a job offer from the local branch of a national car manufacturer. He originally went to work for them as a general purpose IT jockey, fixing everything from network problems and virus infections to changing print cartridges. It didn't take long for Rick's skills to become evident to the higher-ups in the company though, and he soon found himself going through annual promotions far faster than his peers as he took part in larger and more important initiatives.

Like the rest of society, car manufacturers were trying to adapt to the rapid integration of technology in every aspect of life, both through new self-driving technologies and through selling add-ons for older vehicles. Government regulations that mandated that vehicles be able to "talk" to each other were just a few years out from becoming law. While a universal communication specification had already been decided upon, the details were still being hashed out.

Rick wasn't too keen on the new changes or many of the ideas the company had but he worked diligently and faithfully for his employer—after all, he who pays the piper calls the tune. He worked on the team that developed the communication protocols, helped to create automated driving systems and was the lead project manager for a system that made every single new car automatically call for emergency services if the vehicle was reported as stolen or was in an accident. Many of the developments were iterations and improvements on older technology, but there were more than a few that were new as well.

Thanks to the location of his employer's main facility, Rick never left the area he had grown up in. As time passed and he worked his way up the corporate ladder, he began to miss his childhood. Reconciliation with his parents came easily enough and he soon found himself with a plot of land on the outskirts of a small town that was on the eastern edge of the city where he worked.

Rick, along with his wife—whom he had met through the strangest of coincidences—and their three children spent every weekend working to make their plot of land self-sustaining. They grew over a third of their own food, ran half of their household appliances off of solar panels and learned the basics of survival and self-sufficiency skills. Though Rick's job robbed him of his soul every Monday through Friday, it was restored over the weekend, and every moment of those two days made him happy. An absence of technology at home was something Rick had insisted upon. He already had to deal with it far too often at work and was disturbed by how much people were relying on computers to perform even the most basic tasks. It was for that reason that he made it a point to keep things at home as simple and basic as possible.

Rick stopped and sighed as he looked over the vast parking lot where the rental car salesman had assured him his "deluxe" vehicle would be waiting.

Rick hated pavement, glass and steel more than almost anything else, but the presentation he had to give would be the deciding factor in whether or not his company would be selected as the primary partner in an upcoming government contract. His company's future—not to mention a huge promotion—were on the line.

"It's not natural for it to be this hot... at least not at this time of the year." Rick huffed to himself as he jogged across the parking lot. He could feel the sweat pouring down the back of his neck and soaking through his dress shirt. He hoped that the car's air conditioner worked well enough to dry him out by the time he got to his meeting.

After ten minutes of wandering around pushing the alarm button on his key fob, he finally heard the distant beeping of a horn and located the small SUV he had rented. Rick threw his luggage in the back and hopped into the front seat. He glanced at his phone as he turned on the car and saw a new message waiting for him.

Sorry flights were delayed! :(LMK when u get there?

Rick smiled and typed out a fast reply to his wife.

Safe n sound. Just got car. Will call after mtg. <3

As Rick pulled out of the parking lot, he tried to force himself to relax a bit as he thought over the presentation. It wasn't complicated—in fact it was going to be one of the easiest he had ever given—but a car company attempting to move into providing general IT services was a risky move. *Still,* he thought, *everybody's innovating these days.*

Rick ran through the names of the executives and government officials he was going to meet as he pulled onto the spaghetti nest of roads leading out into the city. He repeated them softly, hoping that he had memorized their faces properly the night before. As he mumbled under his breath a loud noise from behind him caught his attention. He glanced at the rearview mirror only to find it filling with the reflection of billowing orange flames and black smoke. Startled, he turned around just as the sound wave from the massive secondary explosion caught up to his car.

KABOOM!

The safety glass in Rick's SUV shattered and cracked into thousands of tiny pieces from the force of the explosion. All of the cars around him experienced the same thing, their horns blaring loudly in unison as their emergency systems kicked in. Rick turned and removed the key in his SUV but the horn continued to blast, so he instead tried to start the engine up again. It sputtered and flared to life, but a few seconds later it died. He tried starting it again, but the engine didn't respond. The radio, however, turned on by itself and began cycling through the local stations at a high rate of speed.

"What on earth?" Rick looked at the indicators on the console of the car, watching the needles and numbers spin and flail around as they randomly changed positions and values. As Rick tried to make sense of what was going on, he noticed that there was a peculiar smell starting to drift through the broken windows.

"Is that…" Rick sniffed, wondering aloud. "Is that gasoline?" He jumped out of the car and knelt down. Underneath his car—and all of the cars next to him that he could see—were trickles of fuel flowing from somewhere beneath their undercarriages. Having worked on a few control systems for the vehicles his company manufactured, Rick suspected that the computer in the vehicle had gone haywire and opened a valve that should have never been opened except in maintenance situations.

As he stood back up and looked at the newly-formed parking lot of vehicles around him, Rick suddenly felt the grip of fear seize hold of his gut. All of the vehicles around him were shut off, yet their horns were still blaring and they all had their radios turned to the maximum volume setting and were cycling through the stations in unison. Something, he realized, was terribly wrong, and he had the strong urge to get as far away from the vehicles as he could.

Rick threw open the door to the back of the SUV and pulled out his luggage before running back to the front and snatching his phone through the window. He began heading back towards the terminal, in the general direction of the thick plume of black smoke that was still rising in the distance, when a far-off whine drew his attention. He looked up into the sky behind the terminal, shielding his eyes from the sun, and saw a white speck growing larger with each passing second.

The whine grew louder as the speck grew larger, and Rick soon made out the shape of a large aircraft hurtling toward the ground. He stared, slack-jawed, as the aircraft impacted with the back side of the terminal building, sending another fireball into the sky. Flaming pieces of wreckage from the impact hurtled through the air and, as Rick watched them begin to descend toward the rows of noisy cars, he realized what was about to happen.

"Run! Get out of here!" Rick screamed at the people around him, but no one paid him any mind as they stared at their non-functional phones and tried to talk to each other over the din. Rick shouted at a few of the people closest to him yet again but they merely looked at him like he was insane.

Not willing to wait any longer, Rick took off running, cutting laterally between the vehicles as he made for a small patch of grass that separated two roads from each other. As a piece of wreckage from the terminal landed a few dozen feet behind him, he could feel the ground shudder from the impact. The vibration and noise were accompanied by a faint *whoosh* as the fire from the wreckage ignited the gasoline fumes that were gathering around and beneath the cars. The *whoosh* was followed a second later by the sound of multiple explosions and the feel of even more intense heat on his hands, the back of his neck and head.

Rick didn't look back as he ran forward, pushing his feet to go even faster, until he finally made it to the grass. He continued running away through the grassy area until he saw a small open garden with a few benches and pieces of art carved into large boulders. He dove into a corner and curled up next to the closest boulder, putting his luggage in front of his face and chest to shield himself from the seemingly infinite explosions that were erupting around him. They continued, growing louder as the fire and flames spread from vehicle to vehicle, drowning out the screams of those burning alive, each of them the first victims of a battle that would engulf the world.

Introduction

Although there are still holdouts, the world's economy is rapidly trending towards becoming completely digitized. The concept of money becomes more abstract with each passing day as credit cards, electronic transfers and digital payment systems become ubiquitous in our everyday lives. Some countries have embraced this change, believing that a one-hundred percent digital economy is the wave of the future. Others aren't so sure and are fearful of the known—and unknown—negative implications that this will have on our future.

The unasked and unanswered question that lurks in the backs of the minds of those who are suspicious is this: what if this all vanishes? Without something tangible like gold, silver or even scraps of paper that hypothetically represent gold or silver, our wealth feels all the more ephemeral and fleeting. So what would happen if someone were to turn off the lights on those 1's and 0's and all of our money was gone overnight? That, however, is only a small piece of the rapidly evolving puzzle.

As the economy moves from the physical to the digital, so too do all other aspects of our lives. Refrigerators, beds and even thermostats are now connected to the Internet as part of what's called the "Internet of Things." These devices are pushed onto the market by corporations so quickly that proper security testing cannot be performed. Exploits are routinely found in home appliances and gadgets that render them vulnerable to attack.

With this in mind, that nagging question becomes even more complicated. What if not just our money—but all aspects of our lives—were turned off in the blink of an eye? Not by an EMP or a nuclear war but by an act of aggression, either war or terrorism or something even more insidious. Some would say we've survived without the Internet before and we can do so again. The fact remains that fundamental parts of our lives depend on this technology. Tractors have built-in security chips that prevent farmers from working on their own equipment. Cars made in the last few decades all have computer chips, and many recent models connect to the Internet.

So what if, overnight, every single device that depends on the Internet to function stopped working? The economy—driven more each year by the Internet than ever before—would fall to pieces. Bank accounts would be zeroed out. Phones, computers, vehicles, airlines, shipping lines, power plants, military defense systems and more could all be rendered virtually useless. Anything containing a sophisticated enough computer along with fuel or a battery could be turned into a bomb and used to maim or injure those nearby. It would be, in a word, chaos.

In a world such as this, only the most prepared and resourceful could survive.

In this world, only the most prepared will survive the fall.

Chapter One

The Waters' Homestead
Ellisville, VA

AUTUMN WAS TRULY in the air, and the leaves on the trees showed it in full force. A cold front had blown through from North Carolina up through New York the previous night, and by the time Dianne Waters woke up the next morning she was shivering. After making an early breakfast of warm oatmeal, toast, eggs and cereal, Dianne cleared the breakfast table and sat down for what she lovingly called "another day on the farm."

Set on the far outskirts of Ellisville—itself on the far outskirts of Blacksburg—the Waters home was a modest-sized two story building set in the dead center of a forty acre plot of land. Thick woods ringed the property and a long, winding driveway passed through them from the house out to a gravel road that, after half a mile, connected up with a country highway.

The property was isolated, charming, beautiful and peaceful—no one ever visited except to deliver the occasional package and piece of mail and, even on a clear day, it was hard to hear any cars or neighbors nearby thanks to the density of the trees. A small spring bubbled into a creek that passed a few hundred feet from the house, meandering down into a three-acre lake at the bottom of a long sloping hill. The area in between the house and the lake had been cleared and turned into a mixture of fields for growing small amounts of crops as well as for keeping a small variety of animals.

Dianne listened to her children as they bumped along upstairs, doing more playing than cleaning, and smiled as she looked out the window. The leaves were finally changing from green to a dazzling display of orange, red and yellow. She sighed and ran her fingers through her dark hair, pulling it into a ponytail as she heard another loud bump followed by the scream of Josie, her youngest at six years old. It was once again time to play the exciting game of "which one of you made your sister cry," starring Josie's older brothers Mark (thirteen) and Jacob (ten).

"Boys!" She shouted up at the ceiling, smiling with some small satisfaction as she heard the whispered panic in her son's voices. "Get your butts down here right now!"

All three of her children showed up a few minutes later, standing in a row at the end of the table. Mark and Jacob both looked solemnly at the floor while Josie, sporting a red bump on her head, fidgeted with her hands and feet as she stood, unable to stay still.

"What is it you boys are supposed to do with your sister?"

"Be nice to her?" Jacob was the first to speak as he tried to gain an advantage over his older brother.

"Correct. Now, I don't know which one of you pushed, poked, tripped or hit your sister, nor do I really want to know. I want you both outside feeding the animals right now, then when you're done, I'll have a few more chores for you before you start on school for the day."

Dianne waved off the pair of "aw, man's" that came next and pointed out the door and at the field beyond. As the boys traipsed off, she watched them for a moment before glancing at Josie. "You're not off the hook, missy. Come on, let's get to your work."

Dianne had been a vocal proponent of homeschooling ever since she was a child, and Rick had gone along with her desire while offering a few suggestions and conditions of his own. In addition to the education they received at home, each of the children spent a few hours every other day with after-school programs, learning to do everything from cooking and basic engine repair to computer maintenance and programming. While Rick wasn't able to participate in their education as much as he wanted due to his job, ensuring that they had a well-rounded childhood and solid foundation were of paramount importance to both him and Dianne.

As the morning turned into the afternoon and all three children took a break for lunch, Dianne began packing their things into the family car to take them into town. One of the perks of being married to someone reasonably far up the food chain at a car manufacturer was getting a new car to test drive every few months. Dianne was particularly happy with the van that was parked in their driveway, especially since it had some of the latest self-driving and collision avoidance features baked in.

"Kids! Let's go or we're going to be late!" Dianne walked out to the car, listening to her children slowly follow after her as they talked to each other about a book they had been reading for the past few nights. When Dianne arrived at the van she opened the door, tossed their backpacks into the front passenger's seat and leaned in to turn on the ignition before heading to the back seat to strap Josie in.

As Dianne buckled Josie's booster seat straps, the soft tones of some local soft rock station abruptly cut off, followed by the sound of the van's engine sputtering a few times before it too, died. A second later the van's horn began to sound and the radio kicked back on at full volume as it cycled through the local radio stations at an increasing rate of speed.

"What the—Mark? Jacob? Did one of you boys mess with the van? Your dad is *not* going to be happy!" Dianne shouted over the sound of the car as she unbuckled Josie, trying to shield her daughter's ears with her arms.

"It wasn't me, mom!"

"Me either!"

Dianne pulled Josie out of the car and yelled. "You three back in the house!"

Dianne waited until the kids were back behind the car before climbing into the driver's seat. She twisted the dial for the radio volume but nothing happened. She inserted the van's key and turned it, but nothing happened there either. She got back out of the car and headed back toward the house, covering her ears with her hands "What's going on with that stupid thing?"

Once she was back inside, Dianne grabbed her cellphone off the counter and tapped in her unlock code. She scrolled through her contact list until she reached the name for the engineer who Rick had told her to call if anything ever broke down on one of the test cars. Wincing at the sound of the still-shrieking vehicle, Dianne shooed her children into the next room before closing the door and sitting down in a nearby chair.

After holding the phone to her ear for several seconds, Dianne pulled it away and glanced at the screen. The call status, instead of reading out as a count of how long the call had been ongoing, merely said "Dialing."

"What?" Dianne hung up and dialed again. She watched the screen of the phone, but nothing changed, even after several more seconds. She sighed and hung up the phone, set it down on the kitchen table and then turned to her children.

"Stay in here. I'm going to go disconnect the battery, then we'll take the old truck into town, okay?"

Jacob, Mark and Josie all nodded and Dianne headed back toward the front door of the house. As she swung the door open, a light breeze picked up, sending the smell of freshly cut grass dancing along. Accompanying it, however, was a foul stench that took Dianne a few seconds to recognize.

"Gasoline?" Dianne mumbled to herself as she turned to look at the car out in the driveway. As she looked at the vehicle, wondering why she was suddenly smelling gasoline, the radio shut off, the horn stopped blowing and the electrical system shorted out. Sparks flew from the bottom of the van, igniting the gasoline vapors with a faint *whoosh* that was quickly followed by an ear-shattering explosion. The van shuddered under the force of the explosion and burst into flames that quickly began to consume it both on the inside and out.

Dianne fell back against the front door of the house, partially from the force of the blast and partially from the shock of watching a vehicle that her children had been climbing in a few minutes earlier explode before her eyes.

"Mom?" Mark's voice came from inside the house. The thirteen-year-old pulled open the front door and all three children gasped as they saw the wreckage of the van in the front driveway. Flames licked out from the vehicle and black smoke filled the air, rising high above the trees. A tire popped from the heat, sending pieces of rubber exploding outward, and Dianne turned and pushed Mark back through the door and into the house. She followed behind him and slammed the door shut before turning to look at the carnage out front.

"Mom, what's going on?"

Dianne could only shake her head and whisper in response.

"I don't know, Mark. I don't know."

Chapter Two

Los Angeles, CA

EVEN AFTER THE explosions around him had slowed to a stop, Rick stayed still in his hiding spot for nearly half an hour. In the distance he could hear screams, car alarms and the sound of chaos as the city began to tear itself apart. The whine of distant engines followed by tremendous explosions indicated that more planes had been downed, and the smell of smoke had increased to a level where it was getting difficult for him to breathe without wheezing.

When Rick finally released the death grip he had on his luggage, opened his eyes and started to sit up, he coughed and grabbed at his eyes as both they and his throat began to sting. He looked up into the sky that had been blue and cloudless only a short time ago. It was filled with acrid black smoke that billowed from innumerable fires and blotted out the sun.

"What the hell happened?" Rick slowly stood to his feet, pulled out a handkerchief from his back pocket and pressed it over his nose and mouth. In the distance the devastation took on an eerily unreal quality, looking like something out of a Saturday morning science fiction film instead of reality. Up close, however, the carnage became all too real.

Twisted and blackened bodies were frozen next to cars along the streets and parking lots surrounding where he was, as fires continued to burn from the engine and passenger compartments of the cars themselves. Most of those who had been far enough from their vehicles to survive the blasts were severely injured, and Rick could see small groups of them huddled on side-walks or beneath the overhangs of small buildings, tending to their wounds.

He turned back and looked at what was left of the airport complex, scarcely able to believe his eyes. Two of the terminals were in flames from the plane that had slammed into the side of the building. Several parked planes were overturned and in pieces, scattered about by the force of the explosion. There were no signs of emergency vehicles in the area, though Rick doubted if anyone in the terminals or aircraft could have survived.

The main building was on fire as well, and several smaller fires had started from the overturned fuel trucks on the tarmac, and were slowly spreading as more fuel continued to leak from storage containers, aircraft and vehicles. He could just make out people running to and fro in front of the main entrance of the airport, and several of them wore firefighter and emergency services uniforms.

Rick walked slowly out from the grassy area he was in, hopping over the slow-burning flames that flickered along the green grass toward the center. The heat from the wrecks of the cars was nearly overwhelming, and every few seconds the wind changed, blowing a fresh wave of smoke and soot into his face. Rick covered his face with his arm and tried to pull his suit jacket closed to shield his torso from the heat. He walked through the maze of wreckage quickly, having to divert his route several times to get past some of the still-burning vehicles.

With no idea of what to do or where to go, Rick looked for the highest ground around, noticing that a small road leading away from the airport turned into an overpass that looked to be the highest point in the area. He headed for the road at a quick pace, keeping a tight hold of his luggage as he went. It wasn't until he broke into a jog and felt his phone in the breast pocket of his jacket bouncing against his chest that his eyes went wide and he stopped to pull it out.

His phone turned on with the touch of a button, though the signal was displaying as far weaker than he would have imagined for where he was located. He frowned, then hit the contacts button before touching the image in the first "Favorites" slot.

"Come on... pick up..." Rick held the phone against his ear, hearing the telltale clicking sounds that indicated that something was happening in the background. It took almost a full minute for him to hear a single ring, which cut short as a message began playing.

We're sorry, this call cannot be completed as dialed. Please try texting your intended recipient instead.

Rick pulled the phone away and scrunched his face in confusion. "Please try texting your intended recipient?" He repeated the phrase to himself, wondering if he had somehow misheard. "I've never heard *that* message before. Still, though, good idea."

Rick brought up his text messaging app and punched in a quick message to his wife.

U ok? I dont know whats going on. Stay inside and away from the car. K?

He was just about to hit the "send" button when he noticed that the phone was rapidly growing warm on the backside. He turned it over and saw, to his horror, that the back case was warped outward like there was a balloon beneath it that was being blown up. Realizing what was happening, Rick didn't hesitate to throw the phone as far as he possibly could, sending it through the air to skitter along the asphalt road before it, too, exploded into flames.

A battery becoming compromised, expanding and then exploding was not a common occurrence, but it had happened before, especially with certain models of phones and batteries that didn't go through stringent quality checks. For it to happen in conjunction with everything else that was going on, though, seemed more than just a coincidence in Rick's mind. He stared at the small phone as flames slowly melted the plastic, reducing it to nothing more than a pile of blackened metal and plastic sludge on the road. Giving the mound of what used to be his phone a wide berth, Rick continued to trudge along the road as it rose steadily and turned into the overpass. When he finally reached the peak, he stopped and turned to look at the city to the east.

"Nope. Definitely not a coincidence." Rick stared, mouth agape, at the destruction before him. At least two other planes had fallen into the city, one striking a skyscraper which was teetering on the edge of falling over. The smoke that filled the sky was fed from fires that were on every street and in most of the buildings he saw. The magnitude of the destruction was over-whelming and Rick turned around and collapsed onto the ground as his mind reeled.

He realized in the back of his mind that he was in shock, and most likely had been since he had started walking away from the airport. As the adren-aline began to wear off, though, he could feel his entire body begin to shake as his thoughts raced, unhindered and uncontrollable. Whatever was going on was not, he determined, a dream, nor was it some sort of freak accident. Cars didn't shut off and start leaking gasoline. Ordinary phones didn't have their batteries short circuit and explode. Planes didn't just fall from the sky.

Rick put his head back against the concrete side of the overpass and closed his eyes, feeling himself sinking into a black pit of unconsciousness. He welcomed it and the relief that he hoped it would bring.

Chapter Three

The Waters' Homestead
Ellisville, VA

"THIS PLACE LOOKS LIKE CRAP!"

"Language, Jacob!"

"Sorry, mom."

"Well it *is* kind of crappy."

"Mark! That's enough from you, too!" Dianne brushed a few strands of hair from her face and took a deep breath as she surveyed the kitchen. Water was everywhere, spreading slowly out over the hardwood floors and soaking into the large rug under the dining room table. Grey smoke and the smell of burning electronics filled the air while a large piece of the edge of the table itself still smoked from the remnants of Dianne's cellphone. She had left it on the table when she went outside, and a few seconds after she came back in to try to make another call, it had burst into flames in front of her. A few baking pans full of water from the sink later and the fire had been put out, though the dining room was a complete wreck as a result.

"Mom? Can I come down now?"

"Not yet, sweetie!" Dianne called up the stairs to her daughter, then turned to her sons. "Mark, I need you to go make sure the animals are okay. The car was pretty loud and they might have been spooked. Give them some extra food to calm them down, all right?"

"Sure thing, mom."

Dianne patted her eldest son on the back as he walked out the back door.

She turned to Jacob, who was sitting on the stairs looking into the kitchen. "I need you to go play with your sister upstairs, okay?"

"But I want—"

"Kiddo. I need your help right now, okay?" Dianne was doing her best to keep the stress out of her voice, but she could feel herself reaching her limit and needed a few minutes alone to figure out what to do.

"Fine…" Jacob's shoulders slouched as he went up the stairs and Dianne sighed at his attitude before turning back to survey the kitchen.

"Right. So. The car exploded. My phone exploded. Just a perfectly normal day here." Dianne stepped gingerly through the water in the kitchen and picked up the landline telephone hanging on the wall. Rick had insisted on having one installed 'just in case there's an emergency' a fact that Dianne was grateful for. She held the phone to her ear and heard a dial tone, then excitedly dialed the number for Rick's cellphone. Her excitement quickly waned as she heard an error message declaring that 'the number you've dialed is currently unavailable.'

"Damn!" Dianne slammed the phone against the receiver and leaned her arm on the wall, putting her head against it and closing her eyes. "Why did you have to go out of town on business on *this* week of all weeks, Rick? Why?"

Dianne quickly dialed another number for their neighbors down the road but got the same message. She dialed another and another and each time the message was the same. 'The number you've dialed is currently unavailable.'

Dianne stood in the kitchen, leaning up against the wall for several more minutes before slowing standing back up and taking in a deep breath. "Right. First things first, clean out the kitchen. Then get the truck out, make sure it still runs. Then we'll head into town and see what's going on there." Dianne nodded to herself and sighed at the mess before her. With a tentative plan in hand she was feeling slightly better about the situation at hand, but there was still a nagging feeling in the back of her head that whatever had happened with the car and the phone was a part of something far, far greater.

Twenty minutes later—and with the help of all three children, a pile of old towels and a mop—the kitchen floor was finally looking better. The water was cleared up relatively quickly after which Dianne ran the mop over everything and took the rug outside to get hosed down by Mark and Jacob and left to dry in the sun. Using a pair of rubber gloves and a few layers of plastic bags, Dianne scraped the remnants of her phone off of the table and dumped it and the bags into a metal trash can at the edge of the driveway. The burned table would have to be dealt with more thoroughly later on, but she scrubbed it for long enough to feel comfortable sitting down at it again. The smoke in the house was the last to be dealt with, after she came back inside and the smell hit her nostrils again. She shooed the three children out onto the back porch before opening several windows both downstairs and upstairs to let everything air out.

With the house in order, Dianne walked out the front door to look at the car again. It was still smoldering in the front driveway, but the fire had long since been put out thanks to the overzealous use of a pair of garden hoses. She hated leaving the burned-out hulk sitting in the driveway, but with no way to move it without getting their tractor out, she decided to leave it for another time.

"All right, kids! Let's go see if the truck'll start up!" Dianne walked around the side of the house and shouted at her children on the back porch. They ran after her as she headed down toward the lake, near where one of their barns was located. The tractor was kept in the barn closest to the house while their old truck was kept in the far barn, along with various tools, old clothes, toys and other odds and ends that had been sitting around in the house.

Dianne glanced at the animals as she went along, noting that Mark had taken care of them just as requested. Their pair of horses had been fed and their trough that they shared with the goats had been filled. The chickens, contained in their fenced-in area, were busy pecking at corn that he had thrown out on the ground for them while the trio of cows munched steadily on a freshly tossed bale of hay.

"Nice work, kiddo." Dianne wrapped her arm around her son and gave him a smile. "Now let's see if this old truck still works."

Dianne had the children stand back from the barn entrance just in case what had happened to their newer car had also affected the truck. Fortunately, though, that was not the case. The bright blue 1972 Ford was a thing of beauty. With ample room in the back plus a crew cab, the truck had more than enough room for their entire family. A gift from Dianne's parents when they first got married, the truck had seen a great deal of use and abuse on the farm before being mostly retired a year back. Rick had the truck detailed and repainted before putting it up in the barn and driving it once a week into work to keep everything running smoothly.

Relieved beyond belief to see the truck in working condition, she grabbed the keys hanging on the wall just inside the barn and threw them to Mark. "You can ride shotgun; Jacob and Josie, I want you two in the back, please. There aren't booster seats so we're going to make sure you're buckled up tight before we get going, okay?"

There was a chorus of grumbled agreements as the three children piled into the truck. Dianne finished sliding open the barn door before walking around the truck, visually inspecting the tires and making sure there was nothing in the back. "All right, you old thing." Dianne whispered to herself as she climbed in and put the key in the ignition. "Let's get going."

The truck roared to life at the turn of the key and Dianne smiled and sighed with relief. "Everybody ready?"

Without waiting for an answer, Dianne glanced at the rearview mirror to make sure Jacob and Josie had their seatbelts on, then threw the truck into gear. She was used to driving an automatic transmission, but had learned how to drive stick years prior, just in case she was ever in a situation where she needed to know how.

The drive up the slope toward the house was bumpy, and Dianne could hear the truck creaking and groaning in protest. After she drove around the house and gave the burned-out hulk in the driveway a wide berth, the ride settled down as she got onto the dirt driveway.

The drive wound through the woods until coming to a metal gate that was erected a hundred feet from the edge of the property. Dianne rolled down the window as she pulled up to the gate, then glanced over at Mark. "Grab the gate, would you?"

Mark hopped out and swung open the gate, pushing it out away from the truck as Dianne rolled through slowly and parked on the other side. As he closed the gate, Dianne leaned out the window and called out to him. "Go ahead and lock it up for me. I don't know how long we'll be gone."

"Sure thing, mom." Mark wrapped a length of chain around the gate and a fencepost before securing it with a large padlock hanging from the fence. It was rare that they locked the gate since they were at home most of the time, but Dianne wasn't sure who might come wandering by while they were out.

After Mark was back in the truck, Dianne pulled forward again until she reached the end of their driveway. The gravel road beyond was a winding one, with the direction to the right leading into town while the other made its way through the country before dead-ending at a state park. Dianne turned right, heading for Ellisville and—hopefully—some answers about what was going on with the car and the phones.

Chapter Four

U S Government Facility
One week before the event

"GENERAL DAVIES?"

"What is it, son?"

A young man wearing a hoodie, blue jeans and sneakers runs down the hall after a tall, white-haired man in a military uniform. The hall is well-lit and sparsely decorated, with no view of the outside world. Offices branch off from the main hall, though the walls for all the rooms are transparent, with no curtains or barriers to keep people from seeing in. People work at computers in the offices, some wearing headphones, some working in small groups, others eating while they type with one hand and some pacing the floor only to rush back and type out a few lines of code. The atmosphere is relaxed, though supervisors and managers stalk the hall, keeping close track of the progress of projects.

General Davies stops in the hall and turns. The young man in front of him wears thick-rimmed glasses, he's slightly overweight and his face is dotted with acne. He takes a couple of deep breaths before talking nervously. He fidgets with his hands and his glasses as he speaks, stuttering and stumbling over his words.

"Sir, you asked me to let you know if there were any intrusions into Damocles."

General Davies raises an eyebrow. "Were there?"

The young man hesitates. "W-well, sir, there… there may have been."

The general frowns. "Follow me."

The pair walk swiftly down the hall until they arrive at one of the lone offices with an opaque door and walls. The general opens the door and walks around to the other side of the desk. *"Close the door and sit."* He motions at the young man, who dutifully obeys. *"Now,"* says the general, *"what about Damocles?"*

The young man pulls a few pieces of folded paper from his pocket and unfolds them. He clears his throat as he skims their contents before looking back at the general. *"This morning at four we picked up an increase in attacks against our Washington facility. It wasn't directed at the Damocles system, but it was in the same area, so I tagged it for further watch. Just before noon, though, the system started getting flooded by a denial of service attack."*

General Davies raised an eyebrow and stroked his chin. *"Who was it from, and what attack were they trying to hide under the denial of service?*

"I'm afraid I don't know who yet, sir. But it was definitely a cover-up. The Damocles security systems triggered ten minutes after the denial of service started, going on high alert and activating the air gap safety systems."

"So Damocles was brought offline?"

The young man shifts uncomfortably in his chair and shuffles the pages in his hand. *"Damocles was brought offline, yes sir."*

The general sighs, closes his eyes and shakes his head. *"I'm sensing a 'but' here."*

"But… it took just over a minute for the systems to kick in after the intrusion was detected."

General Davies opens his eyes in bewilderment. *"Over a minute? What the hell happened?"*

"That's what we're trying to figure out. The entire red and blue teams are working on it, but I think at this point we have to assume that there was at least a partial breach."

General Davies pulls open the bottom left drawer on the desk and takes out a bottle of Jack Daniels Blue Ribbon. He places two shot glasses on the desk, fills both to the brim and slides one across the desk. The young man watches, eyes wide, as the general swallows his shot and follows it by taking a long drink straight from the bottle.

The general closes his eyes, places the bottle down on the desk and leans back in his chair. *"Are there any estimates on how much of Damocles could have leaked out in the breach?"*

*"We don't have any data on how much was—I mean **could** have leaked out, sir."*

"Cut the crap and give it to me straight. Is sixty seconds long enough for a skilled team to get the essential bits of Damocles out of our systems?"

The young man hesitates and licks his lips nervously. *"Nearly all of it, sir. If the attackers had any knowledge on the structure of Damocles they could have extracted the weaponized portions and left the command and control bits behind. That's quite an assumption, though, General. For all we know, they could have—"*

"That's enough." General Davies sits up in his chair, caps the bottle and puts it back into the desk drawer, leaving the full and empty shot glasses on the desk. He rises from his seat and heads to the door, motioning for the young man to follow him.

"What do you want us to do, sir?"

"Divert red and blue teams. Find out what the likely first targets would be and how we can protect them. It doesn't matter who took Damocles anymore. If that much of it could

have been extracted, we're about to have bigger problems on our hands. I'm going to air gap the defense net and tell the President about this situation."

The young man runs off and General Davies pauses in his office, glancing back to the telephone that sits on his desk. He mutters something under his breath as he closes his office door and heads back to slouch in his chair behind the desk.

"Once I decide on how to say it, that is."

Chapter Five

Los Angeles, CA

"HEY MAN, are you alive? Are you okay?"

Rick awoke to the feeling of someone poking him in the shoulder. His eyes flew open and he scrambled upright, wiping the drool from the corner of his mouth and trying to back away from whoever was standing in front of him. A man and a woman, both dressed in singed and blackened business attire, stepped back a few feet at the sight of Rick's wide-eyed expression and flailing limbs.

"Hey, man, take it easy!"

"Wh-who are you?" Rick stumbled over his words as he looked around. The sun had started to fade over the western horizon, casting an unearthly orange glow on the smoke that blanketed the city.

"I'm Jack, this is Samantha. Are you okay?" The man was wearing a suit without a tie, and a piece of his suit had been torn off and wrapped around his wrist. Despite his expensive clothing and shoes, his hair was a mess of dreadlocks and he spoke with the accent of a surfer. The woman standing next to him was wearing a pair of shoes that had the heels broken off, along with a pantsuit that had scorch marks around the edges. Her hair was up in a bun, and her makeup was smudged and stained by the black smoke in the air.

Rick looked down at himself, remembering how he had come to be slumped over on the overpass. He nodded slowly. "I think so. D-do you know what happened?"

The man put his hands on the back of his head and looked around, surveying the city. "You tell me, man. One minute we're on the freeway heading back to the office and the next minute we slam into the car in front of us. The engine shut off and then we saw this bigass plane just *slam* into the building in front of us."

Rick stood up and looked out to the east. The sky was still filled with smoke, but there were fewer fires, visible from buildings and cars on the street. "What time is it?" Rick turned back to the pair and the man shrugged.

"No idea, man. My watch kind of..." The man held up his wrist to show a crude bandage wrapped around his arm.

"It exploded." Samantha jumped in, offering a look of sympathy to Jack.

"Yeah, man. I was trying to make a call through my watch, but I realized my phone was in the car still and it was out of range. I was heading back to the car when *boom!* The car just, like, went up in flames!"

Samantha nodded slowly. "There were a lot of people still in their cars when they caught on fire. We tried to help them out but hardly anybody made it out."

"Then, like, twenty minutes later, or maybe longer, my hand just started burning under the watch. I pulled it off before it caught fire, but it hurt like hell." Jack looked at his wrist, then back to Rick and shrugged. "It's late, though, man. Like, getting dark late. It's going to be rough going here soon without a flashlight."

Rick nodded, then shook his head in confusion. "I'm sorry, but why are you up here, anyway? If you were down on the freeway, why would you come up here?"

Jack pointed down the length of the overpass. "This is the best way out of the city, man. Like, I don't know if we can even get out, but the roads are a *mess* down there."

"There are fires *everywhere*." Samantha jumped in helpfully. "Plus, we heard on the radio that there's been all sorts of looting going on. It's getting insane out there. We figured we'd be better off up here, where there isn't anything to loot to begin with."

Rick spun back around to look at the pair. "A radio? A working radio?"

Jack nodded slowly. "Yeah, man, the city broadcast system. Bunch of speakers hooked up all over the place. It runs off some kind of emergency power, I think. Anyway there were some guys on there talking about how there's looting and the best way out of the city is on the overpass. Oh, and some stuff about the military? I don't know, man, we were busy trying to get away from all the burning cars and stuff."

"Have you all seen any police? Or other emergency personnel?"

Samantha shook her head and shrugged. "We heard a few sirens, but that was a long time ago. I haven't seen a single cop since we've been walking, and I've see a lot of people going by."

As the fog from Rick's mind continued to clear, he looked down the length of the overpass in front of him. The road that had earlier been filled with the burning hulks of cars was now home to people who were trudging along, slowly making their way in the same direction that Rick had been heading. He looked down at the ground where he had been sitting and noticed that his luggage was missing. "Did you see a piece of luggage here? A big black case?"

Samantha frowned. "Sorry, no. But there have been a lot of people going along here. One of them probably took it."

"You did kind of look dead, man." Jack shrugged sympathetically.

Rick sighed, more disappointed over losing the luggage than he would have expected to feel. "Well, thanks for stopping to check on me." He stuck out his hand and Jack shook it enthusiastically. "I appreciate it."

"Right on, man. Hey, if you want to walk with us, feel free. There's a lot of walking to do, and hey, maybe we'll find someone with a working phone!"

Rick looked around, still trying to get his bearings. His body felt weak, his head was still spinning and he was still trying to cope with what he had seen at the airport. "Yeah… yeah I think I'll tag along. Thanks."

As Rick, Jack and Samantha walked on, the pair started talking about their work at a technology startup and wondered what was going to happen the next day. Rick nodded politely as he listened, but his mind was elsewhere, wondering about his family and what was going on in Virginia. He hoped that whatever was happening—which he still couldn't fully comprehend—was isolated to Los Angeles, but knew that was likely just a dream far removed from reality.

Chapter Six

O utside Ellisville, VA

AS THE GRAVEL road turned into a paved one, Dianne began to see signs that the problems with her phones and the car catching fire were only small parts of something much larger. The first sign was the amount of foot traffic along the narrow two-lane road, which normally was devoid of all but the occasional car. Instead, however, there were dozens of people out who were walking, some wearing backpacks and dragging pieces of luggage behind them. There were even a pair of bikers going along that she had to pass, and though they rode what looked like racing bikes, they were bogged down with heavy packs on their backs.

"Mom? What's with all the people?" Mark sat up in his seat as he looked around, a worried look on his face.

Dianne frowned and shook her head as she drove along, giving the cyclists and pedestrians a wide berth. "I don't know, sweetie. Just hang tight and try to stay quiet until we get into town."

The closer Dianne drove into town, the denser the foot traffic grew. She also began to see other cars on the road—just a few, but still a welcome sight —though they, like her truck, were all older models. As the two-lane road grew wider and a shoulder appeared on both sides that indicated she was close to town, she started seeing a more worrying sight.

"Mom are those—"

"Yeah, kiddo. Just like ours." Dianne and the three children stared at the blackened husks of cars that started to appear along the road. A few still had flames flickering from the engine compartment and interior while most were simply smoking. Nearly every vehicle had at least one person standing nearby, their clothing blackened and covered with smoke and soot.

While the density of people was a welcome sight to Dianne, the sight of more burned out cars was worrisome, especially as more and more people began walking, jogging and running toward her truck as she continued on into town.

"Kids, make sure your doors are locked and your seatbelts are tight, okay?"

Dianne glanced around and looked at the doors, then looked at the back window of the cab to make sure it was closed. The people alongside the road, standing next to their vehicles, were beginning to swarm the truck, and Dianne increased her speed to get past them.

"Hey! Stop!" A man jumped out from behind a burned-out sports car and stood directly in the middle of the road, waving his arms in the air. Dianne gritted her teeth and slammed on the brakes, twisted the wheel and then hit the gas again. She heard the man cursing as the truck slid around him, and she glanced back to see him making an obscene gesture at her as she pulled away.

Unfortunately, however, the man wasn't the last to try and stop Dianne's truck. As the trees gave way to fields, houses and shops, people on both sides of the road shouted and pleaded with her to stop and let them in. Without having a clue as to what was going on, Dianne avoided people as best as she could, cutting through a small, sparsely-populated neighborhood on the edge of town as she tried to figure out what to do.

"Mom, what do all those people want?" Jacob piped up from the back seat as Dianne drove along slowly, her mind racing.

"I'm not sure, kiddo. I think they're scared about whatever's going on, though."

"Can't we help them?" Jacob sat up as far as he could, pressing his nose against the window.

"I wish we could, but we've just got the one truck. We can't help everyone we see, at least not right now."

"Where are we going, mom?" Mark asked.

"Good question." A burned out car was parked in nearly every driveway Dianne drove past, and the fire had spread to more than a few yards and houses, as well. Smoke grew thicker the closer she drove towards the center of town, and she started to realize just how serious the situation was. "I think the best thing to do is to see if we can get a few supplies and then head back home."

"What about dad? Is he okay?" Josie piped up from the back seat, and Dianne's gut wrenched at the question.

"I'm sure he's fine, sweetie. He's probably still—oh my..." Dianne's jaw dropped as she turned a corner in the neighborhood and saw what was ahead. Beyond the last few rows of houses sat the town square, the compact yet vibrant cornerstone of the city. The main street wrapped around a small park and gazebo in the center while the edges of the road were lined with shops both large and small. Beyond the center of town, just to the north, was the high school and accompanying stadium, from which a thick cloud of smoke was billowing into the air.

Dianne could make out the flashing lights of fire trucks as they sat near the enormous burning hulk of an airliner that had crashed directly into the stadium, flinging debris for a half mile in diameter. Chunks of metal and remnants of seat cushions were scattered on the rooftops of the buildings around the town square, and Dianne could swear she saw the gruesomely twisted form of someone who had still been in their seat when it hit the road and skidded along for a few dozen yards.

If the debris and victims from the crashed airplane had been the only things wrong with the town square, Dianne wouldn't have been quite as concerned as she was. That, however, was merely the start. A small parking lot on the edge of the square that was normally filled with cars was instead a pile of charred metal, and the fire from the lot had spread to some of the buildings nearby. Owners and patrons of the shops were all standing out in front of their buildings, holding each other as they tended to various burns and other wounds they had suffered.

"He's probably still where, mommy?" From her position behind Dianne's seat, Josie couldn't see the smoke and carnage ahead of the truck, a fact that Dianne was extremely grateful for. Mark, on the other hand, saw it quite clearly, and started to say something when Dianne took another sharp turn, heading for the city's lone grocery store on the back side of the town square.

"Mom, was that an... airplane?"

"I—I don't know, Mark."

"Is dad still in the air? Or did he land? What's going on, mom?"

"Mark!" Dianne snapped at her son harsher than she intended, and she immediately gave him an apologetic glance. "I don't know." Dianne shook her head and lowered her voice to a whisper to avoid upsetting Josie. "I don't know what's going on, but this is bad. This is really, really bad. Let's just get to the store and see if we can get any supplies, then we'll figure out what to do from there."

Chapter Seven

L os Angeles, CA

THE JUXTAPOSITION of Jack's speech patterns, attitude and hair with his suit and shoes was a constant source of amusement to Rick as the trio walked along together. Rick barely had to say anything since Jack was able to talk about seemingly any topic at length and with some degree of knowledge to boot. Originally from Arizona, Jack had traveled to Los Angeles a few years prior and lived on the beach while taking classes online to learn how to program.

After a year of scraping by he managed to get a job offer and upgraded from a hammock between two trees to a single bedroom apartment in the heart of the city. He had never lost his love for the beach, though, as he made clear on more than one occasion. His style of dress, he explained, had been a choice that was quite personal to him. Growing up in poverty meant that he had never owned new clothing, and he used his first paycheck from his new job to buy the best suit and accessories he could afford, making it a point to never be under-dressed again.

Samantha's story was somewhat different than Jack's, and she was quiet until Rick probed gently for her backstory. She had grown up in the area and was the daughter of a local investor who had used his leverage to get her a job at a company he had invested in. The job was as a project manager, and she and Jack had quickly developed a rapport despite their different back-grounds. When the "event" (as the trio soon came to call it) happened, Jack and Samantha had been driving from a meeting that had just wrapped up about a new product they were hoping to launch.

After hearing their stories, Rick shared his own, telling them about his wife and children back in Virginia, the work he did for his—now more than likely former—employer and what he was doing in Los Angeles.

"Dude, you are *super* lucky you were on the ground and not stuck in the air. There were a dozen planes at *least* that came down over the city and the bay!"

Rick nodded solemnly. "Yeah, it was… something else." The thought of the explosions and screams Rick had heard was enough to make him grow quiet, and Jack appeared to feel the same way. The three walked along together in silence, their shoes scraping against the metal, soot and asphalt. Every few cars they passed had another blackened body either in the vehicle or directly next to it, and though Rick felt queasy at the sight of every new body he saw, he could feel his mind starting to numb to the horror.

As night fell, Rick was glad that the sky was starting to clear enough to allow the moon to peek through, which offered up just enough light to illuminate the road ahead while simultaneously hiding many of the horrors. He kept a small penlight and a screwdriver set in his breast pocket which he had thankfully remembered to get out of his luggage as he was first leaving the airport. After being looked over by more than a few people who were escaping the city, though, he didn't want to advertise the fact that he had a light for fear of what someone might do to him to try and take it. Ordinary, good and innocent people can turn violent at the drop of a hat. All it takes is the proper motivation, and even a good man can fall prey to the temptations of evil.

Jack and Samantha continued traveling with Rick until night fell, at which point they decided to stop and rest until the next morning. Rick had nearly stayed with them, but the desire in his gut to escape the city and find a way back home was far too powerful to overcome.

"You sure you don't want to stay here, dude? We might not stay the whole night. Maybe just an hour or two to get some rest."

Rick smiled. "I appreciate the offer, Jack, but I need to keep moving. The sooner I get out of the city, the sooner I'll be able to get in touch with my family."

Samantha and Jack glanced at each other before giving Rick a hug. He stood still, surprised by the sudden embrace, before returning it.

"All the best to you, Rick." Samantha smiled at him. "Stay safe, okay?"

"Yeah, man. Keep your eyes open. Lots of crazies and weirdos around this town, if you know what I mean." Jack made a show of twirling his fingers at the sides of his head, then laughed and shook Rick's hand. Rick gave the pair a final wave as he walked off, still tempted to stay with them and rest, but ultimately determined to keep moving no matter the cost.

As Rick walked along, he saw more and more people stopped on the overpass, clustered together into small groups. There were young, old, women, men, children and elderly; whatever had happened had been no respecter of persons. Rick picked up on pieces of whispered conversations held by those along the overpass as each group discussed and debated their own theories about what had happened. Rick himself still wasn't sure, but the further east he walked along the overpass, the more he hoped that it really was just isolated to the city itself.

Sitting down to give his feet a few moments of rest, Rick sat on a spare tire that had fallen off of a burning vehicle and rolled off to come to a rest against the side barrier of the overpass. With Jack and Samantha far behind him, Rick was starting to feel the effects of isolation begin to set in, as well as feeling the exhaustion from the day's events. As his head began to nod forward, Rick suddenly stood up and started walking again, shaking his shoulders and head around to try and clear the sleepiness from his head. Falling asleep on the overpass wasn't something he wanted to do, especially since there were still so many people wandering by—many of whom eyed his stained and wrinkled suit with no small amount of desire in their eyes.

Rick slipped out of his jacket and rolled up his sleeves, trying to appear more casual and like he didn't have any valuables on his person. *Not like I do anyway, but I'm not sure certain folks would agree with me there.* Another hour's walk transpired in relative silence until, in the distance, Rick saw a faint glow appear on the overpass. As he drew closer he saw crowds of people shuffling off onto a series of exits from the overpass down into the city. "What's going on?" Rick asked a few people walking by. "Why is everyone getting off?"

The fourth person Rick questioned stopped for a moment and pointed at the light in the distance. "A fuel truck overturned on the road; there's no way through." The woman resumed her steady plod down the ramp while Rick stared at the burning wreckage. In the distance, beyond it, he could just barely see the eastern edge of the city, and the hope that it brought with it to escape the burned and blackened hell it had become. "Damn." Rick whispered to himself as he joined the others in their slow walk down the overpass and into the darkened streets below.

As Rick descended into the unfamiliar streets of a city he had never before visited, he became aware of just how vulnerable he was. The streets were sheltered from much of the moonlight and starlight above, necessitating a slower pace to his travels. Although he had exited the overpass in the company of several other people, he soon found himself walking alone as they split off onto other paths, their paths and destinations clear in their minds. Rick's destination was clear, but the path to reach it was vague.

Resisting the urge to use his penlight, Rick stuck to the middle of the street as he walked along, listening to the wind blow past the buildings and along the alleys. He was in a cross between a residential and business area of the city, where signs alternated between advertising apartments for rent and various cuisines. Movement was visible inside many of the buildings as people walked about holding flashlights and lanterns as they tried to end their day with some sense of normalcy.

As Rick walked along his ears began to pick up more sounds from the city. A few distant shouts, the cry of an unhappy baby, the vague and unsettling whispers of figures hiding in the shadows. The further out into the city Rick went, the quieter the city became, until all was still and silent for the longest time. After a good half hour of hearing nothing but the wind and his own footsteps, Rick thought he was hearing things when the sounds of a car engine started drifting along on the breeze. He stopped in the middle of the street and cocked his head, searching for the elusive sound when it echoed through, slightly louder than it was before.

The roar of the engine was growing rapidly closer, and Rick finally realized that it wasn't his imagination—the sound was quite real. He glanced behind him and saw the faint glow of headlights growing rapidly closer, and a strange thought passed through the back of his head. *Hide.* The hairs on the back of Rick's neck prickled as he dashed behind the wreckage of a burned out car sitting on the side of the road.

As the car approached, it became apparent that it wasn't just one car, but three. They were older vehicles, two Cadillacs and a black SUV, and all three had loud music blasting from inside. They drove along the road at a dangerous pace, their tires screeching as they wove between the burned out vehicles in their way and gunned their engines when they had a hundred feet of clear street ahead.

Rick could make out the drivers and passengers of the vehicles as they whizzed by since the cars had their internal lights switched on. Rows of tattoos adorned the skin of each person he saw, and nearly every one of them held a bottle or can in one hand and a gun in the other. There was no particular cohesive ethnic background about the individuals in the vehicles, though they all shared one trait—an excessive amount of maniacal laughter, making Rick exceptionally glad he had listened to his gut.

As the vehicles roared off into the night, Rick slowly stood up from his hiding place and stared at where they had gone, a single question on his mind. "How are their cars still working?"

Chapter Eight

E llisville, VA

DIANNE WAS grateful that there were a few running vehicles going through the town since they helped her truck blend in and be less of a target than it had been while driving in. As she approached the "Eat Rite" grocery store, though, she noticed that there was a distinct lack of vehicles in the parking lot that weren't burned to a crisp, and decided to stop and drive around to the side of the building, parking the truck near a pair of dumpsters.

"All right, kids. Listen up." Dianne looked in the rearview mirror at Jacob and Josie. "I need to run into the store for five minutes. I want you to stay here, with the doors locked, and I want all three of you tucked out of sight in the back cab with a blanket over you, okay?"

Mark looked confusedly at his mom. "Even me?"

"Especially you, bud. I need you back there taking care of your brother and sister, okay?"

"Sure, I guess. But why the blanket?"

"I want all three of you out of sight." Dianne looked around outside the vehicle, seeing a few people walking off in the distance but no one close enough to notice them. "And whatever you do, don't open the door or make a sound for anyone. I don't care who they look or sound like. Unless I unlock and open the door to this truck, you don't move or make a sound. Got it?"

The gravity of the situation was starting to set in for Mark, and he nodded slowly, his eyes wide. As he turned to crawl into the back of the vehicle, he stopped to whisper to Dianne. "Mom, are we going to be okay?"

Dianne put on a brave face, smiled and patted him on the back. "You bet we are. I don't know what's going on, but we're going to be A-Okay."

Mark didn't really believe what his mother was saying, but he crawled into the back seat and helped pull up an old quilt from where it was folded on the floor. Dianne stepped out of the truck and closed the door quietly before turning the key in the lock and pulling on both doors on the left side to ensure they wouldn't open. She checked the doors on the right side as well before casting an eye at the ground nearby, jingling the keys in her hand.

"Where to put you... ah. Here we go." A small stack of cinderblocks sat behind the dumpster on the left side of the truck, and Dianne carefully tucked the keys to the truck inside one of the holes in the bottom block before standing back up and surveying the area. There was still no sign of anyone nearby, and she headed for the front of the grocery store, walking at a quick pace. Hiding the keys in the cinderblock had been a spur-of-the-moment decision, but the condition of the town had her feeling especially worried and paranoid about being robbed. The last thing she wanted to do was give anyone the keys to her vehicle, and she figured that hiding them was better than potentially losing them.

As Dianne rounded the corner to the grocery store and approached the entrance, she started to hear the roar of angry voices and the clatter of carts, cans, and people pushing into each other. As she walked in, she stopped just inside the door, staring in horror at the scene unfolding in the store. Mass panic had gripped the residents of the town, and the store was filled with at least two hundred people—far more than would ever be there on a normal day.

They were crammed into the store like sardines in a can, pushing against each other and smashing their shopping carts together as they ran down the aisles, dumping food into their carts. Fights were breaking out across the store as supplies began running low and shoppers began stealing from each other's baskets. At the front, it was somehow even worse. There were only four cashiers on duty, and they were desperately trying to ring everyone up, though the noise and commotion made it impossible to concentrate.

At the front of the store, on a large television usually reserved for displaying corny advertisements and sales, a newscaster sat behind his desk. Dianne couldn't hear anything over the noise in the store, but closed captioning had been turned on. She stopped for a minute and watching, growing increasingly mortified at what she read.

"Repeating our top story—the US government has confirmed that this is a national emergency. An unknown attack has resulted in the destruction of an estimated hundred and fifty million vehicles in the country, with an unknown additional number in other countries across the world. The key to these attacks appears to be an attack on the vehicle computers that caused them to short circuit and ignite their gas tanks. Similar reports are being confirmed about the mobile phone and airline industries, which have also suffered catastrophic losses. We're also receiving reports that the computer systems in several major power providers have been affected and it is expected that rolling blackouts will occur as the day progresses.

"The human toll is incalculable, but deaths are likely to be in the millions, based on what we're seeing thus far. We have very little solid information to go on at this time, but we encourage you to remain in your homes and away from your vehicles and phones until more information comes in."

Dianne could feel her adrenaline flowing as she turned from the television with a renewed sense of purpose. She grabbed a cart sitting off to the side near the ice cooler and made her way to the center of the store where the canned goods and nonperishables were stocked. She was surprised to see only a handful of people in the two aisles containing the nonperishables loading up their carts. One of them, an older man, glanced at her as she turned the corner and sped down the aisle. "You'd better hurry up; once the bread and meat runs out, that mob's gonna stop being so picky about what they want."

Dianne nodded slowly in thanks at the man, who simply headed off to the next aisle. It was unfathomable to her that people were fighting over things like fresh meat and bread, which would go bad within a few days or less, especially if the power were to go out. Still, she wasn't ungrateful for the mob's foolishness, as it offered her ample time to stock up on what she needed.

First in the cart were sacks of beans; black, red and pinto. Next went every spare bag of rice she could lay her hands on, both white and brown. Once her cart was half-full with rice and beans she pushed the heavy cart to the next aisle and began throwing canned soups, vegetables and fruits into the cart. As she struggled to turn the over-burdened cart towards the front of the store, she heard a faint electrical hum that grew louder by the second until—*POP!*

As the lights in the store blinked out, the screaming began. The only light available to see by came in through the front windows, which were nearly completely covered by advertisements. Realizing that things were about to get extremely hairy, Dianne barreled down the aisle and skidded around the turn at the end, knocking over the endcap as she worked to keep the cart upright. Ahead of her, the chaos had grown to a level she could scarcely believe. The cashiers had all but fled their posts, leaving the customers fighting to push their carts out through the checkout lanes to escape the store. People of all ages fought viciously with each other, though she was somewhat relieved to see that the fighting hadn't escalated past fists and using shopping carts as battering rams.

Since Dianne was off to the side of the checkout and away from the center of the chaos, she took a few seconds to dig through her purse and pull out several twenty-dollar bills. She shouted at the lone clerk who remained at his post, a skinny, scrawny teenager wearing a shirt and pants that were two sizes too large for him.

"Hey!" Dianne shouted at him again, and he turned to look at her, wide-eyed. "Here!" Dianne wasn't about to leave without paying, and she balled up the money and threw it at him. It landed on the floor next to him and he scooped it up quickly. Without power, the cash register refused to open and no one could pay with a credit card, so Dianne wasn't exactly sure what he could do with the money. She still felt better than she would have if she had simply dashed out the front of the store without even trying to pay.

As the cashier picked up Dianne's money, the people who were at the front of the line realized that they weren't going to be able to pay with their cards, and began moving their items back into their carts. Sensing that there was about to be a mad dash for the door, Dianne pushed against the heavy cart and rolled it towards the automatic doors, not bothering to stop. Designed to open on hinges in case of emergencies, the doors gave way as soon as the cart pushed against them, allowing her a quick escape from the store. As she turned the cart to the left, heading for the side of the store where she parked the truck, the screaming and shouting from behind her took on a new, fevered pitch as the hordes of customers decided to abandon their attempts to pay for their goods and resort to simply running out with as much as they could carry.

As Dianne rounded the corner to the side of the building, she looked back and saw the first stream of people exiting the store and running towards the parking lot. Glass shattered behind them as two people absorbed in a fistfight barreled through the front window and tumbled out the front. Shaking her head, Dianne turned back around to look at her truck, only to stop as she saw that she wasn't alone.

Approaching the rear of the truck, Dianne could see two men standing on the left side, both wearing blue jeans and hoodies and wielding crowbars. One of the men stood off to the side while his accomplice alternated between smashing at the driver's side window and the back left window with the crowbar, grunting as it simply bounced off the reinforced glass without leaving so much as a scratch. "Dammit... how the hell are you supposed to get through this?" The man hitting the glass grumbled to the other, who mumbled something unintelligible in return.

"Hey!" Dianne pulled the shopping cart to a stop and shouted at the men. They turned abruptly and stared at her as she reached behind her back and pulled out a snub-nosed .45 revolver and drew down on them. "Get the hell away from my truck! Now!"

Caught unawares, the man who had been beating on the window dropped his crowbar and fled, leaving the other one to shout at him before turning back to Dianne. "Hey! Get back here you idiot! Oh screw off, lady, and give me the keys before I beat your head in." The man took a step towards Dianne and raised the crowbar. She responded by calmly pulling back the hammer on the revolver and taking careful aim at the man's chest.

"I said to get the hell away from my truck." Dianne's tone was menacing, and the man stopped, glancing between her face and the revolver a few times before making his decision. He charged Dianne, getting no further than two steps before she squeezed the trigger. It had been several weeks since she had last practiced firing the revolver, and she had forgotten how much it kicked, not to mention how much noise it made. Her would-be assailant screamed in pain as the hollow point bullet tore along the side of his ribcage, tumbling and rolling as it went.

"Bitch!" He shouted as he scrambled to alter his path and get away, flinging the crowbar in her direction as he ran away from the truck and pursued his accomplice. So focused was Dianne on keeping the revolver trained on him in case he decided to charge her again that she didn't even notice the crowbar arcing through the air until it slammed against the side of her head. The heavy piece of metal hit her skull directly above her right eye, sending an explosion of light cascading through her brain. She nearly dropped to one knee from the force of the impact, but managed to stay upright by grabbing onto the cart with her left hand while her right began to shake as she kept the revolver trained on the man as he ran into the parking lot and soon disappeared.

It took all of Dianne's willpower to fight through the explosive pain in her head without falling to the ground, but she slowly tucked the gun into the holster at the small of her back and pushed the cart up next to the back of the truck. Keeping her blurred vision trained on the direction the two men had run, she started stacking everything from the store into the back of the truck until the cart was empty, then she moved around to the driver's side door. She pulled at the handle twice before remembering that she needed the keys, which she quickly retrieved and used to unlock the truck. She jumped in, locked the doors and took a deep breath.

"Mom?"

Dianne jumped in her seat and let out a short yelp, the pain having momentarily made her forget that her kids were still in the back seat. She turned around and pulled off the blanket that was covering them to reveal their terrified faces as they crouched on the back floor. "Mark! Jacob! Josie! Are you okay?"

"We're fine, mom." Mark got up off the floor and crawled forward into the passenger's seat.

"Those men—they didn't hurt you?"

Mark shook his head. "No; we heard them talking outside the truck for a few minutes before they started trying to break the windows. We stayed still like you told us to, though."

Dianne leaned over and wrapped her arms around Mark, then bent back to squeeze Jacob and Josie's hands as they climbed back into their seats. "Good work, all of you!"

"Were they trying to get into the car?" Jacob was trying to put on a brave face, but his shaking voice betrayed the fact that he was still scared.

Dianne nodded. "They were. But they're gone now." Dianne turned back and looked toward the parking lot, still seeing no sign of the two would-be thieves. "We need to get home, though."

"Mom, are you bleeding?" Mark pointed at the gash above Dianne's eye. The mere mention of the wound caused Dianne to suddenly remember it, and she touched a finger to it, wincing in pain and pulling back a pair of fingers covered with dripping blood.

"Yep, looks like it. Can you find some napkins, or a cloth or something in here for me? You two—" Dianne looked in the rearview mirror. "Got your seatbelts on?" Jacob and Josie nodded and Dianne threw the truck into gear and mumbled to herself. "Then let's get the hell out of here."

As they pulled out of the grocery store parking lot and out onto the road, Mark and Jacob looked out the right-hand windows of the truck at the mayhem in the parking lot. The people who had been inside the store had taken their battle out into the parking lot, where fights were going down for shopping carts full of food and other supplies.

"What are they doing, mom?" Jacob asked from the back seat.

"They're... worried, Jacob. They're worried and scared, and sometimes when people get worried and scared, they act like that."

"Do you know what's going on?" Mark kept his nose pressed to the glass as they made another turn, slowly making their way back to the house.

"Something very bad happened, something to do with people's cars and phones and other things."

"Are we gonna be okay, mommy?" Josie piped up from the back seat.

Dianne adjusted the rearview mirror and smiled bravely at her daughter, who was busy kicking her feet and looking around the truck. "We're going to be just fine, baby. Just fine."

Chapter Nine

L os Angeles, CA

ONCE RICK WAS certain the three cars weren't coming back, he resumed his walk in the direction of what he hoped was the eastern edge of the city. As he went along, he starting mulling over the events of the day, piecing together the clues of what he had learned. While an EMP—an electromagnetic pulse—had been high on his list of possibilities, the sight of the relatively modern vehicles and the lights in windows of various buildings made it clear that was not the answer. Whatever had caused Rick's phone and car to self-destruct and caused planes to fall out of the sky couldn't have been a terrorist attack either, since the scale was far too large and the circumstances had been wrong.

The more Rick thought about the order of the events that had occurred, the more worried he became. Dozens of vehicles all sitting in the road wouldn't start leaking gasoline all at once. And a phone shouldn't just explode in his pocket. Plus planes don't normally fall from the sky—at least not multiple planes at the same time.

"It *was* an attack." Rick spoke out loud to himself as he walked along. "But not an ordinary one. It targeted computer control systems. Vehicles started leaking gasoline, phones shorted out the batteries, the planes were probably diverted intentionally and caused to crash as well. Who would have that sort of ability, though? Russians? Chinese?" Rick stroked his chin and shook his head. He had worked on vehicle control and communication systems for long enough to know that there were always weaknesses in computer systems, no matter how well designed they were. "But what's the connection to them all? Those three cars driving by were only a decade or two old; they would have had computer systems in them. So why weren't they destroyed?"

The answer hit Rick like a bolt of lightning from the smoke-filled sky. "The systems that were destroyed were all interlinked!" He stopped in the middle of the street and ran his hands through his hair as he drew the connections in his mind. "The government's mandate for all newer vehicles to talk to each other necessitates that they have a connection to the Internet. Phones and planes, well of course they would be connected. But if this is something that's wreaking havoc using Internet connectivity, then…" Rick trailed off as he realized the implications. "This isn't something that's confined to the city, is it?"

Rick's question went unanswered by the empty street, and he slowly started walking again, shaking his head in disbelief. "This has to be some sort of terrorist attack; a series of complex viruses designed to infiltrate key networks and wreak havoc across the country. But…how? How could it possibly be done?"

Rick's theory brought him more questions than answers, and after a while he began to doubt himself. He second-guessed, came up with alternate theories and tried to find any other explanation that made an ounce of sense. The more he thought about it, though, the more he became convinced that he was onto something, even if the details weren't necessarily accurate.

Lost in his own thoughts for another hour, Rick didn't notice the city beginning to change around him. He was traveling out of the mixed residential area and into a more commercial one, filled with small shops that crowded in and on top of each other. The shops, unlike the apartments from earlier, were all dark, with no signs of life or light anywhere. Many of the buildings had their windows and doors broken as a result of looting that had occurred hours earlier.

A distant shout snapped Rick out of his thoughts and he looked ahead, seeing two figures stopped in the road that each carried a small light source. Rick's first thought was of the people he had seen in the three vehicles earlier and he started to turn to run down a side street when one of the figures shouted again, loud enough for Rick to hear him.

"Hey, man! Long time no see!" The voice belonged to Jack who, along with Samantha, had just crossed over onto the street that Rick was on, having taken a different exit off the overpass earlier in the evening. Rick smiled at the voice and picked up his pace, heading toward the figures as he shouted back.

"I thought you two were staying for the night!"

"Nah, man, they had some bad vibes coming in there. Figured we'd take a cue from you and get out of dodge!"

As Rick drew closer to Jack and Samantha, a distant noise began to draw rapidly nearer, causing him to freeze in his tracks. After a few seconds of careful listening, his smile dropped as he realized it was the roar of vehicle engines drawing rapidly closer. Still too far from Jack and Samantha to make it to them before the cars reappeared, Rick cupped his hands around his mouth and shouted as loud as he could. "Hide! Quick!"

Jack put a hand up to his ear and shook his head, signaling that he couldn't hear Rick. Jack and Samantha turned and watched as the three vehicles roared by on a cross-street in front of them, then screeched to a halt as the drivers and passengers of the vehicles spotted the couple standing in the road.

"Run!" Rick was crouched down next to a burned-out car, still a few hundred feet away, watching as he whispered under his breath. "For God's sake, run!" Two figures stepped out of each vehicle, six in total, and walked up to Jack and Samantha. The biggest of the six was talking to them, but Rick couldn't hear the conversation due to the distance, the thrum of the engines and the bass from the music inside the vehicles. From what he could see, though, it wasn't a pretty picture. Chains hung from two of the men's hands, while another held what appeared to be a baseball bat or a large piece of wood. The man who Rick presumed was the leader stood in front, waving something around in his hand that Rick couldn't make out, but assumed was a gun.

Rick stayed still for several seconds as he tried to decide what to do. Without a weapon, he would be useless to help defend Jack and Samantha from the unknown men if the situation started to deteriorate. On the other hand, though, he couldn't just sit still and do nothing. Although it made him nervous, Rick started to stand up and began jogging toward the lights and sound down the road, hoping that he could somehow intervene before things turned violent.

"Maybe they're just giving them directions…" Rick muttered to himself. "Maybe I'm misreading this. Maybe—"

A pair of successive gunshots rang out, putting an end to Rick's thoughts on the matter. He stopped in his tracks and watched as Jack and Samantha slowly toppled to the ground, their legs crumpling beneath them as the man who had been talking to them shot them both point blank in their heads. He motioned to his associates who dove on the bodies like vultures, tearing off clothes, jewelry and any other valuables that they could lay their hands on. As his cronies worked, the leader walked around the dead pair slowly, scanning the street as he looked for any other signs of life. Rick lunged to the side and fell to the ground, rolling until he stopped up against the side of a burned out vehicle. He laid still for a long minute, watching the leader stalk around until Jack and Samantha's bodies had been stripped bare. The six then piled back into their cars and drove off, tires screeching as the passengers of the vehicles shouted with demented joy.

Rick slowly rose to his feet and ran down the street to where he had seen Jack and Samantha fall. The street was dark enough that he nearly tripped over their bodies when he got to them, and he pulled out his penlight and held it over their faces as he choked back bile. The man who had shot them had wasted no time, as they both had bloody holes in the center of their foreheads. Their bodies had been stripped down to their undergarments, and their limbs lay at odd angles against the rough asphalt. Rick stepped back from the bodies and shoved his light back into his pocket before covering his face with his hands and shaking his head.

He hadn't known Jack and Samantha at all, but they had seemed like decent enough people who—like him—were stranded due to a disaster that no one could have predicted. To be shot in cold blood for nothing more than the clothes on their backs felt more wrong to Rick than he could put into thoughts or words. He felt the feelings of shock start to overcome him again and he sat down on the sidewalk nearby, staring at the couple's bodies and shaking his head slowly in disbelief. "Thirty seconds more," he whispered to himself, "and I'd be lying there with them."

Rick sat by the side of the road until the first rays of dawn's early light peeked over the horizon. His mind was filled with a swirling kaleidoscope of thoughts that ranged from worrying about his family to imagining how he could have changed the situation with Jack and Samantha. Every time he tried to focus on a thought, his mind wandered, refusing to focus on any particular topic for more than a few seconds.

He watched the black sky turn shades of blue and pink and orange for several minutes, then closed his eyes to wipe away the tears that were gathering. He stood up slowly and spent time scouring the nearby shops, searching until he found a large tablecloth in the back of one of the restaurants. He laid the tablecloth out over Jack and Samantha's bodies, tucking the edges underneath them so that the cloth wouldn't blow away. The gesture felt trite and meaningless, but the idea of simply walking away from them felt even more so. Once he had finished, he turned and headed to the east, not knowing what to think anymore.

Chapter Ten

E llisville, VA

A FEW MINUTES after leaving the grocery store, as they were starting to turn back onto the gravel road, Mark suddenly remembered what his mother had asked him to do earlier when they were distracted by the fighting in the grocery store parking lot. He felt under the front seats of the truck until he came upon an old roll of paper towels, then tore a few of them off and handed them to his mother.

Dianne gratefully accepted the wad of paper towels and pressed them against her forehead, gritting her teeth and drawing in a sharp breath of air as the pain from above her eye reverberated across her entire head. With her left hand on the wheel and her right hand holding the paper towels to her eye, she drove slowly along the gravel road, glad to see that the amount of foot traffic had lessened. There were only a few people out and about still, but they didn't approach the truck, being more concerned with the power going out and trying to find friends and loved ones who hadn't returned home yet.

As the truck started hitting the bumpy portion of the road, Dianne lowered the paper towels and held them out to Mark. "Hold this against my head there, would you?" He accepted the wad of paper towels with a slight grimace, then pressed them up against her forehead as he leaned across the seat.

"Do you think dad's okay?" Mark whispered to his mother as Jacob and Josie sat quietly in the back, staring out their windows at the passing trees.

"I'm sure he's fine, hon. Your dad's a smart guy."

"Yeah, but what if he was on the plane?"

"He wasn't. I got a message from him that he landed just a little while before all of this started."

"But what if his car exploded like ours, or like all the ones in town?"

"Mark, there's no sense in speculating about things like that right now. We need to focus on the task at hand."

Mark sat quietly for a few seconds before responding. "So what are we going to do, anyway?"

Dianne sighed and pursed her lips in thought. "Well, we know that something big is going on. With the power out, we'll need to hook up the extra solar panels in the barn to make sure there's enough juice in the batteries to keep the fridge running. We may need to fire up the generator for a while, too. First, though, we'll see if we can tune in to any of the local TV or radio stations; maybe they'll have some updated news on what's going on. Tomorrow we're going to see if any of the neighbors are home, make sure they're okay and see what they're up to and if they heard any news. Let's make sure we're set at home before we start going out any more, though, okay?"

"What about—"

"Hey. Kiddo." Dianne took the paper towels from Mark's hand and smiled at him. "We're going to be okay, all right? Let's just get home, get all of the supplies inside, and then we'll devise a plan from there. Sound good?" Mark nodded slowly, not completely convinced by his mother's enthusiasm, but satisfied enough to stop asking any further questions.

By the time Dianne started pulling up the winding dirt driveway to their home, the sun was starting to hang low in the sky. She left the children in the truck to unlock the gate herself, casting a wary eye into the woods around them, then secured it again once they were on the other side. After backing the truck up to the front porch of the house, Dianne had Josie and Jacob go inside and play in the living room while she and Mark started carrying the supplies from the back of the truck into the house. The lights in the house didn't work when she tried to turn them on, confirming that the power outage wasn't just confined to the town.

"Mark," she said, "Finish getting everything inside and into the kitchen; I'm going to get the generator started up. We'll use that tonight and see how things look in the morning." Dianne's son dutifully obeyed while Dianne trotted out to the backup generator behind the house. It was an older generator, designed to run off of a tank of propane that was stored nearby since the house was too far out to be connected to the town's natural gas lines. Rick and Dianne had it installed during the first year they moved to their homestead and had used it several times over the years.

Requiring a manual intervention to start, the generator was capable of powering the whole house and then some, and Dianne hated the idea of using it when they had no idea of how long it would be until the power returned. Still, she thought, better to have one night of regular comforts after the day's events before potentially having to transfer to a lifestyle that depended less on electricity. *No, that's foolish. Of course the power will come back on tomorrow.* She tried to shake the feelings of doom and gloom, but the image of the burning wreck of a plane in a field and the terrified look on the newscaster's face still haunted her.

The generator roared to life without hesitation, and Dianne poked her head out of the small outbuilding in which it was housed to see lights blinking on inside the house. She checked the vents on the top and sides of the building before closing the door and then headed back to the house. Inside, Mark and Jacob were busy arranging the supplies they had retrieved from the grocery store on the floor while Josie still played in the living room. Dianne smiled, glad to see that her children seemed to be coping well with what had happened.

"Hang tight here, kids. I'm going to clean up, then we'll get everything put away and make some dinner, okay?"

"You want us to wash up?"

"That'd be great, thanks, Mark." Dianne headed upstairs to the master bathroom and turned on the lights. She stared at her face in the mirror, turning it as she studied the wound above her eye. The blood had dried and crusted over, so she took a wet washcloth and began to gently scrub around the wound, cringing at the pain. It wasn't as bad as she had originally thought—head wounds tend to look worse than they are due to how much they bleed—and after a quick cleaning, some antiseptic and a couple of butterfly bandages, she turned and went back downstairs.

Mark was finishing helping Josie dry her hands off when Dianne walked into the kitchen and put her hands on her hips as she looked at the piles of food on the floor. "Well, then. Let's get all of this put away, shall we?" She quickly divvied up assignments to the children and they got to work, starting with the bags of flour, rice, beans and other staples before moving on to the canned goods. While her kids worked on putting things away, Dianne got out a notebook and pencil and took down notes on the supplies they had just retrieved, along with what was currently on hand in their pantry and in the basement.

There was a solid week's worth of fresh fruit, vegetables, milk, bread and other perishables on hand, and three weeks' worth of pasta, rice, canned and frozen food in the pantry, refrigerator and freezer. The deep freeze—connected to the solar panels and battery backups—held six months' worth of meat, though she figured they could stretch it to eight months with some careful rationing.

The food they had picked up at the store would last for those six to eight months and provide good fillers and nonperishable nutrition along with the meat. She knew the kids (and herself) would get cranky after a while without things like milk, pastries and other comforts, though she could make bread and other baked goods herself in limited batches. The basement, however, held a whole other level of supplies. Collected over the last year and stored in the dark, cool environment were several shelves stuffed with homemade jams and canned vegetables as well as several dozen MREs. She had scoffed at Rick's collection of the military-style all-in-one packaged meals as going a bit too far with the prepper ideology, but as she counted the meals she said a quiet *thank you* that they were available.

The thought of her husband made Dianne pause for a moment and she sat down on the floor next to the shelves and put her head back against the wall. The last she had heard from Rick was that he landed safely, but it was impossible to know how he was doing since the phones weren't working. That thought prompted another and she leapt up and began rummaging around in some boxes behind the basement stairs.

"Ha!" Dianne shouted with excitement as she pulled out a small travel television, an external TV antenna and a wind-up radio from one of the boxes. She ran upstairs with them and dashed into the living room. The antenna was quickly suspended from the curtain rod over the back door and connected to the big TV hanging on the wall. She tucked the smaller TV away for later use, in case the power didn't come back on and she needed to use as little energy as possible. After turning the big TV on and adjusting the input to the tuner, she sat down on the edge of the couch and bit her lip nervously as she flipped through station after station filled with nothing but static. Finally, though, she hit the jackpot as a fuzzy signal from a station in Blacksburg came filtering through. It took a few tries but Dianne finally found the right angle and positioning for the antenna to boost the signal enough to be watchable.

"...we go live to Dale Weatherspoon, in Washington. Dale?"

"Thanks, Tom. As you heard in the President's statement a few minutes ago, we're seeing an unprecedented level of turmoil and chaos across the country. There are an estimated fifty thousand dead from failures associated with aircraft, trains and other mass transportation systems. The White House believes that estimate is just the tip of the iceberg, though, as there are undoubtedly many tens or perhaps hundreds of thousands killed or injured as a result of the personal vehicular detonations. That's a term that the White House is using, and like all of the other problems we're seeing, we have no idea what's causing them. Tom?"

"Dale, what are federal and state authorities doing to try and respond to this national crisis?"

"FEMA, the National Guard and some sections of the US military are responding, but federal and state agencies are crippled by this disaster."

"And there's still no word on what the source is?"

"The White House did say that they do not believe that it's a terrorist attack, but beyond that, there's no explanation for this national—and indeed international—level of destruction and chaos."

"Thanks, Dale. We're going now to a briefing from the director of—"

The image on the television started to shake and the audio became a garbled mess before the signal cut out completely. Dianne picked up the remote and tried changing the channel, but all of them were filled with the same digital static. She turned off the television and threw herself back into a slouch on the couch, sighing in frustration.

"You okay, mom?" Mark wandered into the living room and glanced at the TV before looking at her.

"Yeah, I'm fine."

"Did you find out anything?"

"Nothing useful." Dianne sighed again and shook her head in frustration. "I did find out that this is happening all over the country, or maybe the world. We should probably get settled in if that's the case, and figure out what to do around here to survive long-term."

"Survive?" Mark scrunched up his eyebrows. "You mean living off the land, that kind of thing?"

Dianne smiled as she stood up and embraced her eldest son. "I don't know, kiddo. If things are as bad as they sound, though, then maybe. But we don't need to worry about that tonight. Come on; let's find something for dinner and dig up a movie somewhere."

As Dianne walked back into the kitchen after Mark, she paused at the back door and looked out at the property behind the house. The sun was setting behind the lake and the animals were all grazing in their pens while a gentle breeze rustled the trees, making them shake in a dazzling gold, orange and red display of natural fireworks. She closed her eyes and gritted her teeth as she said a silent prayer.

Rick. Wherever you are out there… come home. Please. Just make it back home.

Chapter Eleven

L os Angeles, CA

BETWEEN RICK AND HIS WIFE, Dianne had always been the one more prone to gravitate toward self-defense. She always carried a small revolver on her person—legally of course—and remembering that fact made Rick extremely grateful. He was no stranger to firearms, having dispatched more than a few injured animals over the years with a bullet to the head and been on several hunting excursions over the years where his prowess had been proved by bringing home three large bucks. He didn't carry a gun normally, though, and being on a business trip meant that he was carrying nothing at all when he landed in Los Angeles.

That's why, as he approached the fringes of the city proper and began to encounter the residential areas, Rick paused at the corner of an intersection, staring at a large warehouse-like store across the street with twin pictures of a hunting rifle and a deer's head sitting on top. The store's windows and doors were smashed open, and the interior was dark. The image of Jack and Samantha laying lifeless on the ground flashed through his mind, and he thought about what—if anything—he might have been able to do if he had been armed and close enough to help.

A show of force? A distraction? Taking one or two of them down with me? As much as Rick wanted to imagine he could have dispatched six armed thieves intent on committing grievous bodily harm, he had to admit that it wasn't very likely he could have changed much about the situation. In spite of that, though, a thought still lingered in his mind.

What if?

Rick approached the store cautiously, peering in through the broken windows and door as he tried to see if anyone was still inside. Glass littered the ground outside the shop and the floor directly inside, and it crunched and crackled with each footstep, making a stealthy approach impossible. He glanced around at the empty streets before calling out softly through the hole where the front window used to be. "Anyone in there?"

Silence was the only response, so Rick took a deep breath and stepped through. He went a few paces to the side, hugging the wall, before stopping so that his eyes could adjust to the darkness. The store, once filled with shooting and hunting gear and accessories of all shapes, types and colors was a disaster zone. Shelves were overturned on the floor and goods were scattered, torn and trampled on, leaving a distinct and obvious pattern of destruction from when the building had been looted. The back and left walls were filled with rows of black pegs that had once held rifles, before every single weapon was removed and absconded with. Most of the glass display cases carrying the few types of pistols still legal in the state of California were shattered, as were the demo cases for the hunting, fishing and camping gear.

The store looked as though a miniature tornado had blown through, leaving very few portions of the building untouched. Rick decided to look for anything that appeared useful anyway, though, since he had no idea what the conditions were outside the city and no clue as to how long it would take for him to find a way back home.

A backpack that had been tossed into a corner was the first item he selected, followed by a shirt, pair of pants and a couple of jackets. He changed out of his suit in a hurry before lashing the jackets to the back of the backpack with some paracord. The food aisle of the building had been mostly cleaned out, but Rick dutifully searched through all of the debris, eventually finding several boxes of energy bars which he dumped into his backpack. A few pairs of socks and underwear followed, then three pairs of shoes—one for his feet and two for spares—that happened to be the last three in his size.

With his immediate food and clothing needs met, Rick turned his attention to the main reason why he had come into the store—a weapon. He went around the glass display cases lining the walls and began searching inside the cases, on the floor, under the counters and in the racks on the walls for any weapons and ammunition he could get his hands on. After a good twenty minutes of searching, Rick had found virtually nothing. There were several boxes of 9mm ammunition, a stack of 5.56 NATO boxes and a few boxes of 12-gauge ammo, but he had seen absolutely nothing in the way of guns.

Rick tucked the ammunition into his backpack and pockets regardless, on the off chance that he might find a gun later down the road. As he picked his way through the back area once again, he paused in front of a door marked "Employees Only" before pushing it open and heading through.

His penlight hadn't been needed in the main section of the store, but as he headed into the back, he pulled it out and switched it on. Much of the back area of the store was taken up by boxes, empty pallets and shelves stocked with supplies meant to be put out on the floor, but there was a small section enclosed in cubical walls that had two large wooden tables with a variety of tools and oils along with a large assortment of firearms.

Rick moved immediately toward the repair benches and firearms, and quickly discovered the small tags hanging off of the guns that marked when they had been brought in along with whether they had been repaired. He grabbed a small 9mm pistol, a hunting rifle chambered in 5.56 NATO with a moderate-sized scope on the top and a pump-action shotgun. He piled the two rifles into a soft gun case, zipped it up and then slung it on his back before ejecting the empty magazine from the pistol, filling it with ammo and then slapping it back into the gun and chambering a round. A pair of knives went next—one into his pack and the other in a sheath hanging from his belt —and then Rick turned his attention to the stacks of pallets behind him.

"How did they miss all of this?" Rick was astonished that the back room of the store had been completely left alone in the mad dash to loot the front area. As he searched through the boxes and pallets of goods, he cut open boxes with his knife, pulling out stacks of batteries, two flashlights, a small one-man tent, more packaged food and—to his relief—a larger backpack to store it all in.

As Rick carefully stuffed the larger of the two backpacks full of supplies, he suddenly felt a twinge of guilt and paused to sit down on the floor and look around at darkened room. "So this is what I'm reduced to? Less than a day after a few cars blow up and some planes fall from the sky, I'm sitting in the back room of a store, stealing from them?" Rick sighed and put his head in his hands as the memory of Jack and Samantha being shot in the heads played through again. "Bastards." Rick whispered softly and continued his packing, pushing the memory aside. He wasn't sure why it was still affecting him so much, but he was determined to make sure he didn't end up dead on the street along with them.

He stood up slowly and put the pack on his back and adjusted the straps before taking the gun case up in his left hand. With his right he tucked the 9mm pistol into a small holster on the inside of his pants, concealing it from view. He felt like a pack mule as he slowly lumbered out of the store, trying to avoid catching himself or anything he was carrying on the overturned shelves as he went.

Standing in front of the store, Rick turned to the east, shielding his eyes from the sun with his right hand. Ahead of him, with any luck, he would discover that his paranoia was unjustified, and he would be able to ditch all of the supplies he had just looted and be on his way back home to his family before dark. As much as Rick tried to tell himself that it was a possibility this could be true, he had the distinct feeling that nothing could be further from the truth and that his journey home would be anything but easy.

With a deep breath, Rick Waters put one foot in front of the other and began his journey home.

Chapter Twelve

L os Angeles

NEW ZONING, tax and building regulations over the previous decade had expanded the city's limits and brought new life and changes to the eastern portion of the city. The Monterey Pass road, once a winding road containing all manner of stores that were squashed between residential neighborhoods to the north and south, had been transformed. Most of the businesses along the road had moved into the neighborhoods to the north and south as part of a new urban planning scheme where grocery stores, banks, restaurants and other similar businesses tried to exist directly in neighborhoods to provide more convenience to residents.

Once the original buildings along the winding path had been destroyed, they were rebuilt into towering monoliths as part of a new "green" industrial design. The interiors of the buildings were sleek and modern in every way possible, but the exteriors had intentionally been designed to look as though the buildings had been built a hundred years prior. Experimental fabrication plants, computer chip designers, 3D printing startups and other companies that needed large amounts of manufacturing space found their home in the new industrial strip.

When the event occurred, however, all of the companies had been hit just as much as any other—and perhaps even more so due to their computerized systems that controlled everything from the temperature and lights to the locks on the doors. Several of the buildings had burned to the ground, but the advanced building designs meant that the fires didn't spread to the neighboring buildings.

As Rick found himself looking down at the Monterey Pass Industrial Row—which was the name emblazoned on the sign leading down the road—he found himself feeling nervous about passing through the large buildings. One of them had toppled over as it burned, strewing debris across the road and making the path look virtually impossible to traverse. The only other option at Rick's disposal, though, was to go around the massive residential neighborhoods that, to his surprise, were still ablaze.

The unique position of the Monterey Pass road and the fire resistant exteriors of the buildings along the row meant that the road acted as a natural firebreak, allowing safe passage through the worst of the fires and out onto a clear section of road beyond that the flames had yet to reach. Rick squinted at the industrial buildings, trying to estimate how much time he would have to get past them before the fires on either side moved far enough east to consume the path he was trying to take.

"Two. Maybe three hours at most." Rick mumbled to himself and shook his head. "This is insane." Still, though, there was nothing else he could think to do, so he forged ahead, moving at a light jog as he tried to make the journey as fast as possible. It took him half an hour to shuffle down from where he was onto the Monterey Pass road. From there he began to move cautiously, watching the towering buildings cautiously. Of all the people he had encountered so far in his journey, those in the three cars had been the only ones who had been violent—so far. There was something about the industrial row that made him uneasy, and he couldn't stop thinking about them as he walked among the buildings.

So focused was Rick on the buildings around him that he didn't notice a low thrum begin to echo in the distance to the west. The sound continued to grow louder by the second, and it was only when it was nearly on top of him that Rick finally noticed it—a blaring of some unidentifiable music coming through overpowered sound systems. He froze in his tracks and turned his head in every direction, trying to identify the direction the music was coming from.

By the time he figured it out, it was too late. Rick was standing in the middle of the road as the three cars drove up, each of them slamming on the brakes and skidding to a halt a hundred or so feet away. Rick nearly froze on the spot from fear and indecision, but the memory of watching Jack and Samantha being gunned down played through his mind. His body reacted to the memory and he leaned to the side, breaking into an all-out run for the buildings directly to his south. The sound of car doors opening came from behind him, though all he could hear was the wind rushing past his ears and the crinkling and jingling of the contents of his backpack as he threw himself forward.

The first shots rang out just as Rick disappeared behind a five-story rectangular structure. Bullets tore chunks of the faux brick siding off of the building, whizzing past Rick as he stumbled, trying to keep from falling over around the sharp corner. Unintelligible shouts came from behind him, and he heard footsteps as the unknown number of assailants began to approach the back of the building.

With nothing to hide behind ahead, a tall wall to his right, the building to his left and the knowledge that stopping or turning around would mean certain death, Rick took the only choice that made sense at the time. He skidded to a stop in front of a door leading into the back of the building and closed his eyes as he turned the handle. He had fully expected it to be locked and for his pursuers to be upon him a few seconds later, which was why he gasped in surprise as the handle turned freely. He pulled the door open and stumbled inside, then stopped as he tried to make out where, exactly, he was.

The building was brighter than he expected, and it took his eyes just a few seconds to adjust to the stark shadows cast from the glass ceiling far above his head. The main floor of the building was filled with manufacturing equipment while catwalks and enormous sections of piping towered high over his head, crisscrossing each other as they reached toward the roof. Rick heard another spray of gunfire as his assailants blindly fired down the side of the building where he had been standing a few seconds earlier. He jumped at the sound and scanned the building for a place to hide before making up his mind about where to go.

Instead of searching for somewhere to take shelter on the ground floor, Rick broke into a run for the closest set of stairs. The stairs wrapped around the interior of the building, providing access to the catwalks that acted as the second, third, fourth and fifth floors of the structure. Rick glanced at the displays and controls that were near the top of the first set of stairs as he ran past, though he was unable to discern what the factory manufactured. He reached the top of the second set of stairs and ran towards the third, his legs burning from exhaustion. He stopped at the base of the third set of stairs and looked out over the railing, craning his neck to try to see the floor below through all of the piping suspended in the air.

Lead ricocheted off of metal and tore through plastic as an unknown number of guns opened fire from below. Rick felt a sharp pain in his right leg as a bullet bounced off of the railing and tore through the edge of his calf. He tried to roll back towards the wall as he fell, but his backpack was too bulky, and he was forced to slip out of it before he could seek some cover. The catwalks and stairs weren't solid but grated, except for a two-foot wide strip that ran along the wall. Rick pressed his back against the cinderblocks, feeling their relative coolness leech the heat from his sweating back. The gunfire continued for another several seconds until a sharp voice cut through it in Spanish, ordering a cease-fire.

"Let's just kill him from down here!" Another voice, this one in English, came next.

"No, not this one." The first voice spoke with a thick accent, purposefully yelling loudly enough so that Rick could hear him. "This one I want to take care of myself."

The implication in the tone of voice of the man Rick assumed was the leader of the group chilled him to the bone, and he began looking around frantically for a way out of the situation. There was no way to get out of the building without going through the men below, and if he stayed where he was, he would soon be captured. "Great." Rick mumbled as he steeled himself for his next move. "Guess the only way to go is up."

Rick pushed himself to his knees before reaching out across the metal grating to grab his backpack and gun bag. With one in each hand, he darted up the third flight of stairs, taking them three at a time as he tried to stay ahead of a spray of bullets. None of them came anywhere close to hitting him, but they did spur him to move faster, and in less than a minute he was squatting at the highest point in the building, panting from exhaustion.

The glass roof above him rose at an angle to meet the glass from the other side, directly over the center of the factory below. Metal supports held the glass in place, and were also the location of large steel fittings to which thick cables were attached that held up the intricate collection of pipes which were suspended above the factory floor. Several of the largest pipes ended at a right angle in a large metal box attached to one side of the building, and on the exterior were a few vents. Rick glanced out at the ground and side of the building he could make out from his location, hoping to spot a ladder or some other means of getting to the ground, but found nothing.

"Come out, come out, little *pollo!*" The leader of the group was taking the stairs one at a time, his men trailing close behind, laughing, jeering and occasionally firing off a shot in the direction where they suspected Rick was located. Rick paid them no mind as he unzipped both his pack and his gun bag and set to work loading up three magazines worth of 5.56 for the hunting rifle.

A few months after buying their home in Virginia, Rick and Dianne had spent a few weeks repairing and rebuilding the fence that stretched around the perimeter of the property. The wooden supports were rotted and the wire was rusted and falling apart. It was long, laborious and boring work, but Rick had enjoyed it immensely due to the time he and Dianne had gotten to spend working together. Three days into their work Rick had heard something rustling in the dead leaves behind him.

He turned to see a large red fox hobbling towards him. The animal had saliva dripping profusely from its mouth and was staggering as it walked, all the while growling and making strange sounds. Rick recognized the signs of rabies immediately and yelled for Dianne to get back to the house. She had refused, though, and instead pulled out the small revolver she carried with her and put three rounds into the creature's torso as it kept heading towards her and Rick. The bullets didn't deter the rabid creature, though, and in fact seemed to make it even more hostile. Not willing to risk waiting any longer, Rick pulled the closest T-post out of the loose soil and jammed it into the creature's skull, killing it instantly.

Rick knew that even with all of the ammunition and firepower in the world, he wouldn't be able to take on every single one of his would-be assailants. If he could take out their leader, though, and do it quickly and professionally, there was a chance—no matter how slim—that it would cause the rest of the men to flee, unwilling to risk being the next to be killed. Rick drove the first magazine home into the rifle and removed the caps from the scope. He laid down on the catwalk, his back to a corner, and rested the barrel of the rifle on the backpack in front of him.

In the moments it took for the gang leader to show his face, Rick felt like time slowed to a dead crawl. He thought about his wife and children, about Jack and Samantha, about the business meeting he had missed and about the fact that he was on the other side of the country from his loved ones. *How is it I go from being on a normal everyday business trip to laying down in an abandoned factory waiting to kill someone?* Rick closed his eyes and licked his lips, trying to control the nervousness that was starting to rise up inside of him. *I'm not a killer. I'm not a killer. I'm **not** a killer.* Rick kept repeating the phrase in his head as the realization about what he was about to do dawned on him. As the nervousness reached its crescendo and he started moving his legs to stand up and try to find another way out, movement down the catwalk caught his eye.

"There you are, *pollo*! Hiding in a corner?" Nearly every bare patch of skin on the man was covered in tattoos, from his bald head and face down to his arms and legs that showed out from underneath his shorts. The man carried a long, gleaming knife in his right hand and a pistol in the other. His grin was maniacal and twisted, his laugh full of cruelty and his eyes filled to the brim with malice. Seeing the man up close made Rick realize that there was no other way out. With that thought, his nervousness vanished without a trace and he squeezed the trigger.

The scope on the rifle had been perfectly aligned when Rick grabbed it from the back room of the sporting goods store. Spending hours in a bag being jostled, tossed and slammed around had moved it slightly out of alignment, though, and it showed with the shot Rick took. Instead of hitting the leader of the gang square in the chest, it hit him in the neck, slicing through his carotid artery and sending a spray of blood out to the side.

The man dropped to his knees in shock, his eyes wide as he held a hand to his neck ineffectually, then pulling it back and staring at the dripping blood in horror. Rick was mortified by the sight, and pulled his head back from the scope to watch as the leader's men stopped in their tracks and ceased their jeering, laughing and shooting. Each of them watched their leader as he pressed his hands against his neck again, trying to stop the flow of blood, but not one of them stepped forward to help him. As the leader turned to his followers and held out his arm, he tried to gasp out a plea for help, but couldn't form the words.

Seconds later, the man fell forward onto the catwalk, blood still pouring from his wound. He raised one hand weakly into the air and then it fell. A shudder went through his body and then he stopped moving all together. The other men were still frozen in shock at the sight, as was Rick, though he came to his senses just before they did.

"Listen up!" Rick shouted as he put his eye back to the scope and swiveled the rifle to look at the next closest face he could see. "Get the hell out of here right now and you can live! Or, you can join your friend there! You have to the count of five to decide!"

Rick didn't even get to "three" before the gang members were falling over each other in their rush to escape. The sight of their leader dying in such a brutal fashion had driven the fight out of them, and each one of was in full-on panic mode. When they reached the bottom of the building they ran out through the back entrance, leaving the door to swing shut. Less than a minute later Rick could hear the sound of car engines starting up, and a few seconds after that two of the three vehicles roared down the road in front of the industrial building, heading off to the east before curving north around the fires and back into the city proper.

Rick didn't get up for a full half hour. He lay motionless on the floor, tilting his head every few minutes as he struggled to pick up any possible sounds he might have missed. When he was satisfied that he was finally alone in the building, he got up slowly and put his backpack on, slipped the hunting rifle back into the soft case along with the shotgun and started walking back toward the stairs.

When he reached the gang leader's body lying face-down on the metal grates, blood dripping down onto the pipes and floor far below, he shook his head and grimaced. He knew that, eventually, he would have to deal with the fact that he had just taken someone's life. When his adrenaline finally wore off there would be more shock to deal with, and hard questions would surface that would have to be answered.

But in that moment, as Rick felt simultaneously elated to be alive and horrified at what he had done, he thought of one thing above all else: justice. He hadn't set out to try and balance the scale of Jack and Samantha's death, and if the gang had left him alone he wouldn't have even tried. In a way he was grateful, though, since the gang leader's death undoubtedly meant that other innocents might be saved from the madness and carnage, and that in some way at least, he had avenged his travel partners' deaths.

"One day." Rick whispered at the body of the man in front of him. "In one day you went from... whoever you were before to this." He held out his right hand and turned it over, looking at his index finger he had used to pull the trigger on his rifle.

"And in one day I turned into *this*."

Rick stepped over the lifeless body and headed down the stairs. He pulled the pistol from his waistband holster and checked to make sure it was loaded, then slipped it back in. He exited through the back of the building, glancing around for any sign of the men that had driven off, and was relieved to see that they were really and truly gone. Rick walked around to the front of the building and saw the third vehicle, the SUV, sitting out on the road with the keys in the ignition and the radio still playing.

Rick opened the front passenger door and threw his bags in, then climbed into the driver's seat and switched off the radio. He ran his hand across the top of steering wheel and sighed. To his left and right the smoke and fire continued inching forward, turning more homes filled with memories and life and joy and happiness into nothing more than piles of ashes. For Rick, his memories, life, joy and happiness were thousands of miles away, and he had no idea if they were intact or if they had perished along with countless others.

If Rick Waters had learned anything in the last day, it was that he was going to make it home no matter the cost. He didn't know how it would happen, but he knew in the deepest corners and recesses of his heart that it would.

"Stay safe." Rick whispered to his wife half a world away as he turned the key and the SUV's engine roared to life. "I'll be there soon."

Author's Notes

May 5, 2017

If you're reading these notes, that means that you most likely read through the entirety of this first book in my new episodic post-apocalyptic series. Whether you're a new reader or you've read books I've written before, I want to thank you for taking some of your valuable time and spending it in the world that I've created. It means a lot to me and I genuinely appreciate it. I really hope you enjoyed the story so far!

I'm writing Surviving the Fall with the idea of making a fast-paced, gripping and somewhat realistic take on the post-apocalyptic genre. I'm tired of the EMP stories that seem to be all the rage these days so I came up with a different take that has some—but not all—of the same effects.

I also wanted to show the end of the world from the perspective of both a typical "lone man struggling to get home" as well as the perspective of someone who's already home and has to fight to protect herself and her family. I really enjoy writing from dual points of view and this lets me do that while also exploring two totally different but complementary perspectives.

When I killed off Jack and Samantha so soon after introducing them, I was torn. They were characters I came up with on a whim and I didn't think much about them at first, but as I wrote their scenes I started to realize that I enjoyed them. They were a fun complement to each other and I sort of wanted them to travel with Jack as he goes on his journey home.

Sadly, though, that wasn't to be. Jack and Samantha's death is as brutal and sudden and meaningless as it is for a reason -- I wanted to show that in the world of Surviving the Fall things are harsh, unforgiving and brutal. I hope I hammered that point home when Rick was backed into a corner and killed the leader of the gang that was chasing him down. There will be more lows coming later in the series, but also a lot of highs, too. After all, what's a story about the end of the world without some hope and good shining through the thick tar coating of the bad?

I came up with the idea for Surviving the Fall at the same time as I came up with the idea for No Sanctuary, another series that's launching in May 2017. Because of my success with publishing Final Dawn a few years back as an episodic series, I wanted to make one of my new series episodic and one of them novel-length. Surviving the Fall is planned to be around 14 books in length while No Sanctuary will be around 7 books in length, with Surviving the Fall books releasing once every 2-3 weeks while NS books release once every 4-6 weeks.

This, I hope, will satisfy post-apocalyptic fans who like episodic series as well as those who like novel-length series. Whichever one you prefer, there's a great new story waiting for you that I really hope you enjoy. When both series conclude I'll of course be releasing them in a "box set" or "omnibus" format. I'm the kind of person who typically doesn't watch a TV series until it concludes and the entire series is available to binge watch, so if you read like that, just watch out for the omnibus at a later date :)

If you enjoyed this story and/or any of my other stories, you should really sign up for my newsletter. I send out quick messages a few times a month and I take a totally different approach to my newsletters than other authors. Where other authors see a newsletter as a selling tool first and foremost I see it as a way to connect with my readers first and foremost. I've met some terrific people (like my AWESOME beta readers) and really enjoy talking to folks who email me.

Don't like email newsletters? I also keep my Facebook page updated and you can message me through there as well if you prefer FB to email. Feel free to drop me a line via email/FB. I'd love to hear from you.

Catch you in the next book!

-Mike

Book 2 - The Gathering Storm

Preface

In the late morning hours on a particularly warm day in Autumn, the world as we know it came to a stop. Every internet-connected device was attacked with an intelligent, adaptive virus that not only caused the devices to stop functioning, but also turned many of them into weapons. Cars with advanced computer systems began leaking fuel which then caught fire thanks to the malfunction and shorting out of their control systems. Cellphone networks began to die and phones began overheating as their batteries were first shorted out and then detonated, turning them into miniature bombs. Aircraft, power plants, manufacturing facilities—anything that had a computer that could connect to the internet was vulnerable and those vulnerabilities were fully exploited.

As the effects of the mysterious disaster begin to take hold, Rick Waters has barely escaped from Los Angeles after a vicious street gang guns down two people he met in cold blood and then nearly kills him as well. Rick's goal? To make it back to his home in Virginia and reunite with his wife and three children.

Meanwhile, at their family homestead, Dianne Waters is grappling with her own set of problems. After watching her family car explode before her eyes, Dianne takes her children with her into the nearby small town in an old truck to visit the grocery store. What she finds is a full-on riot as people are fighting tooth and nail for any scrap they can get and she barely makes it back to their home after a run-in with a couple of miscreants trying to break into her vehicle.

Rick and Dianne have both seen the first stages of society's breakdown, but what they have yet to encounter will test them beyond their limits....

Chapter One

Somewhere between Los Angeles and Las Vegas

RICK WATERS HAD SLEPT in a car exactly twice before in his life. The first time was in the back of a camper van during an ill-advised trip to the beach that was cut short as three people caught a stomach bug. The second time was when he was so sleepy on a road trip that his body shut itself down for a few hours while his wife, Dianne, was driving them up north to visit her parents near D.C. In both cases the vehicles were relatively clean (at least at first, in the camper van scenario) and comfortable.

Sleeping in a car that smelled like a cross between body odor, cheap body spray and various pharmaceuticals was not, however, a pleasant experience. Nevertheless, though, Rick had been forced to crawl into the back seat of the SUV and sleep for a few hours after driving for the entire day. Although he was more alert when he woke up, he wondered if he would ever get the impossible combination of smells out of his clothing.

After leaving Los Angeles, Rick had taken a jaunt to the north until he reached interstate fifteen. From I-15 he planned to drive straight into Las Vegas where he hoped he could find more reliable and solid transportation back to Virginia. Despite what he had seen and heard so far, Rick wasn't convinced that there was no way to get back home without walking or driving.

There's got to be some planes left in the sky. Maybe military flights are still going in and out. I could go to Nellis, see if I can talk someone into letting me on board. Rick knew in the back of his mind that the idea was foolhardy, but he also figured that between Phoenix and Las Vegas, the latter would be more likely to have transportation available. *Big money still means something. Now all I need to do is figure out how to get myself included in whatever that something is.*

While he was driving along Rick was also playing with the radio constantly as he tried to get some sort of update on what was going on. Information was still hard to come by, though, and all he could pick up was static for most of the trip between Los Angeles and Las Vegas. With the gear he scavenged from the sporting goods store he avoided straying from the highway except when absolutely necessary due to blockages from destroyed vehicles. With enough food to last for a few days but no water, he knew he would need to find a source before continuing much farther—especially when the SUV started running low on fuel.

Salvation came in the form of a vending machine that he tipped over at a rest area along the highway. The reinforced plastic front didn't break from the impact but the lock at the back did, and he quickly stuffed as many bottles of water as he could into his backpack while throwing the rest into the back of the car.

With immediate food and water needs taken care of, Rick was feeling upbeat about his progress when the speakers in the car crackled to life and a long series of tones blared over the radio. After the tones finished, a mechanical-sounding voice came next with an announcement that was far too calm for the information it contained.

Attention. Attention. This is the Emergency Broadcast System. We have been informed that a massive cyber attack has taken place against civilian and military assets both in the United States and abroad. Details about the attack are not yet known. Civilians should shelter in place until further instructions are given by federal, state or local authorities. Under no circumstances should any vehicles attempt to be driven, nor should electronic devices be operated. Local law enforcement personnel should remain at their posts. State police and military assets have been directed to areas that are most impacted. More information to follow.

The same tones that came before the message repeated before the message played again. Rick turned down the volume on the radio and shook his head. "Well I guess it's real, huh?"

He drove along contemplating the possible sources of what had happened when he noticed that the wreckage of cars on the highway was starting to thin out. Vehicles that had formerly been in his way were pushed off to the side of the road leaving black scars across the road. They were piled up on both the shoulder to the right and in the leftmost lane, leaving two lanes open and clear for driving.

"What the…" Rick was confused by the sudden change when he realized that he had just crossed the California/Nevada border and was closing in on Las Vegas. "Did the state clear the vehicles off the road? Maybe for emergency services to get through… but still that would take some mammoth equipment working exceptionally quickly." Rick frowned. "It has to be the military doing it. But why?"

Rick's answer came twenty minutes after hitting the border, when he was halfway between Primm and Las Vegas. Large columns of red smoke soared into the sky on the road ahead of him. As he approached, he saw that there were several school buses lined up on the side of the road just on the outskirts of the town. Multiple military Humvees were arranged in front of the buses and there were a few dozen soldiers milling around along with several dozen people clothed in plain clothes.

As Rick approached, the soldiers nearest him on the road held up their hands and he saw a few others readying their weapons. He slowed the SUV and rolled down the windows, then stopped a few dozen feet from the blockade. Four soldiers approached him, two on each side of the car, and one on the driver's side shouted at him.

"Turn off your vehicle and step out of the car!"

Rick felt his heart racing in his chest as he turned off the ignition. There were no guns pointed directly at him that he could see, but he felt extremely nervous about the situation nonetheless.

"What's going on?" Rick asked as he stepped slowly out of the SUV.

The soldier stepped forward and eyed Rick up and down, visibly relaxing as he saw that Rick wasn't posing a threat. He glanced at the SUV and then raised a hand in the air as he shouted at the soldiers back at the blockade. "Older model! Not a threat!" The soldier then turned to Rick and addressed him.

"Sorry about this, sir. We're evacuating civilians from the city to Nellis."

"Why's that?"

The soldier shrugged. "It's orders for now, sir. Are you aware of what's going on?"

Rick chuckled. "Yeah you could say that. I barely made it out of Los Angeles with my life."

The soldier nodded sympathetically. "I understand, sir. Before we take you to Nellis you'll have to leave your car behind. Security reasons."

Rick sighed. "Yeah, that's fine. It's almost out of gas anyway."

"Do you have any weapons on you, sir? You'll need to discard those as well."

Rick hesitated, then glanced at his bags in the front seat of the SUV. "You guys are confiscating all weapons? Why?"

"Base rules, sir. If you're concerned about your safety I can assure you that you'll be fine."

"Ugh." Rick scratched his head. "I think I'd rather just continue on my own. I'm not trying to reach Las Vegas anyway. I'm trying to make it home to Virginia."

The soldier shook his head. "I'm afraid driving through is out of the question, sir."

"How come?"

"There's been some bad gang activity, sir. Orders are to not let any civilians through without loading them into the buses and providing an escort. If you're trying to get back home quickly, I can tell you that we're trying to get transport planes up and running to get civilians like yourself where they need to go."

"Really?" Rick nodded. "How long until the transports get moving?"

"Sorry, sir. I don't have that kind of info." The soldier's patience appeared to be wearing thin as he sighed and motioned at Rick's gear in the passenger seat of the SUV. "Come on, sir. Unless you want to turn around and head back to L.A. I suggest you grab your gear. We'll do a quick search then get you on the—wait... what the hell?"

The soldier stopped talking to Rick and stepped a few paces toward the rear of the SUV. He shouted at the other soldiers with him and they ran past Rick's SUV out on the road. One of them held up a bullhorn and shouted into it. "Stop your vehicle! Stop your vehicle now!"

Behind Rick, farther down the road, a car was blazing down the highway so fast and erratically that Rick was surprised they had managed to avoid flipping over. As the vehicle approached the blockade, Rick ran to the passenger side of his SUV and grabbed his bags before slipping away towards the horde of people clustered around the school buses. By the time he nearly got there, most of the soldiers were out on the road with their weapons raised as they shouted at each other about the car that was approaching.

The car initially seemed to slow down, but at the last second it made one last turn and veered off of the road and into the sand and scrub on the side. The vehicle lurched and flipped through the air sending pieces of plastic and glass flying everywhere. The soldiers scrambled to avoid the twisting mass of the car while shouting at the civilians standing near the buses.

"Get on now! Let's move! Get these people out of here!"

Rick jumped up through an open rear door on the back of the last bus in line and took a seat in the rear. He tucked the rifle case underneath his seat and turned around to watch out the back window. Flames were erupting from the overturned car as the soldiers ran back and forth with fire extinguishers, trying to put out the blaze and rescue whomever was in the car. Rick turned back and shook his head, wondering what on earth he had just gotten himself into.

Out of the frying pan, into the fire I guess.

Chapter Two

The Waters' Homestead
Ellisville, VA

DIANNE WAS NATURALLY AN EARLY RISER, but the morning following the "very bad day," as her daughter put it, was one on which she got up extra early. Before the sun had even cracked over the horizon she was puttering in the kitchen making coffee and setting out breakfast for when her three children got up. She went to the TV in the living room and switched it on, but there was nothing playing except for digital static. She set the TV to automatically switch channels every few seconds and started going through the house and taking notes on what appliances they would be able to run off of the solar panels and which ones they'd have to do without until the power grid was restored. *If it ever gets restored.*

Dianne sighed and tried to push such thoughts out of her head, but it was difficult given what she had seen and heard the day before. If things were really as bad as the newscasts predicted and what she saw in their small town the day before, she wasn't sure if power or normal life would be returning anytime soon.

As Dianne sat at the living room table drinking coffee and listening to the TV static from the other room she started making a mental list of the things she needed to do to get the house, the property, the children and herself ready for whatever might come next.

Living in the country for years had brought about certain benefits when it came to raising her children in terms of enabling them to be largely self-sufficient, at least when it came to Mark and Jacob. At thirteen and ten respectively they routinely carried out chores both inside and outside the house on the homestead and had been taught the basics of survival and preparedness. Much of the teaching had been theoretical rather than practical due to Rick's hectic schedule with his company, but Dianne felt confident that her children would be able to slip into their new roles and duties after a good nights' sleep.

The first task would be to take stock of all the animals and make sure they were fed and that their pens and any equipment associated with them was in good shape. "I'll get Mark and Jacob to take care of that, and Josie can stay with me here in the house." Dianne muttered to herself as she jotted down notes on a three by five card.

"Once we get a list of things that need fixing and take stock of everything here we'll go check on the neighbors. I hope Tina and Sarah's families are okay." The two closest neighbors to the Waters were a pair of older families that Rick and Dianne had met shortly after moving in. With as much emphasis as Dianne kept on the kids pursuing their education and Rick's work at his company they hadn't had time to make too many friends elsewhere except for the children and parents that Dianne, Mark, Jacob and Josie saw each week at the after-school programs.

"I sure hope they weren't traveling." Dianne shook her head, remembering how Tina and her husband liked to spontaneously go on trips cross-country. "Sarah and Jason should be home, though. We'll check on them first and see if they need anything." Sarah and Jason Statler were in their sixties and Dianne had helped them take care of their house and property two years prior when Jason nearly died from a heart attack.

"Once we check on them we need to get back here and start working on getting the solar panels switched on. Hm." Dianne tapped at her teeth with the pen and tried to remember how far Rick had gotten into the project. Both she and Rick had taken an online course in basic and intermediate electronic maintenance targeted towards owners of complex solar panel setups, but it had been a while since she read anything on the subject. "Gotta find my notes. It should come back to me. I hope."

Once the solar panels were hooked up they would need to ensure that only the more critical appliances were running off of the power since there was a somewhat limited battery supply in the basement.

Rick's work at his company afforded him the luxury to test some of their prototype products including advanced batteries designed for in-home usage for long-term storage of power generated from solar or other power sources. The "whole house" batteries wouldn't be able to power the entire house, but as long as she was able to get enough solar panels hooked up and working, she figured they could easily run the refrigerator, deep freezer and a few other devices like a window air conditioner, a few lights and even a space heater if required.

"Won't need the A/C for a while." Dianne crossed the item off her list and wrote in a note about splitting firewood in below it. The winter was forecast to be mild but she wasn't about to take chances when it came to the preparation.

Rick had purchased a bulk load of feed for the animals a month prior that would easily last for two years and Dianne felt confident that they were set in that department. As far as food for her and the children she knew from the prior day's quick stocktaking that they would be fine for around six months—maybe eight if she stretched it—which was good, but not good enough considering that they were at the end of the growing season.

A small cornfield, a patch of green beans, plenty of squash and other assorted odds and ends would add another month or two to the stockpile, but Dianne got the feeling that she needed to be thinking long term when it came to planning. With it already being mid-September, she didn't expect that they could grow anything else in the fields, but she started thinking about a project she and Rick had talked about a few years back.

Rick had always been a proponent of hydroponic gardening ever since he set up his first in their basement using a rubber tote container, an air pump, some grow lights and a few plastic nets and artificial dirt. The idea behind hydroponic gardening is that plants don't need soil to grow—they only need light, food and water. By allowing their roots to grow in water that's infused with nutrients and giving them plenty of light it's possible to grow a lot of plants in a very small amount of space pretty much anywhere.

Dianne remembered Rick talking about commercial vegetable growing operations in places like warehouses in Manhattan and how he wanted to try and replicate something similar in their house or out in the barns so that they could give the soil a year or two off. He had purchased all of the necessary equipment and supplies but had never pursued it beyond that due to a lack of time.

"If he's still got all the nutrients and everything out there I bet we can run the lights off the solar panels during the day and get a sizeable grow setup going in the basement." Dianne furiously wrote down as much as she could remember about what Rick had described and set the idea aside for later perusal.

By the time she got done planning a few more things to do for the day, the three children came stumbling down the stairs and into the kitchen. Mark, the oldest, was still half-asleep though Josie was bouncing off of the walls while Jacob tried not to be annoyed by how much energy she had. "Mom, when is she going to stop waking up so early?"

"NEVER!" Josie yelled at Jacob as she raced around the table and collided into Dianne who was wiping tears of laughter from her eyes.

"Sorry, Jacob. She's got a couple more years before she turns into the sleepy-headed monsters that are you and your brother."

"Ugh." Jacob's response was echoed by Mark though they soon perked up once they started eating. Halfway through their meal Dianne laid out the day's plans for them, adding on a few extra reminders at the end.

"Kids, I don't want you to worry or panic about what's going on. We're going to be just fine and your dad's going to be fine too, okay? I want you to remember, though, that there will be a lot of people who are really scared right now. They're scared, they don't know what to do and when they're like that they can do things that aren't so nice. We need to be extra careful and stick close to each other and watch out for each other. That means if we go out, we stick together and you guys do *exactly* what I tell you. And if we're at home and you see anyone around the house I want you to come running to find me even if you know the person, okay? Mark, I'll have more to talk about with you later, but for now you and Jacob need to get going and take care of your first assignments."

The two boys nodded and ran out the back door of the house down towards the animals, already fighting over which assignments they were going to take for themselves. Josie was still munching on her food when Dianne raised her eyebrows and spoke to her. "As for you, I want you sticking to my side like glue. Got it?"

Josie nodded and grinned. "Like glue on your butt, mom!"

Dianne rolled her eyes and snorted. "Gee, I wonder who taught you *that* one. Come on, kiddo; let's get the dishes done and then get the truck ready to go."

As Josie got changed and ready to go, Dianne went upstairs and unlocked the gun vault in the master bedroom and pulled out a pair of rifles and several magazines of ammunition. She looked at the smaller of the two rifles hesitantly, not wanting to do what she was planning, but knowing that given the circumstances she would need to, despite the dangers involved.

Chapter Three

L as Vegas, NV

RICK WATERS HAD NEVER BEEN to Las Vegas before, but he had read a few articles about it over the years that detailed the changes it had undergone. As the economy in the city shifted and the casinos began to see less and less business the famous strip had shrunk down to less than half of its size. The casinos and other companies that went out of business were demolished and turned into public parks as the city government tried to attract different types of tourists than those just looking to gamble their money away.

The lush green parks around the strip did their job though the increase in tourists never reached the levels it had been when the casinos were at their peak. The result was that, within ten years, the strip and the nearby University of Nevada were the only two places in the city that had any cash flowing to them. Most of the rest of the city devolved into low income areas dominated by gang activity and drug manufacturing, the latter of which helped to partially fuel the influx of tourists due to the state's lax new drug enforcement laws.

The end result of the changes was that the city became more like something out of a movie about a dystopian wasteland than an actual American city. Driving through the city—unless you were coming directly from the airport or going directly back—was heavily discouraged and would easily result in an armed holdup or worse.

As the train of six school buses passed through the city, Rick's nose was glued to the window as he watched the scenery pass by outside. If he hadn't known a bit about the city he would have thought that he had gone to sleep and awakened a month later due to how bad the place looked. *It's like the end of the world's already come for these people. Holy hell, how do they live like this? It looks like a favela in South America or something.*

A pair of Humvees drove ahead of the buses and a single Humvee brought up the rear. All three had fifty caliber machine guns mounted on top and gunners swiveled the weapons in all directions, looking for any potential incoming threats. The rear Humvee was directly behind the bus that Rick was in and every time the guns pointed in his direction he flinched, wondering if they would misfire and send a hailstorm of lead through the back of the bus.

With only a handful of people in the bus, Rick left his two bags near the back and walked up to the front. He clung to one of the railings near the front of the bus and spoke to the driver who was a young man dressed in a military uniform.

"Hey, how long will the ride through the city take?"

The soldier glanced over at Rick before replying. "About half an hour, sir. I'm going to have to ask you to stay behind the yellow line, though, and remain seated."

"Sure thing." Rick sat down in the front row, put his arms on the railing in front of him and rested his chin on his forearms. "How many people have you brought through to Nellis?"

The soldier glanced at Rick again to make sure he was following the previous request before responding. "This is our third run."

"Wow, that many already?"

"A lot of people have been coming out of the Los Angeles area."

"I'll bet. It was like a warzone there when I left. Can't believe how bad it's gotten."

The soldier snorted and shook his head. "It's worse in other places. It's all that damned virus."

Rick felt the hairs on the back of his neck stand on end and he leaned forward in his seat. "Virus? An infection?"

"No, no." The soldier laughed. "No zombies. I mean a computer virus. It was some kind of super virus. Wiped out the stock exchange, destroyed everyone's cars. I heard that a few nukes blew up in their bunkers, too. That might be just rumor, though."

"A computer virus did... all of this?" Rick shook his head. "That shouldn't be possible for a virus to cause this level of damage. These are all systems running on different platforms with different code bases... there's no way."

The soldier shrugged and continued talking, warming up to Rick the more he spoke. "I'm just telling you what I've heard. It doesn't seem possible to me, either, but that's what they've told us."

Rick was lost in thought and shook his head as he tried to wrap his mind around what the soldier was telling him. If it was true—and it was a big "if" in his opinion—then he was having a hard time imagining how such a virus could be created.

Rick was lost in his own thoughts when the bus lurched forward as the soldier hit the brakes. "What happened?" Rick barely caught himself from falling over and pulled himself up to his feet to see what was going on.

The soldier, meanwhile, was completely ignoring Rick and was instead speaking into a walkie-talkie he had pulled from his hip. "Three o'clock and nine o'clock? Roger that. We'll follow you through on route Golf. Out."

The buses ahead began turning off to the right, heading down a side street. Rick held on tightly to the railing in front of him as his bus did the same, and he questioned the soldier again. "What's going on? Are we in trouble?"

"Sir, I'm going to need you to return to your seat." The soldier's voice was rigid again and Rick sensed that their few moments of casual conversation were over.

"Sure thing. Sorry about that." Rick got up and walked to his seat in the back. The few people who were with him on the bus were all looking out the windows and their expressions ranged from exhaustion to fear. When Rick reached his seat the bus lurched again, taking a left down a side street without any warning. Rick was flung to the side and hit his head on the window before he managed to get back into his seat.

He gripped the metal bar on the seat in front of him as he glanced at his bags. Everything was still there aside from a few bottles of water that he had been forced to leave behind in the SUV, though he was worried about the rifle and shotgun in the gun case. The pistol he figured he could hide at the bottom of his backpack, but the long guns would be tough to get into the military base.

"Not that I really want to, mind you." Rick mumbled to himself as he dug through his backpack and stuffed the pistol down inside. He had just finished sealing the bag again when the bus swung to the right, and the soldier driving the vehicle shouted from the front.

"Everyone, please get down onto the floor!" Gunfire from outside the vehicle punctuated the soldier's words and everyone on the bus except Rick obeyed, ducking down onto the floor in front of their seats. Rick, on the other hand, kept turning his head around, trying to identify the source of the gunfire. As he did so he swung the backpack onto his back and strapped it on. He pulled the gun case onto his lap afterwards and checked to make sure that the hunting rifle was loaded.

Another turn and the gun case nearly slipped out of Rick's hands, but he caught it before it hit the floor. Outside, behind the bus, the Humvee driving behind them swiveled its mounted machine gun off to the side and fired a burst at the edge of a building. Brick and mortar turned to dust as the bullets tore apart the building's façade, though Rick couldn't make out who or what they were firing at.

"Get your heads down!" The soldier screamed again and the bus lurched one more time. Instead of steadying and straightening out, though, it continued tipping over to the side. Screams came from the other passengers in the bus as it tipped over, slammed into the ground and proceeded to roll two full times. Rick did his best to hold on to the back of the seat in front of him but without any sort of a seatbelt in place there was little he could do to keep from tumbling along with the bus.

Rick yelped in pain as his chest, legs and arms hit the floor, side, ceiling and seats in the bus as it rolled. His backpack took the brunt of the abuse though, and he could hear the cracking and snapping of the food and water bottles as they broke open. The gun case slipped out of his hand on the last roll and went skidding down the bus which came to rest on its side.

Groans of pain came from down the length of the bus as Rick tried to pull himself up onto his hands and knees. Pain shot through both of his palms as he pressed them against the glass and twisted metal below him and he quickly stood to his feet. Pain shot through his chest and back as he stood, making him instantly regret the movement, and he doubled over, grabbing onto one of the seats next to him for support.

"Help…" The voice from behind Rick was soft and full of agony. He turned to see the soldier trying to pull himself along through the broken glass. Blood poured from wounds on his face and neck, and though Rick was no doctor he could see that the soldier was in rough shape. He hobbled along through the bus, cringing as he passed two of the other passengers whose necks were twisted into odd positions. When he reached the soldier he helped the man to his knees and looked him over.

"Where does it hurt?" Rick pulled off his backpack and dug through it. Pain lanced through his hands from cuts he suffered and blood stained the clothing and supplies, but he pushed through and grabbed a first aid kit. He had just pulled it out of his backpack when the sound of gunfire came from outside the bus. He instinctively ducked down, pushing the soldier backwards and falling on top of him.

"Where are you hurt?" Rick whispered to the man as the gunfire raged outside the bus. The soldier's lips were white and his face pale. Though there was a lot of blood on his face and chest, Rick didn't see any obvious arterial damage until he glanced down at the man's pants. A jagged piece of metal broken off of the steering column of the bus was embedded in the man's inner thigh and his entire pant leg was soaked with blood.

"Oh shit!" Rick fumbled with the first aid kit, his fingers bloody and slipping against the clasp. "Come on, dammit!" Gunfire continued to echo outside the bus from multiple directions as Rick pulled out a wad of gauze from the first aid kit and prepared to try and stop the bleeding.

"Get… moving." The soldier grabbed Rick's jacket and pulled him close. "Nellis is…northeast. Stay off… the strip."

The soldier's breath became rapid and Rick froze with the gauze in one hand, watching as the soldier's life slipped away and he fell backwards, his body landing with a thud against the side of the bus.

"Is he dead?" A woman crawling out of the corner where she was lodged spoke softly as she watched Rick and the soldier. Rick turned and got up, stuffing the gauze and first aid kit back into his backpack. He held out a hand and helped the woman up before looking her over from head to toe for any obvious signs of injury.

"I think so. Are you okay, though?"

The woman felt her body, wincing as she pushed on her stomach. "It hurts some here. I hit the back of the seats pretty hard but I think I'm okay." The woman pulled up her shirt and Rick could see the bruising already starting to appear on her abdomen. It was bad enough that Rick suspected she had suffered some internal bleeding, but it was impossible for him to know how bad it was.

"I think you'll be fine." Rick was lying through his teeth but he didn't want to worry the woman. He was about to suggest that she stay still in the bus while he went out to look for help when a hailstorm of bullets tore through the bus, filling the interior with streams of light.

"What was that?" The woman's eyes were wide and she clung to Rick's arm, trying to get away from where the bullets had entered the bus.

"We need to get out of here right now!" Rick grabbed his backpack and put it on, then laboriously worked his way to the back of the bus and away from where the gunfire was coming from. As he went along he checked under every seat until, finally, he spotted what he was looking for. "There you are!" Rick leaned down and stretched, feeling the pain in his shoulder and upper arm as he grabbed his gun case and pulled it out from behind a seat where one of the straps was caught.

"Come on." Rick looked back at the woman who was caught between looking at the bullet holes and the body of one of the other passengers who had died in the impact. "Come on, leave them. They're already gone. We need to go. Maybe one of the Humvees is out there, or one of the buses."

The woman didn't respond until Rick tapped her on the shoulder. She turned and looked at him with wide, terrified eyes and nodded slowly. Rick grabbed her hand and pulled her to the back of the bus as another burst of gunfire echoed from near the front of the bus. "I'm going to open the back door, then as soon as we get out we need to find some cover, okay?"

The woman nodded again. "Okay." She whispered in response, her voice cracking as she struggled to cope with what was happening.

Rick turned the handle to the back of the bus and steeled himself for whatever was waiting outside. "Ready?" He whispered to the woman and held on to her hand. She nodded and he started his countdown.

"Three... two... one..."

Chapter Four

The Waters' Homestead
Ellisville, VA

"JACOB, help your sister get in the car, okay?"

"Yes, ma'am. Wait... is that rifle for Mark?"

Dianne sighed as she looked at the gun in her left hand. Jacob had always been jealous that Mark was the first to learn how to shoot and she worried about Jacob's overenthusiasm about weapons whenever they were out. "Sure is, kiddo. I'll make sure you get a turn at some practice shooting in the next couple of days. Right now, though, this isn't practice."

"Is Mark gonna kill somebody?"

"No. I just need him to help protect us. With your dad gone on his trip and all of this crazy stuff going on all of you kids are having to pitch in more than ever. For you, that means I need your help with your sister and taking care of our animals. For Mark, that means today I need him to be like a grownup and help me out with some stuff." Dianne smiled and ruffled Jacob's hair. "You'll be there before you know it, buddy. But please trust me —everything I'm asking you to do is stuff that we *need* done. Okay?"

"Yeah, I guess." Jacob crinkled his nose. "As long as you remember that I'm a better shot. Dad even said so."

Dianne smiled and whispered conspiratorially. "Darned straight you are. Now hurry up and help your sister, okay?"

Dianne watched from the front porch as Jacob and Josie got into the rear seats of the truck. Mark came out of the house behind her, keys in hand, and held them out. "Here you go. Everything's locked up and double-checked."

"Thanks, buddy. Hey." Dianne put her hand on Mark's shoulder before he could walk out to the car and lowered her voice. "You remember the four rules of gun safety, right?"

Mark nodded. "Yeah… it's always loaded, don't point it at anything you don't want to destroy, finger off the trigger till you're ready to fire and be aware of your target and anything behind it. Why?"

Dianne nodded proudly and held out the shorter of the two rifles. "I need you to help me out while your dad's away. Keep this unloaded at all times and make sure the safety's on. I'd like you to keep it tucked away in the back of the truck along with a couple magazines of ammunition. If I need your help with shooting something I'll let you know and then I want you to do everything you can to help, okay?"

"Is everything okay, mom?"

Dianne nodded. "I think so. I want you to understand how serious this is, though. This isn't a game. Your sister doesn't really get what's going on and your brother understands to some degree, but right now you're the man of the house and I know you understand how bad things are. Keep your eyes open and remember what we taught you. Got it?"

Dianne felt terrible about talking to her son like she was. She felt as though she was pulling away precious moments of his childhood innocence, but she dearly hoped that her talk with him was the only thing that would have to take place. If situations worsened, though, she knew that he would step up and be there to help—though she hoped and prayed that wouldn't happen.

"Yeah, I got it. You want me to put it in the truck now?"

"Yep, thanks. Here're the mags."

Mark took the rifle and ammunition and piled them carefully in a narrow box bolted in the back of the truck. As he did that, Dianne quickly double checked her rifle and tucked two magazines into the vest she was wearing. She slapped one into the rifle but didn't pull the bolt back, prefer-ring to keep a round out of the chamber for the time being.

We're just going to check on the neighbors. Not to war. Repeating the facts of the situation didn't seem to help and she found herself continuing to worry as she got into the car and glanced back to check on Jacob and Josie.

"Everybody buckled?"

"Good to go, mom."

Dianne glanced at Mark before starting the truck up. "Let's go see if the Statlers are home. Then we'll check and see if the Carsons are there."

The truck started without a hitch and Dianne threw it into gear and began the slow, plodding ride down the driveway and onto the road. Instead of turning right towards Ellisville, though, she turned left and headed farther into the woods and fields of southern Virginia. The thick walls and roof of trees suddenly gave way to a burst of sunlight as the wooded area abruptly ended and wide fields stretched for a good half mile in either direction of the road. Off in the distance, to the left, was the home of Tina and Dave Carson. Ten minutes later, on the right side of the road, Dianne pulled off onto a gravel drive that stretched through field and then through woods as it approached the home of Sarah and Jason Statler.

Sarah and Jason liked to stay close to home just like Dianne did, and though the two families only visited in person occasionally, Dianne and Sarah spoke on the phone nearly every other day. Despite their age and Jason's health, he and Sarah both were aggressive in their work on their land and had some sort of project going on all the time. It was for that particular reason that, as Dianne pulled up to the house and slowed to a stop, she frowned at the lack of apparent activity going on.

"Huh. Usually they're outside working. Did you boys see them when we were driving up?"

Mark shook his head. "No... I saw one of their tractors parked outside the barn but that was it."

"Hm." Dianne furrowed her brow. "All right, let's go see if they're home. Jacob, I want you and Josie to stay right next to each other and follow me. Mark, hang by the truck and if you see anyone give a shout and come running for us, got it?"

Mark nodded and clambered out of the truck with Josie and Jacob following. Dianne grabbed her rifle, stepped out and headed for the front door of the house with Jacob and Josie behind her. She rapped on the front door several times and rang the doorbell twice, then slung the rifle across her back and waited on the porch for an answer.

When none came after a few minutes of waiting, Dianne motioned to Jacob and Josie. "Hang out at the truck with your brother, you two. I'm going to check out back."

Dianne headed around the side of the house to the back and opened the screen door that led onto the large enclosed patio off of the back of the house. The area was open to the air but entirely enclosed with a roof and screen walls, making it the perfect place to sit in the evenings without having to worry about insects getting in.

After rapping on the first set of sliding glass doors and receiving no response, Dianne headed to the other side of the patio and was about to knock on those when she saw a sheet of paper taped to the inside of the glass door.

Dianne/Tina/Judith/Rachel – If any of you stop by, we've gone away for a few days. We'll be back by the weekend, though. If you need us for anything just call us on our mobile phone.

-Sarah & Jason

"Great." Dianne mumbled to herself. "Why on earth did they go out of town?" She shook her head and sighed before heading back around to the front of the house. Josie was sitting down on the rocks in front of the truck playing while Mark and Jacob were leaning up against the side talking when Dianne walked up to them.

"Nobody's home."

"Where did they go?" Mark asked.

Dianne shrugged. "There was a note on the back porch saying they left for a few days. Hopefully they make it back soon, but if they flew anywhere…"

"They might be dead?" Jacob was at that stage in his life where morbid and taboo topics were ones he wanted to discuss more than anything else.

Dianne sighed and shook her head, not wanting to either encourage or antagonize him too much since a neutral approach was usually the one required to get him onto another subject. "No, I'm sure they're fine. It is odd that they would go away without letting anyone know. Maybe if Tina and Dave are home they'll have some more info about it. Let's go check on them."

"What about the animals?" Josie looked up at Dianne from her play at the front of the truck.

"Hey. Good question, kiddo. Let's go take a look. Mark, can you run on ahead and see if they're loose or if Sarah penned them before they left?"

Sarah and Jason hadn't pursued the self-sufficiency and prepper lifestyle as much as Rick and Dianne, but thanks to Dianne's constant encouragement Sarah had eventually persuaded Jason to buy a flock of chickens and start on a small vegetable garden. It wasn't much, but it was enough that Dianne was suddenly worried about what might happen to the chickens if Sarah and Jason had left in a hurry.

As Dianne, Jacob and Josie walked back along a dirt path toward the barn and fenced-in area where the chickens were kept, Mark came racing back toward them.

"They're all locked up inside and the automatic feeder's full."

"Is the outside pen connected to the barn so they can get some sunlight?"

Mark shook his head. "No, they're all inside."

"All right. Let's get the pen dragged over to the side of the barn and hook it up so they can get some fresh air. I'll start on that while you check and make sure the automatic water trough is working."

"What about the garden?" Josie tugged on Dianne's shirt as she trailed along behind.

"That'll be fine until the Statlers get back, sweetie. Right now let's just make sure the chickens are fine and then we'll go check on Mr. and Mrs. Carson."

Josie nodded and ran on ahead after Jacob and Mark. With the clear autumn sky overhead Dianne could almost forget what had transpired over the last couple of days if not for the steady *thunk* of the rifle on her back as she walked along. There was no sign of smoke in the sky, though she wondered if that was simply because they were too far removed from a major city to see any.

Though she had a brief reprieve from her thoughts of Rick for the last few minutes, she once again wondered where he was and if he was still okay. She knew without question that he was working tirelessly to get back to Virginia, but whether or not he was in a position to be doing that was another matter.

"Water's working fine, mom." Mark walked out the front of the barn and wrung out his shirt with a disgruntled look on his face. Dianne laughed at the sight and gave him a smile. "Thanks, bud. Help me get this pen pulled around, will you?"

Mark and Dianne walked to the back of the barn where a ten foot by fifteen foot section of chicken wire caging was sitting atop large rubber wheels. The contraption had been thought of by Rick and built by him and Jason after Sarah had mentioned that they needed a way to get the chickens outside without her or Jason having to run around after them. Rick's solution was to cut a small hole in the side of the barn where the chickens roosted at night and build a fully enclosed cage that could be rolled up to the hole and secured with steel pins to keep it in place. The wheels of the contraption could then be popped off and the cage would sit on the ground, allowing the chickens to get out into the grass without having to worry about them wandering off or being attacked by predators.

Once Dianne and Mark pulled the cage into place and set it up, she called out to Jacob who was inside the barn with Josie playing with the chickens. "Jacob! Pull the door open so these guys can get outside, okay?"

There was a muffled squawk as the one of the chickens got in Jacob's way and then the door opened inward. An explosion of feathers poured out as the chickens fought to squeeze through the narrow opening and get outside. Dianne watched them for a moment before making her way inside to verify that everything was set up properly.

Jacob and Josie were both playing with the chickens inside the barn and Josie held up a chick and squealed with delight. "The eggs hatched! See! He's so cute! Can't we take him home?"

Dianne knelt down with a grin and examined the chick. "Sorry, sweetie, but these are Mrs. Statler's chickens."

"But what if they don't come back? Can we keep them then?"

Dianne felt her gut wrench as she thought about the possibility of Rick not coming back, but forced a smile anyway. "Sure, kiddo. If they're not back soon then we'll have to come pick these guys up and keep them at our place until they get back. But I'm sure they'll be back soon."

Dianne looked at the automatic feeder and the water trough and nodded. "All right, looks like everything's set here. We'll come back and check on them in a few days." Dianne looked at her watch and tapped it. "Come on, we need to get going to check on the Carsons."

After closing the front door to the barn and checking that the cage was secured one last time, Dianne and her children headed back to the truck. "Hands." Dianne intoned, mostly for Josie's benefit, as she had to do every time they finished playing or working with their animals. All three of them quickly coated their hands in alcohol-based sanitizer from a bottle in the front console in the truck as they were climbing in.

As they pulled back onto the road and took a left back towards their home and the Carson's home, Dianne saw that the previously-unmarred sky was now tainted with a thick column of black smoke. While the source of the smoke was initially hard to see, once they got onto the Carson's driveway it became obvious.

"Mom... is that..."

"Hold on, kids!" Dianne mashed down on the accelerator and sent the old truck lurching forward down the bumpy dirt road. As they reached the end of the driveway Dianne hit the brakes and the truck slid forward several feet before coming to a stop. Dianne, Mark, Jacob and Josie all stared in horror at the sight before them.

Chapter Five

L as Vegas, NV

"GO!" Rick spat out the last word and threw himself against the back door of the bus. He expected it to be damaged enough to require a substantial amount of force to open and was surprised when he nearly fell out as it opened smoothly and easily. Outside, the midday sun beat down on the street and the air was hot and dry. Dust swirled around the bus and the stench of gunpowder filled his nostrils.

Boom! Boom! Boom!

The sound of heavy machine gun fire from farther down the street where the bus had been heading made Rick turn to try and locate the source. Behind him the woman from the bus finished stepping out and clung to his arm again. "Where do we go?"

Rick held up his hand as he peeked around one side of the bus and then the other. There was no sign of any of the shooters so he began looking for a building that they could hide in. "There!" Rick pointed at a building down the street with a large overhang and wide glass front doors that were shattered. "Wait a second, first. Hold this!" He handed his gun bag to the woman and unzipped it as she clung to the handles. He pulled out the shotgun and zipped the bag back up before looping the bag around his back. It stuck out like a sore thumb thanks to the thickness of his backpack but it enabled him to shoulder the shotgun which he did before looking at the woman.

"Follow right behind me, okay?" The woman stared at the gun in his hands like she hand never seen one before and nodded slowly. Rick began moving forward quickly, staying as close to the building's wall as possible as he moved along. He continually scanned the area in front of him, behind him and to the side, looking for any signs of movement. Another burst of gunfire down the street made him stop and duck behind a large planter on the sidewalk.

The sounds were farther down the street than they had been before and Rick realized that the fight must have continued down the road. "I guess their convoy moved on. Why the hell would they leave us behind?" Rick shook his head and glanced at the woman who was crouched next to him. "Let's run and get inside that building, okay?"

She nodded and Rick stood up and began running with her close behind. With the blood pumping through his veins and the shotgun in his hand he was beginning to remember some of the years-old self defense and tactical shooting classes he had taken with Dianne long ago. The lessons were simple but the practice had been hard for him to maintain due to his work schedule and he had eventually dropped out, leaving Dianne to finish up. *I'm glad she finished.* The thought of his wife brought a surge of nausea to his stomach and he tried to push the thought from his mind. *Need to survive. Just have to survive for now. Can't help them if I'm dead.*

Rick and the woman made it to the building he had pointed out from the bus and they ducked inside the lobby. It was an office building of some type judging by the décor and layout, though that mattered little to Rick. The only thing he was concerned about was getting off of the street and making sure both he and the woman from the bus were safe.

"Come on, over here." Rick spoke quietly to the woman as he guided her into a chair. "Let me look at your stomach again." The woman lifted up her shirt and Rick gulped as he saw that the bruising was even worse than it looked. "What's your name?" He helped her put her shirt back down before taking off his backpack and gun case.

"Jane." The woman's eyes were still wide and she kept looking around the lobby of the building nervously.

"Nice to meet you, Jane. I'm Rick." Rick dug through his backpack, pulling out wet clothing and supplies until he found a water bottle that was undamaged. "Here, drink this." Jane accepted the water bottle gratefully and took several large gulps before handing it back to Rick.

"Thanks. Where are we?" The look in Jane's eyes made Rick wonder if she was suffering from shock and he then wondered if he was suffering from it as well. His whole body was shaking and he could feel his heart still racing. He closed his eyes and sat down on the floor, taking several deep breaths to calm his nerves before replying.

"I don't know. I'm not even sure where we're at in the city." More gunfire came from down the street as he spoke, though it was far enough away that he didn't jump at the sound. "Are you from Vegas, Jane?"

She shook her head. "No... I've never been here before."

"Hm." Rick pursed his lips. "That makes two of us. If we had a map that'd be extremely helpful. I guess at this point we just have to rely on a compass."

"Where are you going?" A look of concern flashed across Jane's face as Rick started picking through the supplies in his backpack and on the floor, looking for a compass he knew he stuffed inside when he was at the sporting goods store.

"*We* are going to get to the Nellis air base on the Northeast side of the city. I won't leave you behind, especially with how injured you look." *Ha!* Rick grabbed the compass out of the backpack and stuffed it in his pocket. *Here we go!*

"What about all the gunfire out there?"

Rick shook his head. "I wish I knew what was going on. The soldier in the bus said there's been a lot of gang activity. I didn't expect a warzone after only a couple of days, though. Especially in a city this size. Where are you from, anyway?"

Jane was staring off into the distance again and he had to repeat his question before she answered. "I was... visiting L.A. Everybody said to get out of the city so I just started driving east."

"You got anyplace in particular you're trying to get to?"

Jane shook her head at first before nodding slowly. "Colorado. I flew in from Colorado. Wait... my rental car! I left it behind!"

Rick raised an eyebrow as Jane's mutterings became less coherent. "Take it easy, okay? Don't worry about your car or anything else. Just sit there and take it easy. I'm going to see what's going on outside and see if we can get going to Nellis soon, okay?"

Jane nodded but Rick could tell she was barely paying attention to him. He sat his backpack on a chair down from her and put the gun case with the rifle inside of it over his back, picked up his shotgun from the floor and moved toward the front of the building. The sun was still high in the sky and the heat showed no signs of letting up as he scanned the street up and down in front of the building. *So much for that fall weather, huh? Who builds a city in the middle of the desert like this. I mean come on already.*

Rick sighed and headed back inside the building and grabbed his backpack. The jacket he had been wearing went into his backpack and he pulled out one of his last remaining bottles of water and a couple of energy bars. "It looks clear out there. We should get moving and see if we can find the convoy or something. We can at least get moving towards the air base and hopefully get there by tonight or tomorrow."

Jane nodded and stood up slowly, holding her stomach as she walked towards the entrance to the building. "Here." Rick held out one of the energy bars and Jane accepted it gratefully. "Try to take it slow there, okay? No telling how beat up you are inside."

As Jane ate the energy bar, Rick stepped out of the building and into the hot sun. The variation in temperatures—down into the forties the previous night and what felt like the nineties or hundreds in the Vegas sun—turned his stomach. "If you're ready," he said as he put his pack back on, "then we should get going."

Jane nodded and followed Rick out of the building and they started down the street, heading in the general direction of both the convoy and the gunshots from earlier. The shots had died down and Rick hadn't heard any more in the last few minutes, though he was still wary as they walked down the street. "I really wish we had a map. I think we came in at the south or southwest side of the city, though, so as long as we keep heading northeast I would think we'll see signs for Nellis at some point soon."

Rick stayed close to the buildings on their side of the street as he and Jane went along. He kept his walking speed slow, both for his sake and hers. As his adrenaline from running into the building and away from the gunfire started to dissipate he realized that his hands were still hurting. He looked at one of them and grimaced at the myriad of small cuts in it as well as the bits of metal and rock that had been ground into the skin. *Probably should have cleaned that up when we were back there.* Rick sighed and tried to ignore the pain in his hands as he adjusted his grip on the shotgun.

After half an hour of walking passed, Rick finally saw a street sign that indicated they were on the right path. "Hey!" Rick turned to Jane and pointed at the sign. "Nellis is only fifteen miles away. We can make that by tonight if we hurry."

Jane tried to put on a smile but the pain in her eyes was immediately obvious to Rick. "Are you okay?" She put her hand out on the building next to them to prop herself up, but she began to sink down as her knees started to buckle.

"Jane?" Rick ran back to her and grabbed her, then looked for a place where they could rest. A sign across the street caught his eye and he started walking towards it while supporting her on his shoulder. "A lumber yard? I guess it's better than nothing."

Chapter Six

E llisville, VA

THE ENTIRE TWO-STORY house was engulfed in flames that licked toward the sky as they sent torrents of grey and black clouds billowing upward. The conflagration was so intense that Dianne had to back the truck up and park off the side of the driveway before stepping out for fear of the intense heat.

"Jacob, Josie—I want you two in the truck. Mark, you get in the back and get the rifle. Don't load it, just sit in the back with it, okay?"

Mark nodded and jumped out and into the back of the truck. Dianne got out and held her rifle in both hands, her eyes scanning the fields and tree line around the house in search for what could have started the blaze. It had only taken them around thirty minutes to visit the Statler's house and in that time she found it hard to imagine what could have caused the Carson's house to erupt into an inferno.

"Had to have been someone out here." Dianne whispered to herself as she crouched next to the truck. Inside, Jacob and Josie had climbed into the front passenger seat where they were squished together watching the house burn with slack-jawed expressions.

"Kids," Dianne said, keeping her voice low. "Back in your seats now. Mark, stow the rifle and get back in the front. We're getting home right now."

After her children were in their seats, Dianne got back into the driver's seat and started up the truck. She backed down the driveway quickly, wanting to get away from the house as quickly as possible. The nervous feeling that was gnawing at the back of her mind when they pulled up had erupted into full-blown fear as she thought about the implications of the house going up in flames so quickly.

"Mom, what about Mrs. Carson? Shouldn't we check on her and Mr. Carson?" Jacob piped up from the back seat. "Or do you think they were inside the house?"

"I don't think so, bud." The truck skidded as Dianne pulled out onto the road and she threw it into drive. "The Carsons like to go on trips a lot so I bet they weren't even home."

"Their house was fine when we drove by earlier." Mark kept his nose pressed up against the window watching behind them as they hurtled down the road back towards their home. "What happened to it?"

"I don't know. But I don't think it just randomly caught fire and went up like that so quickly. We were only at the Statler's place for half an hour. Somebody had to have set the house on fire."

"Was it an accident, do you think?"

Dianne shrugged. "No idea. But I don't want to take any chances. As soon as we get home I'm going to check our house out to make sure everything's safe inside. I want you three inside once I'm done. Mark, I'm putting you in charge of keeping everyone safe until I get back. Take the rifle and keep a lookout, got it?"

Mark nodded. "Where are you going?"

Dianne chewed on her lip as she zig-zagged along the road, trying to hit as few potholes as possible. "We're back in the woods far enough that I don't think anyone will be coming out here. The Carson's house was pretty close to the road, so if somebody was trying to break in or do... I don't know, whatever they were doing, it was a pretty easy target. I want to check out all the buildings and make sure we start locking them anytime we're not actively outside and using them. At least for the next few days or until we find out more about what's going on."

Mark, Jacob and Josie stayed quiet as Dianne drove the rest of the way home. She, meanwhile, spent the whole way home thinking about how she was going to clear the house, barns and outbuildings. She and Rick had spent a few weeks years ago taking intensive home self-defense classes that included instructions from former Marines and special forces operatives as part of their survival and preparedness mindset. It had been long enough that she had forgotten a few of the details, but the general principles were still firmly lodged in her mind.

Clearing a house with only one person was ill advised, but despite Mark's knowledge and handiness with firearms she wasn't willing to expose him or his siblings to any potential dangers inside. After unlocking and relocking the gate on the driveway, Dianne stopped the car short of the house by a good fifty feet and turned off the engine. She then hopped out, grabbed the rifle and magazines from the back of the truck and passed them to Mark who had followed her around.

"Remember what we taught you, kiddo. And if you hear shots, I want you to take your brother and sister off to your fort in the woods, okay? Don't come up to the house until you get an all-clear signal from me. Got it?"

Dianne could see the nervousness written on Mark's face as she gave him his instructions, but he nodded obediently and took the rifle. "Yes, ma'am. Got it."

Dianne nodded and took off toward the house, keeping to the tree line as far as she could before making a break for the back door. She peeked through the window before unlocking and entering through the back, confirming that the living room was empty. Everything appeared to be untouched and she proceeded from the living room into the kitchen, taking fast but deliberate steps along the way.

Each corner she approached was quickly scanned with her eyes and the barrel of the rifle, her finger resting on the trigger guard and her thumb on a small switch that would engage the flashlight attached to the rail. After the kitchen was cleared she moved through the rest of the rooms on the ground floor, finding no signs of disturbance nor any indication that anyone had broken in. The doors were all secured, the windows were still locked and nothing had been moved or touched.

With all appearances pointing to the house being secure, Dianne relaxed substantially, but still proceeded upstairs and cleared each of the bedrooms and bathrooms before heading back downstairs and going through the basement. She was still on alert, but after double checking every room she finally felt comfortable with declaring the house secure.

After unlocking the front door and stepping out onto the front porch, Dianne looked out at the truck and saw Mark, Jacob and Josie staring back at her expectantly. She gave Mark a thumbs up and jogged out to meet the children as they all got out of the truck and started walking toward the house.

"Jacob and Josie, I want you two upstairs in Mark's room until I get back. Mark, stay upstairs next to a window and make sure it's open. If you hear any vehicles or strange voices outside I want you back in your room with them. Lock the door and do what we taught you, okay?"

Mark nodded and the three children raced inside and up the stairs. Dianne went in after them and locked the front door, then went out the back door and locked it after her. Clearing the house was merely the first step in ensuring that no one was on their property, and she still had quite a bit more work to do. The fact that the house was safe was a big relief, though as she headed down toward the lake and barns with her rifle at the ready, she couldn't shake the image of the Carson's burning house from her mind.

Chapter Seven

L as Vegas, NV

THE SUN HAD NEARLY SET in the sky by the time Jane regained consciousness. She had passed out just as Rick brought her inside the lumberyard and found a few cushions from lawn furniture to lay her on. Her skin was flushed and she felt hot to the touch, and Rick figured that the combination of her injury and them walking in the hot sun for so long had caused her to suffer from heat exhaustion or heatstroke.

"Should've paid more attention in that emergency training course." Rick mumbled to himself as he poured more water onto a rag and dabbed it across Jane's face. He had thought more than once about what the extra time delay might mean in terms of getting safely through the city and to the Air Force base, but he wasn't about to leave Jane behind, especially after what had happened to Jack and Samantha.

"You did a good job." The faintly spoken words surprised Rick and he glanced up at Jane to see her eyes open.

"Hey! You're awake!"

Jane smiled weakly and nodded. "Thank you."

"No problem. By the way, you should probably stay still and keep resting. I think we need to stay here for the night. I don't like the look and sound of the city right now and you're in no condition to travel."

"What's going on?"

Rick stood up and walked past an overturned vending machine from which he had procured several more bottles of water and looked out of a window. "Scattered gunfire, a lot of yelling and a few cars went by."

"Did you see the buses or the soldiers?"

Rick sighed. "Nope. Not so much as a sign of them."

Jane groaned and Rick turned before running back to her as she tried to sit up. "Hey, you need to take it easy."

"I want to sit up."

"Okay, okay. Hang on." Rick grabbed a few more cushions and stuffed them between Jane and the wall behind her to prop her up in a sitting position. "That better?"

Jane nodded. "My stomach hurts, though." Rick lifted her shirt a few inches and nodded. "Yeah, I was looking at the bruising earlier. You probably have some internal bleeding. I don't know what I can do for you except tell you to keep still for at least tonight. We'll see how you're feeling in the morning, okay?"

Jane nodded and closed her eyes as she leaned her head back against the cushion behind her. "That sounds good. Then tomorrow we can get to that base and we can both get home."

"Yeah." Rick forced a smile as he watched Jane wriggle on the pile of cushions, trying to get comfortable. "I sure hope so." After watching Jane for a few more minutes until he was sure she was back asleep, Rick stood up and walked back to the window.

"How the hell did I get myself into this mess?" He mumbled to himself again as he watched the rapidly waning sun. The natural sunlight would normally have been replaced by innumerable artificial lights from Sin City, but the only source of lighting he could see were the flickering twinkles of distant fires. Gunfire and screaming echoed from some far-off portion of the city and he turned to look at the room he had chosen for them to hole up in for the night.

The lumberyard was the type that was mostly outdoors with only a large roof to provide shade and minimal weather protection. The building attached to the roofed area, however, was fully enclosed and consisted of a sales floor, small warehouse, a few offices and a break room. The break room was where Rick had placed Jane before dropping everything except his shotgun and racing onto the sales floor. There he had grabbed the cushions off of several lawn chairs and brought them back to the break room where he arranged a bed for Jane to lay on.

After breaking the plastic on one of the vending machines and tipping the other one over to open it from the back, Rick had pulled out all of the food and drink from both. He then proceeded to use a roll of paper towels and a few bottles of water to make wet rags that he draped on Jane's forehead, arms and legs to try and cool her down. As she had drifted in and out of consciousness he had forced her to drink as much water as he could, though he only managed to get a bottle of it into her.

As he stood with his back to the window watching Jane's slow but steady breathing he realized that they would need a source of light in the next half hour before things got too dark. "Crap." He had a flashlight in his bag but didn't want to use it unless absolutely necessary and decided to see what the building had to offer instead. Rick headed back out onto the sales floor and scoured the place, eventually finding a pair of small battery-powered lanterns on a shelf behind one of the sales counters. He brought them back to the break room and set one on one of the tables before turning it on and stashing the second away in his backpack. The glow wasn't enough to fill the entire room but it was bright enough that Rick could walk around without tripping on anything.

Don't want it too bright anyway. Last thing we need to do is attract attention. He arranged a few more cushions on the opposite side of the room from Jane before checking on her again. *Temperature's going down. Good. Maybe she'll feel better in the morning.*

Chapter Eight

E llisville, VA

AFTER THIRTY MINUTES of careful searching, Dianne sat down on a stump just outside the last outbuilding and breathed an enormous sigh. Her search had been fruitless, and for that she was exceptionally grateful. Not only were there no signs of anyone inside any of the buildings, there were no signs that anyone had been in them except for her and the kids. Not wanting to leave anything to chance, though, Dianne had spent a few minutes in the last building digging around in a collection of junk boxes until she found what she was looking for.

Five large, brass and steel padlocks with matching keys had been stored in one of the boxes. Dianne took four of them and used a Sharpie to mark each key and matching lock with a number. After doing so she tested the locks to make sure they closed and opened smoothly before stuffing the keys in her pocket and hanging the locks on her belt loop.

These should work well. Going to be a pain in the rear for letting all the animals in and out, but maybe we can let up some in a few days. Not knowing the source of the fire at the Carson's house was still eating at her though having a bit of time to not think about it was helping her process the possibilities in a more rational manner.

It could have just been an accident. Their car wasn't there so they had to have been gone. Maybe it was an electrical problem or part of their heat pump failed. The more

Dianne thought about all of the possible sources for the fire the less worried she felt about herself, her property and—most especially—her children.

"Still." Dianne started talking out loud to herself as she stood up and moved back toward the building she had just cleared. "It never hurts to be prepared."

The first of the four brass locks went on a thick piece of chain hanging around the handles of the entrance to the barn. The next three locks went on the next three buildings, including the small shed that was built around their backup generator. Instead of moving the truck into the barn Dianne positioned it behind the house so that it wasn't visible to anyone walking down the driveway and then she popped the hood, disconnected one of the battery cables and closed the hood back down.

"Should keep anyone from driving off with you." Dianne patted the side of the truck and looked down at the buildings, fields and pond as she went through a mental checklist. *All the buildings are safe and secured. Truck's safe. House is safe. Okay, time to try and have a normal evening with the kids.*

Dianne looked up at one of the second story windows and saw Mark peering back at her, the rifle in his hands. She waved at him and he opened the window and shouted down at her. "You coming inside, mom?"

Dianne held a finger to her lips before nodded vigorously. She headed for the back door and was about to unlock it when Mark appeared in the living room and undid the latch and the safety bar before sliding it open for her. "What's wrong?" His face was covered in concern after she had motioned for him to be quiet.

"Nothing, kiddo; everything's clear and safe." Dianne took the rifle from his hands, ejected the magazine and cleared the chamber before nodding at him approvingly. "Well done. How're the other two?"

"They're fine. Jacob's reading, Josie's drawing."

"Thanks for taking care of them. Did you see or hear anyone?"

"Nope." Mark's forehead furrowed. "Why'd you want me to be quiet a minute ago?"

Dianne leaned Mark's rifle up against the wall next to the door and locked up the back door as she answered. "I want to try and keep things as quiet as we can for the next few days, just in case that fire at the Carson's place wasn't an accident. That means no shouting and no playing or working outside unless we absolutely have to."

"Probably shouldn't run the generator or have a fire either, right?"

Dianne smiled and patted Mark on the back. "Good job. That's exactly right. Let's keep things quiet for a few days, okay? Oh, by the way, after dinner can you help me get your dad's night vision cameras set up? I think we've got enough juice in the batteries to run a couple of those, right?"

Mark nodded. "I think so. They just need the router to be working and you can view their feeds from your phone or tablet."

"Cool. Help me out with that after dinner. Speaking of which, I'm going to get your rifle put away in the case above the fridge. Can you tell your brother and sister to come down? I'll put some soup on to heat up." Mark nodded and ran back up the stairs. Dianne picked his rifle back up and took one last look out through the back door before closing the curtains across the door and walking into the kitchen.

Mounted above the refrigerator, the long horizontal cabinet was accessed by a five-digit combination lock. Dianne and Rick were the only ones that knew the combination but as Dianne put away the rifle Mark had been using, she decided that he would need to know the code as well. She was confident in his maturity when it came to the gun, but she didn't want Jacob and Josie to have free access to it. While Josie had shown appropriate levels of respect and care when it came to firearms, Jacob was still careless enough in his day-to-day life that Dianne felt nervous about leaving a rifle out for him to potentially pick up.

After locking Mark's gun and a couple of spare magazines away in the cabinet, Dianne pulled her rifle off of her back and laid it out on top of the refrigerator, keeping it up out of the way while she started on dinner. She thought about turning on the generator out behind the house to make the night's meal slightly easier to prepare but she didn't want to have the noise attract any undue attention. *Plenty of charge in the batteries to keep the freezer and fridge on tonight and the hotplate shouldn't take up much juice, either.*

As Mark, Jacob and Josie came down the stairs, Dianne was opening a large container of canned New England Clam Chowder and dumping it into a saucepan. "Hon, would you get out some crackers and get everyone's drinks ready? I think we've got some apples you can slice, too."

"Sure, mom." Mark and Dianne worked together to get the meal prepared while Jacob and Josie set the table. After everything was laid out and they started eating, Dianne grabbed her notebook and pen and began sketching on the paper in between bites of food.

"What's that, mom?" Josie craned her head in curiosity as she tried to see the pages.

"Well," Dianne said, "I'm trying to come up with some ideas for how to make sure all of us and our house and animals can stay safe."

"Oh." Josie took another bite of soup as she contemplated her mother's response. "Safe from what?"

"Good question. We need to stay warm with the weather getting colder and we need to make sure that if any bad people try to hurt the house or our animals we can keep them away."

"Oh." The answer seemed to satisfy Josie, but Jacob spoke up next.

"What kind of bad people, mom? Did they burn down the house with Mr. and Mrs. Carsons?"

"No, Jacob. The Carsons weren't there."

"But some bad guys burned down their house? What if they come here? Do you think they were, like, from—"

"Ooookay!" Dianne stood up and smiled, speaking over Jacob. "Lots of questions, but we'll get to them tomorrow, okay? There are no bad people here at the house and we're going to keep it that way. Now Jacob and Josie, I want you two to clear the table and rinse the bowls out. Once you're done you can go to the living room and read or play quietly before bed, okay?"

A pair of resigned voices grumbled "yes, ma'am" as they got up from the table, moving as slowly as they possibly could. Mark moved over one seat and looked over his mother's shoulder as she continued jotting notes down on her paper.

"Barbed wire?" Mark raised an eyebrow as he read from the page.

"Just an idea." Dianne shrugged. "We have the fence running around the property but it won't stop anyone from coming in. I think we have a few spools of barbed wire, still. Might be enough to deter people from coming in through the front near the driveway. It won't keep people out but maybe they'll think twice."

Mark waited until his brother and sister were out of the room before whispering his next question. "Do you really think someone burned down their house?"

Dianne sighed. "I'm not really sure. I don't think so, but after what we saw in town I don't want to take any chances. I think we need to be extra careful for the next few days, especially at night. I'll really need your help with this, okay?"

Dianne could tell that Mark was feeling excited about his new role in the ongoing crisis, which helped to reduce the stress of the situation. "Sure thing. What do you want me to do?"

"Help me get those cameras hooked up tonight to start. Mostly I need you to watch over your brother and sister and make sure you're paying attention to what's going on around you. Remember what your dad and I taught you about that, okay?"

Mark nodded and Dianne smiled and ruffled his hair as she stood up. "You're a good kid, kid. Now c'mon; let's go get the cameras hooked up."

While Jacob and Josie played in the living room, Mark located the few pieces of equipment that they would need to have powered on to make the cameras on the outside of the house function properly. Rick had installed a pair of night vision cameras on each of the four corners of the house, near the roof, about a month before leaving on his trip.

The impetus for installing the cameras had been a pack of coyotes that had been in the area, howling away for several nights in a row as they started roaming closer to the Waters' home. When combined with several spotlights and speakers set up throughout the property, Rick had intended on scaring away any of the animals if they started sniffing around the farm at night, but before he could get everything hooked up the howls had stopped. The cameras were installed and wired but lacking power and neither Mark nor Dianne knew whether the spotlights and speakers were functional.

After Dianne and Mark got the power cables for the cameras that were running through the attic plugged in, Mark got the network router online as well. After a few minutes of waiting for both the cameras and the router to power up, Mark powered up a tablet computer from Rick's office and opened a security camera application on the device. It took another half hour of fiddling with cables and settings on the tablet, router and cameras but by the time the sun was starting to set the first image popped up on the tablet and Dianne grinned. "Nice work!"

Mark continued with the setup of the other cameras and before too long he handed the tablet to Dianne. "Here you go, mom. You can push this button to cycle through the cameras and this button changes them from regular video to night vision."

"Well done. This is perfect. Is there a way to make a motion alert on the tablet?"

"Yep!" Mark took the tablet back and showed Dianne how to work the more intricate functions of the app. When everything was said and done Dianne nodded with satisfaction. "Can you set up one of the other tablets around here with this same thing? I think your dad has another one in his office somewhere. I'd like to keep one in the bedroom and one downstairs in the kitchen or living room."

"Sure, I just need to find it."

Dianne nodded. "I'll help you with that tomorrow. I think this'll be perfect for tonight. Why don't you head back downstairs and find something to do. Maybe we can look for the spotlights and speakers tomorrow and see how much work those would be to get hooked up."

Mark nodded and headed downstairs while Dianne flipped through the views of the different cameras on the app. Being able to see the entirety of the outside of the house at a glance made her feel much more at ease. As the night drew on she kept the tablet close to her, glancing at it every few minutes while she worked on preparing the next day's meals and getting a few things cleaned up around the house.

After her children were in bed, Dianne laid on her side and stared at the tablet as she tried to get to sleep. There was no sign of movement anywhere outside but she still felt uneasy despite that fact. She turned over to look at the ceiling and felt the space in the bed next to her. Instead of feeling Rick, though, she felt the cold steel of her rifle tucked just underneath the blanket and sighed, then closed her eyes and drifted off into an uneasy sleep.

Chapter Nine

U S Government Facility
   Six days before the event

THE PRESIDENT of the United States is not having a good day. It has been forty-eight hours since the advanced cyber-warfare system codenamed 'DAMOCLES' was compromised and he has been briefed on the situation by the Joint Chiefs and the head project managers from the NSA who developed the covert application.

The President paces around the conference room table as he listens to the project managers describe the details on what Damocles is capable of before he interrupts them by picking up a lamp and throwing it at the wall. "Will one of you shit-stains kindly explain to me just how the hell Damocles was available for long enough for an intruder to get their hands on it? Why wasn't it air gapped to begin with? Jesus f—"

"Sir?" A secretary peeks her head in through the door of the conference room.

"What is it?" The President roars at her as he storms back to his seat. He grips the back of the chair with both hands, turning his fingertips and knuckles white.

"Michael Evans is here, sir."

"Evans? Who the devil is Evans?"

"The security expert you wanted to see, sir."

"Oh. Right." The President frowns. "Send him in."

A man with disheveled hair, wrinkled shirt, stained khakis and a jacket with leather elbow patches hurries into the room. In his hand is a leather case that he places on the table before sitting down in the closest chair.

"Sorry I'm late, Mr. President."

"We expected you two hours ago. Where've you been?" The President barks in

response. Evans, however, barely pays him any mind as he opens his leather case and pulls out several thick stacks of paper. He stands up and begins hurrying around the conference table, dropping a stack of paper in front of each person as he begins to talk.

"Sorry, the printer ran out of ink when we got to the last few copies. Some of you might have to share."

"What's this?" A man in a military uniform that appears to have a composition breakdown of seventy-five percent cloth and twenty-five percent medals starts thumbing through the stack of papers before passing it to the man to his left.

"This, I'm sorry to say, is an analysis that I just finished running earlier this morning on the effects of Damocles."

A murmur passes across the table as the Generals whisper with one another. The one who asked the initial question speaks up again, looking at the President as he does. "I'm sorry, but who are you exactly? I was under the impression that Damocles knowledge was classified at the highest levels."

The President lets out a smirk as he answers before Evans can. "Dr. Michael Evans is the one who came up with the original theories that brought Damocles into existence. You would know him better as 'Dr. Howard Chu,' an alias he went by to protect his standing in the academic community after we bought everything related to Damocles a few years ago."

"You… you're Dr. Chu?" The man's eyes widen and Dr. Evans nods humbly.

"Yes, sir, I am." He glances down at a copy of the papers he passed around the table. "Now, if you'll direct your attention to page thirty, I can give you a summary on what to expect now that Damocles is in the wild."

Everyone in the room turns to page thirty and Dr. Evans continues. "Thank you. "Now as you can see from the charts on the page, wide-scale attacks are most likely not going to begin for another forty-eight to seventy-two hours. At this point, whoever infiltrated the Damocles system most likely doesn't realize that they were infected with the weapon when they downloaded the source code. If they are working to study and/or weaponized it for their own benefits, as I'm certain they are, then Damocles is learning a hundred times more about them than they are about it."

"Damocles infected them when they stole it?" The same general speaks again and the President answers before Dr. Evans can.

"Damn straight. That's part of why it's so dangerous. It learns from every interaction it has, be it with a system or a human, isn't that right, Evans?"

"Indeed, Mr. President." Dr. Evans pushes his glasses up on his nose and sighs. "Unfortunately, due to Damocles not being completely air gapped as I recommended, page thirty-five lays out the worst-case scenario for what's going to take place over the next week. When I say worst-case scenario, though, you should know that I mean that this is the most likely scenario."

Pages are turned across the table before a series of slight gasps are heard. "This can't be true." Another man in uniform speaks next, his face contorted in horror. "Is this some kind of a joke, sir?"

The President shakes his head grimly. "I'm afraid not. Evans?"

Dr. Evans clears his throat and tugs nervously at his collar. "Gentlemen, what you see before you is what Damocles was designed to do."

"Surely our military systems are hardened against this!" A woman a few seats down nearly shouts and Dr. Evans shakes his head.

"I'm afraid not. Again, if my suggestions had been heeded then we would have had—"

"Evans." The President speaks gruffly, glaring at Dr. Evans. "Stick to what we can do now that it's out in the wild. A lot of people screwed up and I'll personally make sure their heads are on spikes before it's all said and done. But we need options right now. Suggestions?"

Dr. Evans eases back into his chair and runs his hands through his hair, then takes his glasses off and rubs the lenses with the bottom of his shirt. He says nothing for a moment as he stares across the room at a satellite map of the country. When he finally puts his glasses back on he takes a deep breath and turns back to the President.

"Pray, Mr. President. That's the only thing to do at this point. Pray."

Chapter Ten

The Waters' Homestead
Ellisville, VA

NEARLY A WEEK after setting up the security cameras, Dianne and her children fell into an uneasy routine around their home. With no signs of anyone on or near their property during the day or evening, Dianne began to relax her vigilance with watching the cameras and started focusing more on getting the house and property set up for a long-term stay.

Two days of work with Mark in a small clearing out behind the house yielded a fifty percent increase in power availability thanks to the installation of several new solar panels as well as two more batteries that Dianne had found in a box in the basement. There was enough power to keep the deep freezer, refrigerator, cameras, a few lights and a small space heater all running at once during the day. When night rolled around the batteries provided enough power to keep the freezer, refrigerator and cameras running, but Dianne restricted the use of lights and the space heater.

Once the solar panels were set up and hooked up to the house, Dianne started replenishing the stock of firewood outside the house while Mark worked on collecting and cataloguing pieces of a potential greenhouse and aquaponics setup in one of the barns. Jacob and Josie, meanwhile, were tasked with working in the vegetable gardens and the small field where they collected potatoes, corn, squash and other vegetables. After stacking what they collected into paper bags, Jacob and Josie carted them back up to the house and took them down into the basement for Dianne to help sort through at a later point in time.

As Dianne stood up from helping Mark carry a large box full of rubber tubing out of a room in the barn, she realized that she hadn't noticed the additional weight on her back for the last couple of hours. In addition to keeping her pistol tucked into her waistband Dianne also made a point of carrying her rifle on her back anytime she was outside. At first the weapon had been bulky and uncomfortable, but after a few days of work she started to not notice it as much until—finally—it felt almost natural to be carrying it. That realization bothered her more than she cared to admit, but she pushed it from her mind and refocused on the task at hand.

"Do you really think we can grow stuff down in the basement?" Mark scratched his head as he looked at the organized chaos of the supplies laid out on the floor of the barn.

Dianne nodded. "I do, yeah. These LED grow lights barely consume any power and there are enough of them here to fill almost the entire barn. I want to keep things confined to the house at first, though, especially as the weather gets colder."

"How much do you want to grow?"

Dianne shrugged. "As much as we can. I think having some fresh greens all winter long will make things easier on everybody."

Mark shook his head and snorted. "Not me, mom. I hate salads."

Dianne laughed and embraced Mark in a hug before he could pull away. "I know you do, kiddo. Trust me, though, after a month or two of eating canned food you'll be extremely happy to have some fresh veggies."

"What is it we can grow in this, anyway? Just lettuce?"

Dianne scrunched up her nose. "Good question. Your dad's first test was just with greens since it was a system that was full of water all the time. What I'm seeing here looks a lot more complicated, though. I think maybe he upgraded and got a fill and drain system. If so, then I think we can grow other stuff like carrots. I'm not sure, though. I guess we'll find out!"

"Bleh." Mark stuck his tongue out. "I'll help grow everything but I don't want to eat it."

Dianne laughed again and patted Mark on the back. "Come on; let's go see how much actual work the two J's are getting done."

Dianne and Mark headed out of the barn and Dianne locked it up behind them. Outside, Jacob and Josie were walking back from the house down to several rows of paper bags filled with food they had pulled from the gardens. "How's it going, you two?"

"Pretty good, mom."

"Almost finished!"

Dianne nodded approvingly. "Mark, let's help them get the rest of these into the basement and then we'll get a bite of lunch. After that I want to start bringing the aquaponics supplies up into the house and get some more firewood cut."

"What about the Carsons?" Mark picked up a few bags as he asked the question.

"What about them? I'm positive they weren't at home when the fire happened."

"Yeah, but shouldn't we check on them? And go over to the Statler's place and take care of their animals, too?"

Dianne sighed. "I don't know, bud. I don't really like the idea of going out unless we absolutely have to. I'll think about it, though, okay?"

Mark nodded quietly and headed up to the house along with Jacob and Josie. Dianne stood next to the bags of vegetables for a minute, thinking quietly to herself. She realized that she was accepting their new situation far too easily and was bothered by that fact. It had been a full day since she had last checked to see if she could pick up anything on the radio or TV, she didn't want to leave their home to check on the neighbors and had no idea what the general situation was out in the world.

"All right." Dianne sighed as she talked to herself. "Enough of this nonsense. Things may be bad but we still need to see what's going on and check on the neighbors. Maybe things in town have calmed down enough that we can talk to some people there and get updates on what's going on."

Chapter Eleven

L as Vegas, NV

IT WAS JUST after two in the morning when Rick awoke. His heart was racing, he was dripping with sweat and he had the unshakeable feeling that there were other people in the building. He crawled on hands and knees over to the door and pulled it open a few inches, holding his ear up to the crack to listen. For a few seconds there was nothing and he was just about to close the door and go back to sleep when he heard the unmistakable sound of people talking to one another.

"What'd you find?"

"We're at the lumberyard you dipshit. What do you think I found? Bunch of fuckin' wood."

"Hey man, I found wood too. Right here."

"Nah man, that's more like a twig!"

There was a chorus of raucous laughter and Rick slowly closed the door, cringing as the latch softly clicked back into place. While he had no idea who the people in the lumberyard were or what their intentions were, he had no desire to find out, either.

After glancing up to see no locks on the door, Rick glanced around the room, hoping to locate something he could use to block the door. As his gaze landed on the overturned vending machine he had a sudden flash of inspiration and hurried over to it. He got on the end opposite the entrance to the break room and began slowly pushing it towards the door. The plastic front scraped along the floor but didn't make enough noise to cause him any worry.

After nearly a minute of slow, cautious pushing he had the vending machine jammed up against the door. There was still a small window on the door to contend with, but he noticed that the field of view from the door's window was small enough that he could sit next to Jane and no one looking through the window would be able to see them.

The noise from the people walking around in the building grew louder as Rick collected up his gear and stashed it on the far side of the room next to Jane. The light was the last to go, and he turned it off as ran over to Jane. He double-checked his shotgun as he eased down next to her, making sure it was fully loaded before putting the back of his hand on her head. She was finally feeling cool and he sighed in relief. *Thank goodness.* He considered waking her but decided against it, and chose instead to trust that the people would choose to move on after trying the door.

"Hey!" The voice came from outside the break room and Rick felt his heartrate skyrocket. "What's in here?"

"The break room, jackass."

"No shit. I'm gonna see what they're keeping in there."

A few footsteps followed the proclamation. The door handle turned next, then came the sound of the door being shoved. It banged against the vending machine and Rick heard a muffled curse followed by a shout.

"Oy! This thing won't open! Give me a hand!"

Oh shit. Rick's eyes went wide and he flipped the shotgun over to check that it was fully loaded. *Eight shells.* His hunting rifle sat on the ground to his left and his pistol was to his right. Both were also loaded and ready to go.

"What's your problem, asshole?"

"This door's jammed. Gimme a hand."

"Yeah, yeah. Get out of the way."

There was a shuffle outside the door before someone threw his full weight against it. It smashed against the vending machine, moving the object no more than a millimeter in response.

"Damn!" Rick couldn't help but smile at the sound of the frustration in the person's voice. "Something must have fallen in there. Maybe during the quake."

Quake? Rick's eyebrows shot up. *There were earthquakes?*

"Look, there's a window over there. Just go around and see if there's anything worth getting in there, okay?"

Rick's heartrate jumped yet again and he swiveled his head to face the window on the opposite side of the room from the door. It was much wider than the one on the door and anyone looking through it would have a full view on the entirety of the break room and its contents.

"Yeah, yeah. Come give me a boost over the fence, all right?"

"Pansy."

"Shut up."

The two voices grew fainter as the pair walked off, heading around the building to look through the window. Rick's eyes grew wide as he looked around the room, trying to figure out what to do. He thought about trying to hold something up over the window to make it look like it was blocked but realized that was a foolish decision. He then thought about trying to move Jane and his equipment over beneath the window to remain out of sight, but knew he didn't have enough time.

The tables. The idea hit him like a bolt of lightning and he scrambled to his feet. He pulled the tables that were in front of him over, tipping them upward and angling them so that they blocked all sight of the side of the room where Jane and his gear were sitting. He then opened the cupboards near the vending machines and began pulling out wads of napkins, cutlery, creamers and stir sticks and throwing everything onto the ground. *If they think there was an earthquake I'll give them an earthquake.*

Once a sufficiently large mess was spread out across the floor Rick ran back behind the tables and knelt down, not daring to even peek through a crack in between them for fear of being seen. There was silence for several more seconds until he heard a tapping on the window and the same two voices again.

"I think I can break it."

"Then what? You gonna slide through the bars or something? Gonna need a whole lot of butter to get that greased up."

"Shut up. There's nothing in there anyway. Bunch of stuff the quake knocked over. Bah."

"Come on. We'll try down the street next."

The voices faded into the distance quickly as the pair ran off to join their companions. Rick stayed still behind the tables for several minutes after the people left, scarcely daring to breathe for fear of attracting any attention. When he finally peeked out from behind the table and saw that they really were gone he sat up and sighed deeply. His heart was still pumping and though he felt incredibly tired, he dared not close his eyes again for the rest of the night.

Chapter Twelve

The Waters' Homestead
Ellisville, VA

"LET'S GO, KIDS!" Dianne shouted up the stairs and looked at her watch. It was only seven-thirty in the morning but she wanted to get moving as quickly as possible. She heard muffled groans and grumblings signaling that they were waking up and went back to the kitchen to stir the oatmeal, cream of wheat and check on the toast.

Josie was the first down the stairs, scratching her stomach and yawning as she padded into the kitchen and sat down at the table. Jacob and Mark followed soon after, and Jacob was the first to remark on Dianne's appearance. "Are we going somewhere, mom?"

Dressed in blue jeans, hiking boots, a long sleeved flannel shirt and wearing a utility vest with pouches sewn onto every square inch of space, Dianne nodded. "Yep! After you all finish breakfast we're going to head out and check on the Statler's and the Carson's places and see if either of them are back yet. We'll also take a run into town and see how things are going there."

"I thought you didn't want to go out, mom." Mark's voice had the slightest trace of mockery in it and Dianne raised an eyebrow.

"Watch the attitude, kiddo. You were right, though. We need to go check on our neighbors. Plus it wouldn't hurt to take a ride around town and see how everyone's doing. It's been a week since we were out so hopefully things have calmed down since then."

After the children were done with breakfast and had gotten changed, Dianne pulled the truck around to the front of the house. Jacob and Josie ran outside to get in while Dianne had a quick conversation with Mark on the porch.

"Here." Dianne handed Mark his rifle and he looked at her questioningly.

"Do you want me to put this in the back?"

"Nope. Keep it with you in the front. Unloaded, as usual, but you've been doing a good job being responsible the last week. I think it's time you started keeping it with you in the front when we go out."

Mark nodded. "Thanks. I'll be safe."

Dianne smiled and handed him a mag. "Make sure that you are." She pulled on the front door and turned to the truck. "Alrighty! Everybody ready?"

Jack and Josie were bouncing up and down in the back of the truck as Dianne and Mark hopped inside. Dianne handed her rifle to Mark and he leaned them both against his side of the car with the barrels facing down to the floor. Dianne handed him a short bungee cord to loop around the stocks to keep the guns from bouncing around and glanced in the rearview mirror. "Hold on tight!"

After stopping briefly to unlock, open, close and relock the gate on the driveway, Dianne turned left and headed towards their neighbors down the road. The last week had seen a profound change in the color of the leaves on the trees and they were surrounded on all sides by orange and gold as they drove along. Dianne pulled into the Carson's driveway first and gave Mark his instructions as she headed towards the blackened remnants of the building.

"I don't see their car here but I'm going to take a look around and see if anything looks out of place. Stay here with Jacob and Josie and keep an eye out. I'll be back in five minutes. If you hear or see anyone, bring the truck around to the back of the house, okay?" Mark nodded quietly, his eyes—like those of his brother and sister—fixated on the destruction before them.

The fire that consumed the Carson's house had long since extinguished itself but the charred and blackened remains of the building were a testament to the destructive power of the blaze. The building had collapsed in on itself and a few of the walls had fallen outward, resulting in a ring of burned grass that surrounded the building. The Carsons had been exceptionally good about keeping the area outside the building free of debris and brush, though, and the fire hadn't been able to spread anywhere else.

Dianne hopped out of the truck and headed towards what used to be the front door of the home. The beautiful stained glass window atop the door was shattered and the pieces were barely recognizable underneath the ash and soot. Dianne knelt down and picked up a piece of the glass as if doing so could give her some kind of insight into what had happened. She stepped around the house, picking her way through the debris as she kept her eyes open for any signs that someone might have been home when the fire started.

"What am I going to find?" She mumbled to herself as she stepped over piles of brick and pieces of burned lumber. "A pile of bones or something?" After a few minutes of searching Dianne realized that it was fruitless to continue and she went back out front. Mark was standing out beside the truck, keeping his rifle gripped tightly in both hands as he slowly turned around to keep an eye on their surroundings.

"I'm going out back now; back in five!" Mark nodded in response and Dianne jogged out behind the building, not wanting to leave the children by themselves for any longer than was necessary. While Dianne would never admit it out loud, she was at the Carson's house for more than just checking on things. Given their love of travel and the fact that they had clearly not been home when the fire happened, Dianne doubted that they would be back anytime soon—if ever, given what was presumably still going on in the world. Because of this, Dianne decided that she would poke around in the barn behind their house and see if there was anything that might be useful for her and the children as they continued working to set things up for a long-term stay at their farm.

The barn in question was unlocked and Dianne stepped inside cautiously, allowing her eyes to adjust to the dim light before proceeding. Nothing looked particularly out of place and Dianne quickly walked down the two rows of shelving in the center of the building, looking for any tools or supplies that might be useful. She slung her rifle over her shoulder after only a few steps and started pulling boxes and bags off of the shelves and throwing them onto the floor.

"Sorry, Sarah." Dianne shook her head, feeling ashamed over what she was doing. "If you guys make it back I'll reimburse you for every last thing."

Bags of fertilizer, boxes and bags of nails, shingles, tools and other supplies were the first to be pulled off the shelves. Several spools of barbed wire came next, followed by a collection of tee-posts. By the time Dianne was nearly done with pulling things off of the shelves, she heard the hum of the truck's engine out front.

Panicked, Dianne ran to the front of the barn and headed outside, pulling her rifle off her back and looking around frantically for any intruders. Mark stepped out of the truck and Dianne ran to him, whispering to keep her voice low. "Where are they?"

"Where are who?" Mark looked puzzled for a few seconds before he realized what his mother meant. "Oh! No, there's nobody here. You just said you'd be back in five minutes and it's been ten. I wanted to make sure you were okay."

Dianne breathed a sigh of relief and leaned up against the truck as she nodded at Mark. "Jeez. You scared me half to death. Good job, though. I was going to have you pull the truck around here anyway."

"What for?"

Dianne motioned at the barn. "Get your sister and brother out and have them come inside."

Once her children were inside the barn, Dianne put her gun on her back again and spoke to them. "All right kids, listen up. The Carsons aren't here, and they weren't here during the fire. That probably means that they're trapped somewhere just like your dad is. I'm sure they're okay, but it's probably going to take them a while to get back home. Since they're not going to be back for a long time, we're going to borrow a few supplies from them until they get back, okay? I need all of you to help pick up everything I pulled off of the shelves and load it into the back of the truck, okay?"

"Mom?" Josie looked at the piles of supplies on the floor. "Isn't this stealing?"

Dianne crouched down to get on eye level with Josie and sighed, trying to both explain what they were doing to her daughter as well as rationalize her actions internally. "I don't think so, honey. The Carsons probably won't be back for a very long time and right now we need these supplies. When the Carsons do get back then we're going to give them back everything we're borrowing and then some."

"But it's not our stuff, mom."

"I know, sweetie. The Carsons are our friends, though, and they've told your dad and I before that if we needed to borrow anything then we could."

"Hrmph." Josie crossed her arms, looking entirely unsatisfied by Dianne's answer.

"Come on, kiddo; help your brothers get everything loaded up." Dianne patted Josie's back and watched her daughter run off to start helping with the lighter items. As Dianne worked alongside her children she thought about her daughter's question and realized that even she was feeling unsatisfied by the justifications. The feeling that she was probably doing something wrong ate at her but she did her best to push the feeling aside, knowing that whatever they were taking could be replaced and that the Carsons would legitimately want their supplies used in an emergency.

To help make herself feel better Dianne grabbed a piece of paper and a pen from the truck and wrote out a note as Mark, Jacob and Josie finished loading the last of the supplies. The note explained what was going on, what Dianne had seen and what they had taken, though it left out any specific names. *Just in case anyone else happens to come here and read it.* She nailed the note to the inside wall of the barn in a place not easily viewable from the door.

Hurry up and get back, you guys. Dianne sighed as she helped Mark throw the last bag of fertilizer into the truck. *And you too, Rick. Wherever you are.*

Chapter Thirteen

L as Vegas, NV

WHEN THE LIGHT of dawn replaced the flicker of fires in the city, Rick started awake, realizing that he had—contrary to his best efforts—fallen asleep. His head was resting against a cushion on the floor and he lifted it slowly, feeling a twinge in his neck from being in an odd position for so long. After sitting up he looked over at Jane and saw her still sleeping. He put his hand on her head and neck again and was relieved to find that she still felt cool to the touch.

Rick checked his watch, stood up and stretched, walking around the room as he thought about his next move. *Seven in the morning. We need to get moving soon. Got to try and get to Nellis today and see about getting some real medical attention for her and transportation home for me.*

Movement from the other side of the room caught Rick's ear and he turned to see Jane stirring. He walked over and crouched down next to her, opening a bottle of water as her eyes fluttered open.

"Rick?" Jane looked around at the room. "Where are we?" Her voice was hoarse and cracked and Rick handed her the bottle of water.

"Here, drink this. You've been out for a while. We're inside a lumberyard not far from where you collapsed yesterday."

"I... think I remember." Jane took several small sips from the bottle before taking a large gulp.

"Yeah you were awake a time or two but otherwise you've been sleeping. I think the heat got to you."

"Heatstroke in autumn?" Jane smiled weakly and shook her head and Rick laughed.

"I know, it's crazy, isn't it?"

"I think I'm feeling better now. We should start moving again, shouldn't we?"

Rick sighed and nodded. "I don't want to push you with how you're feeling, but we really should."

"How far do we have to go?"

"Fifteen miles."

"Oh." Jane nodded slowly. "Right. I remember that. Okay, let's go." She started to stand up and Rick took her arm, helping her to her feet. She wobbled slightly as she stood but after a few steps her paces became steadier and more sure. "I think I can do this." Jane smiled at Rick as he gathered up his supplies and bags and got everything ready to go.

"We have the whole day ahead of us so I think we should take it slow for the first couple of hours and see how you're feeling and decide from there."

Jane stooped down to pick up a bottle of water and looked at it. "We should try to find an extra bag so I can carry some more water. It'll be invaluable in this heat."

"Good idea." Rick nodded and began searching through the cupboards in the break room until he came upon a simple canvas bag with a wide zipper and single handle. "How's this?" He held it out and Jane took it.

"Perfect." She started filling the bag with bottles of water that were scattered around the room while Rick pushed on the vending machine in front of the door until it was far enough out of the way for both of them to slip through.

"Why'd you put that in front of the door?" Jane looked at the vending machine as she followed Rick out of the break room and he snorted in amusement.

"Oh I had some fun times while you were sleeping." Rick gave Jane the summary of what had happened while she was resting. When he finished with the story she shook her head in amazement.

"Wow. That was quick thinking on your part. What are you, ex-army or something?" Rick noticed Jane looking at his gun bag and the bulging pistol on his hip as she asked the question.

"Hardly. No, I'm a—well, I *was* an engineer."

"Do most engineers carry guns around with them?"

Rick laughed. "Only the ones who nearly get caught by some kind of Mad Max style gang on the outskirts of Los Angeles."

"Oh, that makes—wait, what?"

"It's a long story." Rick chuckled. "Tell me about yourself, though. I live in Virginia, have a wife and three kids and live on a small farm outside Blacksburg."

"A farm? Wow. I'm—well, like you said, I *was* a paralegal. I live in downtown Denver though who knows if it's even there anymore."

"Why were you visiting L.A.?"

Jane smiled wistfully. "Visiting an old friend. We had talked about seeing each other more and one thing led to another. Next thing you know the sky is falling and cars are exploding and I'm stuck trying to get out of the city."

"What made you decide to drive?"

"There was a family who picked me up as I was walking to get out of the city. They were on one of the other buses." Jane's face fell. "I hope their kids are okay. They had four of them."

Rick ground his teeth together as he thought about his own children. "I hope so, too."

The pair were quiet for a few minutes before Jane spoke again. "So you're an engineer?"

"Yeah, of sorts."

"Any idea what's going on?"

"I've heard bits and pieces on the radio. It sounds like an advanced computer virus."

"A virus?" Jane sounded incredulous. "How would a virus make cars blow up?"

"It's a lot easier than you might think. Everything in cars is computerized today to help improve safety and increase efficiency and all that jazz. If someone came up with a virus that could infect the systems on a vehicle they could easily override the safety systems and cause something like that to happen."

"That doesn't seem like an increase in safety at all."

"Nope." Rick shook his head. "Not at all. But that's what we get when a bunch of manufacturers are rushing to be the first to market with the latest and greatest bells and whistles. Nobody thinks about security until it's too late."

"That's terrible!"

"No kidding."

Silence fell once again as the pair continued their slow, trudging walk through the Vegas streets. As they wound their way to the northeast, Rick saw signs that they were getting closer to both Nellis and to a place that stirred feelings of fear inside of him: the Strip. One of the dying words of the solder who was driving the bus was to stay away from the Strip, though he had no idea why.

As Rick and Jane drew closer to the Strip the concentration of smoke and dust in the air started to rise to the point where they were both holding their shirts over their mouths and noses to try and keep it out. Every time the wind changed direction they either lowered their shirts and breathed a sigh of relief or raised them back up and began coughing as waves of smoke were blown towards them.

Nearly three hours after leaving the lumberyard as the sun was getting close to its highest point in the sky, Rick and Jane were walking down a narrow one-way street in between two tall casinos. Shielded from much of the smoke and sun, their shirts were off of their faces and they were chatting quietly as they walked. They were distracted enough that they didn't realize when the one-way street came to an end and they emerged from between the buildings out into the open.

Smoke filled their lungs and they both coughed heavily as they tried to cover their faces against the strong wind. Rick blinked against the dust and smoke several times before managing to clear his eyes enough to see what was before him. He stopped walking and held out a hand to keep Jane from going any farther and she too tried to clear her eyes to see what he was pointing out.

Out in front of them lay the southern end of the famous Las Vegas Strip. The road was several lanes wide on both sides with a wide median in the center and tall, imposing buildings stretching up to the sky on both sides of the road. Off to the left, just a short walk away were the famous Fountains of Bellagio while the Planet Hollywood resort and casino towered directly across the street.

While the scene might have been pleasant at any other point, the condition of the Strip made Rick realize why the soldier had warned them to stay away. The smoke and dust that had been choking Rick and Jane was coming primarily from the buildings on the Strip, many of which were still burning. The shops in front of Planet Hollywood were a pile of twisted metal, plastic and bricks on the ground. The fountains to their left had lost power days prior and while the water was gone there were wrecks of several trucks and cars inside the fountain area from vehicles that had rammed into the bollards and flipped over into where the water had previously been flowing.

Down the street to the left and right Rick could see that every major and minor building in the area had suffered heavy damages. Much of it was related to fires that were still burning inside the wreckage and shells of the buildings but some of it looked like it had been caused from vehicles and an airplane or two that had crashed into them and then exploded. Two days hadn't been nearly enough time for the fuel feeding the fires to be exhausted and the flames licked at the air, sending black smoke billowing into great clouds that drifted on the wind.

Jane leaned in close to Rick and whispered as she stared wide-eyed at the destruction, blinking every few seconds to clear the smoke and dust from her eyes. "What now?"

Chapter Fourteen

E llisville, VA

AFTER LEAVING the Carson's house, Dianne drove to the Statler's, where everything was as they had left it a week ago. The chickens were nearly out of feed, though, and Dianne mused about whether they should take them back home or not.

"You think we can get that cage strapped onto the back of the truck, Mark?" Dianne scratched her chin as she watched the chickens moving about in the cage attached to the outside of the barn.

"I think so, if we strap it down." Mark pulled on the cage, lifting it a couple inches off the ground before releasing it. "Don't we have enough chickens already, though?"

"Yeah, but I don't want to have to keep using gas to come out here and take care of them. We can keep them at our place until the Statlers get back."

Mark groaned. "I guess this means we'll be eating even *more* eggs."

Dianne laughed. The last week had featured more than a few egg-based meals thanks to the chickens they already had at the house. "You'll learn to love them soon enough! Now come on and help me get this lifted onto the back. Jacob, you too! Let's go, boys!"

After closing the small wire mesh door around the narrow portion of the cage that attached to the barn, Dianne unlatched the cage from the barn and picked up one side. Mark and Jacob took the other side and together the three of them walked the cage full of extremely unhappy chickens over to the truck. After making sure everything in the back of the truck was secure, Dianne unfolded a tarp from the storage box in the back of the truck and spread it out over the supplies beneath the cage. She and her sons then lifted the cage onto the back and positioned it as best as they could. With no solid ground under their feet the birds' legs were falling through the narrow holes in the wire, though they eventually settled down into seated positions to try and get comfortable.

With the cage on the back of the truck, Dianne gave Mark and Jacob the job of doing the initial tie-downs while she went with Josie to leave a note for the Statlers.

Sarah – Picked up your chickens to watch out for them. Let us know when you're back. –D

Dianne stuffed the note through the crack between the back door and the doorframe before heading back out to the truck. After getting Josie situated in her seat, Dianne finished helping Mark and Jacob get the cage tied down. "Try not to crap on everything, all right?" Dianne poked at one of the chickens through the wire cage before jumping back into the truck.

"You guys ready to go?" A chorus of affirmatives followed and Dianne put the truck into gear. "Let's go see what's happening in town before we go back home, okay?"

It took Dianne around ten minutes of careful driving to reach the edge of town. As they drove through she saw no signs of anyone like she had a week ago. There were no people walking around, many of the homes appeared deserted and there were no other working vehicles on the road.

After passing through the residential neighborhood on the outskirts of town, Dianne headed for the grocery store and town square. A chill ran down her spine as she pulled into view of the grocery store and saw what it looked like. All of the glass on the front windows had been broken out, shopping carts were overturned and scattered across the parking lot and—from what she could see—there wasn't a single scrap of food left on the shelves inside.

"Wow." Mark whistled softly as he looked at the store. "What happened, mom?"

Dianne was busy scanning the area around him as she replied quietly. "I'm not sure, son. But look at all the other buildings." Every other business that Dianne could see in the small square looked virtually identical in condition to that of the grocery store. Windows were shattered, doors were hanging on half-broken hinges and there were clear signs of looting and intentional damage that had been perpetrated.

Burned out vehicles still littered the area, and though Dianne couldn't remember the exact details of which vehicles had been in which places, the general layout of everything still looked the same. In the distance, even though it was no longer smoking, Dianne could still see the remains of the airplane that had crashed just outside town. Two firetrucks were still parked next to the aircraft, though one of them had rolled over on its side while the other was partially inside the wreckage of the aircraft itself, having clearly been crashed there by someone who attempted to drive it away. Overall the condition of Ellisville was even worse than it had been a week prior, and there were no signs that anyone was around or trying to clean things up.

"I don't understand." Dianne whispered to herself as she drove the truck slowly through town. "Did everyone leave?"

"Shouldn't we get home, mom?" Jacob and Josie were turned around in their seats watching the chickens in the back.

"Soon, kiddos. I want to see if we can find anyone around here who might be able to tell us what's going on." Dianne wound her way through the wreckage of the buildings and vehicles of the town until she got onto the small two-lane highway that led to the main highway that would lead to Blacksburg. As she approached the main highway, though, she eventually had to slow to a stop.

"Well now what?" Dianne opened the door of the truck and stood on the sideboard, peering out at the road ahead. She could see the next few hundred feet of road, the onramp to the highway and a good portion of the highway itself, but there was no possible way for them to drive any farther in the truck.

The wreckage of burned out vehicles sat bumper to bumper, blocking the road and onramp and making it impossible to go anywhere. Dianne had initially considered going off-road in the truck, but looking at the highway from an elevated position made it obvious that the driving conditions there were even worse than on the road leading to it.

As Dianne stood and contemplated her next move, the sound of an engine behind her made her turn and shield her eyes from the sun to figure out the source of the noise. "Mark, rifle!" Dianne ducked down into the truck and grabbed her own rifle before standing back up and holding it to her shoulder. In the distance, back towards town, came the sound of a small engine roaring towards them. As it got closer Dianne could see a man wearing an enormous backpack and sitting on the seat of a motorcycle that was loaded down with all sorts of bags that had been strapped to every square inch of free space on its frame.

The driver of the motorcycle wove the vehicle in between the wrecked vehicles with expert precision, and Dianne realized that he would be able to make it out to the highway without issue. As the motorcycle drew close enough for the details of the driver's clothes to become visible, Josie began shouting from the back of the truck. "Mom! Mom! It's Mr. Sandberg!"

"Who?" Dianne glanced through the back window at her daughter.

"Mr. Sandberg, mom!" Mark opened his door and jumped out of the truck before Dianne could tell him to stop. "He's the biology teacher at the after-school program!"

Dianne hesitated for a split second before jumping down from the truck. "Josie and Jacob, stay there! Mark, stay with me!"

Dianne ran out into the road and held her hands high above her head, waving for the motorcycle driver to slow down. The driver complied, but as he did so the motorcycle started to wobble and Dianne ran forward to catch it before it could fall over.

"Hey there!" Dianne shouted over the sound of the engine as she grabbed the front of the vehicle. The driver held up both thumbs before switching off the engine, laboriously pulling off one of his thick gloves and lifting the visor to his helmet. The man underneath had a soft, kind face with a meticulously groomed mustache and goatee that was salt and pepper in color, and underneath his puffy outer jacket Dianne could see the collar of a checkered dress shirt peeking through.

"Hello!" The rider struggled with his helmet before pulling it off, revealing a short-cropped hairdo and a pair of spectacles atop his nose. "I'm Jim Sandberg! Who are—wait a second, you're Dianne Waters, right?" The rider looked at Mark and grinned broadly. "Mark!"

"Mr. Sandberg!" Mark ran up and gave Jim a high five as Dianne heard the back door to the truck open. Jacob and Josie ran up to the motorcycle and exchanged greetings with their after-school teacher as well before he turned back to address Dianne.

"Mrs. Waters! It's a surprise and a pleasure to see you out here on the road? What are you doing out here, though?"

Dianne hadn't seen Jim Sandberg in the last few weeks due to her schedule, but she had heard all about him from her children who spoke of his kind nature, expert teaching and novel experiments at length every time they came home. "Jim, it's great to see you again." Dianne turned and looked at the highway beyond. "We were going to try to get to Blacksburg to see if we could find out more about what's going on, but it looks like the road's blocked."

Jim's bright smile vanished and the happiness from his voice evaporated. "Do you not know what's going on? I thought I saw your truck in town last week, right after all this... mess happened."

"We've been staying at home for the most part. I heard some things on the television, but I think the power must be out everywhere."

Jim pulled one leg off of his bike before rolling it up next to the wreckage of a vehicle. He leaned the motorcycle against the wreckage and pulled off his other glove. "Dianne, things are very bad. I have a shortwave transmitter in my house and was listening to some emergency broadcasts that were going out before my generator ran out of gas."

Dianne slung her rifle over her shoulder as she glanced around. "How bad is it? Things were getting pretty wild in town last week, but I would have thought that by now..."

Jim shook his head. "No, nothing's gotten better. Maybe you heard on the TV, but this is world-wide. Everyone's affected. I heard that it was some kind of computer super virus, but I don't know enough about that sort of thing to decipher a lot of what I heard." He looked over at Dianne's truck and nodded at it. "Are you and your husband and kids doing okay? Do you need anything?"

Dianne shook her head. "We're okay." She thought about telling him about Rick being in California but decided it was best to keep that information to herself for the time being. "Trying to lay low, mostly, until things get better."

Jim shook his head. "That's a good idea, but I don't know when—or if— things are going to get any better."

"It's awful." Dianne looked around again. "How are you doing, Jim? Are you heading to stay with family?"

Jim looked down at his motorcycle and gear and laughed. "I wish! No, they're too far to reach. I'm heading to one of the federal shelters, up north near D.C."

"Federal shelters?" Dianne furrowed her brow. "The feds are erecting shelters now?"

"Yep." Jim nodded. "The states don't have the capacity to do much right now so the feds are trying to set up shelters for people. I don't know the details but they're providing food and a bed. I'm not equipped to hold out here for very long so I think my best bet is to get there and hope for the best."

"Is that where everyone else in town went?"

Jim shrugged. "I'm not sure. After the insanity in town last week I've been hiding out in my house trying to figure out what to do. I would assume that most folks around here have left, unless they're like your family in which case I bet they're holed up on their property waiting for everything to blow over."

Dianne shook her head. "Damn. I guess I didn't know it was getting that bad."

"I think, based on what I've heard and what's going on, that things aren't going to get better anytime soon." Jim started putting his gloves back on. "You all take care, though, okay? If you have the fuel, you should think about heading up north, too. The shelters are going to fill up fast, I suspect."

Dianne smiled and stepped back from the motorcycle as Jim stepped back on. "Thanks, I appreciate the information. Take care of yourself, okay? Be safe on the roads out there."

Jim nodded and slid his helmet back on, then turned to wave at the children standing behind Dianne. "Take care, you three! You too, Mrs. Waters! I hope to see you again soon!"

Mark, Jacob and Josie all waved goodbye as their teacher pulled away, weaving in and out of the wrecked cars as he made his way to the highway and started heading north. Dianne and her children stood and watched him drive away for a couple of minutes in silence before a chorus of frustrated clucks from the chickens pulled Dianne out of her thoughts and back to reality.

"All right, kids! Back in the truck. Let's get home."

"Mom?" Josie took Dianne's hand as the four walked back to the truck and climbed inside.

"What's up, sweetie?"

"Is Mr. Sandberg going to come back soon?"

"I'm not sure about that. I hope so, though. He's a very nice person."

"And a good teacher, too!"

Dianne smiled at Josie and started up the truck. "I'm sure Mr. Sandberg will be fine and I hope he'll come back soon. For now, though, let's worry about getting all this stuff home and unloaded, okay?"

As Dianne slowly backed up through the tangled mess of cars on the road, she said a silent prayer for Jim Sandberg on his journey. Traveling nearly three hundred miles in the hopes of finding shelter wasn't something she would wish on anyone and she was enormously grateful for the fact that they had enough supplies to last for a long time at their home.

The other related thought that she kept trying to push out of her mind was back yet again as she thought about Jim riding across the state. Dianne's hands clenched the steering wheel as she fought back a tear. *I don't know where you are, Rick. But you've got to make it back. Please make it back.*

Chapter Fifteen

U S Government Facility
Five days before the event

AIR FORCE ONE is in the air, rising to meet a fuel tanker for a midair refueling. The computer systems inside Air Force One have been sealed off from the outside world, and the only access is through a single laptop at the back of the plane. Disconnected from any of the plane's systems or any other computers on the aircraft, the laptop is the only means of communication into and out of Air Force One.

A group of men in suits sit huddled around the computer screen as they watch a streaming broadcast of BBC News. A reporter stands in front of an office building where individuals are pouring out onto the street, each of them carrying a nondescript white box filled with their personal possessions. The President emerges from his private office into the room with the others and takes a seat near the edge.

"Turn the volume up, dammit." He growls and one of his aides hops up and turns the volume up. The voice of the woman is warbled as it comes through the tinny speakers, but even with the distortion it's clear that she is panicked despite her best attempts to remain calm.

"Recapping our top story today, the FTSE had fallen sharply on reports that oil giant BP has suffered catastrophic losses in the Arctic, Russian and South Pacific exploratory platforms. Losses suffered by the company as well as damages are expected to be in the trillions of dollars. As you can see behind me, BP isn't the only one to suffer today as US-based technology giant Computech Incorporated has laid off ninety percent of its workforce in a move that industry experts describe as 'unprecedented, without merit and absolutely mind-boggling.' The exact reason for the layoffs has yet to be publicly disclosed, but—"

The President jabs his finger at the screen and turns to Dr. Evans, who is flipping through a three-ring binder on the other side of the small room. "Evans! What do you make of this?"

Dr. Evans glances over at the screen. "Damocles is experimenting, sir. It's testing its new environments and learning about the systems involved."

"Why the hell would it be tanking companies and getting people fired?"

Dr. Evans looks over his glasses at the President, then glances at the rest of the people crowded around the laptop, all of whom are staring at him. "Sir, Damocles was designed as a learning weapon. It targets for maximum destruction in all areas. Economic destruction certainly counts. The oil platforms are likely its first test of the effects of physical destruction combined with economic destruction."

"Christ." The President looks at the laptop again. "How bad is this going to get before we have some sort of countermeasure?"

"I'm working as quickly as I can, sir. The sooner we get on the ground and I can confer with my colleagues the sooner we can see if it's even possible to create a countermeasure."

"'Possible to create?' Are you telling me we might not be able to fight this thing?"

Dr. Evans puts down his pencil and shakes his head. "Mr. President, what I'm telling you is that you unleashed a superweapon. It has no safeguards. It has no backdoors. It has no magic button that we can press to shut it down. Creating a countermeasure before Damocles decides to start killing people isn't likely to happen."

"Assure me again, General." The President looks at a man seated to his left. "Are the nukes safe?"

"They were air-gapped within minutes of receiving word that Damocles was breached, sir. The only connection into the bunkers is through land-line telephone. Those are isolated and the codes have already been updated."

Dr. Evans shakes his head and laughs. "You think changing codes is enough? If there aren't human beings involved in every single step of the chain, face to face, then Damocles can squeeze into the middle."

Silence—aside from the noise of the television broadcast—persists for nearly a full minute before the President responds. "General, make it happen."

"Sir! Our first and second strike capabilities will be crippled beyond belief!"

"I don't give a flying fuck, General." The President stands up from his seat. "We are not going to be the ones who let this thing launch a nuke. Not happening." The President turns to an aide as he leaves the room and barks at her. "I need the British Prime Minister on a secure line as soon as we touch down. After that I want the Chinese PM and the Russian President on a conference call. Maybe the two of them will start bitching at each other again after I break the news to them."

The President leaves the room and the sound of the news broadcast once again reigns. All except for Dr. Evans are glued to the screen, watching the dramatic events unfold before them in real time. Dr. Evans, though, sits alone with a pencil and paper as he scribbles out line after line of ideas, theories and code to test once he is on the ground.

Hope is fading fast, though not all rays have been extinguished. Not yet.

Chapter Sixteen

T he Strip
    Las Vegas, NV

"NO WONDER he said to stay away." Rick sat at a table inside a nearby restaurant on the Strip that had suffered only minor damage. Behind the glass windows and only partially shattered door the air was easier to breathe and he was able to focus enough to try and come up with a plan.

"Can't we just go across?"

"I think we'll have to. It looks like the fires are all up and down the road. If we try and go around it could take several hours, depending on how far they've spread."

"Why didn't we see all of this before we got there?"

Rick shrugged. "The wind's been changing all day, keeping the smoke mostly away from us. With so many tall buildings between us and the road I'm not all that surprised. Still, I wish we had known."

"It can't be that bad on the other side of the road. It's not all that bad on this side."

Rick shook his head. "It looks like the eastern side took the brunt of whatever tore this place up. The fires are a lot bigger over there than they are here." He sighed and stood up and pressed his nose up against the window. "I think our best bet is to head between those two buildings, right over there. There's a gap in the burned out cars on the highway right in front of that median, then we can climb over that truck and get in between those buildings. We'll just have to hope that the fires back behind those buildings have died down enough to make it easy to get through."

"All right. Let's do it."

Rick raised an eyebrow and looked over at Jane. She, like he, was covered in soot and her face was black except around her lips where she had been gulping water ever since they came into the restaurant. She had been going strong since they started off earlier that morning and Rick was starting to worry about her ability to last much longer in the heat and smoke.

"Are you sure? You passed out yesterday from heatstroke. We might need to rest here for a while, at least until the sun goes down a bit."

"I'd rather get through all of this first, then take a break on the other side."

Rick nodded. "Fair enough. Let's check around in the back and see if we can put some makeshift masks together first. Might help with the smoke and dust."

Ten minutes later both Rick and Jane had found an apron, soaked it with water and cut it off so that they could tie it around their head and have it cover their mouth and nose without impeding their movement. After confirming one last time that Jane was feeling up to moving out, Rick opened the door to the restaurant and headed out into the street.

The wind was kicking up even harder than before and they walked slowly across the road, heading towards the raging fires and thick clouds of smoke on the eastern side of the Strip. The noise from the wind was loud enough that Rick didn't hear the roar of engines at first, and when he did they were already halfway across the road and standing in between the tall palm trees and wide planters in the median.

"Get down!" The sound of the vehicles instantly reminded Rick of Los Angeles and he fell flat on the ground and crawled behind one of the planters. Jane followed his lead and they sat crouched on the grass, waiting to see the source of the noise.

The roar of a pair of diesel engines thrummed through the air and Jane peeked up over the planter. She broke out into a smile and turned to Rick, nearly shouting over the sound of the wind and engines. "It's the army guys! The ones from the convoy! Look, it's their trucks!"

Rick stood up next to Jane and squinted, desperately trying to confirm what she said. He could see a pair of Humvees slowly heading south down the Strip towards them, but the longer he looked at them the more his stomach began to twist.

"Come on!" Jane started to walk out from the median and into the road. "Let's go get them to pick us up!"

"No!" Rick grabbed the canvas bag Jane was carrying on her shoulder and jerked her back, sending her tumbling to the ground. He crouched down next to her and hissed into her ear. "No, stay down!"

"What the hell, Rick?" Jane's face was a mixture of confusion and anger.

"Those are the army Humvees, but they're sure as hell not manned by soldiers in uniform!"

Rick and Jane raised their heads slightly above the planter and he pointed at the lead Humvee. "Look at the guy on the machine gun. He's not wearing a uniform! And the driver doesn't have one on either!"

Jane gulped loudly and sank back down behind the planter, sitting down on the grass and scooting as far away from the road as possible. "Who are they, then?"

Rick continued to watch the vehicles moving closer and shook his head. "I don't know. Maybe they're whoever was shooting at the bus when we flipped over. I sure as hell don't like the look of them, though."

As if on cue, the two Humvees picked up speed and raced down the road before skidding to a stop just in front of the restaurant that Rick and Jane were in only moments before. The pair scooted further behind the trees and planters in the median and Rick laid out on his stomach, watching the vehicles from behind a small gap in between one of the palm trees and one of the planters.

Two men jumped out of the lead Humvee and they were soon joined by three more from the other vehicle. The gunners stayed in their positions, slowly rotating the turrets around as they scanned the road. The five men standing near their vehicles all carried rifles of various types and calibers and each had a bandanna wrapped around their faces and wore thick plastic goggles and hats to shield their eyes and heads.

"Let's check this place out, then head to the Bellagio! Maybe they left the vault door open!" The voice came from one of the three men who hopped out of the second vehicle.

"You idiot." Another man punched the first one in the arm and pointed at the smoldering ruins of the Bellagio hotel. "Do you really think we can get down into the basement? I told you the Strip was a waste of time. We need to stick to the smaller hotels, not these ones! The earthquake tore these apart!"

Earthquake? Rick frowned. *What earthquake are they talking about?*

"Yeah, yeah. Fine. Let's find some food then we'll head out again. How about you two check down the road a block and let us know what you find down in the steakhouse. We'll look here and meet up with you."

"Fine."

Rick stiffened as the five men split up, with two of them walking farther south down the road on foot while the first three went into the restaurant. With the way the two men walking south were going, it was only a matter of time before they were able to see Rick and Jane lying in the median.

Great, he thought. *What the hell are we supposed to do now?*

Author's Notes

May 25, 2017

Welcome to the end of book 2 of Surviving the Fall! I really hope you enjoyed it, and I really appreciate you taking the time to read it. After the fast-paced action sequences of book 1 to set stage for the world of Surviving the Fall I knew I would need to dial it back (just a tad, at least in Rick's case, the poor guy) and start developing the characters and world some more. Things are going to be getting REALLY crazy here soon, both for Rick and for Dianne. If you could see the outlines and notes I have for later down in the story you'd be shocked at what these two are going to go through.

At first when I started writing Surviving the Fall I thought that I would enjoy writing Rick's perspective more. The reality of it, though, is that I enjoy writing Dianne's sections WAY more. I'm still trying to figure out exactly why, but I have some theories. I'm used to writing the crazy conspiracy-theory action and adventure sequences (like those that made up pretty much the entirety of Final Dawn) but I'm really enjoying writing about the more down to earth stuff that's occupying Dianne's time. I'm trying to put a really authentic feel to it and I hope that comes through. As a father to three children (two boys and a girl, but my oldest is only six) I'm thinking a lot about my own wife and children as I put Dianne, Mark, Jacob and Josie through everything they go through.

As you might have guessed I'm ever so slightly paranoid about the types of things that I write about and I often think about what I'd do if the "SHTF" (shit hit the fan). One of the things that I put in this episode is a direct result of personal experimentation that I've done for myself – aquaponics gardening!

I started getting into it last year when I bought one of those overpriced setups that let you grow herbs on your countertop. The plants' roots grow into water that you spike every couple of weeks with nutrients and a LED grow lamp hangs above. I was positively shocked by how well it worked and decided to experiment with a larger setup that I would build myself so that I could save a bunch of money and grow a lot of plants at once.

What I did was take a medium-sized Rubbermaid tub (about two feet long, a foot wide and a foot deep) and cut a couple dozen small circular holes in the top. Into those holes I inserted these mesh cups and substrate plugs (designed specifically for aquaponics gardening). I then filled the tub with water and put in an air pump to ensure the water had plenty of oxygen inside. (All of these supplies are readily available on Amazon and other places. If you're interested in a more detailed write-up, shoot me an email and if there's enough interest I'll start writing some Facebook/blog posts about it.)

Next I hung a pair of grow lights above the container (this, of course, made my wife wonder just *what* I was going to be growing) and then I bought some seeds. I got lettuce, several types of herbs, onions and a few other things I can't remember off the top of my head anymore.

Because the mesh cups hung into the water and the tub was sealed off from any light, the substrate was soaked through with delicious nutrient-filled water and I could just shove the seeds down into the substrate, turn on the lights and wait for the miracle of life to happen.

Sure enough, it only took a few days for my plants to start sprouting. I can't find any pictures of the setup right now (if I do then I'll put them up on my website and Facebook page) but it was amazing. I had a couple HUGE heads of lettuce growing, several enormous basil plants and all sorts of other awesome stuff.

The best part of the setup was that it was completely indoors, there was no need to worry about algae growth since the tub interior was cut off from light sources and I didn't have to mess around with dirt at all. I just had to keep the water topped off, make sure I added nutrient liquid to it once in a while and keep the grow lights on.

Of course, given how awesome that was, I had to add something similar to the story. :D

If you enjoyed that part of the story or any other parts—or heck, if you *didn't* like something—I'd love to hear about it. You can drop me an email or send me a message or leave a comment on Facebook. You can also sign up for my newsletter where I announce new book releases and other cool stuff a few times a month.

Answering emails and messages from my readers is the highlight of my day and every single time I get an email from someone saying how much they enjoyed reading a story it makes that day so much brighter and better.

Thank you so very much for reading my books. Seriously, thank you from the bottom of my heart. I put an enormous amount of effort into the writing and all of the related processes and there's nothing better than knowing that so many people are enjoying my stories.

All the best,
Mike

Book 3 - The Shattered Earth

Preface

After barely escaping Los Angeles, Rick Waters headed east on his quest to return home. He had barely crossed the California/Nevada border when he was stopped outside Las Vegas by a military blockade. Forced to load into a convoy of school buses headed for Nellis AFB, the convoy was attacked by unknown assailants and all but Rick and a young woman named Jane were killed in the crash. Struggling against the abnormally hot autumn weather, Rick and Jane trekked through Las Vegas, trying to make it to Nellis where they assumed they would find safety. After Jane suffered from heat exhaustion the pair took refuge in a hardware store overnight until she recovered enough strength to continue traveling. Unfortunately, as they tried to cross the famous "Strip" they were forced to hide in plain sight as a pair of armed Humvees loaded down with looters appeared.

Meanwhile, in Virginia, Dianne Waters has been working tirelessly to prepare the house, property and her children for what she is slowly starting to realize may not be a temporary situation. The power is still off, there are virtually no people left in the nearby small town and it's nearly impossible to get onto the highway to travel to any other cities. After witnessing a mysterious fire consume a neighbor's home a few miles down the road, Dianne resolves to be more vigilant than ever, ensuring that she and her oldest son are armed virtually all the time.

And now… Surviving the Fall: Book 3.

Chapter One

M ount Weather Emergency Operations Center
One Day Before the Event

A HEAVILY MODIFIED Gulfstream III tears through the bright blue Autumn sky at nearly seven hundred and fifty miles per hour. Reinforcements in the structure of the aircraft enable it to withstand the additional forces generated by flying almost two hundred miles per hour faster than its civilian counterparts. The aircraft has a plain paint job and if the tail numbers were ever searched the aircraft would come back as being owned by a boring face-less corporation.

The truth, however, is another matter. The Gulfstream III is one of several owned and operated by the United States federal government and used as semi-secret transportation for the President, Vice President and other senior members of government. Capable of landing on airstrips where the Boeing 747 cannot, the Gulfstream III—the government modified version of which is referred to as the C-20—carries a very special passenger.

"Mr. Vice President?" A stewardess approaches a man in a suit who is staring nervously out a window. "Sir, would you please fasten your seatbelt? We're about to land."

"Mm?" The man looks up at her questioningly for several seconds before her request finally processes. "Oh. Right. Of course. Thank you."

A portly man of sixty-something years old with drooping jowls, liver spots on his bald head and a smooth baritone voice that captivates his audiences, the Vice President of the United States is in a position he never thought would arrive while he was in office. As he is ferried from an event in New York to the secure underground bunker at Mount Weather, Virginia, he wonders what is happening to the rest of the high levels of government.

Secure communications channels have been down for days and only limited communications are allowed on civilian and insecure channels. He has no idea where the President is, what is being done with the members of Congress or what's happening in the country and the rest of the world. His briefings on Damocles and the effects it is having on the world have been extensive, but he has yet to fully process what it all means.

Ten minutes later, when the wheels of the C-20 have stopped rolling, a black SUV races towards the plane and pulls to a stop. A man in a uniform steps out of the passenger seat and gives the Vice President a quick salute, then motions for him to get into the car. The Vice President obliges, not bothering to ask any questions as the SUV races back toward the Mount Weather buildings and the entrance to the underground bunker.

Hardened against nuclear attack and set a mere fifty miles west of D.C., Mount Weather is the central operations post for FEMA. It is also one of the main relocation sites for the highest military and civilian levels of government and since it is so close to D.C. it is the location of choice for fast evacuations for anyone in, around or near Washington.

Inside the bunker the SUV rolls to a stop and the massive doors begin to slowly close behind it. The Vice President watches the doors close with a raised eyebrow, then finally speaks to the driver. "No one else is coming?"

"They're here already, sir. You're the last."

"Hm." The Vice President steps out of the car and walks down a long corridor that slopes down into the mountain. He passes through two more open vault doors before the décor changes from an industrial look to an office one.

Inside the command center buried beneath Mount Weather the mood is tense. All conversations between the staff are carried on in whispers and the Vice President looks around for someone in command to speak with. After a moment a figure in a suit and tie comes jogging through the door and extends his hand, smiling apologetically.

"Mr. Vice President. I'm so sorry to keep you waiting for so long. Please, come this way."

The man in the suit leads the Vice President through the operations command center into a large room with chairs, couches and tables scattered throughout. The place is decorated like an upscale club with leather furniture, bookcases on the walls and carpeting that keeps the myriad of conversations dulled.

Scattered throughout the room are dozens of high-ranking government officials, all in various states of distress. They are all dressed as though they have just come directly from D.C. and as they catch sight of the Vice President they all approach him and begin to pepper him with questions.

Before the Vice President can raise his hands and ask them to settle down, the man in the suit pulls the Vice President aside and hands him a sealed manila envelope. "The latest briefing, sir. We've severed connectivity with the outside world so everything's on paper now."

The Vice President opens the envelope and reads the single page inside. The color drains from his face as he reads farther down the page and by the time he's done he is white as a sheet. "What can we do about this? Has the President been briefed?"

"We've temporarily lost contact with Air Force One, sir. We're unsure whether or not he's been briefed. As of right now, though, we have to assume that he hasn't."

"What about responses? Surely there are contingency plans?"
The man in the suit shakes his head. "No sir."

Chapter Two

L as Vegas, Nevada

RICK WATCHED the men outside the Humvees carefully as they walked south down the road. After the first three entered the restaurant and vanished from sight, Rick had kept his attention on the remaining pair as they went along, hoping that they wouldn't turn around and see Rick and Jane in the median. Fortunately, though, the pair didn't appear to be interested in situational awareness. Instead of looking around and checking for any signs of trouble, they merely laughed and jabbed at each other as they walked along.

After the pair stopped and entered another building down the road, Rick knew it was his and Jane's best opportunity to get off the median and into cover. The two armed Humvees were the only visible threats, but all it would take is for one of the gunners to spot him and Jane and the two of them would be killed almost immediately.

"Are you ready to run?" Rick whispered to Jane and she nodded, her eyes wide in fright.

"What are you going to do?"

"As soon as both of the gunners are looking away from us we're going to run like hell and try to get inside the casino across the street, okay?"

Jane nodded again, her face creased with worry. "Are you sure we'll make it?"

Rick put on a brave smile, thoroughly unconvinced at his own answer. "Of course we'll make it!"

There was no definitive pattern to how the gunners on top of the Humvees were rotating around and scanning the area, but after a few minutes of watching, Rick finally saw that he and Jane had a window. The gunner farthest away from them had shouted at his partner and pointed at something up the street to the north. Both of them swiveled to face it and Rick jumped up, pulling on Jane's arm. "Let's go!"

Rick and Jane ran full tilt across the road, heading for what used to be a collection of small shops in front of the towering casino. At one point the shops were a neon tourist attraction that had to be seen, but something had damaged them to the point that they were naught but a pile of twisted metal, concrete and broken glass.

As Rick and Jane began to pick their way through the maze of wreckage in front of the casino, Rick thought for a moment that they were in the clear. The metallic whirr and thud of the turrets spinning around and the shouts of surprise from the gunners proved that assumption to be incorrect.

"Hey!" The voice was distant but Rick knew instantly that it was one of the gunners shouting at them. "You two, stop right now!" The shout was followed almost immediately by a burst of machine gun fire that tore into a large slab of concrete and rebar. A plume of concrete sprayed over Rick and he pushed Jane forward, urging her to go faster.

"Come on! They're going to shoot us if we don't move faster!"

Without drivers, the Humvees had a limited range of fire on Rick and Jane, but in between bursts from their guns he could hear the shouting of the other five men as they ran back towards the military vehicles, wondering what was going on. It only took a moment for the men to pile back into the Humvees, start the engines and squeal the tires as they pulled around to head across the street towards Rick and Jane.

"Inside, quickly, quickly! Come on, go!" Rick didn't even bother trying to be stealthy as he shouted at Jane, helping her climb over one last pile of debris that was in front of the casino entrance. A good fifty feet stood between the pair and the front doors to the casino. As they ran Rick cast a backward glance and saw that the Humvees were pulling to a stop at the edge of the road. One of them had a clear shot on the front of the building and Rick pulled Jane to the left to get out of the line of fire.

Lead tore through the air, shattering the few remaining panes of glass hanging in the front entrance of the casino and narrowly missing Rick and Jane. Rick continued heading perpendicularly to the entrance until he and Jane hit the wall of the building, at which point the Humvee on the road no longer had a shot on them.

"Come on, get inside!" Rick continued pushing Jane forward until he saw her stumble, at which point he caught her arm and held her up. "Are you okay?"

Jane turned toward him, her mouth open as she panted, trying to form words with which to reply. She mumbled something incoherent as another blast of fire echoed out. "Dammit!" Rick struggled as he hauled all of his gear and tried to support Jane as they moved closer to the casino entrance. Rick heard a commotion behind him and glanced back to see movement amongst the rubble. Unable to fire on the pair from the road, a few of the men from the Humvees had disembarked and were pushing forward to catch up to Rick before he could get inside.

"Come on, Jane!" Rick shook her by the arm and he felt her begin to walk under her own power again. With a final few steps they crossed over into the entrance of the casino through a broken window and made it inside. Rick steered Jane to the left, behind the wall and dropped his bags onto the floor. He grabbed the shotgun from the bag and whirled back around to face the entrance.

The first of the group to finish making it through the rubble screamed as Rick fired the shotgun. The buckshot spread out in a wide arc at the distance between the two, and while the man wasn't mortally wounded, he clawed at his face and neck as the pellets pierced through his skin. He fell backward into the rubble as the rest of the group paused, suddenly reconsidering their pursuit of Rick and Jane.

While the group had been temporarily halted by Rick's fire, he knew that they wouldn't hold back for long. Once they worked up the nerve to make another move Rick figured that he might be able to take down one or two of them before they killed him. *Got to think of something else.* Rick's eyes flicked across the interior of the casino, his vision slowly adjusting to the darkness.

The interior of the building looked like something had torn it apart. Half of the tables and chairs he could see were knocked over, large sections of the roof had caved in or cracked and the floor was littered with decorations and artwork that had been knocked off of the walls. The evidence of the earthquake that Rick had heard about was plain as day, but he still found the idea difficult to comprehend.

He took a few steps back from the entrance, looking up at the slanted ceiling, when he saw that a large neon sign hanging from the wall was precariously positioned and looked as though it could fall at a moment's notice. Rick stepped back even farther, pointed the shotgun at the sign's supports and fired. Having such low mass, the pellets couldn't do much to damage the metal supports, the wall mounts or the sign itself. At least under normal circumstances they couldn't.

As three shells full of buckshot bounced off of the sign and the supports, Rick heard metal groaning as the tiny vibrations disturbed the delicate balance of the sign and it began to continue its slide downward that had started during the earthquake. The sharp snap of steel breaking preceded the sign shifting down and outward suddenly before coming to a brief halt. The sign swung back towards the entrance and Rick's eyes opened wide and he shook his head, hoping that it would stay in position long enough to swing back in the opposite direction.

A few seconds more was all the sign needed as the bottom swung back towards the interior of the casino. This movement was the final straw for the sign's supports and the massive object came crashing down in a thunderous roar. Because the sign was already angled toward the entrance, instead of falling flat on the inside of the casino it fell at an angle towards the entrance. Light streaming in from the outside was suddenly blotted out as the sign was jammed into the front of the building, completely blocking it off from entry or exit.

"Get through that, assholes." Rick allowed himself a brief smile as he spoke quietly, overjoyed that his ludicrous plan had somehow worked.

Chapter Three

Las Vegas, Nevada

ONLY A FEW SMALL streams of light came through cracks in between the sign and the building and while sounds from outside were muffled, Rick was able to make out the gunfire and shouts and anger as the men outside both shot and threw their body weight at the sign to try and get it out of the way. The commotion outside lasted for several minutes, and after waiting a moment to ensure that the entrance was secured, Rick went over to check on Jane.

The young woman's eyes were closed as she sat on the floor, her head back against the wall as she took long, slow breaths. Rick felt her head and neck and quickly opened a bottle of water for her and helped her take several sips. "Easy there." Rick spoke quietly and splashed water on her forehead. "You're getting too hot again. How are you feeling?"

"I want to live somewhere cold." Jane opened her eyes and forced a smile. "Did you kill them?"

Rick shook his head and glanced back at the sign jammed into the entrance of the casino. Light streaming in through cracks around the sign and through holes and cracks in the ceiling provided just enough light to make out the general shapes inside the building. "No, I didn't. The front door to this building is closed off but I'm sure they'll try to get in here another way."

"Why?" Jane's question caught Rick off guard and he struggled to think of an answer. Why, indeed, was he assuming that the men would try to get into the building?

"I don't know. Maybe they won't, but we should assume the worst given the fact that they stole those army Humvees and tried to kill us."

Jane nodded and slowly started to stand up. "We should keep moving then, shouldn't we?"

Rick helped Jane to her feet and watched her closely, waiting to see if she was going to collapse again. "You sure you're good to move already?"

"I think so. Just feeling a little bit dizzy."

Rick got out one of the lanterns he had taken from the lumberyard and turned it on. The glow was swallowed by the cavernous darkness in the casino, illuminating only a few feet around Rick and Jane. After picking up his gear, Rick and Jane began moving deeper into the building, leaving the noise and commotion of the group outside behind. Before long the shouts and clangs of their efforts to get inside had vanished, leaving only the eerie silence of the casino in their place.

"What happened to this place?" Jane spoke quietly, not wanting to raise her voice above a whisper due to the overwhelming quiet of the building.

Rick shook his head. "Not sure. I heard a group at the lumberyard and that bunch outside talking about earthquakes, though. If there really was a quake that hit the city I guess that would explain all the damage."

"Is this place going to hold together?" Jane nervously looked up at the ceiling, casting a wary eye at the cracks and holes that pervaded it. In the main section of the casino sunlight was visible through the breaks in the ceiling. As they moved into the building and the ceiling dropped to accommodate the floors of the areas above them, they could see that the paint and plaster were cracked there as well. The darkness of the place along with the overturned furniture and gambling equipment and the cracks in the ceilings created an atmosphere where it felt like the entire building could cave in at any second.

"I hope so. Let's just try to get through here quickly, though. I've no idea where the other entrances are here."

Rick and Jane continued on in silence as they walked through the wide halls and expansive rooms of the casino. Rick had stepped foot into two casinos before in his life for business reasons and had been immediately turned off by their maze-like quality. Having large clusters of games and tables jammed next to each other with people standing shoulder to shoulder wasn't something he was a fan of and he never felt the desire to go back.

Even with the darkness and destruction in the building, though, Rick could see that it had been like nothing he had experienced before. The older maze-like layout had been replaced by a wider, more open "playground" style with wide aisles, small clusters of machines and tables and a brighter, cheerier atmosphere. Sunlight streamed in through a collection of windows in one of the next rooms. A few scattered rays of color showed up amongst the white light from the few bits of stained glass that had survived the earthquake.

"This place doesn't look like any casino I've seen before." Rick whispered as he looked around the room, both for a possible exit and for any sign of the men from outside. "It looks more like a resort."

"Think they have any food around here?"

Rick couldn't help but smile at the question and nodded. "Yeah, probably." The thought of having something other than energy bars and water to eat made his stomach growl. "I'm not sure we should be stopping for a meal, but keep your eyes open for a kitchen and we'll grab something to take with us and eat once we get out of here."

Jane nodded and gave Rick a weak smile. "Sounds good."

Rick and Jane continued to pick their way through the large room, heading for the back of the building, when the low rumble of a diesel engine came from outside the nearest wall. Despite the thick walls and layers of carpeting and sound deflection materials, the utter silence of the interior of the building made it possible to just barely pick up on the noise. Jane was the first to hear it and stopped short, grabbing Rick's arm and pulling him to a stop as well.

"Did you hear that?" Jane whispered to Rick and he cocked his head to the side. The engine thrummed as it surged forward and there was a deafening sound as the vehicle hit the side of the building at a high rate of speed.

After failing to get in through the front entrance the two Humvees had split up, with one traveling down each side of the casino, looking for a way in. After locating a service door that was tightly sealed, the group in one of the vehicles decided that trying to ram the side of the building to break down the door was the smartest thing they could do.

In a battle between the armored Humvee and the thick steel door frame and reinforced concrete exterior of the building, the building came out victorious. The Humvee sputtered and choked from the impact and all of the men inside groaned, rubbing their necks to try and relieve the pain from the severe whiplash. The front end of the Humvee was severely dented and one of the tires had nearly popped from the impact, but otherwise it was still drivable.

Inside, Rick listened as the sound of the Humvee's engine receded and he breathed a sigh of relief. "Bunch of idiots. What are they trying to do?"

"Maybe they found a way in?"

"It sounds more like they were trying to ram the building to bring it down on us." Rick snorted and shook his head. "Whatever they're doing, I'd rather not be nearby if they happen to succeed."

Chapter Four

The Waters' Homestead
Ellisville, VA

"MOM! MOM, WAKE UP!"

Dianne groaned and opened her eyes, blinking against the dawning sun's light. She wondered why the curtains in the master bedroom were open until she saw the beaming face of her young daughter pop into view. Josie wore a huge smile on her face as she leaned in close, rubbing her nose against Dianne's nose in an affectionate greeting.

"It snowed, mom! It snowed!" Josie bounced across the bed on her hands and knees and landed on her feet on the floor. Dianne closed her eyes for a few seconds then opened them and sat up, finally processing what Josie had just said.

"It snowed?"

Outside, the sloping field, outbuildings and trees were covered with a thin blanket of snow. It was difficult to see much beyond the small lake at the base of the slope due to the falling snow that was rapidly growing thicker and more intense. Patterns were beginning to form in the snow beneath the trees as it fell from branches and leaves. Beneath the eaves of the outbuildings there was the faintest trace of grass and bare earth, though that was rapidly vanishing as gusts of wind blew the snow every which way.

The peaceful serenity of the unexpected snowfall was punctuated by the shouts of Dianne's three children. She slowly got out of bed and rubbed her arms and hands, realizing just how cold it was in the house.

"Mark?" Dianne called out as she went to stand next to Josie at the window.

"Yeah, mom?" Mark bellowed back from downstairs. Heavy footsteps came pounding up the stairs and he stepped into the bedroom a few seconds later.

Dianne glanced at her son and raised an eyebrow. "Shorts and a t-shirt?"

Mark shrugged. "It's warm downstairs. Jacob and I got a bunch of wood inside and started a fire a little while ago."

Dianne beamed and embraced her son. "Thanks, kiddo! I was going to ask you if you could start getting the wood together for a fire." Dianne looked back out the window and shook her head. "I didn't expect snow this early in the year."

"It's happened this early before, hasn't it?" Mark stepped up next to his mother and crossed his arms.

"Yeah, but not for several years. I hope this doesn't mean a particularly bad winter. So much for checking the weather forecast, huh?"

"Hey mom?" Jacob came running up the stairs next. "Breakfast is… sort of ready."

Mark turned around and glared at his younger brother. "Jacob!"

Dianne turned and raised both eyebrows. "What's this about breakfast?"

"Uh… you can tell her." Jacob raced back out of the room and down the stairs, leaving Mark to sheepishly turn to his mother.

"Mark?"

"We sort of had an accident while making the eggs. You might want to come and see."

Dianne rolled her eyes and gave Mark a playful shove towards the door. "Get whatever mess you made cleaned up and I'll be down there in a few minutes." Josie followed Mark out of the bedroom and Dianne looked back out the window, taking a moment to try and soak up some more of the beauty before she had to turn her attention to more mundane matters.

Chapter Five

F our Days Before the Event

DIANNE AND RICK Waters sit on the couch in their living room. Outside, through the open glass sliding door, they can see and hear their three children playing near the water down by the bottom of their property. It is shortly after dinner, the sun is setting and Dianne and Rick are enjoying a few moments of peace before their children are back inside.

On the television across the room plays a nightly news broadcast that Dianne watches intently. Next to her, Rick browses on his tablet, swiping through news stories and opinion articles from the day while simultaneously replying to mundane emails that have piled up from work. Dianne elbows Rick gently in the side and points at the television.

"What's up?" *Rick looks at her, then at the TV.*

"What's with all this bad stuff going on the last couple days?"

"Hm?" *Rick squints as he reads off the ticker at the bottom of the screen.* "What stuff?"

"There were those oil platforms catching fire, then half a dozen tech companies just went out of business."

Rick shrugs. "No clue. Maybe sabotage on the oil platforms? This is the first I've heard of it."

"What about all the companies going out of business."

"Well, we're near… wait, no." *Rick furrows his brow.* "Huh. That is odd. I haven't heard anything about it at work and they're generally tuned in to the latest that's going on in the tech world."

"You think this could mean trouble for the company?"

Rick shakes his head. "Nah. If there was trouble coming I'm sure I would've heard of it."

"You have been pretty busy lately with that big project and presentation."

"Ugh." Rick rolls his shoulders and cracks his neck. "Don't remind me. I'm trying to forget about that until tomorrow morning."

Dianne smiles and puts an arm around Rick, pulling him in for a kiss. "I'm sure that can be arranged."

Rick lets his tablet slide off his lap onto the couch as he leans in to return the kiss. He is about to say something in return when the sound of three children all shouting "ew" at the same time makes him look up. Mark, Jacob and Josie are standing on the back porch, panting with exertion after charging up the hill back to the house. Josie and Jacob are both soaking wet and covered in dirt and leaves while Mark is standing behind them with a grimace.

"Sorry." Mark speaks sheepishly. "They sort of… fell in."

Dianne laughs at the sight and stands up. "Don't you dare come inside like that. I'll get some old towels for you to dry off with then it's time to get cleaned up before bed."

Rick smiles as he watches Dianne help the children get out of their clothes and upstairs for their showers. After the living room empties out and there are sounds of loud talking, playing and running water from upstairs, he picks up his tablet and glances back at the television. He considers—for a moment—watching to find out more about what's going on before he realizes that he needs to do yet another read-through of his presentation before work in the morning.

Rick leans back on the couch with his tablet and sighs, diving back into his little corner of the world, remaining oblivious to the storm that is approaching.

Chapter Six

L as Vegas, Nevada

"I NEVER THOUGHT stale bread and water would taste so good."

"Anything's better than prepackaged crap at this point."

Jane chuckled and nodded in agreement before taking another bite from her loaf of bread. A few minutes after the sound of the Humvee engines disappeared, the pair had found their way into a nearby kitchen. The smell of rotting food had nearly driven them away, but Rick had insisted they look through the storage shelves to see if anything was still good.

Most of the food was meant to be heated up on a grill or in a pan instead of being cooked from scratch and had been kept in the freezer and fridge. When the power went out, the food spoiled quickly and all that was left were a few canned staples, bread and drinks. Rick packed a couple bottles of high-proof alcohol away in one of his bags along with more canned goods, but he and Jane took a few moments to sit down, eat and rest their feet.

"Ready to go?" Rick stood up and brushed his hands on his pants. Jane nodded as she took another gulp from a bottle of water.

"All set." She stood up and followed Rick out of the kitchen.

After exiting the main floor of the casino, Rick and Jane entered the lobby for the hotel proper. A side entrance to the hotel was caved in, though Rick could see a few shafts of light coming in through the debris. He climbed on the pile of rubble and peered through the crack, squinting in the bright sunlight as he tried to gauge how far back through the building they were.

He was about to say something to Jane when he heard the low rumble of a diesel engine rapidly approaching. Outside, Rick could just make out the next building down the street. In the gap between the buildings was a clear patch of gravel and pavement and as he watched, he suddenly saw the blur of one of the Humvees tearing by.

"Was that one of them?" Jane whispered fearfully behind Rick and he held up a hand, motioning for her to remain quiet. While he couldn't see where the Humvee went from his vantage point, he heard it stop shortly down from the caved-in hotel entrance. The sound of car doors opening and closing followed, along with a group of voices talking.

"Spread out and check the doors. We're getting in there one way or another."

"Why don't we just shoot the doors in with the turrets?"

"Because we've barely got any ammo left. Besides, that only works in the movies, you idiot."

"I have a question. Why are we chasing after these guys, anyway?"

"Because if they happen to run across the Army then they'll tell them where they saw us. Then we'll have to go somewhere else in the city. If you want to go do that and try to deal with the Sureños, then by all means be my guest."

The rest of the conversation grew muffled as the group of men moved down the length of the building and out of earshot. Rick stepped down from the pile of debris and rubbed his chin. "They're still trying to find a way in. Doesn't look like they're going to give up anytime soon."

"Why not?"

"They think we're going to tell the Army about them and ruin their looting." Rick sighed and closed his eyes. "All right. We need to move with a purpose at this point. No more stopping or walking. We have to run. Can you manage that?"

Jane nodded. "It's not hot in here at all. I'll be fine."

"Good. We'll head for the far back of the building and exit through whatever we find. If we hurry then we can beat them there and get out before they realize we're gone."

"Sounds good."

Rick nodded and held the lantern up, searching the hotel lobby for which way to go next. A wide hallway proceeded toward the back of the building from the lobby, passing by elevators and large staircases leading upward into the hotel. While the hall didn't extend for very far, Rick figured that there would be maintenance and staff-only rooms in the back that they could enter to get to the back of the building and continue onward.

After proceeding down the hall, Rick found what he was looking for. A wide door with an opaque window and a "Staff Only" sign on it sat in a small recess in the wall at the end of the hall on the left side. Rick turned the handle and was surprised to find the door unlocked. He pushed it open, holding the lantern in front of him with his left hand while keeping his right hand resting on the pistol on his hip.

What Rick had thought would be a small room turned out to be one of the many entrances to the hotel and casino's maintenance, housekeeping and other facilities. Set into the perimeter of the building around the back half, multiple entrances allowed cleaning and other staff to quickly move about behind the scenes. A portion of the floor off to the side turned into a metal catwalk and Rick could make out the shape of industrial-grade washing machines a floor below, in the basement. Rows of metal racks filled with toilet paper, gallons of cleaners, spare mop heads, buckets and a myriad of other supplies were bolted to the floor and walls of the room for as far as he could see.

"Wow." Jane whispered behind Rick as she looked around. "This is amazing."

"Yeah, it's pretty cool seeing how it looks behind the scenes. I bet it would have been even more amazing while this place was running." Rick stepped forward slowly, forgetting for a moment their commitment to moving quickly through the rest of the building. "It looks like a veritable maze up ahead. Let's stick close together. Let me know if you spot a door leading out or anything else worth checking out."

Jane nodded and took a step closer to Rick as he started heading down through the large utility room. The room expanded and contracted as they went along, taking on the shape of the rooms outside of it. They passed by a new door leading back into the building often enough that they stopped opening them and looking out to see where they were. Some of the doors led to kitchens, others led to offices and some opened into hallways in the hotel.

Each footstep the pair took echoed into the black abyss below them, though Rick's lantern wasn't powerful enough to get a clear view of much that was in the basement. It took the pair another twenty minutes of creeping through the utility area before they entered the true maintenance area of the building. Massive amounts of ductwork, cables and pipes entered through the room and each was labeled with a code that corresponded to its purpose, origination point and exit point from the room. The air smelled intensely of copper, though it was a welcome relief from the chemical scents that pervaded the utility areas.

Rick started getting concerned that they would get lost in the maze of machinery in the maintenance area when Jane tugged on his sleeve and pointed off to the side. "Couple of doors there. Should we check and see where we are?"

"Nice. Good find." Rick headed for the door, opened it and looked out only to immediately turn off the lantern and close the door nearly shut again. He pushed Jane back with his right hand before reaching for his pistol and drawing it.

"What is it?" Jane whispered, her eyes wide with fear. The maintenance room was pitch-black, but outside through the double doors she could see bits of light coming through as they weaved back and forth.

"It's them."

Chapter Seven

L as Vegas, Nevada

RICK PULLED the door closed slowly, keeping the handle turned until it was sealed, then slowly releasing it. He winced as the latch clicked into place, then he checked the flimsy-looking lock to make sure it was engaged.

"How many were there?" Jane whispered again. Rick switched on the lantern and double-checked the lock, then turned to Jane and used his body to shield the lantern so that none of the light would leak out through the cracks around the double doors.

"Three at least. All of them with flashlights and rifles." Rick slid his pistol back into its holster and looked up and around at the room. "We need to find a way out of here. Come on, let's keep going this way. Maybe there's an exit down here somewhere."

Rick and Jane jogged through the maintenance area for a few more minutes until the machinery began to thin out and be replaced by more storage shelves and cleaning supplies again. Upon seeing this, Rick realized that they were at the end of the maintenance area and were now entering another utility area. Instead of having neatly labeled and organized supplies like the previous utility area, though, the new one consisted mostly of unopened boxes with large barcodes and QR codes on them. The extra-wide walkways and strips of yellow tape running down the floor made sense when he saw a pair of small forklifts parked in a corner of the room.

"This must be an unloading area." Rick suddenly grew excited. "We must be near the back of the building. I bet there's an exit around here!" As Rick and Jane rounded a corner, the room grew warmer and brighter and they both increased their speed until they finally arrived at exactly what Rick was hoping they would find.

Three rectangular windows were set into large rolling metal doors of the type used at commercial loading docks. While two of the doors were fully closed, one was halfway open, allowing the relatively cool air inside the building to escape and bringing in the heat from outside. Jane stepped past Rick to start running towards the open door when he put an arm out in front of her, halting her in her tracks.

"Sh." Rick raised a finger to his lips. He gently took off his gun bag and backpack and lowered them to the ground before pulling the shotgun out. He took a few cautious steps forward, not wanting to be on the wrong side of an ambush. The open door was the third of the three and the farthest away, so Rick leaned in towards the first closed door, peeking through the window to see outside.

A thick layer of dust coated the outside of the window and Rick pressed his nose against the wire mesh glass, straining to see what was outside. Behind the casino, a short distance away, was a service road and beyond that was another tall building that Rick couldn't make out very well. A loading dock sat directly beyond the three rolling doors behind the casino but no trucks were parked either in the dock or on the service road.

With no sign or sound of the men inside or the vehicles outside, Rick motioned at Jane. "All right, looks like the coast is clear. Let's get outside and run down this road till we find a place to hide on the other side. Ready?"

Jane nodded and she and Rick both crouched down next to the half-opened doorway. Rick put his backpack back on and was in the process of placing his shotgun down into the gun bag, ready to pull out his pistol instead, when the door leading out into the hotel creaked open. Rick's head jerked up and he looked at the man standing before him.

The man was on the short side, with a solid build and wearing a tank top, camo cargo pants and a bandanna on his head. The gun in his hands—an AK of some sort—was held loosely, and for a long second both he and Rick stared at each other, mouths open, as they both tried to contemplate what was going on.

As the man raised his rifle he fumbled with it just long enough for Rick to stand up and clumsily fire his shotgun from the hip. Pain arced through Rick's wrist and arm and he nearly dropped the shotgun to the floor. As metal clattered against the rough concrete, he heard a howl as the man in front of him clutched at his neck. Blood was pouring from the man's neck and chest and he staggered back through the open door, tripped over his own feet and fell sideways in the hallway beyond.

Rick's fingers burned as he adjusted his grip on the shotgun. He fought through the pain in his wrist as he pulled the weapon tight against his shoulder and prepared to fire again if the man made any aggressive movements. There was a scuffle and a pair of shouts in the hallway and the injured man was suddenly pulled away from the open door. Rick ran to the door and kicked it shut, then twisted the latch and locked it tight. Behind him Jane held her hands to her face and shook her head, her eyes wide as she tried to comprehend what she had just seen.

Acting on pure adrenaline Rick ran back to the open door and turned to her. "Are you ready?" He shouted at her, not bothering with trying to remain quiet any longer. She nodded numbly and he grabbed her by the shoulder. "Let's go, then!"

Rick was halfway under the door and about to help Jane through when he heard the rumble of a diesel engine drawing closer. He backed up into the utility area and pulled Jane to the side of the door. The squeal of tires came from outside and they were quickly followed by the sound of a pair of doors opening and closing again.

"What do we do?" Jane's question was accompanied by the sounds of shouting from the men that were both inside the hotel and waiting outside near the loading dock. Rick racked his brain, trying to figure a way out of their situation. They could retreat back through the hotel and try to lose their pursuers that way, but that solution would be more likely than not to lead to certain death.

"I think they pulled up off to the right. There's a nice bit of cover there if we crawl out. All we have to do is keep them occupied long enough to run down to the left, where I saw an alley leading through the next set of buildings. I think that's our only shot."

"That sounds horrible! How are you going to keep them occupied?"

Rick shook his head and smiled. "Not me, Jane. *Us.*"

Chapter Eight

L as Vegas, Nevada

THE ENTIRETY of the four minutes it took for Jane to unzip Rick's backpack, pull out the twin bottles of vodka, find a box of matches he had put in one of the side pockets, grab a couple of old rags from a nearby shelf and stuff them into the necks of the bottles were pure agony for Rick. He spent that time alternating between peeking out the window to see if the men outside were getting closer and hoping that the ones inside the hotel weren't about to shoot off the hinges to the doors and barge their way in.

When Jane finished, Rick nodded in approval and gave her one last final set of instructions. "Remember, just keep a tight hold on these, okay? When I tell you, throw the first one just inside the door here. I'll take care of the second one."

"Are you sure this will work?"

Rick had no idea whether or not it would, but he felt obligated to lie to her. "Absolutely."

Jane kept a firm hold on the two bottles of vodka as Rick slid under the door and rolled out. He landed in a heap on the ground and groaned in pain before rising to one knee. He peeked over the edge of the walkway and guardrail next to the empty space where a truck would have backed in to the building to offload its cargo. The Humvee was still there and someone was sitting in the turret, swiveling around to watch the end of the building.

From the angle the Humvee was at, Rick realized that anyone in their position wouldn't have been able to see that one of the back doors of the building was open and, thus, they wouldn't have necessarily thought to check down in that direction.

"Hurry up!" Rick whispered at Jane. She handed him both bottles and he set them down on the ground before helping her jump down. "You still have the matches?"

Jane held up the small box and he picked up one of the bottles. "Whatever you do, don't drop this."

The alcohol and chemical-soaked rag caught fire instantly and Jane yelped in surprise. Rick turned and gave her a wide-eyed look but it came too late. A shout down the road accompanied an uptick in the shouting and banging from inside the building and Rick realized that the time for action was either right then or never.

He grabbed the Molotov from Jane's hand and ran halfway down the length of the loading dock with her in tow, then turned and lobbed it expertly through the opening in the loading dock door. The neck of the bottle caught on the lip of the door and broke, then the body of the bottle struck the edge of one of the metal shelves inside. It broke apart, sending the alcohol spilling across the floor.

As the flames licked greedily at the high-proof alcohol, they also found the spilled contents of a few cans of paint thinner that Rick had noticed on the shelf. While Jane had been busy stuffing rags into the throats of the vodka bottles, Rick had quickly punctured and spilled the paint thinner across the floor, all the way up to the interior door that the injured man had retreated behind.

The effects of the Molotov by itself would have been more than enough to give the two men—three if the nearly dead one still counted—behind the door pause once they got it open. The addition of the paint thinner, however, had a profound effect on them before that even happened. The paint thinner, over the course of a few minutes, had leaked underneath the door and into the carpeting on top of which the two men and their nearly-dead companion stood and laid.

Flames wound their way through the offloading area, sending a blast of heat out across Rick and Jane's backs before traveling beneath the door and erupting in the floor on the other side. Rick smiled grimly at the sound of the men's screaming as their feet and legs were suddenly on fire, with nothing they could do to stop it but to flee down the dark halls, the flames and their flashlights the only source of light.

Even though the door in between the hotel hallway and the offloading area was still closed, the screams were loud enough to attract the attention of the gunner in the Humvee and the pair of men who had been walking down one side of the building, checking the doors on the exterior to see if they were open. The gunner swiveled his gun and trained it on the billowing smoke and flames that erupted out through the partially opened loading dock door and the pair of men began jogging towards the sight, wondering what was going on.

"Now or never." Rick whispered quietly and held out the bottle for Jane to light the rag. It, like the first one, also caught fire immediately and Rick peeked up over the edge of the loading dock to see where his target was. The appearance of a new bit of smoke away from the building caught the eye of the gunner in the Humvee who swiveled slightly and fired several rounds that tore through the metal and concrete of the dock. Rick nearly dropped the Molotov as he ducked back down to avoid the fire.

When it stopped he scuttled several feet back down towards the building, masking himself slightly in the billows of smoke pouring out, then stood up and threw the bottle in a long arc, aiming not for the pair of men next to the Humvee, but for the vehicle itself. Rick's hope was that the bottle would shatter on the windshield or front grill of the vehicle which would hopefully distract the men long enough for him and Jane to make their escape.

Rick watched the bottle as it soared end over end through the air as if in slow motion, finally coming to rest not on the front of the vehicle but on the very top. The bottle splintered and shattered across the machine gun turret, dousing the gunner, the exterior and the interior of the vehicle in alcohol and flames. The screams from the two men inside the Humvee were instant and horrifying. The driver kicked open his door and fell out on the ground, rolling around as he tried in vain to extinguish the fire.

The gunner took the brunt of the impact from the Molotov and tried desperately to put out the fire while still being trapped in his seat. Retreating into the Humvee only exposed him to more flames and climbing out was nearly impossible due to the level of trauma he was experiencing. As both of the men in the vehicle screamed out in pain, the two outside the Humvee froze in shock at what they were witnessing.

"Help me!" The driver, still rolling around on the ground, managed to get a couple of words out which snapped the two on foot into action. They both dropped their guns to the ground and one of them started using his hands to try to pat out the flames on the driver. The other one began running around the Humvee, alternating between trying to climb up onto the vehicle and jumping back off as the flames continued to grow more intense. It was obvious that he was trying to find a way to help the gunner, but was unwilling to risk his own life in the process.

As the gunner slowly burned to death, Rick and Jane made their escape. As soon as the first screams came from the direction of the Humvee, Rick had hissed at Jane. "Follow me and don't fall behind!" After that single instruction Rick took off, running full tilt to the left down the service road as he aimed for a small path that led between two buildings on his right. Jane stayed close behind him and as the pair ducked into the path between the buildings, Rick risked stopping for a second to take a glance back.

As he watched the two men burning and their companions half-heartedly trying to help them, he felt a slight twinge of guilt that was immediately assuaged by thinking about what the men had been trying to do to Jane and himself. He briefly thought about getting out the hunting rifle and ensuring that all four of the men were dead, but the knowledge that there was another vehicle and more men somewhere close by made the decision for him.

"Come on." Rick whispered to Jane, tugging at her shirt as she stared slack-jawed at the scene.

"Those men…"

"Tried to kill us. Let's go."

"But…"

"Let's go. *Now.*"

Jane followed behind Rick as he wound his way down the narrow path between the buildings. They traveled parallel to the Strip for a few hundred feet before the path ended at another service road. Rick glanced both ways down the road before pointing to the right. "Nellis is that way. Are you good to keep walking for a while more? I want to get as much distance between them and us before we stop."

Jane nodded but stayed silent, still thinking about the sight of the two burning men. Rick's brutal efficiency in dealing with the attackers frightened her and she wasn't sure what she thought of the strange man anymore.

Chapter Nine

Three Days Before the Event

IN THE OIL *fields a hundred miles north of Las Vegas, a pair of seismologists sit in the back of a camper. They both wear glasses and loose-fitting clothing. Their brows are moist with sweat and a small oscillating fan hung from the ceiling of the camper does little but push the hot air around the room. The pitiful air conditioning unit hanging out of the back window hasn't worked in weeks and there is no time in the schedule to get a new one.*

A pair of monitors are mounted to each wall of the camper, and the seats the seismologists sit in are offset so they can each face in a different direction. One of them, wearing a white shirt and shorts, takes a gulp from a tall glass of water. The other, wearing a grey shirt and shorts, taps furiously on his keyboard. Every few seconds he glances between his two screens, watching as the data displayed on the black and white command line interface changes in response to his inputs.

"Gary?" The man in the grey shirt speaks.

"Hm?" Gary doesn't look away from his screens as he finishes his glass of water.

"Look at this, would you?"

"What is it, Jacob? I'm in the middle of—what the hell is that?" Gary swivels around in his chair with a sigh, rolling his eyes until he catches sight of Jacob's screen. Gary's glass drops from his hand and bounces on the carpet of the camper, rolling under the table and depositing a few stray drops of water on the floor and wall.

"That's what I'd like to know." Jacob taps the back end of his pen against the monitor and shakes his head. "Sure as hell isn't normal, is it?"

Gary stretches his arm out and grabs a mobile phone off the table next to Jacob. He holds it up in front of the monitor and snaps a picture before sending it in a text message. A few moments later the phone's screen lights up and a call comes through.

"Hello?" Gary answers the phone.

"What kind of bullshit games are you two trying to play with me?" The voice on the other end is gruff and annoyed.

"No games. This is the real deal."

"How many sensors are picking it up?"

Gary looks at Jacob and shakes his head. "I don't think you understand. Every single sensor is showing this. Pressure in every single well is building to phenomenal levels."

"Why the hell haven't the safety valves tripped?"

"No idea, sir. We can't access any of the systems."

"God dammit." There is a sound of scuffling from the other end of the line and several more muted curses. "Get your asses out to the closest well and jack in directly. I'll have a crew out there in two hours. As soon as you're at the well call me back and I'll have one of the techs here walk you through accessing the systems."

Gary opens his mouth to argue but the line goes dead. He slowly places the phone back on the table. Next to him, Jacob raises a questioning eyebrow. "That didn't sound good."

"Nope. Not at all."

Chapter Ten

The Waters' Homestead
Ellisville, VA

AFTER CLEANING out the burned egg and scorched toast from behind the stove where they had inexplicably fallen—both boys had no idea how it could have happened, or so they professed—Dianne turned her attention back to the snow.

"All righty, kids. Listen up." Mark, Jacob and Josie were all seated on the living room couch while Dianne paced back and forth in front of the back door. "Since we obviously can't get weather reports anymore and I'm about as good of a meteorologist as I am a circus ringmaster, we need to treat this storm as seriously as possible.

"The heating elements in the solar panels will keep them clear of the worst ice and snow, but we'll need to keep an eye on them and we need to get the rest of them installed as soon as this snow clears. Thankfully we got the bulk of the veggies in, but I want Jacob to help me go through the gardens and clear out any we missed. We'll dump them straight into the freezer and should be able to salvage them."

"What about me and Mark?" Josie kicked her legs against the couch impatiently. Dianne turned and smiled at her.

"You and your brother are going to have quite the assignment. While Jacob and I are taking care of the garden and the vegetables and the animals, you and Mark are going to get the basement cleared out and ready for us to set up the aquaponics."

"We're going to do it in the basement?" Mark asked. "Why not in one of the barns like you were talking about before?" Dianne's original plan had been to set up the aquaponics in one of their outbuildings. Due to complications with running power for the lights and with the onset of the early snow, though, she was glad she had changed her mind.

"Running lines is going to be a hassle and I'd rather not have to make trips back and forth in the snow and cold. Besides, having everything here in the house is going to make things easier overall." Dianne sighed and shook her head. "It's already getting a bit cramped in here, though. Maybe we should think about doing it in an outbuilding after all."

"What about the passageway from the basement?" Mark asked the question meekly, knowing that he wasn't supposed to bring up the subject. Dianne, however, wasn't upset, mostly because she had forgotten about the years-old project that had never been completed.

"The passageway?" Dianne rubbed her chin. "It's been ages since I thought about that. Though as I recall we told you not to talk about it, didn't we?" Mark started to defend himself when Dianne laughed and shook her head. "Relax, Mark. I'm joking. If there was ever a time for everyone in this family to learn about the passageway it would be now."

Started as a project a few months after purchasing the house, the passageway was a pet project entirely of Rick's creation. Obsessed with the idea of houses with secret passages since he was a child, shortly after moving in Rick had created a detailed design for a passage that would lead from the basement of the house to a shed out in the woods. Dianne had initially been against the underground tunnel, but eventually relented once she saw how much it meant to Rick. When she tried to get an answer from him as to what practical purpose it would serve, his response was always the same. He would smile, shrug and say "No reason, just for fun."

Rick's shifting work responsibilities and the growth of their children meant that there was far less time that he could devote to the tunnel project than he had initially hoped. While the length of the tunnel had been dug and partially shored up, the structural supports necessary to ensure it would never collapse had never been put in place. As Rick's free time completely evaporated he finally gave up on the project, sealing off the hatch in the basement so that their children wouldn't inadvertently wander into the passage and hurt themselves.

Forgoing checking the gardens and animals for the moment, Dianne headed for the basement as her three children ran ahead of her. Downstairs, Jacob and Josie ran around the room, shouting about what objects in the room could be connected to the secret passage.

"Maybe if you pull one of these books!"

"No, you have to turn the lights on and off just right!"

"What about the bricks on the wall over there? Maybe one of those will open it!"

Dianne laughed as she headed over to the bookcase and stood on her toes to feel around on the top. Her hand fell on a set of keys and she grabbed them before stepping towards the center of the room. "All right!" Dianne clapped her hands to get the attention of her younger children. "You two, over there by Mark." When all three children were standing together, Dianne adopted a serious expression and tone.

"I want you three to listen very carefully. This tunnel isn't a game. It's not a toy. It's not a place to play. Unless I tell you explicitly that you can go down into it, you're to all stay out, is that clear?"

"Even me?" Mark asked.

"Even you. It's been a couple years since anybody's been down in the tunnel and for all I know it's partially or fully collapsed. Even if it hasn't there's no telling what kind of condition it's in. Everybody understand me?"

A chorus of "yes, ma'ams" were half-heartedly mumbled and Dianne nodded. "Good. Now let's open it up and see what condition it's in." Dianne turned around and pointed to a large rug in the center of the floor. It was a thick piece of carpeting that was covered in stains and tears. The bookcase rested on a corner of it, several boxes were stacked across the back section and an old couch and rocking chair sat in the middle.

"Mark, help me lift that bookcase back. Jacob, pull the carpet out from underneath."

Working together, it only took the four a few minutes to clear off all of the objects resting on the carpet. When they were done, Dianne had Mark and Jacob roll the carpet up into a corner and duct-tape it so it wouldn't unroll.

In the middle of the room, beneath the carpet, was a wide wooden trap-door. Metal bands held the wood together and three thick metal hinges were on the side of the door closest to the back wall of the room. Two large swinging handles and a thick latch and padlock were installed on the opposite side from the hinges, though they were inset into the door itself so that they didn't form bulges that would be visible or tangible through the carpet.

Dianne knelt down, unlocked the padlock and removed it, then motioned for Mark to stand next to her. "Lift on three, all right? One, two, three!" Mark and Dianne pulled at the trapdoor for a few seconds, grunting as they tried to move the wood from where it had sat untouched for so long. The wood groaned in protest as it scraped against the concrete floor of the basement into which it was set until, finally, it came loose.

The door wasn't all that heavy and once it was free of the floor it rotated back smoothly, the hinges giving a slight squeak as rust and dirt were rubbed away. Dianne and Mark carefully leaned the door against the couch and Dianne turned to Jacob. "Grab a couple of flashlights from upstairs, would you?" Jacob nodded and ran up the stairs, taking them two at a time. He was back less than thirty seconds later, excitement written all over his face.

Dianne took one of the flashlights and switched it on before glancing at

Jacob. "Give the other one to your brother. You and Josie stay behind him. Mark, you keep back behind me, okay?" Mark nodded in response.

"Hey." Jacob nudged Mark and whispered as Dianne peered into the hole in the floor of the basement. "How did you know about this place? Did Mom and Dad tell you about it?"

Mark shook his head. "Nope. I walked down here one time years ago when Dad left the basement door unlocked by accident. He and Mom made me promise never to tell you or Josie." Mark shrugged. "I guess they didn't want you two trying to break in and get hurt or something."

"Mark?" Dianne was halfway down the stairs, her body no longer visible.

"Yeah, Mom?"

"Grab your flashlight and come down after me, okay? These steps seem pretty solid so far and I could use the extra light."

Mark grinned as he turned on his flashlight while Jacob and Josie grunted in despair. "Can we come too, Mom?"

"Give us a couple minutes to make sure it's safe first. Mark—watch the ceiling on the third stair. A bit of the wood collapsed. We'll need to shore that up."

Mark stepped cautiously down into the hold, looking at the edges as he went. The sides were covered in dust and cobwebs but instead of being bare dirt they were lined with thick planks. The stairs were wooden as well, though they gave merely the hint of a creak as he stepped on them even after years of disuse. Each step he took downward drew him farther into the darkness beyond, filling his mind with far more exciting thoughts than were worthy of the underground chamber.

"Oh boy." Dianne's voice came from in front of Mark.

"What is it?"

Dianne turned around and shone her light at Mark's feet. His landed on her chest and face and she smiled broadly at him. "Jackpot."

Chapter Eleven

L as Vegas, Nevada

THE NEXT TWO hours of travel went along with very little in the way of conversation. While Rick was concerned with paying attention to their surroundings and ensuring that they didn't run into any of the men who were looking for them, Jane was still frightened by what had happened and didn't know what to say to Rick.

The journey towards where Rick thought Nellis was located was slow and ponderous. The Strip and the areas directly to its east had been hit hardest by the earthquake. Every time Rick thought that they were making progress they had to double back, take a different route and find a way around or through a collapsed building or other large obstacle. Over the course of the two hours they continued hearing the rumble of the diesel engine traveling back and forth and while neither of them commented on it, they both knew what it meant.

When the pair was working to climb through a narrow gap between a partially collapsed bridge linking two buildings together and a group of tractor-trailers parked underneath, they heard a sound that finally caused Rick to break the silence.

"Hey, hold up." Rick turned his head, trying to pinpoint the direction of the noise.

"It's just the engine." Jane gave him a confused look.

"No." Rick shook his head. "It's *two* engines."

"What?" Jane's face went from a calculated calm back to panic. She began turning her head, and after a few seconds realized that the distant rumble she had been hearing had turned into two separate noises. The old one that they had heard for the last two hours was still present, but there was a deeper, throatier rumble behind it that was distinct and separate from the first.

"I guess they put out the fire." Rick sighed. "Not that I expected that whole thing to really stop them, but I was hoping we'd be farther away by now."

"What do you want to do?" Jane looked around nervously, half-expecting their pursuers to appear out of nowhere.

Rick gave Jane a careful once-over as he helped her stand up after their crawl. "You're looking weak and I could use a rest, too. Let's find someplace here to hole up in for the night. Maybe they'll be finished searching by morning and we can carry on then."

"Hey!" Jane put her hands on her hips and scowled at Rick. "I'm not weak."

Rick smiled and nodded. "Sorry, didn't mean it like that."

"And the fact that I'm deliriously tired, feel like I'm about to fall over and might throw up at any moment means absolutely nothing." Jane returned Rick's smile and he chuckled.

"Fair enough. Let's find someplace to hide out and rest."

With the sound of the diesel engines not far away, Rick and Jane soon found themselves creeping quietly through yet another hotel attached to a half-destroyed casino. The building was in slightly worse shape than the one in which they had been previously when they eluded the men. In spite of the risks Rick wanted to head up to the third floor in case the men started searching buildings nearby.

When they got to the third floor via the fire escape staircase, Rick took the lead through the hallway that felt ever so slightly uneven. He guided them to the end of the building and into a room that had a view of the Strip through grimy, dust-covered windows. The room was large, with two beds, a desk, a few chairs and a mini-fridge with a white piece of paper wrapped around it that had the logo for the hotel printed on the side. Rick took off his gun bag and backpack and put them on the bed farthest from the door.

"Think they'll mind?" Jane paused in front of the mini-fridge and pointed at it before kneeling down to open it. Though the fridge was no longer cold on the inside, there were a few bottles of water, sports drinks, small bottles of alcohol and a variety of fruit and candy bars. A few pieces of fruit looked too unappetizing to eat, but Rick grabbed a candy bar, a bottle of water and a banana before easing his aching body onto a chair at the opposite end of the room from the door.

"Good grief." Rick sighed after taking a few bites from the banana. "I had no idea how much I missed fresh fruit."

Jane was already through with her banana and on to sniffing suspiciously at an apple with a few brown spots on it. "I wish this thing was still edible."

"Eh. It's probably fine." Rick tore open the candy bar wrapper and ate it in two bites before guzzling the entire bottle of water. With his hunger momentarily satiated he leaned back in the chair and closed his eyes for a moment, feeling the urge to sleep growing stronger with each passing second. Before he could nod off, though, he heard a faint rumble that steadily grew louder. He jumped up out of his seat and reduced the brightness of his lantern, then set it on the floor under the table.

The windows of the hotel, like the window of the back of the casino, were covered in dirt and dust, but Rick could still see the Humvee rolling along on the street as it wove its way through the wreckage of cars and other debris that littered its path. Following a hundred feet behind the lead vehicle was the second Humvee, its engine running roughly and its paint on the front section blackened from the Molotov Rick had thrown. While the first vehicle had a gunner sitting on the turret, the second vehicle did not, and Rick wondered if the mechanisms on the turret or the gun had been damaged enough that it simply couldn't support a gunner.

"Do you think they'll spot us?" Jane watched through the window next to Rick, crouching on the floor and keeping her body out of sight of the window.

"Nah. They can't search every room in every building and we're doing what they probably least expect. We should stay here till it gets dark. If we go when it's night then it'll be cooler and we'll be able to slip away more easily."

"Do you mind if I close my eyes for a few minutes?" Jane looked back at the bed nearest the door with a longing look in her eyes.

"Nah. Go for it. I'll stay up and listen for any sign of trouble."

Jane nodded and crawled into the bed and under the covers. Within moments she was fast asleep, leaving Rick crouched at the window. He looked out at the once-glamorous Strip and the destruction that reigned in its wake and wondered about the thousands of people who were undoubtedly staying and working in all of the buildings when the event happened. The stretch of destroyed cars along the strip was awe-inspiring, but that would have undoubtedly paled in comparison to the shaking and rumbling from an earthquake.

Thousands—tens of thousands—of screaming voices as buildings swayed and fires raged across the city, people trying to get to their homes and loved ones and out of the city as fast as they could. *Where did they all go, anyway?* Rick had avoided looking for anyone who might have died—his experience in Los Angeles made him not want to repeat the experience of seeing hundreds of charred corpses laid out on the roads. He was sure that many people had to have perished in their vehicles and have been trapped in some of the collapsed buildings, but unless he and Jane had somehow missed seeing thousands of corpses lying about, he wasn't sure what would have happened to them.

Rick's imaginings of the fate of the people who had been in the city weighed heavily on his mind as he eased back into his chair at the back of the room. He reached for his gun case and unzipped it, placing the shotgun across his legs before tucking the case and the hunting rifle beneath the bed. He stared at Jane for a few long moments, watching her back slowly rise and fall with each breath she took. As he watched her he couldn't help but think about his wife and children once again.

It felt like he hadn't seen his family in ages. Without a way to contact them the only thing he could do was keep pushing eastward and pray they were safe. He had complete faith in Dianne's ability to take care of herself and the kids, but what he had seen since the event started shook him to his bones. *Hopefully*, he thought, *they've avoided the worst of it. Hopefully.*

Chapter Twelve

The Day of the Event

THREE HOURS AGO, *the noise and lights of the Las Vegas Strip overwhelmed the intensity of even the sun itself. As the city woke up for yet another day, the unusual heat of the season had no effect on the workers and visitors to the famous location. Thousands poured out of their hotel rooms, heading for air conditioned buildings to eat, spend their money and engage in activities of varying moral standards. Three hours ago it was just another day in Sin City.*

The fires were the first to tear the city apart, spreading through the streets faster than anyone could have imagined. Bumper-to-bumper traffic on nearly every main road didn't help the situation and contributed to the tortuously painful deaths of thousands. As emergency services tried—and failed—to respond to the fires, they quickly spread from the vehicles to buildings, catching homes and businesses ablaze.

In places that were spared from the fires due to their distance from the streets and vehicles, survivors gathered and waited for some word about what to do next. Less than an hour after the fires began, however, the initial survivors would be the next to fall. Earthquakes—small at first, merely rumbles beneath the ground that were dismissed as figments of the imagination—shook the city. At first the buildings merely swayed, but as the rumblings grew louder and more fierce, more people realized that the quakes weren't some sort of side effect of the fires as some had hoped and expressed.

Water mains and gas lines ruptured as the ground buckled, sending explosions of water and fire rocking through the city. The worst of the earthquakes were felt across the Strip and to its east. Buildings that had gone up seemingly overnight in an effort to capi-

talize on a virtual gold rush were the first to fall, crumbling like a gingerbread house set out in the rain. Shoddy construction and cut corners were revealed in the most horrifying of ways as roofs and walls collapsed inward on those seeking shelter from the heat and flames outside.

The larger, older buildings suffered immense structural damage, but most did not fall. Their interiors were left in shambles, their upper floors were unstable and they would have to be demolished and rebuilt, but people who took shelter inside were spared from the worst of the destruction.

Hours after the worst of the quakes are over, aftershocks still ripple through the city and surrounding areas. Most of the dead are buried or burned beyond all recognition. The survivors flee the center of the city for the edges, bartering with the gangs that have risen up and taken power. People sell the clothes off of their back—and more—for the promise of a warm place to sleep and a few scraps of food. The few vehicles that are left intact are used to flee the city for the hope of shelter elsewhere, though there is little to be found.

Small clusters of survivors band together in buildings around the city as they resist the gangs and try to find enough food and water to extend their lives for a few more days. Many who require medication or constant care die within hours. A lack of medical care, the overwhelming heat and stress kill many in the first twenty-four hours.

Some who are close enough to Nellis Air Force Base seek shelter inside. Only a few hundred are allowed inside before the base commander seals the gates and turns everyone else away until he can assess the situation. Fear runs rampant through the base as orders are given from the highest levels.

As groups of vehicles are cleared the base commander begins sending them out in groups to comb the city for survivors. Those who are found are searched, stripped of weapons and brought back to the base. Those who have traveled on foot to the base take longer to process and bring inside, and each new person that appears puts more of a strain on the base resources.

Tents and cots are set up across the base as emergency fuel stores and rations are brought out of storage. The worst contingency plans for the base included the possibility of short-term housing of civilians, but as more people walk and are brought to the base, the commander begins to feel the pressure of having too many mouths to feed.

Word filters down that the federal emergency service departments are establishing shelter cities in key locations across the country. As Nellis continues to clear their vehicles and aircraft of effects from Damocles they are ordered to deploy men and equipment to key locations of the country. Seeking to alleviate the strain on his base, the commander orders that all civilians in the base be questioned to find out which of the shelter cities they wish to relocate to. While not everyone gets to go where they want, more people than not begin to fly out, heading closer to their families and loved ones than they were before.

For the families and individuals who live in the area and don't wish to leave, the commander has no answers. So long as the strain on the base's resources is lightened by shipping off tourists or residents who have family or connections in other areas, those who wish to stay can do so. If, however, too many people wish to stay on base, the commander makes it clear that he will begin forcing people out.

Fear that was lessened by the relief offered by the base now explodes back into the fore-

front of the survivors' minds. Every new bus that pulls in filled with survivors is another reminder that they may be kicked out at any moment. Every new family that walks to the front gates and requests aid is another set of mouths that may become the tipping point that causes everyone to leave. Tensions are rising as quickly as they were eased and there is little that can be done to alleviate them without causing harm to those most in need.

Chapter Thirteen

L as Vegas, Nevada

IT WAS dark when Rick started awake, catching himself in a half-snore and wondering for a few seconds where he was. He hadn't meant to fall asleep but his exhaustion from the last couple of days had worn on him enough that he slept for a few hours. He rubbed his eyes and looked around the room, trying to figure out what would have woken him up.

The lantern was still beneath the table on its lowest setting, Jane was still lying in her bed and the door to the room was shut. Rick realized that what had woken him wasn't what was in the room but what was outside instead. The once-distant roar of the twin diesel engines was far louder and more ferocious than before. In fact, the noise was growing so loud that Rick wondered if they really were on the third floor of the building.

"Th' hell?" Rick whispered to himself as he stood up, holding the shotgun loosely in one hand as he walked over to the window. Outside, down on the street, was a convoy of six Humvees driving along. Each of them had a ring of bright lights around the edge of their roofs that illuminated their surroundings for a few hundred feet. The lights near the front and back of the second, third, fourth and fifth Humvees were angled downward to keep them from interfering with the lead and rear vehicles, but the lights on their sides were angled outward.

The lights made it easy for Rick to make out the shapes of gunners sitting in the turrets of each Humvee, swiveling them around quickly as they scanned their surroundings. They followed a well-defined pattern and ensured that there was always at least one gun pointed in any general direction at any one time.

As the vehicles cruised down the Strip, they suddenly broke their line formation and fanned out to block both sides of the road before shutting their lights off. They halted in the street below the building where Rick and Jane were and he pushed open the glass door leading out onto the balcony just outside. The night air was cold and the wind whipped dust into his eyes as he walked out onto the balcony. With the door open he could hear the engines more clearly and he saw, half a mile down from the Humvees, what they appeared to be waiting for.

Two more Humvees drove along, heading for the line that was waiting for them. The pair of vehicles drove erratically as they swerved around in the road and jumped the median more than once. One of them fired a few bursts from its machine gun at something behind them, but whoever was driving the vehicles seemed more concerned with escaping than anything else.

When the two fleeing Humvees got within a few hundred feet of the six lying in wait, the six turned on their lights and a loudspeaker flared to life.

"Halt the vehicles immediately or we will fire upon you!" The time between the warning and the first burst of fire from the six vehicles seemed improbably short to Rick, though he imagined it seemed shorter than it actually was. The pair of fleeing vehicles showed no signs of halting their advance, though they did turn on the road as they sought somewhere else to flee from their unseen pursuers and the vehicles that had surprised them on the road ahead.

Fire belched from the end of three M2 machine guns as they dispensed fifty-caliber rounds into their targets. Though the Humvees being shot were armored, they stood little chance against the intensity and immensity of the fire. The tires were the first to go on both vehicles and they swerved wildly as their inexperienced drivers fought to keep them under control. Rounds punctured through into the engine and passenger compartments next, spilling vital fluids from both the vehicles and their drivers.

One of the Humvees came to a halt by smashing into a large palm tree in the median of the Strip. The other flipped over as the mortally wounded driver tried to turn into the blocked entrance to a casino across the road. When the vehicle finally skidded to a halt the fire from three of the six Humvees halted and the back doors on each vehicle opened. Soldiers poured out, heading towards the two damaged vehicles with their weapons raised, ready to put down anyone who showed any signs of resistance.

Rick was so absorbed in watching the events unfold behind him that he nearly missed hearing the clatter of the hotel room door opening and slamming shut again. He whirled around, raising his shotgun, but no one was there. His eyes flicked to the bed and, despite the darkness of the room, he could see that the place where Jane had been sleeping was empty. Rick charged back into the room and threw open the door to see Jane jogging down the hall, one of the lanterns in hand.

"Jane!" Rick yelled at her. "Where are you going?"

"To get help from them!" She looked back at Rick and motioned with her hand. "Come on!"

"We don't know who they are for certain! That's a really bad idea!" Rick shouted back at her but she didn't stop. He cursed under his breath before running back and grabbing his backpack from the bed. He tossed the shotgun into the gun bag, looped it over his back, grabbed the other lantern and ran out of the room and down the hall.

Jane was already at the bottom of the stairs and near the front door to the hotel by the time Rick caught up with her. In her hand he could see she was carrying a piece of white cloth, likely one of the pillowcases from the room. "What are you doing?" He shouted at her, but she continued running for the front entrance. She burst out of the door waving the pillowcase and lantern above her head and started shouting at the people outside.

"Hey! Help us! Help!"

The soldiers were busy pulling bodies from the wreckage of the two Humvees when Jane ran out. They turned around, drawing down on her and moving to surround her.

"Drop your weapon!" One of the soldiers screamed at her and she looked at them, confused. Rick slowed down at the entrance to the building, not wanting to further complicate the situation by bursting out after her.

"Please, help us! We've been running for days now!"

"Drop everything in your hands and lay face-down on the ground *now!*" The lead soldier screamed at her and Jane suddenly closed her mouth. The color drained from her face as she realized the magnitude of the situation she was in and she slowly lowered the sheet and lantern to the ground.

"Get down!" The soldier took a step forward and shouted at her again. Jane held her hands up as she dropped to her knees. The lead soldier motioned for his companions to move forward. Two more soldiers stepped forward and grabbed her by the arms and began pulling her toward one of the six Humvees still parked in a row across both lanes of the Strip.

"Hey!" Rick stepped out of the front entrance of the hotel and raised his hands into the air, holding a lantern in his right hand. "Take it easy with her!"

The soldiers turned to Rick and raised their rifles, but he was already dropping down to his knees. "Yeah, yeah." Rick shook his head. "I know, get down on the ground."

Chapter Fourteen

F ive Days Before the Event

"*NOW I KNOW most folks think the undercoating is a giant scam, but before you say no, let me just show you some pictures of the difference between a vehicle that's had undercoating versus one that hasn't.*"

Cold air blows from massive vents inside the Troy Baker Premium Car Lot in Dallas Texas. With three massive walls comprised almost entirely of lightly tinted glass, the autumn heat wave forces the dealership to crank the air conditioning up to high or else risk sweating out all of their customers.

As the salesman pulls out photos showing a car with huge amounts of rust on the undercarriage in an attempt to scare his customer into purchasing the coating, a commotion from the parking lot catches his eye.

Outside, another customer sits in a brand-new SUV. The engine is on and running and the customer and saleswoman helping him are both talking as they look under the hood. A moment after the car turns on, though, the saleswoman and the man looking at the car start coughing. They back up from the vehicle, waving their hands in front of their faces. It doesn't take more than a few seconds for the pair to realize what the smell is.

"Is that... gas?" The saleswoman turns around, looking for one of the service bay technicians. She manages to get a full two steps away from the car in her search before a ball of flames erupts from beneath the vehicle.

Nine minutes later, as the saleswoman and the customer are loaded into an ambulance, a cluster of firefighters, police officers and the owners of the car lot are clustered around the *still-smoldering wreckage. A few of the other customers in the lot and inside the building are standing nearby, watching what's going on, but most of the customers have already left.*

As technicians examine the wreckage of the car over the next few days, a curious tale emerges. Seals around the fuel lines and related components appear to be the first parts that failed. This allowed for a slow leak of fuel that quickly turned to vapor in the afternoon heat. A few moments after the leak began a short-circuit in a computer control chip on the underside of the car caused a spark which ignited the vapors.

As the saleswoman and the customer both survived—albeit with grievous injuries—the story quickly vanishes from the collective consciousness of the area over the next few days. The only people who remain concerned and puzzled by the incident are technicians from both the car dealership and from the manufacturer. Such a dangerous incident should have never happened. Computer control systems are in place in the vehicles to prevent any such situation from occurring.

And yet, somehow, in all of the vehicle's logs, there is no trace to be found of any type of control system malfunction. Everything appears as normal up until the time of the incident when the logs fail to update as though something turned them off.

Chapter Fifteen

Las Vegas, Nevada

THE RIDE to Nellis Air Force Base was uncomfortably long. The stuffy conditions of the Humvees, the menacing looks of the soldiers and the uneasy silence inside the vehicles made Rick wonder if he had made the right decision in going out to try and reason with the soldiers who had been taking Jane away.

After relieving Rick of his weapons and gear, rifling through everything and then throwing it into the back of one of their vehicles, the soldiers had him loaded into a separate vehicle from Jane. He wasn't sure why they were being split up, but his nervousness only increased the longer they took going through the city.

On more than one occasion Rick had tried to strike up a conversation with the pair of soldiers who sat on either side of him in the back seat, but each time he spoke the soldiers either ignored him or gave him a blank stare. With his hands zip-tied in front of him and no idea where he was being taken, all he could do was sit tight and hope for the best.

While Rick had initially guessed that the soldiers had been sent out to retrieve—or destroy—the pair of Humvees that had fallen into the hands of the men who attacked the convoy, he realized halfway through the ride to Nellis that they were doing more than just a retrieval of their assets. The vehicles stopped every quarter mile and each time they did a pair of soldiers jumped out with a small black box in their hands. The soldiers carried the

Book 3 - The Shattered Earth

boxes to a nearby building and disappeared inside for fifteen to twenty minutes before returning. While the men were inside the buildings a brief radio conversation went on between them and the vehicles before they returned and the convoy began moving again.

"Package is set. Lights are green. Confirm, over."

"Showing green lights on remote. Data link secure. NVG is solid. FLIR is solid. Confirmed, over."

"Copy, returning. Out."

This curious series of events occurred a total of thirty times in between when the vehicles picked up Jane and Rick and when they began their final approach to the base. It only took Rick listening to the conversation and watching where the men placed the black box in and on the buildings they entered for him to realize that they were planting surveillance cameras around the city. He had no idea what they were for, but the more he thought about it, the more worried he became.

"You guys not have eyes in the sky anymore?" Rick tried striking up yet another conversation with the soldiers in the car, but they merely stared mutely back at him. He had tried several times to talk to them about their work but all he received in response were a bunch of blank stares. "Come on, fellas. This is one hell of a long ride." Rick smiled, but the soldiers didn't return it.

Why the hell would they need cameras on the streets? The prevalence of civilian and military drones in all roles had been overwhelming during the best of times and while Rick knew very little about satellite imaging, he was certain the military could see virtually anything they wanted with a few clicks of a mouse. Setting up cameras along streets in a city seemed not only downright primitive but somewhat frightening. *If they need cameras set up on streets to keep an eye on what's going on, that can't bode well for whatever's happening.*

Dawn was beginning to break over the city when the convoy rolled up to the entrance to Nellis. Extra fortifications and guards had been deployed and the walls were topped with large bundles of razor wire that had been hastily tacked on. Crowds of people stood near the fence off of the road leading into the base, all of them staring wide-eyed as a man in uniform paced the top of the wall, talking to them through a bullhorn.

The road into the base itself was lined with sandbags, razor wire and HESCO barriers for a few hundred feet out. Three guard towers were positioned on each side of the barriers and there were two Humvees parked at the end with soldiers on the guns and standing nearby wielding rifles. The convoy slowed to a stop at the makeshift entrance to the base and one of the soldiers standing guard walked up to the lead vehicle. Being crunched up in the middle back of the Humvee where the seat was mostly in his imagination, Rick couldn't hear or see any of what was going on. A moment after stopping, though, the convoy sped up again and roared through to the main gate of the base proper.

After another brief stop the convoy passed through into the base and circled around to an aircraft hangar. Rick's Humvee and one other vehicle passed into the hangar while the rest stopped outside. When the two vehicles finally came to a stop inside, the soldiers jumped out and pulled Rick and Jane from the backs of their respective vehicles. Their bags were taken out next and thrown on the floor, though Rick's guns were held back.

"Get your bags and follow me." The soldier who had been driving the Humvee with Rick in the back spoke gruffly to Rick and Jane as he pointed at their gear.

"Where are we going?"

"The Colonel wants to have a word with you."

"Who's that?"

"Colonel Leslie, head of the 99th Air Base Wing."

"With me?" Rick blanched and shook his head. "There must be some mistake."

"No mistake. This way, please." The soldier took out a short pair of scissors and snipped the zip-tie off of Rick's wrists. He placed a hand on Rick's back and guided him forward, deeper into the hangar and through a door at the side. They descended a wide flight of stairs into the subterranean section of the base and the soldier pointed down a hall.

"Keep going that way. One of the airmen will pick you up and take you to the Colonel." The soldier turned and hurried back up the stairs, eager to get back to his companions and off the Air Force base as soon as possible. A battalion of soldiers had been running cooperative drills with the Air Force when the event occurred and while the two areas of the military worked well together on the outside there were still plenty of sub-surface tensions that rubbed members of both branches the wrong way.

A few seconds after the soldier left, a man in a blue uniform came jogging up to Rick. "This way, please." The young man was tall, wore wire-rimmed glasses and spoke quickly as he, too, put a hand on Rick's back to guide him forward.

"You know, I think I can manage to walk without being shoved all over the place." Rick shrugged off the airman's hand and the young man smiled.

"Of course. Sorry about that. Just follow me."

Rick thought briefly about trying to make a run for it, but he had no idea where Jane had been taken and he wasn't about to try running off while in the middle of a military base. Something about that idea sounded positively suicidal.

After a few minutes of wandering through the underground labyrinth, Rick and his escort arrived outside a large door with tinted glass and a sign that read *Conf Rm. 2*. The airman stopped and nodded at the door. "The Colonel's waiting for you inside." With that, the airman was gone and Rick suddenly had to fight the urge to bolt again.

Rick raised his hand to knock on the door but someone inside pulled it open as he raised his hand. He took a timid step forward and was greeted by an outstretched hand that grabbed his and pumped it vigorously.

"Colonel Donald Leslie, but call me Don if you'd like. You're Rick, is that right?" Of all the people Rick had imagined working in the upper echelons of the US military, Colonel Donald Leslie was as far from Rick's expectations as it was possible to get. A portly man in his late forties, the Colonel had hair that was clearly bright red even with as short cropped as it was. His eyebrows were bushy and his face was flushed—either from exertion or excitement, though Rick couldn't tell which.

"Yeah. Rick Waters." Rick shook his head. "I'm sorry; how do you know who I am?"

"The girl you were running with, Jane. She mentioned your name a few times. From what I heard you're the reason she's still alive." Leslie nodded approvingly. "Well done to you."

"Thanks… I think. Colonel, listen, it's been kind of a weird night. Why am I here, talking to you? And where is Jane anyway?"

"She's safe. We have temporary shelters set up here at the base while we're working on relocating civilians from the area."

"Can I see her?"

"Not quite yet." Colonel Leslie stepped back and waved at a chair across the conference table. "Sit down, please."

"What's this about?" Rick walked slowly around the table. "I don't want to sound ungrateful but I was just handcuffed for a few hours in the back of one of your vehicles."

"That was Army, actually, but you have my apologies anyway." Leslie sat down opposite from Rick. The smile on the Colonel's face faded as he glanced through a folder filled with pages and photographs. "I'll cut to the chase, Rick. The grunts that brought you in let it slip that you asked a lot of questions. Questions about the cameras, our satellites and about the… *incident* that's been going on."

Rick couldn't help but chuckle as he sat back in his chair and crossed his arms. "Is that what the feds are calling it now? An 'incident?'"

"Sometimes we overstate things. Sometimes we understate things." Leslie shrugged. "The point is, you've been asking a lot of questions that point to you being someone who may be able to shed some light on what's going on." The Colonel shifted some of his papers around and cleared his throat. "While you're under no official obligation to conform to what I'm about to request, I do want to tell you up front that if you don't agree to the request you'll be held indefinitely until you agree."

Rick's eyes narrowed. "What is it you're going to ask me to do?"

The Colonel slid a piece of paper across the table. Rick skimmed its contents and when he finished Leslie spoke. "This is a national emergency, Rick. The President has requested that anyone who may be able to assist in containing the current crisis be brought to Mount Weather, just outside

Washington. There you'll join others in a think tank of sorts to try and find a solution to whatever the hell is going on."

"What's really going on here, Colonel? I've heard rumors and whispers but I've been running for my life ever since this started and I haven't had much time to sit down and watch the news." Rick pushed the piece of paper back across the table and shook his head. "Besides, I have more important things to do than this."

"More important things to do than helping to save your country?"

"Yeah. It's called getting home to my family."

"Rick, I'm sorry about your family, but what we're facing here is slightly more serious than one man's family."

Rick clenched his jaw. "That's easy for you to say."

Colonel Leslie's face darkened and all of the warmth and kindness that had been present since Rick met him completely vanished. It was as if a spirit took control of the man's mind, the change was so dramatic. The Colonel stood up and planted both palms on the table, leaning forward until he was over halfway across the table. His nostrils flared and his teeth ground as he spoke. Not with a loud voice, but almost with a whisper.

"Your family, Rick, are going to die unless we get this situation under control. So will my family, so will the families of everyone stationed here and so will the families of everyone in this fabulous place we call America."

Rick pushed back in his chair slightly and shook his head. "Intimidating me to try to get me to help you isn't going to work, Colonel. I don't know you, I don't know what's going on and I'm certainly not going to agree to go be part of some think tank and sit around twiddling my thumbs while my family's out there in this mess. Frankly, I find this whole business of you dragging me in here and getting pissy when I refuse to help you do something I don't know anything about to be more than a little bit concerning."

"Then consider this your final chance." Leslie pointed at the document still in front of Rick. "That offer is your only ticket out of here."

Rick shook his head. "Once I know my family is safe I'll be happy to help you. Until then, though, they're my only priority."

Colonel Leslie stood back up. He reached under the table and pressed a small button. A few seconds later the door to the conference room opened and two military police walked in. "Holding area three." The Colonel nearly growled the words as he glared at Rick. "Once you think it over, hopefully you'll change your mind."

"What the hell?" Rick struggled as the MPs grabbed him by the arms and dragged him from the room. "You can't do this! I'm a citizen! Hey, you can't do this you—" The door closed and the Colonel sat back down in his chair. He sighed wearily before flipping back through the paperwork and photographs in front of him. The orders to detain any civilians with skills or suspected skills that could potentially be leveraged to stop Damocles had, in fact, come down from the highest levels of government. The suspension of habeas corpus and the effective implementation of martial law meant that Rick could, in fact, be held indefinitely.

While the Colonel suspected—based on Rick's questions on his ride back to Nellis—that Rick had some passing familiarity with computer systems similar to Damocles, if he had known Rick's actual credentials related to the field he would have had Rick on a plane to Washington twenty minutes after having him hauled into his office. For his part, Rick was starting to understand the gravity of the situation even more as he struggled to remain upright while being pulled down the halls of the base.

In truth the situation was far grimmer than Rick could have imagined. With Damocles having infiltrated and damaged so many vital systems there were virtually no more satellite networks operational. While the satellites were still in orbit and functioning they were nonresponsive to commands from the ground, having been locked out by Damocles. Newer test aircraft and vehicles linked together in experimental systems had also been affected. Each vehicle and aircraft had to be hand-checked and have its firmware flashed and run through a series of offline diagnostics before they could be cleared for use. Of all the scenarios Rick could imagine, none up until that point had been as terrible as reality.

As Rick sat in the brightly-lit cell somewhere in the bowels of Nellis, he contemplated the events that had led him there and began trying to assemble the facts and speculations he had gathered.

"It's a virus," Rick mumbled to himself. "I knew that already. But it's a smart virus. A learning virus. More than a virus, really. It's affected everything… even the military can't fight back against it." Rick snorted. "They sure as hell can't fight it if they're trying to pick up people off the street who sound like they know anything about a computer. Why, though?"

Rick thought back to the piece of paper the Colonel had placed in front of him. The content of the letter was matter-of-fact and got straight to the point. A piece of weaponized computer code that could evolve and change to adapt to a wide variety of situations had been loosed on the country and the world at large. The US government was looking for people with any sort of computing experience to lend their knowledge towards helping find a weakness in the virus so that it could be stopped.

At the bottom of the letter, after a paragraph-long impassioned plea for help, sat the signature of the President of the United States. Rick had nearly laughed upon seeing it, thinking it was some sort of elaborate joke, but the more he sat and thought about it the more he realized that the letter was completely serious.

Rick continued mulling over the conversation between himself and Colonel Leslie when he remembered a detail that had completely escaped him at the time. *Mount Weather. Virginia?* Rick jumped up from his seat at the edge of his metal bed and ran to the door of his cell. He started beating on the bars with his fists while shouting at the top of his lungs. "Hey! Hey, you!

Get the Colonel!" Rick shouted and pointed at an MP who stood down the hall. "I'll do it! I'll do what he said!"

"Shut up down there!" The MP took a few menacing steps forward as he shouted back down the hall.

"No, really! The Colonel said—"

"You're about to find out what he said to do to anyone who doesn't listen!"

Rick backed away from the cell door, clenching his fists into a ball. While he hadn't realized it at the time of the conversation, he had suddenly remembered that Mount Weather was in Virginia, just outside of Washington. He figured that, if he was smart and played his cards right, he could use the Colonel's offer to get to Mount Weather and then slip away down south to reunite with his family.

"Dammit!" Rick hissed to himself as he sat back down at the edge of his bed. Thirty minutes prior he had been handed a golden opportunity to get across the country to within a stone's throw of his family and he had turned it down without realizing it.

Chapter Sixteen

N ellis Air Force Base
        Las Vegas, Nevada

"THAT'LL BE ALL. Thank you, ma'am." Colonel Leslie nods to the young woman. She stands up, nods back and quietly leaves his office. Outside, an MP accompanies her down the halls, up a flight of stairs and to a small tent. In a few hours she'll be strapped into a seat in the back of a C-130 on a flight bound for a shelter city set up hundreds of miles to the east.

As Leslie goes back over the notes of his conversation with Jane, he is interrupted a short time later by the phone on his desk. He picks it up and listens intently, his brow furrowing and his expression darkening with each passing second.

Although Colonel Leslie wasn't originally the highest ranking officer at Nellis Air Force Base, the redistribution and deployment of much of the base's assets have left him as the de facto base commander. In addition to looking out for his men, dealing with the disaster caused by Damocles and trying to get enough planes in the air to meet the constant battery of orders coming his way, Colonel Leslie has had to task a large portion of his men with helping to care for the civilian population.

As thousands upon thousands have come seeking shelter, the Colonel has had to balance caring for them, watching after the men under his command and trying to keep the peace in a situation only ever dreamt of in far-off conference rooms. Finding the proper balance between the extreme of kicking every civilian off the base and denying all aid and the opposite extreme of allowing any and everyone onto the base has been difficult.

The phone call has made things even more difficult. After a few curt replies Colonel Donald Leslie puts the phone back on the receiver and leans back in his chair. He has been at Nellis for eighteen months, but in that amount of time he has grown fond of it like no other assignment he has ever had. The order to abandon the base comes as a shock to him and he struggles to try and process what the implications could be.

A few hours pass, and the Colonel is still in his office drinking another cup of coffee as he works on plans for the withdrawal from the base. The phone rings again and he answers. His eyes grow wide and he slams down the phone, picks it up again and dials another number. After a few minutes of playing phone tag he is finally in a conference call with other Air Force officers. The conversation is fast, furious and more than a little heated.

The discussion and disagreement centers around what to do about the growing population of unruly civilians just outside the base. Other officers are in favor of using lethal force to prevent anyone from making unauthorized entry onto the base. Others, like Colonel Leslie, are unhappy with that option and refuse to fire upon their own countrymen, no matter how bleak the situation may be.

In the end, as the one in command, Leslie makes the decision and hands down the orders. The civilians outside the base are to be kept out for as long as possible. If they do manage to break through the gates and start rioting and looting, the base assets are to be immediately locked down until the people calm down. No one is to fire upon an unarmed civilian unless their life is in immediate danger, and every soldier and airman is to do every-thing in their power to prevent harm from coming to anyone on and around the base.

As Leslie sits in his office, contemplating the worst possible scenarios, he wonders if his decision is the correct one. The temptation to use lethal force on agitated and unruly crowds is strong, but with the situation being as dire as it is and Nellis being abandoned anyway, the last thing he wants is to contribute to even more death and destruction. His authority—and arguably duty—is clear, but the moral argument is a far more pressing one in his mind. He prays that it ends well both for the men and women under his command and for the throngs of desperate people outside the base, desperately trying to get in.

Chapter Seventeen

Nellis Air Force Base
         Las Vegas, Nevada

WHEN COLONEL LESLIE ordered Rick to be thrown into a holding cell, Rick had expected the Colonel to fetch him within a day at most. By the time a week went by Rick was trying to adjust to the fact that he could be in the holding cell indefinitely. Food was brought to him three times a day, and though it was bland it kept him alive. Every day he called out to the MPs multiple times, asking to see the Colonel. At first the pleas were indignant but by the fifth day he was reduced to begging anytime he saw anyone in uniform passing by.

On the eighth day of being held, as Rick was giving up all hope, he was awoken at an unholy hour by a pair of MPs who dragged him off of his bed and ordered him to get moving. As Rick was guided through the base he started realizing that things weren't as they had been merely a week prior. Distant shouts and the roar of engines came from somewhere far above Rick's head and what seemed like an abnormally large amount of soldiers and airmen were running down the corridors with worried looks on their faces.

A shout from down the hall behind Rick and the pair of MPs surprised the three of them. "Get down here! We've got a couple of wounded coming in and need crowd control!" The MPs dropped Rick and one of them ran back down the hall immediately while the other lingered for a moment to help Rick back to his feet and talk to him.

"Take this hall down to the end. When you see the stairs leading up, walk past them, through the door on your right and take *those* stairs up and out." With that the second MP was gone, going after the first at a full-on run.

"Wait!" Rick shouted at the two men but they were gone around a corner in seconds. "What the hell is going on around here?" Rick shook his head and turned around in the empty hall. With no one else in sight and nothing else to do, Rick did as the man had instructed and continued down the hall, watching for a flight of stairs. A few minutes later the sound of boots on the hard floor alerted him to the presence of someone coming from a cross hallway and he stopped, waiting to see who it was.

While Rick expected to see someone from the Army or Air Force coming around the corner, he wasn't expecting to see Colonel Leslie. Based on the expression on the Colonel's face he wasn't expecting to see Rick either.

"What are you still doing here?" The Colonel stopped in his tracks and looked Rick up and down. "I thought I had you released days ago!"

Rick took a step backward, almost ready to turn and run. "Days ago? What are you talking about? A couple of your goons just dragged me out of the cell a few *minutes* ago!"

"What?" The friendliness and charm that Leslie had been wearing like a cheap cologne the first time they had met was completely gone, replaced by a harsh look of frustration and lack of sleep. "No, that's… dammit!" The Colonel started walking and Rick trailed behind him. "I'm sorry, Rick. You're free to go now, though. The exit's back the other way."

"Yeah, the guards told me where it was." Rick shook his head. "I didn't think I'd see you again. What's going on around here? Why was I just dumped in the middle of the hallway?"

Colonel Leslie stopped and turned to face Rick. "I don't have time to stand here and figure out the minutiae of your incarceration. The situation around here has changed quite radically since you arrived."

Rick had to close his eyes, take several deep breaths and clench his jaw to keep from taking a swing at the Colonel. "What, exactly, has changed?"

The Colonel checked his watch and shook his head, muttering to himself before replying. "Fine. I guess I owe you some sort of an explanation considering you've been locked up all this time. Though, really, that's your own damned fault. Of all the people we picked up who were supposed to be sent off to Mount Weather, you were the only one who refused. I figured a couple days in holding would change your tune but that's right about when the shit hit the fan."

"A *couple days*?" Rick could feel the veins on his neck and head bulging. "Are you kidding me?"

"Calm down." The Colonel shook his head. "You can act indignant about your own stupid decisions later, on your own time. The day you were supposed to be hauled back up here to reconsider your decision is, like I was saying, the day the shit hit the fan. One thing led to another and I guess nobody released you. Again, I'm sorry, but you're out now so congratulations."

Rick still didn't know what the Colonel was talking about and he shook his head, confused by Leslie's response. "I... what are you going on about? What shit hit the fan?"

"We've had... let's call it staffing issues here since this whole mess started. Too many problems and too few men spread too thin. I assume you saw the crowds of people outside the base perimeter when they brought you in?"

"Yeah. Looked like a couple hundred, max."

"Try a couple thousand. Which soon blossomed to many more than that. We couldn't hold them here on the base so we told them to seek shelter in the city and started handing out emergency rations a couple times a day.

"The day after those ran out is the day some genius out there got a couple of bulldozers running and plowed through the side of the fence." Leslie shook his head and sighed. "As much of an asshole as you think I am —and I am one, believe me—I'm not about to open fire on citizens of a country I'm supposed to protect."

"The people just swarmed the base, then?"

"Yep. Not like I can blame them. We've got the only food, water and power in the area and it's been hot as balls out here."

"You're a real humanitarian."

Colonel Leslie ignored the jab and continued. "When you've got about ten thousand starving, hot and dehydrated people who are extremely pissed off, you can do one of two things. Let them wear themselves out and break all your toys while they scrounge for food and water or kill them all and live with being a mass murderer the rest of your life. I chose the former. Everyone pulled back inside the secure areas of the base and waited for the looting and rioting above to stop."

Rick shook his head, suddenly confused. "Why is it you're telling me all of this?"

"As of right now, Rick, you're the only civilian left on this base. Everyone else—including that friend you came in with—evacuated days ago. In twenty-four hours we're going to be evacuating the base and moving out to an undisclosed rendezvous location on the west coast." The Colonel looked at his watch again and shook his head. "Look, I feel bad you've been locked up all this time. Your friend went out on a plane the day after you went in there, along with most of the rest of the civilians who were staying on the base. If you hadn't been so stubborn then you'd be most of the way home by now."

"Working in a think tank to fix whatever's going on instead of being home with my family. No thanks."

"Whatever. Look, you have two choices right now. In approximately... three hours we're evacuating. The C130s are loaded and we're abandoning the base and heading for the west coast. If you want to come with us I can spare a seat."

"Head back towards California?" Rick shook his head. "No way. What's the second choice?" A series of distant explosions far above Rick's head punctuated the conversation and he looked up at the ceiling.

"Your second choice is up there." Colonel Leslie pointed upward. "One of the largest street gangs in Las Vegas decided that the civilian takeover of the base would be the perfect time for them to try and steal some more military-grade hardware." He shook his head. "Inbred idiots. Unlike firing on scared, hungry civilians I don't have a problem killing gangsters. Unfortunately they've hidden themselves among the rest of the civilians quite well and I don't have the manpower or time to go hunting for them."

"You want me to… what? Join a gang?"

"Don't be stupid, Rick. In the hangar directly above us there are several Humvees loaded with supplies, weapons and everything needed for a long patrol route. The Army grunts had them ready before everything went to hell and they've just been sitting there. If you're lucky and nobody's broken into the hangar then you can take one and get out of here and keep going east. If you're unlucky then you won't have to worry about traveling anymore."

"You don't have a plane or something?"

Leslie chortled and shook his head. "No. I realize that may come as a surprise given that this is an Air Force base, but we don't typically have planes that an unlicensed civilian is capable of flying and landing just sitting around ready to go."

Another explosion came from above, which was followed by the appearance of a group of airmen at the end of the hall. "Colonel Leslie!" One of them spotted the Colonel and shouted at him. "We have to go!"

"You want to go with option A, you come with me. Otherwise keep going down this hall, turn right and take the narrow stairs up to Hangar Delta. Your call, Rick. Good luck with whatever you choose."

Colonel Leslie turned and ran down the hall towards the airmen, not bothering to look back in Rick's direction. Rick stood in the hall for a long moment, trying to figure out what to do when another explosion shook the underground structure, flickering the lights and shaking the halls.

"Dammit!" Rick turned away from the direction the Colonel had run and continued down his original path, heading for the staircase leading up to the hangar. There was no way he was going to head back west and, while dealing with thousands of rioters and gang members sounded like a terrible choice, it was a choice that was accompanied by a slim chance to continue heading towards home.

That alone made the most difficult decision the easiest in the world.

Chapter Eighteen

N ellis Air Force Base
      Las Vegas, Nevada

AS RICK TOOK the steps up towards the hangar two at a time, the rumbles of heavy equipment, scattered gunfire and people shouting and screaming grew louder. At the top of the stairs sat a thick steel door that he unlatched and pushed open, revealing a hangar similar to the one he had been taken to when he first arrived at the base. The hangar had enough space for several jets to sit comfortably side by side and end to end with room to spare.

Light shone down from the ceiling of the hangar from long bulbs though several of them were flickering, casting eerie shadows across the hangar floor. The room was nearly empty aside from a group of six Humvees lined up near the far entrance to the building. They looked nearly identical to the group that Rick and Jane had been brought in on aside from a slightly different paint job.

Rick hurried across the hangar, wincing every time he heard a gunshot or an explosion outside, wondering if each one was going to be the end of him. As he ran closer to the vehicles, he heard a commotion from outside one of the smaller doors built into the main rolling doors. Three separate smaller doors were built into one another like Russian nesting dolls with the smallest large enough for people and small equipment to pass through, the next for small vehicles to pass through and the next size for large trucks.

A series of small windows were built into the vehicle-sized door at shoulder height, and outside Rick could see several faces peering inward at the interior of the hangar. One of the people swung a sledgehammer at the door, sending a boom echoing through the voluminous space. Rick picked up his pace as the sound came again. Each blow sounded slightly different, and after three or four more he realized that the people outside were succeeding in their attempts to break through the door.

Rick was close enough to the doors to hear what the people were saying and, apparently, for them to see him. One of them pointed at him and shouted at the others. "Hey! Who's that guy?"

"He's not military!"

"Let us in!"

Rick ignored their calls and continued towards the Humvees. When he arrived at the line of them he began opening their doors, looking through them to see which one he wanted to take. Rifles, backpacks and metal cans full of ammunition were loaded into the back of each vehicle, and after looking through the first three he couldn't see any discernable difference between them.

As the noises outside the hangar grew louder, Rick glanced over to see cracks of light shining through the edges of the doors and realized that the crowd outside was close to breaking through. He ran back to the initial vehicle—one of two in the lineup with a gun mounted on the top—and opened the driver's door. The interior was covered with dirt and all of the surfaces looked worn and faded. He slammed the door closed and reached for where he assumed a lock would be, but found nothing. A long metal rod ran the length of the door on the interior with a small indentation three-quarters of the way down. He pushed on the rod, rotating it in place and heard a *thunk* from the door as the rod locked it in place.

"Okay then." Rick muttered to himself and put his hands on the steering wheel. "Where are the keys?" He grasped the side of the steering column, looking for a place where he could even insert a key, and found no sign of the ignition. More pounding and shouting came from the doors and he glanced up to see an arm reaching through a gap, grasping for a lock on the interior.

Rick continued searching for some way to start the vehicle until he finally noticed a large push-button switch sitting near the steering column. Rick jammed his thumb into the button and the engine roared to life, surprising him enough that he slammed his hand down on the small horn in the center of the steering wheel, startling himself with the timid "beep" from the vehicle.

"Crap!" Rick ran his hand over the levers to his right and wiped off a layer of dust that covered the labels for the shifter. "You'd better work, dammit!" Rick looked up to see the smallest door in the stack swing open and a crowd of people began pushing through. He pulled back on the shifter, putting it into drive, and the Humvee lurched forward. He spun the wheel to the right and felt himself push up against the door as the vehicle accelerated into the turn.

Rick looked around the hangar for any other exits, but as the shouting behind him increased in volume and gunfire started to ring out, he realized his only option for escape was in the opposite direction. He turned the wheel again, heading back towards the set of doors and the group of people who were pouring in through them. Rick leaned on the horn as he drove forward though his warning was met with three of the people raising handguns and opening fire.

Rick ducked down behind the dashboard, keeping his foot on the gas pedal, though the Humvee shrugged off the low-caliber shots as though they were confetti. Screams and shouts came from all directions as Rick plowed through the group of people. Some of them were quick enough on their feet to get out of the way while others were injured or killed under the thick treads and massive weight of the military vehicle.

While the hangar doors were reinforced and, under normal circumstances, could have stopped the Humvee in its tracks, the structural damage done by the people breaking in was enough that Rick was able to plow through the door with ease. Metal screamed as it slid together, scraping large gouges in the sides and top of the Humvee. The vehicle began turning as the rear end squeezed through the gap on the hangar door and Rick clung to the wheel, trying to keep the top-heavy piece of machinery from overturning. When he finally got it back under control he headed straight down the middle of the nearest road he saw, cutting across a series of walkways and small areas filled with artificial turf.

Rick hadn't seen much of the massive air base when he and Jane had been brought in over a week prior and as he drove through it searching for a way out he was stunned by its enormity. Most of the fighters that had been cleared for takeoff in the days prior had been evacuated from the base before the looting began. Colonel Leslie, as altruistic and potentially foolhardy as he had been in ceding the base to the nearby civilian population in lieu of killing them, had taken steps to ensure that anything of value was locked away in the specially-built underground bunkers used to store the aircraft when they were being fitted with classified hardware.

The bunkers were a new and relatively unheard of feature of Nellis, as was the entire underground section, which the Colonel had managed to keep secure from the civilians. While the administrative offices would no doubt be overrun relatively quickly, the jets, explosive ordinance and literal tons of ammunition would be kept safe until—or if—the Air Force returned. Colonel Leslie's decision to not fire upon the civilians hadn't been made entirely in a vacuum. Orders to prepare the base for abandonment had come down from the top prior to the civilian overrun. After a brief—yet fierce—debate with others in his chain of command, his argument for leaving them (mostly) alone had won out.

The staggering amount of people running through the secured areas of the base were mind-blowing to Rick, and made him wonder how the base looked prior to being overrun. Another explosion came just off to Rick's right and he turned sharply around a corner, catching a glimpse of a group of people lighting fuses stuck into makeshift explosives. The absence of law enforcement, food and the general panic and horror that the surviving population had been forced to endure was the root cause for the mass rioting and looting. A herd mentality had taken over and there was nothing anyone could do to negotiate with them.

After passing through several streets in the small town situated next to the airfield, Rick groaned as the Humvee bounced out into an open dirt field. Hills rolled upward away from him, stretching out for what seemed like eternity. The bumps and jolts from the rough terrain lanced through Rick's legs and rear end, shooting up his back and jittering his teeth.

"I'd better find a road soon before my fillings rattle themselves loose." Rick mumbled to himself as he struggled with the vehicle, trying to keep it on course to head away from the base before turning east.

As he sat on a helicopter spinning up as it was lifted from a bunker to the surface, Colonel Leslie thought about the strange pair that had come into the base. After throwing Rick into a holding cell the Colonel had a long chat with Jane, finding out a great many details about the mysterious man in the meantime. Jane's stories of Rick's tenacity and compassion over their trip through the city forced the Colonel to consider Rick in a new light. Though Leslie was quickly overtaken by matters more urgent, he gave one last thought to Rick as the helicopter soared westward.

Good luck, you bastard. You'll need it.

Author's Notes

June 30, 2017

With that we reach the end of Episode 3 in the Surviving the Series saga. I hope you enjoyed this episode. It was particularly enjoyable to write for a whole host of reasons and I'm really excited about what's going to happen in the next episode.

You probably noticed that this episode was *very* Rick-heavy with only a couple of chapters devoted to Dianne. The reason why has to do with where the story is going. I need some time to pass in the story (around a week to a week and a half) so that society can really degenerate further. Yikes... that really sounds brutal and morbid, doesn't it?

So far in the story things have degenerated pretty badly. We've had gangs and other groups of people going around looting, but most "regular" people have been right on the edge or far enough back from it that they haven't done anything terrible out of desperation. With another week going by, though, we're not just going to have criminals to deal with. People who would ordinarily be kind and helpful will have turned to horrific acts and society will have broken down to the point of no return.

Now that we're entering that phase of the story you can expect the heat to get turned up on Rick...and Dianne. In fact, Episode 4 will feature Dianne a LOT more as she moves from stockpiling and preparing the homestead to having to deal with active threats. We've seen hints of threats in the form of her neighbor's house burning down and the guys who tried to steal her car at the grocery store. Now we're going to see how she and her kids handle some true adversity. Buckle your seatbelts because it's going to get crazy.

There were a couple parts of this story that were exceptionally fun for me to write and they involved the casino scenes and the hints of the tunnel beneath the Waters' home.

With the casino, since Rick had to pass through Vegas I knew I had to put a casino scene somewhere in there. Since I've never been to Vegas, though, I relied on the extensive catalog of photos from Google Street View, Google Maps and photos tourists have taken inside the various buildings. Combining that with some artistic liberties led me to think up the casino that exists in the story. It's been damaged, it's maze-like and Rick and Jane have to get through it to get out. The tension of having the people outside with the Humvees and forcing Rick and Jane into a showdown with them was also really enjoyable and probably the highlight of that part of the story. (Funny aside – I was actually going to have the heroes in my other series, No Sanctuary, use Molotovs in book 2 but decided that they fit a lot better here.)

My second favorite part of the story and one that's going to see a lot of exposition in Episode 4 and beyond is the tunnel beneath the Waters' house. As a kid I loved the idea of secret passages and underground tunnels. The houses I grew up in never had anything like that in them but that didn't stop me from dreaming about them and imagining their usefulness in all sorts of scenarios. When you combine that with the fact that I've never actually grown up (I've just learned how to behave in public most of the time) and you're left with an adult who gets as giddy as a kid about the thought of a tunnel beneath his house.

I think Rick has a little bit of that child-like wonder in him and that's why he built the tunnel. I'm pretty sure it's going to be used for a lot more than just storage, though....

If you enjoyed this episode of Surviving the Fall or if you *didn't* like something—I'd love to hear about it. You can drop me an email or send me a message or leave a comment on Facebook. You can also sign up for my newsletter where I announce new book releases and other cool stuff a few times a month.

Answering emails and messages from my readers is the highlight of my day and every single time I get an email from someone saying how much they enjoyed reading a story it makes that day so much brighter and better.

Thank you so very much for reading my books. Seriously, thank you from the bottom of my heart. I put an enormous amount of effort into the writing and all of the related processes and there's nothing better than knowing that so many people are enjoying my stories.

All the best,
    Mike

Book 4 - Death of Innocence

Preface

Dianne Waters has spent her time since the Event preparing her house and her family for the end of the world. Living on a homestead far outside a small town in the rural portion of southern Virginia has its benefits during the apocalypse and Dianne is ensuring they are taking full advantage of those benefits. Food is gathered, plans are made to be able to grow fresh vegetables indoors over the approaching winter and the rediscovery of a subterranean passage beneath the house promises new opportunities for storage, defense and potential escape. The storm brewing on the horizon is at Dianne's front door, though, and she will be tested in her commitment to defend her family no matter the cost.

Meanwhile, Dianne's husband Rick has been incarcerated for over a week in a holding cell beneath Nellis Air Force Base just outside Las Vegas. The woman Rick was traveling with was put on a transport aircraft and sent east towards Colorado, but Rick's stubborn refusal to join a government project to try and put an end to Damocles resulted in him being held. After being released and then breaking out of a hangar on the base, he's trying to resume his journey home. But there are many miles between him and his loved ones and there are many more dangers posed by Damocles that have yet to come to fruition.

And now... Surviving the Fall: Book 4.

Chapter One

"JACOB? SEND DOWN ANOTHER BAG!"

"It's on the way!"

The sound of grunts and thumps came from down the way and Mark's face appeared, dripping with sweat as he hauled another overloaded sack of potatoes down through the tunnel. Dianne grinned at him as she took the bag and laid it next to the others, wiping her forehead with the back of her sleeve.

"How many more are there?" Dianne breathed heavily, leaning against the side of the tunnel as she spoke to her son.

"I think that's the last of the potatoes. The rest are odds and ends."

"Gotcha. I'll come up and take a look before we bring them all down. We should try to can anything that won't keep for a long time down here."

"It'd be nice if we had more room in the freezer."

"Yeah, well, the meat's more important to keep in there for now. Come on, let's get upstairs and see what's left."

Mark turned and headed back through the tunnel, ducking his head to keep from hitting it on the ceiling near the entrance. Dianne lingered for a few seconds longer, turning around to take everything in before she headed out as well.

The last week had been a flurry of activity after she opened the old tunnel beneath the house. Built by Rick years ago but never fully finished, they had sealed off the tunnel ages ago and she had all but forgotten about it until one of her sons mentioned it.

It had been so long since Dianne had been down into the tunnel that she had forgotten what it was like. She remembered it as a dingy, dirty, cramped area filled with dirt and bugs and thick with the feeling of claustrophobia. What she found, though, was more akin to an unfinished basement. In his last few months of work Rick had installed structural supports along the ceiling and walls of the passage for the first fifty feet, widening and deepening it so that even a tall person could stand up inside once they got past the entrance.

The floor for the first section of the tunnel was roughly poured concrete, coarse to the touch but extremely solid and stable. A few hairline cracks were visible if one looked closely enough, but the whole thing had held together remarkably well over the years. Beyond the finished section, out past fifty feet, the tunnel turned into more of what Dianne remembered. The size of the passage shrunk and even she had to stoop over to keep from hitting her head.

Ceiling and wall supports only popped up every ten or so feet and she could see that there were places where the supports were straining thanks to the growth of tree roots and the weight of the soil above. The first section of the passage, in contrast, was in near-perfect condition, and she had rescinded her original command to her children forbidding them from coming down and seeing it briefly.

After much discussion between her and her oldest, Mark, Dianne decided that the best use for the subterranean passage was as extra storage for vegetables from their gardens along with any other supplies they didn't want to keep in the barns. The house was feeling cramped and being able to move food, fertilizer, emergency food and other supplies down into the newly opened storage space was a boon for Dianne and the children.

As Dianne followed Mark up the stairs she brushed her fingers against a set of initials carved into the wall. *R.W.* Rick had marked the tunnel as his own creation and seeing the inscription brought a tear to Dianne's eye. It was easy to forget in the moment that he had been gone for close to two weeks. She had kept herself and her children busy in that time, but as preparations began to slow down she found herself thinking more and more about him every day. A few second's thought was all she could spare, though, both for the sake of her sanity and because Josie was calling to her from upstairs.

Chapter Two

N ellis Air Force Base
   Las Vegas, Nevada

THE LONG, wide dirt field sloped upward as Rick drove along, bouncing uncomfortably in the Humvee. It seemed to stretch on forever, an endless array of sand and scrub with almost no features of note. Occasionally Rick would pass by the shell of an aircraft or some land-based vehicle that had been the subject of target practice which made him wonder about the possibility of mines in the field.

"The Air Force wouldn't have a minefield out here... would they?" Rick mumbled to himself. While he had only been driving the Humvee for a short period of time he was already regretting the decision to take the vehicle he had chosen. "Damned springs must be shot in this one. Of course it's the one I picked."

In actuality all of the Humvees were the same way. Rick tried to pull himself up off of the seat with his arms on the steering wheel and bracing his left foot against the floorboards, but all that did was make the bumps harder when he fell back down. After twenty minutes of driving, when his rear end was almost totally numb, Rick crossed over a ridge and slammed on the brakes. Directly in front of him was a set of two chain-link fences topped with razor wire. The fences stretched around the perimeter of the test range and the base property and there was no clear way through them.

On the other side of the fence was a portion of the outer area of Las Vegas, and directly on the other side of the fence from Rick was a junkyard filled with cars, tires and scrap metal piled twenty feet into the air. Rick turned the Humvee to follow the fence and proceeded onward, watching the city to his left as he continued his search for a way off the base. Before long the fence took a turn as well, angling sharply to the right to follow the path of a highway just outside of it. There was still no way through the fence that he could see and he groaned at the prospect of what he would have to do next.

"Watch this thing be electrified and me get electrocuted. That'll be great." Rick turned the vehicle sharply, sliding along the ground as he drove away from the fence. A few seconds later he turned the wheel again and pressed the accelerator down to the floor. The engine roared as the Humvee slowly picked up speed, heading directly for the fence.

The chain-link didn't even slow the Humvee down, but it and the razor wire tore across the top of the Humvee, causing an awful racket and scraping even more paint from the vehicle. Half-expecting the fence to stop the vehicle in its tracks Rick kept his eyes closed as he plowed through, only moving his foot from the accelerator to the brake once he felt the Humvee hit the asphalt on the other side. The tires squealed as the vehicle came to a halt and Rick looked behind him.

The Humvee had torn a gaping hole in both fences and a trail of razor wire stretched from the machine gun on top of the Humvee all the way back to the fence. There wasn't much tension on the wire but he could see that it was still connected to the fence and feared what would happen if he continued trying to drive without getting free.

"Great. Just great." Rick looked in all directions, making sure there was no one nearby before he unlocked his door and hopped out to get a better look at the situation. Without thick gloves or tools he didn't think he could get the razor wire off of the turret so he opened the back door and started rummaging through the bags of supplies.

After a brief search Rick came across a small brown bag underneath the back of the driver's seat. The bag was filled with a variety of miniaturized tools and Rick grabbed a pair of wire cutters and got back out. "Okay… climb up top, snip the wire, don't get shredded by it." Rick climbed up onto the hood of the vehicle and across the windshield, examining where the wire was lodged beneath the gun. Several of the razors were embedded in a thick leather padding beneath the back of the gun's barrel, and he started by cutting the wire around the barrel first. Working slowly to avoid slicing his bare hands, it took Rick several minutes to cut all of the wire loose. There were still bits and pieces wrapped around the turret but given that he was more concerned with making a getaway than he was with immediately using the massive gun, he decided to get back into the vehicle and keep going.

After jumping down from the top of the Humvee Rick stopped to check the front end. The bumper was dented in one corner from when he had rammed through the door in the hangar, but as he looked closer he could see that the tan paint was stained red and brown. He crouched down and looked closer at the stains until he realized what they were.

"Good grief." Rick stood up and closed his eyes, feeling sick to his stomach. Blood, brown hair and bits of skin were stuck to the bumper, trapped in the creases in the metal and coated in sand and dirt. The gore was a grim reminder of Rick's desperate escape from the base and what he had had to do to get out.

A low hum began to fill the air and Rick turned to look back towards the base. Two C-130s were soaring through the air, heading in his direction. As they neared the end of the base property line they tilted sharply in a westerly turn, banking and increasing their pitch to gain altitude. Rick watched the massive aircraft until they were specks on the horizon and the sound of their engines no longer filled his ears, realizing that he was, once again, alone.

"Guess it's time to go, huh?" Rick got back in the Humvee and looked to the left and right. The lonely road outside the north end of Nellis stretched from east to west and Rick briefly checked his heading before turning the Humvee to the right and setting off to the east. He had no knowledge of where he was going, no map to guide him anywhere and no plan on how to get home but he was, finally, back on the road again.

As Rick drove through the desert a windstorm kicked up swirls of sand, reminding him of the city he left behind. Being locked up for over a week with no knowledge of what was going on had been difficult for him, but he worried more for the safety of the young woman he had met. He and Jane had been so busy trying to stay alive in the city that he had learned next to nothing about her, but their survival through multiple near-death experiences made him feel a sense of caring for her that was hard to explain.

Commander Leslie had informed him that Jane had been sent east on a plane, but Rick had no idea what that actually entailed. He doubted he would ever see her again but he hoped that she was safe wherever she was.

Chapter Three

The Waters' Homestead
Outside Ellisville, VA

"MOM!" Josie yelled again as Dianne closed the hatch to the tunnel.

"What did I tell you about shouting?" Dianne yelled back, fully aware of the hypocrisy of the act. There was a brief pause followed by the sound of footsteps on the floor above before Josie appeared at the door at the top of the basement stairs.

"Mom, the tablet is beeping!"

Dianne's attitude instantly transformed from one of slow, plodding reluctance to hasty action. She dashed up the stairs two at a time, grabbing her rifle leaning against the side of the wall as she went. Upstairs, Mark was washing his hands in the kitchen and Dianne tapped him on the shoulder as she dashed by, heading for the living room around the corner.

On the couch, Josie and Jacob were looking at the tablet. Images from the cameras located on the corners of the house appeared on the screen, and one of them aimed at the woods near the front driveway had a red outline that was flashing softly. "Move over, kiddo." Dianne took the tablet and sat down on the couch in between Jacob and Josie. She wiped her fingers on her pants before touching the screen, ignoring the dirt that was falling to the floor as well as smudging her once-pristine floral couch.

The image on the screen appeared normal and Dianne tapped on it, then tapped on the alert notification at the bottom of the screen. A ten-second clip surrounding the event that triggered the alert appeared and

Dianne watched the video replay as she watched for any signs of trouble. Across the room, Mark was peering out the back door, holding his rifle as he watched for anyone out behind the house.

On the screen, nothing happened until halfway through when the branches in the upper section of the trees shook suddenly as a flock of birds ascended. Their action knocked off a large quantity of snow that fell to the ground, offering just enough movement on the camera for the monitoring software to detect. Dianne put the tablet down on the coffee table and breathed a sigh of relief before looking up at Mark.

"False alarm. Just the snow falling."

Mark lowered his rifle and nodded. "That's good."

"You think you can try to tweak the settings again? This is the… what, fifth false alarm? Between the trees shaking, the snow falling and the random animals coming in and out I'm amazed this thing isn't going off all the time."

Mark shrugged. "I can try, but if I turn down the detection much more then it probably won't trigger on somebody walking by."

"Ugh." Dianne pinched the bridge of her nose before pulling her hand back with a look of disgust. She realized that she was still covered in dust and dirt from being down in the passageway beneath the house and stood up quickly to step off of the carpet in the living room. "See what you can do and I'll help you test it later. I don't want it reduced too much, though. I hate all the false alarms but I'd rather have a few of those than miss out on something legitimate."

Dianne went to the kitchen and looked out the window. The snow was still thick on the ground, having received an extra layer thanks to another storm that blew through a few days after the first. She and the kids had spent no small amount of time distracting themselves from the state of the world by playing in the snow and building snowmen for the first couple of days of the original storm. Once the second storm blew in, though, Dianne had slowly transitioned them back into work mode.

With the passageway beneath the house turned into a makeshift root cellar and all-purpose storage area, there was plenty of room in the basement for the aquaponics setup. All of the materials were in the basement and waiting to be assembled and she figured that would be a task for the next day or two. After spending a couple of days organizing and packing the cellar, though, she thought that she and the kids would enjoy taking some time off. *If you can call shoveling the driveway 'time off.' Though I'm sure they'll be doing more snowball throwing than actual shoveling.*

At some point she knew that they would need to go out and check on the neighbors again so she wanted to have a bit of the driveway in front of the house cleared out. *It'd be nice to try and drag that burned-out piece of garbage out of the way, too.*

Dianne sighed and turned back to watch her oldest staring out the window while Jacob and Josie tapped away at the tablet. Mark had changed significantly since that day at the grocery store. He was still only thirteen but he seemed so much older as he stood near the door and watched out back, still holding his rifle.

"Hey kiddos, I'm going to get a shower. Mark, you keep a close lookout, okay?"

Mark turned to look at his mother and nodded. "Will do."

Dianne smiled, gave Mark a thumbs up and headed towards the front door. She pulled off her sneakers and threw them in a pile of shoes before heading upstairs. As she waited for the hot water to arrive, she looked herself over in the mirror. The bags under her eyes were deepening, her hair was frizzled and her skin looked—to her own critical eye, at least—like it was sagging. She turned away and got into the shower, washing out the day's dirt and grime from her hair and skin, trying to empty her mind and avoid thinking about her husband being gone, her son growing up far too fast for his own good and any other depressing thoughts that happened to float past.

Chapter Four

O utside Nellis AFB

RICK DROVE along Interstate 15 for close to an hour before stopping near the outskirts of the Valley of Fire State Park. Not wanting the heavily armed vehicle to draw attention he pulled off to the side of the road and behind a stand of trees before stopping and getting out.

"Time to see what's in here." Rick hadn't wanted to stop anywhere near Nellis or Las Vegas in general for fear of having people from the city show up and surprise him. Out in the middle of nowhere, though, he felt slightly safer.

Rick opened the rear hatch on the Humvee first and grinned at the dozen or so green cans filled with ammunition ranging from 9 millimeter to three boxes of fifty-caliber for the mounted machine gun. Four M4 carbines were stacked next to the ammo containers along with two pistols and a shotgun. All of the weapons had scratches and dents on them but appeared to be thoroughly cleaned and oiled. A satchel of filled magazines for the pistols and rifles sat behind them and Rick grabbed it, one of the rifles, a pistol, the shotgun and a can of ammunition for the shotgun and carried them all around to the front passenger seat.

He loaded and chambered a round into the P320 before sticking it into his waistband at the small of his back. The M4 was loaded next and Rick pulled off the rubber cover from the ACOG scope before pulling the rifle up to his shoulder. The balance felt natural to him and the scope was pristine so he re-covered it and laid the rifle across the seat. Finally Rick picked up the shotgun and studied it, trying to conjure the name of the curious-looking weapon in his hands.

"Oh. M26." Rick snorted in amusement and hefted the weapon. Designed to be attached to the underside of a combat rifle, the M26 was also capable of being mated to a stock and operating independently. The M26 in his hands was in such a configuration complete with a basic sight and a thin strap attached to the base of the short barrel and the rear of the stock. "This thing's gonna hurt like hell with a barrel like that." Rick murmured to himself as he loaded a short magazine with shells and slapped it into the gun. He leaned the rifle up against the passenger seat and looped the strap around a post sticking out of the floor before nodding in satisfaction. "Good. I'm armed again. About time."

After closing the rear hatch to the Humvee, Rick climbed into the back-seat again, unlocked the hatch to the top and stood up. Bits of broken razor wire greeted him as he stood behind the M2, stuck into the thick padding that someone had installed around the edge of the hatch and gun to help stabilize it. He gingerly picked at the wire and razors, pulling a few of them out of the padding and tossing them as far from the vehicle as he could.

There was no ammunition loaded into the gun and Rick thought about figuring out how to load it himself but decided against it for the time being. Operating the gun would take some time to master and with the other weapons at his disposal he was hard-pressed to think of a situation that would require the fifty. *Better to have it and not need it, though.* The old saying flashed through Rick's head and he groaned.

A few minutes later, after retrieving a can of ammo from the back of the Humvee, Rick slid the can into the retaining arm attached to the gun. He fiddled with the gun until he figured out how to open the receiver cover, then placed the first few rounds from the belt into the receiver, wiggled them around until they set in place and then closed the cover with a slap. While he had no intention of firing it without hearing protection unless it was an emergency he at least had the gun loaded and—hopefully—nearly ready to fire.

"Hm." The thought of hearing protection reminded Rick that there was more to the supplies in the vehicle than just the guns and ammo. He slid back down into the back seat, locked the top hatch and began digging through the backpacks and bags between the rear seats and back storage section. Canteens and bottles full of water, MREs and packaged candies and snacks greeted him though there was no sign of any spare clothing, grooming supplies or anything else. His incarceration at Nellis had been accompanied by two cold showers and one washing of his clothes but he hadn't felt clean since the last shower he took before leaving on his trip to Los Angeles.

"At least I've got food for a few days. That's a start." Rick put a candy bar, an MRE and a bottle of water in the front passenger seat before sealing the bags back up and hopping out. He went around the vehicle once again to do a last check before taking off and noticed that what he had previously thought were just bumps on the sides were actually fuel cans. Ten gallons of diesel were strapped to each side of the vehicle, but not knowing how far it could get on a tank or how large of a tank the Humvee had made it impossible to know how far he could go.

"Guess I'll keep an eye on the gauge and play it by ear. I doubt I'll get more than ten miles to the gallon, though." Rick hopped back in the Humvee and shivered involuntarily as he closed the door. In the hour he had driven since leaving Las Vegas the temperature had dropped by several degrees and he was reminded that, despite the unusually warm weather he had experienced, it was still Autumn and things would be getting cold quite rapidly.

Clothing, fuel, water and food were Rick's new priorities. He wasn't sure how he would procure them, but knowing what he needed made it easier to focus on the task at hand. He started up the growling engine and threw the Humvee into reverse, taking it slow over the grass as he wound his way back onto the road. Headed east again, Rick pushed all other thoughts from his mind as he concentrated on thinking of ways to secure his four needed items. If he wanted to get back home, survival was the only thing that he could be concerned with for the time being.

Chapter Five

Three days after the Event

WITH DAMOCLES uncontained and infecting systems across the globe, disastrous effects are felt everywhere. Communication between individuals—let alone countries—is nigh-on impossible. Branches of the military use older equipment without data connections to communicate via voice in an encrypted format, but every time they communicate over long distances they risk broadcasting to a system that is infected with Damocles. If this occurs, Damocles attempts to infiltrate their communication system and destroy it. While this is difficult for the weapon to do to older systems, newer systems that weren't originally infected by the virus are prime targets.

In China, those in rural areas suffer little to no ill effects. Their television, radio and internet capabilities go down in the first day, but any vehicles and other equipment they have is old enough that it can't be affected by Damocles. In the cities and factories and ports, however, it is an entirely different story. Fires tear across the cities, started in the factories by industrial equipment that malfunction. Explosions rock the ports as dangerous chemicals are swept up in the blaze. Towering apartment buildings burn from the ground up, resulting in the deaths of untold numbers of people. Narrow streets that are already crowded at any given time of day are now filled with burning cars and the bodies of the dead.

In London, a tanker filled with fuel and loaded with clothing, electronics and more foreign goods for import smashes through the port at full speed. The captain is flung across the bridge, having stayed on the ship through the end to try and find a way to bring it back under control. The ship begins spilling fuel onto the docks and water surrounding them until a stray spark sets it alight.

In Russia, the Red Square is dark as is the rest of the country. The power grid is the first to go down, removing one way for the people of the country to heat themselves. With the cold of winter pressing in they will have to find another way to find heat or they will die. Trains that crisscross the massive country are stuck on the tracks, their engines locked into place. Engineers work to remove them and replace them with older models without computer systems, but they will not be fast enough. Isolated cities and towns that depend on the trains for food and medicine succumb to panic and infighting within days.

In Brazil, the loss of power and the destruction of an oil refinery near the capital city signals the breakdown of law and order. Riots break out across the country. The police and military organize to quell the rebellion but drug cartels add fuel to the flames, assisting with the decimation of the government and the killing of thousands of innocents. The new government sets up shop within days and quickly establishes a more brutal regime than the one before. It will be only a few weeks before rebellion is once again at the doorstep, if the populace at large manages to find a way to survive for that long.

Chapter Six

The Waters' Homestead
      Outside Ellisville, VA

THE NEXT MORNING, after breakfast, Dianne watched out the back window as a light dusting of fresh snow fell from the sky and settled on the trees and ground. The trees no longer had leaves—having shed them with all of the snow—and their spindly branches cast sharp shadows on each other in the early morning's light.

While she watched out the back window, thinking of nothing in particular, Dianne helped Josie stay upright while the little girl squeezed into a pair of snow pants that were nearly too small. Mark and Jacob were in the kitchen, playfully arguing over some sibling rivalry while they waited for Josie and Dianne to finish getting ready. When Josie was finally dressed Dianne grabbed a jacket and pair of thin work gloves and put them on before looping her rifle around her back. The gloves, while thin and offering little protection from the cold, would ensure that she could easily manipulate the rifle should the need arise.

Once they were outside, Dianne sent Mark and Jacob down to the barns to bring back the snow shovels and feed the animals while she and Josie stayed on the front porch. After a few minutes of whining and wearing her mother down, Josie finally got Dianne to agree to help build yet another snowman.

"He can guard the house!" Josie exclaimed, holding up a short branch that was roughly in the shape of a handgun. Dianne smiled and shook her head as she rolled up a large ball of snow for the base of the snowman.

Fifteen minutes later, when the snowman was nearly done, Jacob and Mark came trudging back through the snow, dragging three snow shovels behind them. "Here you go, mom." Mark held out a shovel before plopping down in the snow, remembering just in time to adjust the rifle on his back so that the barrel didn't hit the ground.

"Thanks, guys. Animals all doing okay?"

"Everybody's fine. They look pretty tired of being cooped up and there's going to be a lot of poop to shovel out, but they're okay."

"We can work on that tomorrow. I need to get the stalls rearranged anyway. For now let's just see what we can do about this driveway."

After a few groans and gripes, Mark and Jacob got to work with helping Dianne clear out the snow in the driveway and parking area in front of the house. The work went relatively quickly and the trio moved on to clearing around the side and back of the house so that the truck would have a clear path to get back around front should they want to go out. Josie busied herself with decorating her snowman near the front porch while the three worked, staying content and quiet until Dianne heard her tumble and roll as she ran around the house.

"Josie?" Dianne turned and helped Josie up to her feet. The little girl's face was masked in fear and Dianne felt her heartbeat increase. "What's wrong, honey?"

"There's a man in the driveway in the woods."

Dianne didn't bother asking any questions. Turning to Jacob, she hissed orders at him in a quiet voice. "You and Josie get inside right now. Get upstairs, in your room with the door locked. Got it?"

Jacob nodded, slightly afraid of the tone in his mother's voice. He took his sister by the hand and they ran through the snow up onto the back porch and inside the house. While they were going inside Dianne started heading back up the slope around the house with Mark in tow. When they neared the front porch Dianne drew her rifle and whispered for Mark to stay back, ready to support her if needed.

Staying close to the house, Dianne scanned the woods in front and to the side before looking over at the driveway. There, just as Josie described, was a man who was walking along the driveway toward the house.

His clothing was dirty and covered in visible stains and he clutched his jacket to his chest, shivering in the cold. His walk through the foot-high snow was more like a shuffle and he stumbled every few steps, barely managing to keep from toppling over. His beard was long and thin, and the hair and skin around his mouth was tinted yellow. His face was gaunt, though he didn't give the appearance of someone who was lacking in food. Overall he looked to be about sixty though that estimate was likely to be far from accurate given the condition of his skin and hair.

"Hold it right there." Dianne spoke loudly and firmly, keeping her rifle at the ready and aiming it just slightly down from the man. The man looked up at Dianne and she shivered involuntarily upon seeing his abnormally large pupils.

"Hello!" The man waved vigorously, then scratched at his neck before tucking his arm back around his chest. He was still shuffling forward when Dianne raised her rifle and switched the safety off.

"I said hold it!" She shouted at the man and he froze in place, swaying unsteadily as he eyed her.

"Whoa, hang on a second!" The man's arms were shaking as he pulled them away from his chest and raised them. His jacket was unzipped and Dianne could see the thin T-shirt he was wearing underneath. It, like the rest of his clothes, was stained as well, though she could make out distinct patterns of red on it.

"What do you want?" Dianne growled at the man, watching his every movement carefully.

"Hey I was just trying to find something to eat! Didn't mean to start anything!"

"We don't have anything here." Dianne motioned behind the man with the barrel of her rifle. "You'd best be moving along. There might be something to scrounge in town."

"Town?" The man laughed nervously and scratched at his neck again. "There's nothing in town, lady. Town's just a bunch of buildings with nobody in 'em and nothing left for anyone!" The man's voice was growing in volume and becoming more erratic as he spoke.

Dianne cast a quick backwards glance, relieve to see Mark crouched by the side of the house with his rifle in hand. "Sorry to hear that. You need to get moving, though. We don't have anything here."

The man cracked a wide smile as he pointed at the snowman near the front porch. "Looks like you've got time for diversions like that! Must have a nice bit of food around here, huh? Can't you just spare a bite or three?"

Dianne pressed the stock of the rifle against her shoulder and leveled the barrel. She leaned into the weapon, letting her cheek rest on it as she lined up the holographic sight square on the man's chest and took one small but menacing step forward. "I won't tell you again. Leave right now. Or you won't live to regret it."

The man's smile turned sour as his lips curled and wrinkled and his eyes narrowed. "What the hell's your problem, lady? Can't afford a guy a bit of food?" He started shuffling backwards down the driveway as Dianne took another step forward. "Fuck you, lady! I don't need your charity!" The man tripped over himself as he tried to turn, sending up a cloud of powder into the air. He cursed and lashed out at the snow itself, grabbing fistfuls and sending them flying as he struggled to get back to his feet.

Dianne continued advancing slowly on him, scanning the trees to her left and right as she went along all while counting on Mark to watch her back. The man jumped over the gate at the end of the drive and staggered down the road back towards town, alternately mumbling and screaming obsceni-ties and gibberish at no one in particular. He seemed to forget that Dianne was even there, not bothering to look back at her as he went along on his way.

Dianne stood at the gate, her rifle at the ready, watching the man until he was out of sight. When he was finally out of sight and earshot she turned back to the house and slowly walked back. She meandered to and fro across the driveway, looking in the woods for signs of footprints from someone other than the man she just ran off. Every few steps was accompanied by a quick glance backwards as she checked to make sure he was really gone.

When she got back to the house Mark was sitting on the front porch glancing around. He stood up as she approached and gave her a questioning look. "Who was that guy and what was wrong with him?"

Dianne shook her head and shrugged. "Beats me. Looks like he was on something."

"On something?"

"Drugs, kiddo. He looked like he was withdrawing." Dianne turned to look back down the driveway. "Someone like that's dangerous."

"You didn't shoot him, though."

Dianne shook her head. "I don't want to kill anyone. Not if I can help it. Besides, by the time he got over the gate his mind was somewhere completely different. You go inside while I go check on the animals again. We'll make an early dinner and trade keeping watch tonight."

"Okay." Mark trotted inside while Dianne lingered, heading around the side of the house and down the slope to the barns. She could tell that Mark was put off by the strange man but she was trying to remain upbeat about the situation to keep him and his siblings from worrying unduly. While Dianne was doing an admirable job of projecting a cool exterior she felt completely nervous and more than a little bit frightened inside.

"Keep it together, Dianne." She whispered to herself as she stalked through the snow, checking the ground for footprints and the barns for any signs of a break-in. "Just keep it together."

Chapter Seven

The Waters' Homestead
Outside Ellisville, VA

STEAMED VEGETABLES, macaroni and cheese and tilapia fillets made for an easy dinner for Dianne to cook. Once she and the children finished their meal she sat Mark and Jacob up with dish duty while she and Josie sat on the couch to read a book. While Josie sat and read the book aloud, Dianne half-listened, keeping part of her attention on the story and part on the tablet sitting next to her on the couch.

Views from the cameras pointed out from the house appeared and vanished from the screen as Dianne kept the camera app full-screened to better make out any and all details. Her rifle sat leaning up against the wall across the room while she felt the comforting bulge of her pistol pressing against her hip.

Dianne had originally thought that going through day-to-day life with a rifle and pistol on her and always on the ready for dangers would be a hard transition. In fact, though, it had been quite easy for her and for her children. Constant, gentle reminders to Jacob and Josie to always respect firearms ensured that the pair never went near the rifles she and Mark carried or the pistol that felt like it was an extension of her body.

When Mark and Jacob finished up with the dishes, she left Jacob and Josie to play in the living room while she took Mark to the front room to go over her plan for the evening. "Basically I want to play it safe for the next couple of nights. I'll plan to stay up most of the night keeping watch, but I'd

Book 4 - Death of Innocence   223

like you to sleep with your clothes and shoes on and be ready to jump up and help me if needed."

"I can do that." Mark nodded. "Are you expecting something bad?"

"Nah." Dianne shook her head in what she hoped was a convincing manner. "That was the first person we've seen in a while, though, and he was pretty messed up. I want to stay extra vigilant without scaring your brother and sister."

"Okay. Just let me know what to do."

"Thanks, kiddo." Dianne smiled and embraced Mark. "Sorry we're going through this. I hate that you three are having to deal with everything."

Mark shrugged. "It's okay. I don't think Josie even notices. And Jacob is… in his own world."

Dianne chuckled. "That he is. He looks up to you, though. I'm proud of you for how much you've stepped up and how many responsibilities you've been taking on." Mark lowered his head and mumbled a thank you as he tried to avert his face. "No, I'm serious, kiddo." Dianne tugged on Mark's chin and looked him in the eye. "You're doing a great job. Your dad would be proud of you, too."

Mark abruptly sat down on the narrow wooden bench in the front entry. "When do you think he'll be home?"

Dianne eased down into the space next to Mark and put her arm around him. He leaned into her and she could feel his chest heaving as he tried to hold back his tears. "I'm not sure, kiddo." Dianne whispered to him, putting her head on his and holding him tightly. "I wish I knew."

"Do you think he's… gone?"

Dianne shook her head and sighed deeply. "No."

"How do you know?" Mark sat up and quickly wiped a tear from the corner of his eye.

Dianne smiled, letting the tear fall freely from her eye and cut a line down her cheek. "Faith, kiddo. Faith."

———

HOURS LATER, after Mark, Jacob and Josie were in their beds, Dianne sat on the stairs with the tablet by her side. The house was quiet aside from the creaks and groans from the appliances that were quietly sipping power from the backup batteries and the drips of water from the snow slowly melting on the eaves. Dianne had spent just over three hours watching the cameras on the tablet before setting it down to take a short break. With her head leaning against the rails of the stairs, Dianne didn't even realize that she was drifting off to sleep until a strange noise roused her from her slumber.

"What the hell?" Dianne mumbled to herself as she sat up straight on the stair. Pain shot through her rear end and she shifted on the uncomfortable wood plank to try and find a more comfortable position. She wasn't sure what the noise was that had awoken her but as each of her senses adjusted to her awakened state she felt the hairs on the back of her neck start to rise.

Something wasn't right in her house.

Dianne looked down at the tablet and tapped the button to go back to the multi-camera view. On the screen, all of the cameras outside the house looked normal. She studied each image intently, listening to the sounds of the house as she tried to figure out what had woken her. The sharp clink of broken glass came a few seconds later and Dianne stood up, her eyes wide as she waited for any further sounds.

When none immediately came Dianne picked up the tablet and backed up the stairs until she was at the top, then swiftly entered the room where Mark was sleeping. A few taps on his chest was all it took to rouse him and when he saw the rifle in her hands and the look in her eyes he was out of bed and on his feet in an instant.

"Mom? What is it?"

"Somebody's in the house. Stay here, at the top of the stairs. I'm going down to check it out. Don't come down unless you hear me telling you to do so. Keep an eye on the outside cameras and through the windows, too."

Dianne tossed the tablet onto Mark's bed before moving back out into the hall. She moved down the stairs quickly, taking each step with the practiced ease of someone who knew exactly where every squeak was. When she reached the bottom of the stairs she stopped and listened. While she expected to hear the sound of more glass breaking or the grunts and shuffling of someone rummaging through drawers in the house, she heard nothing except the soft hum of the refrigerator.

After drawing her pistol, Dianne placed her rifle on a high shelf near the bottom of the stairs. While the rifle was good at a distance, the long barrel would be cumbersome while clearing the rooms as she had learned after her last experience of checking the house. With the very clear presence of someone in or around their dwelling the last thing she wanted to worry about was getting the rifle caught on a doorframe or having someone grab it before she could fire.

Keeping the pistol close to her chest, Dianne padded through the main floor of the house, going from room to room as quickly as she dared. Each empty corner she checked was a welcome sight and in less than two minutes she confirmed that the main floor and basement were clear of intruders.

"What on earth?" Dianne shook her head as she went into the dining room and saw bits of broken glass lying on the floor next to the window looking out the front of the house. She pulled back the curtains to reveal a small hole knocked into the window and a piece of firewood lying on the floor that had been tossed through the glass.

"Dammit!" Dianne cursed herself for, in all of her preparation, forgetting one of the most obvious points of entry into the house. With nothing protecting the windows from the outside world anyone could easily gain entry into the house in spite of the locked doors.

After moving back to the entryway, Dianne grabbed her rifle and started to head outside when she heard Mark trying to get her attention. "Pst! Mom!" Mark whispered down to her from the top of the stairs.

"What is it?"

"There's a guy on the cameras running down the driveway."

"Towards the house or away?"

"Away."

"Stay here and open a window upstairs. Holler down if anything changes."

Dianne moved out onto the front porch and crouched next to one of the pillars, squinting as she tried to see the figure running down the drive. While the cameras had the benefit of infrared spotlights and detectors her eyes did not and all she could see were shadows from the moon and clouds as they passed by overhead.

After waiting outside the front door for several more minutes Dianne crept down the length of the porch until she was standing in front of the broken window. Snow and ice were scattered across the porch along with large drops of dark red blood. Dianne resisted the temptation to examine the scene more carefully with her light as she didn't want to fully reveal her position in case the perpetrator was still out in the woods watching her beyond the sight of the cameras.

Dianne headed back inside the house and upstairs to where Mark was sitting in the hallway watching the tablet. Dianne kneeled down next to him and looked at the screen. "He went up the driveway, eh?"

"Yeah. He was walking funny, too. Like that guy from earlier."

Dianne clenched her jaw, resisted the urge to curse in front of her son. "All right. It doesn't look like he got in the house. There's a piece of firewood on the floor inside and some blood on the porch. He probably cut himself and got scared and ran off."

"What should we do?"

"The sun will be up in a couple hours. We'll have to get some lumber and nails from the barn and seal up the downstairs windows so this can't happen again. You should get back to bed for now, though. Try and get a bit of sleep."

Mark nodded and stood up before heading back to bed. He kicked off his shoes and flopped down, falling asleep seconds after his head hit the pillow. Dianne took the tablet and went back to sit on the stairs. Unlike before, however, she wasn't tired at all and she doubted that she would be sleeping well for a very long time.

Chapter Eight

S omewhere in Utah

AFTER PASSING BRIEFLY through Arizona Rick found himself in Utah, continuing on along Interstate 15. He stuck to the main road as much as possible but frequently found himself having to either take alternate routes or go off-road when passing through towns and cities. The high volume of destroyed vehicles sitting in the road played havoc with the Humvee which was substantially more difficult to drive and maneuver through tight spaces than the SUV Rick had picked up in Los Angeles.

While on a back road trying to get back to the Interstate Rick came across a large, formerly well-maintained gas station. The pumps had caught fire and burned down but the building looked intact and Rick decided to stop and see what they might have in the way of clothing and food. He drove around the building slowly, watching through the windows for any sign of movement. When none came he parked behind the station and hopped out, taking a rifle and pistol with him.

The air was still chilled and he shivered again as he moved into the building, checking each corner as he went. A flashlight was attached to the end of the rifle and he flicked it on once he got fully inside. The illuminated interior was a complete disaster and looked like a herd of elephants had stampeded through the place. Shelves were knocked over, food and other supplies were trampled on the floor and the drink cases had their glass doors smashed in. Behind the counter the cigarette displays had been torn apart by people stealing as many cartons as they could get their hands on.

Rick wrinkled his nose at the smell of rotting milk and meat as he stepped gingerly through the mess in the store. He scanned the ground and the few upright shelves for anything of use, but anything that hadn't been taken was either crushed to bits or torn open and rotting. Dismayed and disappointed, Rick started to head towards the back door to the building when a pile of tipped-over boxes caught his eye near the front.

He crouched down over the stack of boxes and picked one up, turning it over to see the front. "GPS, eh?" Rick raised an eyebrow as he looked out the front window at the darkening sky. "I doubt any satellites are still working. But maybe…hm." Rick took the box back outside to the Humvee and sat in the driver's seat. He opened it up and popped the included batteries into the back of the unit and switched it on. A pleasant chime accompanied a woman's voice as a greeting while the device initialized. When it began searching for a signal Rick stepped back out of the Humvee and held it flat in the palm of his hand, staring up at the sky.

"There's no way you'll pick anything up. No possible way." After a few minutes of waiting for the device to try and locate any GPS signals the unit flashed an error message on the screen.

No GPS signal acquired. Defaulting to static maps. Please try to re-acquire GPS signal later.

Rick grinned at the error message text and got back into the Humvee, setting the GPS unit on his leg as he turned the vehicle back on. "Now that's what I'm talking about!" As he pulled out of the gas station he manipulated the touchscreen with his fingers, zooming in and out to see the level of detail offered by the device. It appeared to contain details for the entire country down to the smallest street and back-country roads. It was possible that the maps were a few years out of date but having something was better than nothing.

A thought passed through Rick's head and he slammed on the brake pedal, put the Humvee into reverse and stopped in front of the gas station's front entrance. He hopped out, picked up the rest of the intact boxes and threw them into the back of the Humvee before getting back in and continuing on his way. He hadn't seen any batteries in the store but since the units each came with a set he figured it would be a good idea to have as many as possible along with a spare unit in case the first one he picked up got broken.

Using the unit's street search feature it only took Rick another ten minutes of driving to find his exact location on the map. Zooming out he saw that the road he was on would turn north soon as he went deeper into Utah but if he passed through Fishlake National Forest he could cut east onto Interstate 70 and head directly for Colorado. It wasn't the most direct easterly route he could have taken from Nellis but under the circumstances it was the best he could manage.

Rick stared at the screen as he zoomed out, the roads and highways disappearing as state borders and names were drawn. He felt like he had traveled so far already but Virginia was still so distant. The view of the vast distance he still had yet to cross made him feel like an insignificant speck, breaking down the mental barrier he had put up to try and keep from worrying about his family back home.

He slowed the Humvee to a stop in the middle of the road and closed his eyes, sighing deeply as he tried to keep his emotions under control. "We can do this." Rick whispered to himself. "We can do this. They're okay. Dianne's okay, Mark's okay, Jacob's okay and Josie's okay. We can do this. We can get home." Squaring his shoulders, Rick gritted his teeth and grabbed the steering wheel with an iron grip.

"I'm coming home."

Chapter Nine

Three days after the Event
Mount Weather, Virginia

"WILL someone please tell me why the hell I wasn't informed about this... this weapon?!" The Vice President of the United States, deep within a bunker at Mount Weather, is furious. He paces the conference room like a lion, pouncing on every hesitant answer as he struggles to understand what is going on.

"The development of Damocles was classified at the highest level, sir. The President himself had limited knowledge of the weapon until—"

"I don't give two shits what information you held from the President. Have you even heard from Air Force One?"

A man near the end of the table looks around nervously. "No sir. Not yet."

"Then you'd better give me some answers right now. What is Damocles? Why was it developed? How did it get loose? How do we stop the damned thing?"

A report given to the President six days before the event is produced by another man at the table and copies are passed around. The Vice President snatches one up and flips through it, then shakes his head and tosses it back on the table. "I don't have time to read this shit right now. Give me what I need to know to make a decision."

"Well, sir." A man near the end of the table clears his throat. "Damocles originated as a privately-developed system to experiment with advanced command and control techniques."

"In English?"

"Damocles knows how to talk to just about any device or system that has a computer.

It knows this because it's a learning system. It teaches itself based on human and computer interactions and learns how to find and exploit weaknesses in systems."

The Vice President narrows his eyes. "You mean it's just a computer virus?"

The man speaking looks around the table nervously. "Damocles is to a computer virus what we are to chimpanzees. A computer virus—even the best and most well-designed one —is a bulky, unwieldy tool compared to Damocles. The power of Damocles is that it constantly alters itself depending on the system it attacks. It can change and alter itself to attack... well, as I said, sir. Anything."

"Why, exactly, was a private entity developing such a thing?"

More nervous looks. "Damocles didn't start out as a weapon, per se. The NSA bought out the project, classified it and then went to work with the CIA under the umbrella of a new project called Cerberus. They turned Damocles into... well, Damocles."

"Christ. So the spooks created this? For what purpose?"

Another man, farther up the table, answers. "For the protection of our country, sir."

"Well it doesn't look like that went all that well, now does it?!" The Vice President explodes, slamming his palms down on the table. "We're not going to have a country left if this shit keeps going on! How did this thing get loose anyway?"

"There was a break-in. A virtual break-in. A system in the Cerberus network was compromised. That system happened to be linked to the development systems where Damocles was being tested and the source code was housed. The code was downloaded and then we believe it was compiled and inadvertently activated by whomever broke into the system."

"And that let this thing run rampant?"

"The code was in a testing state at the time. Under normal circumstances its capabilities would have been severely limited. Whoever broke in did so at the moment in time when the capabilities were all unlocked by default. That's why it's infecting every system it can without any discrimination."

The Vice President sits down in his chair, his shoulders sagging as he rubs the bridge of his nose. He turns back and forth in the chair for a moment, trying to process the information he's just been given. "You developed the most advanced cyber-weapon imaginable. Left it unlocked, on a system that was connected to the outside world. Someone broke in and stole the weapon and then turned it on." He looks up at the man who was speaking a moment earlier. "Is that about right?"

"Yes sir."

"And now we and everybody else in the world who're not in the stone age is undergoing a total societal collapse." The Vice President shakes his head and claps his hands together slowly in a mocking fashion. "Well done to you all. Well fucking done."

An awkward silence fills the room and everyone avoids eye contact with the Vice President until he speaks again. "So what do we do now? Wipe this thing from our systems and reboot? Is that a thing? Can we do that?"

More nervous glances bounce between the people at the table before the man farther down the table speaks again. "That's... not really possible, sir. Damocles has replicated itself across the globe. It's infected every system there is. If we clean a system but it touches an infected system it'll simply become infected again. We've tried getting in touch with the Cerberus team but they were in an area that was extremely hard hit."

"Are they the most likely ones to know how to stop this?"

"Unless we can locate Dr. Evans, yes."

"The one on Air Force One?"

"Yes, sir."

The Vice President shakes his head and speaks to a man in a military uniform. "General, I want soldiers scouring the Cerberus facility. Work with these eggheads and do what they tell you. Find the people, computers, documents or whatever else we need." He turns and looks at the man near the end of the table. "There are millions of people dying across the globe and we're the ones responsible. You figure out how to stop this thing. I don't care how. Figure it out, tell the General what you need and his men will get it for you."

The Vice President stands up and turns to walk out of the room. "The rest of you figure out how we can salvage this country before it's too far gone to do so. And find the President for God's sake!"

Chapter Ten

The Waters' Homestead
Outside Ellisville, VA

WHEN MORNING CAME and Mark went downstairs, Dianne was already down at the barns feeding the animals and finding the spare lumber, nails and a couple of hammers. The tablet was perched on a shelf near the door to the barn with the motion alarm for the camera in front of the house turned to its highest setting. The tablet was nearly out of range of the wireless signal in the house but enough data came through that Dianne could see the view on the camera change every few seconds.

Once the animals were taken care of and Dianne picked out enough boards to cover all of the windows on the bottom floor she headed back to the house, musing about the one weakness left that she wasn't sure how to deal with. The sliding back door was all glass and while she initially thought about closing it off completely she realized that would cut off one of the three doors into the house that she and the kids might need in case of an emergency. *Plus*, she thought, *it'd be nice to still have a good view of the property from the living room.*

Dianne stood on the back porch for a few minutes before going inside, mulling over various options in her mind before coming to one that she found reasonably acceptable. Nailing boards over the stationary side of the door would cover up half of it and if she created a rudimentary door with more boards she could attach it to the others to create a makeshift door. Locking it would be solved by attaching a thick rope or piece of chain to the wood and threading it to something inside to keep it secure. It wouldn't be pretty but it would allow them to retain the functionality of the back door.

Dianne headed back inside to find Mark in the kitchen cleaning up the table while Josie and Jacob finished the last few bites of their breakfast. Since the chickens were still producing more than enough eggs the go-to breakfast meal had become eggs, crackers and a can of fruit. Mark pulled a plate from the oven and put it on the table for Dianne and spooned out a couple slices of peaches that were sitting in the bottom of one of the cans. "I saved this for you."

"Thanks, kiddo!" Dianne smiled and sat down. After quickly devouring her food she helped Mark finish cleaning up before sending Josie and Jacob to clean the upstairs of dirty clothes and toys. Once they were distracted she sat down with Mark and went over her plan with him.

"Clearly we still have some issues with security around the place."

Mark giggled before trying to turn his expression serious. "Er, yeah. Sorry."

Dianne smiled and shook her head. "No, you're right to laugh. Of all the things we prepared for and got ready I never thought to secure the easiest way into the house. There's no excuse for it." Dianne's smile faded. "That could have been a lot worse than it was."

"I saw you were out at the barn when I got up. Did you find enough boards and stuff to close up the windows?"

"Yep, everything's down there. We just have to bring it all up." Dianne shook her head again. "We really need to get the aquaponics rolling down in the basement. Adding some nice leafy greens to our diets would be good. Today's not that day, though, I guess."

Over the next few hours Mark, Jacob, Josie and Dianne worked to move the lumber from the barn to the back porch of the house. The sun was bright and the temperature warmer than Dianne had expected which resulted in the snow starting to vanish before their very eyes. Trudging across the wet grass and dirt wasn't that much more pleasant than going through the snow, though, and before long each of the four had mud streaking across their shoes, pants and—in Josie's case—face.

Mark worked a small handsaw to cut misshapen boards to size while Jacob carried them back and forth to Dianne. Josie was in charge of handing Dianne the nails, four of which were used on each board. Dianne cringed at the first few boards she pounded into place across the beautiful siding of her house, but she knew that the actions were necessary to help ensure her family's survival. *Besides,* she thought, *it'll add extra character for when Rick gets back.*

It was mid-afternoon by the time they were done boarding up all of the windows. Dianne sat them all down on the back porch and went inside to heat up an early dinner while Mark sketched out a design for the covering on the rear sliding door. Dianne hadn't realized how much darker the house was going to be with the windows boarded up, but she tried to keep a positive attitude despite the darkness. With soup in hand she headed out to the back patio and passed around bowls before sitting down to see what Mark had drawn.

"I think if we put the boards up vertically on the left side of the door like this, then add in a couple of horizontal ones for stability, we can just mount the hinges directly onto the horizontal boards."

Dianne turned around to look at the sliding door and nodded. "I think that's the best idea, yeah. Then we'll just have the same setup on the right side, except it won't get nailed in."

"Yeah and I think we could mount some sort of hook on the inside door-frame to loop a rope or chain around. The only problem with that is the glass door won't be able to shut all the way."

"Hm. Well, with the hinges mounted so far out there's going to be a gap there between the wood door and the sliding one. What if we just put an actual lock onto the doorframe in between the two doors. Just a slide lock or maybe a hook lock. We could put a couple of those on there, one at the top and one at the bottom."

"I think we have some of those in the barn somewhere. At least I think we do."

"Yep, I think you're right. That would be from Jacob's six-month obses-sion with all types of locks." Dianne smiled and tussled her younger son's hair as she stood up. "All right, this sounds like a plan. Jacob, how about you and your sister get things cleaned up while Mark and I get started on this? Turn on an extra light in there, though. It's pretty dark."

With a few grumbles Josie and Jacob got to work as requested. While they washed and put away the bowls and pot Dianne started hammering in the vertical boards to the left outer side of the sliding doorframe. Mark ran down to the barn while she worked and dug around in old boxes until he found a plastic baggie filled with locks of various types and levels of rust and brought them back to the porch along with three heavy-duty hinges from a workbench.

"Think these'll work?"

Dianne glanced at the baggie as she plucked a nail from between her lips and rested it against a board. "Yup. Perfect."

In the span of two hours the finished section covering the left side of the glass door was completed and the right side was preassembled on the floor of the patio and ready to be put into place. Inside, on the couch, Dianne listened as Josie and Jacob watched a recorded TV show before glancing at the tablet propped up on a chair that showed the view of the security cameras. "Everything's been really quiet today. No sign of that guy."

"Maybe he won't come back?" Mark offered the suggestion half-heart-edly, believing in it about as much as Dianne did.

"I doubt that. But maybe. Okay, come on. Let's lift this up and get it attached." The solid iron hinges were one of the weak points of the back door, but Dianne knew full well that all of the wooden barricades around the windows and back door would mean nothing to someone who was determined to break in. They were designed to both obscure views inside the house from trespassers as well as offer Dianne and the children a few extra precious seconds to prepare a defense should an invasion become imminent. Someone could just as easily use a crowbar and elbow grease to pry off the boards from one of the windows as they could remove the hinges from the door.

"Up we go!" Dianne lifted the door up and Mark hammered in a couple of temporary nails through the hinges into the door to keep it in place. When he was done Dianne let go of the door slowly and helped him screw it to the hinges.

After another hour of adjusting hinges, adding more reinforcements and a pair of locks that attached to the frame of the sliding glass door, Jacob and Josie stood on the porch holding flashlights up as Mark and Dianne drove in the final nails and screws. When they were done, Dianne and Mark stepped back to admire what they built.

"All right, Jacob. Head inside, pull the door shut and lock it." Dianne watched as Jacob did as she asked. The makeshift door covered the entirety of the sliding glass door and a small handle mounted on the inside of the wood made pulling it closed easy. A few seconds later, once both locks were engaged, Dianne stepped forward and began prying at the door to test how well it would hold. Even after jamming a screwdriver into the cracks between the boards to gain leverage she still couldn't do more than pry the door out by a millimeter or two. Satisfied that the door would do she released it and stepped back.

"Okay, looks good from out here. Open it up again." Jacob opened the locks and pushed the door open and Dianne nudged Mark and smiled at him.

"Well done, kiddo. We did a good job today."

Mark nodded and smiled back as he looked at the door. "It's not the best looking thing in the world, is it?"

"Nah, but that's okay. It works and that's what matters." Dianne patted Mark on the back. "Come on, let's get inside. I'm beat."

After sending Josie and Jacob upstairs to get themselves ready for bed Dianne and Mark cleaned up the tools from the back porch and stacked the spare lumber along the side. There was enough left between what was on the porch and what she didn't pull from the barn that she started thinking about shoring up more of the tunnel beneath the house. That, however, would be a project for a different day.

Chapter Eleven

_____

S omewhere in Utah

DRIVING NORTH along I-15 was an exercise in boredom. The land was mostly flat and covered with sparse patches of grass, dirt and low hills that jutted out of the ground. The lack of deep ditches or any semblance of uneven terrain made it easy for Rick to go off-road when he was in between cities. Passing through cities had become a thousand times easier thanks to the GPS unit he picked up and he could tell that he was making much better time than before.

Rick had never been in the military, but after driving for a few hours in the Humvee he concluded that people who drove and rode in Humvees all day must stuff their pants with pillows or very small mattresses. Even when driving on the highway Rick could feel every single imperfection in the road. The few minor bumps off-road reminded him time and time again that all of the painkillers he had taken from a first aid kit beneath one of the seats were doing absolutely no good.

As the Humvee started running low on fuel Rick began studying the GPS along long open stretches of road to decide where he would stop to try and get more diesel. Large cities were out of the question as he knew they would have already been ransacked. Smaller towns and isolated stations would likely have been hit as well, but he figured there would be a slightly higher chance of finding something there.

He settled on Paragonah, a tiny town that was located just off of the

Interstate a few miles down the road. There weren't more than two dozen intersections in the entire town and it was just outside a larger city by the name of Parowan. He hoped that if people were evacuating and escaping from the area that they would go to the larger city instead of the smaller, or that there would at least be a few less people around in Paragonah than in Parowan. After driving through Parowan, Rick pulled off the highway and smashed through a low wooden fence on his way to Paragonah. The detour caused him slightly more pain but saved several minutes of weaving around destroyed cars along the highway.

Although Rick had noticed the level of destruction in the towns and cities he passed by, it wasn't until he was actually driving through one of them that he realized just how bad things had gotten. In the small town with a population of less than five hundred there were dozens of destroyed cars in the streets, swaths of houses and small shops that had burned to the ground and a feeling of unease that accompanies disasters of all types and sizes.

When Rick got about halfway through the small town he spotted one of the two things he was looking for the most: a gas station. Like the other station he stopped at the pumps at the station in town had burned to the ground but there was a dump truck parked nearby that looked untouched. Rick pulled up next to the truck and turned off the Humvee. Grabbing his rifle he climbed into the back and opened the hatch to the top where he stood, holding the rifle in both hands while he surveyed the area around him.

Burned buildings dotted the view on the side of the street opposite the gas station. On Rick's side, however, most of them looked relatively intact, or at least they didn't appear burned. Windows were broken, façades had been torn down and trash and debris was scattered everywhere. A chilled wind cut through the street, sending old newspapers and plastic bags tumbling and soaring, but there was no sign of any other movement anywhere he looked.

"Nice and creepy." Rick shook his head and sighed. "Just what I hate the most. A creepy-ass town that's completely deserted. Only *slightly* better than one where everyone's trying to kill you or steal your stuff."

Rick slithered back down inside the Humvee and sealed the hatch before jumping out. Keeping the rifle in hand he went over to the dump truck and opened one of the fuel tanks on the side, then shone the light at the end of the rifle down inside. He kicked the tank and saw liquid sloshing around close to the top and nodded with satisfaction. "Excellent. Now to get that stuff into the tank." After another glance around Rick headed down a side street, looking into the front yards of each house he passed. The third house on his side of the road contained exactly what he was looking for. He trotted across the yard up to the side of the house, unscrewed the garden hose coiled up next to some bushes and carried it back to the Humvee.

Once there he opened up the Humvee and grabbed the tool bag out of the back. Using a knife inside the bag he cut a length of the garden hose about four feet long and another length about six inches long. Setting the lengths of hose to the side on the ground he unstrapped one of the cans of diesel fuel from the side of the Humvee and began filling the Humvee with the fuel from the can. Once both cans were emptied and he checked the fuel level of the vehicle and saw it was nearly full again he brought the empty cans over to the truck.

Rick pushed the longer length of hose down into the open tank and stuck the other end into one of the open jerry cans. He then opened the cab of the truck and searched around until he found a particularly filthy looking undershirt, wrapped it around the middle of the shorter piece of tubing and then stuck the shorter piece of tubing into the tank. With the old undershirt jammed up against the gap between the two hoses to form a makeshift seal he put his mouth around the short length of hose and gave a sharp, powerful blow.

The change in pressure inside the tank forced the fuel to rise up through the garden hose, and a second later it was siphoning into the empty fuel can. Rick flashed a grin, pleased that a video he had watched on the internet at two in the morning years ago had finally come in handy. Once the first can was half full Rick stuck the hose into the second can and used the first to completely fill the Humvee. As the second can continued filling he went inside the gas station, emboldened by his success, and began searching for any more containers that he could use to turn into makeshift jerry cans.

The only bottles he could find that were suitable were water bottles, and they were full and intact, sitting in the back room of the gas station on a shelf. He briefly considered dumping half of them out and filling them with fuel but decided against it, knowing full well that the water could be desperately needed later down the road.

Chapter Twelve

The Waters' Homestead
Outside Ellisville, VA

DIANNE AND MARK spent the night sitting in the upstairs hall near the stairs, taking turns dozing, watching the cameras and listening for signs of intruders. Dianne had insisted more than once that Mark needed to sleep in his bed but she was tired enough that she nearly nodded off while talking to him so he took it upon himself to ensure she got a few hours of sleep. The night passed uneventfully and when the morning light broke over the horizon Dianne and Mark slowly trudged downstairs and sat at the kitchen table.

"I can't believe your brother and sister are still asleep." Dianne looked at her watch and put her head in her hands. "Ugh. I'm getting too old for this."

Across from her, Mark took his mother's coffee cup and sniffed at it before taking a sip and making a face. "How can you stand that stuff?"

Dianne looked at her son through a crack between her fingers and snorted. "Believe me, when you reach my age you'll learn to love it."

"Yuck. I hope not." Dianne and Mark sat quietly for a few minutes while Dianne sipped her coffee, then her son spoke again. "The windows look good. I don't think anyone will be able to get in very easily."

Dianne turned around in her chair to look at the dark space in the wall that used to offer a view out onto the lake behind the house. Only a few cracks of light were visible through the boards covering the window. "Yeah it does look good. I wish we didn't have to do it but it's safer this way."

"Should we board up the windows upstairs?"

"Nah." Dianne shook her head. "If we're worried about people scaling the house and coming in through the upstairs then I don't think a couple boards will stop them." She took a long sip from her mug and set it back down on the table.

"There is something else we need to talk about, though."

Mark looked at her warily. "What did I do?"

"No, nothing you did. It's about the tunnel." Mark stayed quiet as Dianne continued. "I've been thinking about this since we opened it up and I decided that we need to make it more than just a storage area."

"What do you mean?"

"Well, the house is a bit more secure now but there's always the chance that one or more people could get in. If something like that happens, and something happens to me, you're going to be in charge of taking care of Jacob and Josie."

Mark shifted in his chair, clearly uncomfortable about where the conversation was leading. "Mom, nothing's going to—"

"Just listen up, kiddo." Dianne's expression grew serious. "If something happens, you're in charge of your brother and sister. If we're inside the house and you can get them to the basement, I want you to get them into the tunnel. Lock the door and haul ass down through the tunnel to the other end."

"Are you sure it comes out in the shed in the woods?"

"Yep. I went out there a few days ago while you were all inside and checked it out. It looks clear. The tunnel's a bit iffy at the end but we'll get it shored up enough that it'll function as an emergency escape should the need arise."

"Nothing's going to happen to you, though." Mark insisted, declaring it a statement of fact.

"You're darned right." Dianne smiled and stood up, holding out her arms. Mark stood up and gave her a hug and she held him tight. "I'm sorry about all this, kiddo. I never wanted you to grow up so fast." Dianne whispered and closed her eyes, holding her eldest son for a long moment until she heard the clatter of feet on the stairs. She stepped back and clapped Mark on the shoulders, noticing but not mentioning the tears she could see him trying to hide in his eyes. "Chin up. We're going to be just fine around here, okay?"

Mark nodded and turned away, wiping his eyes while Dianne greeted Jacob and Josie with a big smile. "Hey you two! Finally up?"

⊏⊐

AFTER BREAKFAST, a stroll around to check on the outbuildings and animals and a brief slushball fight with the last bits of melting snow, Dianne decided it was time to get back to work. She and Mark worked on carrying lumber up into the house, down into the basement and through into the tunnel while Jacob and Josie were put on house-cleaning duty. Floors were swept, bathrooms were scrubbed and toys were put away while Dianne and Mark sweated it out hauling building supplies.

Lunch came and went and Dianne got to work on assembling the aquaponics stands in the basement while Mark worked in the tunnel, cutting the boards down to size. Once they were done Dianne planned to fix them to the sides and ceiling of the tunnel every ten feet or so to help stabilize the passage and keep it from suddenly collapsing should they need to use it. Every so often Mark would trot up the passage stairs and help Dianne with her work and she would head down into the passage to take new measurements in the tunnel for Mark to use for his sawing.

By the time it started to get dark Jacob and Josie had long since abandoned their cleaning tasks and were instead running full-tilt around the house getting into trouble. Dianne decided that it was time for another break and made dinner before surprising the children with a movie in the living room while they ate. While Mark, Jacob and Josie ate and got lost in an animated film on the couch, Dianne sat at the kitchen table and kept an eye on the security camera feeds on the tablet.

Dianne's habit of watching the security cameras whenever she could had become so routine that it was blending into the normalcy of everyday life. After the first day of the event, when she realized what was going on, she had desperately tried to make life for her children as normal as possible but the more time that passed the more she realized that "normal" was forever gone.

When the movie was over Dianne gathered up the dishes and sent her children upstairs to play and read while she cleaned. Once done, she sat on the couch and opened a notebook to write out the day's activities. She had started the journal a few days after the event in an attempt to chronicle what was undoubtedly the most unusual part of her entire life.

After Jacob and Josie were asleep Dianne and Mark resumed what was beginning to become their nightly watch. Mark slept for the first few hours before Dianne roused him, then she sat up against the wall in the hallway with her gun at her side and her eyes closed while he flipped through the security cameras and padded softly between the windows.

Dianne was woken an hour into Mark's watch by him tapping on her shoulder. "Mom. Wake up." Mark's voice was quiet but urgent.

"Hm?" Dianne rubbed her eyes and sat up. "What is it?"

"There's movement out back."

Dianne grabbed the tablet from out of Mark's hands and stared at the screen. One of the cameras on the back of the house pointed out at the barns and lake, offering a wide—if slightly blurry—view of the entire back property. Even with the distortion and pixilation caused by the camera's night vision mode Dianne could make out a dark figure moving around in front of the barns. The sight of the figure chilled her and she dropped the tablet into Mark's lap and stood up.

"Stay here and keep watch. If things go bad you need to do like we talked about before, okay?" Mark nodded and Dianne put her hand on his shoulder. "Mark, I need you to do this, okay? If someone comes in the house and they aren't me, you need to shoot them. Aim for the chest and don't stop pulling the trigger until it clicks, okay?"

Mark visibly gulped as Dianne picked up her rifle and headed down the stairs. She muttered to herself as she went, trying to psych herself up for whatever confrontation lay ahead and steel herself for what she suspected she might have to do. Killing another person, no matter the situation, was not a choice she wanted to make lightly.

When it came to protecting her children and her home, though, there was no "lightly" about it. The choice would be swift, decisive and permanent.

Chapter Thirteen

Somewhere in Utah

THIRTY MINUTES LATER, after Rick filled and secured both fuel cans and his siphoning hoses, loaded the water into the back of the Humvee and packed one of the back seats full of as much non-perishable food as he could find in the storeroom of the gas station, he got back into the driver's seat and nodded with satisfaction. "Now all I need is some clothing." While he had no objection to scrounging around in an open, obviously empty gas station, the idea of searching through people's houses made him extremely nervous and he decided to continue driving rather than risk being shot in the face by someone who had stayed cooped up in their home.

After sitting still for a moment as he drove slowly down the street, though, Rick realized just how cold he had become during the refueling process. Even with all of the exertion he put out he felt very cold and knew he needed to do something about it. A small diner on the side of the road caught his eye as he was driving past and he pulled his vehicle up to the front door and looked inside. The windows in the front were all smashed in and the interior looked like a tornado had blown through but the one thing he was looking for—a series of red and white checkered pieces of cloth—were still there.

Wielding just his pistol this time Rick jumped out and ran inside the restaurant. He went around to each table, tugging the tablecloths off of each table and draping them over one arm. Once all sixteen cloths were in his possession he hauled them back out to the car, threw them into the passenger's seat and got back in.

"There." He looked at the cloths with a squeamish expression. A handful of them were relatively clean looking but most had a variety of stains on them of all different shapes and colors. They smelled vaguely of smoke and old sandwiches but there were enough that he could easily use them as blankets or fashion them into horrendously-colored ponchos. "It's better than freezing to death, I guess."

Rick looked out at the sky, noting the rapidly encroaching darkness. With a full tank of fuel he figured he could make it north on Interstate 15 and east on Interstate 70 all the way to Green River—another small town off the Interstate—without having to stop for fuel or use any of his reserve. If he wasn't able to get any more diesel there then he would have to start searching at every rest stop, town and big city he could come across. Unfortunately there didn't seem to be any more big cities until Grand Junction, Colorado and he hoped he'd be able to find some more fuel before getting there.

"Assuming I can find diesel for this guzzler I'll go over the Rockies, bypass Denver and keep going across the plains." Rick shook his head and looked back at the sky. The weather didn't look friendly and with as cold as it was getting he started wondering if snow was in his future. The Humvee was capable of handling just about any terrain but he wouldn't want to be stuck driving it over the Rocky Mountains in a snowstorm.

An hour later, as Rick was nearing the turn-off from Interstate 15 to Interstate 70, his fears came true. The flakes were light and soft at first, making him think that they were just flurries. When they started sticking to the ground instead of melting, forcing him to slow down to avoid slipping on the slick roads, he realized that the snow was accumulating in a frighteningly rapid manner. In the time it took for him to get a few miles through Fishlake National Forest on Interstate 70 a full six inches of snow had fallen on the ground, covering the Interstate and disguising the obstacles in his path with a dangerous—albeit beautiful—coating.

The Humvee had a surprisingly powerful air conditioning system with enough coolant in it to keep the interior of the vehicle in the eighties even in the heat of a Middle Eastern desert. This had surprised Rick to no small degree when he had turned it on after leaving Nellis as he had assumed that military vehicles lacked such amenities. While the air conditioning on the vehicle worked well the heater was, sadly, not up to the same standards. Rick could barely get a trickle of warm air out of the vents and he found himself wrapping his legs and torso with the tablecloths from the restaurant to try and keep warm.

Rick tried valiantly to press forward in the snowstorm, but the lack of visibility became too much for him to handle after he lost track of the number of times he had a low-speed collision with the remnants of a burned-out car in the middle of the road. "Dammit!" Rick squinted as he looked through the windows looking for a place where he could seek shelter. There were no buildings nearby, no underpasses to stay beneath and the only place he could see that would help protect him from the driving wind was parking next to an eighteen-wheeler along the side of the road.

Rick pulled up next to the massive truck and shut off the Humvee, concluding that it was probably better to save some fuel given how little heat was getting into the passenger compartment. He moved the food and supplies in the back seats to the floors and crawled into the back, curling up against a backpack pressed up on the door and covering himself with layer after layer of the tablecloths. He wasn't tired in the least but with nowhere to go and nothing else to do he figured that rest was his best option.

Rick's mind wandered as he stayed still in the back of the Humvee, the swirling snow and biting wind cutting through the imperfections of the Humvee and bringing the chill outside to the interior. With no distractions to occupy himself he started thinking about home again.

The level of destruction, both of things and of basic humanity itself, terrified him. Not because he feared for his own safety or the safety of those he had met, though he worried about those people and himself as well. It was his wife and children who he felt the most concern over. If the smallest of towns in the middle of Nowhere, Utah could be burned half to the ground and look like a horde of zombies came through, what did that mean for Ellisville?

What did it mean for the few neighbors near his house? Would they have turned hostile as well? What about the people from town? Would they have sought refuge—forcibly, perhaps—farther out in the country? How long would it take, he wondered, for friends to become enemies? Rick closed his eyes and pictured his wife and children seated in the kitchen the morning he left on his business trip. He refused to believe that they had been killed or injured, for their survival was the only thing keeping him going. He said a quiet prayer for them, hoping against all hope that they were alive and well and continuing their fight against the encroaching darkness.

Chapter Fourteen

One day after the Event
Deep in the Republic of Bashkortostan, Russia

DEEP BENEATH AN ISOLATED MOUNTAIN, far beyond the reach of conventional and non-conventional weapons, sits a massive bunker that covers over five hundred square miles of real estate. Built as part of a decades-long project involving tens of thousands of workers, the bunker beneath Mount Yamantau—known as Mezhgorye—is the lynchpin in the Russian continuity of government plans.

While Russian intelligence services detected the Damocles infiltration of networks external to their own, they—like most other countries—did not realize the threat it posed to their own internal networks until it was too late. Most government systems were affected by the virus and were quickly shut down and destroyed along with many civil systems as well.

Inside Mezhgorye, however, life for the twenty thousand government employees and support staff goes on as normal. The only portion of the Mezhgorye network that is infected by Damocles is an isolated and air-gapped system used to communicate with the outside world. The rest of the site's systems are left untouched, including the three dozen ICBMs, the massive generators that power the complex, the bunker's computer systems and the pair of satellites used by the bunker for specific spy operations.

After being evacuated to Mezhgorye, the senior Russian leadership set to work analyzing Damocles and attempting to discover both its origins and how to disable it. Each attempt to study the virus ends with yet another infected system, however, and by the second day after the Event they are forced to admit that there may not be a way to analyze and disable the virus through traditional means.

This revelation paves the way for discussions about non-traditional means of disabling the virus. Based on a flawed analysis of the way Damocles operates, the technical experts performing an analysis of the virus believe that it is being controlled by a central system somewhere within the United States. The fact that the USA is being ravaged by the virus as much or more than the rest of the countries across the world is the only thing keeping Russia from launching missiles in an attempt to destroy what they believe to be the nexus of the virus's control systems.

With communications channels down across the globe, though, there is no way for the Russian government to contact their American counterparts to discuss the situation and find out more information about what is going on. Arguments in favor of the nuclear solution are strong and persuasive and as the days go by and the situation in the country worsens it begins to look more and more like the solution that they will be forced to attempt.

Chapter Fifteen

The Waters' Homestead
Outside Ellisville, VA

THE GRASS WAS STILL DAMP from the melted snow and Dianne headed quickly down the slope towards the barns. She kept low, crouching to try and avoid being seen, though she needn't have bothered. By the time she got halfway between the house and barns she could see the shadowy figure in front of the closest building kicking at the barn door and talking.

"Dammit open it up already!" The voice belonged to a man, and she recognized it as the man who had approached their house previously. Not taking any chances she stayed quiet as she snuck up behind him, stopping when she was a little over thirty feet away.

Dianne stood up and flicked on the flashlight attachment on her rifle, sending twenty-five hundred lumens of blinding, flashing brightness at the man. He turned and raised his arms in surprise, shielding his eyes from the unexpected blast of light. With the light at the end of her rifle set to rapidly pulse the light on and off, the man was disoriented by the beam. He backed up, keeping his right hand over his eyes while his left felt along the face of the barn for support.

"What the fuck?" The man shouted. "Turn that off!"

"Stop right there!" Dianne fired a shot past the man into the dirt. The rifle's crack echoed across the stillness of the night and the man stopped in place, expressions of anger and fear washing over him.

"What're you doing, lady? I only wanted some food!"

"You're the one who showed up the other day, right? And tried to break in the other night?"

The man lowered his arm briefly but immediately raised it again to shield his eyes. "Yes! Damn you, yes! Turn that shit off!"

"Why did you try and break in? I told you to get off our property. Why would you come back?"

"I had to! I had to get *something* for them!"

Dianne shook her head. "For who?"

"For Rogers! For him! For all of them! I haven't brought back anything in three days! They'll kill me if I don't bring something back tomorrow!"

For a brief, fleeting moment, Dianne felt bad for the man. He sounded scared, alone and desperate. He was clearly in some sort of bad situation and needed a way to get by. Dianne dropped her rifle slightly, illuminating the man's chest instead of his face.

"I'm sorry."

Dianne fired seven shots in rapid succession. Five of them found their mark on her target while two narrowly missed, going into the trees and ground. The man screamed in pain as he dropped to the ground, blood soaking through his clothes and forming a small puddle beneath him that rapidly increased in size. Dianne stood still for several seconds, her rifle aimed at the man as she took in quick shallow breaths. She started to feel dizzy and moved over next to the barn, leaning on the building for support as she tried to get her breathing under control.

A few minutes later, when she was breathing normally and her head was clear again, Dianne stood up straight and slowly approached the man's body. She nudged at his outstretched arm with her foot, but he didn't respond, remaining face-down on the ground. She glanced at the area around him, confirming what she already knew—the amount of blood on the ground clearly indicated that he was dead.

Dianne crouched down next to the man, put her head in her hand and sighed. "I'm sorry, whoever you are." She reached out and brushed a hand over his back and shook her head. "You could have just stayed away. But you didn't."

Dianne stood slowly, her knees feeling weak, and plodded back to the house. Mark was waiting for her on the back porch, having watched the altercation from afar. "Mom? Are you okay?"

Dianne looked at him without stopping and nodded slowly. "Yeah. Go ahead back inside. I need to take care of some things. Keep an eye on the cameras and fire off a shot if you see anyone else around, okay?" She grabbed a shovel that was leaning against the back patio and turned around, heading back down towards the barns. Beyond them, in the woods, she stopped and detached the light from her rifle, leaning the gun up against a nearby tree. She balanced the light on a nearby log and got to work digging.

Two hours passed before Dianne was satisfied with the depth of the grave. It was only three feet down, but with the addition of a thick layer of rocks she was confident that the body would be well out of the reach of any local predators. Dragging the man's body into the woods was easier than she thought it would be. He was thinner than he appeared and his pants slipped off as she pulled him by his wrists.

After pulling him into the hole Dianne piled earth atop his body and headed to the side of the closest barn. There, next to it, was a large pile of stones weighing twenty to thirty pounds each. They had been intended for making a decorative edge around a portion of the lake but their new purpose was much more utilitarian. The appropriateness of that fact given the state of the world didn't escape Dianne's notice and it somehow made her feel slightly better about what she was doing.

The soft glow of pre-dawn set the bare trees alight as Dianne finished putting the final stone atop the unknown man's grave. Dianne gave the site a final look as she walked around it, checking her work, before she picked up her rifle, shovel and flashlight and headed back to the house. She was covered in sweat and dirt as she trudged up onto the back porch and flopped down into a chair to watch as the sun slowly rose above the horizon.

A moment later she heard the soft hiss of the back door sliding across its track and turned to find Mark coming out onto the porch with a glass of water in hand. He gave it to her wordlessly before sitting down next to her. They were both quiet for nearly twenty minutes as Dianne sipped on the water and rested before she finally spoke.

"I can't believe I did that."

"Why did you kill him, Mom?" Mark's question came a few seconds later, quiet and reserved.

Dianne mulled the question over in her mind, probing it and picking it apart before answering. "I had no choice."

"But he was unarmed."

"Was he?" Dianne glanced at her son.

"I… I mean I watched him standing there and then you just… murdered him."

"Self-defense isn't murder, son."

"But he wasn't attacking you!" Mark's voice grew louder.

"Mark." The tone in Dianne's voice made Mark shrink back into his chair. "He trespassed on our property. Tried to break into our house. Tried to break into the barns. He was desperate and wouldn't leave us alone. I gave him more of a chance than I should have."

"But—"

"And he wasn't, in fact, unarmed." Dianne reached down to the ground beside her chair and dropped a long rusty kitchen knife and a small two-shot Derringer on the table. "He had these in his back pocket, Mark. And he was talking about someone who he had to bring things to." Dianne looked out over the lake and shook her head. "I don't like what I did. Believe me. I hate that I had to do it. But he wasn't some innocent person who was lost and needed help and wasn't going to hurt us. Just because he didn't hurt us doesn't mean he wasn't going to. And I'm not letting this family get hurt."

Mark sat quietly in his seat, staring at the knife and gun his mother had tossed onto the table. He licked his lips and whispered a reply after a long moment. "I wish you hadn't had to do it."

Dianne stretched out her hand and Mark accepted it, holding onto her hand and arm. "Me too, kiddo." She sighed as she watched the morning sun play across the slight ripples in the lake. The peacefulness was a stark contrast to the dark events of the night. The new day brought a glimmer of hope with it as well.

"Me too."

Chapter Sixteen

Two days after the Event
    Deep in the Republic of Bashkortostan, Russia

IN A CONFERENCE ROOM that is both lavish and Spartan, the senior members of the Russian government sit at a large round table. The Russian President listens intently as the last two days' worth of compiled analyses are laid out before him. The situation is grim and the solution—if it can even be called that—is grimmer.

The country is in shambles, the cities burning and the countryside flooded with refugees seeking shelter and food they will not find. Modern and old computer systems alike are suffering at the hand of the mysterious virus that has torn across the globe. The twin spy satellites operated by Mezhgorye pass over the country, watching the migration and destruction of the population as the military fails to contain riots and uprisings.

People already half-starved from years of a downward spiraling economy have nothing left to lose and throw their lives away for the chance that their children might get a morsel of food. Vast curtains of smoke drift across the cities from the burning chemical fires, killing thousands and mortally injuring tens of thousands more.

There is no hope left. No way of countering the assault from every direction. The military has started to fracture, splintering into groups based on regional assignment and what resources are stockpiled in which regions. It will be another week at most before territorial wars break out and the country is consumed by infighting.

"You believe the command and control center is in NORAD?" The Russian president speaks softly, his narrowed eyes flicking around the table as he listens to the response.

"It is either there or in the capitol."

"You understand the repercussions we will suffer from taking such an action, yes?"

"If we do not take some sort of action then the repercussions will be far more damaging."

The Russian president rubs his eyes and wearily sighs. *"What new analysis supports this type of an escalation?"*

"The analysis we performed yesterday shows—"

"New. Analysis." The President's tone reflects a hint of the frustration he feels. *"Not yesterday's analysis. New analysis."*

The man who answered the President sits back in his chair, looking as though he wishes he could burrow straight through the chair and wall to escape. *"It is difficult to perform new analysis, sir. Every system that we attempt to use to analyze the virus becomes, itself, infected and—"*

"If we drop an ICBM on top of NORAD then they will retaliate and we will have nuclear winter on top of everything else. There cannot be any mistake in this. Perform more analysis. Find a way to contact the Americans. Do whatever it takes. We will not launch until the facts are on our side."

"Yes sir."

The Russian president stands up and leaves the room without another word. As the others in the room slowly leave whispered conversations are held between the leaders of small factions that have formed over the last forty-eight hours. The chief subject of the conversations is, naturally, the virus. The distinction is in how the factions wish to deal with it.

Some believe the Russian president is moving too slowly on the subject. Others believe the fact that an ICBM launch even being on the table is a dangerous sign. What every faction knows and agrees with, though, is that the President has ears in every faction and knows precisely what everyone is thinking at all times. They all tread carefully as they speak, each of them keenly aware that the person they speak to next may deliver a report to the President directly after the conversation concludes.

Chapter Seventeen

The Waters' Homestead
Outside Ellisville, VA

TWO DAYS after killing the stranger trying to break into their property, Dianne sat on the back patio and watched her three children playing by the edge of the lake. A brief burst of warm weather meant she was able to break out the shorts and t-shirts for what was possibly the last time of the season. She hadn't spoken to Mark about the incident two days prior since their brief conversation on the patio, but she had noticed him avoiding talking to her at every possible opportunity. Dianne didn't want to pressure him to discuss the subject since she didn't know what he was trying to work out in his mind, so when he came walking up from the lake to sit down beside her she was surprised.

"Mom?"

"Hey kiddo. You guys done?"

"Nah. They want to keep playing. I'll go back down there in a minute. I wanted to talk to you first."

"What's up?"

"You were right."

Dianne raised an eyebrow, trying to tread cautiously. "Right about what?"

"About... the other night. With what you had to do. I didn't understand it then but I think I do now."

"Oh yeah? What do you understand?"

"We are incredibly blessed to have all of this stuff." Mark gestured out at the property and barns behind the house. "I doubt there are many people who have all of this after what happened."

"You're probably right. We're living halfway normal lives right now, for the most part."

"Yeah." Mark scratched his head and shifted in his seat. "I guess I just wanted to say that I understand. If we don't defend what's ours then some-body's just going to take it away from us. There's nobody out there to stop them."

"Not that I'm aware of."

"Right. Well... I get it." Mark nodded.

Dianne smiled wistfully at him and stood up to give him a hug. "Thanks, kiddo. Are you okay now? You've been kind of stand-offish the last couple days."

"I think so, yeah." Mark started heading off of the porch and back down towards the lake. "It's kind of a lot to think about though, you know?"

"Try not to think about it. Just relax and enjoy yourself."

Mark nodded and turned to jog back down to join his siblings. Dianne watched him go before sitting back down in her chair. The smile she had forced for Mark's sake withered, turning her face into a mask of sorrow.

The Event had robbed her of her husband, of normalcy, of the everyday lives of her and her children. It had shattered her world and forced her to adopt a kill-or-be-killed mentality that was beginning to bleed over into her children. Jacob and Josie had remained mostly untainted by what was going on. Mark, though, was different. She was glad that he understood what she had done but his understanding was the source of her sadness. In his under-standing came the loss of more of his innocence, stripped away from him before she was prepared for it to happen.

As Dianne sat and thought about what was happening to her family, another thought floated through her mind that she had picked at on and off for the last two days. The man she killed had mentioned that he was tasked by someone named "Rogers" to gather supplies and that there was more than just the one other person involved. If this "Rogers" person happened to wonder where his missing man had gotten to, he might send more people out in search of him. That, in turn, could lead to a very messy situation at the homestead.

Try as she might, though, Dianne couldn't think of anything they could do to fortify their house and property more than they already had. The house was boarded up, the animals were kept indoors or under close guard when they were outside and the children were under strict instructions to keep their voices low whenever they were outside playing.

She had already been giving Jacob and Josie refresher instructions on how to use some of the smaller, more balanced pistols in the house in case worse came to worse. The idea of using a portion of the tunnel as a firing range to help Mark practice without worrying about attracting attention above ground had occurred to her, but only if she could figure out a way to ventilate the space. There was a lot still left to do and Dianne had no idea how much time was left to do it all before action would take the place of preparation.

One fact burned in the center of her mind above all others, though: there would be no quarter or surrender given to anyone who tried to invade. If more people arrived at the house looking to steal and kill, Dianne would do everything in her power to keep her family and property safe.

Chapter Eighteen

Three days after the Event
Somewhere in the Wyoming wilderness

THE FLAT PLAINS, rolling hills and sheer mountain cliffs are covered in lush green vegetation in spite of the early winter season. Pine trees dot the landscape with swaths of dark green, carving out enormous sections of the rolling hills and mountains and filling them with an impenetrable cover of soft needles. Gentle waves lap at the shore of wide lakes fed by trickling creeks and rushing rivers. Upstream, in the mountains, still-melting snow adds to the volume of water rushing down the mountainsides.

The stillness of the late morning air is broken by three MV-22 Ospreys screaming through the air, their horizontally-aligned blades pulling them forward at three hundred miles per hour. They follow the features of the terrain below, cutting through tree-covered valleys and soaring above lakes and vast unbroken fields.

Flying only a few hundred feet above the ground, each Osprey has its rear door open. Half a dozen Marines stand near each open door, their harnesses the only things keeping them from tumbling to their doom. The Marines scan the ground behind them while the pilots scan the ground in front. Radio contact is constant between the three Ospreys as they update each other in real time.

Their search for the Boeing 747 designated as Air Force One has been going on for sixteen hours and there is very little solid information to go on. A garbled radio transmission was received seventeen hours ago from the pilot and co-pilot of the aircraft, announcing that the plane was plummeting towards the earth. The reasons for the crash are not known to the Marines, but one of the Secret Service agents on board the lead Osprey has privileged information.

An inadvertent activation of the 747's backup communications system opened the computer systems of the aircraft to communication with the outside world for eleven seconds. Damocles took ten seconds to discover the communication connection, exploit it and insert a copy of itself into various firmware on the plane before the backup communications system was switched off. Twenty minutes after infection the aircraft began to malfunction in the skies over Wyoming and started its swift descent to the ground.

With no solid information on where the aircraft went down, small groups of aircraft that were not infected by Damocles have converged on Wyoming. They scour the state in miles-long grids, searching for any clue of its whereabouts. The sight of smoke in a long, flat valley comes over the radio and the three Ospreys break off from their search pattern and head for the location. No external navigational data or communications over any system except locked-down and encrypted voice-only communications is allowed and the pilots rely on their training and paper maps to guide them.

It takes fifteen minutes before the Ospreys spot the smoke. The lead aircraft, carrying the Secret Service agents, slows down while the other two break off and increase their altitude to get a visual confirmation on the exact location of the crash. The lead Osprey's rotors tilt into the vertical position as it nears the location, turning the aircraft from a plane into a massive, awkward helicopter. In a clearing a few hundred yards from the crash site the Osprey sets down into the soft grass.

Before the blades can even begin spinning down the Secret Service agents and Marines deploy from the back of the craft. They sprint across the field and head for the nearby woods. A hundred yards inside the woods the broken and battered nose of the 747 leers at them. The cockpit windows are smashed and broken, the metal is dented and torn in multiple locations and one of the reinforced wings was sheared off long before the main body came to a rest.

The Secret Service agent in charge barks orders at the Marines, ordering them to fan out across the woods and begin searching for anyone who escaped the wreckage. He and the other agents descend upon the plane itself, accompanied by a pair of Marines and two medics. All of the doors and hatches on the plane are open and several bodies are lying on the ground around the aircraft. Fire has consumed much of the remaining wing and though fire suppression systems prevented the flames from entering the interior the plane is filled with thick acrid smoke.

The Secret Service agents move through the 747 swiftly, checking each compartment for the commander-in-chief. The small living, dining and lounge areas are all empty, but the President's private office door is sealed shut. The agents force open the door and find a dozen people crowded together on the floor, many suffering from injuries ranging from superficial to serious. After determining that the President is not in the room the agents leave one medic to tend to the wounded and proceed farther down to the back of the plane.

In the rear of the aircraft sits a small chamber that is armored, padded and locked. A separate air supply is built into the room with enough oxygen to last for twenty-four hours. The room is still sealed shut and appears intact. The agents open an access panel on the outside of the room and the head agent enters in a long code. The panel glows green and several thick bolts inside the door disengage. The door mechanism slowly pulls the door open and the agents peer in to find the bloodied and bruised form of the President of the United States.

The medics rush forward and check him over before one of them turns back to the head Secret Service agent. "He's alive. Pulse is weak, though and his breathing is bad. Smoke probably got in here when they crashed."

"Can you move him?"

"It should be safe, yes."

"We're getting him out of here now." The agent directs his men to help the medics before running down the length of the plane. He calls out commands into his radio, pulling the Marines back from their searches. A small group of them will return to the Osprey with the President while the remaining force stays on the ground and works with the other two Ospreys to pull any survivors and sensitive equipment and information from the crash.

One of the survivors, ordered along with several other staff and crew into the President's private office before the crash, is Dr. Michael Evans. He clutches his left arm as he is led out of the plane by a Marine, looking around at the wreckage in awe. Once outside he receives basic medical treatment before being guided to the Osprey. On board he asks to speak to the person in charge, telling them he has vital information about the Event. He is assured that he will be able to speak to someone soon, but in the chaos of the rescue operation his request is quickly forgotten.

Author's Notes

July 10, 2017

Holy cow, if you're reading this that means you've probably read *four* books in the Surviving the Fall series! I can't express how awesome that is and how much it means to me. Thank you SO very much! In the last couple of weeks Surviving the Fall and No Sanctuary have been selling far better than I ever imagined they would. That's all thanks to YOU, the reader who decided to take a chance and try reading my books.

I've been taking turns writing books from Surviving the Fall and No Sanctuary by alternating back and forth but I decided that I needed to write Surviving the Fall Episode 4 before moving back to No Sanctuary. Part of that was because I got behind in my schedule for writing Episode 3 and part of it was because Dianne and Rick needed some extra love and attention sooner rather than later.

For Rick, he's getting a break for this book. Sort of. Instead of dealing with people trying to kill him, being locked up in a military holding cell for over a week or trying to survive in the desert heat he now gets to worry about *slightly* less immediate threats. He has weapons and transportation (for now). He has a bit of food and water. He has a few scraps of clothing to keep him warm. His struggles have temporarily shifted from being active to passive ones. Unfortunately things don't stay still for long, as he's going to find out when he hits Colorado.

For Dianne we're finally getting to the part of the story that I'm *super* excited about. There's a lot I want to talk about with regards to Dianne here, so strap in and get ready.

First off, the title. "Death of Innocence." I have three children (ages 6 [nearly 7], four and two) and they mean the world to me. There are certain movies and books (*The Road* springs to mind) that I can't bear to watch or read because of the effect they have. So, of course, I'm trying to put some of that into this series. Yeesh. The title references Mark mostly, since this book is where he goes from someone who's been trained and prepared by his parents for this sort of eventuality—but is still a fairly innocent young man— to someone who has his world turned upside down. He watched his mother kill a person. That's going to screw with his head and continue screwing with it.

One of my hopes for my children is to preserve their child-like innocence for as long as possible but I know that it won't last forever. Imagining a TEOTWAWKI situation where the innocence is ripped apart like wrapping paper on a present at Christmas is difficult but powerful at the same time. Dianne doesn't just have to cope with survival against the elements and enemies. Now she has to cope with holding her family together, protecting her two younger children and helping her oldest as he grows up *way* faster than she ever wanted.

And there's plenty more to come. The Waters family is going to be stretched to their breaking point before this series ends. We can only hope that Rick and Dianne put enough into their children for them to withstand the pressure.

Talk about a downer! Let's talk about some other stuff now. This book is also about moving Dianne from a more passive situation to an active one. Rick gets to move from active to passive but Dianne's in the opposite situation. The house is ready, the food is gathered and things are going okay. But now that she has to deal with an external element she's seeing the cracks in her defenses (like forgetting to board up the first floor windows). And there's still the mystery of the neighbor's house that burned down. And now we find out that there is some group of people out there who sent the guy she killed off to gather supplies. Not good!

The one upside about this episode is that I finally got to explore the tunnel. Ah the tunnel. Something I was SO excited about having in the story. It's a bit implausible, I know, but I don't think it stretches the suspension of disbelief *too* much. And trust me, it's going to be a LOT of fun near the end of the series.

I originally got idea from Brian Jacques' *Redwall* series that I read as a child. That was probably my favorite series to read and I vividly remember going to book sales and libraries and seeing new books in the series and reading them nearly all the way through on the drive back home.

In one of the books (I think it was in the first one, simply titled *Redwall*) there are scenes where the moles (this is a series where all the characters are anthropomorphic animals by the way) dig underground passages around the grounds of a walled-in abbey to get around while they're under assault from enemies. The idea of having a tunnel beneath the Waters' home was too good to pass up and I intend to make full use of it—both for good *and* bad—in the coming books.

If you enjoyed this episode of Surviving the Fall or if you *didn't* like something—I'd love to hear about it. You can drop me an email or send me a message or leave a comment on Facebook. You can also sign up for my newsletter where I announce new book releases and other cool stuff a few times a month.

Answering emails and messages from my readers is the highlight of my day and every single time I get an email from someone saying how much they enjoyed reading a story it makes that day so much brighter and better.

Thank you so very much for reading my books. Seriously, thank you from the bottom of my heart. I put an enormous amount of effort into the writing and all of the related processes and there's nothing better than knowing that so many people are enjoying my stories.

All the best,
    Mike

Book 5 – The Burning Fields

Preface

Last time, on Surviving the Fall. ...

Rick left Nellis Air Force Base and headed east in a Humvee provided to him by the commander of said base. His journey east was, thankfully, much calmer than his journey through the city of Las Vegas. The unusually warm Autumn weather soon turned sour as a blizzard blew in, catching Rick by surprise and forcing him to take shelter in the Humvee using a pile of stained tablecloths to keep warm.

Meanwhile, in Virginia, Dianne and her children upped the ante on their preparations as a strange man appeared. After fortifying their house against attacks the man returned and Dianne was forced to shoot him or risk having him grow violent and harm them in his attempts to steal from them.

Mark, Dianne's eldest son, witnessed the shooting and is having some trouble coming to terms with what happened. In addition to trying to help her son cope with what he witnessed Dianne is disturbed by something the man said before she killed him. Something about there being "others" whom he was working for.

And now, Surviving the Fall Episode 5.

Chapter One

T he last few miles of any trip are always filled with a mixed bag of emotions. The excitement of being at the destination—especially if it's home and it's been a long time since the last visit—mixes with the uncertainty of whether things will be exactly as they were before. If the road to the destination is a familiar one that hasn't been tread in many days, weeks, months or years there's a sense of nostalgia as every similarity and difference between the last visit and the current one are illuminated in stark detail.

For Rick the differences were more startling this time than ever before. The usually clear road was covered in snow and burned-out wrecks of cars stretched across the small town of Ellisville. Homes were boarded up and some had been demolished by fire. As he crossed from the town onto the country road the destruction became less pronounced but there were still signs that the effects of the event had reached to even the smallest and most remote corners of the world.

Rick turned off of the main road, feeling his stomach jump in anticipation of finally being back. When he got to the gate on his driveway he stopped, got out of his car and smiled. *They're still here*. Snow was thick on the ground but someone had shoveled the driveway between the house and the gate. He opened the gate and swung it around, then got back in his car and drove through, taking his time so that the tires wouldn't spin out and kick rocks and dirt into the air as he headed down the drive.

The house was beautiful. It had a sort of glow to it that made him feel completely at peace. He could see smoke coming from the chimney and grinned again. Rick stopped his car in front of the house and turned off the engine before stepping out. It had been a long journey but he was, finally, home. There was laughter coming from his children inside that he could hear even through the closed door and he ran up onto the porch and rapped loudly on the front window.

The face of his wife appeared down the hall through the window as she turned to see who was outside. She wore a look that was a combination of shock, surprise and absolute glee. She dropped the dish in her hand to the floor and it shattered, but she paid it no mind as she ran down the hall towards the front door.

Rick went over to the front door and waited for his wife to open it, an ear-to-ear smile plastered across his face. As the seconds ticked past he noticed that the cloudless day was turning darker and he glanced out at the sky. Dark clouds began rolling in, driven by an ill wind that cut through the spaces between the trees like an expertly sharpened blade. Rick pulled his jacket tight around his body in an attempt to guard against the dropping temperatures but the action did little to alleviate his discomfort.

The sky continued to darken as he turned around to look through the small windows at the top of the front door. He noticed then that the door was slightly ajar. He blinked several times, wondering if it had been like that when he first arrived. He pushed on the door slightly, peeking into the shadowy entry and shouted out.

"Hello? Dianne? Kids?" Silence was his only answer. He pushed on the door more, opening it fully to step inside, each step he took emboldening him to move faster and with more determination. When he had seen Dianne through the window from the porch the interior had been fully lit with sprigs of holly and red berries shaped into wreaths and hanging from the walls. Now, though, the inside of the house was dark and the only sign of the decorations were curled brown leaves lying on the floor.

"Dianne?" Rick reached into his waistband and slowly withdrew his pistol. Floorboards that he remembered being solid and firm squeaked and protested under each slow footstep he took down the hall. The walls were covered in dirt and dark red and black stains, some of which looked too much like blood for his comfort.

"Where are you?" Rick shouted again. The idea of his wife and children possibly playing a practical joke on him had crossed his mind but the disparity between the state of the house as he saw it and how it was just moments before confirmed that something else was going on.

Glass crunched underfoot as Rick entered the kitchen and he glanced down at the floor. The room was dark but he could make out the dish he had watched Dianne drop—along with dozens of other dishes, too. Plates, cups and bowls had been shattered on the hardwood floor while the dining room table was flipped on its side and two of the chairs were broken into pieces.

Rick turned around and pushed open the door to the basement. He gagged at the smell that came rushing out. The scent of death overwhelmed him and he turned and ran to the sink as his stomach and chest heaved in disgust. A moment later, when he had evacuated the contents of his stomach, Rick turned back and pulled his shirt up over his mouth and nose and headed back to the basement door.

Rick's eyes grew wide as he padded down the stairs, seeing more destruction like that in the kitchen. The basement was oddly lit, not with a white or yellow light but with a red one that illuminated and highlighted a thick pool of blood that was spreading across the floor. He looked off to his right and saw four bodies lying together on the floor, blood still trickling from them. He opened his mouth to scream in terror as he stumbled forward down the stairs when a sharp pain lanced through his forehead.

Rick's eyes fluttered open and he held a hand to his throbbing skull as he tried to figure out what was going on. He was lying on his side having just started awake and smashed his head against a strip of metal on the back of the seat in front of him. Light from the morning sun was peeking through patches of melted snow on the windshield of the Humvee. Rick looked down the length of his body, patting the layers of stained tablecloths as he tried to slow his rapid breathing and heartbeat.

It took several seconds for his brain to register what was going on and when he did his head slumped back down and he let out a sigh. It had been years since he last had a nightmare and he couldn't remember a single time since setting out from Los Angeles when he had even dreamed. The stress and struggle of the journey had gotten to him in more ways than one and the briefest respite had resulted in a dream that quickly devolved into something far worse. The relief at realizing that it had been just a dream slowly trickled away as Rick thought more about his wife and children and everything that could be happening to them.

Chapter Two

The Waters' Homestead
Outside Ellisville, VA

"HOW'S THE WATER LEVEL?" Jacob squatted down next to his mother.

"We're looking good here." Dianne rolled out from under a table in the basement and looked at her son. "Go ahead and tell him to shut it off."

Jacob raced back up the stairs, down the hall, through the living room and out the back door. He waved at Mark who was standing near a faucet. Mark nodded in confirmation before turning the faucet off and heading inside and back downstairs with his brother.

While Dianne waited for Mark and Jacob to return she looked over at Josie who was busy at the far end of the table performing the task Dianne had given her. "How's it going, sweetie?"

Josie didn't look up at Dianne as she replied. "Good." Josie's concentration showed in her every movement as she carefully deposited a single seed into the hole of each piece of substrate.

Dianne smiled and stood up, brushing the dirt off of her legs and arms as she surveyed the hydroponic setup. A pair of long collapsible tables served as the base for the setup. Dianne had drilled holes into the tables just big enough for plastic nets to sit in. The nets held the substrate, the material that the seeds would sit in and both absorb water from and use as a stable structure through which to grow their roots.

Beneath each table sat a pair of short, wide plastic tubs which were filled with water and nutrients. The tubs had been raised so that their tops were pressed up against the bottom of the tables. Dark pieces of cloth were stapled along the edges of the tables and draped down to the floor, protecting the transparent plastic tubs full of water from receiving any excess light. The growth of algae and mold was a pressing concern in such a setup and cutting off light to the tubs was a key element in managing its growth.

While Dianne filled the containers she had given her daughter, Josie, the task of placing a seed into each of the holes in the substrate nets. The substrate was completely soaked through since the nets sat down in the water and they gently bumped against the edges of the holes in the table thanks to the air pumps that were quietly gurgling away as they provided oxygen to the water in each tub.

Dianne picked up a large piece of paper she had covered with strips of packing tape to protect it against water damage. On the paper was a diagram of the tables and holes along with labels showing which plants were going into each location. "You've been following this exactly, right?" Dianne glanced at her daughter who nodded in affirmation.

"Okay, great." Dianne patted her daughter on the back as she leaned down to examine one of the seeds. Nestled down in the small hole in the piece of rough substrate material—a mixture of mineral wool and lava rocks—sat a tiny black seed barely visible even in the brightness of the grow lights overhead. With oxygenated and nutrient-filled water and grow lights the seeds would germinate and begin to grow within just a few days. As long as they took care of the water and ensured that the plants got plenty of food and light then they would be eating fresh greens inside of a month.

Dianne smiled at the thought before turning at the sound of her sons thumping down the stairs. "Everything look good outside?" Dianne asked Mark, noting that his rifle was still slung on his shoulder.

"All clear."

"Sky still getting dark?"

"Yeah, it looks and feels like a storm's coming soon."

Dianne sighed. "Well, we might as well turn off all the non-essentials. I think tonight's going to be a fireplace reading night for everyone after dinner."

"But what about the movie?" Josie still didn't look up from her task.

"Another night. We won't have enough juice to run the freezers if we keep using non-essentials while the clouds and storms are bad."

Josie shrugged. "Okay."

Dianne turned to Jacob. "When she's done, can you both head upstairs and get started on dinner? Mark and I need to organize some in the tunnel before we shut the lights off." Jacob nodded and headed over to watch his sister while she finished up her planting. Dianne and Mark, meanwhile, headed down the stairs into the tunnel.

It had been four days since Dianne had shot the strange man who had been harassing them and Mark seemed like he was back to normal. It had taken him a couple of days to work past witnessing his mother shoot the man point-blank but aside from catching him staring off into space more often than usual she hadn't noticed anything wrong with him. She hadn't had a chance to privately check and see how he was doing since yesterday, though, and figured she'd take the opportunity to do so before everyone got wrapped up in dinner.

"What is it you wanted help with?" Mark looked around the tunnel as he took his rifle off of his shoulder and leaned it up against the wall. The weapon that Dianne had been hesitant to give to him at first had become a natural extension of his person.

Dianne pointed to a pile of extra lumber and enough supplies to build out three more tables worth of garden beds. "Help me get these organized and stacked up neatly. I want to wait to set any more up until we're sure the ones up there will grow without any issues."

Mark nodded and got to work next to his mother. The two shifted the supplies in silence for a few minutes until Dianne finally spoke. "How are you doing?"

"Mom." Mark's tone had the stereotypical teenage whine around the edges. "You don't need to keep asking me that. I'm fine."

"Yes I do need to keep asking you that. I know you seem fine but I want to hear about what's going on up there in your head. You still thinking about what you saw?"

Mark shrugged. "Not really."

"What's up, then? You've been a bit distant the last day or two."

Mark didn't reply for several seconds as he moved a box of substrate from one side of the tunnel to the other. "I guess... you said he said something about there being other people he was working for, or with, right?"

"Yeah." Dianne remembered every syllable of her short conversation with the stranger. "He said that he 'had to get something for them.'"

"*Them.*" Mark shook his head and sat down on an overturned plastic tub. "What do you think he meant by that?"

Dianne sat down on the ground across from Mark. She had considered the implication of "them" often since the events a few nights prior. "There must be a group of people nearby who—"

"How close? In Ellisville? Or Blacksburg?"

"If I knew that, I could get a job as a psychic." Dianne chuckled and shrugged. "I have no idea. But if they're sending people out to scout around then we probably have more trouble coming our way soon."

"Do you think they're the ones that burned down the Carson's house?"

"I don't know why someone would do that and not burn the Statler's place down as well."

"Maybe they accidentally did it?" Mark closed his eyes, trying to imagine what a group of people could have done to burn down a home. "Like they broke a gas pipe or something?"

"No idea. It's certainly possible, though. Maybe burning it down spooked them and they decided to stay away from the area for a while."

"So we should secure the property?"

Dianne smiled. "You read my mind. Come on, let's head upstairs. After dinner I'll show you the plans I've been drawing up. I think we should get to work on them tomorrow."

Mark and Dianne stood up and Mark replied as he followed his mother up the stairs. "How are we going to secure the whole property?"

Dianne smiled. "We'll figure it out."

Chapter Three

S omewhere in Utah

"WHY DOES the flipping weather have to change so fast around here?"

Rick spoke to no one in particular as he climbed out the wreck of a nearby car and dusted snow and soot off of his clothes. The weather which had changed from unbearably hot to frigidly cold in the course of a day was already starting to warm back up. The two feet worth of snow that had fallen while he was huddled in the back of the Humvee was melting quickly, leaving a soft slush base on the road beneath the deceptively wet top layer.

After waking up from his nightmare and realizing that the new day had brought warm weather Rick decided to do a bit of scouting in the nearby vehicles before taking off again. He was only a few miles inside the Fishlake National Forest but the change in scenery had been noticeable. The barren desert and small hills gave way to taller, more defined peaks and patches of green and various shades of brown though the colors were still mostly covered in white.

The main highway, Interstate 70, was a two-lane highway in each direction split down the middle by a wide median. It wound and meandered back and forth through the national forest, occasionally splitting off into dirt and paved paths that branched out to the north and south. Rick could see a fair distance down the road ahead of him thanks to his elevation and the road looked clear for the most part with only a few vehicles scattered here and there.

Rick sighed as he climbed back into the Humvee and started the engine. "Guess I'd better get moving." He mumbled to himself as he buckled his seatbelt and set off through the snow. Off to the side of the road where the land dipped down, he could see streams of water from the melting snow as they carved paths through the dirt and grass.

With no real plan except to head east, Rick turned on one of the GPS units he had acquired and zoomed in on the static map of the region. Interstate 70 looked like his best bet for not only getting through the national forest but beyond. After passing through the forest there would be a fair way to go before hitting the city of Grand Junction where his next great obstacle would begin to rear its head.

Stretching from British Columbia down through New Mexico, the Rocky Mountains were a breathtaking sight to behold. Rick had seen them from the air a few times while in a plane but the only true way to appreciate their majesty was from the ground. He could still remember being in a car with his family when he was a child as they drove across the plains of Kansas towards Colorado. The sight of the cloud-like mountains rising above the plains reminded him of white-capped giants standing tall on the horizon, frozen in place for all of time.

While the snowstorm in the national forest and the travel across the desert in the military vehicle had been uncomfortable he was more concerned about what would happen when he started having to cross through the mountains. Not being familiar with how the Humvee would perform at high altitudes or in deep snow he was unsure of the best place to cross or what the best destination was.

Continuing on I-70 to the north would take him into Denver but the terrain looked exceptionally steep along the road based on what he could tell from his GPS. Breaking off in Grand Junction onto I-50, though, would dump him out near Pueblo and south of Colorado Springs.

The idea of heading into Denver had its appeal given the size of the city and his admittedly misguided hope that things would have settled down some in the day or two it could take to get there. As he scanned the map near Colorado Springs, though, he noticed a label for Cheyenne Mountain and remembered where he had heard that name before.

"That's... that's where NORAD is." Indeed, as he zoomed in on the map, he saw a label for the North American Aerospace Defense command as well as Fort Carson, a military base just down the road from the facility. Built deep within Cheyenne Mountain and designed as both a strategic command post and one of many shelters of last resort for high-ranking government officials, NORAD would undoubtedly be staffed and well-protected from anyone looking to take advantage of the current situation.

Thinking about visiting yet another military facility made Rick's stomach turn after his experience at Nellis but the more he thought about it the more it started to make sense. The commander at the Nellis Air Force Base had

wanted to send Rick to northern Virginia to join a task force whose purpose
was to figure out a way to solve what was going on. It had only been Rick's
refusal to be pressed into service that had landed him behind bars while Jane
had been sent on her way in a transport craft shortly after she and Rick had
arrived at the base. With many miles to go before the decision would have to
be made, Rick verified his route one last time before shutting off the GPS to
conserve battery power and give his full attention to the road.

His journey through the national forest was peaceful and serene, far
more so than he had expected. Aside from the occasional vehicle that had to
be avoided he encountered almost no issues related to driving in the wet
snow and slush. By early afternoon the snow on the highway was nearly
gone and there were bare patches in many of the fields as well. Fuel was, as
it had been ever since nearly running out after leaving Nellis, his primary
concern. The lack of vehicles along the road was troublesome particularly
since every one he encountered was either destroyed, ran on gasoline instead
of diesel or both.

Rick drove as conservatively as possible, trying his best to balance speed
with efficiency. By the time he exited the national forest, though, he had
burned through a full tank of fuel and half of his reserves. He was starting
to get worried about the lack of fuel when a small gas station appeared
immediately after the "Thanks for Visiting" sign at the edge of the national
forest.

With no guardrail in place and a clear path between the highway and the
gas station Rick turned the wheel and bounced across an open field as he
made for the station. He was about to pull in and park in front of the station
when an uneasy feeling crept its way up his back and made him turn sharply
to give the station a wide berth.

With the evening sun hanging low in the west Rick circled around the
gas station at a decent clip, leaning down and looking through the narrow
passenger window and front windshield at the station. Instead of a darkened
interior like he had expected the inside of the station was lit with a wavering
glow like that from a fire, candles or some other non-electric source.

A short sign sitting near the gas station that would have normally
contained prices was instead covered with thick pieces of cardboard onto
which a message had been written by hand in black marker.

**We have fuel. Do not come inside. Park in front and we will
trade. Try anything funny and you won't live to regret it.**

The last sentence made Rick snort in amusement but his smile quickly
faded when he saw a metal barrel that had been set up next to the sign. The
barrel was obviously meant as a warning to those who might try to take
advantage of the station's owner as it was riddled with bullet holes that
varied in both size and pattern.

"Oh yeah." Rick shook his head as he circled the building again. "This is
legit. Let's just stop at a place that promises to shoot me if I do anything

'funny.' Great. Just great." Rick flicked on his GPS unit and thumbed through the options to look at the stored database of information about food, rest stops and gas stations along his route. The station he was at was the only one for another fifty miles or so and given his lack of fuel he wasn't sure he had any choice but to stop and hope that the author of the sign was sincere.

Chapter Four

The Water's Homestead
Outside Ellisville, VA

DINNER and the time spent reading and quietly talking with her three children afterward ended up taking far longer than Dianne had initially thought it would. By the time she was ready to talk about her fortification plans with Mark it was late enough that she decided to save it for early the next morning.

Mark dutifully took the first watch shift, staying awake and watching through the upper windows and the security cameras for almost four hours. When his time was up he woke Dianne and she continued the watch through to the next morning. The storm that she had anticipated arriving overnight never manifested and, much to her relief, the morning brought a cloudless sky with plenty of light for the solar panels.

After a quick breakfast and setting up Josie and Jacob with their schoolwork and cleaning tasks for the day she sat down with Mark at the kitchen table and broke out a spiral-bound notebook from a drawer. "I've been keeping notes on possible fortifications we can make around here. We probably should have started them before that guy ever showed up but I keep thinking every day that…" Dianne trailed off and sighed, gritting her teeth as she fought back a tear.

"I'm sure he's fine out there. He's probably trying to get back here right now."

"Yeah." Dianne wiped the edge of her eye with her shirt sleeve and focused her attention back on the notebook. "Anyway, we don't have enough supplies to try and surround the entire property with something to keep people out. I think that would be pointless anyway given how much square footage there is and how few of us there are. So things like tall fences, walls or razor wire extending all the way around everything are all out of the picture."

Dianne flipped through her notebook and Mark pointed at a sketch of the property she had drawn. "So you think we should fortify each building individually instead?"

"Yeah. Or the entrances at a minimum. Basically make it a huge pain in the rear end for someone to break in and steal stuff."

"How so?"

"Reinforcing the barns' big sliding doors and the smaller doors with lumber and extra locks. Make it so that they'd have to bring in a bulldozer to get through the doors. We could also take some of the razor wire we picked up and staple it to the outer windows on the house to make anyone think twice about breaking through the boards."

Mark tapped on the edges of the sketch. "What if we took some of the long pieces of lumber and made moveable half-wall type things with whatever wire and spikes we can come up with? We can put those out in the driveway and around the generator shed and the solar panels."

Dianne uncapped a blue ballpoint pen and drew in some squiggles along the driveway and around one of the small buildings behind the depiction of the house. "That's a very good idea. I don't want to put anything too far out on the driveway, though, because anything visible from the end of the road would just draw more attention to us.

"I think if we put some nails and razor wire on boards and stretch them across the drive after the gate that would be great. And we definitely need to add them around the generator and solar panels." Dianne wrote a few notes to herself on the page and patted Mark on the back. "Nice thinking, kiddo."

"Where do you want to start?" Mark stood up from his chair and grabbed his shoes from near the back door.

"I think our safety is the first priority so let's start with the house. Jacob and Josie will be busy for a few hours with school and cleaning. We should be able to get the windows reinforced and then we'll all get to work on the outbuildings after lunch."

Twenty minutes later, after changing into double-layered shirts with jackets and thick leather gloves, the pair set to work unraveling the razor wire. A staple gun made it easy to attach to the boards on the windows and after a few mishaps and a short time of experimenting to figure out the best way to coil and attach the wire they were soon moving along at a rapid pace. It took the rest of an hour for Mark and Dianne to finish up and when they were through they walked around the house to examine their work.

Each of the several windows on the ground floor had been completely covered in thick, looping strands of overlapping razor wire. The wire was stapled to the boards and to the siding of the house as well, making it so that anyone who wanted to try and break through would have to risk getting cut up first. The back porch was left as-is though Dianne noted that she wanted to reinforce the front door later in the afternoon before taking care of the outbuildings. With only two entrances to the house free of impediments and deterrents the building was beginning to look less like a home and more like a fortress.

"Mom." Mark scratched his head as he talked. "This place looks like a prison camp now."

Dianne laughed and nodded. "Yeah, it does, doesn't it? Still, it should make someone think twice about coming in."

I hope it does, anyway. Dianne left her last thought unspoken as she followed her son around the house and towards the outbuildings to start planning out how they would secure those as well.

Chapter Five

Somewhere in Utah

"ALL RIGHTY, THEN. HERE WE GO." Rick mumbled to himself as he slowly pulled around to the front of the gas station as instructed by the sign. The doors and windows of the Humvee were armored and reinforced against small arms fire and he kept them locked and rolled up. His pistol sat on the seat next to him within easy reach and he unbuckled his seatbelt in case he needed to duck down and hide.

The metal canopy extending from the front of the building over the pumps was lower than on most gas stations due to the building's age. Rick wondered as he pulled in whether the turret would scrape against the top of the awning but, thankfully, it did not. He watched through the passenger window at the building, looking for movement inside when the sound of an engine firing up behind the building caught his attention. A moment later he heard the sharp squeal of feedback through speakers before an older man's voice cut through.

"You out there! You need fuel? Honk once for yes. Two for no."

Rick considered the question for a few seconds before deciding that honesty was the best choice given the current circumstances. He leaned on the horn, giving it a quick honk, then waited for a reply.

"What're you doing all the way out here by yourself? Your convoy passed by here yesterday. Oh... for...." There was the sound of fumbling and crashing as the microphone was presumably dropped to the floor. Instead of the voice coming back, though, Rick saw movement through the front window of the station before the front door eased open.

A man who looked to be in his late seventies pushed open the door. He clutched a shotgun in his weathered hands and his wrinkled face was set in an expression of suspicion. He approached the Humvee cautiously until he caught sight of the camo jacket Rick was wearing and then relaxed, standing up taller and lowering his gun. Rick reached over and rolled down the passenger window a few inches and waved at the man in a friendly manner.

"Hey there! You got any diesel?"

The man stopped several feet from the Humvee and looked it over, nodding approvingly at it. "Yeah, still got some. Your convoy sucked up most of it. You get separated from them or something?"

Rick was about to ask what the man was talking about when he realized that the man thought Rick was with the military. That assumption was likely part of why he was being so friendly and Rick didn't want to disrupt his friendliness by surprising him.

"I wasn't part of that convoy. I'm coming straight out of Nellis, heading for Fort Carson."

"Carson? That's where the convoy was going, too." The man sniffed and ran a hand through his hair. "They were talkin' about some kind of computer virus causing all of this nonsense. You know if that's true?"

"That's the story right now, yes sir."

The man nodded and pursed his lips. "Knew I should have joined up when I was young and had the chance. Not that it would have made a lick of difference today, though." He sighed. "Well I won't keep you. I'm sure you've got important things to do. Just pull over to the diesel pump and I'll get your cans and tank filled up for you."

Rick nodded in appreciation. He drove over to the pump and turned on his GPS unit again, attempting to look busy while still keeping an eye on the man. Under any other circumstances he would have hopped out and helped the man fuel up the Humvee but he was already feeling nervous enough with his partial deception. If the man started asking details about Rick's supposed service or anything else he feared the truth would come out in an ugly and confrontational way.

It took the man just over ten minutes to fill the empty can on the side of the vehicle and its tank. When he was done he walked up to the driver's door and tapped on the window. Rick glanced down at the man and saw that his shotgun was leaning up against the pump. He rolled the window all the way down and nodded at the man.

"Thanks very much. What do I owe you?"

The man shook his head. "Not a damned thing."

"You sure?"

"Absolutely."

Rick smiled. "Well, thank you. It's much appreciated. You out here all by yourself?"

"That's right."

"Nobody helping you?"

"Nope."

"Do… do you want a ride somewhere?"

The man laughed and did a half turn as he raised his arm to gesture at the gas station and the land behind it. "I've been living out here for my whole life. Just because the power's out, the internet's down and people are going a bit crazy doesn't mean I'm going to up and leave."

"So you're just waiting here to help people?"

The man cocked his head to the side and looked Rick in the eyes. "If we don't help each other, what's the point? Someone tries to steal from me I'll shoot him. No questions asked. Someone needs help and asks politely, though? I'll do whatever I can."

Rick nodded slowly. "That's a noble attitude. I admire it, for whatever that's worth, but I just hope you don't end up—"

"End up what?" The man interrupted Rick. "Dead? Taken advantage of?" He reached over and hefted his shotgun, his voice growing dark. "I've helped out a dozen more besides you and your fellow soldiers. And I've buried three so far who tried to take advantage of me."

Rick felt his heart race at the matter-of-fact statement and nodded, slowly reaching down to put the Humvee in gear. "Well, I appreciate the help."

"No problem at all." The man smiled and gave a salute to Rick. "Stay safe out there! And be careful crossing the mountains. No telling who or what's up there."

Rick gave the man as much of a smile as he could muster and eased onto the accelerator. He rolled up the front windows and pulled back out onto the highway, checking his rearview mirror frequently as he went. Behind him he saw the man walk slowly back into the gas station, head down and gun in his hands as he returned to his self-imposed watch.

"What the hell was with *that* guy?" Rick wondered aloud as he sped along, wanting to put as much distance between himself and the gas station as possible. Though the encounter had ended without an altercation the man's statement about killing and burying three people disturbed him to no end. He felt fortunate that the man had mistaken him for a member of the military and hadn't asked any questions, either, otherwise he felt certain that the whole encounter would have gone in an entirely different direction.

Wearing only a camo jacket, Rick didn't exactly look the part of a soldier. He figured that since he was driving a Humvee that was armed to the teeth he was close enough in appearance to a soldier for casual observers to make the assumption.

"Fresh tank and full reserves." Rick nodded as he tapped on the GPS.

"That should get me close enough to Grand Junction to find more fuel." He was no closer to a decision about where to go after Grand Junction but trusted that he would make the right choice once he got there. Until then he just had to keep pressing forward.

Chapter Six

The Water's Homestead
Outside Ellisville, VA

DIANNE AND MARK continued working on moving around supplies and stacking them in front of the various outbuildings. Once they were finished they started working on the mobile razor wire fencing units out in the driveway in front of the house. Mark started by hammering nails of various lengths and widths into the boards and placing them point-up on the ground. Dianne then went back and crafted tight loops of razor wire, stapling it down to the boards so that it coiled up and around in a six to twelve inch radius around the top and sides of the boards.

Individually each board posed little threat to those on foot but when laid in a staggered row they became dangerous to both foot and vehicular traffic. The nails on at least one of the boards were guaranteed to puncture a tire while the rows of razor wire would cause anyone stepping over them some moderate amount of pain or hassle. Short and darkly colored knots of rope on the ends of the boards made it possible to drag them around without risking harm but the color of the rope would make it hard for others to even tell that they were present.

With the boards complete Dianne and Mark laid them out twenty or so feet back from the gate, at the start of a turn in the drive. The curvature of the ground in the drive made it nearly impossible to see them from the gate and completely impossible to spot from the road. The number of boards on the drive made Dianne feel slightly better since anyone coming in with a vehicle would have to use the driveway and they would, at a minimum, be slowed down by them.

With the initial work to the driveway complete, Dianne and Mark set to work crafting another set of boards. Instead of long narrow ones, though, they took a large piece of plywood and completely covered it with razor wire. They moved the plywood down near the generator shed and stapled lengths of razor wire to the outer walls of the outbuilding. Once that step was complete the pair used their experience in creating the reinforced back door to the house to mount the plywood to the exterior of the shed door, in effect creating a secondary layer. A padlock went on last before Dianne walked around the generator building to survey their work.

"I think you're right, Mark."

"About what?"

Dianne grinned. "This place *is* starting to look like a prison."

"See!" Mark threw his hands up in the air. "I told you!"

"It's good, though. If we do this to all of the buildings then we'll make it a bit more of a challenge for intruders to get at anything."

"That's good. If somebody comes on the property again maybe they'll just leave."

"You know, I was thinking about that." Dianne sat down on the ground and pulled off her work gloves. "If I was someone who really wanted to break in and steal something, would I go for the building that's the most fortified or the least?"

"What do you mean?" Mark sat down beside her, idly picking at the brown grass as she continued.

"Imagine you're someone who wants to take something we have. You wander in and find a bunch of buildings with razor wire and extra locks and everything on them. Would you try to break into the building that's the least protected or the most protected? The least protected would be the easiest but the most protected would theoretically have the most valuables for you to take."

"I'm not sure—" Mark's response was cut off as Dianne continued talking.

"See, I started thinking about this a little while ago and my first thought is that someone would go for the building that has the *most* security because they want the most valuable stuff. But I don't think so anymore."

"Why not?"

"The guy who showed up here was skittish. He wasn't looking for a fight. He wanted an easy target, something to take without a struggle. I think that if someone comes out here again and sees a bunch of heavily fortified buildings they'll want to go for the ones that are least fortified." Dianne paused for a few seconds and smiled. "So that's what we'll do."

"You... you want to leave one of the buildings unprotected? Why?"

Dianne stood up and brushed the dry grass and dirt off of her pants and hands. "Because that's the building we're going to fill with traps and alarms."

Mark's eyes widened as an unknown childhood fantasy was simultaneously discovered and on the verge of being fulfilled. "Traps?"

"And alarms." Dianne shrugged her shoulders. "But mostly traps."

Chapter Seven

S omewhere in Colorado

RICK PULLED hard on the steering wheel, grunting as he tried to keep from falling out of his seat. The behemoth of a vehicle skidded along the road, feeling as though it might tip over right up until when he finally straightened it back out. Rick glanced in the side mirror and saw the last exit for the city of Grand Junction fading in the distance. A pair of dilapidated old cars came barreling down the off-ramp and onto the highway after Rick but they were too late to catch up to him.

Rick sighed and glanced at the fuel gauge again, relieved that he had been able to fill it up before he had been forced to leave the city. After passing through the majority of it via an overpass without incident he had chosen an out-of-the-way gas station near the edge to fill up the cans and tank before making his climb over the Rockies.

Just as he was finishing up with filling the tank he had noticed movement in a nearby building as the hairs on the back of his neck started to stand on end. Rick had barely been able to get back into the Humvee before all hell broke loose. Shots rang out at the Humvee from the building across the street, though they were all small caliber and bounced harmlessly off of the armor and reinforced glass.

Rick had calmed down slightly once he realized he wasn't in immediate danger. He drove away from the buildings as quickly as he could, feeling exceptionally grateful for the protection offered to him by the Humvee. On his way back towards the highway he noticed the two old cars pursuing him and accelerated. His drive around the obstacles on the on-ramp to the highway was not without peril but thanks to his deft driving he was able to quickly evade his pursuers.

Rick's encounter with the gang in Los Angeles and his experience in Las Vegas left him wanting to avoid conflict wherever possible. He was exercising extreme caution while around cities and constantly scanning his surroundings even while on the road. The close call at Grand Junction did, however, help him in one way—deciding which route to take.

Although Rick had spent a week in a cell at Nellis Air Force Base his treatment there was far superior to what he had experienced in the city proper. With Denver being such a large, sprawling city he had no doubt that there would still be large numbers of people there and he didn't want to find out how they were behaving or what condition the city was in. Even if he were to be detained at the fort he figured that there was a greater than fifty percent chance of the conditions there being better than any of the other cities, including Denver.

For that reason he had turned off of Interstate 70 and onto Highway 50. The route would take him south through desert and farmland and would − after crossing over the Rockies—dump him out near Colorado Springs, Fort Carson and NORAD. The suggested route from his GPS unit had him following I-50 all the way around the majority of the mountainous terrain but the distance was significantly longer than going straight through.

With a full tank of gas and both reserve cans full Rick calculated that he could just make it to the military base if he took a few smaller roads through the mountains. The extra benefit of doing so was that he would avoid many of the cities and towns along the way that no doubt held many more people who were more interested in shooting first and asking questions later.

With a final glance in the side mirror Rick relaxed and sank back as far as he could into his uncomfortable seat. *This*, he thought, *is going to suck.*

⊂⊃

RICK WAS four hours into an estimated five-and-a-half hour trip when the snowstorm blew in. The darkening clouds behind him had formed shortly after he left Grand Junction but he had managed to stay ahead of them through most of the mountains. The sheer cliffs, staggering peaks and array of wildlife and natural beauty had tempted him to stop to rest and enjoy the views but the encroaching threat of a storm spurred him to dangerous speeds along the mountain roads.

Following both natural and man-made paths through the mountains, the roads through the Rockies varied between life threatening and serene moment to moment. Exposed rock faces with loose rocks and gravel were interspersed with cliffs that dropped off into valleys filled with pines. The only protection offered against hurtling off to a certain death was a short and rusty guardrail that Rick had no doubt would offer little resistance to the Humvee. Driving along and avoiding the occasional destroyed car was relatively easy, though, since he could simply drive in the middle of the road without fear of running into any other cars.

The easy and fast drive quickly turned treacherous and ponderous with the arrival of a storm that made the blizzard he had encountered previously look like a few flurries. Wind battered at the heavy vehicle, jolting it from side to side. Rick tried to keep the vehicle's speed up for the first twenty minutes or so but eventually had to slow down after his first turn resulted in him sliding the vehicle up against a rock face. Ten minutes later the tires began slipping on the ice and snow and he had to slow down again. While much of his journey was uphill he was starting to worry about what would happen when he reached the apex of his climb and had to start going down again.

It was at that apex, when Rick was driving along a flat open area in a small valley between the peaks that the storm began to weaken. The driving snow turned into flurries and the clouds broke, revealing the blue sky above. The next corner offered Rick a view of some of the deep valleys below him and he slowed the Humvee to a crawl partially to ensure he didn't go flying off the edge and partially to gape in awe at the view.

Rows of pine trees that had yet to be covered in snow stretched out far towards the horizon. They rose again on the opposite side of the valley, stopping at the timberline where the bare rock and perpetual snow began to take over. The area off to the east was clear enough that Rick was astounded to be able to see the vague outline of distant cities.

"It's beautiful." Rick whispered the first words he had spoken all day, captivated by the sight in front of him. The majesty of the landscape left him dumbfounded and barely able to think. He slowed the Humvee from a crawl to a stop, parking it near a rock face opposite the steep cliff that sloped down into the valley. He grabbed his rifle and got out of the vehicle, running to the opposite side of the three-lane road.

Rick stopped at the guard rail and marveled at the sight for several minutes, taking in the frigid mountain air with deep breaths. Each one seemed to imbue him with a renewed sense of energy and purpose. By the time he noticed that the storm was beginning to pick up strength again he was already covered with snow and shivering uncontrollably. Despite his discomfort he remained elated and encouraged by the pristine sights as he ran back to the Humvee to dry off and get back on the road.

The natural wonder and beauty of the mountains and valleys had been the reminder Rick needed that not all was lost. His relative numbness towards being shot at in Grand Junction and how mildly he had reacted towards the incident made him realize that he was starting to get used to what was going on. Seeing something as close to perfection as what he was witnessing while traversing the mountains was both refreshing and palate cleansing. The horrors and disasters in the world weren't all-encompassing, after all.

Exactly two minutes later Rick's brightened mood darkened again as he heard the distant sound of engines drawing closer, their powerful whines cutting through the noise of the storm. The din of the engines sounded at first like enormous trucks but once Rick noticed that the sound was actually coming from *above* him he realized that his very life was in danger of being snuffed out.

Chapter Eight

The Water's Homestead
Outside Ellisville, VA

IT WAS in the mid-afternoon after lunch when Dianne and her three children were hard at work out behind the house when they heard the faint rumble of an engine through the trees. Jacob had been the first to hear it and he had dutifully charged across the small field from where he was busy measuring panels on a barn door.

"Mom! I heard a car!"

Dianne dropped the roll of razor wire and the staple gun to the ground and grabbed the rifle off of her back. Next to her Mark did the same thing and she glanced at him as they both started running back to the house. "Get them inside through the back door then I want you providing overwatch from upstairs. Got it?"

Mark nodded and motioned for his brother and sister to follow him. Dianne could hear the vehicle as well, though it wasn't from the direction she would have expected. Instead of driving from the nearby town of Ellisville towards the house it was driving from the opposite direction towards the house, as though it had come from somewhere farther off in the country. The roads in that direction were rough and winding and only someone with knowledge of the area—or an extremely up-to-date map—could have navigated their way in from any other major areas.

As Dianne rounded the house she heard the sound of the engine growing louder as the driver accelerated. The dirt road connected to the driveway ran in front of the Waters' property before going around the side. It was up the side she heard the engine as it continued growing louder before slowly getting quieter. A quiet squeal was audible and the engine shifted down, reducing the noise as the vehicle decelerated. Bits of white paint were visible through the thick stand of trees though they weren't moving.

Dianne ran to the edge of the woods in front of the house and turned back. One of the upstairs windows was open and she could see a form standing at it, rifle in hand. She waved to Mark and he waved back, then she pointed at the driveway to indicate where she was going next. She walked parallel with the driveway, keeping to the trees both for camouflage and to avoid the spiked boards sitting out on the dirt. She was near to the gate when she heard the sound of the engine rev up again. The vehicle appeared beyond the gate a few seconds later, visible in between the trunks of the trees.

It was a large white pickup, covered in dirt and dents and rolling slowly down the dirt path towards the gate. From her position Dianne couldn't make out how many people were in the cab but the back of the truck looked to be filled with boxes and covered containers. She half-expected the truck to accelerate and plow through the gate but it slowed to a stop instead. The truck shuddered slightly as the driver shifted into park and Dianne heard the click of a door opening on the driver's side of the truck, opposite the side of the driveway where she was hiding.

Dianne shifted over towards the driveway by a few feet, keeping low to the ground and hiding herself behind trees. She leaned out to see who had gotten out of the truck when she caught sight of the figure. It was an older man wearing a jacket with tufts of white hair poking out from underneath a worn baseball cap. The man moved slowly, looking around in all directions as he kept a firm hold on the pistol in his right hand.

The man stopped at the gate and Dianne watched as he reached for the thick chain and padlock. He held it and turned the lock over a few times before dropping it and sighing. There were enough tree branches between Dianne and the man that she couldn't make out who he was but she decided that—given that he was the only one out of the car—she needed to make her move.

"Hey!" Dianne ran through the woods to the edge of the driveway and pressed her body up against a thick oak tree that was a few feet away from the gate. "You at the truck! Drop the gun and put your hands up!" Dianne swung her rifle around and braced her shoulder against the tree, exposing as little of herself as possible. She had expected to see the man standing in front of the truck, surprised by her aggressiveness but instead she saw him ducking out of sight behind the front of his truck. Before she could say anything else he raised his pistol and fired three times towards her.

Each shot wildly missed its mark and Dianne immediately returned fire, dropping down as she did in order to present a moving target to her opponent. Her bullets ricocheted off of the gate and penetrated through the thin sheet metal of the edge of the truck's hood and she heard the man yell as he retreated farther behind the vehicle.

"Get down, Sarah! Get down!" The man's voice was familiar to Dianne, though it took her several seconds to place it. When she did she immediately lowered her rifle and shouted at the man.

"Jason? Jason Statler? Is that you?" There was a long moment of silence before Dianne heard a reply.

"Dianne? What the hell do you think you're doing, shooting at us?" The man coughed loudly as he talked before cautiously peeking over the hood of the truck. Dianne poked her head out and waved sheepishly at Jason before stepping out onto the driveway.

"Jason!" Dianne shook her head and smiled at the man. "You are a shit shot. You know that, right?"

Jason coughed again as he walked towards the gate. "You haven't missed your range days by the looks of it."

Dianne swung her leg over the gate and hopped onto the opposite side. She grabbed Jason's arms as if to reassure herself that he was real and smiled again. "You have no idea how glad I am to see you."

Dianne embraced Jason in a hug that nearly toppled the older man over. A second later Dianne heard the door to the truck open and another figure, more lively than Jason, jumped out. "Dianne? You're still alive!"

Dianne turned and ran over to Sarah Statler. She, like her husband, was in her early sixties but still active and as lively as she had been when she was twenty. Jason's health had diminished over the years but that fact never seemed to keep Sarah from being as vibrant and chipper as she had when the pair had first been married.

"Of course I'm still alive!" Dianne squeezed Sarah tight in a hug as Sarah's husband came walking over. Dianne stepped back, wearing an ear-to-ear grin as she looked at her friends before giving them each another hug. "You two have *no* idea how happy I am to see you."

"You have no idea how glad I am you missed me." Jason rubbed one of the holes in the hood of the truck where one of Dianne's shots had penetrated through the metal. "The engine's still running so I guess you didn't hit anything vital there, either."

"Oh, be quiet!" Sarah thumped her husband's back before looking at Dianne. "How are the children? And Rick?"

The mention of her husband dimmed Dianne's overwhelming happiness and Sarah suddenly looked concerned at Dianne's abrupt change in attitude. "What's the matter, D?"

Dianne patted Sarah and Jason on the arms and nodded towards their truck. "Get in and I'll open the gate and clear the drive for you. Let's get out of sight of the road and into the house where we can talk."

Chapter Nine

E ight days after the event
London, England

"THIS WAY. QUICKLY!" A small child, a girl, follows her father and mother. The three run swiftly down cobblestone streets, sticking to the shadows and pressing themselves up against the sides of buildings anytime they hear the slightest movement. The father holds his finger to his lips as he wraps his arm around his wife who, in turn, pulls their daughter close to her. "Keep very quiet." The man whispers to his wife and she relays the message to their little girl.

After running out of food the family tried to beg, borrow and steal what they could from local corner shops. Unfortunately the shops had already been ravaged by other survivors and the family was left with no other choice but seek out what the flyers taped to the lampposts in their neighborhood called "Emergency Services Food Relief." The program was crude but effective. By turning certain restaurants in neighborhoods into food distribution points the government has come up with a way to quickly get supplies to where they are needed without dealing with the issues caused by mass transportation and delivery.

"Across the street now. And hurry!" The father pushes his wife and child ahead as he turns to locate the source of a noise behind. Nothing is immediately visible so he follows them as they head down an alley. Distant shouts and screams are accompanied by the occasional burst of gunfire, though most of the more violent noises seem to be coming from a fair distance away.

"Mama, I'm hungry." The little girl tugs on her mother's coat and whispers softly.

"I know, darling. Just a little longer." The mother picks up her daughter and looks at her husband. "How much farther do you think?

"Just up the next street." He holds a tattered flyer in his hand and taps at the address printed on the bottom. *"We can only get enough for three days but that should tide us over until we can get out of the city."*

As the trio cross the last street before their destination they look off to their right, seeing the iconic image of Big Ben towering over the city below. The clock has not rung in days, though, and while the mother and child are too busy watching where they are going to notice, the father sees that large pieces of the clocktower have been torn out by some sort of attack. The father grinds his teeth at the sight but says nothing as he follows his wife and daughter to their destination.

Outside the small fish and chip shop the street is barren without a soul in sight. The father looks around, confused by the lack of other people, and talks quietly to his wife. *"This is the right place… right?"*

His wife takes the flyer and looks at the address before nodding. *"This is the place."*

"So where is everyone?"

The man's wife points at the window. *"There's a light on in the back. I guess someone's home after all."*

The man looks through the window and nods. *"All right. Let's get inside quickly, get our food and go."*

The tables and chairs in the small shop have all been moved to one side. Large stacks of plastic containers dyed bright yellow sit next to the tables and chairs, all of them filled with discarded food packaging and wrappers. Two boxes that are partially full of food sit near the back of the shop and the father nearly runs toward them before resolving to maintain his decorum even in the face of hunger and tragedy.

He walks up to the counter and hits the small bell with his hand, sending a shrill ring echoing through every room of the building. There is no answer and, after several seconds of waiting, he rings the bell again. His wife and daughter stand close to him and his wife whispers after another several seconds pass.

"Where is everyone?"

The man shakes his head. *"I don't know. This seems…odd."* The man walks around and peeks behind the counter, noticing too late that there are two men crouched in hiding. The father staggers back as the two men jump out, each of them wielding large butcher's knives in their right hands.

"Get down on the floor!" One of the men screams at the father and pushes the father over, knocking him to the ground. The other man leaps over the counter and runs to the front door, bolting it before the mother and daughter can even think about leaving. A flurry of words are exchanged between the men before the one nearest the door begins pushing the child and wife into the back of the shop.

"Stop! What are you doing?" The father struggles to his feet but the man standing over him with the knife kicks him in the head, knocking him back down to the floor.

"You stay down!" The man runs behind the counter and leers at his companion. The other man pushes the small girl to the ground and tears at the mother's clothing, ignoring the screams of terror and panic from both her and her child.

The father crawls along the floor, his head spinning and his vision blurry as he desperately tries to stop what is unfolding in the back room. He pulls himself up to his knees just *as the man who kicked him comes back out of the room. The man sees the father and snarls at him before raising the butcher knife and running forward.*

Crack!

The sound of glass breaking accompanies a stagger in the knife-wielder's gait. He goes from charging at the father to starting to fall over, grasping at the wall as he drops the knife. Several more cracks sound out as the front glass windows shatter and blood pours from gaping wounds in the man's chest. The father turns to look at the front window as a dozen men dressed head to toe in black enter through the window and the door, breaking through wood and glass as they storm the building.

The noise and commotion draws the attention of the man in the back room who steps out, his knife having been forgotten on a shelf. He sees the body of his companion first and his eyes grow large. He screams and tries to escape back into the room but the loud snaps of suppressed weapons fill the shop with noise. The man drops to the floor, having taken sixteen rounds through his back and head.

The father tries to pull himself to his feet but he is interrupted by two of the men in black. They pull him up and pat him down, pulling his legs and arms apart to ensure he isn't hiding weapons of any type. One of them pulls the father's wallet from his pocket and opens it before showing the photograph on the ID card to one of the other men.

"Civilian." The voice of the man in black is muffled by his mask but his companion understands him nonetheless.

"Get the child and the woman outside with him. Load up. We need to move." The order comes from one of the other men in the shop. The command is swiftly carried out and the father soon sees his wife and daughter being helped out of the back room.

The father is confused by what is going on, his head still spinning from the blow he sustained. "What are you doing with us?" His speech is slurred and the words don't come out properly but one of the men in black helping him out into the street replies anyway.

"Emergency evacuation. Door-to-door sweeps."

"Evacuation? To… to where?"

"North. We're pulling out of the city."

"Leaving the city?" The father shakes his head and instantly regrets it. "Why?"

"It's overrun. Nationalist groups merged with the Fascist Liberation Party by the looks of it. They're waging an all-out war on any and everyone they've ever disliked. Today's the day of their big cleansing from the looks of it." The man in black points to a military truck a few feet away. "Up inside you go, sir. Your wife and daughter, too."

"Thank you." The father doesn't know what else to say. He tries to process what the man is saying as he helps his wife and daughter into the truck. There are several other families in the back, each of them looking terrified beyond belief. The father finally notices his wife's condition and embraces her as she holds her daughter to her chest while trying to pull the scraps of cloth that used to be her shirt up around herself.

One of the men sitting across from the trio stands up and takes off his jacket and sweater before passing the sweater to the father. He nods in thanks and helps his wife put on the sweater before sitting back and holding her in his arms once again. Outside the truck come the sounds of more shouting as the men in black clear more shops and flats. They move quickly down the street, pausing every once in a while to move the truck along behind them.

When the back of the truck is filled to the breaking point it is escorted through the city to the north. There, well outside the city, a stronghold has been erected. Families are assigned to tents and given food, water and—if necessary—medical attention. The conditions in the camps are borderline to say the least but all that matters to the father is the fact that his family is, for the time being, safe.

Chapter Ten

The Water's Homestead
Outside Ellisville, VA

IT TOOK the better part of an hour for Dianne to regale Jason and Sarah with the story of the last couple of weeks. They had insisted on hearing about what had happened to her before telling their own story and they hung on her every word and description from start to finish.

"D, I am so incredibly sorry. I'm sure he's fine, though. Just you wait; he'll be walking through that front door one day soon with a story to tell that you can't even imagine." Sarah reached out and put her hand on Dianne's leg.

Jason, standing at the back door looking out at the half-finished fortifications on the outbuildings, shook his head and snorted. "Damn straight he's fine. If we can make it back from Maryland and you can turn this place into a cross between a castle and a prison camp I'm sure Rick can handle a little walk."

"Jason…" Sarah's tone carried a note of warning in it.

"It's okay, Sarah." Dianne nodded and sighed. "Jason's right. I'm sure Rick's fine. It's just so far away and there's nothing I can do to help him or even try to find him, you know?" Dianne took a deep breath and glanced at her watch before raising her voice to call to Mark in the kitchen.

"Hey Mark? Can you get some water boiling for dinner?"

"Sure thing, mom."

"Now listen here," Jason turned from the door. "We don't need you to use any of your supplies on us. We've got our own food and we aren't about to take anything from your mouths."

"He's right." Sarah looked over at Dianne. "We don't want you to—"

"Jason. Sarah." Dianne looked at the both of them as she stood up. "I won't take 'no' for an answer. You're staying for dinner and for the night and that's final." Jason opened his mouth to argue and Dianne pointed a finger in his direction. "And if you try to argue with me I'll put holes into all four of your tires."

"Fine." Jason tried to feign annoyance though Dianne could tell he wasn't the least bit unhappy about it.

"Good. Now that you've listened to me babble on for an hour I want to hear every detail about what you two went through. We went over to check on you and saw your note but you two aren't the types to take spontaneous trips anywhere. What happened?"

Sarah stood up and patted Jason on the back as she walked into the kitchen to help Dianne with the dinner preparations. "This old man is what happened."

"Hey, it's not my fault!" Jason protested as he followed the pair into the kitchen.

"So what happened?" Dianne asked. "You two don't usually go away on trips."

"Jason's had some health issues lately and we got an appointment with a doctor at the Mayo Clinic." Sarah patted her husband's hand as she sat down next to him. "We expected it to take several months to get one but this one opened up and we had to take it."

"Why didn't you let us know you were going?" Dianne looked at Sarah.

"We figured it was just overnight. Head up there, stay at a hotel for the night, see the doctor the next morning and then pop back down." Sarah sighed. "Then everything went south."

"The morning of your appointment?"

"Yep." Jason put his fork down and wiped his mouth with his napkin. "We were in the middle of talking to the doctor when the lights went out. Everybody at the office figured it was just a temporary blackout so we finished up talking to him and headed out to the truck." Jason shook his head. "Thank goodness their parking lot was empty that morning or we probably never would have made it back."

Dianne took a drink of water and helped Josie cut up some of her larger pieces of broccoli. "You're talking about the exploding cars, right?"

"Yeah, but it was worse than that." Sarah nodded. "Well, you said you went into Ellisville. You saw what it was like there."

"And on the ramp out to the highway, too. I can't imagine what it would have been like up there."

"It was hell on earth." Jason stared into space as he recalled the morning of the event. "There were fires everywhere. Smoke was filling the air. We thought about just driving off but that would have been suicide so we went back into the doctor's office and stayed there for a while. A few hours later, when the fires from the cars had died down, everyone in the office went outside and saw that the buildings were starting to burn. We had the only working vehicle in the area so we loaded the doctor and his nurses and staff and a couple other patients up and took them to their homes."

"I really hope they made it out of there." Sarah had a sad look on her face. "That nurse, especially. She was particularly nice."

"What happened then?"

Jason and Sarah looked at each other, then Jason spoke. "Then things got worse. I figured whatever was going on would blow over so we went back to the hotel. That turned out to be in flames which sort of signaled that something really bad was going on. The couple of radio stations that were working for the first day or two said that whatever was going on was happening across the world."

"And," Sarah clarified, "that it was getting worse."

Dinner was long over and night was fast approaching before Jason and Sarah finished their story. After spending a day and night in their truck in Maryland they had started driving south in an attempt to head back home. Impassable roads and the presence of looters in the cities had forced them off of the main roads but they soon found themselves stymied as they tried to get around Washington.

The capital was under complete lockdown and the pair were turned away and forced to go a hundred miles out of their way in order to get around it. While Jason had his pistol in a lockbox in the truck to keep them safe they hadn't brought more than the few day's worth of food that was contained within their go bag. This combined with the new route they had to take had forced them to loot from more than a few homes and businesses to get enough food for their journey back.

All in all the pair had actually encountered less trouble than Dianne would have guessed. They only ran into a few unfriendly people though that was because they stayed as far away from populated areas as possible. There was one close call involving a group of young men and women who had surrounded their truck in the region of Fredericksburg but a few well-placed shots from Jason had driven them off.

"I still can't believe you managed to make it all the way back here in that old piece of junk. Though that's probably the only reason you made it back."

"How's that?" Jason sat on the couch next to his wife, gratefully accepting a cup of coffee from Dianne. Mark, Jacob and Josie had gone upstairs to read while Jason, Sarah and Dianne talked and Dianne finally felt comfortable speaking as openly and frankly as she wanted.

"Didn't you wonder why your truck wasn't damaged while so many others were?"

Sarah looked at Jason and poked him in the side. "See! I told you there was something weird going on."

Jason gave Sarah a sideways glance and rolled his eyes. "Yeah, yeah. I guess you were right."

"Anyway." Dianne steered the conversation back on track. "The reason why is because your car is old. Old enough, anyway."

"What does that mean?"

"When all of this first happened I went into town. The Eat Rite had a newscast playing on the TV while everyone was freaking out and panicking. The reporter said something about it being a computer-based attack."

"Huh." Jason nodded in understanding. "The truck's old enough it doesn't have any computer systems that would be affected."

"Exactly. And that's also why there's a burned-out wreck out front."

"I was wondering about that when we came in." Jason stroked his white beard and let out a soft whistle. "That's something else. Explains why the power's off, doesn't it?"

"Yep. The TV still works, as do the tablets the kids have been using, but I bet this attack was designed to hit big systems first. Things like cars and power stations and airplanes."

"We saw a hell of a lot of downed planes around D.C. A *hell* of a lot." Jason looked at Sarah and sighed. "I guess we should be glad we never bothered to get that new car, huh?"

Sarah nodded and the trio sat in silence for a few minutes, digesting both their dinner and the information they had shared over the last couple of hours. It was Jason who finally spoke, glancing at his watch as he did. "Well, I guess we should be getting back home. We need to get unpacked and figure out what we're going to do to shore things up over there starting in the morning."

"Go?" Dianne shook her head. "No way. You two are staying tonight. And tomorrow we're going to have a long talk about next steps."

Jason started to argue when Sarah elbowed him gently in the side. "Just nod and say thank you so we can both get some sleep, you big oaf."

Chapter Eleven

S omewhere in the Colorado Rockies

RICK JUMPED out of the Humvee and looked behind him only to dive back into the vehicle as he shouted in terror. "Holy shit!" The Humvee shook like a toy as a massive aircraft descended out of the clouds. Flames and black smoke engulfed the left wing, lighting up the side of the mountain like the sun itself.

Only one of the C-130's turboprop engines on the right wing was operational. The two engines on the left wing were both on fire while the other engine on the right wing was sputtering and smoking. The enormous cargo door was open and through the fire and smoke Rick could make out the forms of dozens of people all seated inside. He only caught a glimpse of them for a split second but the look of panic and horror in their body language as they thrashed around in their seats made him incredibly glad that the sound of the plane's engine was loud enough to drown out their voices.

A piece of aluminum from the wing bounced off the road in front of Rick as he ran back across to the guardrail, nearly causing him to slip in the snow as he abruptly changed directions to avoid the flaming piece of debris. A shower of fuel fell from the sky behind the plane as the pilots desperately tried to get rid of all that they possibly could.

Once he was back at the edge of the road, Rick watched as the plane banked hard in the valley, barely missing the edge of a row of trees with its left wing. It cut low over the treetops and pulled up for a brief second in which Rick thought it might make it over the next mountain. Gravity, however, had different plans.

The plane's upward climb slowed dramatically to a halt. Time paused for a fraction of a second as the one remaining engine struggled to pull the mammoth piece of metal up and over the mountain. The herculean efforts put out by both the machinery and the pilots inside were to no avail and the plane drifted back and sideways, plunging its right wing directly into the valley floor. The wing collapsed instantly under the weight of the body and remaining wing. Metal screeched and trees snapped like toothpicks. The smell of fuel hung thickly in the air and Rick wondered for a moment if the pilots had managed to dump out enough fuel to keep the craft from turning into a fireball.

Pressure, fuel and flame met and intermingled, causing an explosion that tore across the valley. Rick could feel faint heat from the explosion on his exposed face and hands and he watched in horror as the still-moving aircraft was completely and utterly destroyed along with everyone on board. He was shivering again by the time he realized that the storm was intensifying and he ran back to the Humvee and threw it into gear.

Rick tore down the mountain road, bouncing in his seat as he drove far faster than was safe under the current weather conditions. The Humvee slid back and forth on the snow, glancing off of the guardrail more than once. Rick was no longer concerned over his safety, though, as he wanted to get closer to the wreck and see if—somehow—there were any survivors.

The ride down the mountain in the Humvee took several minutes but the flames and smoke were still as intense as they had been when he started. A small "scenic view" pull-off and dirt path leading down into the valley were near the wreckage and he skidded to a stop, nearly turning the Humvee all the way around due to how far it slid on the snow-covered pavement. Rick grabbed a jacket from the Humvee and his pistol and ran towards the dirt path to see how far he would have to go to get to the wreckage.

Rick stopped near a simple wooden structure at the start of the dirt path with a pair of bathroom signs out front and looked out over the valley. He was near the bottom of it but the view was spectacular—or it would have been had the storm not gotten worse. He could see smoke rising from the wreck several hundred feet out along the path but the flames appeared to be slowly dying down due to a lack of easily combustible fuel and the steadily increasing snowfall. Rick looked back at the Humvee hesitantly before running down the dirt path and plunging headfirst into the unknown.

It didn't take more than a few minutes for Rick to get close enough to the wreck to realize that his attempt at rescuing survivors was a fool's errand. Smoldering pieces of the plane littered the ground for hundreds of feet in all directions. Dozens of trees had been virtually vaporized from the impact of the crash but there were hundreds more that had been knocked over, snapped in half and turned into splinters. Rick stepped over and under the wreckage and the trees, trying to figure out where to start searching for survivors. He stopped in a small clearing to rest for a moment and happened to glance down at the ground in front of him.

A small hand rested on the ground, severed just above the wrist and covered in burns and soot. It was smaller than Ricks by a significant amount and the sight of the extremity made Rick's stomach turn. He knelt down and reached out, getting ready to touch the hand when he noticed a small form lying a dozen feet farther away amongst the trees. Rick's face turned ashen at the sight and he vomited uncontrollably onto the ground.

AN HOUR LATER, though his stomach was devoid of all food and liquid, Rick's stomach and throat muscles still heaved as they tried to expel contents that were not present. He had spent the time combing through the wreckage for survivors but his search was in vain. Sixteen intact bodies and pieces of several more had turned up and each time he saw one the image of the small child's body flashed across his mind, causing him to retch uncontrollably.

Night was falling, the fires from the wreckage were nearly extinguished and darkness was settling in over the valley when Rick finally worked up the fortitude to give up his search. His body was soaked from the snow, he was trembling and shivered from head to toe and he felt more hollow inside than he could ever remember feeling before in his life. He walked up the dirt path back towards the road slowly, casting weary glances in every direction in one last-ditch effort to find anyone who could have survived.

After changing his clothes and huddling underneath his pile of table-cloths it took Rick two hours to warm up with the help of three heating packs taken from MREs from the back of the Humvee. Once he stopped shivering and started getting the feeling back in his fingers and toes he returned to the driver's seat and slowly started moving his vehicle down the road. The darkness obscured the smoke still drifting into the sky from the wreckage and the fires that still burned were small enough that they appeared only as the faintest glow through the trees.

Rick paid no attention to the wreckage as he drove on, feeling completely and utterly defeated by his fruitless search. The joy and wonder he felt at seeing the beauty of the valley and surrounding mountains was gone, replaced only by an emptiness that was as deep and wide as the valley itself. Each person he found—and the many he didn't—served as a reminder of the horrors of the world he lived in.

For one fleeting moment he had found peace and a semblance of hope but as he left the valley behind he felt only numbness inside his heart and soul.

Chapter Twelve

The Water's Homestead
  Outside Ellisville, VA

FRESHLY SCRAMBLED EGGS, sausages, slightly stale toast—made from frozen bread—and a bit of butter and jam made for a surprise breakfast for the children. Jason, Sarah and Dianne were all up and cooking when Mark, Jacob and Josie got up. The six ate a relaxing breakfast before getting on with the business of the day.

"So." Dianne wiped her mouth with a napkin and passed her plate to Jacob. "What do we need to get from your house to get you all set up to stay here?"

"Stay?" Jason raised one of his bushy eyebrows. "Dianne, while we appreciate the hospitality we can't be an imposition like that during times like this. You have three to watch out for and feed. We can't add to that."

Dianne glanced at Sarah and gave her a slight grin. "You really don't have to argue with every single thing. You know that, right?" Jason gave a harrumph and tossed his napkin on his plate as Dianne continued. "We're all set up here with power, food, defenses and more. We have room for you both and we could all stand to help each other out during this… whatever it is. We've known each other for long enough that I trust you both and I know you can both handle a gun."

"I can." Sarah spoke softly and Dianne could barely catch herself from laughing at the remark. "My husband here couldn't hit the broad side of a barn based on how he was shooting yesterday."

Jason harrumphed again and was about to say something when Dianne interrupted. "Now listen. I'm not going to take 'no' for an answer. We need to pool our resources with each other. You can take the spare room upstairs and help us out with tending to the hydroponics, cooking, taking care of the animals and keeping watch and on and on. That's going to be a hell of a lot easier than you two trying to fortify and take care of yourselves and us trying to do things on our own, too."

Josie, who had been listening to the conversation more than her brothers, ran over to her mother and nearly shouted in excitement. "Are Mr. and Mrs. Statler going to stay with us?"

Dianne ruffled Josie's hair and smiled at Jason. "They're thinking about it, sweetie. Go back and keep helping your brothers, okay?"

"Okay." Josie smiled at Sarah. "I really want you both to stay here with us. It'd be so much fun!"

Josie ran back to the sink to keep helping with the dishes. Sarah leaned forward and lowered her voice as she spoke to Dianne. "I'm glad to see they're holding up well."

Dianne leaned forward as well and spoke quietly and candidly to both Jason and Sarah. "Cards on the table here, you two. We could really use someone else around here. Not just to pool resources and share the workload but just for general company. Those kids are going stir-crazy with just me here and I'm starting to talk to myself more and more. I understand if you want to do something else but as far as I'm concerned—and if Rick were here I know he'd agree with me—you two are welcome here like family." Dianne paused and grinned at Jason. "So long as you don't shoot at me again."

Jason couldn't repress his smile as he shook his head and tried to keep a straight face. Sarah, meanwhile, smiled and nodded. "As long as this one agrees then we'd be happy to stay. We're not going to freeload, though."

"Damn straight." Jason clapped his hand to his mouth apologetically as he looked over at the kids. "Sorry. Darned straight. We've got a lot of dry goods at the house and some spare clothes, bedding and pillows. Lots of books, tools and other equipment, too. Oh, and guns and ammo of course. If we take one of the trucks over we can probably get most of it in one go. We might be able to get the fuel cans, too. I added stabilizer to them when I filled them last and we'll probably need them at some point in the near future."

Dianne nodded, impressed by Jason's short list of supplies. "You know, I grabbed a few things from your place a while back when we got the chickens but left most of it there. It's been a while, though, so hopefully nobody's looted it."

"That reminds me—I'd like to see the Carson's house, maybe see if there are any clues as to what happened." Jason stood up from the table.

"We can do that, sure." Dianne looked at Sarah. "You're okay staying here with the kids?"

Sarah stood up and headed into the living room to retrieve one of her bags from the truck. "Better than okay."

Jason realized what Sarah was getting and smiled. "You'll like this, D."

Sarah pulled a rectangular block from the bag and threw it across the room. Dianne caught it with one hand and flipped it over, immediately recognizing what it was. "What's the range on this baby?"

"Twenty miles or so. With the trees around the house it'll be cut down by a fair amount but I can just sit upstairs at a window to keep in touch."

"Nice thinking, Sarah." Dianne clipped the long range two-way radio to her belt and looked at Jason. "You want to take your truck or mine?"

"It's been a while since I've seen it but I think yours has more room in the back, right?"

"Yeah, I think so." Dianne grabbed the keys for the truck from the top of the refrigerator and passed them to Jason. "Go ahead and bring it around out front. Jacob, would you and your sister take this chair upstairs and show Mrs. Statler the best place to put it so she can see out over the driveway?"

Sarah, Jacob and Josie headed upstairs while Jason walked out the front door and around to the back of the house to get Dianne's truck. Taking advantage of the moment of privacy she stood next to Mark and talked to him in a soft voice so that no one could overhear their conversation.

"I want you to keep a close eye on everything here, okay?"

Mark cocked his head, slightly confused by the request. "Mr. and Mrs. Statler are okay, aren't they?"

"They're fantastic. I can think of few other people I'd trust to have here with us more than them." Dianne hesitated. "But you're still the man around here till your dad gets back. So I need you alert and watching out for all of us. Especially your brother and sister while I'm gone. Got it?"

Mark nodded. "Got it. Do you want me to show her the security cameras?"

"Absolutely." Dianne nodded vigorously. "Don't misunderstand me, kiddo. I'm not worried about Sarah and Jason. I just need you to keep your eyes open. Having them drive out here to the house has me a little more nervous since I'm thinking more about the guy from a few days ago."

"Oh." Mark nodded, understanding what she meant. "I'll keep my eyes peeled."

Dianne smiled and patted him on the back. "Good. We'll be back in an hour or two. Make sure you or Sarah are near the radio, okay? Don't hesitate to call if you need something."

"Will do." Mark watched his mother as she grabbed her jacket, slipped on her shoes and shouldered her rifle. She slipped a few extra magazines for the rifle into her jacket pockets and headed out front where Jason was waiting with the truck.

Dianne hopped into the driver's seat as Jason slid over into the passenger's seat. "You ready for this, Jason?"

Jason held his pistol in his hands with a firm grip, keeping the weapon pointed at the floorboard as he scanned the driveway ahead of them. "Damn straight I am."

Chapter Thirteen

Three days after the event
  Near the border of Oregon and Idaho

THE V-22 OSPREY *tears through the sky at over three hundred and fifty miles per hour. The massive twin rotors slice through the air, pulling the aircraft forward as it sails westward towards its destination. In the back sits the most important person in the world, guarded by a group of Secret Service and Marines. The man they protect is breathing laboriously as two medics work to stabilize his condition and clear his airway.*

"Status?" The Secret Service agent in command grasps a handrail as he leans in to check on the medics.

"The same. Smoke inhalation with potential internal injuries. We're treating the smoke inhalation but we can't do a lot till we get him under a scanner to see what's bleeding inside."

The agent turns and walks wordlessly to the front of the aircraft. "How long?"

"Twenty minutes."

"Dammit." The agent seethes but there is nothing he can do. He sits back down and stares at the two medics as they provide oxygen to the President. The flight time to the mountains near the border of Idaho and Oregon turns out to be eighteen minutes. Near the end of the flight the V-22 descends and its twin rotors tilt upward. The craft uses its navigational lights to visually signal that it is approaching for a landing as the risk of using any type of communication system is too great with the passenger they have on board.

The visual signal is acknowledged by a series of lights embedded in wide slab of concrete sitting in the middle of nowhere near the Seven Devils Mountains. The V-22 sets down on the pad and its rotors spin down. Two hundred feet in front of the pad, the face of the mountain cracks open as the visually camouflaged doors to one of the government's top-secret continuity-of-government bunkers open.

Threat analysis conducted while Air Force One was still in the air indicated that well-known facilities—even those hardened against a strike—were not viable options for the President given the state of the world. After the crash the decision was made to fly him to the Devil's Mountain Complex, one of the newest and least heard of facilities. Like Cheyenne Mountain, Mount Weather and Raven Rock, the Devil's Mountain bunker is buried deep beneath the earth, hardened against an attack and designed to house senior members of the government for months or years if necessary.

Before the doors can open all the way a trio of small vehicles come racing out of the complex. One of them stops at the back of the Osprey and the President, the two medics and several Secret Service agents get on board and are whisked away. Marines and more Secret Service agents get on board one of the other vehicles which follows the first into the bunker.

The third vehicle is equipped with a tow arm that attaches to the front of the Osprey. It quickly brings the craft inside and the doors are shut again. The total time that the Osprey spends sitting out on the landing pad is eleven minutes. Once it is inside and the camouflaged doors are closed the bunker returns to a state of virtual nonexistence as far as the outside world is concerned.

Inside the bunker the V-22 Osprey is towed into a small space used for storing aircraft. Two helicopters and another V-22 sit in the space, each of them fueled up and ready to be towed out to the front pad at a moment's notice.

A wide tunnel—larger than the main entrance to the Cheyenne Mountain bunker—slopes downward into the earth. The tunnel and complex took three years of round-the-clock work to complete and it is the most advanced bunker facility in the government's arsenal. Two nuclear reactors provide power, a natural spring provides water and a limestone cavern carved over centuries by the spring provided several thousand square feet of open space that formed the initial backbone of the facility.

Excavation outward from the limestone cavern increased the facility to three square miles of floor space spread over twelve levels and housing a standard rotation of two hundred workers and government employees. The occupancy limit for the facility is in the thousands, though, and the Devil's Mountain Complex is nearly at the seventy percent level.

A full hospital with imaging technology, an operating room and three permanent doctors quickly go to work on the President. Tests soon reveal that he has suffered damage to his kidneys and one of his lungs received a minor puncture due to multiple rib fractures from the force of the plane crash. All in all, though, his condition is stable and the doctors expect him to recover enough to return to his duties within a few days.

In the meantime, with no way of communicating with the outside world for fear of infecting more systems with Damocles, there is no one able to take the senior leadership role. Even when the President awakens he will be faced with the startling reality that there isn't much left that he can do to change what is going on.

Chapter Fourteen

The Water's Homestead
Outside Ellisville, VA

JASON INITIALLY WANTED to go see the remains of the Carson's house before doing anything else but Dianne persuaded him that getting supplies was the first and most important priority. The drive to the Statler's house didn't take long and when they arrived Dianne was exceptionally relieved to see that the place was still intact and untouched.

"Pull around to the barn first. I've got some beans and rice double bagged and sealed in some airtight canisters." Jason scratched his nose and beard. "I think it's about a hundred pounds or so of both if I remember right."

"Got it. You got the keys to the house handy?"

"Ha. I wish. We lost those days ago. I had to hotwire the damn truck. I'll grab the spare key from up in the rafters on the back porch."

"Excellent. Let's get the rice and beans in along with whatever tools, then we'll cover everything with a tarp if you've got a clean one sitting around. We can stack the stuff from inside the house on top of that and cram whatever else we need into the back cab."

"Sounds like a plan to me."

Dianne and Jason hopped out of the truck and immediately got to work. The full night's sleep on a soft bed after a full meal had energized him like he hadn't experienced since the event took place. He and Dianne moved quickly, loading the rice and beans first before getting hand tools, boxes of nails, a burlap sack filled with screws and other miscellaneous odds and ends. By the time they finished it had taken just over thirty minutes and half of the back of the truck was filled with supplies.

Dianne secured the tarp in place while Jason headed over to the house. He retrieved the key and opened the back door before quickly sweeping the darkened building for intruders. A thin layer of dust covered all of the horizontal surfaces and there was the distinct smell of rotting fruit in the house. Aside from that, though, everything in his home appeared untouched and unchanged.

Dianne pulled the truck around to the back of the house, hopped out and went inside to meet Jason in the kitchen. "Where should we start?" She looked around, suddenly wishing she had brought a flashlight with her.

"I know Sarah's got a fair number of cans in these cabinets. How about you look for any more food that's still good while I get clothes, toiletries, spare sheets and the like." Jason frowned. "Well now wait a minute. I guess we can leave some stuff here, right? We'll just come back for it if we need it."

Dianne shook her head. "I wouldn't leave anything here that you can't live without. If somebody comes around and torches this place like they did the Carson's house then there wouldn't be anything to come back for."

"Hm." Jason gave a disappointed grunt. "You're right. Give me twenty minutes or so. I'll stack everything here on the table so we can carry it all out at once."

Dianne nodded and started pulling back the shades from the windows, both to make it easier to see in the dark cabinets and so she could have a better view outside the house. Cans, jars and boxes of food went into cardboard boxes brought to her by Jason and before he was done Dianne had finished filling three of them with nonperishables or food that could last for at least a couple months before it would go bad.

While Dianne was cleaning out the cabinets Jason scoured the closets, prioritizing undergarments, socks and spare pairs of shoes. These were stuffed into duffel bags and spare suitcases along with shirts, jackets and long pants before the bags were carried to the kitchen and placed next to the suitcases.

He opened his closet-sized gun safe next, pulling out three long rifles, two shotguns and half a dozen pistols that he and his wife were the most comfortable with shooting. These—along with several thousand rounds of ammunition—were carried directly into the truck where they were tucked beneath the tarp. Dianne helped Jason finish up by gathering any and all toiletries from the bathrooms before they stood together to look at the pile of goods in the kitchen.

"Think we have room for some nonessentials?" Jason mused as he looked at the pile.

"Definitely. Grab any books or CDs you have. If you've got a laptop computer you should bring that, too."

"I'm on it." Jason hurried into the living room while Dianne started loading boxes and bags into the back of the truck. It didn't take Jason long to gather several dozen books, a stack of CDs and his computer, all of which went into the rear cab of the truck. When he was done he helped Dianne load the rest of the boxes and bags into the truck before folding the tarp over everything and tying it tight.

When they were finished Dianne snapped her fingers and turned to Jason. "You said you had gas, right?"

"Yep." He nodded. "Back in the barn. I'm glad you remembered."

"We've got room for it. Let's stick it at the back away from everything else and get back to the house."

Jason and Dianne got back into the truck and she pulled it back around to the barn. They both quickly loaded the metal jerry cans into the back, making sure that they were completely sealed to prevent leakage. With the fuel, supplies from the barn and extras from the house loaded, Dianne nodded in approval. "I think we're set here, don't you?"

Jason walked alongside the back of the truck, running his hand along the tarp as he mentally went through his checklist. "Yep, I think we're good." He turned to look at the rest of the contents of the barn. "There's lots more useful stuff here but I think we got the most important things."

"Good. We can swing back by here again and make another trip but I don't want to count on that happening just in case something bad goes down."

Jason nodded. "Agreed."

"All right. Let's stop by what's left of the Carson's house before we head back and get all of this put away."

Chapter Fifteen

S omewhere in the Colorado Rockies

RICK TRAVELED SLOWLY through the storm, stopping frequently when the winds picked up and continuing on when they died down. He focused entirely on his journey, paying attention to the road and his driving as he worked his way down out of the mountains. Thoughts of his family and the plane crash intermingled and tugged at the corners of his mind but he pushed them away as he chose to hold tight to the numbness instead.

So focused was Rick on the road that he didn't notice the headlights on the road ahead of him until they were nearly upon him. A dozen vehicles were driving along on the left side of the road in a convoy formation until their lights fell upon his Humvee. As soon as the driver of the lead vehicle realized that the person coming towards them was in a military vehicle he radioed the drivers of the rest of the vehicles and slid his truck around to block the road.

Rick slammed on the brakes and blinked several times as he struggled to pull himself back to reality. He looked around frantically, wondering what was going on until he heard a voice over a loudspeaker.

"You in the vehicle! Douse your lights and put your hands on the steering wheel!"

Rick could see that the vehicles in front of him were painted with the same camouflage patterns as his Humvee and he realized with a sinking feeling in his stomach that he was dealing with the military again.

"Douse your lights now, driver! Or we'll fire upon you!" A burst of fire cracked and echoed across the mountainside as one of the soldiers standing in front of the truck fired several rounds into the air. Rick responded immediately by turning off the Humvee's headlights and rolling down his side window before putting his hands on the front windshield.

"They're out, dammit!" Rick stuck his head halfway out the window and shouted as loudly as he could. "The lights are out!"

"Turn off the vehicle, open the door and step out slowly! Keep your hands where we can see them!" Rick detected an undertone of panic in the man's voice and quickly obeyed, not wanting to be shot just because the soldier was feeling nervous. He cut off the engine and opened his door slowly before depositing his pistol on the passenger seat. Rick then slid out of the car and raised his hands above his head while slowly walking a few paces away from the vehicle.

Half a dozen soldiers ran forward, their rifles raised. Two of them grabbed Rick and forced him to the ground as they groped the entirety of his body. The rest of the soldiers scoured the Humvee, pointing out Rick's weapons and supplies to one another before running back to the truck to give a report. After a couple of minutes on the ground Rick was pulled to his feet and shoved unceremoniously towards the truck.

"Get moving!"

Finally able to catch his breath Rick looked around and shouted at the soldiers who were pushing him. "Hey! What are you doing?"

"Misappropriation of government property during a national emergency is a *very* serious charge." The answer came from in front of Rick, from a figure standing near the back of the truck. "Tie him up and throw him in the back. He can ride with us till we secure the crash site, then he'll go with us back to base."

"Yes, sir!" The answer came from the two soldiers dragging Rick. He struggled against them as he shouted at the figure who had spoken to him.

"Wait a second, I didn't misappropriate that thing! The commander of Nellis told me to take it!"

The officer stopped and turned, raising his eyebrow at Rick. "Nellis was overrun. Everything that was left there was stolen. You really expect me to believe that the commander specifically gave you one of their vehicles?" The officer walked back over to Rick and cocked his head to the side. "Just who do you think you are?"

"My name's Rick Waters. I'm not in the military. I was in Los Angeles when... *whatever* happened. I'm just trying to get home. I made it to Nellis and got out just as it was overrun." Rick took a deep breath as he stumbled over his words. "I'm just trying to get home."

The officer laughed and turned away and Rick tried one last attempt. "I know about the virus! I know about Damocles!"

Rick's mention of the virus made the officer stop again. He stalked back to Rick, his face dark as he pulled Rick away from the two soldiers and hissed at him. "How do you know about Damocles?"

"I told you I was at Nellis. The Colonel's name there was Leslie. He tried to get me to sign an agreement to be flown to Virginia as part of some emergency task force to stop whatever this thing is."

"And you didn't go?"

"I'm trying to get home to my family. So no. I didn't go. Though I realized too late that if I had I probably could have gotten to them a lot sooner."

"Or you would have died in a plane crash." The officer's tone was softer and he thought about what Rick said for several long seconds before nodding curtly. "Get in the back of the truck and stay put. We've got search and rescue to perform before we head back to base."

"You're doing a search and rescue on the plane crash out in the valley?" Rick shook his head. "I saw that crash happen. The plane nearly came down right on top of me."

"You saw the crash?" The officer's eyes lit up. "Where is it?"

"Bottom of the valley. Just keep going straight up the mountain and you'll find it by the smoke and the downed trees. It's no good, though."

The officer narrowed his eyes. "What do you mean?"

Rick shook his head. "I went down there to search for survivors. It's... there's nothing left." Rick felt his stomach turning and he tried to force the image of the bodies out of his mind. "Just bits and pieces."

The officer's shoulders visibly slumped. He turned around and cursed under his breath before waving at the soldiers. "Get him in the front of the truck. Don't bother tying him up. He's going to show us where the crash is."

"But I said—" Rick's protest was met by a raised hand from the officer.

"Doesn't matter. We're on a search and rescue mission. So that's what we're going to do." The officer walked away, muttering quietly enough that no one else could hear him. "Or one part of it at least."

⸺

RICK'S STATEMENT about the crashed plane and the status of the passengers on board turned out to be accurate. He guided the soldiers to the pull-off along the road and guided them down the path and into the woods. The soldiers fanned out in a search formation, searching through the woods with powerful spotlights as they tried to locate anyone who could have survived the crash. Rick hung back on the path, choosing to lean up against a tree and look at the sky rather than involve himself in the search yet again.

After a few hours the officer in charge called the search off and ordered everyone back to the vehicles. Rick trudged along with the soldiers, noticing that their palpable disappointment over the result of the search was mixed with another emotion: hopelessness. Barely anyone talked to each other and when they did it was in hushed tones and bleak expressions.

The ride back to Fort Carson was slow and plodding and Rick nearly fell asleep by the end of it. When they did arrive, though, the officer ordered him out of the truck. "Get out and follow me."

"Where are we going?" Rick looked around at the Fort in the dim rays of the early sun.

"You're going to get a few hours sleep before you go see the general up at the base."

"Base?" Rick raised a quizzical eyebrow. "I thought we were at the base."

"No, you get to go up there." The officer pointed at the nearby mountain. "The generals are all holed up there. We got word on the radio on the way back that one of them wants to talk to you. Apparently your story checks out. Sort of." The officer shrugged and motioned for Rick to follow him. "Not that it'll do much good anyway. The world's gone to hell and there's no coming back from that."

"What do you mean?"

The officer shook his head. "If you think you've seen some shit in the last couple of weeks... well. You don't know the half of it."

Chapter Sixteen

The Water's Homestead
     Outside Ellisville, VA

"WHO IS THAT?" Dianne slammed on the brakes and Jason was relieved they weren't traveling more than a few miles per hour. He looked out the side window to see a dark green SUV parked near the charred remains of the Carson's home.

"That is not their car."

"No it's not. It sure as hell is not." Dianne veered off the road into the field opposite the Carson's house, heading for a rotten old half-collapsed barn sitting near a grove of trees.

"What are you doing?" Jason looked at Dianne before turning back to try and see the SUV again.

"Getting us out of sight so we can go see what's going on."

"Sweet mother of mercy…" Jason grabbed the rifle and two full mags that he had quickly loaded back at his house and hopped out of the truck. Dianne was already at the edge of the road, crouched down as she ran across and knelt down in the tall grass at the edge of the Carson's property.

Jason joined her a moment later, fumbling with the rubber cover on his red dot optic. "What is it you're planning on doing here?" Jason whispered in Dianne's ear. She waved him off, cocking her head to listen to the voices she could hear down near the house.

"Come on. Let's get closer and see what they're doing." Dianne crept through the grass, heading for a line of trees that followed the Carson's driveway. She and Jason used the trees as cover as they moved toward the house before they finally stopped a few dozen feet away.

The driver's side front and back doors of the SUV were open as was the trunk. One person was sitting in the passenger's seat though Dianne couldn't make out any details about them. The voices were coming from behind the remains of the Carson's house, near the barn, and Dianne listened intently as they slowly came back towards the SUV.

"…all your fault we have to deal with this, asshole."

"If you say that one more time I swear I'll put another hole in your head!"

"Not like he'll notice it."

"Ha! Nice one."

Three men and two women walked slowly around the edge of the house, all dressed in loose-fitting pants and light jackets. Dianne didn't recognize the women and the three men had hoodies pulled over their heads making them impossible to identify. The two women and one of the men carried pistols while the other two men had AR-style rifles slung casually on their shoulders. The figure in the SUV turned out to be a large man with a deep voice. He stepped out of the vehicle upon seeing the figures and began speaking with a confident tone that indicated he was the leader of the group.

"Anything?" The man from the car spoke, but it was hard to tell precisely who of the rest of the group was replying to him.

"Not a flipping thing."

"They told us something was here." The large man spoke again.

"Yeah well maybe they lied."

"Hmph." The large man grunted and shook his head. "Not possible that she could have lied to him. No, there's something here. If it's not in the barn then it's in the house. It would have made it through the fire. That's what they said."

"Maybe if Tim here hadn't burned the place to the—"

"I told you to shut up!" The one called 'Tim' raised his rifle and threatened the man holding the other rifle. "Do you *want* another hole in your head?"

"Gentlemen." The deep-voiced man raised his hands and the rest of the group turned to look at him. "Let's not assign blame for who fucked up and burned this place down. The old bitch said that her safe is here so we're going to keep looking till we find it."

The man with the pistol shook his hand. "We scoured the barn. If it's here then it's in the house and we need tools to get this debris moved."

The large man remained quiet for a few moments before waving his hand. "Fine. Load up. We'll come back when we have time to let you idiots dig around. We need to finish our rounds and get back to the boss before it gets too much later. Maybe he can talk the old bat into giving up some more specifics about her little stash in the house. Ha!"

Two of the men threw back their hoodies as they walked to the SUV and Dianne gave Jason a wide-eyed look. The group crammed themselves into the SUV, talking quietly about something neither Dianne nor Jason could hear. The vehicle's frame sagged low to the ground under the weight of so many people and it slowly turned around in the drive before heading back out to the road. Dianne and Jason pressed their bodies to the ground, keeping out of sight as the vehicle headed down the driveway. It paused at the end of the road before turning off and heading away from Ellisville and farther out into the country.

Dianne let out a rush of air, her spinning head making her realize that she had been holding her breath for the last few minutes. She looked at Jason as they slowly stood up, not wanting to run out to the road until they were sure the vehicle was gone.

"Who were they?" Jason leaned around the tree, watching as the back of the SUV vanished behind a row of trees.

"Two of them I recognize. They tried to steal the truck back when this all started." Dianne started walking slowly down towards the road, keeping her eyes peeled. She stopped at the edge of the road, watching the trail of dust from the SUV disappear from sight. "I think we know who burned down the Carson's house."

Jason stroked his beard as he stood next to Dianne. "What do you want to do now?"

Dianne nodded in the direction of the collapsed barn and the truck hidden behind it. "Let's get these supplies home. We have a lot to figure out."

Chapter Seventeen

F̲our days after the Event
       Cheyenne Mountain, Colorado

DR. MICHAEL EVANS steps onto the back of the small electric vehicle. He adjusts his satchel on his shoulder as he looks up at the ceiling of the mile-long tunnel that leads from the outside of the mountain into its very heart. With Dr. Evans being the last person who can fit on the vehicle it takes off abruptly, nearly throwing him off. He sits down in his seat and adjusts his satchel on his lap. He looks to his left at the two people sitting next to him, both of whom are wearing suits that look like they've been through hell.

The tunnel is well-lit and there is a constant flow of air blowing through it. A small nuclear reactor buried deep beneath the underground complex keeps the lights on and the exhaust fans running as well as providing enough excess electricity to run half of the nearby military base. Built in in the 1960's, the Cheyenne Mountain Complex took five years to complete—at least the portion known to the public. The other, secret portions of the complex took an additional seven years to complete though some construction never really stopped.

It takes several minutes for the electric vehicle to pass through the tunnel as it has to stop periodically to make room for other, more urgent transports. Several trucks zoom by, turning off into side tunnels and small parking areas as they load and unload supplies and personnel. The chaos in the underground tunnel is strangely ordered and though Dr. Evans feels overwhelmed by what is going on he never feels like it's out of control.

"Dr. Evans?" A man in an Air Force uniform approaches Dr. Evans, extending his hand.

"Yes?" Dr. Evans realizes that the vehicle has come to a stop and steps off, accepting the handshake.

"I'm Lieutenant Shulman. Would you follow me? We have a room prepared for you."

"A room?" Dr. Evans looks up at the massive metal structure standing in front of him that is built into the tunnel. The three-story metal building is the original structure that was part of the first five years of construction. While it appears from some angles to be built directly into the rock, none of the structure actually touches the mountain directly. Thousand-pound solid steel springs line the exterior of the structure, keeping it safe in case of an earthquake or a nuclear strike.

"Yes. Right this way, please." Lieutenant Shulman hurries towards the building before turning abruptly and heading down a long, sloping tunnel farther into the earth. "You'll have a private room and we're working on getting your belongings that were pulled from the crash back to you. That may take some time but you're marked as a priority asset."

"Priority asset?" Dr. Evans shakes his head. "I'm sorry... I don't understand what's going on. I was in Air Force One with the President before we crashed, then we were pulled from the wreckage and flown here. I haven't been briefed or anything."

"Continuity of government, Dr. Evans. The President and all other surviving high-ranking members of the United States government have been evacuated to secure locations. You were marked as a high priority asset due to your traveling with the President which is why you were brought here."

Dr. Evans has been in a fog of sorts ever since the crash a day prior. His mind has been clouded and his thoughts impaired due to shock from the crash and exhaustion from working for days prior. Hardly anyone has spoken to him during his transit from the crash to the Cheyenne Mountain Complex as his physical well-being meant he was tagged as low priority in terms of needing medical attention.

As he speaks to Lieutenant Shulman, though, he starts to remember details about his work. His research and study of the Damocles virus had progressed to advanced stages before Air Force One crashed and he wonders in the back of his head whether it was his work that led to the destruction of the plane.

'Impossible.' Dr. Evans thinks to himself as he shakes his head. 'It's a coincidence. But a damned scary one.'

As Dr. Evans thinks more about Damocles and his work while walking with Lieutenant Shulman he speaks to the Air Force officer. "Lieutenant? While I was on the plane I was working on some research into the cause of all this mess. I don't suppose my laptop or research notes survived the crash, did they?"

"I'm afraid I don't know, sir. Transport of the gear recovered from the crash has been held up due to issues at the base. As soon as they're able to offload everything and bring it up, though, I'll personally take care of searching for your things for you." Lieutenant pulls a small notebook from his breast pocket and uncaps a pen. "You say it was a laptop and research notes?"

Dr. Evans holds up his leather satchel. "Yes, they would have been in a case like this one, except larger."

Lieutenant Shulman looks at Dr. Evans' bag and nods. "As soon as the gear arrives I'll look through it."

"Thank you. It's extremely important. I was working on ways to combat the cause of this destruction and I believe I was on the verge of some important revelations, so—"

Lieutenant Shulman interrupts Dr. Evans as he stops and opens a large metal door. "Of course, sir. I'll do everything I can. In the meantime your room is through here, number eighty three. You'll find a common room down the hall. Your room has a shower inside and you can pick up food and toiletries from the supply room down the opposite hall. We'll announce meals at regular intervals but if you want to make something yourself we have MREs and other packaged food in the kitchen just off the common room." The Lieutenant motions for Dr. Evans to step through into the building. "If you'll excuse me, sir, I need to get back."

"Oh. Right. Of course." Dr. Evans steps up into the building and the door slowly closes behind him. He walks down the hall and finds his room after a few minutes of searching. The door opens to reveal a simple bed built into the wall, a small closet with a few shirts and a pair of pants that appear too large for him to wear and a shower that looks frighteningly narrow. A tiny desk sits behind the door with a small metal chair. He sighs wearily at the small accommodations before turning around to head out and explore more of the building.

"Hi there!" A young woman sits on a grey couch at the back of the common room when Dr. Evans walks in. She stands up and waves at him before walking over to him and shaking his hand. "Thank God. I thought I was alone in here!"

"You haven't seen anyone else?"

The woman shakes her head, her short ponytail bouncing back and forth. "Nope. Nobody else is living here yet. I've seen others for meals and stuff but that's all."

"Well, it's a pleasure to meet you." Dr. Evans only had to half-force a smile as the woman's bright personality had already caused the other half to form on his face. "I'm Dr. Michael Evans. And you are?"

"Nice to meet you, Dr. Evans! I'm Jane. Jane Leverett."

Author's Notes

August 20, 2017

We are now FIVE books in to this episodic roller coaster of an adventure and I can't thank you enough for being here. These last few months have been absolutely INCREDIBLE as my books have taken hold on Amazon and sold like gangbusters. I'm in awe of how many people are reading No Sanctuary and Surviving the Fall each and every day and I can't thank you all enough.

In case you're wondering… yes. The Jane at the end of this book is the same Jane that Rick helped through Las Vegas. Say WHAT??? Yep. She's back. And, what's even better is that she's going to be able to help Rick with a pretty big task coming up here soon. When I came up with this portion of the story I was so elated that I was able to tie her back into the story and I'm really looking forward to sharing it!

For my two current post-apocalyptic series (No Sanctuary and Surviving the Fall) I wanted to ground them in a healthy dose of reality which is why they have general plots that I more or less ripped from the headlines. In Surviving the Fall we learned that a secret government computer virus was inadvertently unleashed on the world and while that may have sounded outlandish a few years ago I wouldn't be surprised if something very close to Damocles exists (or is in the works) right now.

When I write about real-world locations I try to keep things relatively realistic, too. Google Maps and Street View help a *lot* with this for regions I've never visited but there are times when some creative liberties must be taken. A perfect example of this is the route Rick takes from Grand Junction to NORAD which is just outside Colorado Springs.

I based a lot of the imagery for those sections on a trip I took with my father to Wolf Creek when I was much, much younger than I am now. It's been a long time but the views of the Rockies on that trip have been burned into my memory. Two stand out in particular. The first is the view of the Rockies across Kansas. It was a particularly clear day when we were driving there and seeing the Rockies off in the distance was a magical experience. They're so well-defined against the flat ground and the blue sky that you'd think they're not real.

The second was when we were deep in the mountains, driving along narrow roads. There were several times where sheer drop-offs were inches away from the wheels of the car or when a high cliff rose up on the other side. Snow covered every horizontal surface and we even had a bit of a storm blow in near the end of the drive that nearly required putting chains on the car.

I realize that the geography of Rick's drive from Grand Junction to Colorado Springs doesn't really fit with the real-world roads that are on the map right now. When I looked at the street view of the roads nothing was interesting enough for me so I made an executive decision to suspend a bit of reality instead. :) I think that despite the inaccuracies the spirit of the region was kept intact and the overall story was helped enormously by the change.

Something else I did was take some liberties with the interior of the NORAD—The Cheyenne Mountain Complex—facility. After searching for photos of the interior of the facility I was surprised to find a couple of sets though they didn't give me much to go on. I drew on movies, TV shows and my imagination to come up with an idea for what a modern or near-future NORAD complex could look like if there had been a bunch of secretive construction going on.

As far as I'm aware there isn't a hidden bunker in the Seven Devils Mountains. I needed a west coast location to evacuate the President to, though, and after searching around through satellite imagery for a while (I *love* these random parts of being an author!) I figured that the Seven Devils would make for a neat location both because of their name and they appear to be relatively out of the way. It probably wouldn't work in real life but hey, this is fiction!

If you enjoyed this episode of Surviving the Fall or if you *didn't* like something—I'd love to hear about it. You can drop me an email or send me a message or leave a comment on Facebook. You can also sign up for my newsletter where I announce new book releases and other cool stuff a few times a month.

Answering emails and messages from my readers is the highlight of my day and every single time I get an email from someone saying how much they enjoyed reading a story it makes that day so much brighter and better.

Thank you so very much for reading my books. Seriously, thank you from the bottom of my heart. I put an enormous amount of effort into the writing and all of the related processes and there's nothing better than knowing that so many people are enjoying my stories.

All the best,
Mike

Book 6 - The Long Road

Preface

Last time, on Surviving the Fall . . .

Rick Waters, having successfully survived his journey through Utah, found himself deep in the Rocky Mountains. After struggling through storms and seeing the terror and majesty of nature he was nearly killed by a crashing cargo plane as it plummeted into the side of a mountain. He runs to the crash site and searches for survivors but finds nothing but death and destruction instead. As he wearily prepares to continue onward he is taken into custody by the military out of the nearby Cheyenne Mountain Complex where he is about to run into someone he thought he would never see again.

Meanwhile, in Virginia, Dianne Waters and her three children continue to strengthen their homestead after being alerted to the existence of other nefarious people in the area by the man Dianne had to kill. One day, as they are working, Dianne nearly kills—and is nearly killed—in a brief gunfight with a person she initially thought was another would-be robber but instead turned out to be her neighbors, Jason and Sarah Statler. After Jason and Dianne go to the Statler's house to procure more supplies they see a large vehicle full of people at the Carson's burned out house and learn that Mrs. Carson is being held captive.

And now, Surviving the Fall Episode 6.

Chapter One

C heyenne Mountain Complex
    Outside Colorado Springs, CO

ALTHOUGH IT WAS dark when the convoy in which Rick was riding pulled in to Fort Carson, there was still power to much of the base. Lights on and around the runway showed planes and helicopters parked out of their normal positions. Several of the hangars were open and had people and vehicles going back and forth between the aircraft. Two of the helicopters— older models that looked like they had flown in straight out of Vietnam— had their rotors spinning and their lights were on. The rest of the aircraft that Rick could see, however, looked like they were non-functional.

He rode from the base to the Cheyenne complex in the back of an armored transport vehicle along with several other individuals. A few of them were soldiers but others were in suits that looked like they had been worn without being taken off for the last week or three. No one inside the vehicle spoke to each other except for the driver who had a brief conversation with two guards stationed outside the entrance to the Cheyenne complex.

The attitude of the people inside the vehicle and those Rick had seen on the base was the thing that stood out the most to him. In Las Vegas and Nellis he had gotten a sense from the survivor and military populations that they were scared and desperate but they still had hope. The attitude from everyone he had met since walking back to the road from the C-130 crash was of utter despair. There was no sense of hope left in anyone's faces or voices and they all kept to themselves, staring at the floor of the vehicle in silence. Hope was no longer present in the minds of most.

"ID." The second guard sounded much like the first, asking the driver of the armored vehicle for his identification in a rote, robotic tone. The driver displayed his card and the guard glanced through the small window at the passengers in the back. "More of 'em, eh? Any of these from the crash?"

The driver shook his head. "No survivors."

"Shit. Third one in the last day. What the hell's going on? An escalation?"

The driver shrugged. "That's way above my pay grade."

The guard nodded and sighed. "Yeah, same. Good luck. Drive safe."

The driver nodded and put the vehicle back into gear, revving the diesel engine. The armored transport continued up the winding road towards the base of Cheyenne Mountain. While the rest of the passengers in the transport stayed still in their seats Rick leaned forward, looking past the others to watch out the front window. The transport headed down the mile-long tunnel quickly, stopping only a few times to pull to the side and let other vehicles pass. When they reached the end where the tunnel branched off, the transport stopped and the back door slowly opened.

Rick turned to see a pair of soldiers at the back of the transport. Each of them carried assault rifles and flashlights. The pair ran their flashlights over the faces of each person in the transport before stopping on one in particular.

"Rick Waters?"

Rick felt his stomach churn and he wondered if the soldiers could hear his gulp. He raised his hand tentatively and gave the soldiers a half-smile. "That's me…"

"Come with us please, sir." One of the soldiers tucked away a small scrap of paper into his pocket and waved at Rick to step forward.

Rick looked around at his fellow passengers with wide eyes as he rose from his seat and made his way out of the vehicle. The soldiers pointed at a massive doorway beyond the vehicle and one of them touched his back, prompting him to move. "This way, sir." Though the soldiers stuck close to Rick he was somewhat relieved to find that they weren't making any overt moves to detain him. He knew that there was no way he could escape but not being put into handcuffs or having them physically restrain him made the situation slightly more bearable.

The first door into the labyrinth beyond weighed twenty-five tons and looked to be a good three feet thick based on Rick's quick estimation as he walked past. The door was only ajar enough for two people walking side by side to squeeze through. While the door could be opened and closed electronically there were several soldiers standing nearby ready to seal it manually if needed.

"Why are you guys leaving the door open?" Rick looked at one of the soldiers escorting him after they passed through the door and entered the facility proper.

"Orders." The answer was abrupt and left Rick with a confused expression.

Rick and the soldiers pressed on, winding their way through the main facility and up three levels until the soldier stopped outside a wooden door that looked oddly out of place in the beige metal hall.

"In here, sir. The general's ready to see you now."

"Who is this? I don't remember making an appointment." Rick's attempt at a joke fell flat as the soldiers didn't do so much as blink as one of them replied.

"General Black, United States Army. He's in temporary command."

"Temporary?" Before Rick could ask the soldier to clarify there was a voice from beyond the door.

"Is that him?" The question was as brusque as the voice was gravely.

"Yes, sir!" One of the soldiers straightened his back slightly as the other responded.

"Well get him in here now, dammit!"

Rick gave one final look at the soldiers before pushing open the door and entering the office beyond. The soldiers pulled the door closed behind him and he found himself in a surprisingly small office, half of which was taken up by old cardboard boxes filled with reams of paper. The other half was devoted to a tiny L-shaped desk, a couple of chairs that looked like they had fallen through a time machine from the 40's and a man the size of a bear wearing a uniform that looked like it could pop at any moment.

"General?" Rick took a half-step forward, bumping his foot on a chair and almost tripping in the process. He stuck out his hand and the General nodded at him, ignoring his attempt at a handshake.

"Correct. General Black. Sit down, Mr. Waters. I'll get straight to the point." The general continued to talk before Rick could make an attempt to sit down in one of the chairs. "I was informed that you were heading in this direction. Glad to see we could catch you before you got past."

Rick tilted his head, confused by what the general was saying. "Am I… in trouble for something? The commander at Nellis gave me the Humvee and—"

"Who would that be?" The general picked up a pen and held the tip to a piece of paper.

Rick squinted, trying to remember the man's name. "It was Leslie, I believe. Yeah, that was it. Colonel Leslie."

"Hm." General Black scribbled down the name and placed his pen back on his desk. "So why is it you didn't head east to Mount Weather when you had a chance?"

"How did you know about that?"

"We do actually talk to each other, Mr. Waters." The general spoke in a condescending tone and Rick suddenly felt like he was back in his father's office undergoing a combination lecture and interrogation. "Would you care to answer the question?"

Rick shrugged. "I didn't feel like going. My family's more important to me than trying to be a hero so I decided not to go. Seeing that C-130 go down in the mountains makes me glad I didn't, though."

General Black frowned again. "That was an unfortunate oversight on the part of the flight crew. And, for what it's worth, you're much better off for not having gone to Mount Weather." He sighed and shuffled a few papers before interlacing his fingers and placing them on the desk in front of him. "Mr. Waters. You've come here in a military vehicle from a base that was overrun. You were in the vicinity of a crashed aircraft. We know nothing of your background or history and yet here you sit in the heart of a military base. Explain to me why I shouldn't kick you out on your ass and hope a nuke drops on top of you to spare me the trouble of wasting a bullet."

Rick's stomach sank and his heartrate skyrocketed as he realized that the general was being very serious. He blinked several times and cleared his throat as he thought about the ridiculous question, trying to come up with a satisfactory answer. Finally he decided on one that he hoped the general wouldn't be expecting. "Actually, I'd prefer to be kicked out. Just give me my vehicle and supplies and I'll be on my way."

General Black's face was frozen and he sat still, not sure what to do. Finally, after a few seconds, he opened his mouth only to shut it again before finally finding the words to speak. "I... what?"

"Kick me out on my ass, General." Rick resisted the urge to sound smug though he knew he had the man sitting across the desk on the ropes. "I have a very long trip ahead of me and I'd prefer to continue over arguing or being interrogated."

The general shook his head and ran his tongue over his gums as he looked down at the paperwork on his desk. "That, uh... no. Impossible." He held up a piece of paper and Rick squinted at it.

"What's this?"

"Orders. You're tagged as a 'Class A' asset. You and all the other civvies who managed to wrangle their way onto our transports."

"I... don't follow."

General Black leaned forward, his face solemn and his tone as serious as a heart attack. "Civilian search and rescue attempts have been largely suspended. We're in full-on damage control mode at this point. The only reason the Russians haven't nuked us to hell and back is because they probably can't even point their damned missiles in our direction due to Damocles."

"What on earth does that have to do with me and whether I can travel or not?"

"You were approved for transport to Mount Weather and you were given a military vehicle. You're now officially required to be held in a secure facility until such time as the situation can be brought under control." The general kept glancing down at the paper as he recited a passage from it. "The period of this detention is indeterminate but is up to the discretion of the superior officer." He looked up from the paper. "That's me."

"So you're going to hold me?" Rick rolled his eyes and slumped back in his chair. "Great. I knew I should have gone to Denver instead."

"I sincerely doubt you would want to be in Denver right now. The place makes hell look like a resort."

Rick shook his head. "Just let me go. I'll leave now and I won't bother you or anyone else. I'm just trying to get home to my family."

"These orders come down from the top, Rick. Part of some of the extreme emergency measures that were devised back in the 60's. If you were a Class B or C then I'd consider it. But you were tagged for the think tank at Mount Weather. You're Class A whether you like it or not." General Black pressed a button on his desk and the door opened a few seconds later to reveal a pair of MPs standing outside.

General Black motioned to the MPs and one of them stepped inside to stand next to Rick. "You'll be taken to your room down below. Meals will be delivered and you'll have full use of our library. Once I figure out what to do with you then we'll go from there."

The MP reached for Rick's arm and Rick pulled away as he leaned forward to try and continue the conversation. "This is bullshit, General! I'm a United States citizen! I have rights, guaranteed to me under the—"

"Under the what, Mr. Waters?" The general stood up, his nostrils flaring as he glared at Rick. "Under the constitution? Under a piece of paper that formed the basis for a country and a civilization? There is no more country or civilization, Mr. Waters. There is death and destruction and if we don't secure every able body and—more importantly—every able-bodied *mind* available then we will fall into the abyss and never climb out." The general nodded at the MP. "Take him to his room. Make sure he has food and what-ever else he needs. Rick struggled as the MPs took him out of the general's office, still protesting even after the door was shut in his face.

Chapter Two

The Water's Homestead
Outside Ellisville, VA

"MOM! We were starting to get worried!" Mark ran out the front door as Dianne and Jason pulled into the driveway. He carried his rifle on his shoulder and glanced around as he headed across the porch and drive to the truck.

"Hey, Mark." Dianne's smile was forced though she was fairly certain Mark wasn't picking up on it. "Everything go okay here?"

Mark nodded. "Yep! We tried calling you on the radio but you didn't answer."

"Oh, crap. The radio!" Dianne got out of the truck and fished around in the back, finally finding the device. "Yep, looks like I forgot to turn it on."

"Dianne?" The front door opened and Sarah Statler came walking out with Jacob and Josie in tow. "Jason! What on earth are you doing not answering the radio like that?"

Mark leaned close to his mother and whispered in her ear as Sarah continued to fuss at Jason. "Mrs. Statler's been kind of on edge ever since she tried to call you guys on the radio."

Dianne covered a slight grin with her hand as she coughed loudly to interrupt Jason and Sarah's argument. "Hey, we've got a lot of stuff in here. How about you kids get started moving it inside? Leave the fuel in the back of the truck but get everything else in the house, okay?"

Mark gave Dianne a curious look but shrugged and nodded. "Will do."

He, Jacob and Josie got to work while Dianne steered Jason and Sarah over to the side of the house where they could talk in relative privacy.

"You still should have remembered to turn it on!" Sarah was still talking about the radio when Dianne turned to her.

"Sarah, it was my fault, okay? Besides, we have much bigger problems than forgetting to turn on a radio." Sarah was about to say something else when she finally caught the undercurrent in Dianne's tone and saw her serious expression.

"What?" Sarah looked between Jason and Dianne. "What happened?"

"After we got the supplies we went over to the Carson's place. We saw a car there so we parked across the road behind the old barn at the end of your property and snuck back across."

"A car at the Carson's? Are they there?"

Jason shook his head. "I'm afraid not. Whoever was in that car was…"

Jason trailed off and Dianne finished his sentence. "Bad. Very, very bad. They were talking about looting the house, looting other people's houses and Tina, too."

"They were talking about Tina? Tina Carson?" Sarah's eyes grew wide. "Is she okay?"

Jason and Dianne looked at each other and Dianne cleared her throat. "She uh… I think she's alive. But I think they have her."

"They kidnapped her?" Sarah's face was a mask of horror and Dianne motioned for her to quiet down.

"That's what it sounded like. I think the group was trying to get to a safe or some other valuables in the house but they couldn't find anything."

"What about Dave? Did they mention him?"

Dianne shook her head slowly. "Nothing. They didn't stay at the house long, though. We were lucky to miss them when they arrived."

"I don't mean to speak out of turn here, Dianne." Jason shifted back and forth on his feet as he spoke. "But I think the biggest issue right now is making sure that the house and everyone in it is kept safe from these people. Especially… well. You know." Jason was watching Mark and Jacob carry suitcases into the house. "Once we're certain everything here is secure then we can try to find these people."

"Agreed. I'm not sure how these people don't know where we are already, though. We've burned enough fires and gone out a few times. You'd think we would have run into them by now." Dianne snorted. "Though I've run into two of them before."

"You have?" Jason raised an eyebrow and Dianne nodded.

"Mhm. Back when all this started I went to the grocery store to get some staples. They were trying to break into the truck when I got back. I ran them off and figured that was the last I had seen of them. I guess they fell in with this group."

"Whoever they are there's more than just the ones we saw." Jason scratched his head. "I wonder where they're holing up. We went through quite a few back roads out to the east when we were driving in. That sort of makes me think they're somewhere out between Ellisville and Blacksburg. Unless you've been out that far recently, that is."

"Nope." Dianne shook her head. "We've mostly kept to ourselves here. We were going to head out but the roads were blocked enough that I didn't want to risk it."

"What are you two going on about?" Sarah interjected herself back into the conversation. "Tina's being held by a group of vagabonds, Dave's missing and you two are talking about blocked roads and Blacksburg?"

"Sarah, we have to figure out what to do here."

"Damn right you do, Jason! You need to figure out how to get Tina out and see if you can find Dave, too!"

Dianne cocked her head. "That's… exactly what we're doing. First we have to figure out where they're holed up, though. They have to have a base close by if they're driving around on what I assume is a regular basis."

"Oh." Sarah nodded. "Good. That's… good. Sorry."

Dianne smiled and chuckled. "Did you think we wouldn't go after one of our friends?"

"Well. I mean, you were talking about securing the house and then looking for the people and I figured you were just talking about avoiding them or something." Sarah threw her hands up in the air and gave an exasperated sigh. "Sorry. Ignore me. Carry on."

Jason laughed and held out his arms, wrapping them around his wife and giving her a hug. "We're not going to leave Tina—or Dave, if he's still out there—in the hands of those people if we can help it."

"We do need to finish securing everything here. Then I think we can go out scouting for them." Dianne looked at Jason. "Agreed?"

He gave a definitive nod. "Agreed."

Chapter Three

M ount Weather, Virginia

THE VICE PRESIDENT of the United States is exhausted. He's been up for over thirty hours straight talking to politicians, military leaders and a variety of civilians who've flown in from across the country.

The politicians were the first to be dismissed by the Vice President. Relegated to a lower floor in the Mount Weather complex their initial cries of unity quickly dissolve into partisan bickering. Arguments fly back and forth over which bill was responsible for the creation of Damocles, whose districts have been worst hit, how long the recovery efforts will take and what the disaster will do to their poll numbers.

The military leaders have been both less and more helpful than he expected. They have continually approached him with solutions to a variety of problems facing the country, though many of them rely on overwhelming firepower instead than finesse. The threat of Damocles is global and the military fears that foreign countries will soon target the United States with any functional weaponry as a retaliation for developing Damocles and allowing it to escape out into the wild.

The civilians, whom the Vice President initially thought would be helpful, have failed to come up with any solutions that are workable. Each of their plans has failed in the conceptual or practical phases and resulted in yet another device becoming infected or more wasted hours attacking Damocles in a way in which it can't be affected.

With no solutions to the problem on the horizon the Vice President retreats to the Presidential Suite, located in a far corner of the bunker. He sits down on the edge of the bed and loosens his necktie, takes off his jacket and flops down on the bed.

He closes his eyes, wishing for the thousandth time since he last slept that the President would show up somewhere. If the President is, indeed, alive then there has been no communication to Mount Weather of that fact. The personnel in the complex have deferred to the Vice President for all decisions given that he is the ranking member of government. Despite the pressure from both political parties he refuses to officially assume the Presidency until another day or two passes.

"Sir! Sir, wake up!"

The Vice President opens his eyes and groans. He realizes that he fell asleep some time ago, though he doesn't know how long he's been out. As his eyes focus on the figures standing around the bed he realizes that they are comprised of military personnel and staff from the bunker.

"What? What's going on?" He runs his tongue on the roof of his mouth as he tries to rid it of the awful taste inside.

"Something's wrong with the bunker, sir. We need you to come with us right now."

The Vice President sits up on the bed and processes the statement for a few seconds before replying. "What's going on with the bunker? Be specific."

Someone high up in the Navy steps forward into the Vice President's line of sight. "Sir, we believe that one of the civilians was trying an experiment on a Damocles-infected system. The infection jumped from the infected device to the bunker's network."

The fog that had settled over the Vice President's brain immediately lifts. "They did what? What's that mean for us?"

"Technicians are already at work isolating the infected equipment but it may be too late."

"Too late?"

The lights flicker as the Vice President speaks. A few seconds later they go out and the suite is plunged into darkness. The military brass remain calm though a few staffers at the edges of the room make muffled groans and cries as they feel around, trying to keep from being overwhelmed by the claustrophobic nightmare they have been plunged into.

"Who's got a light?" Someone calls out.

"Here, I have a penlight." Another answers.

A few moments later, after half a dozen flashlights have been pulled from the pockets of the most prepared, the Vice President leads the group out of the suite and down the hall to the main command room of the bunker. When he arrives, though, he wonders if he made a wrong turn somewhere along the way.

"Hello?" The Vice President shouts into the dark room, its cavernous volume too large for the penlights to pierce its depths. A chorus of replies follow and a few small flashlights slowly emerge as clusters of people group up together. "Do we not have any emergency lights?"

"Flint said she was going to start the backup generator." The reply comes from somewhere else in the room. "It should be on any minute."

The minutes tick by slowly until the distant sound of a throaty diesel engine comes to life. The lights flicker to life a moment later, revealing the throngs of people who have gathered together in the room. As their voices surge the Vice President raises his hands and shouts above the din.

"*Everyone, quiet down! We don't know what happened yet but with the generators on we'll be just fine. I need everyone to return to your assigned rooms or jobs while we sort this out. I'll have a further announcement on the situation shortly. Thank you!*" Though the Vice President's short statement sounds hopeful, half an hour later he finds himself facing a dearth of hope.

"*Damocles is in the entirety of the systems here? Everything?*" He closes his eyes and sighs.

"*I'm afraid so, sir.*" A man with a scruffy beard, glasses and a stained dress shirt sits in front of the Vice President. "*The only reason the backup generator is working is because it's old enough to not have computer controls on it. Our HVAC system is offline, the reactor automatically shut down—thank goodness—and we have zero comms or computer systems online.*"

"*Can we open the bunker doors at least?*"

"*We can do that, yes.*"

"*What about water?*"

"*The pumps were all computer-controlled. There is a backup pump but it's tied to the backup generator and the capacity is minimal. We'll have drinking water but that's about it.*"

"*Well.*" The Vice President shakes his head, overwhelmed by frustration and helplessness. "*So much for the think tank.*"

Chapter Four

Cheyenne Mountain Complex
    Outside Colorado Springs, CO

RICK COULDN'T SLEEP.

According to the simple wall clock in his room, it had been hours since he had been deep underground and placed into a room the size of a large walk-in closet. The door had been locked from the outside when the MPs left and try as he might Rick hadn't been able to get it to budge.

He passed the hours through a variety of monotonous activities. First on the list had been looking for any alternate ways out. The only one he was able to find was an air vent that a small child would have had difficulties crawling through.

With no way to get out Rick turned his attention to going through his bag that the MPs dropped off shortly after delivering him to his room. There were some changes of clothing, a couple of MREs, a flashlight and a few empty shell casings but the majority of what he had stored in the Humvee had been thrown out or confiscated. Rick was grateful for the extra changes of clothes that someone had kindly stuffed into the bag and he almost felt bad for how good he felt over having a hot shower for the first time in weeks.

Once he was clean and changed Rick felt drowsy but no matter how hard he tried to go to sleep he just wasn't able to do so. The bed was hard, the pillow thin and the sheets on the narrow bed were coarse but Rick had slept in so many uncomfortable positions and locations lately that those things didn't bother him in the slightest.

With sleep eluding him and the reasoning behind it a mystery as well, Rick got up and did the only thing left to him: pacing. Back and forth he went, taking a few steps forward before stopping, turning around and pacing back the other way.

Rick had been pacing for close to an hour when some noises from the hallway attracted his attention. The window to his room was small but there was a thick mesh screen just beneath it that enabled him to hear the approach of anyone outside. After the MPs deposited him and his bag in the room he hadn't heard anything else—until a person shouted.

"Get your hands *off* me!" The voice was a woman's, full of indignation and a level of irritation that made Rick smile.

Jeez, he thought, *I wouldn't want to be on the receiving end of that.* Rick strained at the window, looking down both sides of the hall until he finally caught a glimpse of the source of the ongoing noise. A woman with shoulder-length brown hair and wearing jeans and a T-shirt was standing with her back to his room. Two MPs—not those who had brought him to his cell—were in front of her. A thin man who was balding in the back stood next to the woman, though based on his body language he was trying to blend in with the background more than he was trying to engage in the argument.

"Miss." The word came from one of the MPs and Rick swore he could feel the woman tensing up. "We can't let you in to see him."

"What part of *your commanding officer said we could* don't you understand?"

"Ma'am," said the other MP, "we'd need to speak with him directly before—"

"How about a letter from him, signed and dated today?" the woman reached into her back pocket and withdrew a piece of paper. She unfolded it and held it up in front of the MPs. The one who had spoken first took the paper and held it, examining it closely before letting out a deflated sigh.

"I guess... this is signed by the general. So I guess you can see him."

"And he's to be let out."

The MP shook his head. "He's to be released to the personal recognizance of Dr. Evans." The MP looked at the thin man standing next to the woman. "You're okay with this, Dr. Evans?"

"Oh yes." The man nodded vigorously. "Quite."

The first MP passed the paper to the second and shrugged. "Everything checks out, then. He's at the end of the hall. Just keep an eye on him, the both of you. If anything happens the general's going to have our asses for dinner and yours for dessert."

The MPs turned around and walked off, leaving the woman and the thin man standing in the hall next to each other. They held a brief whispered conversation before turning to look in the direction of Rick's room. Rick didn't recognize the man heading towards him but the face of the woman was extremely familiar. It took Rick a few seconds to place it but once he did his eyes widened and his mouth dropped open in shock.

"Jane?!"

After not having seen Rick for well over a week, Jane grinned wildly at the sight of his face through the small window. She ran to the door and threw open the bolt holding it shut. Rick tugged the door open and stood in shock as he looked Jane over from head to toe. "Are you…" Rick shook his head, wondering if he was dreaming.

"Rick! I can't believe you made it out here!" Jane ran into the room and embraced him. Rick returned her embrace before holding her at arm's length to look her over again. "I thought I'd never see you again."

"Me too! When they put me on that plane heading east I figured that you were being shipped out to Mount Weather. So much for that, huh? How on earth did you make it out here, anyway?" She grinned as she asked the question before shaking her head. "No, don't tell me right now. That's bound to be a story for later."

Behind her the thin man pushed up his glasses and smiled at the reunion. "So this is the famous 'Rick,' eh?"

Rick held out his hand and nodded. "I had no idea I was famous, but I suppose so. Rick Waters."

"Dr. Michael Evans." Dr. Evans gave Rick a firm handshake and looked over at Jane who was still grinning from ear to ear as she looked at Rick. "This young lady told me you got her through the hellhole that is Las Vegas. That's impressive."

Rick shrugged and looked down at his feet, unsure what to say in the face of the praise. "Nothing much to it. Just doing what needed to be done."

"Bullshit." Jane cut in, grinning again. "Rick singlehandedly saved us more times than I care to remember. He took care of me when I got over-heated and he didn't leave me behind even when I slowed him down to a crawl.

Dr. Evans nodded, glanced behind him and took a step forward, lowering his voice to a whisper. "Rumor through the grapevine is that you were supposed to go to Mount Weather. Part of that think tank they put together."

"That's what they told me at Nellis, yes."

"And you declined?"

"Yep."

Dr. Evans nodded again. "Good."

"Why is that good?"

Dr. Evans looked out into the hall again as though he expected someone to be listening. "Partly because there are rumors about something bad happening at Mount Weather. Nobody really knows what, though. And partly because if you know enough to be taken to Mount Weather then you'll be the first person here who knows enough to not only believe me but help me stop this madness." Dr. Evans glanced at Jane apologetically. "No offense intended. I meant only that Rick probably has the skills necessary to help unravel the technic—"

Jane shook her head and smiled at Dr. Evans' awkward stammering. "None taken."

Rick shifted on his feet and gave Dr. Evans a quizzical look. "I'm afraid I don't know what you're talking about. Is it Damocles?"

Dr. Evans held a finger to his lips and shook his head, whispering again. "Not now. Tonight, after dinner. There's a community room in the building just down the hall. No one ever uses it after dinner, though. We'll meet there, the three of us, and Jane and I will tell you everything."

Rick looked at Jane. "What are you guys talking about?"

Jane smiled at him again and patted his arm. "You'll see. We've got a lot to figure out."

Chapter Five

The Water's Homestead
   Outside Ellisville, VA

DIANNE WAITED until after dinner when Jacob and Josie were busy cleaning up the dishes to tell Mark about the conversation she had with Jason and Sarah. His response was relatively muted though he asked a few questions here and there as Dianne explained things. When Dianne told him that she and Jason would most likely be going out to search for the group—which she had started calling 'the gang'—Mark grew antsy.

"I want to come with you and help."

Dianne smiled at the response and reached across the dining room table to hold his hand. "I know you do, kiddo. I need someone here to help watch the house and keep your brother and sister safe."

"Let Mr. Statler stay here. He and Mrs. Statler can watch the place, right?"

"Of course they could. But I want you here." A muffled thump and a pair of voices arguing upstairs made her smile. "Besides if we leave the two of them here they'll be arguing too much to pay attention to anyone approaching."

A smile briefly passed across Mark's lips before he forced it back down. "I don't know, mom. I don't like this. I don't like you going out and leaving again. It doesn't seem safe."

"I don't like it either." Dianne shrugged. "But we can't just leave Tina out there. I would take all of you with us in the truck but there's no way I'm letting your brother and sister get anywhere close to those people."

"Were two of them really those guys from the grocery store?"

"Yep. So I want you to stay on your toes here. Keep the security cameras up at all times. Minimize the time spent outside. Keep the fires to a minimum, too. No loud noises, no engines except in an emergency. Above all, though, remember this: don't hesitate to shoot. If you don't know the people and they're on our property then you need to shoot. If they do anything threatening, shoot. Don't shoot to frighten, either. This isn't a game or a movie where warning shots will scare them off."

Mark gulped and Dianne squeezed his hand. "Don't worry; you'll do great. And I highly doubt anyone will be coming out here while we're out scouting. It's more likely that we'll run into someone since… well, we'll be looking for them."

"I don't really like the sound of that."

"Don't worry about it. I'll have Jason with me. He may not look it sometimes but that guy's tougher than nails. If we get into a rough spot we'll be fine."

"Mrs. Statler seems pretty handy with a gun. Once you guys left she kept one on her till you got back. I don't think she wanted to be seen holding one or something, at least by you guys."

Dianne smiled. "Sarah's a bit of an oddball, but she'll take care of you all." She stood up, carrying her coffee cup over to the sink and handing it to Jacob to wash. "Besides, it's not like we're going out for very long. We'll leave in the morning and be back sometime after lunch or near dinner."

"Hopefully."

"Hey." Dianne frowned. "Don't be a pessimist. Have some faith, okay?"

Mark nodded and stood up from the table. Another thump came from upstairs along with more arguing. "Should I go see if they need some help up there?"

Dianne looked at the ceiling and shook her head. "Nah. They're fine. They just need to get settled in."

<hr />

AN HOUR LATER, after Mark, Jacob and Josie were sitting quietly in the living room reading, Sarah and Jason came downstairs, still having a friendly argument along the way. Dianne was sitting in the recliner in the living room watching out the back window with a tablet on her lap with the security cameras pulled up on it.

"Hey you two!" She smiled as Jason and Sarah walked in, poking at each other. "We heard you rattling around up there. You get settled in okay?"

Sarah nodded. "This bag of bones won't cooperate. But yes, we're good." Sarah smiled at Jacob and Mark. "We appreciate you two letting us stay in your room."

Mark nodded. "You're welcome. Mom's had us all in the same room since this started, though, so it's no big deal."

"Well we appreciate it regardless." Jason chimed in before taking a seat on the floor. "So, D, you ready for tomorrow?"

"I think so. What time do you think we should leave?"

"Seven or so should be good. I'll get the guns and ammo loaded up when I get up at six if you'll take care of the food and water."

"Sure thing. Let's bring enough supplies to last for a couple days. We're coming back by the evening but who knows what could happen out there."

"Absolutely."

"What are you two planning on doing, anyway?" Sarah looked at Jason and Dianne. "Just searching for these people or trying to rescue Tina or what?"

"Scouting is the primary goal." Dianne replied. "We need to find out where they are, how many people are in their group and what kind of weapons and transportation they have. And we should probably figure out their general disposition. Maybe the ones we saw were… misunderstood?"

Jason chortled. "Please. Don't give them that much credit."

"Yeah, yeah. I know. Stranger things have happened, but it's not likely." Dianne's smile faded. "I hope Tina and Dave are okay."

"We'll find out tomorrow, hopefully. If we can locate them."

"What's the plan for that again? Dianne got up and walked over to the kitchen table. Jason followed and the pair stood looking over a large map of the area that they had talked over earlier while making their plans for where to go.

"We should go west first. Head along the highway or the service road as much as possible. I'm betting they're set up somewhere between Ellisville and Blacksburg. If not, though, then we should get to a high point—maybe the old water tower or radio tower—and keep watch for a few hours. If we see a vehicle we'll try to follow them to see where they go."

Dianne nodded. "Good. If we run into trouble we'll head north and east and lose them in the back roads before swinging around and coming back here. Whatever we do we can't let them know where we are."

"You know, I was thinking about that." Jason jerked his thumb in the direction of the fireplace. "I think I know why they haven't found you from the smoke."

"Why's that?"

"The house is set down far enough and the lay of your land is such that most of it's dissipated by the time it rises over the trees. The smell of the burning wood probably draws their attention sometimes but when they're driving in the area they'd have a hard time seeing any smoke at all."

"Huh. You're probably right about that. Thank goodness for small favors." She turned to Mark, who was listening in on the conversation. "I still don't want any more fires than are necessary, okay? No sense in taking risks when we'll be away."

"Yes, ma'am." He nodded and Dianne turned back to Jason.

"What else should we bring?"

"Couple of thick coats, extra pair of socks and shoes and a couple blankets in case we get stuck in the truck. Other than that, though, I think we're good."

"Which truck do you want to take? I think yours is probably a bit quieter."

"Yeah, I think so. Let's do that."

Dianne clapped her hands together. "I think we're set, then. We'll head out first thing, scout and see if we can find these people and figure out what the situation is with the Carsons."

"Sounds like a plan."

Chapter Six

S omewhere in Russia

THE RUSSIAN PRESIDENT sits at the head of the conference table, idly playing with a cap from a bottle of water sitting in front of him. He barely listens as his military leaders drone on with justifications for why they believe a missile strike on the United States is a prudent course of action. He has already decided that a strike will do nothing but lead to further bloodshed but given the influence the military leaders have he must take a more diplomatic approach.

"Gentlemen." After twenty minutes, when they finally finish speaking, he addresses them. "I appreciate your concerns. I share them. The fact of the matter is that we will gain nothing from this strike." He holds up his hands to silence the initial vocal objections. "I have given you the courtesy of speaking uninterrupted. You will do me the same courtesy, yes?" The question isn't a question at all, but a statement. Despite the heavy influence each of the leaders wields they are still subject to the whims of the man at the head of the table.

"Now. As I was saying." He stands up and begins a slow walk around the table, brushing and nudging up against the chairs of the others as a way to ensure they recognize his authority. "I share your concerns. This weapon is nothing other than a doomsday device that was created to overthrow their enemies and ensure their fading empire would remain relevant in modern society. However, there are a number of problems with lobbing missiles across the globe.

"Chief among these problems is the fact that the USA is suffering far worse than some countries. There is absolutely no sign that they have remained uninfected by the weapon or that they are using this release as some sort of cover. They are affected quite profoundly."

"Who cares?!" A man with medals across half his chest shouts from down near the end of the table, pounding his fist on its surface. "We must strike at them now, before it's too late! We have the advantage here! Fifty-two of our missiles still stand at the ready!"

"So we use them. What then? Who's to say how many they have ready to send back? Or Germany. Or Israel. Or France. Or Britain. Or China, for that matter. Perhaps they would decide it's time to add a bit of land to their collection."

"So you want us to cower in fear?"

"Do you truly believe that?" The President's tone is icy cold and full of menace.

"Of... of course not. Sir."

"What I propose is simple. We watch and we wait. We still have an eye in the sky and we will use it to our advantage. We will sit, quietly, watching and gathering information until the time is right. Then—and only then—we will make our move."

"And what will that move be?"

The President, having arrived back at his seat, places his hands on the chair. "The one most advantageous to ourselves."

Chapter Seven

C heyenne Mountain Complex
      Outside Colorado Springs, CO

IT WAS after dinner the following day when Rick, Jane and Dr. Evans met up in the common room of the building where the three of them were staying. The day had been largely uneventful and Rick had managed to catch a couple hours of sleep before his curiosity got the better of him. After exploring the entirety of the building he was housed in—an exercise that turned out to be frightfully boring—he went back to his room until an alert sounded over the base's intercom alerting everyone that it was time to eat.

Dinner was devoured in haste and once Rick and Jane finished they quickly headed back to the common room. Dr Evans arrived twenty minutes later and after walking inside he sealed the door by jamming a folding chair underneath the handle.

"Those bureaucratic fools!" Dr. Evans nearly shouted as he stalked over to a seat near Rick and Jane who looked at him with wide-eyed expressions.

"What's the matter?" Jane asked. "Trying to get them to let you run some tests again?"

"It's not even that!" Dr. Evans flopped down in the chair, his display of anger quickly dissipating as his expression turned from upset to exhausted. "It's like they've all given up hope up there. They're all just sitting around talking about survival probabilities." He scoffed and shook his head. "What do they expect us to do? Hide in a cave and wait till the food and water runs out or the Russians decide to see if they can solve the problem with a few well-placed nukes?"

Rick snorted and nodded. "You've been talking to General Black, I take it?"

"He is, without a doubt, the most asinine excuse for a military leader I've ever seen in my life. And that's saying something given how many I've worked alongside."

Rick smiled. "I couldn't agree more, Dr. Evans."

Dr. Evans abruptly changed the subject as he pulled a satchel close to his side, cradling it like it was his own child. "Rick. You were asked to go to Mount Weather."

"That's right. We talked about that yesterday?"

"And you're aware of what they were trying to do there."

Rick leaned back in his chair and thought back to his meeting with Colonel Leslie. "Well, yeah. When I was at Nellis Air Force Base the commander there showed me a paper with a brief description of what was going on. It also described a think tank they were assembling at Mount Weather to try and combat the virus."

"Damocles. Yes. I know it... quite well."

"Are you one of the scientists working on finding a way of stopping it?"

Dr. Evans glanced at Jane with a slightly worried expression before answering Rick's question. "I suppose. I was—well, I suppose I still am— better known as Dr. Howard Chu."

Rick's eyes narrowed as he tried to remember where he had heard the name before. "That sounds very familiar. I can't quite place it, though."

Dr. Evans nodded. "I'm not surprised. My false name was all over research papers and theories that were developed related to practical artificial applications, specifically with a focus on—"

"Distributed applications. Right?" Rick finished Dr. Evans' sentence.

"Exactly. You heard of it?"

"You could say that. My teams referenced your work a lot when we were furthering our development on car-to-car communications. Your work influenced a lot of what we did."

"So *that's* why they wanted you at Mount Weather." Dr. Evans rubbed his chin, his eyes lighting up as he realized what Rick's area of expertise was.

"I don't think so, no. I think it was because I was asking too many questions about what they were doing with their imaging setups in Las Vegas. They heard me use a few technical terms and figured they stick me on a plane to their think tank."

"Little did they know that you were probably one of the best people to actually be on that think tank." Dr. Evans shook his head. "What a small world."

"I wouldn't say the best but... yeah. I don't know."

Dr. Evans sat quietly for a moment before he continued. "So you know about my alter-ego's work. That's good. But that's only half of it."

"Oh?"

"Yes." Dr. Evans nervously picked at a seam on his satchel as he spoke. "I was one of the principle researchers who first developed what the government purchased and turned into Damocles."

Rick raised an eyebrow. "You? You developed Damocles?"

"The concept of it, yes. That's why I had to use a false identity. When the federal government found out what we were doing they bought us out lock, stock and barrel. We stayed on to help them develop it further for a year or two and then they let us all go to continue development in-house."

Rick ran a hand over his hair and down the side of his face. "Damn. I'm impressed."

"You shouldn't be. My work was the genesis for this weapon and what's happening today."

"Boys?" Jane interrupted. "If you're done being humble about your accomplishments you two might want to turn your attention toward something useful." She looked at Dr. Evans. "You were telling me a couple days ago about some ideas you had for stopping Damocles. Maybe Rick here can help?"

Rick shrugged. "I'll certainly try. I don't think I'm necessarily the best but hey, if you want to bounce ideas off of me I'm all ears."

Dr. Evans felt as though a weight was lifted off of his shoulders and he released his death grip on his satchel. "You have no idea how glad I am to hear that. Everyone I've talked to has either been a politician or a monkey with a gun and medals on their chest." He opened his satchel and pulled out a stack of papers that he placed on the table in front of Rick, Jane and himself. "Give me a minute to get this organized and I'll walk you through exactly what Damocles is, what it does and why all of the current attempts to stop it have failed."

Rick snorted nervously and glanced at Jane and Dr. Evans. "That sounds... ominous."

"Believe me, Rick, once you know what I know you'll wonder why anyone's still alive."

"DAMOCLES DIDN'T START out as Damocles." Dr. Evans slid a few pieces of paper over toward Rick. "Before the feds bought us out we developed the idea of a mutagenic language through which different machines could talk to each other even if the base hardware and software was radically different. The idea was to make the 'Internet of Things' easier to develop for."

Rick flipped through the papers. "A mutagenic language, eh? How would that work?"

"We'd have a very basic set of parameters through which the machines could talk to each other. Because the code was mutagenic it could adapt to conform to whatever rigors were enforced by the system which it was on. So if you loaded it onto a smart refrigerator it would automatically figure out how to use the refrigerator's networking commands to talk to a central server, for example."

"That sounds *incredibly* useful. And also incredibly dangerous. How advanced was the mutagenic code?"

"Not very. Not at first, anyway." Dr. Evans took off his glasses to clean them and massage the bridge of his nose. "We used learning algorithms to study the underlying structure of a few dozen different embedded operating systems to form basic rules that the code would follow. From there we let it learn on its own. By the time the feds kicked us out I think we were up to several hundred unique permutations of hardware and software combinations."

"That's a lot." Rick shook his head. "But not nearly enough to cause this type of damage. Not when you've got military-grade hardened systems that are encrypted and protected against intrusion."

"You'd think so, wouldn't you?" Dr. Evans flipped through his stack of papers until he found the folder he was looking for. "Before we got kicked out I was accidentally blind-carbon-copied on an internal email. The email was vague but it heavily implied that the NSA was absorbing our work. What they were doing with it I don't know but it was... well, you can read it for yourself."

Rick read through the pages in the folder, his eyes growing wide as he gently shook his head. "Wow. This is huge. But what's this reference to an 'internal learning matrix' all about?"

Dr. Evans shrugged. "Hard to say for certain but based on how much they love collecting data I bet they have—well, *had*—some pretty wild learning algorithms."

"Hey, guys?" Jane interrupted again. "Can I get some English words thrown in here and there?"

Dr. Evans looked over at Jane as Rick responded. "A learning algorithm would be like a computer that can learn from what it sees. You input data and it learns and adjusts itself based on that data." Rick looked back at Dr. Evans. "The stuff we had in the private sector was truly wild. I shudder to imagine what the feds have had locked away."

"That's what I think happened." Dr. Evans shifted in his seat to address both Rick and Jane at the same time. "I think they took our base and then integrated their advanced learning machine algorithms and pointed them at every computer system they could."

"And thus Damocles was born."

"Maybe." Dr. Evans shrugged. "I'm not sure it was that fast, though. I think that perhaps they started with the intent to use it as a spying technique.

A way to infiltrate systems quickly and covertly no matter what those systems were built on. Then someone recognized other potentials and weaponized it."

"I'm going to guess that a few folks have tried shutting it down to no avail, eh?"

Dr. Evans nodded solemnly. "The version that was let loose was—and I'm not being hyperbolic here—the worst, most dangerous version of the program imaginable. There were no restrictions placed on it whatsoever."

"Why would they even have something like that in their system? And who would steal it and let it loose?"

"They were probably running testing simulations. Whoever let it be exposed to a networked system in that state—or any other, quite frankly—needs to be shot in the head if they're still alive." Dr. Evans reached into his satchel, pulled out a metal water bottle and took a long drink. "As to who would steal it I doubt we'll ever know. A foreign government? A teenager with too much time on their hands? Or maybe the software jumped out on its own. That doesn't really matter anymore, though. What matters is stopping it."

"Why? It seems like things have kind of slowed down here lately, right?" Jane glanced between the two men as she looked for a confirmation.

"That," Dr. Evans said as he nervously cleaned his glasses again, "is precisely what worries me so much at this particular moment in time."

"Why is that?" Rick had a feeling that he wouldn't like Dr. Evans' answer and he was correct.

"Damocles, from the start, was built to slowly ramp up its attempts to assimilate within a system in a steadily increasing fashion. When I was on Air Force One I was given all the data they had on the changes to Damocles and I'm afraid that design characteristic was significantly increased and improved upon."

"So the virus ramps up its attacks? Is that what you mean?"

"More than that. Each new level of attack seems to bring something else. It's designed to disrupt key parts of a particular target on a vast range of scales. It could be used to attack a company or a country. Damocles scales based on what's required to complete its tasks at hand. On a country scale—like we see right now—it's going after key sectors of the economy and infrastructure, like with the vehicles and phone networks and drilling operations. The stock market was one of the first things to get hit." Dr. Evans wiped a bead of sweat from his forehead. His face was red from talking so quickly and passionately and he sat back in his chair to take a few deep breaths.

"So this little lull here probably isn't a lull?"

"I doubt it very much. You'll notice that we aren't at nuclear war. Yet. I suspect measures that extreme were left as a measure of last resort to be executed only when all other measures had been carried out. Given this lull, though, it may be that Damocles is evaluating what to do next and deciding whether or not those final measures should be executed."

"Dr. Evans," Jane interjected, "you make this thing sound like it's alive. Like a robot or something."

"No, no, no." Dr. Evans shook his head firmly. "It's most certainly not sentient, if that's what you're implying. We're decades or more away from anything of that nature. No, Damocles is an extremely sophisticated piece of software with a huge number of choices it can make based on an equally large number of inputs it takes in. It's complicated beyond belief but it has no thoughts of its own. It is following its directives to the letter."

"That's good." Rick sighed. "But still doesn't help us very much."

"I know. When I was on Air Force One I was in the beginning stages of figuring out some potential solutions to shutting Damocles down in a way that wouldn't require frying every computer on the planet. The inability to communicate with anyone else who is informed on the topic and the crash both hampered my work."

Rick saw where Dr. Evans was going and nodded. "Let's put our heads together and see what we can come up with."

Chapter Eight

Outside Ellisville, VA

"ARE you sure they'll be okay?" Dianne found herself asking Jason the same question for the fourth time as they drove down the dirt road. She hadn't expected to feel so nervous about leaving her children at the house for half the day but as they headed out she had felt a twinge of pain in her heart for doing what she felt like was abandoning them.

"D. Come on now." Jason kept his eyes on the road as he talked. "You've done a hell of a job training Mark and I'm pretty sure Jacob could handle himself in a pinch, too. Sarah's a better shot than I am. They'll all be fine for the day. I promise."

Dianne snorted and laughed. "I hope she's a better shot than you. Otherwise it'd be her I'd have to worry about, not the gang."

"Hey now, just give me a place to sit or lie down and watch me go to work. I'll be able to handle myself just fine."

"I know, I know. I'm just teasing." Dianne smiled at Jason before looking out at the road ahead of them. "It's funny how normal things look right here."

"Why wouldn't it? It's just a bunch of trees."

"I don't know. When I think about the end of the world I think about fires, meteors and rivers of lava. Not trees and snow and clouds in the sky."

"Not everything's terrible at the end of the world."

"No." Dianne pointed ahead of them. "But some things are."

A few hundred feet away at the edge of Ellisville sat the remnants of several burned out vehicles. Rust was rapidly accumulating on their twisted frames and though they had only been there for a couple weeks they looked as though they had been sitting out for years. Jason took the truck through town slowly, keeping the engine as quiet as possible as they listened out through the open windows for any other vehicles.

Dianne assumed that there were still a few people left in town but after thirty minutes of driving and searching she was beginning to think that everyone up and left. "Where is everybody?"

"Gone to the big cities. Trying to get food and shelter from the government, I suspect. Not that there's much food and shelter to go around anymore."

"This reminds me of some natural disasters, like earthquakes and hurricanes. Everybody up and leaving due to floodwaters or something like that."

"Does anything look different in town compared to the last time you came out?"

Dianne shook her head. "It's been a while and we didn't explore very much so I have no idea."

"Hm. I'm not seeing anything out of the ordinary. Besides, you know, the place looking like a tornado blew through.

"We should head west towards Blacksburg and see what's out that way. If you're up for some off-roading."

"I think I can handle it." Jason smiled and turned the corner, heading in the general direction of the highway leading out towards Blacksburg. He followed the same route that Dianne had taken just after the event, when she and the children had run into one of their after-school teachers who was leaving the city on a motorcycle. She had considered trying to go off-road to search for other people but decided instead to head back to the house.

With her and Jason now in pursuit of a gang who had burned down the Carson's house she was glad that she had made her original choice. She was also looking forward to inflicting no small amount of revenge upon the people who had taken Tina and done who-knows-what with Dave.

Intended to help relieve the stress on the smaller roads and the main US-460 highway, the 460 business highway was split into north and south routes with the southern one being the original and the northern one being the new one. The new northern road took a westerly route past Ellisville and through into Blacksburg where it merged with US-460 proper. Dubbed "the slow-way" by those in the area, the highway passed by Ellisville, went through Blacksburg and out to the northwest. Though it was relatively new it was under constant repairs due to the haste that had gone into its original construction. Traffic was nearly always backed up along all sections of the road including the on and off ramps near Ellisville.

"Wow." Jason whistled softly as he saw the piles of destroyed cars clogging the ramp onto the highway.

"Yeah. It's pretty bad, isn't it?"

"If you think this is bad you should see what it's like in the bigger cities." Jason revved the engine as he went off-road into the soft dirt and grass, driving in a wide circle around the vehicles and the guardrail near the ramp. "Bodies everywhere, cities burning, more vehicles than this scattered everywhere. I can't believe all of this devastation could be caused by some sort of malfunction."

"Tell that to my phone and my car."

"Damn. I forgot about what happened to our phone. Same thing happened to yours, huh?"

"If yours burned to a crisp then yes, exactly the same."

"Hm." Jason shook his head, focusing away from the conversation and back on where he was driving. The guardrail stretched for a good half mile and the ground was soft enough that the large truck felt like it was going to get stuck or slip into the rail at any second. Once Jason got them onto the highway Dianne breathed a sigh of relief before groaning at the sight before them.

"Holy cow. How... how are there so many cars here?" Before them stretched four lanes of burned-out vehicles as far as Dianne could see.

"They don't call it the slow-way for nothing. Must have been bumper-to-bumper when it happened."

"Huh." Dianne sat back in her seat and thought for a few long seconds. "Then those guys can't be based out along this way now can they?"

Jason's eyes widened and he nodded thoughtfully. "That is a very good point. Where else would they go, though?"

Dianne opened up the map they had been studying at the house the day before and flattened out the section around Ellisville. "What if they're using one of the back roads? One that would give them unrestricted movement while simultaneously keeping them away from major highways that would be too obstructed to use."

"Like 407?"

"Exactly." Dianne traced the path of the road out to the west. "It has plenty of connections between Ellisville and Blacksburg, it runs the whole way and it doesn't see much traffic on account of how narrow and twisty it is."

"Interesting. I would have assumed they'd choose a major highway to be on, though. Just in case there was any foot traffic."

"What about here?" Dianne pointed to a spot on the map where 407 and the northern 460 business routes came very close to each other. "There's one of those big gas stations out there that..." Dianne trailed off, then looked over at Jason. "That has to be it."

"Absolutely. It's slightly elevated, there's already a structure there—well, if it didn't explode like everything else—and it's close to a highway and road they could actually use to get around on. Yes. Yes that has to be it."

Dianne nodded. "Okay, we'll check there."

"One problem, though." Jason scratched his chin. "How are we supposed to get close to it without being heard or seen? If we take 407 they'll spot us half a mile away. We can't exactly take the highway."

Dianne held her thumb and index finger close to each other over the scale on the map and estimated out the distance between the spot where they were currently sitting and the spot where they thought the gang might be hiding. "Looks like we're three, maybe four miles away. Think you can make it half that distance off-road?"

Jason grunted. "Hm. Is that a challenge?"

Chapter Nine

S omewhere in China

THE GREAT FIREWALL is no more. It took Damocles less than thirty seconds to identify a weakness in the firewall's infrastructure and another sixty seconds to spread to the
network of devices on which it operates. Billions of internet-connected devices were next to
fall. Those with batteries were overheated and destroyed. Those without were shorted out,
locked up or otherwise rendered inoperable. For some of the one point five billion residents
of the country their lives are upended. Those living in and around the most populated areas
suffer from catastrophic losses as the power goes out and fires rage unchecked through overbuilt cities.

For others, though, their lives continue on much as they normally have. Blackouts—a
staple of life in many parts of the country—are thought to be the reason for the loss of
electricity. With no cellphone towers up and running Damocles cannot spread to any mobile
phones that were not previously infiltrated so the number of injuries and fires from destroyed
phones is much lower than in the cities.

Life carries on for the rural residents. They gather together, help each other out,
continue to till their fields and go about their daily routines. The first signs of trouble come
when the military sends out convoys to collect food. The collections are larger than normal
and the farmers cannot get the soldiers to say anything about what's going on. The farmers
are warned at gunpoint not to enter the cities and the soldiers leave, carrying the food back
to the cities to be distributed amongst the residents.

The lack of preparation by most of the civilian population for such a catastrophe
means that residents not in rural areas begin to suffer immediately. Medicine and food runs

out in less than a day. Transportation systems are jammed or destroyed, stranding millions of workers far from their homes and loved ones. Fires bring down miles worth of city blocks, killing many and inconveniencing even more. Starvation looms on the horizon, approaching like a rider on a pale horse.

While the government deploys troops to keep its citizens alive it also works on a solution to the Damocles problem. Uninfected systems are thrown against the virus and different measures are taken to destroy, block or delay it. None of the measures are effective. The best only buy a few extra seconds while the virus analyzes the new set of parameters and adjusts, quickly routing around the blocks and destruction attempts.

Hidden away in isolated bases and bunkers, the leaders of China struggle to cope with the situation. The redistribution of food can only work for so long and with millions upon millions left without homes, jobs or a way of lasting for more than a few days on their own the country is looking at a decimation of its population in less than a week. Looting, rioting and outright civil war has not yet begun but the government knows this is bound to happen before too long given what is going on in other countries.

Three satellites owned by China still operate, sending back images to computers deep underground that have yet to be discovered and infected by Damocles. The operators of the satellites are not in positions of authority and the senior government members are not close enough to reach by any functional communication systems. The operators resolved themselves to documenting the unfolding apocalypse, using the imaging sensors on the satellites to produce highly detailed pictures of as many countries as possible.

One day the images may prove useful to historians. For now, though, they are simply a way to keep boredom and the thoughts of death at bay.

Chapter Ten

Cheyenne Mountain Complex
Outside Colorado Springs, CO

IT WAS four in the morning before Dr. Evans had finished giving Rick a crash-course in the details about Damocles. Jane had gone back to her room for a few hours of sleep before bringing in a pot of coffee, three mugs and a few packs of food that were a cross between a breakfast casserole and a pile of mush.

"Any progress?" Jane poured herself a cup of coffee and sat down in a chair, curling her legs up underneath herself.

Rick poured a cup of coffee for himself and Dr. Evans and shook his head. "Not a lot. I understand quite a bit more about this thing but the more I understand the more potential solutions I think of keep going out the window."

"It is vexing, isn't it?" Dr. Evans sipped from his mug.

Rick flipped over some papers onto which he had scribbled notes while Dr. Evans was talking. "If Damocles is in pretty much every internet-connected device then that means those devices will infect anything that connects to them. So beyond the fact that destroying every infected device would be impossible from the get-go, once devices started talking to one another all it would take would be one infection to cause the virus to spread all over again."

"Precisely."

Rick scratched his head. "Isn't there a back door into the system? The feds have used back doors into private systems enough times that you'd think they'd have a few into their own."

"I'm afraid not. Damocles *can* be accessed but it requires an authentication using a 2048-bit encryption key."

"Wait. What?" Rick nearly dropped his cup of coffee in surprise. "It can?"

Dr. Evans nodded slowly. "Of course. Damocles has a communications interface that monitors for signals from all sources, including itself. If a shutdown command is sent and successfully authenticated then the command spreads to all other instances of Damocles the next time they monitor an affected version of Damocles."

"Why didn't you tell me this before?" Rick flipped through the pages on the table and Dr. Evans shrugged.

"It's a bulletproof system. It didn't seem important to bring up, sorry."

"Everything's important, Dr. Evans. You know that. And that's a very clever way to propagate commands. Why has no one issued a shutdown command to it yet?"

Dr. Evans shrugged. "I don't know. Once I figured out that the weapon had this capability built in to it I started asking people why we couldn't send a shutdown signal but nobody seemed to know why. One of the President's aides sounded like he was going to help but that was right before the crash. Then I was brought here and I've spent days trying to get these idiots to help but nobody seemed like they thought it was a viable solution because nobody even knows where to start with getting the encryption key or the proper interface protocols to give it a shutdown command. I sort of gave up on that solution myself, to be frank." Dr. Evans' voice was hollow and he had the look of a man who had been utterly defeated.

Rick shook his head. "No. No way. A propagating shutdown command is the only way this would work. Otherwise, like you said, even if you could destroy or maybe even clean this stuff off of systems all it would take is one infected system touching them and everything would go down again."

"Of course. But without the key—"

"Michael." Rick put his mug down on the table and locked eyes with Dr. Evans. "I flew from Virginia to California on a business trip right before this all started. I was barely on the ground before planes and cars started exploding around me. I've faced down the military, bloodthirsty gangs and mother nature herself. I've watched people die in front of me, some of them by my own hand. I've made it this far to get back home to my family and I'm not about to stop." Rick's voice shook slightly as it increased in volume and intensity. "If I can do all of that then I'm pretty sure you and I can figure out a way to stop this damned thing before it gets any worse. If this is the only surefire way to stop this weapon then I promise you we're going to figure out how to make it happen."

Dr. Evans closed his eyes and shook his head. "That's a good speech,

Rick. But it doesn't change the fact that we don't have what we need to even talk to Damocles much less authenticate a conversation."

Rick began pacing across the room, talking as he walked. "I have to imagine the key would be stored on a secured system. Maybe even an air-gapped one, right?"

Dr. Evans shrugged. "I suppose so. That would make sense, given who developed it."

"You said the communications protocol is bulletproof, right?"

"Absolutely." Dr. Evans nodded.

"How can you be sure?"

Dr. Evans hesitated for a second, glancing between Rick and Jane. "Because they used software I wrote for it. I know it inside and out. It's completely foolproof. No holes, no gaps, no tricks. Nothing you can exploit."

"Damn." Rick scratched his chin and tilted his head back and forth, letting out a contented sigh as he heard and felt his neck and back crack. "Okay, so if we want to stop this then we have to get the private key somehow."

"But no one knows where it is!"

"Irrelevant." Rick shook his head. "We can't wipe it out and we can't bypass its security. The only option available is to obtain the private key so we can encrypt a shutdown message." Dr. Evans tried to argue again and Rick shut him down. "I understand the challenges involved here, Dr. Evans, but we have to come to grips with reality. If there are no other possible paths forward then we *must* take the only one available to us. Now come on, work with me here. Let's say we figure out the key. What then?"

Dr. Evans sat back in his chair, working through the scenario in his mind. "We… we would need to know the precise communication protocols. Exactly how to tell it to shut down and propagate that command to all other instances of the virus that are seen. We couldn't tell it to erase itself because that wouldn't further the spread of the shutdown command."

"Okay, so that kind of information is probably going to be found some-where close to the key. We'll deal with that later, too. Let's say we have the key and we have the commands. What comes after that?"

"We'd need a system that Damocles hasn't totally trashed. We'll give the command to that system and the system will talk to other systems that are affected and it'll spread outward from there."

"And it won't reinfect those systems?"

"No." Dr. Evans shook his head firmly. "Damocles will still be on the clean systems, but it'll be in a shutdown state. If any live versions of the virus try to reach out and infect a clean system they'll receive the shutdown command from the clean system instead."

"Okay, great. Again, it shouldn't be hard to find something like that close to where we find the key and command instructions. Now we know what we need to do."

Jane smiled and nodded, having been listening intently the whole time. "That's great, Rick. But how do we do it?"

Rick looked at her. "We?"

Jane nodded. "What, do you think I'm going to sit around here?"

"I, uh… well no." Rick stammered. "I guess I didn't peg you as the adventuring type.

"Oh come on, now." Jane gave Rick a wry smile. "After Las Vegas you'd have to strap me down to keep me from tagging along with you again."

"You had… fun?" Rick raised an eyebrow.

"The nearly dying from heatstroke part wasn't that much fun, no. And I guess the other parts weren't 'fun' in the conventional sense." Jane uncurled her legs and shifted forward in her seat. "But that had to have been the most exhilarating time of my life." She looked at Dr. Evans and back at Rick. "So if you two are planning something to save the world you can count me in."

Dr. Evans laughed and clapped his hands on his knees. "Now *that's* the spirit!" He looked over at Rick. "I'll add my two cents to this as well, if you don't mind. Jane's been absolutely incredible since I got here. Helping me obtain a computer to perform some research, distracting some of the soldiers when I needed to get some data from their archives and that sort of thing."

"Huh." Rick nodded approvingly. "Color me surprised and impressed."

"So what's the plan, gentlemen?" Jane took another sip from her mug and watched Rick and Dr. Evans intently.

"Good question." Rick glanced upward and sighed. "The first thing we should do is see if General Black will listen to both Dr. Evans and me try to explain what we have to do to stop Damocles. If he'll listen then he might be able to help us figure out where to go to get the data we need."

"Another question." Jane put a finger up in the air. "What's the plan for when he says no, laughs in your faces and tosses you back into your rooms?"

Rick looked at Jane and Dr. Evans with a determined expression set in stone on his face. "Then we find our own path."

Chapter Eleven

─────────────

S omewhere between Ellisville, VA and Blacksburg, VA

WHEN JASON finally pulled the truck to a stop, Dianne slowly released her death grips on the overhead handle and her left armrest. It had taken nearly three-quarters of an hour for Jason to get them to within half a mile of the gas station and Dianne had been holding on for dear life most of the way. The journey off-road had resulted in three near misses at rolling the truck over on its side, two instances where they had nearly gotten stuck in the soft dirt and at least seventeen new dents and scratches in the vehicle's paint.

"Jason?" Dianne whispered his name as she stared out the front windshield.

"Yeah?"

"Can we find a different way back next time?"

"I'd like that."

"Yeah." Dianne nodded. "Me too."

After taking a few minutes to collect themselves the pair got out and retrieved their gear from the truck bed and the back seats. Once everything was set Dianne turned up the volume on the radio and pressed down on the microphone button.

"Dianne to Sarah. Dianne to Mark. Anybody home?" A few seconds of silence passed before the radio screeched and a static-laden voice replied. "Hey mom, we're here. Any updates?"

"None yet. We think we may have figured out where they are but we won't know for certain until we get there. We've got half a mile of walking to do and we'll know then. We're going to go quiet on the radio for now and we'll call you in a couple hours or so."

"Sounds good. Stay safe out there."

"You too."

Dianne switched off the radio and slipped it into her backpack before hoisting the bag onto her shoulders. "You ready for this, Jason?"

"Ready as I can ever be, D."

"Let's get going."

Leaving the truck parked far off the side of the road hidden in a dense cluster of trees and bushes, Dianne and Jason headed out. They followed the path of the highway, staying well clear of the road as they crossed the rolling hills, open fields and occasional lightly forested areas of southern Virginia. Their pace was slow—mostly due to Jason—but after an hour or so they finally found themselves approaching the location of the gas station.

From their vantage several hundred feet across the street on a hill it was easy to see that what used to be a large, clean and well-lit building had been radically altered and turned into something completely different.

Sandbags were piled high along the perimeter of the property around the gas station, surrounding both the main building and a few sheds that were located to the sides and back. Barbed wire had been crudely attached to the sandbags which stood about four feet tall and were at least four or five bags in thickness. Burned-out cars had apparently been pulled into position around certain parts of the sandbag interior, helping to shore up sections where the ground sloped sharply in one direction or another. The roof of the building and the covering over the pumps had been transformed as well, with a single row of sandbags three layers high stretching around the edge. A ramp constructed of scrap lumber stretched from the ground up to the roof, looking like it could collapse at any moment.

The windows of the main building were covered with plywood and boards, but only halfway up. The top half of the windows had been left exposed likely to aid those inside by providing natural lighting and allowing them to see out of the building. A handful of fires had been built inside rings of cinderblocks across the property of the gas station with two of them being particularly large and having dishes suspended over them. A few people sat near the fires, talking as they tended to the dishes which Dianne assumed were filled with food for a late lunch or early dinner.

Two entrances to the gas station—one off of the highway and the other off of the country road—were visible and a handful of people Dianne assumed were guards standing around them. Each of the guards carried a rifle of some sort and were dressed in normal street clothes, though they appeared more tattered and dirty than normal. A handful of people stood outside the country road entrance talking to the guards about something in an animated fashion.

The look of the compound had a very end-of-the-world feel to it and Dianne couldn't help but feel reminded of Mad Max as she studied its layout and the people walking around inside. "I think we found it." She whispered to Jason as she crouched on the hill behind a tree.

"No kidding." Jason took off his backpack and sat down next to her before pulling two pairs of small binoculars out of his backpack. "Here."

"Good thinking. I was just going to use the rifle scope."

"Easy there, trigger finger. I don't need binoculars to tell me there's way too many people down there for us to take on alone. Besides, we don't even know if these are the same people or not."

"Oh they are the same people. Look off to the right side, near that big shed." Dianne pointed and Jason swiveled his head to peer at the location. A few cars were parked near the shed at the far end of the parking lot along with a pair of large fuel trucks. One of the vehicles, a large SUV, appeared to be the same vehicle they had seen at the Carson's house the previous day.

"Oh." Jason whispered. "I guess we did find them." Both he and Dianne were quiet for a few minutes as they watched the compound, studying its layout and the people inside intently.

"Hey, hey!" Dianne reached out and slapped at Jason with her left hand while watching through the binoculars. "Check out that small shack behind the building. Three people just walked out. Is that her?"

Jason turned his gaze on the location Dianne was talking about and gasped softly. "Wow. Yep. That's Tina all right. She looks like hell, though!"

"What a pack of assholes, beating up an old lady like that." Dianne paused for half a second and glanced at Jason. "Sorry. No offense."

Jason chuckled. "Tina and Dave have ten years on Sarah and I. None taken." His laugh was short-lived as he watched Tina being taken out of the small shed behind the gas station and unceremoniously lowered to the ground out next to one of the fires where food was being prepared. The pair of men that had carried her over left and one of the women tending to the fire squatted down next to Tina and appeared to be speaking to her.

"I really wish I could hear what's going on." Dianne sighed in frustration.

"Don't need to hear it to know they're doing something bad down there."

"True enough. What do you think we should do?"

"Sit our asses right here and keep watching."

"What about Tina?"

"We know she's alive. She looks relatively unharmed and she's still coherent. Look, she's eating something right now. We can't go off half-cocked on this. We need to gather as much information as we possibly can before we do anything."

The sight of her friend being treated roughly in what looked like an enemy encampment boiled Dianne's blood and made her want to take her rifle and start putting holes into every person she could see. Jason was right, though, and she knew it so she pulled out a pen and notebook from her backpack, got into a comfortable position on the grass and propped the binoculars up on her knees.

"Let the watching begin."

Chapter Twelve

Cheyenne Mountain Complex
Outside Colorado Springs, CO

RICK HAD FORGOTTEN about how small General Black's office was until he, Jane and Dr. Evans were standing shoulder to shoulder inside of it. They had given up on trying to squeeze into the chairs across from the general and elected to remain standing instead. Across the desk General Black eyed them with a look that was a combination of suspicion and irritation.

The general glanced at his watch and shook his head. "It's been fifteen minutes since you barged into my office demanding to tell me about a solution to the Damocles virus. All I've heard in the last fifteen minutes are theories about how maybe, possibly, if you can find a magical deus ex machina, then you can shut down Damocles and things will go back to normal."

Rick looked over at Jane and Dr. Evans, then back at General Black. "General, that's not at all what we're saying. There are no guarantees here and this is far from a bulletproof solution even if we do find it. Dr. Evans and I have spent the last several hours working on this and—"

"Oh my." General Black made a face of mock horror and put his hands to his cheeks. "*Hours? Several* of them? Well goodness gracious me, I'm *so* sorry I doubted you!" His look returned to one of pure annoyance. "Greater minds than the two of yours have been working on this problem since it started."

"That's just it, General." Dr. Evans spoke next. "Everyone—including myself—was looking for a loophole. A way to beat this thing the easy way.

There are no easy ways, General. The sooner we accept that the sooner we can start looking for a way to attack it head-on which is exactly what we want to do."

"And you want me to give you a vehicle and enough supplies to head... where, exactly?"

"That's what we're hoping you can tell us, sir." Rick pointed at a small stack of papers on General Black's desk that they had given to him when they first came in. "That's a summary of the information we think would be useful to have in order to locate the center where the NSA was working on Damocles before it was unleashed."

General Black chortled as he picked up the pages and made a show of pretending to thumb through them. "What makes you think I would give you that kind of information if I even had it?"

"A sense of patriotic duty to your country?" Jane crossed her arms. "Or maybe you want to be heralded as a hero who helped save the world."

General Black nodded upward at the ceiling and raised an eyebrow as he gave a slight smile. "There's a mile of solid rock between the outside world and us. I am the king of this underground domain and quite happy to remain that way for the time being. I have my orders and they say for me to stay put, seal off the mountain in just under forty-eight hours and ensure that every soldier and civilian in here is kept safe until this situation is resolved." He leaned forward in his chair, steepling his fingers together. "*That* is my job. Not to save the world. Not to listen to crackpot theories. Not to do anything except for my job."

"But General, this is crazy!" Rick shook his head. "If we don't do something soon then Damocles will escalate things and then—"

"And if things do escalate then you'll be relieved to know that we've got five years' worth of supplies down here so you'll be alive through whatever happens."

"General." Dr. Evans took off his glasses and cleaned them on his shirt before replacing them again. "I'm aware of a few of the particulars of this base having been—as a child—a secret admirer of the place."

"I'm elated. What's your point?"

"I know that this complex can't survive a direct nuclear strike. An indirect one, sure. But a direct one? With today's missile technology? No."

For the first time since meeting the man Rick noticed that General Black was visibly disturbed by what he was hearing. Dr. Evans noticed it as well and pressed his advantage. "I believe that Damocles is trying to decide what to do next. Nuclear weapons may be on the table. If that's true then we have to move right now. Otherwise if we're too late..." Dr. Evans trailed off and shrugged.

General Black's eyes turned to darkened slits and his chest expanded as he took in long, deep breaths. Rick could feel the general's rage as the uniformed man stood up from his desk and pointed a long finger at the opposite side of the room. "Get out of my office."

"But General—"

"One. More. Word. And all three of you will find yourselves in cells eating bread and water for the next *month!*"

Dr. Evans opened his mouth to speak again but Rick elbowed him in the side and turned to the door. The trio slowly walked out, with Rick being the last. He turned to give General Black one final look before closing the door. "Asshole." Rick mumbled to Dr. Evans and Jane as he stood next to them.

"Time for Plan B?" Jane looked at Dr. Evans and Rick. "Or do you two think you could wrestle him down and beat some sense into him?"

Rick shook his head and looked around in the hallway before whispering to the others. "No. We need to move on and it sounds like we have a limited window. Only forty-eight hours till they lock this place down."

"We must find a way out of here by tomorrow." Dr. Evans gulped nervously. "Knowing where to search for the information we need would be helpful as well."

Rick put his hand to his head, rubbing away sweat and grease. "We all need some sleep. We've been at this far too long. Come on, let's head back and get showers and a few hours of rest. We'll reconvene in the morning and figure something out."

As the trio headed back down the hall towards the building that housed their rooms a uniformed figure approached from a nearby cross-hallway. "Mr. Waters?"

Rick turned to look at the man and nodded. "Yeah, that's me."

The uniformed soldier glanced at Jane and Dr. Evans before looking back to Rick. "I need to speak with you privately for a moment, sir. It's about your gear from your vehicle."

"Oh thank goodness. Finally!" He turned and waved at Dr. Evans and Jane. "You two head back. I'll take care of this before I head back."

The three exchanged quick goodbyes before Rick turned back to the soldier. "You said something about my gear?" The soldier looked both ways down the hallway before ducking into a nearby office and pulling Rick along with him.

"Ow! What the hell?" Rick pushed the soldier back and gave him a confused and angry look. "What's your problem?"

"Mr. Waters! Please, keep quiet." The soldier was whispering as he approached Rick again. "We don't have more than a minute before I'm missed." Rick, sensing that something important was about to be communicated, kept his mouth shut and nodded in understanding.

"I'm a technician, Mr. Waters. I work on the scanners and have had the opportunity to work with other agencies as part of interdisciplinary studies. I've learned... a lot. A lot about how different systems work. The observational ones in particular." The soldier licked his lips nervously. "I love my country, Mr. Waters. I love it dearly. I can't stand to watch things happen like this."

"What are you talking about? Rick whispered. The soldier reached into his pocket and pulled out a small black box about the size of a large cellphone.

"I've done a bit of sleuthing myself, Mr. Waters. Dr. Evans is right. The only way to defeat this virus is to attack it head-on." The man held out the black box and Rick gingerly accepted it.

"What's this?"

"It has a thirty-day battery life on standby and eight days if you're using it at full capacity. I've disabled the network connectivity so it won't get infected. But it will help you get to the systems you need to have a shot at ending this."

Rick fiddled with the box for a few seconds before looking at the soldier. "Who are you? Why are you helping us?"

The soldier ignored the questions. "Your best bet to leave is early in the morning. The shift change is at zero four hundred. Take the General's car. You won't get as many questions that way. Just tell them you're running an errand for him."

A shout from down the corridor made the soldier freeze in fright before stepping around Rick, a nervous expression painted on his face. "Please, Mr. Waters. Don't let it end like this." With that final statement the soldier was gone, running down the corridor before Rick could get another word in. Utterly confused by what had just happened Rick looked down at the small box in his hand for a long moment before slipping it back into his pocket and hurrying out of the office, down the hall and back towards his room.

This just keeps getting stranger and stranger.

Chapter Thirteen

Somewhere between Ellisville, VA and Blacksburg, VA

TWO HOURS and three pages of notes later and Dianne was beginning to feel like she understood the dynamics of the encampment. While she and Jason weren't able to hear anything anyone was saying the body language and habits of the people residing in the fortified gas station made it clear who they were and what they were doing.

The people of the camp were divided into two categories: those with the guns and those without. The people with the guns spent most of their time guarding the place while those without spent most of their time cooking, working on vehicles and performing menial labor. Dianne wasn't sure if the people who didn't have weapons had been pressed into servitude or whether they were there by choice but regardless they were treated with no small amount of contempt and dismissal by those who did have weapons.

Tina Carson, meanwhile, appeared to be a unique anomaly. She—unlike the other people sans weapons—was constantly under watch though she wasn't tasked with any laborious activities. After getting food near one of the fires she had been hauled back into the shed behind the gas station. There were no signs of overt violent activities going on and Dianne wasn't entirely certain what to make of Tina's situation.

"Hey." Dianne heard a whisper behind her and turned to see Jason slinking through the brush.

"Heyo. Everybody good?"

"Yep. Mark said the cameras have been clear and they've not heard or seen a thing today."

"Good." Dianne nodded. "Thanks for checking in on them."

"No problem. Anything new about the camp down there?"

Dianne looked down at her notebook and shrugged. "Nothing really. I've got a few more notes on red shirt and blue shirt. They seem to be the leaders but they spend so much time inside I couldn't tell you more than that. The guards traded a few gallons of gasoline with another group that came up."

"What'd they want for it this time?"

"I think the group handed over a cage with some chickens inside. Seems like a bad trade to me."

"No kidding. That's a horrible trade!"

"Somebody drove up in an older car and unloaded several sacks of… something. I'm not sure what it was. Grain or something, maybe. They got several gallons of gas and left."

"So these guys have set up a trading post?"

"It makes sense, doesn't it? They've got a bunch of gasoline and that's got to be in hot demand. With two full fuel trucks and who knows how much underground they can keep this trading system up for weeks or months more before running out. That's long enough to branch out into other goods if they need or want to."

"So they're capitalists?"

Dianne laughed. "Well, don't go giving capitalists a bad name. They're still scum of the earth. I'm nearly one hundred percent sure that they keep the people without guns there as slave labor or something. Maybe labor in exchange for safety. They aren't treated right, whatever they're there as."

Jason shifted into a sitting position and scanned the camp with his binoculars. "What about Tina or Dave? Anything new there?"

"No sign of Dave at all. I haven't seen Tina since they took her back into that shed. Speaking of which, the sheds are definitely dormitories. The large one out front may be storage but the ones in back probably have mattresses all over the floors."

"What do they use the main building for, then?"

"Who knows. They have a generator back behind it, though."

"Really?"

"Yeah. Must be a small one since we can't hear it. But they carried some gas around back after the lights inside flicked off and they went back on a minute later."

"Maybe those two guys you pegged as the ringleaders are keeping the main building to themselves."

"Wouldn't surprise me. I wish I could get more information on them."

Jason pulled out a pack of crackers from his backpack and passed one to Dianne. "What about the two you remember from the grocery store?"

I think they're either out or they're sleeping. I saw the guy who looked like the leader of the group from yesterday wandering around but haven't seen the two from the grocery store."

Jason continued munching on his crackers and chasing them down with swigs from a bottle of water. When he finished he belched, crumpled up the wrapper and threw it in his bag and stretched his back and shoulders. "What's the plan, then? Any thoughts?"

"I'm just doing what you said, watching and waiting."

"We've done plenty of that. Now it's time to figure out a plan."

Dianne flipped through her notebook to a sketch of the encampment she had drawn as a reference for her notes. "There are too many of them for us to take on in a direct assault."

"I like how you're already talking about assaulting their encampment." Jason grinned.

"Do you want to go down there and negotiate?" Dianne turned to look at Jason. "There've been more than a few people who've traded with them and gone their way without any issues."

"Hm." Jason got his binoculars back out. "I was joking but now that you mention it, that might not be a terrible idea."

"Jason. *I* was joking. There's no way in hell we should go down there and talk to them. Even with our weapons we'd be no match for their numbers. I mean, sure, we might get them to talk to us and everything would be okay. But the risk of dying is big enough that I don't think we should even attempt it."

"So what's your idea?"

Dianne pointed at the sketch of the compound in her notebook. "See there near the left side at the back where they have those burned out cars on the slope? A few of them don't look like they were shored up very well. I bet we could sneak in back there at night, go through the cars and head for the shed where they're keeping Tina."

"What then?"

"I assume we'd sneak back out, go around the compound and hike back to the truck."

"Hm." Jason grunted again. "I like the core concept but I think it needs some work."

Dianne laughed. "Okay, Mr. Expert. You tell me what we should do."

"Yeah, yeah. Give me a few minutes. I'm thinking."

Jason and Dianne sat quietly while Jason looked at both the compound and Dianne's sketch. After a few minutes of pondering he pointed out across the road. "We need to distract them. Get their attention off of the back of the compound and out towards the front."

"How do you propose we do that?"

Jason looked up at the sky. "It'll be dark in a few hours. Once the sun goes down I'll head down and position myself a few hundred feet to the right, along the east side. You'll head down to the west side near those burned out cars along the fence. I'll set up enough noise to pull every single one of them over to the east side while you go in, get Tina and get out. We'll meet back up at the truck and get out of here."

"That sounds incredibly risky for you."

Jason chuckled. "Risky? You're the one who'll have to go inside the compound and get her out!"

Dianne thought about Jason's proposal before finally nodding her approval. "Fine. We'll do it. But if anything goes wrong I want you to get out of there. I'm going to do the same. We can't help her or anyone else if we're dead."

"All joking aside I really think this is the least risky solution. I'll be far enough from the compound that I can just slip away and head back to the truck. You're going to be the one in real danger. If you end up getting stuck and need help just fire off three quick shots and I'll head back."

"I sure as hell hope I don't need to do that."

"Me too, D. Me too."

Chapter Fourteen

Cheyenne Mountain Complex
Outside Colorado Springs, CO

"DID you at least get his name?"

Rick rubbed his eyes and groaned. "No. Again. I did not get his name. Or his rank."

"Well what did he look like?"

"I don't know... like a soldier? Average height, average weight, wearing a uniform."

Jane stopped her pacing and sat down in a huff. "Well it would have been nice if you had been paying attention to the only person who's so far acted like they could help us."

"Even if we found him again I wouldn't want to ask him for anything else."

"Why not?"

Rick sat up in his bed and swung his legs over the side. Jane sat in a chair near the shower while Dr. Evans was perched on top of the desk, gently kicking his legs back and forth as he watched Jane and Rick talk. In his hands was the small black object Rick had received from the soldier.

"Because," Dr. Evans said, holding up the object in his hands, "if someone finds out he gave this to us then he will never see the light of day again. Ever."

"You figured out what it is?" Jane looked over at Dr. Evans.

"It's just a miniaturized computer. Nothing all that fancy. Protective shell hides the screen and small keyboard. It's like those old phones more than anything else, really."

"Great." Jane rolled her eyes. "Why don't you order us a pizza before we all get thrown in a cell."

Dr. Evans smiled as he popped open the computer to reveal the small display. "As with many things it's not what's on the outside that matters quite as much as what's inside."

Rick hopped out of his bed and crossed the room. He took the computer from Dr. Evans and looked at the screen, tapping at it and on the keyboard. "What is all of this?"

"Information."

"That's kind of vague. What type of information?"

"I'm not entirely certain yet. But if this soldier gave it to you after our conversation with General Black and the soldier mentioned Damocles then it must have something here to help us."

As Dr. Evans talked Rick continued to browse through the files on the device. His eyes widened as he reached a folder full of filenames that started to make sense. "These look like military bunker locations. They're all marked as top secret."

"Bunker locations?" Jane got up from her chair and circled around to look at the device alongside Rick and Dr. Evans. "What good does that do?"

"That's just one small fraction of the information on this thing." Rick closed the device and handed it back to Dr. Evans. "I bet that soldier dumped everything that might even be tangentially related to Damocles onto this. He probably stole it from their archives here."

Dr. Evans nodded. "Agreed. I'll look through it and see if I can find anything that'll be immediately useful in our search. You two should figure out how we're going to get out of here. I'm not entirely comfortable with using the General's car."

Rick shrugged. "The soldier said that would be the easiest thing to do. I'm inclined to believe him until we see otherwise."

"Just be safe. Both of you."

Rick and Jane nodded before Rick turned towards the door. "Come on, let's look around a bit and see what kind of trouble we can get into."

Jane rubbed her hands together and grinned. "Now you're talking!"

⸻

WHILE DR. EVANS toiled away on the uncomfortably small computer, Rick and Jane did their best to look like two normal people out for a stroll inside an underground military complex. The oldest part of the complex was larger than Rick had initially expected, with multiple buildings beyond the initial one that he had seen and that housed General Black's office. The deeper sections of the complex were obviously newer and there were ones that were even farther underground than the structure where he, Jane and Dr. Evans were being housed.

Cheyenne Mountain had never been originally intended as a place for civilians to be housed for long periods of time. Over the years, though, as the threat of global wars based on nuclear, chemical and biological attacks grew, the government revised some of its plans. Predictions based on civilian casualty numbers ranging from mild to extreme were created and a general guideline was drawn up that would be enacted should the situation warrant it.

At its most basic level this guideline directed military teams to secure and protect civilians that happened to fall within their local jurisdictions. For places like Nellis that had huge populations next door this directive didn't work very well given that the civilian population could overwhelm and overrun the base. For Cheyenne Mountain and other underground locations, though, it worked much better.

So long as the situation didn't require that the bases "button-up" they would remain open to collect as many people as they could hold. Once full, however, they would close their doors and keep anyone from moving in or out until the threat levels dropped. The Cheyenne Mountain Complex, while not near capacity, had other protocols to follow and thus would be closing in less than two days. Being equipped with enough food and water for the residents inside to wait things out for up to five years meant that Rick and Jane had to find a way out of the base and fast.

"Where are we? Haven't we just gone deeper into the complex?" Rick turned around and looked at the multi-colored stripes painted on the wall. Different colors branched off into different tunnels though none of them were marked by name.

"I'm not sure. I think red means the hospital area." Jane stopped and looked down a long tunnel. "Did we pass the hospital before?"

Rick shrugged. "I have no idea. It's insane how deep this place goes."

"I heard a couple of airmen talking when they were coming in the other day. They were going on about these huge limestone caverns beneath the complex that were filled with food and water. I guess that's where General Black is going to get the supplies to keep everyone alive."

"I'm not sure I'd want to be alive if I would have to be trapped underground with General Black."

Jane snorted in amusement. "Fair point. Come on, let's head back and see if we can find a way up."

After another forty-five minutes of wandering Rick and Jane rounded a corner and found themselves staring down a short corridor leading to the main doors for the complex. The activity in the corridor was frenetic with soldiers, airmen, marines and sailors running back and forth as they delivered messages and carried pallets of supplies and equipment from vehicles in the tunnel through the main doors.

Rick watched the commotion for a moment before nudging Jane and whispering. "We should get outside into the tunnel and see what it's like out there. We'll have to get through the main doors if we want to leave anyway so we might as well test it now."

Rick was about to walk towards the gates when Jane pulled at his jacket to stop him. "Hang back a second." She pointed across the hallway at a red sign hanging from the wall.

EMERGENCY EXIT ONLY – KEEP SEALED AT ALL TIMES

"What do you think that is?"

Rick shrugged. "An emergency exit?"

Jane rolled her eyes and gave him a playful punch on the side of his arm. "No kidding. Don't you think it's worth checking out?"

"Probably so, yeah. Let's see if we can make it through the main doors without being stopped. On our way back in we'll head over there and see what's up with the emergency exit."

"Sounds good. Lead on."

Rick took a deep breath, straightened his back and walked briskly out into the main hallway with Jane following close behind. Rick kept his eyes forward, ignoring the occasional sideways glance he got from a few of the uniformed men and women. He made it through the first door easily enough but had to stop in between the first and second while the soldiers pushed both doors open a few more feet to make room for several large pallets that were being pulled into the complex.

The delay was enough that Rick was starting to feel nervous about standing there doing nothing but he did his best to keep a passive look on his face until the path was open again. As he and Jane stepped forward one of the soldiers manning the door turned and glanced at him. "Sir? Where are you going?"

Crap. Rick glanced at the soldier as he and Jane slowed down. "General Black sent us out here. Said our gear was being brought in and we should go collect it so it doesn't get lost."

The soldier glanced back and forth at Rick and Jane for a second before nodding. "Go ahead."

Rick smiled and sped back up and he and Jane quickly passed through the second door. Outside, in the tunnel, the noise and commotion was through the roof. Vehicles full of crates and people were lined up through the entirety of the entrance tunnel and halfway down the side of the mountain. Rick turned and headed down the tunnel, stopping once he reached a large stack of crates.

"What are we doing here?" Jane whispered to Rick.

"Watching." Rick nodded at the commotion. "My guess is that they're going to be bringing in people and supplies like this right up until the point when they seal those doors. We might be able to steal one of their trucks while they're unloading it and just drive it out of here."

"I thought that guy told you that the General's car was the best thing to take, though."

Rick shrugged. "I don't see anything other than Humvees and these big haulers, do you?"

Jane looked out from behind the stack of crates and pointed back down at the direction from which they came. "It looks like everything's turning around in front of the main doors but the tunnel keeps going past that. Maybe there's a parking area or something down there."

"Huh. Good point. Let's check it out."

The pair received almost no questioning glances as they walked along, though Rick chalked that up to the fact that they were blending in well with the sea of civilians and soldiers who were heading through towards the main doors. As they neared the doors Rick pulled Jane along with him as he slipped to the side out of the throng and between a pair of parked trucks. After heading to the other side of the tunnel Rick picked up the pace and jogged along until he reached the spot where the vehicles were turning around.

"Ha! Told you!" Jane grinned and walked past Rick. Parked up against the wall inside a small painted-off area sat a small two-door black sports car. A few other vehicles were parked behind the sports car but none of them looked anything like it.

"Huh. I didn't take General Black as the type to drive something like this." Rick circled around the car and cupped his hands around his eyes as he peered in through the heavily tinted passenger window. "You think all three of us can fit inside this thing?"

Jane was standing on the driver's side of the vehicle, up against the wall of the tunnel, and gently tugged on the handle. The door opened with a soft whoosh and she peeked in. "The backseat's a bit small but I can squeeze in there. Oh, hey! Look at this!" Jane reached in and pulled out a set of keys that were sitting in the center console.

"Nice. Leave them there, though." Rick glanced back toward the gate and stepped away from the car. "We don't need those on us in case we get searched or something."

"Got it." Jane tossed the keys back into the car and closed the door before walking around to stand next to Rick. "So this is our escape route, huh? We'll come out here, get the car and head down through the tunnel and to... wherever Dr. Evans says, I guess."

Rick nodded. "Yep. Exactly. Hopefully the sight of the general's car driving along will confuse the soldiers enough to let us slip by without them making too much of a fuss." Rick kicked one of the car's tires and sighed. "I'd prefer to have something a bit beefier but being able to outrun anyone chasing us isn't bad, either."

"Are you two lost?" The soldier that had spoken to them on their way out into the tunnel was now standing in front of the main door shouting at them.

Rick waved at the man as he whispered out of the side of his mouth at Jane. *"Follow my lead."* They walked towards the soldier who had his hand on his sidearm while he narrowed his eyes at them.

"I thought you two were going out to get your gear."

Rick sighed and threw his hands up in the air. "We were supposed to. But it wasn't out here. We were just taking a walk while we waited to see if it was being unloaded." Rick turned to Jane. "I still don't see it, do you?"

"Nope, nothing." Jane shook her head.

"We'll head back in, I suppose." Rick spoke again before the soldier had a chance to reply. "I don't want to get in the way any more than we have." Rick smiled and walked past the soldier, leaving the man to stand there and watch the pair as they went back inside the complex.

Chapter Fifteen

Somewhere between Ellisville, VA and Blacksburg, VA

AFTER WALKING a fair distance away from the hill to answer the call of nature and radio the house to give Sarah and Mark an update, Dianne headed back to rejoin Jason. The sun had all but vanished on the horizon and the pair were checking their gear yet again in preparation for heading down to the compound.

"I'll leave my bag up here," Dianne said, "and Tina and I can pick it up on the way out."

"How much stuff do you have in there?" Jason hefted the bag with one hand and rolled his eyes. "Just give it to me. I'll tie it onto my pack."

"Are you sure?"

"Yeah, you two are going to have to loop around far enough from the compound that you don't need any excess weight on you."

"And you're going to be running from people who know where you are. You don't either."

"Quiet, you." Jason shook his head. "I'll be fine. Just remember the plan and make sure you don't get caught. No noise, no gunfire, no flashlights. Just get her out and go. I'm going to catch hell if you get hurt while we're out here."

"Yeah, Sarah wanted to talk to you when I called in earlier. I told her you weren't near the radio. She didn't sound happy."

Jason grinned. "Why do you think I made *you* go call in?"

Dianne chuckled and stood up, taking in a deep breath and letting it out in a long sigh. "You ready for this?"

"Ready as I can be."

"All right. I'll expect the shots in fifteen minutes."

"Starting my countdown now."

Dianne reached out and gave Jason a hug before turning and running down the hill, heading for the western side of the compound where the back of the gas station—and the shed holding Tina—was located. Jason went in the other direction, circling around to the eastern side and aiming for a rise from which he would have a clear angle on the front of the compound.

It took Dianne ten minutes to get in position at the back of the compound and she realized that getting in and out was going to be easier than she thought. One of the burned out cars was a large truck with a gaping hole through the center that had been filled with several sandbags. With no guards in sight she was able to pull the sandbags out before ducking down behind the vehicle to await Jason's distraction.

Jason, meanwhile, reached his location in just over five minutes, giving him plenty of time to contemplate the plan he and Dianne had set up and think of ways to improve it. Instead of merely firing off several shots to draw the attention of those inside the compound he would put the rounds through a few objects instead. Dianne had insisted that he not kill anyone since it was impossible for them to know the details of those who appeared to be the captors and the captives, so that was out. Shooting out some lights and putting holes in the fuel trucks, though? That sounded like it would provide an excellent distraction.

Jason swept the scope of his rifle across the compound, making mental notes as he went of various objects that would make for good targets. When his gaze passed over the north side of the compound—the side that had been impossible for them to see when they were perched on the hill to the south—he noted that there was a small object with several cables leading away from it. The generator wasn't all that powerful but it looked like the only thing providing light in the compound aside from flashlights carried by the occupants and the fires that were still burning.

He glanced at his watch and took a deep breath. *Almost time.* Once the first shot rang out he figured that he would have two minutes at most to continue firing before they identified his position and started out after him. Jason had already scouted the path down from his position and found the quickest way that would allow him to evade his eventual pursuers and make it back to the truck before they spotted him.

When the fifteen minutes was up Jason pressed his rifle up against his shoulder and steadied his breathing. The wood paneling on the stock felt rough on his cheek and the metal was cold in the autumn air. He squeezed the trigger on the rifle slowly, relaxing his body as he sunk into the weapon to make it as much of an extension of himself as he could.

The shot was loud, more so than Jason had expected with the foam earplugs he had dug out of his bag and placed in his ears a few minutes prior. The crack of the rifle echoed through the still night, cutting across the compound like a flaming blade. By the time the noise of the rifle reached the ears of those in the compound the damage it dealt had already been done.

The generator coughed and sputtered for a few seconds before going out. The lights around and inside the gas station blinked out along with it. Even as far out as he was Jason could hear the shouts of panic from the people inside the compound. *Time to up the ante.*

He fired six more shots, three of which were just to make noise and the other three of which were to further incite panic. One of the metal pots over a fire clanged as the bullet passed through, spilling the contents of the container out into the flames. Another bullet pierced the bottom of one of the fuel trucks sending a slow but steady trickle of gasoline pouring out into the dirt. The final shot went through the glass on the front door of the gas station, turning the safety glass into small chunks that fell with a loud crash into a heap on the ground.

Satisfied with the level of distress he had caused to the people in the compound, Jason scanned it again with his scope to make sure there was nothing he was missing. As he panned over to the south side of the compound he took in a sharp breath as he saw a man with a gun running for cover at the back of the building where Dianne was presumably rescuing Tina.

BEHIND THE COMPOUND Dianne jumped up at the sound of the first shot and headed through the burned out SUV. She glanced around to look for any guards before hopping out and running headlong for the shed at the back of the gas station. While the lights in the compound had gone off there was still just enough residual sunlight left for her to see the crude latch on the outside of the shed. She opened it, threw open the door and hissed inside.

"Tina? Tina! Are you there?!"

"Who's that?" The tired voice came from the depths of the shed and a small form came shuffling forward. "Dianne?" Dianne held out her hand to Tina to help her down when a deep shout came from off to her right.

"Hey! What the hell do you think you're doing?" Dianne turned her head to see a large man carrying a rifle in his hand skid to a stop. He looked just as surprised to see Dianne as she did to see him and both of them stood stock-still for a long second as each tried to figure out their next move.

Chapter Sixteen

Cheyenne Mountain Complex
    Outside Colorado Springs, CO

"A SPORTS CAR?" Dr. Evans asked the question again. "Are you sure?"

"It was either that, a white sedan or an SUV that looked like the back bumper was about to fall off."

"Hm." Dr. Evans scratched his chin. "I wouldn't think the general would be a sports car type of person."

"That's what I said." Rick chuckled. "I know it's not ideal but the more I think about it the more it makes sense that it'll be the best way to escape. The guards will recognize it so they won't be as prone to stopping it and it'll be fast enough to get away from whatever they send after us."

"You think they'll send people after us?" Dr. Evans' eyes widened and he gulped nervously.

"I don't know for certain but I wouldn't be surprised." Rick sat down across from Dr. Evans and gestured at the small computer in the man's hands. "How's it coming with this?"

"Hm?" Dr. Evans seemed to be lost in thought and took a few seconds to respond. "Oh, yes. The data. I'm afraid I've found nothing yet. Bits and pieces here and there but nothing new. Everything I've seen so far mirrors what I already know."

"Do you think you'll find anything?"

Dr. Evans shrugged. "There is an enormous amount of data on this device and its configuration makes it difficult to quickly search through it. I am thankful, though, that the power port is the same for other mobile devices. At least I won't run down the battery while using it."

Rick stood up, patted Dr. Evans on the back and nodded. "Excellent. Keep at it, please." He glanced over at Jane. "Do either of you want anything to eat? It's just after lunchtime, apparently. You wouldn't know it without looking at a clock, though."

"Yeah, I could do with a bite." Jane nodded.

"Hm? Yes, yes. Excellent. Please." Dr. Evans nodded without looking up from the miniature computer.

Rick chuckled and turned toward the door. "I'll be back in a bit."

AFTER TAKING a break to eat a quick meal Dr. Evans returned to his work. He sat at the desk in Rick's room, hunched over the computer tapping away at the small touchscreen and keyboard as he tried to locate information relating to Damocles. The archives in Cheyenne Mountain were enormous and contained data from dozens of government agencies of all types. Every once in a while he would come across a folder, document or search results relating to Damocles that looked worthwhile but ended up revealing nothing new.

The clues and hints of something larger buried in the data prompted Dr. Evans to continue working while Rick and Jane rested. It was around seven in the evening when Rick woke up and decided to take a stroll around the complex to relax his nerves and work some of the pent-up energy out of his system. He headed up to the main entrance into the complex to watch the people going back and forth. When he got there he noticed a strange uptick in the stress levels coming from everyone he saw.

"Hey!" Rick waved at a soldier who was running by and the woman slowed down.

"Can I help you?"

"Yeah, what's going on? Is something wrong?"

"Didn't you hear?"

"Hear... what?" Rick shook his head slowly.

"The general's closing the doors early. We're buttoning-up in three hours."

Once again Rick felt his stomach lurch. "They're closing the doors early? But what happened to the forty-eight hours?"

The woman shrugged. "No idea. If you'll excuse me, though." She dashed off before Rick could ask another question. He stood there for a moment, pondering what she said before he realized that the change was going to profoundly affect their chances of escaping from the complex.

"Shit!" Rick hissed under his breath as he turned and ran back down to get Jane and Dr. Evans. As he burst into his room they both looked up at him, smiling broadly.

"Hey! Perfect timing!" Jane jumped up from her seat next to Dr. Evans. "I think we've got something here!"

"That's great, but—"

"Yes, yes!" Dr. Evans nodded furiously. "We most definitely have something here. It was all Jane's suggestion that led to the discovery, too. See, we were—"

"Michael!" Rick shouted and Dr. Evans stopped talking. Before he or Jane could say anything, Rick continued. "They're buttoning-up in less than three hours!"

Jane and Dr. Evans both remained quiet for several seconds before Jane raised her hand. "Question. What's buttoning-up?"

"They're going to close the main doors." Dr. Evans removed his glasses and rubbed his eyes. "Damn. Did anyone tell you why?"

"No. It's busy as hell up there, though. Everyone seems to be in a mild state of panic about it."

"No doubt." Dr. Evans sighed. "We should get our things together. Jane and I were able to find some information that will prove useful once we're on the road."

Rick nodded. "Good. Explain it to me when we're in the car. For now let's get our bags and as much food and water packed up as we can fit without looking overly suspicious."

"How are we going to get back out there with our bags without getting stopped, though?" Jane asked.

Rick gave a sly smile. "Don't worry. I think I've got that covered."

⬜

"YOU HAVE *GOT* TO BE KIDDING!" Jane hissed at Rick as they walked down the corridor in plain view of a large number of military personnel.

"Keep quiet and smile!" Rick whispered back to her through gritted teeth.

Jane shook her head and forced a smile that she wasn't feeling on any level. Walking a few feet behind Rick she carried two large black trash bags, one in each hand. Dr. Evans was behind her carrying the same while Rick had a large green wooden box in his arms. After watching a few people carrying empty boxes and more than a few black bags out earlier in the day, Rick had come up with the idea of sneaking their gear out via the same means. Though the plan was basic and seemed obvious he was glad to see that they were getting even less sideways glances than they had earlier in the day when they walked in and out while carrying nothing.

Look like you belong and nobody questions anything. I guess that works in NORAD, too. Rick suppressed a chuckle and stepped to the side to avoid running into someone coming through the interior door. He, Jane and Dr. Evans then passed by the twenty-five ton vault door and headed for the exit when Rick heard a familiar voice.

"Hey, what are you doing out here this time?" Rick lowered the box and saw the same soldier who had stopped them earlier. He flashed a smile and hefted the box back up.

"Somebody has to get all this out so we volunteered to help. The less trash inside makes it better for everyone, am I right?" Rick tried not to sound *too* overly enthusiastic about the task but he could tell that the soldier wasn't completely convinced.

"Go ahead and set that down. I need to check it first."

Rick kept his smile steady as he lowered the box to the floor. He glanced at the outer door, mentally going through the plan for what they would have to do if they were caught.

"Go ahead and open it up for me." The soldier kicked at the box with his boot. Rick bent over, grabbed the top of the box and gently pulled it open. Inside sat a pile of refuse that he and Jane had collected from several garbage cans around the buildings while Dr. Evans had been busy finishing his packing. While not overly smelly the garbage had a definitive odor to it with the lid to the box open and the guard crinkled his nose. He stepped back and shook his head with a sour look on his face. "Better you than me. Go on, get it through."

Rick nodded and picked the box back up, glanced back at Jane and Dr. Evans and continued on through the outer door. The soldier barely gave Jane and Dr. Evans a passing glance as they walked by and in a matter of seconds all three were standing out in the tunnel.

As soon as they had passed the vault door they headed to the right, going deeper into the tunnel towards the general's car. Instead of stopping at it, though, they went past it and gathered together at the back of the sedan. Rick lowered the box gently to the ground to avoid any excess noise while Jane and Dr. Evans dropped their black plastic bags and tore them open. Each of the plastic sacks held one of their bags of gear at the bottom with a large pile of crumpled-up paper at the top. Rick quickly glanced through the bags to verify everything was there and nodded at Jane and Dr. Evans.

"Nice work, you two."

"No way." Jane shook her head. "That was all you. Brilliant thinking, filling that box with garbage like that."

"I figured that guy would want to see something so I made sure he had a show." Rick picked up his bag and peeked around the side of the sedan. "Dr. Evans, you've got the computer, right?"

"I do, yes."

"Good. If you're both ready to go then let's get the hell out of here. We'll throw the bags in the trunk, Jane will get in the back seat while Dr. Evans gets in the passenger seat then I'll get in the front and we'll take off. Sound good?"

"Let's blow this joint." Rick smiled at Jane's reply. He stood up and hurried toward the sports car, opened the driver's side door and got the keys off of the center console. He went around to the trunk, unlocked it with the key and threw his bag in. Jane and Dr. Evans threw theirs in next and went around to get into the car while Rick gently closed the trunk. Once Jane and Dr. Evans were seated Rick went back around, climbed into the driver's seat and pulled his door closed.

"Good grief!" Rick reached for the controls to the seat on the left side, adjusting it forward and upward. "I guess this is his car. The seat's practically sitting in the trunk."

"Hallelujah! I see some leg room starting to appear back here!"

"All righty." Rick buckled his seatbelt and looked at his companions. "Fasten your belts and hold on to your butts. This might get bumpy."

Author's Notes

September 8, 2017

You're still reading this story? Wow! Thank you so very much for continuing on; it's readers like you who have made this an incredible experience. I'm pretty sure you're going to like where the story goes from here. :)

Chekhov's Gun is a principle in in writing that says that every story element should be relevant. If a story talks about a gun in the first chapter then that gun needs to be fired in the second or third chapter. If it's not going to be fired then it shouldn't be in the story in the first place. So… basically it's foreshadowing. But the term "Chekhov's Gun" sounds way cooler.

With episode 6 of Surviving the Fall we're finally starting to see some big guns firing that have been hanging around since the beginning of the series. I've been patiently waiting to bring the Carsons and Statlers back into the story as well as re-introduce the two jerks that tried to steal Dianne's truck. There's also the bit about Rick's job that gave him the right type of expertise to be able to work with Dr. Evans to figure out what to do about Damocles. That's pretty handy, eh?

Tying story threads together throughout a multi-book series is challenging and despite writing down my plans and doing frequent checks to make sure I keep up with things, sometimes something will slip through the cracks. While I'm hesitant to admit some of the larger changes I've made in the story for fear of pulling the curtain back too far I thought this might be interesting.

Okay, so, if you were to peek at my original overall outline for Surviving the Fall you'd see that the people who were going to arrive to help Dianne weren't actually supposed to be the Statlers. They were originally going to be her parents. What I realized when I got into book 5, though, was that I hadn't talked enough about Dianne's parents to make this a storyline that would make any sense whatsoever. I would have just been bringing in some random people halfway through and introducing them with no context.

When I realized I had backed myself into this corner I tried to figure out what I thought would be the next best answer (but which I think actually turned out to be a far better one). Enter Jason and Sarah. They (and the Carsons) were mentioned multiple time at the start of the story and there was context to them coming back in. I won't disclose their original fate (except to say that it was not dissimilar to what the Carsons have gone through) but them acting as helpers to Dianne and the kids was a much better story idea than the one I originally had.

While Jason and Sarah were introduced originally as longtime friends of Dianne and Rick, there's still a bit of wariness with having new people involved who aren't blood relatives. It's the apocalypse after all and people are going to do whatever they need to do to survive. Thankfully the Statlers have nothing but kindness in their hearts (so far, anyway). This particular storyline also really fits with what we learned in previous books about the Statlers being out of town and since they know the Waters and the Carsons then it becomes natural that Jason and Sarah would band together with Dianne to help figure out what happened to Tina and Dave.

My point is that in the end my original mistake turned out to be better for the story than my original plan would have been. That happens to me a lot when I'm writing and is one reason why my books can sometimes take a while to write. I'll be writing along, making good progress when I'll realize that a story element that I had originally planned would be far better if I changed it to something else. Sometimes that change is small and sometimes it can be large enough to affect the rest of the series.

Episode 6 of Surviving the Fall was definitely the easiest to write of all of them so far. I've reached the point in the story where it's almost writing itself and when I sit down to add to it the words just flow onto the page. With the end of this book we've now reached what is essentially the point of no return in the story. Rick and Dianne have both been set on paths that will demand the very best from them. If they don't provide their best, there will be very real long-term consequences for them and for the world at large.

If you enjoyed this episode of Surviving the Fall or if you *didn't* like something—I'd love to hear about it. You can drop me an email or send me a message or leave a comment on Facebook. You can also sign up for my newsletter where I announce new book releases and other cool stuff a few times a month.

Answering emails and messages from my readers is the highlight of my day and every single time I get an email from someone saying how much they enjoyed reading a story it makes that day so much brighter and better.

Thank you so very much for reading my books. Seriously, thank you from the bottom of my heart. I put an enormous amount of effort into the writing and all of the related processes and there's nothing better than knowing that so many people are enjoying my stories.

All the best,
  Mike

Book 7 - The Darkest Night

Preface

Last time, on Surviving the Fall....

Rick Waters has finally found a familiar face. Jane, the woman he helped in Las Vegas, turned out to be staying with many other civilians in the Cheyenne Mountain Complex (NORAD). She happened to meet and befriend Dr. Evans, the man who originally worked on the precursor program that became Damocles and who was on Air Force One with the President when the plane crashed. After meeting and discussing Damocles, Rick and Dr. Evans decided that they needed to get out of NORAD and try to stop the program before things got worse. After a daring escape they stole the commander's vehicle and together with Jane fled the base, though they may be jumping from the frying pan into the fire....

Meanwhile, back in Virginia, Dianne and Jason have gone off in search of Tina Carson, who they learned had been taken captive by a band of ne'er-do-wells, some of whom are very familiar to Dianne. After locating the people who kidnapped Tina they discovered that they were woefully outnumbered and worked to come up with a plan to rescue Tina. As they begin their assault on the group's compound, Dianne works her way toward where Tina is being held while Jason provides overwatch. Their plan seems to be going well until Dianne is discovered and must quickly adapt to the situation....

And now, Surviving the Fall Episode 7.

Chapter One

"NO GUNFIRE." That had been one of Jason's statements before he and Dianne split up. She had gone into the compound with the full intention of making no noise whatsoever. Slip in, grab Tina, slip out. That was the plan. Unfortunately, as Dianne was learning all over again, the best laid plans do indeed often go awry.

"Hey!" As Dianne reached up to help Tina down the steps from the shed where she was being held, a loud voice boomed from behind. "What the hell do you think you're doing?!" Dianne whirled around to face the source of the noise. A large man who had been charging around the corner of the gas station to avoid Jason's gunfire was skidding to a stop, a rifle held loosely in his hands. He stared at Dianne with wide eyes, unsure whether she was a stranger to the compound or one of the people that the group at the compound had either outright kidnapped or coerced into working for them.

Dianne's pistol was tucked into her waistband holster and her rifle was slung over her back. Her left hand was still held out to Tina as she dropped to the ground, allowing her legs to buckle beneath her as she braced her left arm for an impact with the ground. Her right hand darted toward her holster and drew her weapon, flicking off the safety as she pulled it from its holster.

Five shots went out in rapid succession, three of which hit home in the man's chest and one which sliced through his neck. He dropped his rifle as he clawed at his neck, trying to scream out in pain but managing only to summon a horrible gurgling as blood poured unhindered through the jagged hole in his neck.

Dianne turned around to help Tina down but found her friend already halfway down the steps, holding onto one of the shed doors for support. She was dressed in a dirty, torn nightgown and wearing slippers, both of which had holes in the top, sides and front. She bore a scowl that was plainly visible even in the moonlight as she shuffled over to the dying man, trying not to slip on the grass and dirt.

"Asshole!" Tina shouted as she kicked the man in the side. He reached towards her and Dianne pulled her away before grabbing the man's rifle and tossing it as far away from his body as she could.

"Tina!" Dianne held her friend by the shoulders and looked her up and down. The older woman's short form looked even shorter, her skin was filthy and she appeared to have lost a significant amount of weight. "Quiet down; this is a rescue!"

"You could've been a bit quieter about it." Tina raised an eyebrow and smiled at Dianne. "Thank you, though. I was getting tired of being here."

"No sweat. Let's get out of here." Dianne turned away and Tina took the opportunity to kick the dying man one last time before following Dianne.

Dianne's eyes widened in an exasperated expression at Tina's action. "Do you have to?"

"Yeah." Tina nodded. "He was an asshole."

Dianne rolled her eyes. "Come on. We need to get out of here." She led Tina down through the makeshift fence at the back of the compound formed by the shells of old cars. The pair crawled through the fence and made their way out behind the compound, circling around to the side as they followed the path Dianne had taken on her way in.

The lack of artificial lighting in the compound made their getaway smoother than Dianne had anticipated though she wondered in the back of her mind why no one had investigated the gunfire behind the gas station. The thought was almost immediately followed by the sound of voices along the side fence of the compound.

"John's dead! Who shot him?!"

"Is it the sniper?"

"It couldn't be! That was from inside the perimeter!"

"Get to searching, you idiots! The woman's gone!" The last voice made Dianne's skin crawl. She pushed Tina forward into the brush, whispering at her to crouch down so that they could hide from the searching lights of the people inside the compound. As the lights and sounds of people running around started drawing closer to the area outside the compound where Dianne and Tina were walking, Dianne cringed as a gunshot rang out. The light that had been drawing closer to her and Tina suddenly vanished but before she could try and think about where the shot came from the sky erupted into fire. Light and heat poured out from the front area of the compound, accompanied by the sound of a massive explosion. Dianne, acting purely on instinctual self-preservation, threw herself to the ground, pulling Tina along with her.

⸻

JASON CURSED SILENTLY as he watched the man disappear behind the back of the gas station. A few seconds later the sound of several rapid gunshots echoed out from the compound. Fearing the worst he debated getting up and heading down into the compound to try and save Dianne but decided to wait a moment to see if the shots had been from her.

A wave of relief washed over Jason as he saw the outline of two figures outside the compound, moving through the trees and brush as they slowly made their way away from the fence. *Hallelujah.* Jason breathed a sigh of relief and turned his attention back to the compound and the people therein.

The man wearing the blue shirt—the same one who had been the leader of the group he and Dianne saw at the Carson's house—was peeking out from inside the gas station. The man wearing the red shirt—whom Jason and Dianne had decided was the leader of the group as a whole—was standing next to "Blue Shirt" and the pair appeared to be holding a conversation. Outside the gas station in the compound several people had gotten their hands on flashlights and appeared to be searching around the front, back and sides of the building.

"They're going to see that Tina's gone missing. Damn!" Jason whispered to himself as he panned across the compound with his rifle scope, trying to decide what to do next. Blue Shirt and Red Shirt ran out of the gas station and held a hasty conversation with a couple of men standing near the fence a short distance from where Dianne and Tina were walking. The man with the red shirt gesticulated wildly and the meeting was apparently disbanded as everyone who had been standing there dispersed and began running through the compound with their flashlights, presumably looking for Tina.

As one of the searchers ran along the inside of the fence he shone his flashlight outside the compound, its beam drawing closer to where Jason could see Tina and Dianne running along. He gritted his teeth and screamed internally, wishing there was some way he could get Dianne and Tina to lay down in the brush or otherwise hide until the man passed them by. With no other options Jason let out a low growl as he zeroed in on the man, aiming for his center of mass.

The bullet cracked as it broke the sound barrier, whizzing across the darkness and penetrating through two layers of cloth before shredding both flesh and bone. The man who had been close to discovering Dianne and

Tina dropped his flashlight and screamed, though his cry for help was quickly overshadowed by what occurred a few seconds later.

The fuel truck out in front of the gas station—the same one that Jason had punctured with his rifle with the intent of depriving the group of the valuable gasoline contained within—had been leaking throughout the events of the last several minutes. As the liquid spread along the ground through the compound the fuel evaporated, creating a cloud of explosive fumes. When the fuel finally hit the campfire near the fuel truck the flames ignited the fumes, sending a wave of fire along the ground and back to the truck.

Considering the poor quality of care given to the fuel trucks that the group had been bringing into the compound it was a wonder that they hadn't had an accident with them. The tops were left off of the trucks, allowing the fuel to slowly evaporate, and they hadn't done any checks on the valves and seals. The result was a truck that was dangerously explosive and when the flames finally spread to the vehicle its explosiveness was demonstrated in spades.

Although Jason was a significant distance from the compound he still flinched from the light and the faint heat generated by the explosion of the truck. Fire and metal wreckage rained down from the sky across the compound and the area surrounding. Several members of the group in the compound who were unfortunate enough to be close to the truck were instantly killed by the blast and the flames. Those far enough away to not be killed instantly were seriously injured and began screaming as they tried to put out the fire that clung to their clothing.

The explosion of the fuel truck immediately diverted the attention of the group inside the compound from both Tina's disappearance and Jason's gunfire. He watched as Dianne and Tina slowly stood up outside the compound and continued moving, relieved that they hadn't been injured by the explosion. As they moved off from the compound Jason turned his gaze back to the gas station, still performing overwatch for the two women until he was confident they were far enough from the compound to be relatively safe.

Safety, however, is always relative. As Jason panned over the compound again he noticed that, near the back, Red Shirt and Blue Shirt were not only still standing but were pointing in Jason's general direction. Jason had just enough time to notice that the pair were holding rifles and squirm backwards a few inches before a burst of gunfire began hammering his position on the hill. He grabbed his rifle and his bags and rolled backwards along the hill, trying to get into cover.

When he finally made it behind a small dip at the top of the hill he put his head back on the grass and groaned before putting on his backpack. He crawled away from the hill, keeping the tree at his back and his rifle in one hand, getting away as fast as possible while hoping that he had distracted the group long enough for Dianne and Tina to get away.

Chapter Two

S omewhere near the border of Colorado and Kansas

"OF ALL THE cars I've ridden in this has to be the absolute *worst.*" Dr. Michael Evans groaned as he shifted position yet again, trying to find a comfortable spot to sit in the back seat of the small sports car. Every swerve and bump in the road was magnified tenfold in the back of the vehicle; though up front Jane and Rick weren't having quite as many difficulties.

"You kept making fun of me for complaining! Now you get to see what it's like!" Jane grinned in the rearview mirror, glancing back for a second as she drove along. Rick sat next to her and shook his head, feeling more like a father on a road trip than a man on his way to either save the world or meet his maker.

"Quiet down, you two. We're all taking turns riding in the torture chamber. Make the best of it and keep the complaints to a minimum." Dr. Evans rolled his eyes but said nothing, merely grunting with each new movement of the car.

It was late in the morning as the small sports car tore along the open Kansas highway at just under a hundred miles an hour. The sky was surprisingly clear, offering a breathtaking view of the Rocky Mountains in the background and an uninterrupted horizon of green and brown ahead. The flat, featureless plains along both sides of the road offered a somewhat comforting view on a world that seemed remarkably unchanged.

The number of vehicles on the highway was surprisingly small and the lanes were clear of debris. This made it easy to maintain a high rate of speed without worrying about coming up on a burned-out wreck or having to somehow go off-road in a vehicle that barely had enough clearance to handle a speed bump.

The escape from the Cheyenne Mountain Complex had been relatively easy, surprisingly enough. The guards at the main gate had it partially open at the sight of the General's car and Rick had sped through before they realized their mistake. If the General even knew about the theft he either didn't care or had bigger things to deal with since, as they sped along through the base and out toward the highway, they didn't see a single vehicle coming after them in pursuit. After driving for a few hours Rick handed over the reins to Jane. She kept them going as dawn broke over the horizon and continued going along well into the late morning.

"You know," Rick said, "as uncomfortable as this car is we really are lucky to have gotten our hands on it."

"Why's that?" Dr. Evans piped up from the back seat.

"It's still intact for one thing. I never thought I'd see an Edison still working after what Damocles did to all of the modern vehicles. The fact that the General had the computer systems disconnected is a minor miracle. I don't know how we'd make it all the way across the plains in a Humvee or something."

"Security precautions, I'd guess. He wanted something fancy and modern but in his position he couldn't be all connected up to everything if he's working in the complex."

Rick leaned over and looked at the fuel gauge, shaking his head in amazement. "We haven't even used a fifth of the tank so far. It's incredible."

"You work—well, *worked* in the auto industry, right?" Jane said. "Why do you find it so incredible?"

Rick smiled. "For all I complained about my job and automation coming in and being a harbinger of doom—I was right by the way—stuff like this still fascinates me. I also hadn't realized how far Edison had come in improving the efficiencies of their solar panels. Once we run out of gas we should only have to stop every few hours to let the batteries catch up. They're *almost* providing enough power to fully run the car."

Jane glanced over at the large LCD panel embedded in the center dash of the vehicle. Rick had been tapping at the screen for the last hour and every time she or Dr. Evans asked him what he was doing his only response was 'working.' "Would you please just tell us what you're doing with that thing?"

"Yes, please!" Dr. Evans spoke up from the back seat. "Anything to break up the monotony of this dreadful ride!"

Rick pointed at the display which was showing an overhead image of the car on the top half and a black and white command-line window and keyboard in the bottom half. "Trying to access the root administrative systems. Some of our internal developers found backdoors into Edison's software a year or so ago when they first went to market. If I can access that then I might be able to figure out how to get more drive time out of the gasoline engine and maybe even the solar panels."

"Do you think some of the features were artificially locked away?" Dr. Evans leaned up, suddenly intrigued by what Rick was doing.

"That's something Edison and a few other manufacturers were doing with their hybrid and full electric vehicles, yes. General Black strikes me as the type who would rather spend the money on the full feature set versus skimping but you never know." Rick shrugged. "Not that it really matters. None of the old backdoors I remember still work so I can't get into the computer and muck around with things."

Dr. Evans slouched back in his seat and sighed. "Pity. Still, if what you say is true about what'll happen when we run out of gas then I suppose I can continue suffering through the complete lack of suspension and cushioning back here."

"Boys," Jane said, "I hate to change the subject, but we should really discuss what we're going to do now that we're away from the complex and aren't being chased. Speaking of which, I still can't believe we're not being chased."

Rick instinctively looked in the side mirror, seeing nothing but empty fields and road stretching out to the pale Rocky Mountains. "Whatever their reason for buttoning-up was, it must have been serious." He turned in his seat as much as possible to look at Dr. Evans in the back. "Jane's right, though. We haven't talked much about what you found in that database. Where exactly are we going?"

"We still need an authentication key to tell Damocles to shut itself off. I think, based on what I found in the database given to you by that soldier, our best chance is going to be heading to Washington and locating someone with access to it."

Rick stared at Dr. Evans for a few seconds before bursting out laughing. "Seriously? What do you want to do, just walk up to the NSA's front door and knock? I doubt anyone's still home there and even if there was someone left they wouldn't listen to us."

"Be that as it may, this is the only path forward I see for us. You said you'd do whatever it takes, right?"

Rick's smile slowly vanished and he nodded. "Yes. We have to stop this before it gets any worse. If nuclear options are coming soon on Damocles's list then we have to act fast."

"Then I don't know what else to do. The only way to tell Damocles to stop is by communicating with it directly. That's easy enough to do. But we need that encryption key. Without it we won't be able to do anything."

Rick sighed. "Okay. Washington it is. What if nobody's around who can help us?"

"I spent a little bit of time at the complex the NSA used when they were working on the project. I can probably remember where to go and from there we'll have to search individual servers—assuming we can even access them—until we find what we're looking for."

"How do you know the NSA was in charge?" Rick furrowed his brow. "I don't doubt that they were but that seems like the kind of information they'd want to keep secret."

Dr. Evans snorted. "You work with spooks long enough and you start to be able to tell them apart at a glance. The code monkeys they brought in had fresh NSA recruit written all over their faces, plus a couple of higher-ups were clearly working there too."

"You think the facility will still have power?"

"Undoubtedly. Maybe not active but they have several different backup power mechanisms at their high-security locations. Damocles might have shut down one or two of them but not all. The quickest way we'll be able to resolve this is by finding someone to help, so let's hope for that."

"Or maybe we'll find a yellow sticky note on a monitor somewhere with the password we need."

"Ha!" Dr. Evans laughed. "I doubt it. We should find all of the equipment we need to connect to enough Damocles systems to make the propagation of the shutdown command fairly fast." He shrugged apologetically. "I know it sounds bleak but it's the best we've got to go on."

Rick turned back around in his seat and nodded. "Sounds like a plan. A terrible, rudimentary, fly-by-the-seat-of-your-pants plan. But still a plan."

Chapter Three

D allas, TX

THE ORANGE and yellow hues of a seemingly neverending firestorm blot out all other colors. The hellish glow is made all the more real by the addition of an intense heat that radiates through the streets, swept along by the wind and the buildings themselves.

The fires started a short time ago on the western edge of the city as gas mains cracked and burst, sending explosions rippling beneath three blocks' worth of commercial buildings before automatic safeties kicked in. The safeties stopped the explosions from spreading to other sections of the city but did nothing to contain the fires that began to jump from building to building. Years worth of strategic dismemberment of building safety codes, as government and business colluded to make legal and illegal profits their number one priority, have resulted in a fire of unimaginable proportions.

As the fires spread people begin to panic. A few find temporary shelter underground but the lack of oxygen—all that is available is consumed by the fires—quickly leads to their demise. Most flee on the surface, running along streets, alleys and sidewalks as they leave everything but the clothes on their back to try and save themselves.

Mothers and fathers carry young children in their arms, cradling them and pushing their faces against their chests to try and protect them from the smoke, ash and violence. People shout at each other as they discover new routes they believe will save them. Some cross through a shopping mall, hoping that it proves to be a shortcut. Others descend into the sewers to try and find protection from the flames. Many try to cross a pedestrian bridge over an artificial canal, overloading it in the process and sending it—and themselves—crashing down onto the concrete below.

It is impossible to get out of the city with a vehicle. Most of them were destroyed in primary or secondary explosions before the gas fires began. The few vehicles that are left are unable to get out because there is no room for them to drive. The streets are clogged with the smoldering wreckage of all manner of cars, trucks and more.

A few who have bicycles, skateboards and even roller skates use them to great effect, at least initially. They are quickly overpowered by those without and their faster modes of transport are stolen and re-stolen again and again. Those who move too slowly in choke points are shot without hesitation, their broken and dying bodies acting as nothing more than an inconvenience to be trampled upon by those who are trying to escape.

For all of the fighting, screaming, crying, begging and pleading that goes on there is no salvation for most of the one million people who try to escape the flames. Driven by the winds and moving at speeds that cannot be matched by sheer force of will the intense heat and lack of oxygen kills all in its path. Those who survive are at the edges of the city, far from the explosions and left with escape routes both on foot and by vehicle. They flee before the approaching firestorm, seeking shelter beyond the city as they try to understand what is happening and what, if anything, they did to deserve such a torment.

The initial explosions killed two hundred and eighty people. Tens of thousands more have perished in the firestorm since. A million more will die before the day is out. There is no salvation for those in the city or in countless others across the globe. All the victims can hope for is a quick death, free from pain and suffering.

Most will experience the opposite.

Chapter Four

Somewhere between Ellisville, VA and Blacksburg, VA

"WE'VE GOT to pick up the—"

"If you tell me to pick up the pace one more time I'm going to take these slippers off and jam them where the sun doesn't shine!"

Dianne stifled a snicker at Tina's annoyed response. Dianne had been encouraging Tina to try and walk faster ever since they got away from the compound but Tina's footwear made traveling quickly over the rough terrain difficult to say the least. Moving through the trees, brush and open fields in the dark was challenging enough during the times Dianne dared to turn her flashlight on. She did so sparingly, though, as she wanted to try and avoid any possibility of being spotted by the group at the gas station.

The pair walked along mostly in silence except for the occasional whispers and huffing and puffing from Tina. A lifetime of working as a nurse meant she had been on her feet far more than she ever wanted and after retiring she confined her walking to an indoor treadmill, at the mall or while on vacation. Hiking through the woods—especially while wearing slippers—was not on her itinerary.

"How much farther till we get to your truck?"

"Not long. Five, ten minutes maybe." Dianne turned and looked back at the orange glow behind them. "Good grief. You can still see the fire back there."

Tina didn't bother looking back as she replied in a gruff tone. "I'm not surprised. Jason nearly killed all of us with that explosion."

"He also saved our lives."

"Fair point." Tina shrugged and called back to Dianne who was standing still staring at the glow and smoke over the hills. "You coming or not?"

A little under ten minutes later Dianne and Tina crested a hill, went down the other side and found the truck in the cluster of trees and bushes where Jason and Dianne had left it. It appeared to be untouched and there was no sign of anyone else in the vicinity. While that normally would have been a comfort to Dianne she suddenly grew worried.

"Where's Jason?" Dianne turned on her flashlight and scanned the woods and field nearby. "Jason?" She hissed loudly, not wanting to yell for fear of attracting unwanted attention. "Where are you?"

"Where was he? When you were getting me out, I mean." Tina opened the passenger door to the truck and climbed in, groaning as she rubbed her sore feet.

"On a hill overlooking the compound. He should have gotten here first, though. He had a faster path to the truck than we did.

"Maybe he had to take a different direction to draw them off or something? There were those gunshots coming from the gas station."

"Maybe…" Dianne opened the truck and reached into the back, grabbing a couple of bottles of water and two energy bars from under the seat. She handed one of each to Tina and they both ate and drank, finishing their impromptu meal in haste. After Dianne finished draining the bottle she threw it into the back seat of the truck and closed the driver's side door. "I'm going to look for him."

"Not a bad idea." Tina nodded. "I'd come with you except…" She motioned down at her bathrobe and slippers as she trailed off.

Dianne nodded. "There's a pistol in the glovebox and more food in the back. Just stay in the truck and you'll be fine. I'll be back in t—wait. Did you hear that?" Dianne turned and crouched next to the truck, moving down to the back and through the trees to peer out into the field beyond. The sound of a faint groan had caught her ear and she scanned the dark field, looking for any sign of movement.

Off to the right of the field, near the road, Dianne finally spotted the source of the noise. A lone figure was walking towards the truck. The figure moved slowly, staggering along as they went, all while carrying a pair of packs on their back and a gun in one hand. Dianne stared at the figure for several seconds, trying to make sure it was who she thought it was before running forward.

"It's Jason!" A voice in Dianne's ear made her jump in surprise and she turned to see Tina crouched next to her.

Dianne ran out into the field, meeting Jason a good fifty feet from the truck. It was dark enough that Dianne could just barely make out the contours of his face, but as soon as she reached him she realized that something was terribly wrong.

"Jason? What happened?" Dianne whispered to Jason as he stopped and dropped to his knees. He slowly fell backward, letting the backpacks break his fall. His breathing was labored and slow and his shirt and jacket clung to his side awkwardly, like he had fallen in a puddle. Dianne flicked on her flashlight as she leaned down to see what was wrong with her friend only to gasp in surprise and shock at what she saw.

Dried blood caked Jason's face, smeared across by his own hand as he wiped sweat from his forehead and cheeks. The blood appeared to originate from his right side, where his shirt and jacket were sticking to his torso and stained a dark red. Jason's skin was exceptionally pale, looking a near-white in color. His eyes fluttered as he struggled to speak, barely able to pass more than a few breaths of air across his lips.

"What the hell happened to him?!" Tina stood over Jason and Dianne, pushing Dianne to the side to get a better view of the man lying on the ground. "Get that gear off of him and get him to the truck, quick! You got any supplies in the back of that truck?" A nurse for over thirty years of her life, Tina wasn't about to let a little thing like being kidnapped stand in the way of her helping one of her friends.

Dianne nodded and looked up at Tina. "In the back seat. And our packs, too. Do we move him, though?"

"Of course we move him! And by 'we' I mean you! Get him in the truck, quick!" Tina was already heading back towards the truck as Dianne slipped the packs off of Jason and grabbed his rifle.

"Hang on there, Jason. I'll be right back." Dianne bolted for the truck and threw the gear into the back before running back. She pulled Jason up, feeling him struggle with every muscle in his body to keep from collapsing again. They walked back toward the truck with Dianne grunting under Jason's weight as she held him upright. When they arrived Tina opened the door and got inside, then helped pull Jason in while Dianne pushed from the outside.

As they were finishing up getting him maneuvered into a lying position in the backseat Dianne heard a distant shout. She turned and saw the bouncing beams of half a dozen flashlights on the far side of the field. Wielded by six running figures the lights were drawing closer to the truck. Dianne swore under her breath and finished pushing Jason into the back before looking at Tina.

"Do what you can for him. We have to get out of here."

Tina nodded, not bothering to look up at Dianne as she flicked on the overhead dome light in the truck. "Just try not to get shot, okay?"

Dianne closed the door and hopped into the driver's seat. She twisted the key and cringed as the engine roared to life, signaling their exact location to all who were near. With no choice but to continue on she flicked on the lights, put the truck into gear and hit the gas. The truck lurched forward across the rough terrain, tree branches and overgrown bushes lashing at the sides and top of the vehicle. Dianne tried valiantly to keep the truck from bouncing around as they drove across a field away from the six men but as gunshots started to ring out she abandoned any hope of a smooth drive and focused on getting away as quickly as possible.

A total of four shots happened to connect with the truck but the worst of the damage was from the last one which took out one of the taillights. The rest embedded in the rear and side paneling, hitting nothing of importance and merely adding accents to the truck that Dianne hoped Jason would soon be able to fume and fuss about.

"How's he doing?" Dianne glanced in the rearview mirror to see Tina bent over Jason with blood on her gloved hands as she worked on his side.

"Not good! Get us to wherever we're going as fast as you can!"

AS THE WHITE truck pulled away and vanished into the distance, the six men stopped giving chase and stood still in the field, panting as they tried to catch their collective breath. The first one to speak was tall, broad-shouldered and wearing a red shirt.

"Find them." The statement was short and to the point.

"How are—" One of the other men started to ask a question when the man in the red shirt turned and stared him down.

"I don't care how or how much trouble or anything else. I want solutions, not excuses. Find. Them."

"It could take days… maybe weeks."

"They have a truck. That means they have a place where they're living. Maybe fuel and stockpiles of food, too." He turned to look at the other five. "Which is kind of important now that we *lost all of our shit!*" Flecks of spit shot from the man's mouth as he screamed, his face turning a similar shade of red as his shirt.

The other five men nodded and turned to head back toward the compound to salvage what they could. Preparations would be made to leave at dawn to start searching for the people in the white truck and the hours of darkness left were going to be filled with a great deal of toil.

The man in the red shirt stayed in the field for a moment, watching off into the distance in the direction where the white truck had disappeared. His mind was devoid of thoughts about the truck and its occupants; the only thing that passed through was the anticipation of his satisfaction when they caught the truck and its occupants and made them pay for what they had done.

It wouldn't just be wonderful. It would be *glorious.*

Chapter Five

N ear the Kansas/Missouri Border

WITH AN UNEVENTFUL DRIVE across the Kansas plains behind them, Rick and his two companions drew closer to the border of Kansas and Missouri and the massive sprawling metropolis of Kansas City. With a population of nearly one million people the technology and oil boom of the last few years had nearly doubled the city's residents overnight, putting enormous strain on infrastructure and support systems.

The selection of Kansas City as one of three worldwide test centers for a new type of solar cell meant there was excess cheap power for residents and businesses alike. This, in turn, fueled the growth of massive datacenters as internet-based companies added new datacenters in the area to take advantage of nearly zero power costs and attractive tax cut incentives. The discovery of a new source of oil less than thirty miles north of the city merely added to the boom as drilling, pipeline and other associated equipment was brought in and built to support the new industry.

Not one to turn down the influx of new commerce into the area the mayor of Kansas City worked with the governors of both states to aggressively expand the area, adding new office parks, power stations, oil refineries and more. Not everyone was happy with the changes to the area, though. Small businesses and residents suffered the most, enduring bumper-to-bumper traffic at all hours of the day, an increase in competition from newly built big-box retailers and a loss of unique character and charm as the population grew and changed in such a short span of time.

The seventeen massive, newly-built skyscrapers near the center of Kansas City were famous across the country as testaments to the rapid changes that had taken place. As Rick, Jane and Dr. Evans neared the city though, Rick cocked his head in confusion. "Aren't there supposed to be seventeen of those?"

"The skyscrapers?" Jane opened her eyes and leaned up in the back seat, peering through the windshield. "Uh... where are they?"

"I count seven. Not seventeen." Dr. Evans rubbed his eyes and looked again, wondering if he had somehow miscounted. "Yes. Definitely seven. What on earth could have happened to the others?"

Rick shook his head, a feeling of dread rising in his gut. "I don't know. Should we just go around?"

"That will add a significant delay to our journey." Dr. Evans scrolled through the map built into the car's central display. "If this is anywhere close to a recent version of the layout of the area then most of the roads will pass through the greater Kansas City metropolitan area no matter what. We'd need to backtrack a hundred miles to find a fast route to go around." Dr. Evans shook his head. "No, we must press on through the city and out on the other side."

"Great." Rick swallowed hard and sighed. "Find me the best way through the city."

"That... may be difficult." Dr. Evans peered out the window at a highway that branched off from the one they were on. It slowly rose into the sky, passing over homes and businesses on the outskirts of town. What he was looking at wasn't the elevated highway itself, though, but the massive chunks of it that had come loose from the structure as a whole, crashing to the ground and crushing everything beneath them.

"What the..." Rick took his eyes off the road for a few seconds, staring at amazement at the highway before the bump strip at the edge of the road brought his attention back on driving.

Jane pressed her nose against the back window. "What happened out there?"

"I have no earthly idea." Dr. Evans whispered as he studied the massive structure. "An earthquake, perhaps?"

"That'd have to be a pretty major earthquake, wouldn't it?"

Dr. Evans nodded. "It would indeed."

"So where should I go?"

"I would stay on this road as long as possible. It should pass through the city and out the other side without getting us stuck in the mishmash of small streets."

As the trio drove along they all stared in wonder and fear as the signs of destruction increased both in scope and magnitude. Long cracks ran along large buildings and roadways, pieces of buildings' facades lay strewn along the streets and strange shallow holes were visible in more than a few locations. Thin trails of smoke rose across the landscape, though whether they were from fires started by survivors or remnants of whatever disaster had befallen the area was impossible to say.

"This is creepy as hell." Jane whispered from the back of the car, switching between the left and right windows as she gazed out at the destruction. "It looks like somebody shook the city half apart."

"Is Kansas City on a fault line?" Rick wondered aloud.

"No idea." Dr. Evans shrugged. "But this type of tectonic activity is less surprising than you might think."

"Come again?" Rick glanced at Dr. Evans.

"When I was on Air Force One, before we crashed, I remember hearing people talking about mild to moderate earthquakes that were happening around the country. I have to wonder if Damocles had something to do with it. Perhaps by reversing pipeline flows, increasing the flow rate of fluids being pumped into the ground in exploratory wells or pressurized oil retrieval operations or other similar things."

"Oh, great." Jane rolled her eyes. "So this thing can cause earthquakes now, too?"

"That's not entirely accurate." Dr. Evans replied. "Damocles is an asymmetric weapon of war. It's designed with countless types of attack methods ranging from direct to subtle. We know that certain types of widespread artificial underground activity can manifest earth tremors so it's well within the realm of possibility that Damocles decided to ramp up that type of attack in some areas of the country."

"At least the main road through the city seems relatively clear." Rick said. While Jane and Dr. Evans had been busy watching their surroundings Rick had been focused on getting them through the city as quickly as possible. As they approached the center of the city Rick noticed that the number of intact vehicles was starting to increase. Most of them were burned out but there were more than a few that were still intact, which made him realize that they should take full advantage of the opportunity.

"Have you all seen anyone as we've been driving through?" Rick started easing up on the gas as he looked for a likely candidate vehicle in a safe location.

"Nobody. Unless that smoke is people, but I'm not convinced." Jane put her chin on the back of Rick's seat. "Why? You got an idea?"

"I'm just noticing that there are a decent number of vehicles that look intact around here. I know this thing only sips fuel but I hate letting a good stash of the stuff go to waste. What if we stop, siphon some gas from one of these cars and look around for some more supplies and maybe a gun or two while we're at it? It's a long drive to Washington and I don't know how long it'll be till we have an opportunity to stop again."

Dr. Evans nodded. "Excellent point. I loathe the idea of stopping here but I think you're right."

"Jane?" Rick looked in the rearview mirror, not wanting to make a decision on stopping without it being unanimous.

"Absolutely. I need to stretch my legs anyway."

"Perfect." Rick pointed out through the right window. "I saw a cluster of vehicles over there a minute ago. I'll swing back around. It looked like there were a few shops nearby so we can do a bit of supply searching, too."

Rick tapped on the touchscreen and turned off the gasoline engine, switching their car over to run solely off of the electric batteries so that they could move around without being heard as easily. At the next intersection he turned right off of the main road and wound the car along the street until he got to the parking lot he had seen previously. When he pulled in he realized why there were so many intact cars and he laughed at the sight.

"Ha! Look at those!" Half the parking lot was filled with burned-out wrecks of modern vehicles that had been destroyed by Damocles. The other half, though, was filled with pristine—albeit filthy from all the soot and smoke in the air—cars from the thirties through the seventies. The classic car meetup was a staple for the downtown area and it had gone from a once-per-month tradition to something that was almost continuously ongoing in some form or fashion.

Rick drove slowly down the line of cars, soaking in the sharp edges and gorgeous curves that were staples of the older designs. Dr. Evans and Jane had their eyes glued to the windows as well and Dr. Evans finally spoke up. "Can't we take one of these instead?"

"I sure as hell wish we could." Rick nodded. "The gas mileage on them is going to be abysmal, though. Plus this electric motor and our solar panels—"

"Yes, yes." Dr. Evans sighed. "I know. These things are just gorgeous, though."

"You won't get any argument from me on that one. Come on, let's find a hose and get to siphoning."

"Should we split up?" Jane asked. "One of us can get the tank topped off while the other two go look for supplies?"

"No." Rick's reply was firm and immediate. "We're sticking together, not splitting up. The last thing we need is to have one of us get hurt or into a bad situation on their own. That's doubly true because we've got no weapons to speak of right now."

"That's not entirely true." Dr. Evans reached under his seat and pulled out a thin, narrow plastic case. He popped it open to reveal a small semiautomatic pistol along with two seven-round magazines. "I found this under the seat while you were napping in the back earlier today."

Rick's eyes widened at the sight of the gun. "And you were just going to tell me about it now?!"

Dr. Evans shrugged as he closed the case back up. "It slipped my mind. My apologies. But at least we have something, right?"

"Absolutely! You know how to handle a gun?"

"Not… very well." Dr. Evans shifted uncomfortably in his seat. "I've never been a big fan of them. I suppose there's no better time to change that point of view than now, eh?"

"Yeah, I'd say so." Rick eased to a stop and shut off the car, unbuckled his seatbelt and accepted the case from Dr. Evans as he looked between him and Jane in the backseat. "Look, here are the basics. Just in case we get into trouble." Rick popped open the case and demonstrated how to load the pistol, eject a round from the magazine, where the safety was and how to hold and fire the weapon. When he finished he slipped the small .380 into his right pants pocket and put the spare magazine into the left. "First priority right now is fuel. We won't make it to DC without it. Once we have that we'll go look for more food, water and weapons. I doubt we'll find much of anything but given that all these cars are still here it's possible there are small pockets of the city that have been untouched."

It took less than an hour for the trio to locate some plastic tubing—taken from the fish section of a pet supply store—and siphon out enough gas to fill up the tank on the general's car. When they finished they began searching the shops in the area surrounding the parking lot. Water and food were their priorities but Rick knew how much more valuable weapons would be especially since they had a working vehicle with enormous range.

Rick took point on the search, leading them up and down streets and sidewalks as they searched through the area. Every once in a while they found a bottle of water here or an unopened candy bar there; nothing could be found in large quantities but the small finds slowly began to add up. It was the early evening when they had strayed half a mile from the original parking lot when they found themselves standing in front of a big-box grocery store set smack dab in the middle of the downtown district. While normally a bargain-priced store filled with cheap, shoddy overseas merchandise and food with questionable origins, the store had received fresh branding for its location in the heart of the metro area. The parent company was experimenting with offering its usual products with an upscale feel and a higher price-point and had decked out the building in spades.

An underground parking garage with a thousand spaces sat beneath the store, ensuring that customers would be able to visit with ease. The store itself was four stories tall and encompassed nearly a full city block. Constructed of brown brick and large glass panels, Rick was taken in by the pleasantness of the design until he noticed the cracks and broken glass in various places.

"Looks like the same kind of damage we saw on other buildings." Dr. Evans pointed at the cracks. "This absolutely looks like seismic activity."

"I haven't felt any tremors since we got here. Have you?" Rick replied.

"No, but that doesn't mean anything. If we're going to search inside for supplies then we should be quick about it. We don't want the place coming down on top of our heads."

"Shouldn't we have brought the car?" Jane looked both directions down the street. "We've got a bit of a hike to get back."

Rick shook his head. "I'd rather not get cornered somewhere while driving it. On foot we can move faster in all of the mess on the roads. Plus, while the electric motor doesn't make any noise, the three of us on foot will attract less attention than that thing will."

"Let's get inside, then." Jane rubbed her arms through her jacket, feeling a chill despite its warmth. "I don't like being out here."

As they walked into the store Rick was taken aback by the amount of natural sunlight inside. As he looked up at the ceiling and walls, though, he quickly discovered the source. A transparent roof coupled with a complex mirror system redirected and redistributed sunlight through the building. What was once a feature that provided shoppers with a feeling of being in a natural environment now ensured that Rick, Jane and Dr. Evans could browse through the store at ease despite their lack of flashlights.

"Okay, now we spread out a bit. No more than an aisle or three between us, though." Rick looked at Jane and Dr. Evans. "Stay on the same floor. Let's try to keep the noise down, too. No telling who might be around."

The trio each grabbed a shopping cart near the front of the store and began browsing, staying close to each other and communicating through loud whispers instead of shouts. It was apparent that the store had been looted, though whoever had done so hadn't been very thorough about it. Stacks of batteries and flashlights went into their carts along with the occasional package or can of food, a few jugs of water and clothing that—while dirty and smelling vaguely of smoke—was still in good condition.

While the bounty of the store was more than welcome, the more time they spent inside the building the more nervous Rick and Dr. Evans grew about the integrity of the structure. The cracks to the outside of the building were just as pronounced inside and in some areas they ran from the floor all the way to the ceiling. Bits of glass and metal from the roof and levels above were scattered across the floor though there had thankfully been no sign of anything fresh falling while they were walking around inside.

"Dr. Evans." Rick stopped his cart at the end of the aisle and whispered. "Let's get Jane and consolidate what we've found. I don't like the look of this place and we need to get out of here soon."

"Agreed." Dr. Evans stood from where he was pawing through a pile of sweaters and pushed his cart, following Rick down a couple more aisles. Jane was standing at the end of the aisle going through an endcap when Rick tapped on her shoulder.

"Get your cart and let's consolidate what we have."

Jane nodded and retrieved her cart and the three of them stood whispering while they compared what they found. There hadn't been much food but with what they found and what they already had there was enough to make it all the way to Washington and back. Water was more plentiful, though, and they had an adequate amount to see them through at least the next few days. Dr. Evans had picked up a few dozen disposable lighters and a couple packs of firestarters and Rick found some empty containers that could be used to store some excess gasoline. Jane's cart was mostly empty, but when she pushed aside the underwear, socks and shirts she grabbed, she revealed a find that made Rick's eyes grow wide with excitement.

"Where did you find these?!" Rick reached down into her cart and pulled out a pair of 9mm pistols along with five boxes of ammunition. He passed one of the guns to Dr. Evans and looked at Jane. "Seriously, where did you get these?"

Jane shrugged. "You two seemed like you had the food and water in hand so I headed over to sporting goods."

"You went off by yourself?" Rick shook his head. "Dammit, we were supposed to stick together."

"Yeah, yeah. You didn't even notice. Anyway, all the display cases were smashed in and looted. They even took the stuff near the paintball section. These and the ammo boxes, though, were in a locked cabinet underneath the counter with a note on them saying they were being held for some guy who I guess never came in."

"Wow." Rick nodded, impressed by Jane's attention to detail and creative thinking. "Nicely done on this find. Five hundred rounds will go a long way, too. We can spare a couple magazines for you two to get used to shooting them."

"Oh yeah. There were some other things under there, too. I guess whoever wanted this stuff put on hold needed the whole kit and caboodle." Jane lifted a pair of waistband holsters from the cart, four extra magazines, two flashlight and laser sight attachments and a pack of spare batteries.

Rick quickly loaded both pistols and slipped one of them into his waistband before looking at Jane and Dr. Evans. "Which of you feels more comfortable with this?"

Dr. Evans held out his hand. "I'll carry it, if you like."

"Sure thing." Rick passed the weapon to Dr. Evans before pulling out his pocket .380 and holding it out to Jane. "That means you get this."

"It's cute!" She took the pistol and turned it over in her hand.

"Cute but deadly." Rick eyed Jane as she examined the pistol. "Just keep it tucked away and don't shoot anything unless it's a life or death situation. We only have a couple of mags for it."

Jane nodded and put it into her back pocket. The three then picked through the supplies in the carts as they tried to decide what to take with them. They stood over the carts talking in low voices for several minutes before a low, barely perceptible rumble was swiftly followed by the distant sound of breaking glass.

"What was that?" Rick whirled around, looking in all directions for the source of the sound. It was far enough away that he couldn't pinpoint the source and he looked at Jane and Dr. Evans. "Any idea where that came from?" Before either of them could answer there was another crash, this one of glass and metal together, and much closer than the first.

"Spread out!" Dr. Evans whispered, pointing down the main aisle of the store. "Don't all stand in one place in case it's an earthquake!"

Jane and Rick moved several feet away from Dr. Evans and then Jane moved even farther down and squatted next to the broken remains of a center display that, before the event, once held hundreds of cans of fruit. As Jane looked warily between the ceiling and the entrance of the store on the opposite side of the building she swore she saw something moving near the front doors where she, Dr. Evans and Rick had entered.

"Rick!" Jane swiveled her head and whispered, her expression a cross between confusion and outright fear.

"What is it?" Rick felt goosebumps rising on his arms as she spoke.

"I saw something down there!"

Chapter Six

The Water's Homestead
        Outside Ellisville, VA

"JASON!" Sarah ran from the front porch of Dianne's house, shouting at the sight of her husband being pulled from the truck. Somehow Dianne had managed to get them back to the house in just under thirty minutes despite both the rough terrain and having to drive in the dark. She had radioed Sarah on the way back in the hopes of preparing her for what was coming but the line had been spotty as they drove through thick trees and behind hills and she hadn't been able to get a clear message back. Tina had managed to slow Jason's bleeding during the drive but he was still doing poorly and as Sarah ran to Jason and tried to grab him Dianne had to hold up a hand to stop her.

"Sarah! Help us get him inside, quick!" Dianne's stern voice broke through to Sarah and she nodded numbly and took Tina's place on the other side from Dianne.

"Mom?" Mark stepped off the porch, his rifle in his hands. "What happened?" He smiled and waved as he saw Tina hurrying toward the house. "Mrs. Carson! You're okay!"

Tina, still wearing her dirty bathrobe and slippers, nodded at him and smiled grimly. "Good to see you, Mark. Jason got hurt pretty badly. Can you round up any hand sanitizer you've got and clear off your dining room table? I also need lights. As many as you've got. I'll need to clean out his wound and stitch it."

"Yeah, I think we've—"

"Don't tell me, just get everything together, okay? We have to hurry if we're going to save him." The combination of Tina's serious tone and her disheveled appearance made Mark realize just how serious the situation was. He nodded and ran back into the house to start getting things ready while Tina followed behind.

"Do you all have running water?" Tina asked Mark. He flipped on a light switch to the hall and Tina squinted at the sudden brightness.

"Water and lights, yeah. We're running off solar."

"Fantastic. I'll wash up at the sink. Can you get me a big plastic trash bag or something? I just need something to wear over this stupid robe while I'm working on him."

"Yep, got it." Mark pulled out a black plastic trash bag from beneath the sink.

"Perfect. Cut a hole in the top and sides for my arms. Make sure you clean the table off with hand sanitizer. I want it to be as sterile as possible." Tina stood in front of the faucet and began scrubbing her hands under hot water, washing off layers of dirt and grime. After Mark finished with the trash bag he hurried into the dining room and cleared off the table before spreading out a plastic tablecloth across the top. Tina pulled her makeshift covering on and started washing her hands again as Mark quickly wiped down the tablecloth with alcohol-based hand sanitizer.

By the time Tina was finishing up with her final round of hand washing Dianne and Sarah had brought Jason into the house. Tina directed them to get him up on the table as she rummaged through a bag of medical supplies given to her by Mark. She pulled out a pair of scissors and quickly cut Jason's shirt off, having already taken off his jacket when they were in the truck. With the dining room lights and a couple of tall lamps brought in by Mark she could finally get a good look at what was going on.

"Christ. Looks like they nicked his liver. No wonder he's been bleeding like a stuck pig." She looked at Sarah. "Do you know his blood type?"

"B positive, I think." Sarah stood on the other side of Jason, clutching his pale, cold hand.

"Anybody here B positive?"

"I'm O negative." Dianne stepped closer to Tina. "It's the universal donor, right? That's what they tell me when they call me twice a month to pester me about giving even more blood than I already do."

Tina threw a bony thumb over her shoulder in the direction of the kitchen. "Get in there and get cleaned up. I want both of your arms washed and ready to go. Mark, dig around in that kit some more; I'm pretty sure I saw a line and a couple of needles in a packet in there."

Dianne pulled off her jacket and rolled up both sleeves as she went into the kitchen to wash her arms. Tina focused back on Jason's wound, cleaning it out with a sealed bottle of water she had found sitting on the floor in the kitchen.

"Shouldn't you use something else to clean that out?" Sarah spoke up from across the table as she stood on her toes to watch Tina work.

"Nope. Alcohol or hydrogen peroxide can do more harm than good. Just need to wash it out thoroughly, seal it up and get him started on some antibiotics. Hey, Dianne?" Tina shouted into the next room.

"Yes?" Dianne called back as she walked back in, drying water from her hands but leaving her arms wet to air dry until Tina told her what to do next.

"You have general antibiotics around, right?"

Dianne nodded. "Some old stuff, yeah. We don't have a lot, though."

"Can Mark go look for them?"

Dianne looked at her son. "In the big box we put away, remember? The pill bottles. Grab all—well, no. Just bring the whole box in. Set it on the table in the kitchen and we'll go through it in a bit."

Mark nodded and ran off to find the box of supplies. Dianne walked over near Tina and looked at Jason's side before wincing and turning away. "That looks bad. How's he looking?"

"The wound's not terrible. He's not doing well, though. He needs blood right now." She looked at Dianne. "You ready?"

Dianne nodded. "How are we doing this?"

Mark, having already retrieved the box of medicine, was standing quietly in the corner holding a pair of sealed plastic tubes, IV needles and small bags used for saline or medicine. Tina motioned at Mark. "Give those to your mom. Dianne, open both bags, take the needle out of the end of one of the lines and jam it into the other line. We need a line with a needle at both ends. This'll be a direct blood transfusion."

"Are you sure it'll work?" Dianne spoke as she worked, manipulating the plastic tubing and the sealed needles as requested.

"Gravity works in mysterious ways." Tina looked over the line that Dianne had put together and nodded. "Okay. I need to wash up real quick then we'll do this. Sarah, come around the side here and hold this compress in place. I'll tape it up once we finish the transfusion. We should have done this right away but it would have been difficult to do in the truck." Tina hurried to the kitchen to dispose of her gloves and wash the blood from her arms. She returned and rummaged through the medicine box until she found a couple packs of alcohol wipes and pointed at where she wanted Dianne to stand before putting on a fresh set of gloves.

"Stand there, on the left side. Sarah and Mark, you two need to stand next to her. You're going to feel woozy once we get into this but I need you to be elevated so we make sure the blood flows through, okay?"

Dianne nodded and stepped over next to Jason. She put her hand on his bare shoulder, shuddering at how cold he felt. She wanted to ask Tina for the details on how Jason was doing and what she thought his chances at survival were but with Sarah in the room—and very close to breaking down over the condition of her husband—she held her tongue. Tina inserted the tip of the needle into Dianne's arm smoothly and swiftly, working off of years of experience of performing dozens of similar operations nearly every day.

Blood filled the line, quickly running down to the opposite end where it began to dribble out. Tina used a piece of scotch tape to hold the line and needle down on Dianne's arm and began tapping the tube and the needle at the other end gently to ensure there weren't any large air bubbles in the line. Once she was satisfied, she inserted the other needle into Jason's arm and taped it down before turning to Dianne. "This is crude as hell but it'll do."

"How long will it take?"

"Should be about half a liter every fifteen minutes or so. I'd like to give him two liters, if you're up for it."

"That sounds like a lot."

"Yep." Tina nodded. "He lost a lot, though."

Dianne sighed and nodded. "Whatever it takes. I'll stay up for as long as I can but I don't mind telling you I'm already starting to feel a little bit dizzy."

"Hang in there. You've got this."

Chapter Seven

S omewhere in Russia

"SIR?" The man steps into the wood-paneled room with trepidation. Tchaikovsky pours from speakers built into the walls, turned to a high enough volume that the man cannot be heard. He clears his throat and speaks again, trying to attract the attention of the man in the leather chair near the side of the room.

"Sir? I have news." The man in the leather chair takes in a mouthful of smoke, letting it swirl against his cheeks and tongue before expelling it in a gentle plume.

"What is it?" The man in the leather chair doesn't bother turning or looking up as he asks the question. His attention is divided equally between his cigar and the projected image of a roaring fire on a television screen in front of him. The screen is a poor substitute for the real thing but so far beneath the earth there is little chance of seeing a proper fire in a fireplace.

"The technicians found something in the code of the virus, sir. A communications protocol. They say that the virus can receive commands, potentially even a shutdown command."

The Russian president has his cigar halfway back to his mouth when his body freezes in place. A slight trail of smoke rises from the end of the cigar, tracing a lazy path to the ceiling where a smoke detector has been conveniently disconnected. "Communications protocol? How did they discover this?"

"They outfitted a device to log what happened to it as the virus took control, then they infected the device. Near the end, when the infection process was completing, there was a block of data that quite clearly checked for a remote command input."

"Did they try giving it a command?"

"It's… it's encrypted, sir. Impossible to crack. Even if we still had access to the Galileo project we still wouldn't be able to do it."

While most would be deterred by the disappointing news, the Russian president sees the new information as an opportunity in spite of the obstacles still in the way. He rolls his cigar between his thumb and forefinger, pondering the discovery in silence for a few moments before responding. *"Do they still believe the software to originate from the NSA?"*

"That is who developed this iteration of it, yes. It shares traits from numerous other projects but the fingerprints of that agency are all over it."

"Then it stands to reason that the NSA would have the means to interface with the virus. They would have the key required, yes?"

"Undoubtedly. Which begs the question of why they wouldn't shut it down themselves."

"They are a bureaucracy a kilometer thick. I can think of a dozen reasons why they would have neglected to shut down the virus after it escaped into the wild. All of them are equally plausible." The president sighs and looks at his cigar. The embers in the end have gone out, leaving the stick of tobacco to grow cold. He places it down on a table next to his chair and stands up. *"Follow me."* The younger officer dutifully follows the president, scribbling everything his commander asks and tells him into a small notebook.

"How many aircraft are operational that can reach the eastern coast of the United States?"

"One… no, two, perhaps. One undoubtedly. I am not sure about the second."

"One is all we'll need. Which is it?"

"The Tupolev. Stationed two hundred miles away from us. With external tanks it can make the journey, but it will not be able to return."

"It won't have to. Which special forces teams do we have close to the air base where it's stationed?"

"That I do not know, sir."

"Find out. I want a team—a small team, two at most who will protect two technicians—on the aircraft within the next forty-eight hours. They will insert into American airspace above Washington, DC and parachute in. Once there they will proceed to the NSA headquarters and extract the necessary information required to communicate with the virus. They are authorized to use any means necessary to secure and extract the information—I want this point made clear to the guards especially.

"Once the information is secure, they will transmit it to us via satellite and then prepare for a long-term stay in hostile territory." The president glances at the young man, watching the officer's face to see just how shaken he has become.

To his credit the officer holds himself together, though he is having difficulties processing what he is hearing. *"Sir… forgive me, but… you intend to send a four-man team to infiltrate the headquarters of one of the premiere intelligence agencies in the United States? And not even four men if two of them are technicians."* The officer shakes his head in confusion. *"I don't see how this could possibly succeed."*

"Did you know that the Americans have all but abandoned their capitol? There are some forces still in place, but they are guarding the symbolic locations. The other locations,

including the NSA, have been left unguarded. We assume they purged the data from those locations but they will not have purged it all. There will be information left about this virus. The team will find that information and deliver it back to us." The president's lips draw tight into a thin, cold smile. "And once we are free of this weapon we will be happy to help others regain their freedom as well. For a price, of course."

Chapter Eight

K ansas City, Missouri

WHEN RICK first heard the ominous sounds of glass breaking and metal falling he half-expected the building to cave in on top of them. The gunfire coming from the front of the store, the panicked screams from Jane as she ran for cover and the shouting from Dr. Evans as he tried to get everyone back together were not at all what he had anticipated hearing and experiencing. Bullets whizzed past, snapping as they hit metal shelving and ricocheted off of the polished concrete floor. Whoever was firing on them had a miserable aim and Rick wondered how they could miss every single shot on three targets in the relative open in broad daylight.

"Back here, hurry!" Dr. Evans waved at Jane and Rick from an aisle in front of the store's empty pharmacy department. They ran to him, finding him holding open a door into the employees-only area as he tried to maneuver their cart full of consolidated supplies through the narrow opening.

Rick pushed Jane ahead while he hung back, drawing his pistol and racking the slide in one smooth motion. He listened as the sounds of gunfire stopped and were replaced by the shouts of a group of people at least five strong. Looking around at the layout of the back of the pharmacy, Rick decided that retreat wasn't their best option.

"Hey! Hold up back there." Rick whispered to Jane and Dr. Evans as the two tried to push the cart past piles of boxes in the hall.

"What? We have to get out of here!" Dr. Evans exclaimed.

"Nope. We're staying and fighting this one." Rick shook his head defiantly.

"Are you insane?!" Jane looked at him, her eyes wide and her face covered in fear.

"They're terrible shots. And listen—they're running straight down here at us. We have to get out through the main entrance if we want a clear shot back at our car. Our best bet is to challenge them, kill as many as we can and push them back. Once we do that we'll take the cart and run straight out the front of the building."

"What if there are more out there?"

"There won't be."

"How can you possibly know that?" Dr. Evans huffed as he watched out into the store, nervously awaiting the imminent arrival of the hostile group.

"Because people who attack willy-nilly like this don't think strategically."

"Are you willing to bet our lives on it?" Jane asked quietly.

"One hundred percent." Rick nodded, confident not so much in his assessment of the situation but in the knowledge that if they didn't put up a strong defense against their attackers then they'd be at a serious disadvantage trying to retreat farther into the store.

"Okay, what do we do?"

"Dr. Evans, you stay here. Keep the door closed and locked. If you see anyone coming close, shoot through the glass. Aim for the chest and prepare yourself for the recoil of the gun. I need you waiting there with the supplies ready to move out on my signal. Jane, you come with me." Rick pushed open the door into the area of the pharmacy where the pharmacists and assistants spent their time, stepping over empty shelves and pill bottles that had long since been ransacked. "Stay here, under the counter. Keep your gun ready but don't shoot unless I tell you. We need to conserve ammo for that thing."

Jane nodded, squatting down so that she could just barely see over the pickup counter. Rick scurried down and around to the drop-off counter and knelt down. He took two of the spare magazines for the pistol from his pocket and dumped a few dozen rounds of ammunition onto the ground from one of the boxes he had grabbed from the shopping cart. He quickly loaded one of the magazines and put it back into his pocket. He was halfway through loading the second when he heard the sound of nearby footsteps and paused, placing the half-filled magazine on the ground and gripping his weapon firmly with both hands.

The first figure to pop out was a young woman, her face covered with dirt and her clothes both torn and a size or two too large for her frame. She ran along, holding a rifle in her hands as she looked to the left and right, searching for Rick, Jane and Dr. Evans. Rick popped up from behind the counter and squeezed the trigger, emptying his magazine in the woman's direction. At least three of the rounds connected with the torso and legs and she screamed in pain as she fell, her body making a sound like a sack of mashed potatoes hitting the ground.

Rick dropped back behind the counter and ejected the magazine before popping a fresh one in and popping the slide forward. He glanced over at Jane who had her hands over her ears as she watched him. "Come here!" He waved at her as he whispered and she crawled to him. "See this?" He held up the partially filled magazine and pointed at the bullets on the floor. "Push them in from the top and line them up with the others like this. Once you do this one, fill this empty one, too. Make sure you put them in correctly, though!"

Jane nodded and got to work while Rick glanced back up over the counter. The woman he had shot was gone, but there was a long streak of blood on the main aisle twenty feet away where she had fallen. As he glanced around two more people ran out into the main aisle, though they were slightly more prepared than the first had been. They tried to stay in cover, ducking behind display stands and flimsy metal shelves, mimicking what Jane, Rick and Dr. Evans had done when they were escaping from the initial assault.

Seriously? Rick popped up again and dumped half of his magazine into the metal shelf where one of the people was trying to hide. The thin sheet metal offered practically no resistance to the bullets and the person shouted out in pain. Rick then turned his attention to the other person who was across the main aisle, hiding behind a cardboard center display unit. Rick finished emptying his magazine into the cardboard, spreading out his shots to magnify his chances of landing one on his target. He was rewarded with yet another scream and the hasty retreat of someone clutching their wounded arm.

Stung by the vicious counterattack by their "victims," the group beat a hasty and noisy retreat across the store, away from both the main entrance and the pharmacy. Rick watched them as they ran and realized that he, Jane and Dr. Evans wouldn't get a better chance to escape.

"Here!" Jane held out the full magazine as Rick popped out the empty one. He slammed the fresh one home and turned to look across the room and down the hallway at Dr. Evans.

"You ready?" Dr. Evans gulped nervously and nodded. "Good. Jane, you stay behind me and help him with the cart. Collect any guns, ammo or supplies from anyone we drop along the way." Jane nodded numbly and followed Rick as he ran back to Dr. Evans.

Rick pushed open the door and held it while Dr. Evans and Jane got the cart out of the hall and back into the store. They made a beeline through the pharmacy area, stopping briefly at the body of the first person Rick had shot so that they could collect the woman's backpack and rifle. After they finished they continued on towards the entrance of the store and emerged unscathed out into the street.

"Which way to the car?" Jane looked around, realizing that she couldn't remember where to go.

"That way!" Dr. Evans pointed down the street and the trio took off running. Jane and Dr. Evans stayed in the lead, navigating the shopping cart full of supplies through the cracked and debris-riddled sidewalks and streets. Rick took up a position as a rearguard, watching their back and flanks for any signs of their attackers.

The three moved through the streets quickly and neither saw nor heard any signs of anyone ahead or behind. The distant, unsettling rumbling that they had heard while inside the store came back three times on the way back to the car and each time it was accompanied by the sound of distant metal and glass shifting and breaking.

"What the hell is that? An aftershock or something?" Rick spoke quietly to Dr. Evans.

"Possibly."

"Great. All the more reason to get out of here."

When they arrived at the parking lot they saw that their car was sitting where they had left it, untouched and ready to go. "How long do you think we have till they follow us here?" Rick whispered to Dr. Evans, not wanting to draw the attention of anyone who might be lurking in the area.

"You killed at least one, perhaps two of them. I don't think they'd follow us."

Rick shook his head. "No, they'll follow us." He looked at the car and back at the contents of the shopping cart that Jane was swiftly unloading into the trunk of the sports car. "Dammit. I'm going to fill one of the five-gallon containers. Just so we have some emergency fuel." He pointed at Dr. Evans's waistband as he grabbed the plastic tubing and the empty container and ran to one of the nearby vehicles. "Get your gun out, get behind some cover and keep your eyes open."

Despite the cold weather Rick felt beads of sweat run down his chest as he squatted over the container, watching the amber-colored liquid slowly drain from the vehicle's gas tank into the container. Without a pour spout they'd have to siphon the fuel out of the container and into their own vehicle but having to go through a bit of trouble would be far better than not having any should they need it.

"Car's loaded and ready to go." Jane sat down on the ground next to Rick, her head constantly moving as she scanned the buildings surrounding them.

"Have you seen any sign of people?"

Jane shook her head hesitantly. "I don't think so, no."

Rick looked at her with a raised eyebrow. "You don't *think* so?"

"The shadows and the light are playing funny tricks with all that broken glass and metal. I keep thinking I'm seeing something moving around in the tall buildings but so far it's turning out to be nothing."

"As soon as I get this filled and stowed away we'll get out of here." Rick leaned his head against the side of the car, watching the thin stream of liquid slowly fill the container. When it was nearly to the top Rick pulled out the tube, coiled it up and capped the container. He hauled it over to the car and stared at the vehicle for a long moment, trying to figure out where to put the flammable liquid.

"The frunk." Dr. Evans said, still kneeling behind a nearby car.

"Say what?" Rick looked at him, not sure if he had misunderstood what Dr. Evans was saying.

"The frunk? Front trunk?" Dr. Evans pointed at the front of the vehicle and Rick instantly understood what he meant. While fully electric vehicles had helped bring the term "frunk" into the mainstream the recent surge of fully electric vehicles with backup gasoline engines had lessened the use of the phrase. In fully electric vehicles the entire space normally taken up by the engine under the hood was generally available for use as a second trunk to store items. Since new hybrid vehicles still had a gasoline engine—albeit a much smaller one than normal gas-powered cars—the "frunk" was significantly smaller but, in some models, still present.

Rick pulled a lever next to the driver's seat to open the hood and walked around to the front of the car. The gasoline engine sat on the left side under the hood as he faced it, taking up about two-thirds of the available space. The third on the right was a deep well protected by a thick firewall and heat shield and received a small supply of cool air courtesy of the vehicle's air conditioning system. This ensured that anything placed in the front storage space wouldn't become too hot if the vehicle's engine was engaged.

Rick placed the container of gasoline down into the recess, giving the engine a suspicious glance as he closed the hood. "I know that thing's got a firewall two inches thick all around it but having that much gas next to an engine makes me nervous as hell."

"Better than in the back seat or trunk to get fumes or liquid all over us." Dr. Evans replied.

"I guess. Do we even need it, though? We can just run full electric and —" Rick's musing was cut short by a metal *ping* next to him, followed a half-second later by the cracking echo of a rifle shot. He looked at the raised hood of the car, seeing a small hole that had been punched through the metal.

"Let's go!" Rick shouted and slammed the hood closed, jumping and ducking around to try and avoid getting shot. Jane ran for the vehicle and jumped into the back seat, curling her body into a ball on the seat to try and present as small of a target as possible. Puffs of dust and more metallic pings were accompanied by gunfire from multiple sources as Dr. Evans and Rick piled into the car.

Rick switched on the motor and the lights inside sprang to life. He threw the vehicle into reverse and swiveled around to look out the back window.

The street they had driven on to get to the parking lot was rapidly approaching and Rick spun the wheel as they got close, sliding the sports car around and bringing it to a halt on the road.

He then put the car into drive and pushed the accelerator all the way down to the floor. With no internal combustion necessary to deliver torque to the wheels the car instantly sprung forward like it was trying its hardest to imitate a rocket. Rick clung to the steering wheel, trying to make corrections to their course as small and as smooth as possible to keep from running off the road or causing the vehicle to fishtail. As they pulled away from the parking lot and back down the road the gunfire grew quieter and more sporadic until it either stopped completely or was too far away to hear.

Rick eased up on the accelerator and looked over at Dr. Evans then back at Jane. Both had their fingernails digging into the leather interior as they braced themselves against the sides and roof in an attempt to compensate for the lightning-fast maneuvers they had just experienced. Rick grinned at them and tugged at his seatbelt. "Should have put yours on!"

"No kidding!" Jane shouted at Rick from the back seat as Dr. Evans let out the breath he had been holding since they first started moving.

"That… was incredible." Dr. Evans whispered, shaking his head in disbelief.

"Maximum torque at zero speed." Rick smiled again and patted the car's dashboard like it was alive. "It's been a while since I drove an electric like that. I used to… wait… do you hear that?" Rick looked questioningly at Dr. Evans and Jane before rolling down his window and slowing down the car. Because the electric motor made essentially no noise Rick could hear what was going on in the city quite well.

"Is that more rumbling?" Jane asked.

Rick nodded. "A lot more." He stopped the car on the highway, put it in park, opened his door and stepped out onto the pavement. The low rumbling they had been hearing was considerably louder and—worst of all —Rick could actually feel it in his feet. He looked back at Dr. Evans, a note of panic in his voice. "I'm no earthquake expert but I'd say this feels like more than just an aftershock!"

"Then we need to move! Quickly!" Dr. Evans motioned for Rick to get back in the car. Rick jumped back in and Dr. Evans cast a wary eye up at their surroundings. "We're not even halfway through the city and we're still surrounded by buildings. If this is an earthquake then we need to get out of here as fast as possible. Also I'd recommend getting to surface streets instead of this elevated highway."

"No kidding!" Rick pressed down on the accelerator again and the car zipped down the road once again. The rumbling that had only been audible when they were quiet and motionless was now coming through even with the road noise and motion from the car.

"There!" Jane stuck her arm forward between the seats as she pointed at an off-ramp from the elevated highway. "Pull off there!"

"I have no idea where that goes!" Rick glanced between the highway ahead and the off-ramp, trying to make up his mind about where to go. An instant later his decision was made for him. Rick, Jane and Dr. Evans all stared slack-jawed as one of the buildings half a mile down the way they were driving, just off to the left of the elevated highway, began to sway back and forth. Rick slowed down as they watched the building's movement grow more and more violent until it began to topple, twisting over the elevated highway as it went and carrying a huge chunk of the road with it.

Rick accelerated the car again and moved into the right-hand lane, taking the off-ramp down to ground level as quick as humanly possible. "Nice call." He nodded at Jane in appreciation. "Now the only question is… where on earth do we go from here?"

Chapter Nine

The Water's Homestead
   Outside Ellisville, VA

DIANNE AWOKE WITH A GROAN, waving a hand in front of her eyes to try and block out the light. As her vision became clear she realized she was lying on her side on the couch in the living room, a light blanket draped over her and the wooden covering for the back door open. Her feet were propped up on several pillows and light was streaming in through the back window and a broad ray covered her chest, neck and most of her face. She looked around the room, trying to piece together how she got onto the couch when the events of the morning and previous night came flooding back.

Midway through the blood transfusion Dianne started to feel weak enough that she needed to sit down. After bringing her a stool Mark and Sarah had helped to keep Dianne upright until Tina was satisfied that Jason had received enough blood to give him the best possible chance at survival. With Dianne too dizzy and weak to do anything else she had gone to sleep on the couch, exhausted both from the transfusion and from the overwhelmingly intense time she and Jason had faced during their rescue of Tina.

While Dianne slept Tina, Sarah and Mark made a pallet on the floor in the dining room next to the table and gently put Jason on it to rest. Some of his color had returned as a result of the transfusion and while his breathing was still slow the bleeding had stopped and he appeared to be stable. Leaving the cleanup of the table for the next day Tina went to sleep on a separate pallet near Jason while Sarah and Mark took turns keeping watch throughout the night. Sarah never strayed too far from the dining room, keeping a concerned eye trained on her husband at all times.

"Mark?" Dianne spoke softly, her throat and lips feeling too dry and coarse to do much more than squeeze out a whisper. "Sarah?"

The sound of footsteps came from the kitchen and Josie's smiling face came around the corner. "Mom!" The young girl ran forward and squeezed Dianne tightly before recoiling with a terrified expression. "I'm sorry! Are you okay?"

Dianne smiled and pulled her daughter in for another hug. "Of course I'm okay! You didn't hurt me at all. I just got really tired from last night."

"Did you help Mrs. Carson save Mr. Statler's life last night?"

Dianne nodded and squeezed her daughter tightly. "I think so." Dianne held Josie at arm's length, fighting to keep tears from forming in her eyes. "Now where are your brothers? And everyone else, for that matter?"

"Mark and Jacob are outside with Mrs. Carson showing her around. I think Mrs. Statler's in the dining room with Mr. Statler, but she's probably taking a nap. You want me to go wake her up?"

Dianne shook her head. "Nah. She could probably use the sleep after dealing with you three while Mr. Statler and I were out. Tell you what, though. I could use something to drink. Could you get me some water and something to eat, too?"

"Sure!" Josie bounded off into the kitchen while Dianne rose to her feet. Talking to her daughter had made her temporarily forget about the condition of her mouth and throat, but she quickly rediscovered the dryness as she slowly shuffled toward the kitchen. She felt weak all over her body and her head hurt but she continued on, heading into the dining room to check on Jason.

The dining room table—parts of which were stained a dark crimson red—had been pushed to one side. Jason was resting on his back up against the wall while Sarah was on her side next to him, her hand resting on his hip. They both appeared to be sleeping and Dianne eased down onto the floor near Jason's head and whispered in his ear.

"Hey. You still alive?" Jason's eyes slowly opened, proving Dianne's hunch right. Jason swallowed hard and nodded slowly, whispered so as to not wake up Sarah.

"I think so. It hurts like the dickens, though, so I'm not too sure."

Dianne smiled and nodded. "I'm glad to hear it. Just stay still and rest some more. We'll get some food in you here soon."

Jason nodded again and closed his eyes, returning to a state of pain and restlessness that was keeping him from fully falling asleep. Dianne stood back up and headed back into the kitchen, fighting against the urge to fall over with every step. She sat down at the kitchen table and smiled at Josie as the young girl brought over a glass of water and a plate with a few pieces of toast with butter, some crackers and a bowl of canned fruit.

"Mrs. Carson said you should have plain toast for your first meal along with a vitamin. Just until you start feeling a little bit better."

Dianne nodded sagely and took a bite and a sip of water. She quickly found that there was a raging appetite beneath the dizziness and exhaustion and finished the toast in another few bites. "That was fantastic. Got any more?"

Josie shook her head. "She said just one piece."

"That's exactly right. Just one piece for now. You can have more in a bit." The back door slid open and Tina poked her head in, jumping into the conversation before Dianne had a chance to reply.

Dianne turned in her chair and smiled at Tina as the older woman stepped inside, taking her shoes off at the door. She was dressed in somewhat ill-fitting clothing that looked like a combination from both Dianne's and Sarah's closets. Tina caught Dianne looking at her outfit and gestured to it, rolling her eyes and throwing her arms into the air. "Yes, yes, I know. I look ridiculous."

"No," Dianne said, shaking her head, "I was just thinking how much better that looks than that ratty pink bathrobe and slippers you were in."

"Your shoes are a bit large but it's nice to have socks on, I will say." Tina smiled and walked over to the kitchen table as Mark and Jacob looked in and waved at their mother.

"Hey mom! We showed Mrs. Carson all around. We're gonna go make sure everything's fed, okay?"

"Take Josie with you, will you? And stay safe out there. Keep the noise levels down. Any sign of something strange and you two head back."

Both boys nodded as Josie grabbed her jacket and ran out back with her brothers. Jacob closed the door before they ran back down the steps of the back porch, heading for the barns. Tina reached down and picked up a small plastic pail off of the floor that she had been carrying and placed it onto the table. "You guys have a *lot* of chickens. Also, we have more eggs if anyone wants any."

"Tina." Dianne put her hand on Tina's and spoke softly. "What happened? Where's Dave?"

Tina Carson was a tough woman. She had been through a lot in her life and thirty years of being a nurse had both exposed her to a massive amount of pain and suffering while simultaneously teaching her how to step back and isolate herself from it so that she could function on a daily basis. Applying those skills to her personal life wasn't something she had ever anticipated doing… up until when she did.

"It was… I don't even remember when it was." Tina closed her eyes, trying to think back to the day of the event. "We were in the house when the lights went out. We figured out pretty quickly something bad was happening when the phone caught fire, though."

"Is that what happened to the house?"

"Yeah. Well, sort of." Tina shook her head. "It feels like a dream."

"Is Dave… was he…"

Tina ignored the question. "We were outside on the porch trying to decide if we should call the power company or wait for them to fix whatever was wrong. We smelled smoke and realized it was coming through the door. Dave went inside and saw flames all up the wall in the living room, starting from where the phone was." She shook her head. "Damned smoke detector never went off. Piece of crap.

"Anyway, it burned a good chunk of the living room before we got it under control. A pair of industrial-sized fire extinguishers took care of that. We sort of forgot about the source of the fire at that point as we just tried to get things cleaned up. We headed into town to get some supplies, realized that something terrible was going on and came back here to get our things together in case we needed to leave."

"You went into town the day it all started?" Dianne's jaw dropped. "We did too! We went to the grocery and had a run-in with a couple of the guys who Jason and I saw at your house the other day."

Tina shook her head. "Unbelievable. So we must have just missed crossing paths."

"I guess so. We went out to your house the day after to see if you were okay but everything was… well. Gone."

"Yeah. That happened later the first day. When we left town and headed back home we were followed."

Dianne felt her heart skip a beat and the hairs on the back of her neck stood on end. "Followed?"

"Yep." Tina spoke matter-of-factly, trying to distance herself from the emotional impact of that fateful day. "We went into the barn to get our emergency supplies out to check them and everything. When we went out of the barn to go back into the house there was an SUV pulling up. The doors opened and a group of assholes stepped out all armed to the teeth. Dave pulled out his concealed carry and dropped one of them but the others…" Tina shook her head. "They threw me in the back of the SUV and torched the house with his body inside. They piled our supplies in with me and drove off to the gas station."

"Tina. I'm… I'm so incredibly—"

"Sorry?" Tina sniffed, wiping a finger along the edge of her eye. "Nothing for you to be sorry about. Bad things happen every day. It's their fault Dave's gone. Not yours."

"I know, but still."

Tina forced a half-hearted chuckle and plucked at the shirt she was wearing. "You want to know the funny thing? I had on all my regular clothes when they dragged me there. But I grabbed my robe and slippers out of the things they stole and wore them all the time just to mess with those assholes. Just like how I told them there was a safe on the property. Between that and wearing the bathrobe in this weather they thought I was insane. I'm pretty sure one of them felt bad for me because he threw me a blanket to help keep me warm in the shed." Tina laughed, this time with genuine humor. "From what they said every time they got back to their compound I had them crawling all over the barn and the house looking for that safe. Idiots. It was the least I could do to keep them busy and waste some of their time so they'd have less to spend on doing to others what they did to me."

Dianne shook her head in amazement. "You are one stubborn son of a gun. You know that, right?" Dianne had forgotten about how refreshing Tina's no-nonsense attitude and blunt way of speaking could be. She also realized that Tina was either not ready to talk about her husband's death or had already, somehow, gotten past it and Dianne didn't want to press the issue any further.

Tina snorted and her expression grew serious again. "How many of them did you and Jason kill? I know you shot one while you were pulling me out of that shed."

"I don't know. There was him, yes. I'm sure several died in the explosion. Jason might have shot some more of them but I don't know."

"There's one, he always wore a red shirt. He's their leader. He's a sly one. I wanted to ditch the bathrobe and slippers bit days ago but it was all I could do to keep him on his toes. If he died during your rescue attempt—which was nicely done by the way—then their whole little wannabe-gang would go crashing down with him."

"I don't think he died, but I'm not sure. I know the guy you're talking about. He and a guy in a blue shirt seemed like they were the ringleaders when we were scouting their compound."

"Scouting the compound? Listen to you. A regular Army Ranger."

Dianne rolled her eyes. "Yeah, sure. Look, we need to talk more about this gang later. Anything you learned about them would be good to know."

"You want to know about them? Sure. I can tell you that." Tina pantomimed writing out a checklist on the table with her finger and thumb. "They seem to be interested in two things. First: being the biggest assholes possible. Second: exerting as much control as their pitiful little operation can manage. They want to be 'kings of the highway' based on what they said, though since the highway is mostly filled with burned out cars I'm not sure they totally thought that through."

"You think they'll come after us?"

"After what you two did? Absolutely." Tina grew serious again and leaned forward. "I, uh... haven't really said 'thank you' to you yet. I'm honestly not sure how, given what you and Jason did. Especially with him in the condition he's in. But... thank you."

Dianne shrugged. "You're welcome, but you would have done the same thing." Dianne hesitated. "Dave would have too."

Tina nodded. "Yeah."

The pair sat in silence for a few seconds before Dianne cleared her throat. "We'll talk with Sarah and Jason when he gets up later and figure out a plan of defense going forward. I talked to him earlier, by the way. Just for a second. He's in pain but he's still trying to rest, though that's largely been unsuccessful from what he said and looks like."

"Mm. Not surprising. You don't have much in the way of pain management."

"Yeah we didn't get our pharmacy renewal license in time so I had to throw out all the morphine." Dianne made an exaggerated expression. "Sorry about that."

A slight smile, one that appeared genuinely spontaneous, appeared on the corners of Tina's mouth before she replied. "I'll dose him up again here soon with what you do have. His liver's already having a rough enough time. I don't want to be stressing it too much with a bunch of pain meds in his system."

Dianne leaned in and whispered to Tina. "What do you think his chances are? Truthfully?"

"If he was lucid and talking to you? Pretty good. I'm most worried about the infection. He's bound to have one and most of the antibiotics you have aren't really what I was hoping for. I'll have to keep a close eye on him and make sure nothing serious develops."

"What if it does?"

"Then things get a lot worse. For all of us."

Chapter Ten

K ansas City, Missouri

SITTING in the cramped car surrounded by shaking buildings and the ever-present threat of being crushed was not a pleasant experience for Rick, Jane and Dr. Evans. Going through all of that while trying to find a path out of the city that was least likely to wind up with one or more of them being killed was even less pleasant. While the vehicle's navigation system had onboard street-level maps of pretty much every city in the country without regular updates the maps quickly fell out of date. This was especially true for places like Kansas City which were going through rapid growth and expansion phases and thus had near-constant changes to their streets both physically and in name.

"This isn't West 34th anymore." Jane pointed out the side window as they zipped across an intersection. "It just turned into Malone Parkway."

"Malone?" Dr. Evans typed in the name into a search box on the center console and a pair of streets on the map became highlighted in yellow. "That's not for another block. I guess that's another change."

"Do I still take a right-hand turn at 19th?" Rick kept his eyes on the road.

"Yes. I think so." Dr. Evans zoomed in on the map. "Yes, definitely. We'll see if that dumps out where it should."

Rick ground his teeth together, trying desperately not to let his emotions get the better of him. Driving the small car through the streets of a crowded, overbuilt city would be challenging on a regular day. Adding in the fact that the tremors were continuing to grow in frequency and severity made the drive so much worse. They had nearly crashed several times already, either because a tremor took them by surprise or because part of a building or overpass had collapsed in their path. They had also nearly been the victim of falling debris two times, but Rick hoped that keeping them going at a high rate of speed would considerably reduce the chances of that occurring.

Based on Dr. Evans and Jane's readings of the map on the center console they were approaching the middle of the city and would soon be halfway to getting out. With the sole intact elevated highway becoming too compromised to use in moving throughout the city they were forced to stick to the surface-level roads as they wove between hordes of burned out or abandoned vehicles and collapsed or partially collapsed buildings.

The question they had upon first approaching the area—wondering what had happened to most of the skyscrapers that the region was famous for—was soon answered as they entered into the heart of the city. The downtown area was centered around a large park approximately four square blocks in size. The seventeen newly constructed skyscrapers had been built around the park, turning it into both a focal point and a natural island in the midst of a sea of metal and glass. Unfortunately the island itself had been consumed by the metal and glass, sucked under by a tidal wave caused by the earthquakes.

Seven skyscrapers stood around the park, six on the east side and one on the north. The other ten that had been on the north, west and southern sides of the park had all collapsed, leaving no more than a few stories of their structures still standing. Millions of tons of debris from the ten buildings lay strewn around the area, though most of it covered the park at the center of where they used to stand.

A few had toppled over onto nearby buildings, though the majority of the damage caused to the other buildings in the area was from the earthquakes and not from the impact of the skyscrapers. While many of the buildings on the outskirts of town had shown signs of damage in the form of cracks on their interiors and exteriors the ones in the center were much more heavily damaged—if they were even standing at all.

Even though only a small fraction of the downtown area was visible to the trio, Rick immediately realized that they would have to find a path around the center of the city if they wanted to escape. "Damn!" Dr. Evans cursed as he looked up and saw the swath of destruction laid out before them. "Give me a minute here." He looked back down at the map while Rick turned around to start getting them away from the center of the city.

As Rick drove along he felt another tremor, but unlike the others that merely caused the car to vibrate and shake the one they were experiencing was actually making the car buck off of the ground by an inch or so. "Guys?" Rick looked at Jane and Dr. Evans. "Can I get some help here?" Jane and Dr. Evans were frantically arguing as they looked at the map, trying to decide which route to take when a particularly powerful tremor hit. The car bounced off the ground and landed with the tires slightly off-center, causing them to veer off of the road. Rick barely managed to keep them from smashing into the side of a building and he shouted as he continued accelerating. "Just choose a road already!"

Jane leaned forward and jabbed her finger at the screen, causing it to ripple with rainbow hues as she pressed on the panel. "Go there! Take a left at the next intersection! The buildings aren't as tall, so maybe we'll be safer!"

"Left at the next intersection. Got it." Rick held tight to the steering wheel, feeling it and the entire car fight him with each tremor. Jane and Dr. Evans watched the buildings on both sides of the road as they tore past, growing more alarmed at how much the structures were swaying and shaking. Bricks and glass fell off onto the sidewalk and street and dust began to fill the air. While the other tremors had slowed down and even stopped after a while there was no sign of that occurring anytime soon.

"Look out!" Dr. Evans shouted and Rick hit the brakes, spinning the wheel to take an immediate right. A mess of cables and stoplights were falling into the street just ahead of where they had been driving. Rick turned left again at the next street and kept going forward, not certain that the path they were taking would lead them anywhere useful.

As they continued winding their way around the center of the city on the northern side, Jane kept watching as the lone northern skyscraper drew ever closer. Standing at ninety-six stories tall with another hundred feet worth of antennas on top, the building was swaying back and forth like a tower built —and about to be destroyed—by a child.

The movements of the tower seemed like they were taking place in slow motion due to how large the structure was, and while she thought at first that it would slow down and stop she soon realized that the shaking was only getting worse, not better. "Rick?" Jane said, quietly. "Rick!" She said his name again, more forcefully.

"What?!" Rick's attention was focused completely on driving and he didn't bother looking back at her as he replied.

"That skyscraper's going to collapse."

"What?" Dr. Evans leaned forward and gasped as he looked up at the building. "Holy shit... Rick, we have to move faster!"

"I'm trying!" With a clear, open stretch of road for what looked like a good mile ahead, Rick was pushing the car to its absolute limits while simultaneously fighting against the shaking and rumbling beneath the earth. As he glanced up at the skyscraper to see what was going on for himself he felt a sickening squeeze in his stomach as the building wobbled slightly too far towards the left in the direction of where they were driving.

Chapter Eleven

The Water's Homestead
Outside Ellisville, VA

JASON DOZED on and off throughout the rest of the day and into the evening hours. Tina, Sarah and Dianne continued to check on him while Mark stayed busy instructing his brother and sister with cleaning and maintaining the hydroponics in the basement and with feeding and caring for the animals. Mark, Tina and Dianne took the main watches throughout the day and night so that Sarah could spend as much time with Jason as possible.

Not wanting to trouble Jason given his condition, Dianne and Tina kept their discussions regarding their response to the gang between themselves, Sarah and Mark. The conclusion, after hours of on and off discussion, was to keep the status quo largely unchanged. The property and the house was largely protected against surprise assault and there wasn't much else they could do that didn't involve completely surrounding the property which, as they had talked about before, was not within the realm of feasibility.

The cold weather and the concerns over keeping a fire going and having the smoke be seen by the gang was a constant worry. Near the end of the day as the sun started going down they agreed that they would need to make the best of the situation by running a single, small space heater in the dining room. Everyone who was sleeping would be on pallets in the room to help conserve warmth while those who were on watch would double down on the blankets and warm clothing. The temperature over the last few nights had been warmer than expected which helped with the situation and Jacob and

Josie were overjoyed at the change in scenery despite the direness of the whole situation.

It was in the early morning hours when Dianne, who was trying to get a couple hours of sleep, was awoken by Tina's rapid tapping on her arm and whispering in her ear. "Dianne. Get up. I need to talk to you."

"Wha…huh?" Dianne blinked several times and nodded slowly. "Sure. Talk."

"Not here. In the kitchen." Tina stood up and hurried to the kitchen while Dianne slowly stood up and padded from the moderate warmth of the dining room through the blanket hung in the doorway and into the cold of the kitchen.

Mark was standing at the back door as Dianne sat down across from Tina who passed the bleary-eyed mother a cup of coffee. "Here. Drink this. You need to be awake."

"Tina, while I appreciate the coffee, I really hope this is an emergency." Dianne croaked out the words as she sipped on the hot drink, both hoping that the caffeine would wake her up and wishing she could be back on the floor sleeping.

"Jason's not doing well." Tina spoke quietly, not wanting anyone else to hear. Dianne's eyes widened and she put the cup down on the table, her brain suddenly kick-started into high gear.

"Come again?"

"Jason. He's not well." Tina shook her head. "His temperature's going up pretty rapidly and he's starting to have trouble breathing. I talked to him earlier and he seems… confused. Definitely not himself."

"He seemed okay when I talked to him last night."

"I know." Tina nodded. "That's what's worrying. He's getting worse."

"What do you think it is?"

Tina sighed and scratched her head. "I… don't know. My best guess is an infection. Maybe a bad one. Sepsis, possibly."

"Sepsis? That sounds bad."

"Yeah, it's a whole-body infection. If that's it—and I'll be honest, I'm pretty sure it is—he needs real antibiotics very soon or he's going to die." The frank declaration sat in the air, hovering over the table as Dianne tried to make sense of it.

"Okay… so what do we do? Try more antibiotics?"

"Nothing you've got here is going to help. Mark helped me go through every last bit of meds you've got. They're fine for small wounds and infections but something this serious needs something real."

Dianne took in a deep breath. "Where do we find what he needs?"

Tina ran her hands through her greying hair and exhaled sharply. "That's what I needed to talk to you about. The only places that will have something like this are hospitals or LTAC hospitals."

"What's an—"

Tina interrupted Dianne, answering her question before she could finish. "Long-Term Acute Care. It's kind of like a mix between a normal hospital and a nursing home. We send folks there who need weeks or months' worth of hospital-level care."

"And a place like that is going to have antibiotics?"

Tina nodded rapidly. "Yes. More than a normal hospital, most likely. They'll have mass quantities of broad-spectrum antibiotics and fluids that he's going to need to survive. He'll need to be on an IV for a while. Couple of weeks, maybe. Possibly less, maybe more."

"Shit." Dianne cursed under her breath before glancing over at Mark who was still focused on watching out through a crack in the covering over the back door. "How long does he have?"

"Twelve hours at most. Beyond that he could go at any minute. As it is it'll be a struggle to keep him functional for that long."

"How did this happen? Was it something with the wound?"

"It was probably contamination from something. We cleaned everything as best as we could but given the situation and what I had to work with I'm not surprised it happened. That was a pretty nasty shot he took. A few inches over and he'd be six feet under right now."

Dianne shook her head, both in disbelief at what was happening and with amazement at how casual Tina could be about Jason's condition especially given that she had so recently lost her husband. *You are going to need so much therapy when this is all said and done.* Dianne thought about how much Tina was keeping bottled up inside, wondering how long she'd be able to hold it in before she lost control. After a few seconds she pushed the thoughts from her mind and focused on the task at hand.

"Okay, so somebody has to get to a hospital or this laser thing."

"LTAC. Long-Term—"

"Right, right. LTAC. Got it."

"I think there's one in Blacksburg, on the western side, but I don't remember the address." Tina furrowed her brow as she tried to remember the location of the facility. Dianne, meanwhile, stood up and walked over to a kitchen drawer, opened it and pulled out a tattered book from inside. She tossed it on the table, sat down, opened it up and began flipping through the yellow-colored pages. Tina nodded and smiled at the sight.

"Everyone says to just get rid of your phone books because cellphones and the internet's where it's all at. I'm glad to see you hung onto yours, too, because mine's part of a giant pile of ash."

"Absolutely I kept one around." Dianne continued flipping through the pages, searching through the medical care section. "The phone numbers are out of date but if this LTAC you're talking about was a major facility then they probably haven't changed locations in a few years. Wait. Here we go." Dianne pointed at a faded advertisement on the right side of one of the pages. "Regency Long-Term Acute Care Facility. That the place?"

Tina nodded. "Yes. Bingo. That's it."

Dianne retrieved her notebook, tore out a piece of paper and scribbled down the address two times. She tore the page in half and stuffed one copy of the address in her pants pocket and left the second copy on the table. "Okay. So this place will have meds, you say. If they don't, where do I go?"

"Try Montgomery or Hillendale. My guess is that looters would have targeted them first given that they're very obviously hospitals and would have stuff like opiates on the premises. Regency, though..." Tina shrugged. "I think it's the best bet."

"Okay." Dianne took a deep breath and pinched the bridge of her nose. "I'm exhausted. But I'll leave in twenty minutes."

Tina stood up. "I'll go with you. I can leave instructions with Sarah and Mark for taking care of Jason and—"

"No way." Dianne held up her hands, stopping Tina from coming around to the other side of the table. "You're staying right here."

"You can't go out there alone. You're tired, you've been through hell and if that group finds you then you'll need backup."

"You need to stay here and hold things down. Sarah's an absolute wreck and completely out of it. If Jason takes a turn for the worse, you'll be the only one who can help him. Mark, Jacob and Josie can handle most of the lookout and cooking jobs. Just trade lookout shifts with Mark, keep an eye on Sarah and keep Jason alive. I'll be fine on my own." Dianne put on a smile that she knew was completely unconvincing.

Tina slowly sat back down in her chair, turning over their options in her mind before finally nodding in agreement. "You're right. I hate it, but you're right." She grabbed Dianne's notebook and began writing in it.

"What's this, a shopping list?" Dianne turned in her seat to read Tina's scribbles.

"Yep. The names of all the different antibiotics that will work. We'll also need bags of fluids to help rehydrate him and I want more lines and needles. If you can find all of this then you can get these things, too." Tina spent a full five minutes thinking of a laundry list of supplies for Dianne to get. When she was finished she tore out the page and handed it to Dianne.

"These are in order of importance, right?" Dianne looked at Tina.

"Yes. The top five are absolutely required. The rest would be good to have."

Dianne grabbed a permanent marker from a drawer and wrote out the names of the top five items on the list on the inside of her left arm, along with the address of the facility. She then folded the paper and tucked it into her pocket before looking around and taking a deep breath.

"Seems like I just got back here a few minutes ago and now I have to leave again."

Tina took a step forward and lowered her voice to a whisper. "You really aren't in a good condition to go out there right now. You're exhausted, you gave all that blood, there are people out there searching for us. It's a bad situation all around."

"What choice do I have?" Dianne sat down and began putting on her shoes. "We can't let Jason die if there's a chance to save him."

"That's beyond question. I just…" Tina hesitated. "I just don't know what I can do to help you." She looked down at the table and shook her head. "You two risked everything to pull me out of that compound and now you're having to go back out again."

"You do what you do best. Keep Jason alive. I'll be fast and as soon as I find what we need I'll radio back." She shook her head. "Though based on how well that worked the other day I don't know that you'll even get my message."

"Just be safe, Dianne. If you see even a hint of trouble you need to get out of there and forget about all of this. I know I sound like a cold-hearted machine saying this but losing another person just isn't worth it. Especially when that person's you."

Dianne took a deep breath and nodded before turning to look at the blanket covering the entrance to the dining room. "I'm going to give them a kiss goodbye and let Mark know what's going on before I go."

"I'll get food, water and ammo together for you."

As Dianne crawled along the floor to kiss Josie and Jacob's sleeping forms, she felt an intense wave of emotion rise up inside of her. She had barely gotten to see and interact with them after returning with Tina and Jason and the very idea of leaving again made her want to snatch up her children, run away and hide somewhere where they could live in peace and no one would ever bother any of them again.

Reality, however, is a harsh and cruel mistress, and Dianne had to settle for a kiss on Josie and Jacob's cheeks before standing up and walking out into the front hall. She sat on the bench in the entryway with Mark for a few minutes, holding a whispered conversation with him about what was going on, before she gave him a hug and a kiss as well. She was surprised by how well he took the news of her having to leave again, but she chalked up his lack of a reaction to him trying to be the new man of the household.

The last thing she wanted to see was for him to grow up so quickly but the days of his innocence and being able to just be a kid were long and far away. She was perpetually sad for how quickly all three of her children had to grow up but was also incredibly proud at how well they—and especially Mark—were rising to the challenge.

As she walked out across the driveway and around the house to get in her truck and start her journey she cast a quick glance back to see Mark's face in the window, watching her go. In that moment she saw the face of his father staring back and wondered for the thousandth time where Rick was and if he would ever come home to see her and his children again. She looked up at the twinkling stars in the sky, shining like an infinite array of diamonds and whispered her perpetual prayer.

"Come back home, Rick. Please come back home."

Chapter Twelve

K ansas City, Missouri

JANE AND DR. EVANS stared out the right side of the car, watching in horror at the building that was toppling over above them. Window panes were breaking into individual shards from the strain they were under and the metal twisted and snapped, slowing the rate at which the building fell over but not by enough to matter. Shorter buildings that were in the way between the skyscraper and the road helped to slow the building's fall as well, but it was clear that nothing would make much of a difference if they didn't get out of the path of destruction.

Rick didn't allow himself to glance over at the falling building, though he could tell based on the ever-widening shadow that they were far too close to for comfort. He kept the accelerator pressed down to the floor and engaged the gasoline engine, trying to eke out a slight boost in speed to get them past where the structure was about to hit. "Come on...." Rick mumbled to himself, still fighting against the tremors to keep them on the road.

As the toppling skyscraper came crashing down onto the road, Jane and Dr. Evans both closed their eyes and turned away, each of them convinced that their lives would be snuffed out within seconds. An earth-shattering crash was accompanied by a fiercely blowing wind, a cloud of dust and debris and the sound of Rick shouting at the top of his lungs as he grinned from ear to ear. "YES!" Their car had cleared the edge of the falling skyscraper by less than twenty feet. The margin of error was far too close for comfort and the experience wasn't one that any of them wanted to repeat, but they had managed to survive.

Before Jane and Dr. Evans could join in on Rick's celebration of their escape from near death, Rick's face darkened. "Look, up ahead. Is that... are those people?" Due to their speed the cloud of dust and debris had only partially overtaken the car so they could still see out the windshield well enough to discern that there were people moving farther down the street.

"I think so... yes." Dr. Evans nodded. "Most definitely, yes. It looks like they're running."

"Probably from the quakes." Another tremor struck as Rick was speaking and he let off of the accelerator as he fought with the steering wheel. The car's tires squealed as it slipped to the right and the left, then Rick pushed down on the accelerator again to straighten out the rear and stop the fish-tailing from getting any worse. Once they had straightened out again he slowed down even more. "Yeah, they must be trying to escape. Why would they still be here, though? This place has been totally demolished!"

"Where else do they have to go?" Dr. Evans shook his head. The people were spread out along the side of the road with some walking and some running away from the center of the city. As the car passed by they gasped in shock, many of them reaching out as if to try and grab hold. "If they can't get to a vehicle and use it to get somewhere then this may be their best chance of survival. There aren't that many options outside of the city."

The ground shook again and Rick cursed as the car nearly spun out of control yet again. "Nobody's going to survive here if these earthquakes don't stop!"

"Can't we help them?" Jane watched the people as they drove past, her sympathy strengthening since the people weren't trying to shoot at them. "They seem harmless enough. We could pick up one, maybe two?"

Rick shook his head. "No."

"Why not?"

Rick sighed. "I appreciate what you want to do with helping these people, but the answer's no."

Jane crossed her arms and took on an indignant tone. "I didn't realize this suddenly became your sole decision."

Dr. Evans licked his lips and spoke hesitantly. "Perhaps we could... maybe just one of the children?"

Rick ground his teeth together again. "I said no. I mean no."

"Then can you explain why not?"

Rick looked at Dr. Evans and Jane. "Have you two not been paying any attention to what's going on? Or have you not seen the people trying to kill us? Just because they're not openly shooting at us doesn't mean—dammit!" Rick struggled again as the car fishtailed from another tremor. "It doesn't mean that they're friendly!"

"But what if they are?" Dr. Evans replied quietly.

"If we stop for these people they might turn on us, mob us, steal our vehicle and supplies and leave us with nothing. Tell me, either of you, how that helps us. Because I'm pretty sure it helps no one."

"They have children!" Jane implored.

"So do I." Rick's tone grew dark. "My family's out there waiting for me. And I'm potentially giving up on ever seeing them again to try and stop this madness. That's not a decision I make lightly and there's not a chance in *hell* that I'm going to jeopardize what we're doing. Some risks we have to take. Others we don't. Right now we don't have to take this risk.

"I know that's hard to swallow and believe me, if we had room for every one of them and a way to ensure everyone's safety I'd stop in a heartbeat to pick them up. But we don't. And we have something bigger and more important to focus on. So that's what we're going to do. Got it?"

Jane and Dr. Evans both sat quietly after Rick's response, watching as the car went around a bend in the road and the people disappeared. With nothing but silence and tension filling the car, each of the trio was left to their own thoughts, each of them wondering if the decisions they were making were actually the correct ones. Mistakes were easy to make but difficult to correct in their current environment. None of them wanted to be the one to make a call that could potentially destroy their fragile attempt at stopping Damocles.

Author's Notes

October 22, 2017

Hoo boy. Things are really starting to heat up for Dianne and Rick. We've moved into the part of the story where the action is going to continue pretty much non-stop. I like that part of the story. The slow build-up (particularly on Dianne's part) earlier in the series is going to pay off here soon as the defenses she and the kids have set up will be tested. Hopefully everyone makes it out alive.

One of the hard parts about writing a story like this is coming up with a "big bad" that is interesting, engaging, powerful (but not overly so) and fits in well enough with the storyline that it doesn't completely yank away your willing suspension of disbelief. Coming up with Damocles as the main "bad guy" for Surviving the Fall took a lot of thinking and an even greater amount of time was spent thinking about how he/it can be defeated.

If you've read my Final Dawn series then you'll know that the "big bad" there had a few similarities to Damocles but was ultimately a bit more in the science fiction realm than in the realm of reality. When I came up with Damocles I took a hard look at where we are right now with our technological capabilities, thought about where we might be in 10-20 years and figured 'yep, this actually seems pretty realistic.'

We've already got self-driving cars and one of the future requirements of them will be that they can communicate with each other. We've seen in the past that super-secret viruses have penetrated government and commercial networks and sat undetected for long periods of time. We're more connected than ever with the Internet of Things growing larger every single day. How long will it be until all of the bugs and security holes are exploited by a nefarious person or persons? Couple that with the startling advancements being made in artificial intelligence projects and you don't need a sentient program to bring out a huge swath of disasters. You just need someone with a chip on their shoulder who knows what they're doing to bring about serious harm on a lot of innocent people.

Okay, enough about the potential realism in the book. Let's talk about Ruskies. :D

In case you haven't noticed from reading my other books, I sort of have a thing for putting Russians in my stories. When I decided to make the Russians play more than a minor role in Surviving the Fall (as we saw here in Episode #7), I thought more about why I like putting Russians in and I think a lot of it has to do with the cultural stereotypes surrounding their people and their culture. This was reinforced in me by watching Star Trek (The Original Series) a *lot* when I was younger.

What I saw (both in Star Trek and in cultural stereotypes) was that Americans/Federation were generally the more technologically advanced, more sophisticated and "better" people while the Russians/Klingons were less advanced, less sophisticated and morally grey in a lot of what they did. What stuck out to me, though, was this idea that despite the lack of sophistication on the part of the Russians/Klingons, when they made something it tended to work no matter what. The AK-47 is a great example like that. You can drop it, freeze it, heat it up, pour sand into it, drag it through the mud but it'll still fire.

I know that view of things isn't completely accurate, but it's the kind of thinking that makes for a nifty narrative in stories. That's why the *Arkhangelsk* (from Final Dawn) was able to do what it did, that's why the Russians in Surviving the Fall still have assets to commit to traveling to the USA to stop Damocles and it's why I'm sure they'll feature in my stories again in the future. When it comes down to it… they're just so darned fun to write about!

If you enjoyed this episode of Surviving the Fall or if you *didn't* like something—I'd love to hear about it. You can drop me an email or send me a message or leave a comment on Facebook. You can also sign up for my newsletter where I announce new book releases and other cool stuff a few times a month.

Answering emails and messages from my readers is the highlight of my day and every single time I get an email from someone saying how much they enjoyed reading a story it makes that day so much brighter and better.

Thank you so very much for reading my books. Seriously, thank you from the bottom of my heart. I put an enormous amount of effort into the writing and all of the related processes and there's nothing better than knowing that so many people are enjoying my stories.

All the best,
    Mike

Book 8 - The Edge of
the Knife

Preface

Last time, on Surviving the Fall….

Rick, Jane and Dr. Evans are continuing their journey across the country as they seek to travel to Washington, D.C. to—hopefully—stop Damocles before the situation escalates. As they pass through Kansas City, they realize that there are more than just human dangers to contend with. Massive earthquakes have torn apart the city and the surrounding landscape, giving them an entirely new hazard to deal with. As the ferocity of the tremors continues to increase they barely escape the city with their lives.

Meanwhile, Dianne successfully pulled Tina out of the encampment where she was being held prisoner, though the price for doing so was substantial. After being wounded while covering Dianne and Tina's escape, Jason lost a tremendous amount of blood. Tina's former job working as a nurse was the only thing that kept him alive—that at a healthy amount of Dianne's blood that was donated through a person-to-person transfusion. After thinking Jason was in the clear they soon realized that his condition was worsening again due to a serious infection that wasn't treatable with any medications on hand at the house. Someone has to go find the medication necessary to treat him and return in less than twelve hours or Jason will undoubtedly die.

And now, Surviving the Fall Episode 8.

Chapter One

S omewhere between Ellisville, VA and Blacksburg, VA

DIANNE SLOWED TO A STOP, rubbed her eyes and tried to fight back a yawn. After failing in her fight, she stretched and looked at her watch before sighing and putting her truck back into gear. It had taken her the better part of an hour to get as far as she had, though she still wasn't in Blacksburg proper. Winding her way around the main highway—to give as wide of a berth to the gas station compound and those inside as possible—had taken more time than she thought, and though she was still heading in the right direction she wasn't sure when she'd actually arrive in the city.

Keeping the use of the truck's headlights to a minimum had slowed her down, though the terrain had done more than anything else. Going over fields and hills had nearly gotten the truck stuck multiple times and she wasn't sure what she'd do if that finally happened. When she felt that she had bypassed the gas station compound by a wide enough margin she made her way back to the highway only to find it largely taken up by the burned-out wrecks of vehicles that had been destroyed.

Even with the journey taking as long as it was, Dianne pressed forward. Any thoughts of abandoning her task and heading back home were immediately dismissed. Dianne's primary responsibility was to her family, but Jason, Sarah and Tina were as much a part of her family as Rick, Mark, Jacob and Josie. The arrival of what felt like the end of the world brought with it an upheaval of priorities and reinforced exactly who could be trusted and who couldn't. A friend—even if they weren't a blood relative—who was loyal in spite of everything going on was still family, and Dianne was determined to do anything she could to keep her family alive and healthy.

So lost was Dianne in her thoughts about her children and friends back at the house that she had to slam on the brakes to keep from running into a line of vehicles that branched off of the main highway onto an off-ramp and out towards the first exit into Blacksburg. Grass and dirt were ejected from the ground as the tires sought traction, finally finding it as Dianne pulled the wheel to the right and the rear left tire caught hard on the gravel and asphalt of the off-ramp's shoulder. She took several deep breaths, her heart racing as she flicked on the headlights and squinted to read the sign at the end of the off-ramp showing which restaurants and amenities were available.

"Looks like I'm here." Dianne closed her eyes and put her head back against the seat, taking another deep breath while saying a silent prayer of thanks that she hadn't just crashed the truck. After collecting her wits she starting moving forward again along the grass to the side of the off-ramp. A clear spot in the road up ahead was revealed as she crested the hill and she gratefully got off of the grass and back onto solid pavement.

With a population of nearly one hundred thousand people, Blacksburg had exploded in size in recent years thanks to both the local university and the relocation of several technology and manufacturing companies to the area. Being within driving distance of Washington while simultaneously being outside of the sphere of influence of Northern Virginia had helped to spur growth in the city.

Huge swaths of industrial real estate were repurposed into green manufacturing spaces, commercial and office buildings were constructed and homes, townhomes and apartments were filled as quickly as they could be built. While the growth had meant good things for the businesses and people working for them, the city's infrastructure had been overwhelmed and the city was in near-constant gridlock between six in the morning and eight in the evening. Construction projects meant to widen and add new roads had only added to the commotion.

The sheer amount of wreckage on the road leading into the city was mind-blowing to Dianne and she shook her head as she looked at it, trying to figure out how she could possibly get through. Only small sections of the road were wide enough for the truck to pass through and the others were blocked by burned-out vehicles. Dianne looked at the map she had pulled out of the truck's glove compartment earlier and double-checked to see if there were any alternate paths to get where she needed to go. "Nothing." She sighed and looked back at the road ahead. With no places for her to go off-road she put the truck into gear and moved forward, cringing at the thought of what was about to happen to the old truck.

A loud screech came from the front right panel as the truck collided with its first obstacle. The engine didn't even strain, though, as the weight of the wreck was inconsequential when compared to the power propelling the truck. The wreck moved to the side as Dianne kept moving, all while the screeching continued down half the length of the right side. The sounds grew louder and more consistent as Dianne pressed forward, using the truck as a makeshift bulldozer to push her way down the street.

She tried not to imagine how the sides and front of the truck would look after being scratched up one side and down the other, instead focusing on the task at hand. She was surprised at how well the strategy worked, though, and continued pushing through, thankful that the headlights were high and protected enough that they hadn't yet been broken by any of the debris she was pushing out of the way.

The initial group of vehicles soon gave way to an intersection that was relatively clear. Dianne stopped the truck in the middle of the intersection, grabbed her flashlight and the map from the passenger seat and hopped out. She circled around the truck, examining the damage and checking the tires to make sure they weren't suffering too much damage. While the paint on the front edges and sides of the vehicle was scratched and the metal suffered from small tears in a few places, everything was holding together better than she had anticipated.

Dianne unfolded the map onto the hood of the truck and looked around at the street signs, orienting herself and figuring out where to go next. As she looked at the darkened, burned buildings around her and the signs that still stood, she saw a billboard advertisement nearby for a walk-in clinic that was a quarter-mile down the road. Checking her map she saw that if she made a slight detour down a side street she'd be able to visit the clinic on her way to the Long-Term Acute Care facility.

"Doubt they'll have much of anything but it's worth a shot." Dianne mumbled to herself as she folded the map up and hopped back in the truck. The road ahead looked clearer than the section she had driven on getting from the off-ramp into town so she pressed on, all while keeping a close eye on her surroundings. Everything appeared calm and quiet and she sensed no signs of danger, but she still watched the road and buildings with a wary gaze.

⊂⊃

"WHERE DO you think that one's going?"

"Th' hell would I know?"

"I'm just looking for an opinion!"

"My opinion's that you need mouthwash."

"Up yours."

"Should we follow them?"

"Let 'em get closer. See how many they are inside."

The two men sitting in the front of a small hatchback on the top of a hill off the highway watched as the blue truck drove through the grass just outside Blacksburg. They spoke quietly, puffing away at cigarettes and blowing smoke out the windows of the car as they studied the truck. As the vehicle passed close by the hill the man in the driver's seat sat up abruptly, his cigarette and warm bottle of beer forgotten.

"What color jacket did that lady have?"

"Which one?"

"The one who was at the station the other day. She came in while all that gunfire was going on and took that old woman away."

"Hm." The man in the passenger seat frowned. "Green and white? Maybe?"

"I think that's her."

"But the truck they drove off in was white."

"Yeah, but they might have more than one truck."

Both men watched the truck drive up alongside the off-ramp and onto the road before it turned in towards the city and vanished behind a building.

"She was the only one in the truck, right?"

"Yup."

The man in the driver's seat turned on the engine of their hatchback. "Call it in while the engine warms up."

The man in the passenger seat picked up a portable two-way radio from the floor near his feet. "Base, this is unit three. We need to speak to the boss. Got a sighting on someone he'll be interested to hear about."

The voice of the man in the red shirt came back a few seconds later, full of annoyance and frustration that seems to be ever-present. "What is it, unit three?"

"Lady driving a blue truck just went into Blacksburg off the first exit. She had the same color jacket as the one who was at the compound the other night."

"Did you stop her?!" The red-shirted man's voice grows even more strained.

"No, but we saw where she went."

"Then get after her you idiots! Hurry up!"

"Yeah, we're on it."

"Don't get 'on it!' I want her caught right this second!" The man in the red shirt screamed into the radio while the man in the passenger seat looked at his compatriot. They shrugged at each other before the man in the passenger seat finally sent back a reply. "We're going after her now. Will radio back soon."

Before the transmission was severed, the pair could hear the man in the red shirt shouting obscenities at someone in the background. The man in the passenger seat replaced the radio in its spot on the floor and pulled out a handgun and flashlight while the man in the driver's seat put the car into gear.

"You ready for this?"

"Absolutely."

Chapter Two

S omewhere in Missouri

THE CAMPFIRE CRACKED and spat into the darkness, sending sparks up into the air that merged with the twinkling of an infinite field of stars. The air was bitingly cold, making each breath drawn too far from the flames feel like icicles stabbing down through the throat and lungs. The smell of pine was heavy, carried by the chilled breeze that shook needles on limbs and carried away the dark trail of smoke.

Rick had always enjoyed autumn and winter nights, particularly those that could be experienced outdoors. The chill of the cold air on his back while the heat of a roaring campfire kept him warm was a magical combination. Even as far from home as he was, sitting on the side of the road in the middle of nowhere during the apocalypse, he still found himself enjoying the fire and the cold autumn air. It was a guilty pleasure, though, as with any sort of stillness came the thoughts of his wife and children and the 'what-ifs' that plagued his mind.

What if I had just delayed the trip?
What if I had gotten on a later flight?
What if I had taken them with me?

In the back of his mind Rick knew that such questions were futile and ultimately a waste of time. The situation was as it was and no amount of wondering and questioning could change that. His only path forward was to do his best to get back to them, though even that goal was temporarily on the sidelines in favor of a larger, bigger one that would ultimately provide more protection and safety than his mere presence.

Weapons used to be simple. Rocks and clubs. Swords and spears. Bullets and bombs. The digital age had created an entirely new battlefield out of thin air and while defenses were few and far between, weaponry was abundant. *Damocles. Typical doomsday-sounding name for a weapon that should never have been created.* Rick sighed and poked at the fire with a long branch, stirring up a wave of sparks as more sap from the pine wood was discovered by the flames.

"Hey, give us a hand?" Rick looked up to see Jane and Dr. Evans appear through the trees. Jane had a flashlight in one hand but she, like Dr. Evans, was carrying an armful of firewood and appeared to be on the verge of dropping it. Rick jumped up and grabbed several pieces of wood out of her arms and dropped it near the fire before helping Dr. Evans as well.

"Looks like you two got a nice haul out there." Rick nodded approvingly at the small pile of fuel. Jane brushed her hands on her pants before sitting near the fire and holding them out, her whole body shivering.

"Indeed." Dr. Evans replied as he sat near the fire as well. "This should keep us through the night."

"Absolutely." Rick picked up a few pieces of wood and stacked them on the fire, shielding his eyes from the sparks. "We could do with something a bit less sappy but it's better than freezing to death." Rick sat down when he finished as an uncomfortable silence fell over the trio. He let the silence persist for a few long minutes before sighing and breaking it.

"I get the feeling that we need to have a talk here. I don't want to let this go any further than it has."

Jane didn't look at Rick as he spoke, but Rick caught Dr. Evans glancing between them. After the argument that had occurred—primarily between Rick and Jane—as they were escaping from Kansas City, Jane had hardly said anything to Rick. The city had been collapsing around them as they drove out and Jane had wanted to stop to try and rescue anyone who they could cram into their vehicle. Rick had refused, pointing out that they had neither the room nor the time to stop, not to mention the potential dangers involved even if they had the time or space.

Dr. Evans had stayed out of the argument for the most part. He initially agreed with Jane but soon changed his mind to side with Rick that they needed to focus on their plan to disrupt Damocles before the program started wreaking any more havoc. Jane and Rick hadn't talked much over the couple hundred miles they had gone since leaving Kansas City and Rick was tired of the silence.

"Jane, look." Rick stared at the fire, trying to find the words he was looking for.

"No." Jane spoke quietly and Rick looked up at her.

"No what?"

"We don't need to talk about it." She took a deep breath and looked at him, then over at Dr. Evans, then back at Rick. "I was... letting my emotions get the better of me. You're right. Both of you. We can't let anything jeopardize this crazy plan of ours."

Rick shook his head. "Don't sell yourself short. I don't think what you wanted to do was a bad thing at all. In fact we *need* that kind of thinking now more than ever. When we were at Nellis and they wanted to send me to Mount Weather to join in their think tank I refused because I just wanted to get home to my family. The idea of doing anything else was just foreign to me. The more I've learned about Damocles the more I've realized that stopping it needs to be my—*our*—priority. If it's not... if people like us don't step up and try to fix what's going on, then things will get worse for everyone. My family included."

Jane furrowed her brow. "What's that got to do with the people in Kansas City?"

Rick leaned back. "I have been so caught up in getting back home—and now I'm so caught up in this plan—that it's easy to forget about things like compassion. This is the kind of situation when it's natural to retreat from other people and try to protect oneself and focus solely on the objective at hand but we can't do that all the time. Well, I guess we *can*, but if we do, what does that say about us?"

"So... you're saying we should have stopped?" Jane looked confused.

"No." Rick shook his head firmly. "Discernment is important, too. We were attacked in the city and we have no idea if those people we saw fleeing were part of the group that attacked us, or really anything else about them. We know they were running to escape the earthquakes and that's about it. If we had just been trying to escape and if we had a different vehicle then maybe we could have helped in some way. But in our situation we couldn't afford to stop. We can't afford to stop for anything. Not until we finish this. That's how we help those people and countless others. We finish this."

"I know." Jane nodded. "It really sucks, though."

"I can agree with that." Dr. Evans chimed in.

"Ditto." Rick looked at Jane and paused briefly. "We still good?"

Jane nodded slowly and smiled. "Yeah. We're good."

Rick smiled and looked at her and Dr. Evans. "I'm glad. I can't do this nonsense on my own and you two haven't stabbed me in my sleep yet so I need both of you alive, well and not completely pissed off at me."

Jane and Dr. Evans both chuckled, then Dr. Evans spoke. "Speaking of this 'nonsense', as you put it, our experience in Kansas City has led me to believe that we should steer clear of any large cities from now on. We have fuel and supplies to get all the way to Washington. The potential benefits of further searching are, in my opinion, vastly outweighed by the downsides."

"I'm with him." Jane nodded in agreement.

"Same." Rick nodded as well. "We'll stick to the highways where we can but we'll divert around any large cities. They're not worth the risk."

"How much longer do you think it'll take us to get there?" Jane asked.

"A couple more days, most likely. Maybe longer, though." Rick shrugged. "It depends on the roads and if anything else happens along the way."

"I hope not."

"You and me both."

Chapter Three

S omewhere over the North Pole

THE BEAR IS COLD.

Flying at an altitude of forty-five thousand feet, the modified Tupolev Tu-95—nicknamed the Bear—has a small cabin with room for two pilots and five additional crew. The thin metal separating the interior of the aircraft from the exterior does nothing to keep the cold out while the small space heater in the middle of the aircraft serves mostly as a decorative accessory. Threadbare cushions sag against the rough wood and metal seats, providing little comfort as the aircraft bumps and bucks in the turbulence. The men riding inside the aircraft are wrapped in warm clothing from head to toe but the cold still pierces through, a constant reminder that they are unwelcome strangers in the land they are passing through.

While the Bear is pressurized, the age and lack of regular maintenance of the aircraft mean that the air is not quite as thick as it should be. For the two pilots and special forces operatives who have spent the last fifteen years of their life at high altitudes, this means nothing. For the two technicians who have spent their lives in a bunker staring at computer screens it means everything. The technicians keep their oxygen bottles and masks on their laps, taking deep breaths from them every few minutes as their bodies struggle to adjust to the change.

The four men are just over five hours into their eleven-hour journey and despite their discomfort the flight is going well. One of the four engines is leaking fuel, though this was anticipated ahead of time and the external fuel tanks will be more than adequate to ensure the aircraft reaches its destination.

Spetsnaz officer Ostap Isayev, the pilot and leader of the expedition, comes over the internal communications channel of the plane. "We are less than six hours out, assuming the weather holds. At one hour out we will begin final preparations and parachute checks."

Carl Aliyev—the co-pilot and another Spetsnaz officer—sits next to Isayev while the two technicians sit in the seats behind the pilot and co-pilot chairs. After Isayev's announcement there is silence on the channel until Oles Belov looks at Jacob Yermakov and thumbs his microphone.

"This weather is shit, eh Jacob?"

Yermakov swallows hard, the Dramamine he had when they took off starting to lose its potency. He nods slowly and grimaces as he replies. "I don't think I can take another six hours."

"Just wait till we have to drop in!" Though Belov is a technician he relishes the opportunity to get out of the bunker where he was debugging lines of code. Being selected to fly across the globe and potentially save his homeland from this mysterious digital weapon is both an honor and the fulfillment of several of his long-held fantasies all at once.

Though Belov and Yermakov hadn't met before they were taken to the bunker shortly after the event, their similar personalities and taste in music and animated television programs meant that they quickly formed a bond with each other. The pair would often work together, trying to find ways to thwart or protect against Damocles. While they—like everyone else on the planet—were unsuccessful, they still learned a great deal about certain aspects of how Damocles functioned. This knowledge, no matter how limited it was, was enough to ensure that they were the two technicians selected for the mission to America.

"I don't think I can handle a parachute." Yermakov swallows hard again, tasting acid in the back of his throat. He reaches for a canteen of water but grabs a wax-lined paper bag at the last second. Up front, Isayev and Aliyev glance back at the sound of the retching. They both roll their eyes at each other then turn their attention back to their tasks.

Chapter Four

Blacksburg, VA

HALF of the strip mall that contained—among other things—a Chinese restaurant, a dry-cleaner, a dollar store and the First Med Walk-In Clinic was charred to a crisp. The fire had inexplicably stopped halfway through its destruction of the Panda Inn, leaving the clinic and dollar store to the left of the restaurant intact. The blackened roof and walls had collapsed inward on the restaurant while to the right of it there was nothing left of whatever businesses had been located there.

The parking lot in front of the strip mall was completely filled with scorched vehicles. Dianne thought that she might be able to get into the lot by pushing some of the wreckage out of the way but getting back out would likely prove to be impossible.

Forgoing parking directly in front of the walk-in clinic Dianne turned left, pulling off in front of what had once been an oil change service station. The beams of the truck passed over the collapsed structure, revealing that there had been two vehicles inside when the place caught fire. Dianne wondered if the vehicles themselves had been the source of the blaze as she thought back to the sight of her own SUV catching fire and exploding in front of her house.

Dianne eased to a stop in an open area between the street and the service station, keeping the lights on the truck off as she navigated by moonlight. Before leaving the house Sarah had warned Dianne about the likelihood of looters around hospitals due to the opiates and other drugs stored in those locations. Dianne wasn't certain that there would be any substances in a walk-in clinic that people would want to loot but decided to take the cautious approach regardless.

She grabbed her flashlight and pistol and got out of the truck, crouching next to the vehicle as she scanned the clinic, dollar store and the rest of the surrounding area. A gentle breeze drifted between the buildings, carrying the faint noise of insects from the grass and trees just outside the city. There were no signs of movement in the area except for the brief flutter of half-burned paper and plastic sheeting that was stuck amongst the ashen ruins. Once Dianne was satisfied that she was alone she retrieved her bag and headed for the walk-in clinic.

The strip mall had obviously been in need of repair and upkeep even before the event, as evidenced by the cracks in the sidewalk, support pillars and underside of the roof. A thick layer of soot and ash lay on every surface, giving the place an unearthly look and feel. The front windows and glass doors of both the dollar store and the clinic had been smashed in and there were traces of dried blood on the ground in front of the clinic.

"Looks like somebody got themselves all cut up." Dianne murmured to herself as she crouched down to examine the bloody shards of glass. "Not fresh though." She looked up and pointed her flashlight at the interior of the clinic, the beam casting stark shadows from the frame of the door and the furniture that had been knocked over inside.

Dianne thumbed her pistol's safety off as she stepped inside the clinic. She scanned the front room with her light and weapon, wincing as the glass beneath her feet cracked and crunched. After confirming that the front of the building was clear of other people she moved into the back rooms, checking each office and waiting room before moving past them. When she reached a large area with cabinets—most of which had been broken open— she stopped and slipped off her backpack and jacket.

Most of the contents of the cabinets had been taken, but Dianne dutifully rolled up her left sleeve and consulted the sharpie-written list of must-haves she had jotted down on her arm before leaving the house. It only took a few minutes for her to check the cabinets and by the end she was disappointed. While there were a few bandages and basic antiseptics she located on some bottom shelves there was nothing left that could be used to help Jason.

Dianne clenched her teeth as she checked through the cabinets and rooms in the clinic one last time. She didn't know why she thought the walk-in would be a good place to stop considering Sarah had told her what locations would have the medications and fluids they would need for Jason. Wasting even a few minutes on a fruitless search could prove to be fatal for her ill friend.

All right. Time to go. Dianne hurried back to the room with the cabinets to get her jacket and backpack. As she leaned over to grab them she heard a faint noise coming from the back of the building. She froze, turning her head towards the sound as she strained to make out the source. It sounded at first like a distant groaning, perhaps coming from the building's structure as it shifted, but as she listened she began to realize that it was actually coming from two people who were bickering with each other. Dianne crept towards the back door to the clinic, keeping her body pressed against the wall as she moved cautiously, trying her best not to make any noise.

"...did she go, anyway?"

"I don't know."

"Haven't we looked around here long enough?"

"No! Her lights went off around here. We keep looking till we find her or see that she moved off. You head that way, I'll go down the street this way."

"Ugh. I hate going on foot."

"Get used to it. If we don't find her then our asses'll be in a sling."

As the two men talked with one another Dianne slowly peeked through the hole in the back door where the window had once been located before someone shattered it. Across the back parking lot, standing in front of a row of buildings behind the clinic, stood two men whom she recognized. They were just starting to separate and walk in different directions down the street but Dianne could still see their faces enough to realize who they were.

Them again? Dianne groaned and moved away from the window, closing her eyes as she realized that the two men were the ones who had tried to steal her truck at the grocery store at the start of the event. They were also two of the group who had been present at the Carson's home when she and Jason heard about Tina's kidnapping. As she thought about the conversation she just overhead she realized that the "he" they were talking about was most likely the red-shirted individual who was the leader of the group at the gas station.

If he's got people looking for me... this is bad. Very, very bad.

Chapter Five

S omewhere in Indiana

SMOKE WAS thick in the air, robbing the sky of color and dampening the spirits of Rick, Jane and Dr. Evans. While the drive through Missouri and the southern half of Illinois had been smoother than the trio could have asked for, when they entered Indiana things started taking a turn for the worse. The first sign of trouble ahead came in the form of light swirls of ashes that came and went with the wind. The ash quickly grew in density and was accompanied by thick, acrid smoke that reduced visibility and made it uncomfortable to breathe.

By the time an hour had passed Rick had been forced to reduce their speed from over ninety miles an hour to around thirty just so that he wouldn't inadvertently collide with any obstacles in the road. The slowdown in pace was infuriating and no matter what road or direction they took they couldn't escape from the smoke and ash.

"What's causing all this?" Jane looked out through the windshield and passenger window, shaking her head in frustration.

"Fire. A lot of it." Dr. Evans answered from the back seat.

"No kidding." Jane rolled her eyes, her patience wearing thin from spending so much time cooped up in the car. "What kind of fire, though?"

"The hot, burning kind?" Rick snickered at his joke though he was the only one of the trio to do so.

"A massive fire, perhaps of a nearby forest. To produce this much ash and smoke in this volume the fires would have to be absolutely enormous."

"Sure would be nice if the wind would change." Rick swerved to avoid a hole in the highway. "Then maybe we could see more than a few inches beyond our faces."

"Hey guys?" Jane was staring out the windshield. "Is it just me or is the smoke and ash getting… more orange?"

It took a moment for Rick and Dr. Evans to notice the change, but they slowly realized that Jane wasn't just seeing things. The sky was, indeed, beginning to take on an orange hue that was backdropped by a glow that would look good on the cover of a horror novel but when viewed in reality was terrifying in ways that Rick couldn't even begin to express. As the car began to crest a hill, the breeze picked up and the trees by the side of the road swayed back and forth. The ash and smoke swirled, rising and falling as it dispersed slightly, just enough to extend the visibility by enough to see what was causing the glow.

When Rick had taken family vacations with his parents to visit his grand-parents in Oklahoma, one of his favorite memories was spending each after-noon watching a movie with his grandfather. Rick's grandfather liked older movies and his favorite actor was John Wayne. Many westerns were consumed over the years, but Rick's favorite John Wayne movie wasn't a western at all. Rick didn't remember much about the plot of *Hellfighters* but one thing was cemented in his mind forever: the image of burning oil wells that looked like fountains of pure flame.

Beyond the road, out in a distant field, sat the infrastructure that supported the local oil mining operations. Dozens of pumps and drills littered the field, some covered in rust from years of use while others had been installed mere months prior. Instead of slowly pumping away, though, the oil wells were on fire, and just like in *Hellfighters*, they looked like fountains spitting out flames.

Smoke billowed into the sky, blocking out the blue for miles in every direction. Even from the extreme distance they were sitting Rick could swear he felt the heat from the fires. It took no small amount of concentration to keep from backing the car up, turning around and finding a path that would take them far, far from the field. The oil wells, however, were not the only things that were on fire.

Past the field, barely visible through the cloud of smoke and the torrents of flame was a veritable ocean of fire. The side of the distant mountain, covered a month prior by a dazzling mixture of red, yellow and green was now pure orange. The fire was moving slowly through the trees, speeding up when the wind picked up and slowing down when it faded away. Rick's mouth silently opened and closed several times as he kept trying to find the words to describe the landscape laid out before them.

"It's as if hell itself has come to earth." Dr. Evans whispered from the back seat. "Look, out among the fields. You see the cracks in the ground? More like what we saw in Kansas City."

"You still think Damocles did it?"

"A handful of examples is scarcely proof positive but I think I can say with absolute certainty that the weapon is responsible for this." Dr. Evans looked at Rick. "This is only going to get worse. We must continue with all possible speed."

Rick nodded and set their car in motion again, taking advantage of the temporary clearing of the air to get past the area as quickly as possible. It didn't take more than a mile or so more of traveling before Rick realized that they wouldn't be able to continue without taking some serious risks.

"Look, out there." Rick slowed the car as he pointed out the left window to the north. "See that fire?"

Dr. Evans and Jane craned their necks, seeing another distant forest fire that was a few miles off. "What about it? It's still a ways out, right?" Jane looked at Rick.

"Yeah, but look at where we have to go." Rick tapped on the screen in the car and zoomed in on the map to their approximate location. "This road curves north for the next leg of the journey. We're going to be driving straight into that inferno."

"Why can't we take one of these back roads out to the east?" Jane pointed at the screen.

"We could. But it's risky. Most of them wind all through the hills and loop back on themselves. If the wind changes direction and pushes the fires closer to us we'll have no way to escape."

"What if we backtrack and go back around?" Dr. Evans chimed in. "We're only a few miles in here and we could go back, divert straight east, cross the Ohio River and then start heading northeast again after that."

Rick nodded slowly. "All right, then. We'll turn around and head around this mess. Better safe than sorry. Are you sure we'll be able to get across the river, though?"

"I don't see why not."

As Rick turned around and headed back the way they came, he was glad to see the fires receding into the distance. Dealing with the wind, rain, cold and even people was child's play compared to dealing with a fire as big and as menacing as the one sweeping across the fields and forests. He hoped it would eventually die out but there was no telling where or when that would happen—if it happened at all.

Chapter Six

B lacksburg, VA

DIANNE SAT near the back door of the walk-in clinic for a few more minutes as she listened and occasionally leaned up to peek out the window. With the two men prowling around behind the strip mall she didn't want to take any chances on making sounds that might lead them to her. The more she thought about how she could get away, though, the more she realized that she would—at some point—have to get to the truck and take off. That amount of noise would certainly draw their attention, but there was nothing else that could be done.

How am I supposed to get away, though? Dianne thought back to her inspection of the map as she tried to remember how to get to the LTAC facility from where she was. With nothing of worth inside the walk-in clinic it was clearly time for her to move on to the LTAC. Getting away would undoubtedly prove problematic. With the two men nearby she could either stand her ground and fight them—perhaps overpowering one before the other realized what was going on—or she could wait for the opportune moment to flee and hope that they couldn't follow her or get a lucky shot off before she got away.

Already angered by Jason's injury caused by the gang, Dianne seriously considered ambushing the two men to both keep them from following her and to exact a measure of vengeance for Jason's injury, Tina's kidnapping and whatever other horrors the two men and their compatriots had inflicted on other people. While Dianne wasn't dissuaded by the thought of killing the two men she did have to weigh what it could potentially mean for Jason.

If she spent a lot of time on a plan that wasn't successful—or even if it was—then that would be less time that she could devote to finding the medication that Jason so desperately needed. After wrestling with the decision for a few minutes Dianne gave up on the idea of trying to take the men out and instead began moving back towards the entrance to the clinic. Inside the front lobby she stared out into the parking lot, looking for any signs of the men that were searching for her. They were likely still searching the buildings behind the strip mall, though as she caught sight of her truck across the street she groaned and wished she had parked it in a slightly less obvious spot.

Dianne ran out of the entrance to the clinic, jumping over large piles of glass as she tried to minimize the noise she was creating. She stopped halfway through the parking lot, pushing herself down between the remnants of two cars as she paused again to watch and listen for the men. The noise she made going out the front door didn't seem to attract their attention so she moved forward again, keeping as low to the ground as possible and sticking close to objects she could use for cover in case she started taking fire.

After glancing both ways down the street and seeing nothing, Dianne gave up on her stealthy tactics and ran full-tilt across the road. She shrugged off her backpack halfway to the truck and ran around to the driver's side. She tossed her pack onto the passenger seat and hopped in, closing the door as softly as possible.

"So far so good…" Dianne whispered to herself as she inserted the key into the ignition. She hesitated before turning it, double checking that there was a round in the chamber of her pistol before proceeding.

When the engine coughed to life Dianne could swear that it was louder than it had ever been before in all the years they had owned it. With the windows rolled down Dianne could hear the echo of the engine carry across the streets and parking lots, bouncing off the buildings and the pavement as it seemingly called out for everyone in the area to come investigate the source of the sound. Certain the pair of men had heard the truck, Dianne didn't waste any time getting moving. She threw it into gear and tore forward down the street, passing by the clinic and the back street where the men had been walking as she flicked on the headlights to keep from running into any obstacles along her way.

The bright beams caught the reflection of pale skin and startled eyes as one of the men ran out from a building to see where the noise was coming from. He nearly fell into the street as he stopped abruptly, staring dumbfounded at the truck as he tried to make sense of what was going on. Seizing upon an opportunity Dianne held fast to the steering wheel with her right hand while she swung open the driver's side door with her left, bracing it with her left leg and arm. She jerked the steering wheel to the left and pushed outward on the door with her leg and arm, feeling a loud thud as it struck the man who was standing on the pavement.

Dianne pulled the door closed and pulled the truck back to the right as the man cried out in pain, falling to the ground and tumbling forward from the force of the collision. His partner emerged from a building on the opposite side of the street a second later. He glanced at his fallen cohort before he looked up at the truck and started firing at it with his pistol. Fortunately for Dianne, though, she was far enough down the road and his aim was bad enough that he had no chance of hitting her.

"MY ARM!" The man lying on the ground screamed as his partner continued firing round after round at the truck. He knew there was little chance of hitting the vehicle or the passenger inside but he felt obligated to try anyway. Once the truck was out of sight he ran over to the man on the ground and knelt down next to him.

"You okay?"

The man on the ground spat at the one standing above him, then cried out in pain as the movement caused a wave of pain to travel from his shoulder down to his wrist. "Do I *look* okay? What the hell's wrong with you?! Help me up!"

The uninjured man helped the one on the ground to his feet, then the injured man took off his jacket to see the extent of his injuries. He could still move his fingers and had some limited movement, but whenever anything below his left shoulder moved around he felt pain wash over him.

"Did she break it?"

"Maybe." The injured man tried to form a fist but gave up as the agony made tears well up in his eyes. "Let's just get in the car and go after her."

"What was she doing, anyway? She was close by."

"I don't know. I don't care, either." The injured man growled. "But that bitch is going to pay."

Chapter Seven

ISS-2, International Space Station 2
Three Hours After the Event

"HOUSTON? Houston, can you hear us? Jacksonville? Can anyone hear us?"

"Anything?"

Ted Wilkins shakes his head. "Nothing. It's like the satellite relay system is gone."

Jackie Frey looks back out the window as she watches the surface of the earth. "The fires are spreading. There's smoke all across the panhandle now."

"What could be going on? We had comms until, what? Three hours ago?"

Jackie nods. "I think so."

"Got anything yet?" Commander Devin Palmer drifts into the room, reaching out and grabbing onto a handhold to stop his forward momentum.

"Nothing yet. I think something's wrong with the TDRS. I'm getting nothing from any of the satellites. No static, no keepalive signal, no nothing. It's like they're just... gone."

"I was able to get a visual lock on four of the relay satellites and seven others in higher orbits. They all appear dead, though."

"Dead?"

"They're tumbling. Orbits are destabilizing. Some'll burn up in a few days. Probably a few weeks for the others I saw."

Ted's eyes widen as he realizes what Devin is saying. "Did someone send them kill commands?"

Commander Palmer shrugs. "No clue." He looks over in the corner of the room. "Did you try the emergency radio bands?"

Jackie nods, still looking out the window. "For an hour straight. No response. There's plenty of static out there but nobody's transmitting on anything that we can pick up."

Commander Palmer gently pushes himself toward the window and whistles at the sight of the southeastern United States below. "Look at that smoke out in the gulf. Are those rigs that are burning?"

Jackie nods again. "I think so."

"Holy hellfire. What's going on down there?"

"Uh… Commander Palmer? You want to come take a look at this?" Ted wipes his arm across his brow, his nervousness and trepidation growing by the second.

"What's going on?"

Ted points to an image on the screen of the laptop he's working at. "I just saw a flicker in the O2 tank sensors. They were showing empty for a split second, then they were back. Then there was a surge in the main computer controls, like it was working overtime for a minute before going back to normal."

"Hm." Commander Palmer pulls himself in front of the computer as Ted drifts to the side. "You run a diagnostic?"

"Not yet. This happened just now, when you two were talking."

Commander Palmer taps on the keyboard, paging through the software that shows readouts on all of the systems running on the space station. At first glance everything appears normal, at least until Palmer starts digging deeper into the systems. Strange fluctuations in pressurized tanks, voltage changes in key electrical systems and seemingly random spikes appear in the main computer system.

Twice the size of the ISS, the ISS-2 has been online and manned for six months and has already served as host to several civilian and politician visits and countless scientific experiments. The original ISS is still in orbit, though it is unmanned and offline, with plans to decommission it in the works. Only three astronauts—all American—are onboard the ISS-2, though five more were scheduled to arrive from Venezuela, Russia and China within the next four to six weeks. Being slightly understaffed on the ISS-2 has not proven to be a problem for the three astronauts as they have had many automated and upgraded systems at their disposal, making the ISS's systems look primitive in comparison.

"I don't understand what's going on." Commander Palmer turns back to look out the window. "But it's got to be related to that. Maybe war?"

"It doesn't look like it." Jackie shakes her head. "There are fires across the globe. Most of the major cities look like something bad is happening. It seems to be country-agnostic."

"Terrorist attacks?"

Jackie shrugs. "I don't see how. Maybe? But how could it be coordinated world-wide?"

Palmer is about to respond when the lights in the room flicker for a few seconds before shutting off entirely. The whine of a compressor in some distant part of the space station slowly dies off, leaving the room shrouded in darkness and silence.

"What the hell? Where are the emergency lights?" Using the bit of light coming from outside the station Palmer makes his way to a small cabinet on the wall. He pulls out a pair of flashlights, throwing one of the lights to Ted while motioning to Jackie to follow

him. *"Ted, get on the computer and see what's going on. Jackie, I need you with me. Let's see if we can get some lights on in here."*

"Computer's dead, Commander." Ted slaps at the keys and pushes the power button for the monitor on and off but nothing happens.

"Merde." Palmer curses under his breath. *"Okay, with system power offline we need to check the breakers and relays first. Ted, you head down and check those. Jackie, get your eyes on the reactor and see if there's a problem with it. I'll go up to control and see if anything is showing up there. Use the pipes to communicate."*

"On it." Ted and Jackie pull themselves through a tube in the 'floor' of the room, heading to the panels that house the main power breakers for the space station. Commander Palmer, meanwhile, proceeds up into the control room. He pulls a flexible tube close to his face and speaks into it.

"Got anything down there?"

A hollow, tinny voice echoes back through the tube. *"Give us just a second. We're checking the last row of them now."* There is silence for a few more seconds and Ted's voice comes through again. *"Nothing. Absolutely nothing. No problems, no issues, no nothing."*

Palmer glances across the instrument panels, toggling switches as he flips through a thick notebook filled with emergency checklists. *"I'm getting nothing from up here, either."*

"Commander?" Jackie's voice is distant, but filled with stress and alarm. *"I think I found the problem."*

Chapter Eight

S omewhere Near the Indiana/Kentucky State Border

"SERIOUSLY? Again? What is that, the third one that's been down?"

"There was the one that was still standing back at the start."

"Technically standing doesn't really count for our purposes. I wouldn't trust that thing to hold up a housefly."

"Do we keep going?"

"What other choice do we have? They can't *all* be out. I hope."

Rick sighed, and waved dramatically at the car. "After you." Jane grumbled as she climbed into the back seat, then Rick and Dr. Evans got in. Rick started the car, put it into gear and backed away from the remnants of the bridge that once stretched across the Ohio River, linking the west and east sides together.

They had been following the river's course for over an hour, starting down near Louisville and working their way north along the western bank. Avoiding major cities like Louisville was a priority for them given the unpredictable shifts in the ground in the area and they had hoped to use a smaller bridge in between Louisville and Cincinnati to cross over the water.

Unfortunately, though, the earthquakes that had caused them to avoid the larger cities had caused other, more urgent problems as well. They had started just outside Louisville, looking for a bridge to cross the river. The first one they saw was an older, two-lane bridge that had only a simple guardrail on both sides. They were about to cross the bridge when Jane yelled at Rick to stop, having noticed something wrong just as they were about to cross over the threshold of the bridge.

The trio had stopped, gotten out and walked to the bridge to find that the bridge was splintered and cracked with long fissures running on the road's surface as well as on the support beams that held it up. With collapsed buildings visible in the distance at the edge of Louisville, they all agreed that they should continue north and try to find a crossing that looked like it wouldn't plummet into the water if they drove across.

An hour and two collapsed bridges later and Rick was beginning to wish they had risked the first crossing. Evidence of intense tectonic activity dotted the area, affecting both man-made structures and the natural landscape. Structures never designed to be subjected to earthquakes had either completely collapsed or were a strong gust of wind away from falling into a heap. Clusters of trees and sections of open fields were completely gone in some places, replaced only by dark crevices and holes in the ground. The two bridges the group came across were likewise destroyed with small pieces of cement and steel sticking out of the water like gravestones.

Rick crossed his hands on the top of the steering wheel and rested his chin on them as they sat in front of where the third bridge once stood, looking out across the water. "It's so close. So. Close."

"We could sw—no, wait. Duh." Jane rolled her eyes at herself. "Can't exactly take the car across the water even if we did swim, could we?"

Rick blinked a few times as he crinkled his nose. "What if we could, though?"

"This car is a wonder of modern technology, Rick, but it can't fly." Dr. Evans replied.

"Not fly. But float."

Jane laughed. "Is this James Bond's car or something?"

"No, no; listen, just hear me out." Rick lifted his head and zoomed out on the map on the center console. "Back when we were outside Louisville, did either of you take a look down the river toward the city?"

Dr. Evans and Jane looked at each other, shrugged, shook their heads and replied in unison. "Not really."

Rick began tapping his fingers against the steering wheel as the threads of a plan began to slowly weave themselves into a tapestry in his mind. "The Ohio River sees—or saw, at least—a lot of barge traffic. Goods going up and down the river. I remember looking down the river toward the city and seeing a bunch of barges and tugboats down there."

"What's that got to do with us?"

Rick put the car into reverse, glancing nervously at the fading sun. "We need to find a barge or a big boat or something on the river. If we do, we can bring it to shore, load the car on board, get the barge across and we're home free." Rick stepped on the accelerator, pressing the three of them into their seats as the car jumped forward.

Jane looked out the back window. "Not to disparage your plan or anything, but shouldn't we be going back towards Louisville if you want to get a boat?"

Rick shook his head. "Nope. We keep pressing forward and head north. If we're lucky we'll find an intact bridge. If not, then hopefully we'll find a barge adrift or run aground or something."

"I don't particularly like the sound of this plan, Rick." Dr. Evans clung to the handholds inside the car as it sped along.

Rick shrugged. "It's the same plan, more or less. The bridge would be best, but if not... well, we have a backup plan."

***

ANOTHER HOUR and a half's worth of driving brought with it the discovery of two more bridges across the river—one for road traffic and one for trains—that had been completely destroyed. No boats or barges or water-craft of any kind had been spotted and the trio's morale, while temporarily boosted by Rick's new plan, was steadily dropping. The sky was a mixture of dark red, orange and purple with the sun sitting low over the horizon when Jane shouted, startling Dr. Evans and nearly causing Rick to swerve off the road. "There!" She pointed out to the right at the river and Rick slowed down.

"What? What is it?"

"You wanted a boat; there's a boat!"

Rick turned the nose of the car towards the water as he stopped, the white headlights casting a wide beam across the river. The water was muddy and filled with various parts of trees, likely a result of the earthquakes that were stirring up sediment and causing trees to fall in. Out on the other side of the river, past the debris and barely illuminated by the headlights, was the vague outline of a long, flat rectangular object. The object was large and looked like it was stuck on the eastern bank. Rick stared at it for a long moment before nodding slowly, a smile spreading across his face. "Yes. Yes, it is."

A pair of binoculars and some careful studying of the shadow-shrouded barge revealed that it was tied up to a small dock on the opposite bank, held in place by a single line that had somehow not broken or become dislodged. The pièce de résistance, though, was what was attached to the far end of the barge, gently rocking in the current of the river. A tugboat—a "pusher" boat —was still attached by cables and lines, and it had been tied off on a large tree that was a couple dozen feet up away from the edge of the river. Together the barge and the pusher kept each other from drifting away from shore while also providing two points of contact with land, reinforcing each other's tie-offs and helping to keep the precarious pair relatively stable.

Whoever had been piloting the pusher had done an admirable job in securing both the barge and the pusher despite there being very little to work with. What had caused the pilots to want to abandon the craft was anyone's guess, but Rick knew that unless he, Jane and Dr. Evans were to get lucky enough to find an intact bridge hours or perhaps days further up the river, the best shot they had at crossing in any reasonable amount of time was to use the barge and pusher.

Rick took a deep breath and unzipped his jacket, the rapidly cooling night air piercing through his shirt and prickling his skin. "Which one of you is the best swimmer?"

Jane's eyes widened and she took a step back towards the car, shaking her head and raising her hands. "No way."

"Doctor?" Rick looked at Dr. Evans.

"Ugh." Dr. Evans groaned and nodded slowly. "I did swim competitively for a few years when I was in college."

"Hey, that's awesome! I haven't dipped a toe in anything deeper than a puddle in years so if I go under you can just carry me on your back." Rick grinned as he pulled his boots off.

"Couldn't you just make a raft or something?" Jane watched as the two men disrobed down to their underwear. "Swimming in this weather at night across all of *that* sounds like a death wish."

Rick grinned. "Not if we plan ahead."

Chapter Nine

B lacksburg, VA

"OKAY. JUST BREATHE. JUST BREATHE." Dianne closed her eyes and put her head back, taking a deep breath to calm her nerves and her racing heart-beat. For some reason that she couldn't quite put her finger on, she was having more trouble coping with the two men chasing after her than she had when she had walked into the metaphorical lion's den to rescue Tina. She had been nervous then, but for some reason her narrow escape from the two men chasing her in Blacksburg had her even more on edge than before.

Should I just go home? The thought passed through Dianne's mind once again and she didn't immediately dismiss it. Despite her fortitude and will to press on she was forced to admit that she was starting to get scared by the prospect of facing the two men—and whoever else might be with them— again. Heading home without the medication Jason needed was a daunting option, and while she might be able to make up an excuse that would stand up to scrutiny for why she turned tail and ran, Dianne knew she wouldn't be able to live with herself if she didn't continue pressing on.

"Okay." Dianne took another deep breath, talking to herself again. "Hold it together. You just have to get to the LTAC and get the medication. Besides, it's only two of them and you lost them. They don't know where you're going." Dianne opened her eyes and looked at herself in the rearview mirror. "There's only two of them. Of course... there's only one of you." She furrowed her brow as she realized that was the likely reason for what she was feeling. Being away from home with no one to assist her was a new experience and was the likely source for her increased levels of worry.

"Buck up, buttercup." Dianne squared her shoulders and started moving again, weaving the truck farther into the city. She knew that the two men would likely continue to try and track her down, but she had a job to do. The sooner she finished doing it the sooner she could get back home, get Jason fixed up and then start planning on how to eliminate the threat to her and her family once and for all.

It took another half hour of slow driving to finally get to a point in the city where Dianne could see the LTAC. She spotted the large, rectangular building when she was still several blocks away. It sat above the surrounding structures, both because of its height and because it was the only building undamaged by fire in the area. Located in the midst of an oasis of green, the LTAC sat in the middle of one of the few spots of green grass and trees left in the city.

The Regency Long-Term Acute Care center was a combination of a nursing home and a hospital. Patients in need of moderate to intensive care for long periods of time—weeks to months—would be transferred from a hospital to the LTAC where their needs would be better served. Part of Regency's amenities included its location inside a major city and well-manicured lawns and gardens on-site that allowed residents to relax, hopefully helping to accelerate the healing process.

With the autumn weather in full-swing most of the green grass had faded and the leaves on all but the pine trees were covering the ground instead of the branches. The first rays of the rising sun illuminated many of the details of the grounds and the building, though there was much still shrouded in shadow. What Dianne could see quite clearly, though, was that there was no easy path forward to the facility from where she was sitting.

While the grounds of the LTAC looked clear—except for the parking lot out front which was covered in the blackened remains of the vehicles that had been parked there—the roads around it were some of the most clogged Dianne had seen so far in her journey through the city. Melted and charred wreckage sat bumper to bumper on both lanes with only small breaks and gaps in between that might afford the possibility of passage through.

Dianne considered trying to push her way through the wreckage anyway, but the time and noise involved made her wary. Not only were there the two men who were searching for her to consider, but there could be any number of people left alive in the city who might seize on the opportunity to attack her. *Got to get off the street and go on foot.* Dianne's stomach churned at the idea of leaving the relative safety of the truck but there was no other option. She pushed forward in the vehicle, circling around the area surrounding the LTAC as she looked for a place where she could park it out of sight.

Halfway through her drive she spotted a four-story parking garage located just off of the street she was on. The remains of a few cars blocked the entrance but inside the garage she could see that the path was relatively clear on the ground floor. She turned the truck towards the entrance, pushing through the vehicles in front and breaking the flimsy wooden gate that stood in her way.

Inside the front of the parking garage were dozens of spaces marked with blue paint, signifying that they were handicapped parking areas. Most of them were empty, aside from an intact white panel van that had a wheel-chair ramp attachment mounted to the back. As Dianne looked through the rest of the garage she saw what she was expecting near the back, where the rest of the parking spaces began. Dozens of vehicles, all of them burned to the ground, were lined up in neat rows. There were undoubtedly more of them on the floors above, but Dianne didn't bother driving up to check.

Taking one of the handicapped spaces to the far right of the inside of the garage, Dianne backed the truck up next to a wall, positioning it so that it was impossible to see from outside the structure and difficult to see even once inside. She double-checked her gear and glanced at her watch again, feeling her heartbeat quicken as she realized how much time had passed.

It had taken around an hour to get into the city, then getting to the LTAC had taken another two and a half. With nearly three hours down there were just over nine left to locate the medications Jason would need, get back out of the city and return home. She stepped out of the truck and slipped on her backpack, put her pistol in a waistband holster and grabbed her rifle out of the back seat. She verified that the rifle was loaded— including one in the chamber—and took a deep breath. "All right," she whis-pered. "Let's do this."

Dianne jogged out of the parking garage, stopped at the entrance to briefly look down the street and continued running out across the road towards the LTAC. A couple block's worth of buildings, roads and destroyed vehicles were between her and the edge of the facility and she wanted to get out of the open and inside the building as soon as possible. As she ran around and jumped over vehicles and debris scattered along the road she grew more and more thankful that she was going on foot. Seeing the destruc-tion up close made her realize that there would have been no possible way for her to get the truck up to the facility and she would have likely gotten stuck less than a quarter of the way there.

As Dianne picked her way through the clogged street and sidewalks, she heard the sound of an engine off in the distance. Panic seized her by the throat and she pushed forward, moving as quickly as she could. Whatever vehicle was approaching was still a ways out but if it was the two men again she knew that they might stop and start searching for her again at any moment.

The climb up the hill to the LTAC facility was steeper than she thought and Dianne slipped more than once on the dormant grass and dirt. She knelt down at a chain-link fence surrounding the facility and pulled a pair of wire cutters from her backpack. After extending the handles and locking them into place she cut away half of the fence and folded it open before slipping through, putting the cutters into her backpack and resuming her climb.

As the hill leveled off and the grass and dirt turned to gravel paths and well-manicured trees, Dianne heard the engine grow louder. She crouched down next to a nearby bench and stared out into the ruins of the city, looking for the source of the sound. The sun's rays were reaching farther across the city, their slender fingers of light gently peeling back the shadows and revealing the true extent of the devastation. Dianne scarcely had time to shake her head in awe at what lay below before she saw a flash of movement along the road near the parking garage where she stashed the truck.

A silver hatchback made its way down the street as Dianne watched, its small size allowing it to traverse the difficult terrain without resorting to pushing obstacles out of its way. Though Dianne was far enough from the vehicle that she didn't think she would be seen she still flattened herself against the ground, peeking her head just high enough to watch the vehicle as it continued driving along. After several minutes of watching, Dianne realized that the car would be blocked from sight by a tall building in the next few seconds. She seized upon the opportunity and leapt up the instant the car was no longer visible. She turned and ran towards the LTAC, feet pounding across gravel, grass and pavement as she headed for the nearest doorway.

Dianne stopped at the front door and pulled a knife from her pocket. She flipped it around and pressed the base of the handle against the door, pushing with all of her strength until the glass door snapped under the pressure of the glass breaker and shattered. Dianne stepped in over the pile of glass, dropped to one knee and rapidly scanned the area, breathing a sigh of relief both at the fact that she was now completely out of sight of the car and that the room appeared to be empty. She slowly stood up, taking a closer look at her surroundings as she started to realize what type of a place she had walked into.

She stood in front of a welcome desk inside of a wraparound atrium that extended all the way around one side of the structure. The roof of the building was transparent and each of the floors above the ground level had open-air balconies that looked out onto the open space, affording the staff and residents a spectacular view not just of the outside of the building but of the inside as well. The exterior walls on the front appeared to be made completely of glass, though it was heavily coated with reflective film to the point that even the morning sunlight was just starting to illuminate the interior of the structure.

Couches, chairs, recliners and benches were scattered across the length and breadth of the bottom floor as far as Dianne could see. A café and a small restaurant stood near the side about halfway down the length of the building and a large grand piano sat off in the corner by itself, the lid still raised from the last time someone had played it. Dianne walked slowly through the rows of seats as she thought back to the times she had been in the hospital giving birth and she realized that the LTAC was hands down the nicest looking medical facility she had ever seen.

It looks more like a luxury spa than a hospital. Sarah's explanation for what the place was—a cross between a hospital and a nursing home—crossed her mind again and she nodded in understanding. *If you're spending weeks or months here, you want it to be nice.* Not only did the facility appear luxurious but she could tell by the architecture that it was modern, as well, and doubtless offered patients the latest in treatment methodologies.

Dianne's footsteps echoed through the atrium as she walked along, speaking softly to herself in the wide, empty space. "So. If I were a bunch of powerful antibiotics, where would I be hiding?"

Chapter Ten

I nternational Space Station 2 (ISS-2)
Four Hours After the Event

COMMANDER PALMER'S *brow wrinkled as he stared through the viewport of the small reactor housed in one of the ISS-2's habitats. An experimental small-scale fusion reactor, the device provided the station with more than enough power to run all of its systems twice over. The solar panels that the station periodically deployed were originally intended for use as the primary source of power, but the unparalleled success of the reactor meant that the solar panels had been relegated to act as an emergency power source.*

That was, at least, until approximately two hours ago. Palmer scans the logs that Jackie Frey pulled from the reactor's computer just before it went offline. The results are not pretty.

"This command has no source. How is that possible?" Palmer looks up at Jackie. "Is that even possible to do?"

"Not that I'm aware of. I guess it's possible that ground control could have gotten in through a back door and initiated the power-down sequence but we lost communications a couple hours before the command was issued."

"So then it had to come from on board the station?"

Jackie shrugs. "I don't know. These records don't seem like they tell the whole story."

"What'd I miss?" Ted Wilkins floats into the reactor room and glances between Jackie and Commander Palmer.

Palmer tosses the printout through the air before turning to look through the viewport at the interior of the reactor chamber. "A power-down command was issued to the reactor around two hours ago. At the same time the solar panels were extended, almost like whoever issued the power-down command wanted it to go unnoticed."

"Is that where the computer problems came from?"

Jackie shakes her head. "I thought so at first, but now… no. I don't think so."

Palmer is about to ask a question when a deep shudder runs through the length of the station. The groan of metal and crack of materials that should not be cracking while in space echoes through the room and the three astronauts look at each other with wide eyes. Several alarms go off a second later, each of them a different tone and frequency. The worse, by far, is accompanied by a bright orange light that flashes from the corner of each room in the station.

"We're losing O2! Get your suits on now!" Commander Palmer doesn't hesitate to bellow out the order even as the station shakes again as it lurches to one side. Ted reaches out for a handhold on the wall and looks at it with a horrified expression.

"Did someone turn on the thrusters?"

Palmer kicks against the exterior of the reactor, pushing himself toward the nearest wall. He grabs hold, feeling the vibration of the station's thrusters and shakes his head. "Negative. What's going on here, some kind of computer glitch?" Before either Jackie or Ted can answer he waves them off. "It doesn't matter; first we get in our suits then we'll see what's going on!"

The three astronauts sail through the rooms of the station, quickly reaching the area where their suits are stored. They crack open the back of the suits, step inside and the back seals automatically as they flex their muscles. A small green light illuminates at the bottom of their helmets' heads-up displays to indicate that the seal is complete.

Ted, the first to get into his suit, is about to press a button on his left wrist display to connect the suit to the station's computer system when Palmer grabs his right hand and pulls it away. "No!" Palmer says, looking at Ted and Jackie both. "If this is a computer glitch it could affect the suits, too. Don't connect them to the station. We'll do this all manually."

The trio spend the next twenty minutes sweating—in spite of their suits' on-board cooling systems—as they attempt to find out why the station's thrusters started firing. The reason why is not forthcoming but the end result is soon discovered, though it generates more questions than answers.

"Who would want to de-orbit us?!" Jackie pounds her fist against the bulkhead as she stares at the rough set of calculations drawn out on a notepad by Commander Palmer. Ted is furiously scribbling on a separate pad and, once he finishes, he compares his calculations to Palmer's.

"Confirmed. We're de-orbiting and should reach the point of no return in about… an hour. Maybe less. Hard to tell with how the systems are acting."

"And all the fuel's expended?"

"Every drop. They burned hard and fast."

"It has to be sabotage." Palmer taps his pen against the notepad and shakes his head. "Or a terrorist attack."

"If we could pick up any sort of transmissions then maybe we could figure out what's going on."

Palmer frowns, feeling a chill run down his spine. "Our emergency radio equipment. Does it run completely separate from the station's systems? Or is it tied in to everything here?"

"Tied in. Wh—oh. Oh God." *Jackie slowly shakes her head.* "No…"

"Oh yes." *Palmer nods slowly and Ted's eyes widen as he realizes what they're talking about.*

"Do you think… maybe the computer problems are affecting the backup radio systems, too?"

"They're tied directly into the main computer. Which is currently having some sort of psychotic break."

Commander Palmer snorts at Jackie's morbid sense of humor before his face grows serious again. "Unless someone here has a magic switch to flip and turn off the thrusters we're going to have to abandon the station if we want to live."

"Where are we going to go? We're too low to use the lifeboat to perform an emergency splashdown, aren't we?"

"We would have had to leave six minutes ago to do that." *Commander Palmer grits his teeth.* "We should have, though. I didn't realize that all the fuel was gone. Even if we were to pull something out of our asses that would start pushing us back out we've got too much momentum in the wrong direction."

Silence descends over the three as they each contemplate the repercussions of what Palmer has said. Space travel is a dangerous endeavor and each of them has understood that death waits around the corner. Facing it head-on isn't what they were expecting when they woke up that morning, though.

"Commander?" *Ted is staring out the window, watching across the vastness of space as he speaks.*

"What's up?"

"How far away is the ISS?"

"I don't know, a few hundred kilometers?"

"It's at roughly the same orbit we were at before this started, right?"

"Uh, yeah, we're…" *Commander Palmer stares at the banks of switches and monitors, looking through them as he tries to process Ted's question. After several long seconds he whirls around, his eyes wide and his mouth open.* "Yes! It could work!"

"What could work?" *Jackie looks at Ted and Palmer in confusion as they start talking excitedly over one another.*

"The ISS!" *Ted turns to her.* "We're too far down and are carrying too much mass and momentum to slow our descent or try a safe splashdown in the lifeboat."

"But if we use the lifeboat to carry us to the ISS, we should have full control over all the systems there." *Commander Palmer continued.* "The computers were taken offline but they still have power. Everything's just dormant!"

"Does the lifeboat have enough thrust to get us there, though?" *Jackie asked.*

"Not on its own." *Palmer shook his head.* "But it uses a different fuel source than the station thrusters. There's a spare tank for the lifeboat down in the cargo section. Back of the napkin math says that plus what's on board will get us and all the supplies we can carry over to the ISS."

"What do we do from there?"

"We sit tight and wait for a rescue. Or pray there's another fuel tank and use that to get back home."

Jackie shakes her head. "This sounds insane."

Palmer nods. "It's absolutely insane and we will probably die due to some sort of unforeseen variable involved in flying by the seat of our pants."

"Sounds way better than sitting here waiting to die, though." Ted replies.

Jackie hesitates for a second before nodding in agreement. "I can't argue with that. Let's do it."

Chapter Eleven

Somewhere Along the Indiana/Kentucky State Border
The Ohio River

JANE HELD a flashlight in each hand, using them to illuminate Rick and Dr. Evans while she shook her head and loudly complained at them. "You two are positively insane. I can't believe you think this is going to work."

Rick and Dr. Evans sat on the ground, their shirts and pants off as they tore black plastic trash bags off of a roll Rick had dug out of the back of the car. He had picked up the bags when they were in the shopping center previously and while he didn't know at the time how he was going to use them he realized that they would be perfect for helping himself and Dr. Evans cross the river.

Rick looked up from his work, sweat beading across his forehead despite his lack of clothes. "It'll work. Trust me. Right, Doc?" Dr. Evans glanced over at Rick and nodded as he blew air into a group of bags five layers thick that were all stuffed inside one another.

"It should help provide some much-needed buoyancy in the water, yes."

"Plus we can wrap up our clothes and shoes and have them when we get over there."

"And a blanket, to dry ourselves off with."

Rick nodded enthusiastically. "Good call. Jane, could you grab the blue one out of the back seat? It's light enough to take with us, I think."

"You're crazy, both of you." Jane hurried back to the car, grabbed the blanket and ran back to Rick and Dr. Evans. Rick folded the blanket tightly and sealed it inside one of the trash bags, squishing all the air out of the bag and then tying it tightly to keep water from getting inside. Dr. Evans did the same with his and Rick's clothing while Rick stuffed their shoes, a flashlight and some food and bottles of water into another bag.

"Perhaps, but if it works then we'll save a bunch of time over continuing to drive." Rick stood up and examined the makeshift floatation device he had constructed. The bag was nearly full but not completely so which would allow him to rest his chest on it while kicking with his feet to both propel himself forward and keep him afloat. Dr. Evans had inflated his bags the same way and with a full five layers of plastic on both they felt confident that an errant branch or rock wouldn't instantly tear and deflate the bags.

"What if the boat doesn't work or you can't get it loose?"

"We'll swim back and keep going." Rick shrugged. "It'll take us twenty minutes to cross over, another twenty to check out the boat and then we'll know if this was worth the time expenditure or not. I know this is crazy, stupid and whatever else you want to call it but I'm tired of sitting in that car trying to find a bridge to cross. We're losing so much time it's not funny. This could work, so we're going to give it a shot."

Jane nodded solemnly and followed Rick and Dr. Evans to the water's edge. Rick turned to her and pointed out at the barge and boat across the river. "All right, just remember to stay here and keep the light pointed at the barge. We'll walk upriver a bit before jumping in so that we don't end up down too far away from the barge. As long as you keep the light over there we'll know where to swim."

"Don't worry about me." Jane said. "You two just worry about not drowning or coming down with hypothermia."

Dr. Evans nodded. "It's fortunate that it's not quite as cold tonight as it was last night. But the water's going to make the air temperature a moot point."

"Let's just get going and try not to think about that right now, okay?" Rick turned and headed along the bank upstream. Jane had positioned the car near the edge of the river facing upstream with the lights on which made it slightly easier for the pair to navigate through the trees and brush along the edge of the river. Dr. Evans and Rick's primary goal during the walk was to keep their air-filled bags intact, which they managed to do with only a few close calls.

"Okay." A few hundred feet up the river Rick stopped and looked at Dr. Evans. "You think this is far enough?"

"It depends on how well you can swim." Dr. Evans smiled.

"Yeah, yeah." Rick sighed and looped the bags containing their shoes, the flashlight and the food and water around his neck. "She was right, you know."

"About what?"

"This is a really, *really* stupid idea."

RICK KEPT his head and chest up as he leapt from the bank into the river, trying to put as little pressure on the fragile bag of air as he could. His toes scraped against the soft mud of the river's bottom and he gasped in shock at the water's temperature. His body started to shiver almost immediately and he nearly lost the bag around his neck before re-adjusting it and positioning himself on the makeshift float.

Dr. Evans jumped in after Rick and, after arranging himself on his bag, shouted out to Rick who was already several feet down the river. "Kick! Kick as hard as you can! This current is strong!" Rick put his head down and began kicking his legs, as quickly as he could without thrashing them. He looked up occasionally to try and see how much progress he and Dr. Evans were making but from his position in the river it was nigh-on impossible to tell where the water stopped and the land began.

"Stop looking up and kick harder! We're nearly there!" Dr. Evans' voice was much closer than it had been a moment ago and Rick had to fight the urge to stop kicking and look over to see where his companion was. His calves and thighs burned as he pushed harder and he could feel the bag he was resting his chest on beginning to slowly sink further into the water, likely due to a leak in one of the layers of plastic.

After kicking for what felt like forever Rick noticed that there was a yellow glow out of the corner of one eye. He risked a quick glance up to see that the barge was around fifty feet off to the right and he had nearly crossed the breadth of the river. Not wanting to miss the boat and be forced to come ashore downriver, Rick put his head back down and grunted as he kicked even harder. His muscles screamed in agony and the last several feet felt longer than the rest of the swim combined. Finally, though, he heard Dr. Evans shout again, and relief washed over him.

"Look out, you'll hit your head on the barge!" Rick stopped swimming and looked up as he floated past the front of the barge. The pusher boat was next and Rick saw a thick metal chain hanging down into the water from the deck of the craft. He reached out and grabbed the chain and his body swung slowly around in the current until his legs and waist bumped up against the hull of the craft. Rick tried to pull himself up into the boat but even though he thought he hadn't used his arms during the swim he found that they felt just as worn out as his legs.

"Hey, Dr. Evans!" Rick called out. "Give me a hand?" No response came, but after a few seconds there was the sound of thumping and rustling plastic above Rick's head. He looked up as a hand and arm shot down and Dr. Evans' smiling face appeared.

"Come on, Rick! Come aboard!" Rick used his last bit of strength as he clung to Dr. Evans' arm, using it and the side of the boat to pull himself up onto the deck. When he finally pulled his legs in over the side he collapsed to the deck, panting heavily and shivering uncontrollably.

"H-h-holy c-cow." Rick's teeth chattered and Dr. Evans quickly opened the plastic backs they had both hung from their necks and got out the blue blanket. He dried Rick off first before drying himself, then they both put their socks, pants, jackets and shoes on. They were still damp all over but as Rick continued to shiver inside his clothes he felt himself slowly starting to feel better.

"That was insane." Rick whispered to Dr. Evans.

"It was fantastic!" Dr. Evans smiled broadly as he rubbed his hands together. "What you're feeling is perfectly natural. The cold of the water combined with the intense physical exertion has left your body sapped of strength. Be sure to drink some water and eat something. You'll feel better soon."

"How is it you're doing just fine while I'm the one suffering?" Rick's hands shook as he opened up an energy bar and ground it beneath his chattering teeth.

Dr. Evans shrugged. "When I used to swim competitively I would train during the winter using a lake behind my parent's house. That plus living in cold climates most of my life got me used to it, I guess."

Rick stood up slowly and gave Dr. Evans an envious look. "Thanks for the help out there. I appreciate it."

"No worries."

Rick was about to suggest that they check out the pusher boat when they heard Jane yelling faintly from across the river. "You two okay?!" Rick turned to see her standing near the car—with its lights now off—waving her flashlight at them. Rick raised both arms and gave her two thumbs up, which she replied to by raising a thumb and switching off the flashlight.

"Okay, then." Rick turned back to Dr. Evans. "Let's see if this thing works."

<hr />

THE ESTIMATE of twenty minutes for checking out the pusher boat turned out to be reasonably accurate, as it took the two men fifteen minutes to break open the lock leading into the control room on the deck. Two minutes later they located all the necessary switches and buttons required to turn on the lights, raise the anchor and switch on the engine. The pusher boat roared to life with one turn of the key, its well-maintained diesel engine none the worse for wear after having sat out in the weather ever since it was abandoned.

Whoever was manning the boat had either left in a hurry or was exceptionally messy. There were food wrappers, empty soda bottles, discarded newspapers and a stack of books scattered inside the small cabin that housed the control room. The boat's logbook was stuffed in a small drawer on one side of the room but there was nothing written inside that gave any information about why the people working the pusher boat had decided to anchor it next to the bank of the river.

"Maybe they wanted to use it again?" Rick speculated aloud as he thumbed through the logbook again before tossing it back into the drawer.

"I feel sorry for them." Dr. Evans surveyed the controls and nodded. "I believe I understand how this all works."

"Fantastic. Do you think we can get the barge across the river and back?"

"I'm not familiar with how these things work, but moving perpendicular to the regular motion of travel would seem to me to be a difficult endeavor. However, given that this boat is designed to maneuver the barge in all sorts of areas I think we'll be able to get it at some point or another."

"Good." Rick stepped up to the controls. "You want me to drive or do you want to take a crack at it?"

Dr. Evans took a step back. "Please, by all means. I'd rather have you at the wheel in case something goes wrong."

"No problem. Just guide me on what does what since you figured it all out already."

Rick and Dr. Evans spent the next thirty minutes working to get the barge from the east side of the river over to the west. A three-hundred-foot length of the river was traversed numerous times as they experimented with controlling the pusher and the barge, gradually working their way across the water while dealing with the current, the ungainly barge and the darkness.

One factor that Rick was exceptionally thankful for was that the barge was empty except for trace amounts of coal that had apparently been the last thing it was hauling. If the barge had been fully loaded there would have been little to no room for the car and it would have been much more difficult to push it across the river. He and Dr. Evans guessed that the barge had been on its way back down the river after delivering a shipment of coal upriver when the event occurred. The operators of the boat most likely abandoned the craft at that point, though where they went was anyone's guess.

Jane stood on the western bank the entire time, watching carefully as Rick and Dr. Evans got the barge closer and closer to shore. When they were within a few feet of the edge Rick jumped from the boat to the shore, carrying with him one of the ropes attached to the barge. He and Jane ran north along the river until they reached a particularly thick oak tree which they proceeded to use as a tie-down point for the barge.

"All good?" Dr. Evans leaned out of the control room, shouting at Rick and Jane.

"It's secure!" Rick shouted back. Dr. Evans pushed a button that lowered the pusher's anchor over the side where it quickly dropped into the relatively shallow water near the bank, sinking deep into the silt and mud.

"Anchor's down!" Dr. Evans called out from inside the control room. He eased the throttle back on the boat, allowing the current to gently push the barge and the boat down the river until the rope holding the barge to the tree went taut. Both the boat and the barge bumped up against the shore and Rick ran back to the barge and pointed at a coil of rope.

"Jane, grab that and loop it around that tree. I'm going to take this one and do the same down here."

While Rick and Jane secured the barge to the shore, Dr. Evans shut off the boat's engine and jumped on shore, glad to be off of the boat and back on dry land. He grabbed a rope from the boat and tied it to a nearby tree as well before walking over to the barge and examining it with a flashlight. Rick and Jane walked over and stood next to him once they finished their tasks and Dr. Evans looked at Rick.

"How should we do this?"

Rick looked at the car parked nearby and back at the barge again, crossing his arms as he thought. "The deck's a good foot lower than the bank. Maybe we use those boards at the front of the barge to make a ramp? Drive the car on board with those, head across to a clear spot and drive it off the same way?"

Dr. Evans nodded. "Exactly what I was thinking. Let's do that, unless anyone has a better idea."

Jane shrugged and took a step back. "Sounds good to me. I'm going to stay over here out of the way until you tell me what to do."

"All right, then." Rick nodded. "Let's do it."

While the idea of rolling the car onto the barge and back off again on the other side sounded simple enough, the execution was decidedly not. The risk of losing their only method of fast transportation caused Rick to lapse into his risk-avoidance mode where he triple-checked every possible outcome of everything they were doing to make sure nothing bad would happen.

The loading process itself took a good forty-five minutes. Once the car was aboard it took another twenty to get across to the other side and secure the barge and boat in relatively the same location they had originally found it. The denseness of the trees and slope of the eastern bank of the river made the offloading process substantially riskier than the loading process had been. After a few close encounters—including one where one of the planks slipped and fell into the water—Rick breathed a huge sigh of relief as he felt the back wheels of the car hit the grass and dirt and keep moving forward.

He drove the car slowly through the trees as Jane and Dr. Evans helped guide him from alongside the vehicle. When they arrived at the edge of a road that ran alongside the trees on the bank of the river Rick stopped the car and the trio headed back to the boat to make sure they weren't leaving anything of value behind.

While Dr. Evans and Jane were keen to get moving as quickly as possible again, Rick insisted on staying a few extra minutes to put the boat back the way they found it—minus the broken lock on the cabin door. When they finished, they stood on the shore taking a final look at the boat before heading back to pile in the small vehicle.

"I can't believe that worked." Jane smiled as she spoke. "You two did a good job."

"Nah," Rick shook his head. "We all did. Excellent work all around. And yeah, I'm a little bit surprised that worked as well as it did."

"I rather enjoyed it." Dr. Evans replied. "It was better than riding in that car for the last few hours."

"Very true." Rick sighed. "Unfortunately I think that break's just about come to an end."

Chapter Twelve

Blacksburg, VA

DIANNE'S first stop in her search for Jason's medication was the welcome desk near the door where she entered the building. A large poster hung from a stand behind the desk with a floor plan of the facility. Labels were printed over each section of the building, showing where everything from the main cafeteria to the surgical suites were located. Most of the building was taken up by single-occupancy rooms on every floor but the top that were used for housing and treating patients. Exam, surgical, administrative and other rooms and offices were primarily located around the edge of each floor with three elevators and three sets of stairs—one at each end and one in the middle—acting as the means to traverse through the different floors of the building.

Dianne studied the poster for a few minutes as she looked for any mention of a pharmacy or other section of the building but discovered nothing. *Maybe it's not labeled for security purposes?* She decided to head up two floors to the main nurses station where she hoped she'd find a lead that would point her to where the medication was stored.

As Dianne moved through the facility she was struck by the realization that the place looked remarkably clean in spite of the destruction surrounding it in the city. None of the windows or exterior doors had been broken, there was no sign of looting on the ground floor and she had seen no sign that there were other people in the area. The oddity of the place being both untouched by the fire and left alone by any survivors was a good thing but it was also slightly nerve-wracking.

In an effort to ensure she really was alone Dianne didn't take the stairs near where she came in nor did she take the set in the middle of the building. Instead she walked all the way down the length of the atrium, checking the windows and doors along the way, until she reached the far staircase.

Why would anyone leave this place alone? Maybe they didn't realize this is basically just a hospital. The sign out front indicated that it was a long-term care facility and she assumed that anyone looking to loot medical supplies would put two and two together and realize the place could be a goldmine. *Apparently they didn't.*

She looked up the stairs, took a deep breath and ascended slowly. As it was located at the end of the building the staircase was surrounded on three sides by tall, wide panes of glass. The stairs themselves were wide and deep, though they were only a few inches high and covered with slip-proof carpet to help accommodate the needs of the older patients. The stairs looped back on themselves twice for each floor with a wide landing after each loop. Dianne paused on the first landing and looked out through the window, shielding her eyes from the glare as she marveled at the beauty of the building.

The effect of the sun coming through the glass box on the stairs was almost enough to keep her from noticing the city that stretched out as far as she could see. The longer she looked, though, the more its destruction began to overwhelm her. Fire had consumed huge portions of the city, swallowing Virginia Tech, the Blacksburg Zoo and many of the new apartment complexes that had been built over the last several months.

In areas where the fires hadn't completely destroyed the buildings there were hundreds and thousands of destroyed vehicles along with shops and homes that had been broken into and looted. The city resembled something out of a zombie or disaster movie, though all Dianne could think about was how much worse it could potentially be in other areas of the country—like wherever Rick was.

⬜

"YOU'RE SPILLING IT!"

"How is that my fault? My arm's broken!"

"You couldn't do *anything* with it if it was broken. It's probably just fractured."

"Isn't a fracture a break?"

"Just shut up and give me the jug."

The man with the injured arm passed the jug of water over to his companion, intentionally spilling some of it on the ground in the process. The uninjured man growled but decided not to escalate the situation. He grabbed the jug and took a long drink before wiping his mouth on the back of his sleeve and sighing.

"How are we supposed to find her in this mess?"

"I don't know. Why would I know?"

"I'd rather find a needle in a haystack. At least then I could sit down while searching."

The injured man slid off of the hood of the hatchback where he had been resting and pulled back his coat to look at his arm. He had used a strip of cloth to fashion a makeshift sling but keeping it immobilized had done nothing to dull the pain or reduce the swelling that was still growing around his elbow, wrist and shoulder. He could still move his fingers, but doing so caused a tremendous amount of pain to shoot up through his entire arm and down the side of his chest.

"You should call in. Tell him we haven't found anything."

The uninjured man shook his head. "What good will that do? He'll just get even more pissed off."

The injured man picked up a pair of binoculars off of the hood of the car and looked out across the city. "I don't see how that's possible. He's already... wait. What's that building up there?"

"What building?"

"That one, up there, with all the glass windows."

"Nursing home, I think. My grandmother was there for a few months before she died. I went there once. The cafeteria had good food."

"Look at the end of the building on the right. Second floor. Do you see what I'm seeing?" The injured man held out the binoculars. His companion took them and focused on the location, studying it closely for several seconds. The faint image of a figure wearing a white and green jacket was just barely visible through the heavily tinted glass. She was standing still, looking out on the city for a moment before she turned away and vanished from sight.

"Well I'll be." The uninjured man lowered the binoculars and grinned. "She went to a nursing home? What the hell for?"

"You really want to look a gift horse in the mouth?" The injured man walked around the car and opened the passenger door before reaching in to get the radio sitting on the seat. "Base, unit three here. Put him on. We've got something." He looked at his companion as he lifted his finger off of the transmit button. "You sure it's a nursing home?"

"Pretty sure. They call it something else but yeah. That's what it was."

"Hm." The injured man waited a few seconds until the man with the red shirt came on the radio.

"I hope you have some good news."

"We found her."

"Have you apprehended her?"

"No, but we know where she is and she's currently cornered in a building. We need some backup here, though. It's a big building."

"Where at?"

"In the city. It's a bigass glass complex sitting on a little hill surrounded by trees and stuff. Sticks out like a sore thumb. Have them come in off the first exit and keep heading straight. They won't be able to miss it."

"Get inside and make sure she doesn't escape. They'll be there shortly."

The radio went dead and the injured man tossed it back in the car. He pulled his pistol out of his waistband, wincing as he bumped it against his arm. "You ready?"

The uninjured man lowered the binoculars again and nodded. "Let's do it."

Chapter Thirteen

Twenty Minutes North of Washington, D.C.

"DERR'MO!" Isayev curses in his native tongue as he fights with the Bear's controls, desperately trying to keep them level and on course. Without a functional long-range radar system on board the aircraft, the storm cell had appeared almost without warning. The storm buffets the aircraft, causing the metal to groan and strain as opposing air forces stretch it to its limits. Hail beats against the metal and the windows, the ice still soft enough to be chopped up by the propellers but hard enough to put dents in the roof.

Designed for high-altitude flight, the Tupolev Tu-95 is a long, narrow cylinder with wide wings and four super-sonic propellers. It is designed for smooth sailing high-altitude flight, not for low-altitude work in the middle of a thunderstorm. Isayev and Aliyev work in unison, trying to respond to the changes in wind speed as they pass through the storm without losing too much altitude.

Blov and Yermakov sit behind Isayev and Aliyev, their eyes closed as they cling to their seats and harnesses, trying desperately not to throw up. Their silent prayer is that the turbulence they experienced earlier in the flight will return to replace the storm that feels like it will yank them out of the sky and throw them into the ground at any moment.

"Engine three is out! That makes two!" Sitting in the co-pilot seat, Aliyev shouts at Isayev through his headset. "How close are we to the destination?"

"Not close enough. Besides, we can't bail out in the middle of the storm!" Isayev shouts back.

"If we lose another engine we won't—" Aliyev's reply is cut short by a deafening crack of thunder. The sky directly outside the plane is, for a brief instant, illuminated like the

surface of the sun as a bolt of lighting appears directly off the starboard side of the plane. The two technicians who had been holding themselves together admirably in the face of the storm have now resorted to shouting into their headsets, trying desperately to tell the two Spetsnaz officers that they should land the plane as quickly as possible. Aliyev merely rolls his eyes at the technicians' hysterics and switches off their headset microphones remotely, focusing back on the task of keeping everyone alive.

"As soon as we get clear of the worst of this storm we'll need to jump, okay?" Isayev doesn't look up from his controls as he yells at his co-pilot over the noise.

"You want me to get them ready now?"

Isayev nods. "Yes. We'll have to be fast about this; we're nearly out of fuel anyway."

Aliyev groans as he unbuckles his harness, a particularly brutal piece of wind nearly tossing him out of his seat and onto the floor. He holds tight to straps hanging from the ceiling and sides of the aircraft as he moves back until he's face-to-face with the technicians. Both of them have their eyes screwed shut and he taps them on the chest until they reply.

"Gentlemen!" Aliyev crouches down, keys his microphone and shouts into it. The technicians look at him, their eyes wide with fear.

"Your parachutes are still on, correct?" Both men nod.

"You remember how to use them, yes?" Both men nod.

Aliyev points at a hatch on the side of the plane, behind the right wing. "We'll be jumping as soon as we clear the storm. I will go first, then you two will go, then Isayev will go. Do you understand?" Both men nod.

"Good. Be ready! We jump soon!" Aliyev starts to move back to the front of the plane when the craft violently shudders. He stumbles, loses his grip and slams into the side of the craft before pushing himself back upright. He ignores the pain in his arm and side as he stumbles back to his seat. "What happened?!"

"Engine one is out! Number four is the last one!"

"That's the one leaking fuel, isn't it!"

Isayev nods. "We have to jump soon; I won't be able to maintain altitude much longer!"

"The storm's still terrible!"

"We won't have much of a choice! We can keep her up for a few more minutes at most, then we must go otherwise we'll be too low!"

Isayev and Aliyev work the controls of the aircraft furiously coaxing every bit of power they can from the leaking engine as they fight against the storm. They hold their own for another two minutes, enough to bring them closer to the edge of the clouds, when the final engine coughs and sputters. Aliyev glances out the window at the engine and shouts at Isayev.

"We have to go! Altitude is dropping fast!"

Isayev is about to answer when a blinding light fills the cabin. He throws his hands up in front of his face until his eyes adjust to the sunlight. From outside, the plane looks like some sort of dying monster as it bursts forth from the storm, ribbons of cloud rippling off the tips of the wings. "Go! Go!" Isayev shouts at Aliyev and reaches beneath the controls, pulling a lever to lock them in place. With the worst of the storm behind them the plane *can glide for a fair distance, enough to put it several miles or more away from where the four men will land.*

Once the plane is set Isayev climbs out of his chair and into the back compartment where Aliyev and the two technicians are waiting. Aliyev raises his thumb into the air and the gesture is returned by Isayev. Aliyev turns, pulls the emergency lever on the door and it falls off the plane, spinning violently as it disappears behind them. Aliyev walks up to the door, braces his arms against his chest and steps out without hesitation, disappearing for a few seconds only to show up again once his parachute deploys.

Belov and Yermakov stand at the edge of the door, neither of them wanting to be the first out when Isayev walks up behind them, braces himself with two leather straps and kicks them out through the door one after the other. He shouts at them as they go, reminding them to pull their cords and sure enough he sees two more parachutes open up. With one final look around the cabin Isayev straps himself to a large canvas bag filled with supplies and pushes it out the door as he jumps into the unknown.

The Bear flies for nearly fifteen more miles, its fourth engine occasionally sputtering back to life along the way, but it eventually crashes on the far western side of the capital, far from where its four temporary inhabitants eventually land. The eyes that see the plane crash are few and far between and the mission, as far as the two Spetsnaz officers can determine, is still successful. Whether it will remain so is anyone's guess.

Chapter Fourteen

B lacksburg, VA

WHAT ON EARTH is that smell? Dianne wrinkled her nose as she ascended to the second floor of the building. When she had first walked in she had dismissed the faint foul odor as coming from rotten food in the café, but the deeper she walked into the second floor's hallways the stronger it became. Without the benefit of direct sunlight to penetrate into the inner halls, Dianne was finally forced to switch on her flashlight. She scanned back and forth with it, looking down the hall and at the rooms around her before panning down to the carpet. She held the beam on the carpet for a second before kneeling down to get a closer look at it. *What on earth…*

The carpet was dark grey in color but it looked like there was a pattern on some parts of it that made no sense. When she walked on the pattern the carpet felt different, like it was stiffer than the parts that were plain grey. Dianne swallowed hard, fighting back against the rising bile in her throat as the smell continued to grow stronger with each step she took down the hall. Finally, as she reached a large open area where the main nurses station was located, she realized that the smell wasn't coming from rotten food. "Dear sweet merciful…" Dianne's eyes opened wide and she pressed her arm up against her face, swallowing the saliva that felt like it was pouring into her mouth.

When she was in college all those years ago her roommate had been a fan of horror movies. She was a particular fan of horror movies that relied on gore and on-screen violence to induce fear in movie-goers. While Dianne had never been a fan of such films she had agreed to watch a movie simply titled *The One* with her roommate late one October evening. The first twenty minutes of the movie were tense, but bearable. The remainder of the movie left Dianne with nightmares for days on end and cemented in her mind the fact that she was *not* a fan of the gory horror movie genre.

As Dianne's eyes flicked across the scene laid out in front of her she couldn't help but think back to that night with her roommate and the nightmares that had followed. The same surreal, visceral fear gripped her stomach, twisting it into knots and sending more bile rising up her throat. Her brain felt like it was short-circuiting, simultaneously telling her to run and fight and hide all at the same time. Her limbs felt frozen as she stepped back, nearly falling over as she reached out and grabbed the wall for support.

"What... what happened here?" Dianne whispered to herself, scarcely able to believe her eyes. The bodies of at least four individuals were strewn across the floor in front of the nurses station, the smell from their rotting flesh stinging Dianne's eyes and the back of her throat. Two appeared to be wearing nurse uniforms while one lying on his back near an overturned wheelchair looked like he was a patient. A fourth body wearing a police uniform was across the room near a wall with a pistol on the ground nearby.

The grey flooring was soaked through with blood and other bodily fluids that had leaked from the corpses and soaked into the carpet. Dianne slowly realized that the fluid mixture must have been causing the stains she had seen elsewhere on the carpet in the hallway, though she hadn't seen any bodies lying in the hall.

After dry heaving for a moment and taking a long drink of water to try and wash down the bile Dianne pulled her shirt up over her mouth and nose and stepped gingerly through the carnage. She saw two more bodies behind the nurses station, both with bandannas over their faces and white undershirts that had been stained with blood. One of the figures was on his face while the other was on his back, the handle of a pistol-grip shotgun still in his hand.

The more Dianne saw of the bodies and how they were laid out, the more she began to ignore the smell and gore and focus on deducing what had happened. At first she thought that it was a simple robbery gone wrong, but after stepping behind the nurses station and picking up a logbook she found on the desk, she saw that the situation was far more complicated—and horrifying—than she first imagined. Someone—one of the nurses or doctors from the looks of it—had kept a record of what had happened on the day of the event and for the four days following.

- SOMETHING HAPPENED EARLIER. Giant explosions in the parking lot and in

the streets. Almost everyone's car went up in flames. Dr. Landrum and a couple of the nurses from upstairs left, said they needed to walk home to their families. The Internet's down, phones aren't working and the TV just cut out. What's going on.??

- A couple of people showed up to pick up their relatives. They were armed and didn't want to answer any questions. Another one showed up after that, said The BBQ place down the street's up in flames. A couple of the apartment towers downtown are smoking pretty badly. Saw a plane going down near the airport, hard. We're all talking about leaving but there are too many people here.

- The fires are unbelievable. We seem to be safe for the moment, but it's like hell on earth out there. Emergency generator's half out of fuel, or that's what the pair who went to check on it said. Couple of cops showed up earlier in a beat-up cruiser. One of them was hurt pretty bad from a gunshot to his gut. His partner told us it's anarchy in the streets. All the doors are locked and we've consolidated the patients to this floor so we're okay for now.

- Fires are dying down but there's still a bunch of smoke and ash in the air. Generator went down in the middle of the night and we lost six. The police officer's partner was one of them. There's no power for the refrigeration units so not sure what to do.

- Another five went last night. We're running out of what we need to keep them alive. Two more cops showed up, armed to the teeth. Rough shape. Said looters are running rampant.

- Saw an ambulance out in the street, lights flashing. It stopped and a few people got out and started running up. Cops met them at the door and one of them went down. They killed a few of the people but there are more coming.

- Why oh why no no no more dying, lots of gunshots

- Holed up upstairs but they're down a floor below. They want drugs and we're mostly out. Only a few bags left but they're not happy with that. They're shooting patients trying to make us give them what we don't have. One officer alive. He's going to try something he said is crazy and stupid. I hope we make it out.

THE REST of the pages were illegible, a mixture of scrawled and smeared pen along with droplets of dried blood. Dianne closed the book and looked at the bodies on the floor. "So they were trapped here, trying to take care of the patients when you idiots arrived and started shooting the place up so that you could get high?" She shook her head. "I wonder if there's anyone still alive here?"

She hurried away from the nurses station and stopped at the first room down the hall. She opened it slowly, keeping her gun at the ready, when she was nearly bowled over by more foul odors than she had already experienced. Already overwhelmed by the sight and smells outside the nurses station she barely managed to pull down her shirt off of her face before vomiting onto the floor. Dianne wiped her mouth on the sleeve of her jacket and took a hasty drink of water before looking for the source of the fresh odor.

Inside the room, lying on the two beds that were sitting next to each other, were the bodies of a man and woman that had been dead for more than a few days. They were dressed in plain off-white clothes that had the appearance of being standard issue for patients in the facility. Dianne realized with no small amount of horror that the patients must have died after the event, either from lack of medication or food, from injuries inflicted by the looters or something even worse.

Was anyone alive to take care of you people? Dianne choked down more water, fighting the urge to vomit again as she closed the door. She checked several more rooms along the hall, finding similar scenes in each of them. In some the patients had been in their beds when they died. In others the doors had been jammed from the inside, but she could see through the window on the door that a few patients had crawled out of their beds and died near the door, either trying to keep it closed to keep out the looters or because they had been trying to escape.

The more rooms Dianne checked the more she grew used to the sights and smells and by the time she reached the end of the hall she was convinced she knew what had happened. "They couldn't get out of the city after the fires broke out, so they hunkered down here. Probably their best move at the time but they couldn't have accounted for the looters. A few cops happened to show up and fought with the looters but it looks like most everyone involved died. With no doctors or nurses to take care of the patients they died too." Dianne tried not to think about what life must have been like for the staff and patients at the facility in the final few days and focused instead on the job at hand.

"Jason's still alive and still needs help. I need to see if I can find anything that the looters didn't manage to carry off before all of this went down." Dianne continued talking to herself as she headed back to the nurses station. She searched through the notebooks, folders and paperwork there until she found a laminated sheet that had a list of floor and room numbers along with some names that looked familiar. After rolling up her sleeve and comparing some of what was listed on the sheet to the names of the medications Dianne had written on her arm she headed back towards the stairwell, ready to ascend to the next floor. She didn't know if what someone had written in the logbook about running out of medications applied to what she was looking for but she finally had a good lead on where to potentially find them.

Dianne stopped on the landing of the staircase briefly, taking a moment to savor the relatively fresh air and try to clear her mind of the images she had seen on the second floor. She looked out into the city, finding a measure of peace in the stillness of the devastation when a hint of movement caught her eye. She looked down the hill, near where she had last seen the hatchback, and saw—passing behind a cluster of buildings—the glint of red, silver and green. She froze in place as she watched the area until she finally located the source of the movement.

Three vehicles stopped along the street behind the hatchback and a dozen people got out of the SUV and two sedans. Most of them milled around while two went up to the hatchback. Dianne scrambled to get her rifle up to her shoulder and she focused her scope on the hatchback. Two men—the same two that had been chasing her—stood near the hatchback talking to a woman and a man who had arrived in the new vehicles. Their conversation was animated and one of the men from the hatchback pointed at the LTAC facility. The other three turned and looked at it, nodding in some sort of agreement. The pairs broke up after that and the entire group of people began moving through the city, fanning out as they approached the building.

"Oh, come on!" Dianne shook her head in frustration, shouting at no one in particular. "You've *got* to be kidding me!"

Chapter Fifteen

Somewhere in Northern Virginia

RICK PEEKED out from beneath the overpass, grimacing at the dark clouds still roiling overhead. "When on earth is this going to let up?" He sighed, walked back over to the car and sat down on the hood next to Jane. Dr. Evans was sprawled out on a small rise in the concrete, a rolled-up jacket tucked under his head as he tried to catch a few minutes of sleep. Thunder boomed, rain crashed and hail thudded against the overpass above, but the trio and their vehicle were safe and dry under its protection.

After crossing over the Ohio River they had driven through the night and the rest of the next day, stopping only for a few hours in the evening to rest and warm up some food over a fire. The rest of the night was spent driving again as they took turns making their way across wide highways and single-lane backwoods roads. The storm had rolled in from the west in the late morning, as they were crossing over the state line between West Virginia and Virginia.

Rick took charge of the driving at that point, keeping them going at a steady clip through the rain and lighting until the hail started to get dense and forceful enough to force them to pull over and find shelter. The car's rooftop solar panels were designed to stand up to the harshest weather conditions but Rick knew full well that they wouldn't be able to last long in a hailstorm no matter how well they were designed.

Finding the overpass had been a stroke of luck given that none of the group wanted to travel any farther into a city than necessary. With nothing around except for open fields and winding highways, the spot provided safety and security while simultaneously ensuring that they couldn't easily be snuck up on.

The storm continued raging on for a full hour before it began to die down. As soon as the hail gave way to rain Rick was back behind the wheel, ready to get them going again. Jane and Dr. Evans were less enthusiastic about resuming their trip given that they had spent more hours than they wanted to think about crammed together in what felt like a shoebox on wheels.

"Have I mentioned," Jane said as she squirmed in the back seat. "That I *hate* this car? Because I do. I really do."

"I think you've brought it up once or twice, yeah." Rick laughed as he pulled out from beneath the overpass and accelerated along the highway. "Look on the bright side, though. We're almost to Washington. Once we get there we'll be out of the car. Of course we'll be digging through what very well may be the rubble of the USA's foremost spy agency trying to find a way into their systems to get the access key that will let us issue a shutdown command to the most sophisticated cyberweapon ever developed."

"I'd rather stay in the car, if that's an option." Dr. Evans deadpanned his response and Jane couldn't help but shake her head and chuckle.

"Boy, you two really know how to show a girl a good time. Do we get to have more gunfights, too?"

Rick shook his head, his response more serious than not. "I sure hope not. We've barely got any firepower."

"Rick?" Dr. Evans was leaning forward, staring intently at the sky through the windshield. "I may be hallucinating. Can you look up at the sky and tell me what you see?"

Rick lifted his foot off the accelerator and leaned forward as well. He scanned the sky for a moment, not immediately seeing what Dr. Evans was talking about. When he did, though, he gasped in shock. "Is that…"

"A plane? Yes. Yes it is. A Russian plane. A Tupolev Tu-95, if I'm not terribly mistaken."

"Dr. Evans?" Rick brought the car to a halt and they all stared at the silver plane soaring through the sky. "Why is there a Russian plane flying over Washington?"

"It's more than a Russian plane. It's actually a bomber. A long-range bomber."

"Sweet mother of mercy." Rick whispered, swallowing hard to push down the lump in his throat. "How do you know?"

"I used to be obsessed with model aircraft. The Bear—that's the ninety-five's NATO reporting name—is an older bomber, originally flown in the fifties."

"Is it… going down?" Jane watched the aircraft tilt slightly to the side as it continue heading from east to west, somehow growing larger the farther it traveled.

"Holy crap, yes it is." The tires of the car squealed in protest as Rick pulled the vehicle around to head west and follow the plane's path.

"You want to chase it?!" Jane shouted from the back seat. "It's crashing!"

"Maybe!" Rick replied, dividing his attention between the road and the plane. "Or maybe they're trying to land it nearby! It's people, though, possibly from a government agency."

"Russians, though! Not exactly our friends!" Jane shouted.

"I think you'll find that anyone not actively shooting at us could be considered our friend." Dr. Evans glanced back at Jane. "Besides, whoever has the resources to send a plane to the other side of the globe may also have resources that can aid us in stopping this global threat. Maybe they're even here to try and do what we're doing."

Rick shook his head and slowed the car back down. "Not like that they're not; watch!" He pointed out the window as the plane took a steep dive downward, plummeting toward the ground like a wounded bird. For a split second, as it vanished behind some buildings in the distance, Rick wondered if the pilots on board had managed to pull up. The massive ball of black smoke and fire shot down Rick's faint hope.

"So much for that, then." Dr. Evans slumped back in his seat.

"You're sure it was a Russian plane?" Rick watched as the smoke rose into the sky and the orange flames began to fade away.

"One-hundred percent. Perhaps someone parachuted out of the plane earlier in the flight?"

Rick shrugged and slowly turned the car around once again. "Maybe. They would have been coming out of that storm not too long ago. I wonder if that tore them up and downed them. Can you imagine trying to parachute out in something like that?"

"Guys, I hate to butt in, but can we talk about how weird it is that a Russian plane potentially dropped Russian soldiers into Washington?" Jane leaned forward from the back seat. "Is no one thinking about what that could mean?"

It was Dr. Evans' turn to shrug. "We don't know that the plane was carrying soldiers or that anyone made it out before it crashed. You are right about one thing, though. It's incredibly odd to see a Bear flying over Washington. The reasons for them being here are myriad and, frankly, none of them make that much sense."

"So what should we do?"

Rick answered this time, his expression hardened into a mask of determination as he drove them towards the city. "We do what we set out to do. If someone else is here to do the same thing then we work with them. If they're not... well, we'll burn that bridge when we come to it."

Author's Notes

November 8, 2017

Hi there! If you're reading this then you've made it to the end of episode 8 of Surviving the Fall and I can't thank you enough for coming along on this awesome journey. As you can probably tell we're entering the final stages of the story and it's probably only going to be a few more books before everything is done. There's still a lot of ground to cover, though, and things are going to be intense both for Dianne and Rick.

When planned out Dianne's final story arc, I wanted something that would showcase her willingness to do anything for her loved ones as well as how fed up she is with putting up with the nonsense she and her family are going through. When she shot the intruder who was repeatedly trespassing on her farm and trying to break into her house and barns she was merely defending her family and property. Tina's capture and Jason's wounding have made it all too clear that their enemy is willing to do anything. Now she has to do the same.

When I write about the motivations and actions of both heroes and foes in my stories I try to keep it relatively grounded. Writing about a fictional overlord who rises to power in a wasteland and amasses an army or a hero who manages to put together his own large fighting force is a trope that's been done more times than not. I like to keep things more personal and down to earth, at least on some levels. That's why Dianne and her kids were completely alone at their house for the first chunk of the story and why there are only three other people there with them now.

That smaller, more intimate and personal feeling of survival is something

I find supremely interesting. Imagining and even acting out what you might do in a situation like is occurring in Surviving the Fall is something I find to be both a good thought exercise and something that's fun, too. If Dianne and her kids were part of a large collective of random people who banded together then the stakes, in my opinion, would be lower. Right now they're living on the edge, surviving because of their own personal preparedness and forethought. If they were part of a larger collective then I think it wouldn't be quite as interesting.

I debated for a while about whether I wanted Rick to have traveling companions on his journey home or not. If you'll recall, in the first part of the story Rick met a couple of people in Los Angeles who traveled with him briefly but the pair was ultimately gunned down in front of Rick. The point I wanted to hammer home there was that the world in this story is brutal. It's unexpected. Bad things *do* happen, even to people who do nothing wrong. Forcing Rick to travel alone didn't quite feel right, though. For one thing it would be difficult for him to figure out everything about Damocles on his own. Enter Jane and Dr. Evans. Two characters who became unlikely friends and one of which has a personal connection to Rick thanks to the events of Las Vegas.

These three have the resolve necessary to carry out their plan. Whether it works or not—and what the four Russians who parachuted in over D.C. will do if they run into Rick, Jane and Dr. Evans—is a subject best left for the next book. :)

If you enjoyed this episode of Surviving the Fall or if you *didn't* like something—I'd love to hear about it. You can drop me an email or send me a message or leave a comment on Facebook. You can also sign up for my newsletter where I announce new book releases and other cool stuff a few times a month.

Answering emails and messages from my readers is the highlight of my day and every single time I get an email from someone saying how much they enjoyed reading a story it makes that day so much brighter and better.

Thank you so very much for reading my books. Seriously, thank you from the bottom of my heart. I put an enormous amount of effort into the writing and all of the related processes and there's nothing better than knowing that so many people are enjoying my stories.

All the best,
Mike

Book 9 – The Tipping Point

Preface

Last time, on Surviving the Fall....

After escaping Kansas City, Rick, Jane and Dr. Evans continue their journey to the east, with their destination of Washington, D.C. growing ever closer. Their struggles grow larger as the effects from Damocles become more pronounced. Massive earthquakes and raging forest fires have ravaged the land, and they are forced to deal not with human opposition but opposition from nature itself. After managing to get through the worst of it, they see a Russian bomber crash on the western edge of the city, with no apparent survivors to be seen. They continue forward, trying to find a way to get to the information they need to shut down Damocles, all while wondering in the back of their minds what final trials are waiting for them.

Meanwhile, with Jason at death's door, Dianne travels to the nearby city of Blacksburg, VA in search of medication he needs in order to pull through. Her first stop yields little fruit, but she has a run-in with a pair of individuals affiliated with the gang that she and Jason fought against to rescue Tina. After escaping from them she makes her way to a long-term acute care facility deeper in the city where Tina was positive she would be able to find medication. Though there was no one left alive in the facility, a scene of utter carnage and horror awaits her. As she struggles to locate the necessary medication, she realizes that she has been tailed and is now surrounded as multiple members of the gang descend upon the facility, rendering her trapped and leaving her with nowhere to go.

And now, Surviving the Fall Episode 9.

Chapter One

Washington, D.C.

"WE'VE BEEN GOING AROUND in circles for an hour, guys." Jane groaned from the back seat, arching her back and shifting her weight around to try and find a more comfortable position in which to sit. "Can't we just take a break?"

Rick was about to reply with an explanation that stopping would result in yet another unacceptable delay when Dr. Evans cut in. "That's not a bad idea, my dear. Rick, would you mind?" Rick glanced over at Dr. Evans, ready to argue with him about it, but the look on his face made Rick reconsider.

"Uh... yeah, sure." He glanced around the vehicle and pointed to a nearby building that was around seven stories tall. "I'll stop over there. If the structure's not too damaged on the interior maybe we can get to the roof and spot a path through the destruction while we're at it."

"Sounds great," Jane replied, "Whatever it takes to get us to pull over. These bumps and turns are killing my back."

Three hours of circling the south and western edges of Washington, D.C. later and the trio was still no closer to finding a way into the deeper portions of the city without abandoning their vehicle. The high number of vehicles and the tightly packed buildings meant that, like other urban centers, the city went up like a book of matches once the Damocles virus destroyed most of the vehicles in the area. Fires tore through structures old and new alike faster than first responders could mobilize and over ninety percent of the nearly 1.1 million people living and working in the city died within hours of when the fires began.

Of course, anyone with moderate to high level connections in the city was nowhere nearby when things hit the fan. High ranking government and military officials, their families, their friends and friends of their friends all slipped away in the days and hours before the zeroth hour. The workers—both in private and government sectors—whose ceaseless labor enabled those at the top to do their jobs weren't so lucky.

Back of the napkin math done by a small group of senators, an active Army general and a Navy admiral showed that there simply was no way to evacuate any decent sized number of people from the city without inciting panic across the globe and potentially causing more deaths than they antici-pated might occur. While their assumption about panic was correct, their assumption that only ten percent of the city would perish was a gross under-statement. After the first wave of explosions destroyed most of the vehicles in the city, most survivors tried to flee on foot. The swiftly spreading fires ensured that those staying in their homes and those on the streets were killed.

There was no possible way in which large numbers of people could have survived—though that was the entire point of Damocles. A weapon of war that could turn a country's own resources against it was an invaluable tool. In the right hands it could quickly bring about an end to conflicts, topple dictators and help to ensure peace and stability. There are very few 'right hands,' though, and most hands that start out right either turn wrong or die out and are replaced by the wrong hands anyway.

"Looks like that highway there acted as a firebreak." Rick held his right hand over his eyes while pointing with his left. "It's clogged with vehicles but we might be able to go around on this western edge and weave between the buildings." With most of the city in ashes and a potentially long journey ahead of them, neither Rick, Jane nor Dr. Evans were keen on leaving their only mode of transportation behind.

"Maybe," Dr. Evans replied. "Or we could try going all the way around to the north."

"And what about the bridges?" Rick shook his head. "The railroad bridge was completely broken up and the regular one next to it was covered in burned-out vehicles."

"Guys, I hate to be a downer, but is it possible that we might *have* to leave the car behind and go on foot from here?" Jane inserted herself into the conversation as she emerged onto the roof from the floor below.

Rick sighed and looked back over the city, most of which was charred and giving off thin wisps of smoke. "That does not look like a fun place to walk. Besides, we don't know where the facility is. We could spend days walking around from potential location to potential location."

"That sounds like hell," she replied. "But if that's our only option then the fact that we hate it doesn't really matter, does it?"

Dr. Evans looked at Rick, wearing a slight smile and an amused expression. "She does make a good point, you know."

"Ugh." Rick sat down on a large metal duct running along the roof and closed his eyes. "I started this whole nightmare walking through a city on fire. I hate walking. I really, really hate it."

"Cheer up, Rick." Jane smiled as she sat down next to him and gave him a hug. "Besides, I don't think the city's technically on fire. So it's got that going for it."

Rick snorted, laughed and shook his head. "All right, fine. Let's take one more hour and search along this western edge, where the fire didn't jump the highway. If we can't find a way into the city after that then we'll move in on foot. Okay?"

Dr. Evans and Jane both nodded as Rick stood to his feet and the trio headed back down through the building and out to their car for what they hoped wouldn't be the last time.

⬜

"I MISS THE CAR." Since leaving the vehicle tucked away in the garage of a small lube shop fifteen minutes prior, none of the three had spoken a word until Dr. Evans finally broke the silence.

"I don't," Jane replied immediately. "Sitting in the front seat was torture. Sitting in the back was somehow worse."

"General Black," Rick intoned in a deep, mocking voice, "Thank you for the use of your automobile. Might I suggest something a little roomier next time, with a better suspension and some off-road capabilities, though?"

Dr. Evans chuckled while Jane rolled her eyes. "That thing is such a piece of garbage. I'll be glad to never see it again."

"I look forward to using it to get back to my family once this is all said and done," Rick replied.

"Where's your family at again, Rick?" Dr. Evans asked.

"Down near Blacksburg."

"My goodness," he replied. "They're very close, then."

"Don't remind me unless you want me leaving you two and never coming back." Rick's reply carried a hint of humor around the edges, but it was obvious that he was actually quite serious.

Chapter Two

B lacksburg, VA

DIANNE'S EYES flicked back and forth as she watched the group of a dozen men approaching the building. Two she recognized—both from earlier in the city when they had hounded her at the clinic and from when they had tried to steal her car when the event started—but most of the rest she did not. A couple of the faces looked familiar, and after a few seconds of racking her brain she realized that she remembered them from when she and Jason had infiltrated the gas station to rescue Tina.

"I don't see red shirt anywhere," she mumbled to herself, referring to the leader of the group at the gas station, though she hadn't seen his face and realized that he could easily be in the group.

As the men closed in on the LTAC building, Dianne turned around and ran up the stairs, her remembrance of why she was there in the first place finally kicking in. While she would have to deal with the gang at some point, finding the medication for Jason was crucial and without it her journey to the LTAC would be wasted. She took the stairs two at a time and threw open the door to the next floor, disregarding all pretense of stealth. She was in a race against time before the group got into the building, and every second delayed was a second wasted.

Dianne ran down the hall, looking for the room number that had been written in the notebook at the nurse's station, her flashlight bouncing back and forth as she scanned the walls. She finally arrived at a small alcove in the hall and stopped, double-checking the number next to the space and nodding before tugging on the door set just inside. There was resistance to the pull, and Dianne tried again before realizing that it was locked—likely for good reason given the medications that lay just inside.

She instinctively glanced down the hall in both directions, listening carefully for any signs of the men who were approaching. After confirming that she was alone for the moment, Dianne took off her backpack and rummaged around inside before pulling out a small five-pound sledgehammer that she had thrown inside before leaving the house. The wire mesh safety glass was tough and designed to stand up to a fair amount of abuse, but several swings with the hammer obliterated it, leaving a narrow gap for Dianne to reach in and unlock the door so that she could open it up.

The room tucked away in between patient rooms and small offices had neither windows nor decorations. Several shelves lined the walls and they were divided up into sections. Each shelf contained a myriad of bins, all of which had labels on them with a few words and several numbers and letters that designated what they were, along with a barcode. A barcode scanner hung just inside the door, used by the staff to keep track of every single item that was removed from the storeroom.

The bins on the shelves were filled with all manner of supplies, and Dianne quickly began rifling through them while occasionally glancing at the scribbled words on her arm. She had written the list of must-haves on her arm both in case she lost the full list that was still tucked in her pocket and so that she could quickly refer to it without having to fumble for a paper. The decision had been spontaneous but turned out to be an enormous timesaver in a situation where every second was potentially a difference between life and death.

"Yes!" Dianne whispered to herself, pumping her arm as she finally found the bin she was looking for. Several small vials were inside, each of them with the name of one of the antibiotics Tina had requested to help cure Jason. Given that the top choice on Tina's list was nowhere to be found in the room and the ones she did find were second, Dianne decided that they would have to be good enough. She grabbed her backpack from the floor where she had placed it after entering the room and took several rolls of gauze from a bin on a nearby shelf. After quickly rolling all of the vials up in thick layers of gauze she placed them in her pack before returning to the shelves to find the other items she needed.

"Needles, tubing and saline… check, check and check." The other items were easy to find, and she stuffed them into her pack along with as many other useful-looking supplies as she could find. Large adhesive bandages went in next, then several different types of needles, bottles of over-the-counter pain medication in blister packs, a thick roll of medical tape and several sealed scalpels and pairs of tweezers. Diane's backpack was almost bursting at the seams as the tried to fit the tape, scalpels and tweezers inside and she shoved them into the pockets of her jacket, not wanting to abandon anything she had picked up. The entire room was a gold mine and she wished that she had time to ransack the entire place and fill her truck to the brim, but a faraway noise reminded her of the perils of her situation.

"What the hell happened here?!" The shout was loud, but distant, echoing through the halls of the facility and alerting to the fact that the men were inside and likely on the floor just below her.

"Did that bitch do this?" Another voice asked, equally as loud as the first.

"They've been dead for days, you idiot. Calm down and keep searching!"

Dianne slipped her backpack on as she stood near the door to the room, then made sure her rifle was secure across her back before drawing her pistol with her right hand and gripping the small sledgehammer with her left. "All right, Dianne," she whispered, trying to psych herself up for what was coming next. "You just have to get down a few floors past a dozen people who want to hurt or kill you. No biggie."

With a deep breath, Dianne moved out of the room and slunk down the hall, her flashlight off and in her pocket to avoid the chance of the men seeing the light. She walked lightly, going ball to heel with each step, hoping that there weren't any loose floorboards or large objects in her way that might give away her position. She reached the end of the hall without incident and stood next to the stairwell, breathing as quietly as possible as she listened to the noise below.

Footsteps, the sounds of hushed conversations and the occasional banging of a door or some unknown piece of equipment were constant, and were drawing closer to the stairwell with each passing second. Knowing that the men were likely searching room by room for her, Dianne looked around and did the only thing she could think to do: hide.

The single patient room next to the stairwell was small and sparse, with a neatly made up bed in the corner, a television on the opposite wall and an uncomfortable-looking recliner near the window. Dianne eased the door open quickly, relieved that the hinges didn't let off so much as a creak, then swiftly closed it and turned to look for a place to conceal herself. The only place inside the room that she could hide in was the bathroom, which—like the room itself—had a door without a lock on it. The shower was built into a deep recess in the wall, though, and the curtain was thick, tall and permanently affixed on rollers to a bar mounted into the wall itself.

Dianne eased into the shower and closed the curtain on the side closest to her, wrinkling it up a bit to try and make things look natural. She leaned to the side and took several deep breaths, the backpack, weapons and supplies stuffed in her jacket all contributing to a slowly growing feeling of claustrophobia.

"Breathe, Dianne. Breathe." She whispered to herself again as she clenched her eyes shut and took slow, steady breaths, willing the feeling away before it could overwhelm her.

There, in that small bathroom inside a small patient's room on the third or fourth floor—she could no longer remember how far up she was—she leaned against the cold tile wall and waited for what she fully expected to be death to come for her. Her death, in that moment, was inconsequential. Her thoughts instead turned to Jason, and how he was in pain and suffering from a fever and infection that would soon consume him. She thought of her children and wondered if Tina and Sarah would be able to take care of Mark, Jacob and Josie or whether they would succumb to the cold, thieves or some other threat.

With no word from Rick and no way to get in touch with him, giving up seemed easier than ever. She was one woman against a dozen armed men, all of whom were undoubtedly angered beyond belief and would kill her— or worse. Dianne flicked on her light and looked down at the pistol in her hand and at the strap of the rifle hanging over her shoulder. Going down fighting was the honorable way out, and she figured she could take at least three or four of them with her, and perhaps wound a few others along the way.

The scrape of footsteps on the stairs outside the room was faint, but caused Dianne's thoughts to seize up and her body to tense. She held her breath, listening as a pair of feet plodded up the last few steps and stopped just outside her room.

"We've got to stop for a few minutes. This walking and climbing nonsense is killing my back."

"Yeah, just be glad we're not back at the gas station. That fire killed a few of the workers. He is *pissed*. His best bitch was one of them. Died in the first explosion."

"That one with the long blonde hair?"

"Yup."

"That was his favorite?" The voice chortled. "Did he not know she was getting used by everyone and their brother, too?"

The other voice laughed. "Nope. Best hope he doesn't find out, either, otherwise he'll start killing all the rest of 'em and leave us with nothing at all."

"He won't kill the kids. They're good for labor if nothing else."

"Until they get to a certain age, am I right?"

As Dianne listened to the two men carry on with their conversation, she felt herself growing angrier by the second. With all of the drama surrounding Tina's capture and subsequent liberation and Jason's injury, Dianne hadn't given much thought to the other people not part of the gang who had been at the gas station. While she wasn't all that surprised to hear what the men were saying, she was nonetheless infuriated by it.

She glanced down at her pistol again before slipping it into its holster, then carefully put the small sledgehammer in between her thighs to keep from bumping it onto the floor of the shower. She rummaged through her pockets, pulling out the medical tape and a few of the sealed scalpels. She unwrapped them slowly, wincing at every crinkle in their packaging as she wondered when the men would hear, but they were too absorbed in their conversation to pay her any mind.

Once she had three of the scalpels unwrapped, she pressed them together and carefully wound a long piece of medical tape around them, both strengthening them as a weapon and giving herself extra grip when holding on to their handles. The three blades were lethally sharp and shimmered in the glow of her flashlight, and though they weren't meant to be used as offensive tools, she had no doubt that they'd stand up to at least a few slashes and stabs.

Dianne's hands shook as she worked, both from adrenaline and rage, and when she finished working on the scalpels she picked up her flashlight from the small shelf in the shower where she had placed it, slipped it into her pocket and took the sledgehammer back into her left hand. Using the gun would virtually guarantee that she would be able to kill both men, but mere escape was no longer her objective. Her mind was clouded with a red mist, obscuring common sense and reason and her sense of self-preservation. She would kill as many of the men in the facility as she possibly could, and with each death there would be one less terror afflicting the innocent.

Chapter Three

W ashington, D.C.

RICK HAD EXPECTED the city to be quiet, but it was quite the opposite. A soft whistling wind carried through the devastated streets of Washington, sending swirls of ash and bits of trash tumbling and floating along. The wind played a backdrop to a chorus of groans, creaks and snaps as the buildings in the city settled into their new existence. Foundations warped by the intense heat popped and snapped as they cooled while bits of roofs and walls that hadn't completely collapsed slowly moved around in the wind, parts of them occasionally crashing down.

The steady crunch of Jane's, Dr. Evans' and Rick's footsteps echoed through the rubble as they stepped over the remains of cars and buildings, picking their way slowly toward the center of the city. The sun was sinking slowly in the sky behind them, making each step more difficult than the last and forcing them to slow down so that they wouldn't trip and fall.

The Capital Beltway (Interstate 495) and other roads that intersected with it helped to form fire breaks that kept large swaths of buildings and neighborhoods intact from the fires that raged nearby. The timing of the initial explosions meant that most vehicles were away from residences at the time, which further helped to keep those sections from being completely destroyed in the initial fires.

After crossing the beltway near Falls Church, the trio made their way east, with their goal being to make it to Arlington by the following night. From there they would strike out across the Potomac River, either by bridge or by boat, and they would then be inside Washington proper. Dr. Evans first wanted to visit Foggy Bottom, one of the oldest neighborhoods in Washington and the home of the United States State Department, a choice that struck Rick as more than a little odd.

"Dr. Evans, I'm not an expert on politics or the federal government or anything of that nature, but why would the NSA have a facility there?"

Dr. Evans grunted as he jumped over a telephone pole lying in the street. "My suggestions are based entirely off of what I overheard and read during the initial attacks. There was a lot of talk going on about a 'control center' in Washington, and Foggy Bottom popped up as one of three potential locations, though again, it's all based on what I overheard and caught glimpses of in paperwork I shouldn't have been looking at."

Jane chuckled and clicked her tongue against her teeth. "Tsk tsk, Doc. Reading things you shouldn't have?"

"Yes, well, at the time I was scared that I might go to jail. Little did I realize there was a fate in store for me that's far, far worse."

"You said three locations, right?" Rick tried to steer the conversation back on track. "What were the other two?"

"The NSA cooperated on the project with the CIA after they bought it out."

"The CIA headquarters is north of us quite a way, though, isn't it?" Rick asked. "Shouldn't we have gone there by car first?"

"Nope," Dr. Evans shook his head. "Damocles wasn't the first project that the CIA and NSA collaborated on. They had a dedicated facility in the heart of D.C. that housed that work since they wanted it to be crystal clear that they were projects owned by both agencies."

"Why would the NSA work with the CIA, though?" Jane asked. "Wasn't the NSA in charge of all of the virtual, computer espionage stuff?"

Well," Dr. Evans said, "The NSA's primary functions are in code-breaking and code-making. They operate primarily in the digital realm, yes, with very few field agents. Developing a weapon of war that can strike at physical assets through a digital medium is a challenge, though. You have to have intelligence on those systems, understanding not only how they work but how they support a country. That's where the CIA comes in. They're the big kahuna of the agencies in some sense, but their primary role for a project like Damocles would be their extensive network of intelligence agents and assets. Where the NSA exists primarily in the digital space, the CIA exists primarily in the physical space."

"So the CIA would collect intel that the NSA would then use to build out Damocles?" Rick nodded. "Sounds about right. I still want to know who let Damocles out into the wild."

"Nobody was sure, from what I heard," Dr. Evans replied. "It could have been a foreign government, but it also could have been a hacker who was poking around and released it by accident as they were trying to access secure systems. We may never know."

"I don't buy that it was a government. They'd be crazy to unleash something like this on purpose since it would affect them as much as anyone else."

"Not if it was a country that was lagging behind on the technological scale. We and other heavily industrialized countries have put so much of our 'stuff' on the web and connected everything together which made things easy for Damocles. A country that isn't as interconnected or reliant on computer-controlled systems wouldn't experience the same effects. But they also wouldn't have the resources to do this, so… yeah. It's a mystery."

Jane shook her head. "Regardless of who started it, as long as we can stop it then that'll be good. I can't imagine what it'll take to rebuild, though."

"An enormous amou—hang on. What was that?" Rick stopped short in the street and cocked his head to the side, angling it to try and pick up on something. "Did you guys hear that?"

"Hear what?" Dr. Evans and Jane stopped, and he turned to look at Rick as he replied.

"It sounded like an engine starting up, but I don't… wait. There it is again!" Rick's voice dropped to a whisper and he looked intently at Jane and Dr. Evans, both of whom had their heads back, rotating them around as they tried to pick up on what he was hearing. Jane was the first to nod, confirming that whatever Rick thought he heard wasn't just in his imagination.

"Yep, that's an engine. No question." She glanced at Dr. Evans, then back at Rick with a worried expression. "That can't be good, can it?"

"Very few things seem to be good these days," Rick replied. He unslung the rifle he had been carrying from his shoulder and slipped off his backpack. "Check your weapons, you two. Make sure they're loaded and you have your spare mags close at hand." The rifle had been one of the handful of weapons they had taken from the group attacking them in the Kansas City store, along with a few pistols and boxes of ammunition for both the rifle and pistols. An AR-type rifle chambered in .556, it was equipped with an off-brand scope that Rick was certain was nowhere close to being properly zeroed but they had neither the time nor the spare ammunition to do it.

While Rick collected the magazines for the rifle and the 9mm pistol in his waistband, Jane made sure that the magazines for her .380 were easily accessible while Dr. Evans did the same for his 9mm pistol. None of them were happy with their armament but it was better than nothing and would have to do in a pinch.

"It's getting louder," Jane whispered as Rick stood up and put his backpack on. He gripped the rifle tightly and gulped as he tried to calm his racing heart. He had known that they would be more likely than not to run into yet another conflict before arriving at their destination, but that knowledge did nothing to make him feel less nervous.

"Yep. Follow me and let's keep going. We'll stick as close to the buildings as possible and try to get around these guys, whoever they are. Hopefully we can slip past them and avoid any problems."

Chapter Four

E arth Orbit
         Seven Hours After the Event

"GIVE IT ANOTHER HALF SECOND."

"Direction?"

"Same as before."

"Got it. Waiting for your mark."

"Three… two… one… mark."

The small capsule shudders as its engine kicks on for exactly one half of one second, increasing its speed and making the three occupants tense up involuntarily. When the burn completes, there is another jolt and the cabin of the capsule is once again enveloped by silence. The three crewmembers hold their breath as Commander Palmer studies their position, waiting to see if the burn was executed properly or not.

"We're in the pipe." His words are accompanied by exhalations of relief from Ted and Jackie as they look at each other, hopeful for the first time since leaving ISS-2. "We're synchronized with the ISS's orbit. Thirty minutes till visual acquisition, then another hour or so till we can make contact." Commander Palmer extends his arms, bumping them against the wall of the capsule as he tries in vain to stretch.

Built as a lifeboat to escape the ISS-2 in case of catastrophic emergencies, the small capsule was never designed to cross the vast distances separating the second and first space stations. When faced with certain death in a space station whose orbit is rapidly decaying, though, designs are thrown out the window and every effort is made to survive, no matter what. Thus, as the ISS-2 continued its dive towards the earth, the small capsule ejected, heading for the *International Space Station* – a place that has been empty and dormant for a full six months, ever since the ISS-2 was brought online.

"Either of you ever been to the ISS?" Commander Palmer leans forward and looks to his left at Ted and Jackie. All three crewmembers are dressed in full EVA suits and are wearing extra oxygen tanks. The capsule barely has enough room to fit them, to say nothing of the hoards of food and other supplies they stuffed into every nook and cranny.

"Never."

"Nope. You did, though, right?"

Commander Palmer nods. "I was part of the decommissioning crew. We shut everything down and prepped her for long-term storage. She was supposed to be kept in orbit till her station-keeping thrusters ran out of fuel, then she'd burn up."

"How long was that supposed to take?"

"A year or so, give or take."

A long pause passes over the conversation before Jackie replies. "So we'll have plenty of time there to figure out our next move. Assuming we make it."

Commander Palmer smiles at her from behind his thick visor. "We'll make it."

<hr>

ONE AND A HALF HOURS LATER, the capsule shudders again. This time, though, it's not from the thrusters, but from an impact with its destination.

"Clamps?!" Commander Palmer shouts.

"Secure! Green lights across the board. We did it!" Ted, Jackie and Commander Palmer let off cheers of joy and elation as they celebrate their safe arrival at the International Space Station. Their arrival is both welcome and slightly unexpected, but they are all thrilled beyond belief that they made it. The real challenge, however, is about to begin.

"All right, listen up you two. We're secured to the station but we still have to get inside. The downside with all of this is that we can't afford to expend the fuel to dock the capsule properly so we're just going to leave it hanging and EVA everything in."

"Should be fun," Jackie replied with a nervous laugh. "I've only done three EVAs before this."

"No time like now to do your fourth, eh?" Commander Palmer unbuckled himself from his seat and slowly floated toward the top of the capsule. "Make sure everything's secured. I'm going to pop the hatch in thirty."

The sharp hiss of escaping air went away a second after Palmer unsealed the hatch at the top of the capsule, opening up the interior to the vacuum of space. Ted and Jackie stayed in their seats while Commander Palmer floated through the hatch, checking his oxygen levels in his suit for what felt like the hundredth time since putting it on. "I've got two hours of air left. We need to hustle to get inside and get the scrubbers turned on."

"You want us to wait here and monitor your progress or follow behind with supplies?" Ted asked.

Commander Palmer hesitated with his answer at first, weighing the risks they were

taking with the greater ones associated with running out of air. "Under any other circum-
stances we wouldn't be grappling the outer structure of a decommissioned space station
with a lifeboat while we try to EVA to the other side, force open an airlock and get inside
all before running out of O2. So, yeah, you two gather the supplies and let's do this as fast
as possible."

Chapter Five

B lacksburg, VA

DIANNE SWUNG OPEN the bathroom door and looked out into the small room, checking to make sure that the two men hadn't walked in without her hearing. They were still just outside the room, though, and based on their voices it sounded as if they were sitting on the floor with their backs to the wall. She tried to ignore their vulgar language as they continued going on about the various things they had done with and to the "workers" at the gas station, but everything she heard served to raise her blood pressure even more.

Bracing herself at the door, she listened to the position of their voices outside, trying to picture where they were in the hall. *One to the right, and one leaning directly against it, I think.* Killing didn't come naturally to the home-schooling mother of three, but desperate times called for desperate measures, and evil had to be snuffed out.

Dianne threw her weight down on the door handle and pulled inward, stepping to the side as the door flew open and bounced against a rubber stopper on the wall. A man wearing a filthy coat that was once the color blue fell backwards, his eyes wide and his arms flailing as he tried to grab for the doorframe to hold himself up. The rifle that had been in his right hand slipped and fell forward into the hall, landing with a light clatter as the back of his head smacked against the hard floor behind him.

The man just barely had time to open his eyes as Dianne stepped over him, bringing down the small sledgehammer in her right hand directly into the center of his face. The sound was horrific. Flesh, cartilage and bone all snapped and squished and squelched as the sledgehammer drove the man's nose into his brain. His body jerked and twisted as his muscles spasmed, but no noise emanated from his throat as he lay on the floor, the plastic handle of the sledgehammer sticking out from where his mouth and nose used to be.

Though Dianne was sickened by the sounds of the man's death, she didn't hesitate to make her next move. Opening the door and slamming the sledge into the first man's face had taken him and his partner by surprise, but in another few seconds she knew the second man would be fully aware of what was going on and would try to fight back. She wasn't about to give him that chance.

She took a step out into the hall over the first man's twitching body, glancing to the right and locking eyes with the second man, who was still looking over at his partner, trying to figure out what was going on. He started pulling up the rifle lying across his lap to aim it in Dianne's direction, but she ducked low, pushing her body into his and pressing her knees on his hands to keep the rifle and his arms down and out of the way.

At the same time, she slashed forward and to the side with the taped-together scalpels, cutting at the man's throat as hard and fast as possible. If he had a chance to let off a shout or a cry for help, her position would be compromised and it would be that much harder for her to escape. While she wasn't an expert at quietly assassinating people, she reasonably assumed that if his throat was cut wide open he wouldn't be able to make much noise—at least nothing above a gurgle.

The sun's rays through the window at the end of the hall glinted off of the silver tips of the scalpels as they whirled towards and through the man's neck, cutting three deep gouges through his carotid artery on the left side of his neck, through the upper portion of his trachea and just barely nicking his right carotid as she pulled the scalpels free. He tried to gasp in surprise and pain as the blades sliced through his flesh, but Dianne was fast enough with her movements that there was no time for him to react—at least not at first.

Blood spilled freely from the left side of the man's neck and his face turned from one of surprise to one of shock and disbelief. Rivers of red ran across his skin, barely visible in the shadows, but leaving a trail of warmth and stickiness wherever they went. Dianne could feel his hands moving beneath her legs as he struggled to bring them up to his wounds, trying in vain to staunch the flow of blood. He choked and wheezed as blood poured out of his neck, flowing into his damaged trachea as well as down his front and onto Dianne's right hand and arm. The warm wetness wasn't something she was expecting and she nearly jumped off of him, but instead clamped down on his chest with her right arm, putting her face up next to his. She dropped the scalpels from her left hand before clamping her hand over his mouth and nose, stifling his gurgling cries to ensure no one could hear them.

As she stared into the eyes of the man who only moments prior had been talking about the captives in the gas station camp as though they were so much cattle, she saw fear. Pure, unadulterated, raw fear. His pupils dilated and contracted as he looked between her and the brighter parts of the hall, searching for some way out of his situation. There was nothing he could do, though. Death's wings were wrapping themselves around his body.

While she had expected him to pass out relatively quickly due to the loss of blood, it took just over a minute for his body to go limp, though he grew progressively weaker throughout the time she sat on him, keeping him from moving or making any sounds. As the blood flow slowed and his head sagged forward, bumping into her chest, she jerked her hands back and stood up, stumbling backward until she hit the wall. She stared at the man's body in disgust for another long moment before the sound of distant talking voices broke her from her morbid preoccupation with the man's corpse.

As she picked up the scalpels and went over to retrieve the sledgehammer from the first man's face, she was overwhelmed with a sense of satisfaction—a feeling that was entirely unexpected. There was a sense of disgust and shame over the fact that she had just taken the lives of two people in a wholly violent and nauseating way, but at the same time she felt immense relief at knowing that there were now two less people who could hurt her.

"Two down," she whispered to herself as she pulled the sledgehammer free with a quick and squelchy tug, "ten to go." Dianne didn't really expect to kill each and every one of the twelve men in the building, but there were undoubtedly at least a few more in between her and the exit. Whatever it took to escape and get back to her friends and family was what she was going to do—no matter how many stood in her way.

"Okay, Dianne." She clenched the blades in her left hand and hefted the sledge in her right. "Ten more to go. You can do this. You can do this."

Chapter Six

W ashington, D.C.

WHILE RICK, Jane and Dr. Evans tried to give a wide berth to the location where the engine noises were coming from, the destruction in the city and the direction they had to walk to reach their destination forced them on a more or less direct path towards the sounds. With the residential neighborhoods far behind them and commercial, government and industrial buildings on all sides, they were close to the river when they finally spotted what was causing the ruckus.

A couple blocks down the street, just on the close side of the river, were a collection of people with rifles on their backs wearing black and blue jackets with the words "Capitol Police" emblazoned on the back in white lettering. A few of them wore simple seamed caps while the rest had on baseball caps, and all of the headwear carried the same lettering as the jackets. Upon seeing how the people were dressed, Dr. Evans and Jane's first reactions were to sigh with relief and start moving into a position where they could call out to them. Rick, however, grabbed them both by the arms and pulled them back into a nearby building where they could observe the people working without being spotted.

"What the hell, Rick?" Jane pulled her arm away from him, giving him a dirty look in the process. "They're the good guys!"

"Are you sure about that?" Rick snapped back at her. "How do you know they're not some gang that killed a bunch of cops and stole their clothing?

Or even if they are police, that they're not just going to try and take every-thing we have under some pretense?

"I... I don't—"

"Exactly. We don't know. Which is why we're going to take our time, watch them carefully, and then figure out what to do once we have more information." He looked at Dr. Evans, seeking confirmation and backup, and the man sighed and nodded slowly.

"Rick's right, Jane. We're three versus what looks like at least a dozen or more."

"Son of a..." Jane cursed under her breath, looked around the room they were in and then sat down on a chair that was covered in dust. "Fine. But don't say I didn't warn you."

Rick stood close to the front of the building, peeking out through the large window that had long since been smashed in, either by a person or by the event. He could see clearly down the length of the street, and watched carefully as the men dressed in police outfits continued walking down the road. They didn't seem particularly concerned about their surroundings as only a few of them had their weapons out and at the ready. Most of them gestured and spoke with each other, spending a great deal of time pointing at scorched vehicles in the road that were blocking their path.

After ten or so minutes of watching, the source of the engine noise that the trio had heard finally came into view. A pair of massive bulldozers, both of them painted orange, drove side by side next to each other as they went down the street. They turned the corner in unison, their tracks rolling along effortlessly across the pavement. As the bulldozers neared the men they slowed down and the men scattered to the sides of the street, making way for the massive vehicles to do their thing.

With plows nearly as tall as the cabs on the bulldozers, they pushed forward with the blades at opposite angles, working together as they drove headlong into the crowd of vehicles blocking their path. The horrible sound of groaning, screeching metal echoed down the street, causing Rick to wince and cover his ears as the wreckage in the road was pushed aside by the powerful machines. The men dressed in police uniforms walked beside and behind the bulldozers, staying clear of the debris they pushed out of the way and checking to make sure nothing was getting caught up in the treads.

While the pace of the bulldozers was slow, they were nothing if not powerful and they continued moving along in a steady fashion. It wasn't until the bulldozers and the men were less than a block away from the building where Rick, Jane and Dr. Evans were hiding that Rick realized that they had a problem. Turning around, he looked at Jane and Dr. Evans, both of whom were standing and watching just beside him.

"We need to get out of the building," Rick whispered.

"What?" Dr. Evans looked at him. "What for?"

"They're checking buildings as they're going by. We need to ease into a back room or something so we don't get spotted."

Jane turned and headed behind the counter of the shop they were in, only to stop and look at the wall. "That… might be a problem."

Rick slipped back from the window and stood next to her. Behind the counter, where the outline of a doorway leading into the back of the shop was visible, was a pile of debris from where the back half of the building had collapsed in on itself. Rick glanced around the rest of the small establishment, looking for a place for them to hide, when he realized there was only one option.

"We need to try and break through before they get any closer. Then we can escape out the back and head around them." Rick motioned at Jane and Dr. Evans. "Come on, let's try to clear a path!"

As Rick and Dr. Evans moved towards the counter, intending to circle around and start work, Jane began tugging at a large cinderblock sticking out from the wall. As she pulled, the block and the rubble above it shifted, tumbling down towards her. She jumped back, trying to get out of the way, but tripped and fell down in a corner behind the counter as the rubble rained down on her legs, pinning her down and trapping her in place. Rick and Dr. Evans ran to her side and she groaned in pain, gritting her teeth together to try and keep from making any noise that might attract attention.

Rick knelt down next to Jane and took her hand as he looked at the piles of wood and rubble covering her lower half. "Are you okay?!"

Jane nodded slowly, closing her eyes and keeping her jaw clenched shut from the pain as she hissed through her teeth. "I think so. It hurts like hell, though!"

"Grab the bags," Rick whispered to Dr. Evans, "And bring them back behind the counter. We'll have to hide out back here while we try to get her free."

Dr. Evans did as Rick asked, tossing their bags near the front of the shop over the counter before heading around behind it with Rick and Jane. Rick was already working on pulling the rubble off of Jane, setting it gently to the side to keep from making too much noise, and Dr. Evans joined in. With their limited weaponry they knew that if they were discovered and the men in the street were hostile, things weren't going to go well.

Minutes ticked slowly by as Rick and Dr. Evans worked together in the shop, hearing the rumble of diesel engines and screeching metal growing closer. Dust billowed into the air as one of the bulldozers disturbed a large pile of ash, sending a cloud of it flying past the shop and up into the air. The vehicles drove by slowly, barely visible through the dust and ash as they rumbled along, the sound from their engines rattling the few intact pieces of glass still left in the shop. Dr. Evans and Rick stopped moving rubble and Dr. Evans crouched down low next to Jane while Rick stayed sitting up, peeking over the counter as he watched for the men who would be walking behind the bulldozers.

"You're almost free," Dr. Evans whispered to Jane, "As soon as they pass by we'll get you out. Can you still move your legs and feet?"

There was still a moderately-sized pile of broken wood, cinderblocks and bricks on Jane's legs, but she tried moving them nonetheless, wincing only slightly as she did. "Yeah. I can still move them. I think something's stuck in my leg but I can feel my toes and move them."

Dr. Evans patted her on the shoulder. "Good, good. Just stay still. We'll get you out in a moment or two."

While they hadn't been able to hear the men talking before, once the bulldozers got just beyond their building their sound faded enough that Rick was able to hear the shouts of the men walking behind the vehicles. Rick cocked his head and listened intently, trying to discern not only their words but their tone and intent behind them as well.

"Unit three reports they found a cache of food and water, all unspoiled. They're near capacity and will be heading to us shortly."

"What about unit four? Any luck?"

"Nothing since their last report an hour ago. They're gathering bits and pieces but nothing solid. Unit two's still trying to resurrect that crane they found but it doesn't look promising."

"Using these 'dozers as battering rams isn't going to work if the doors on that facility are as big as they're supposed to be. We're going to need something more."

"We need a bunker-buster."

"Ha!"

Rick looked back and saw his own confused expression mirrored in both Dr. Evans and Jane's faces. The conversation between the men walking outside the shop made no sense, and sounded like a mix between some sort of nefarious plotting and a group of rescuers trying to help people out. Rick sank beneath the counter as the voices drew close to the shop, trying to stay out of sight. The crunching of boots on the pavement outside grew louder until were walking past. Rick could hear the steps of no less than six individuals outside the shop, and he held his breath and put a finger to his lips as he remained motionless, hoping that the men would keep walking by without stopping.

"Rogers, isn't this where you got your wife that ring last year?" The voice came from the entrance of the shop where Rick, Jane and Dr. Evans were hiding. Rick felt his heart rate explode and he wondered offhand why the men hadn't heard it beating.

"Hm. Yeah." More bootsteps crunched, this time closer than before. One or more of the men were inside the shop. "Nice couple ran this place. I wonder what happened to them."

"Same thing as everyone else, probably."

The other man kicked at a pile of debris on the floor, sending bits of metal and wood flying up and over the counter. "Yep. Come on, let's go."

Rick felt his whole body relax at the man's words. Dr. Evans and Jane's faces were pictures of relief as they all listened to the pair exit the shop—until Rick felt a sharp pain in his awkwardly positioned leg. A cramp throbbed in his thigh unexpectedly and he kicked his leg outward, straightening it to try and relieve the pain. The motion did not come without consequence, though, and there was a loud clatter as he kicked the pile of rubble behind the counter and near Jane's legs.

Rick felt his face flush red and he closed his eyes, praying that the sound was either quieter than he thought or that it would be lost in the rumble of the diesel engines a short distance away. As the footsteps stopped near the front of the shop and he heard a pair of bodies abruptly turn around, he knew that it wasn't going to be. Half a second later, a loud voice called out, causing a sinking feeling in his stomach as he realized he had just doomed them all.

"Who the hell is in there?!"

Chapter Seven

I SS, International Space Station

COMMANDER PALMER GLANCES at his watch. Twenty-five minutes of oxygen left and counting.

"Hurry up!" He bellows over the comms as he and Ted stand inside the airlock, looking out at Jackie. She is floating through space, the thrusters on her EVA suit firing at short intervals to keep her on track with the airlock. When she finally arrives, Ted and Commander Palmer help her pull in the string of equipment lashed to her arm and Commander Palmer begins operating the manual controls to seal the outer door. Once the door closes, he motions toward the inner door.

"Ted, use the manual controls to get the inner hatch open. Once we're inside, I'll head for engineering control station and get everything booted up. You two get everything in, seal the airlock and then get up to the main controls and see if there are any critically damaged components. We've all but used up our air so we've got to hustle."

Ted nods, though the motion is imperceptible inside his bulky suit. He works the control for the inner hatch as quickly as his gloved hands allows, and soon it opens with a quick whoosh as air from inside the station rushes in to fill the void in the airlock. Shedding the large thruster portion of his EVA suit, Commander Palmer pushes himself past Ted and Jackie, calling out to them as he goes by. "Sounds like the skin of the station is intact, at least, so that's good. Cross your fingers, guys; I'll be back in a jiffy!"

As Ted and Jackie work to get the equipment and supplies into the narrow tubes and passageways of the station, Commander Palmer flies toward the center of the maze, where the main engineering controls are located. A row of massive batteries sits in the center of the station, the energy within kept topped off by solar panels on the outside of the station that were never fully retracted. While the batteries have kept core systems in the station online ever since the last astronaut left, the main power source for the station is a combination of an experimental micro fusion reactor developed by MIT and the main solar panels which are still safely tucked away.

While the station possesses air scrubbers and tanks of reserve oxygen, the batteries in the station are not enough to process and distribute the air. Either the reactor or the solar panels—or, ideally, both—must be activated. The only question is which one is more liable to still function.

"How's it going down there, Commander?" Ted comes in over the comms, his voice calm with just a touch of concern.

"Twelve minutes of air left," Commander Palmer replies. "How's it look at command? Do the reactor or panels show any signs of damage?"

"Negative, commander. Both systems show as green based on the passive sensors."

Commander Palmer takes a deep breath and looks at the controls in front of him for a few seconds before responding. "Heads or tails, Jackie?"

"Commander?"

"Heads or tails? Don't think about it; just pick one."

"T—No, heads."

"Reactor it is." Commander palmer enters the command to start up the reactor, then pushes himself back from the console and watches the screen with trepidation. "Startup time for both is roughly the same, about ten minutes. With both systems showing green it's a shot in the dark over which one will work. Maybe both will. Maybe one won't. Maybe both won't."

"That's certainly comforting, Commander," Ted replies.

The trio of astronauts float quietly for the next nine minutes and thirty seconds, anxiously awaiting some sign that the correct choice was made. As the startup sequence for the reactor completes, Commander Palmer hears a slight hum as a vibration begins to build within the center of the station. A few seconds later, Ted comes over the comms, nearly breathless with excitement.

"We've got systems coming online across the board up here! Environmental systems are starting up now and we should have breathable air any second!"

Commander Palmer sighs with relief and takes a moment to compose himself before responding. "Excellent. It needs a bit of tuning so I'll be down here for a while. Make sure all of the vital systems are online; there should be a checklist up in command somewhere for this type of scenario. Run it." Palmer pauses for a few seconds, thinking about what happened on the ISS-2. "Don't bring up the communications channels yet, though."

"Don't... you don't want to call home?"

"I've got a funny feeling about it. Call it a hunch. Just wait for me before booting any sort of ground comms up, okay?"

Ted and Jackie look at each other skeptically before Ted shrugs, accepting Commander Palmer's instruction. "Will do. See you on the command deck soon."

Commander Palmer peers through the thick glass at the small reactor, watching as the lights across its surface blink out status codes. He lifts a hand to his helmet and slowly *releases the latch before twisting it and taking it off. The air on the station is stale but breathable, and he can feel a slight breeze of freshly processed air from somewhere off to the side.*

The three astronauts from ISS-2 are still alive. It's more than a minor miracle that they've survived, but there is still much to be done. The older station needs maintenance and upkeep to house them long-term, and the options for getting back to Earth must be carefully studied and calculated to ensure success. And, in the background, there's still the question of what exactly happened. Commander Palmer's mind begins to race with possibilities before he catches himself and focuses on the task at hand.

"Survival now," he mutters. "Answers later."

Chapter Eight

W ashington, D.C.

"MERDE!" Dr. Evans hissed, shaking his head at Rick. "What now?"

As Rick sat behind the counter, hand on his pistol, contemplating whether to try and engage the men in and outside the shop, he took a deep breath and listened as the man in the doorway shouted again.

"I said who's in there? Put your hands up and come out now, or we'll consider you a threat and open fire!"

Rick grabbed his pistol and passed it to Dr. Evans before whispering in his ear. "If this goes south, make sure you take two or three of them out, okay?" Rick ignored Dr. Evans' wide-eyed expression and slowly raised his hands over the counter, shouting as he began rising to his feet.

"Take it easy! I'm coming out!"

"Drop your weapons!"

"They're dropped, they're dropped!" Rick shouted back at the man as he stood up, wincing and closing his eyes in anticipation of the bullets he expected to come flying toward him. The bullets did not come, though, and he opened one eye and then the other to see three of the men standing in front of him, rifles aimed at his chest as the one closest spoke again.

"Are you alone? What are you doing in here?"

Rick glanced between the men, studying their expressions in the fraction of a second he knew he had to respond. He sensed no malice in their faces, only nervousness and exhaustion. In that instant, Rick decided to try and trust them, hoping desperately that it wouldn't backfire.

"We have someone wounded back here; she's trapped under rubble!" He kept his hands in the air even as he turned and looked down towards Jane. Next to her, Dr. Evans looked back at him, his eyes wide as he shook his head.

"'We?'" The man responded. "How many is 'we'?"

"Three in total," Rick said. "Myself, a doctor and our friend. We're just passing through the city; we heard you coming and didn't know what your intentions were so we hid in here. We were going to try to get out when we realized you were coming closer but the back wall collapsed partially and trapped her."

The lead man looked back at his companions, exchanging questioning glances with them before turning back to Rick. He lowered his rifle slightly and stepped forward. "Move back. I want to see behind the counter."

Rick shuffled to the side, nearly tripping over the rubble, and looked down at the others. "Dr. Evans, put the gun down and keep your hands on your head, okay?" Dr. Evans shook his head again, but Rick nodded and persisted. "Just trust me, okay?"

Rick wasn't sure why he was putting his trust in the men standing in the shop with their rifles aimed in his direction. It could have been because the men didn't immediately open fire or call him a liar or do any number of other things that would indicate that they didn't really care about Rick or his companions, or it could have been because he really didn't have much of any other choice. Relief flooded him, though as Dr. Evans slowly put the pistol on the ground and put his hands on his head, just as the lead man stepped up and looked over the counter.

"Shit." The man stepped back and looked over his shoulder. "We've got one wounded here. Get a medic and some backup to help shift this crap off of her legs."

The man standing at the very edge of the shop nodded and headed out into the street, calling out to his companions. The one closest to Rick turned to him and looked him up and down carefully before turning to Dr. Evans. "You, get up and stand next to your friend there, okay? Don't make any sudden movements."

Dr. Evans complied with the instruction, glancing longingly at the discarded pistol on the ground as he stood up. He still had one tucked into his back waistband, but there was no possible way he could fish it out and use it without getting all of them killed. Like Rick, he had little choice but to trust that the men in the shop weren't going to kill them, though that was of little comfort to him.

"You armed?" The man asked Dr. Evans, who glanced at Rick before answering.

"Y—yes."

"Where at?"

"Behind me, in my belt. A pistol."

The man nodded, tightening his grip on his rifle while his companion near the door did the same. "Pull it out slowly and put it on the floor." As Dr. Evans did what the man told him, Rick spoke up.

"We've got a rifle and a couple more handguns behind the counter. It's not much, but you're welcome to take them in exchange for our lives."

"In… what?" The man looked confused as he turned to his companion. The other man dressed in a police jacket shook his head and replied.

"They think we're bandits or something, Lance."

"Oh for…" The leader shook his head and sighed. "We're not going to hurt you so long as you don't make any movements against us." He extended his hand to Rick while his companion watched warily, his rifle still up. "I'm Captain Lance Recker, Capitol Police."

"You—you're really with the Capitol Police?" Dr. Evans blurted out, his hands still on his head even while Rick cautiously shook Lance's hand.

"Of course we are," Recker replied. "Who else would we be with the hats and jackets?"

Rick shook his head. "If you've seen some of the things we've seen, you'd have a whole host of ideas running through your head." He sighed with relief before turning to Jane as she groaned.

"Hey, you idiots, I'm still trapped under here. And it still hurts like hell."

"Jane!" Rick started moving toward her before stopping and looking at the captain. "We need to get her out."

Recker glanced at the other officer standing closer to the doorway before tossing him his rifle. "Here. Keep an eye on them." The officer near the door looked like he was about to argue, but Recker shut him down with a narrowing of the eyes and a shake of his head. He and Rick hurried to Jane's side and began shifting rubble while Dr. Evans moved the pile from behind the counter to out front, all while doing his best not to make eye contact with the officer still standing near the door.

After a few minutes, three officers ran up to the shop and looked inside, their hands immediately jumping to their weapons before Recker raised his hand and shook his head. "Stand down. Jackson, get back here and look at her legs. She had a lot of rubble fall on them."

Rick and Captain Recker moved aside while an officer carrying a large red bag slipped behind the counter, eying Rick and Dr. Evans warily. "You good here, sir?" He looked at Recker as he asked the question, trying to figure out if his captain was somehow on the wrong end of a hostage situation.

"All good here. Take care of her, okay?"

Satisfied with the answer, Jackson knelt down and turned his attention to Jane, who was lying still on the ground with her eyes closed. Her breathing was shallow and hoarse, and she groaned as Jackson gently probed her dirt and blood-covered legs.

"What's your name?" Jackson spoke quietly to Jane as he felt for breaks and watched her reactions, trying to gauge how much pain she was feeling.

"Jane." She whispered the answer through gritted teeth.

"Nice to meet you, Jane. I'm Scott. Can you describe how much pain you're feeling right now on a scale of one to ten?"

"Nineteen?" Jane whispered again, though this time there was a hint of a smile playing at her lips. Scott smiled back and shook his head.

"That doesn't sound good. Can you feel this?" He reached down and pulled off her shoes, then pinched her toes. She nodded in reply. "Okay, great. Can you wiggle them?"

"Yeah. I tried earlier. Hurts like hell, though."

"Yep, understandable." Jackson gingerly lifted one of her legs and Jane groaned in pain. "You've got some pretty big shards of metal lodged in here. Captain?" He turned and looked for Recker, who leaned over the counter.

"How is she?"

"We need to get her out of here and to somewhere where I can get this stuff out of her leg."

"You two," Recker said, motioning at Rick and Dr. Evans, "Let's get her moved."

"Gently, please," cautioned Jackson. "Nothing appears to be broken but there's some slivers resting way too close to an artery."

After a minute of shuffling under the watchful eye of the officer near the door—his rifle now pointed down, but still at the ready—Rick, Dr. Evans, Jackson and Recker got Jane lifted up and onto a thick mat that one of the other newly-arrived officers spread out across the top of the counter. As soon as she was set, he waved off the others. "Give me some space here. Mitchell? Get the trauma kit and assist."

In less than a minute Jane was hooked up to an IV and both Jackson and the officer he had called over to help him were wearing gloves and starting to work on Jane's legs. Recker led Rick and Dr. Evans away out into the street where Rick had his first chance to look around since they entered the small shop.

The pair of bulldozers were stopped a block down from the shop and a handful of officers were milling around them, watching Recker and the two new strangers with interest. Each of the officers looked battle-worn; their faces were covered with dirt and grime, their eyes had bags and their demeanor spoke of a lot of walking and very little rest. Like with Recker, Jackson and the other officers inside the shop, Rick detected no trace of malice or ill intent in the men and women in uniform. They looked exhausted and near their breaking point, but not like they wanted to steal from or kill Rick and his companions.

"So, tell me, Rick." Recker stretched his neck back and forth until he felt it crack deep inside and a wave of relaxation flooded it and his upper back. "What are you and your two friends doing here?"

Rick glanced at Dr. Evans, trying to figure out how much to tell the leader of the group he had just met. There were potential positives and negatives to any choice he might make, and it was impossible to tell which was the correct one in the moment.

Chapter Nine

B lacksburg, VA

DIANNE WATERS WAS A GHOST. She crept along the stairs to the next floor down, keeping as close to the wall as possible and taking special care that she didn't rub her backpack or her body up against anything that might make any noise. Her heart was racing and her breaths came rapidly through her nose, her nostrils flaring as she tried to keep herself calm.

Dark red blood clung to her skin and clothes, feeling sticky as she adjusted her grip on the five-pound sledgehammer in her right hand. In her left, the scalpels still shone in the light coming through the windows as she kept her fingers tightly grasped around them, ready to slice at any targets that might try to surprise her. Strands of hair pulled from her ponytail in the brief fight with the two men hung in her face, though she dared not move them for fear of smearing blood on her forehead.

Gore still clung to the sledgehammer even after she tried to shake it off a few times. Bits of flesh and bone and blood covered the front half of the cylindrical head of the tool and the handle was stained and tacky from the blood covering her right hand. Pausing to think about the violence she had wrought would lead to hesitation, and hesitation would invariably lead to her demise. She had to keep moving forward, slinking through the shadows to become an angel of death so that she might return and ensure that her family would continue to live.

So that is what she became.

The third man to die to her hand was at the bottom of the stairs, his back to Dianne as she crept up on him. Her footsteps were quiet enough that all he heard of her was the faint whooshing of the sledgehammer as she swung it through the air, smashing into his temple and knocking him to the floor. His body was still moving after his fall so she struck him again, then he lay still, motionless as blood pooled from the hole in the side of his head.

Not bothering to stop to catch her breath, Dianne stepped over his body and hurried down the next flight of stairs, heading for the ground floor. She heard voices talking in the hallways nearby, but no one was close enough to see her so she continued forward, her weapons ready to strike at a moment's notice.

When Dianne turned the corner on the landing to the last set of stairs leading onto the ground floor she stopped and froze for an instant before hastily backing up into a corner near the window where the shadow from the wall could conceal her presence. Three figures stood in the wide open first floor of the facility, each of them carrying a rifle in their hands and bearing grimaces on their faces. While she could only see three figures at first, the one closest to her was talking to a fourth who she couldn't see. However, based on their conversation, that one was searching through the back closets and rooms near the cafeteria and administrative offices. The man closest to her was blocking her exit through a nearby side exit while the other two men were wandering around near the other two visible exits from the building.

Crouched down on one knee in the shadows, Dianne watched the men carefully, trying to figure out if there was a pattern to their movements that she could exploit to get past them. They wandered and turned and talked at random but there was no apparent order to their actions. Glancing at the scalpels in her left hand, she placed them gently on the floor, transferred the sledge from her right hand to her left and then drew her pistol from its holster. She began tensing her legs, preparing to fire on the man in front of her before making a mad dash for the closest door when the frantic shouts of someone a few floors up caught the attention of everyone in the building.

"Holy shit! They're dead! They're dead!!" The shouts echoed through the quiet corridors of the facility and Dianne glanced upward, realizing that the two men she had killed in the hallway had just been discovered. She glanced at the man who was near the stairs at the same time he focused on the stairwell and began running toward it. He was so distracted by the shouts from above that he didn't even notice Dianne at first. Only when he was three steps up did he see her still crouching in the corner, a pistol in one hand and the small sledge in the other.

Dianne stood and swung the hammer at his head, but he brought his rifle up reflexively and blocked the blow. The sledge slipped from Dianne's hand and crashed to the ground, bouncing off of the carpeted stairs and away from where it could be easily retrieved. With his aim ruined by the force of the blow to the rifle barrel, the man lunged forward at Dianne, grabbing at her throat as he shouted at her.

"I've got you now!"

Dianne felt herself toppling over backward under the weight of the man, her left arm held out to try and shield herself from his attack while her right arm came up, still holding the pistol. She pressed the end of the gun into the man's gut and pulled the trigger five times, each round snapping loudly in the confined space. The man's eyes grew wide and he screamed in pain after he realized what was going on. His body became dead weight as he fought to get away from Dianne and he rolled off of her, tumbling to the ground as he writhed and shouted, calling both for help and to alert his comrades of Dianne's presence.

"She's here! Help!" The man called out with a gurgled voice as Dianne got back to her feet and half ran, half slipped down the remaining stairs. The other two men in the lobby turned at the sound of the gunshots and the man's cries and started running in her direction. After glancing around to see that the nearest exit from the building was too far to run without fear of being caught, Dianne turned to the closest window and squeezed off three shots. The rounds easily punctured the thick glass, causing spiderwebs to spread across from top to bottom and side to side.

The panes of safety glass were nearly ten feet high and wide and were designed to be nearly unbreakable, though if their structural integrity were to ever be compromised, they were supposed to shatter into small, dull pieces that wouldn't hurt anyone nearby. As Dianne ran for the glass, gunshots echoing loudly in the lobby of the building and shouts of alarm and pain coming from both the bottom and upper floors, she held both arms up in front of her head and braced for an entirely different impact than that which arrived.

Dianne cried out in pain, not from the impact with the glass, but from the sudden blow to her upper legs. The fourth man who had been prowling through the back offices had come out just in time to see her running for the window. He gave chase and tackled her, sending her tumbling through the window and out onto the rough dirt and soil just outside. Even through the pain and the chaos, Dianne's priority was still the medication in her backpack, and she resisted rolling onto her back despite how that movement would have alleviated her pain.

Instead, she kept her head and chin high to avoid smashing her face against the ground. She kicked furiously with her legs, freeing her right one and slamming the heel of her boot into her attacker's face. He yowled in pain and she felt his grip loosen, then she repeated the motion to dislodge him fully. As she came to a stop she raised her pistol and fired at him, pulling the trigger as many times as it took for the slide to pop back and stick. The man's head blossomed blood onto the ground and she pushed herself to her feet as she glanced from him to back inside the facility.

From the bottom and upper floors a hailstorm of gunfire rang out, splintering multiple windows open and raining glass down onto Dianne. She heard and felt the whistle and pop of rounds landing all around her, but she bobbed and weaved as she ran along, ducking to the left and right to keep trees, benches, fences and other obstacles between her and her attackers. She had no specific goal in mind as she ran from the facility; she was just trying to escape.

As Dianne tripped and stumbled down the hill from the LTAC building and neared the road, the shots from behind her gradually lessened, but she still heard the occasional crack of a rifle and the shouts of the men who were scrambling to get out of the building and pursue her. When she reached the chain-link she glanced back and forth, trying to orient herself to find the break in the fence she had made when she arrived. She finally found it and slipped through, snagging her backpack and rifle in the process which forced her to waste precious seconds getting them free.

"There she is!" Just as Dianne freed herself and her gear she heard the roar of one of the men from farther up the hill. He charged down toward her, firing his rifle wildly as fast as he could pull the trigger and sending the shots careening in every direction. Dianne bolted away from the man and his companions, making a beeline for the parking garage where she stashed her truck. With stealth no longer an option it was a footrace, with the grand prize being life itself. Faced with that grim reality, Dianne ignored the pain in her legs and pushed herself faster, hoping beyond hope that she could still make it out of the city in one piece.

Chapter Ten

W ashington, D.C.

"UHH..." Rick ran his hands through his hair before looking around and motioning to a couple of ash-covered benches sitting on the sidewalk. "Mind if we sit down?" Recker nodded and the trio sat, with Dr. Evans at one end of one bench, Rick at the other end and Recker leaning against the arm of the other bench, his leg half propped up across its length.

"I have a feeling you're about to tell me that I won't believe what you're about to tell me," Recker said. "So I'll start by telling you that I probably will. We're on our way to Mount Weather, part of a rescue mission to save a bunch of eggheads trapped there."

"Mount Weather?" Rick's eyes grew wide as he recognized the name.

"Rick, that's where—" Dr. Evans started.

"I know, I know. They wanted to send me there." Rick shook his head before looking back at Recker. "You say there are people trapped there?"

Recker nodded slowly. "A bunch of scientists and government officials. They were working on trying to fix all of, well, *this*." He gestured to their surroundings. "How do you know about Mount Weather? You were supposed to get sent there?"

Rick glanced at Dr. Evans. "You think we can tell him everything?"

Dr. Evans shrugged. "I don't see why not."

"All right," Rick said, then turned to Recker. "Back before this all started, I was at home down in Ellisville, VA, outside of Blacksburg. I left my wife and three children to fly to Los Angeles and give a presentation for the company I worked for. I landed probably thirty minutes before the cars started exploding."

"Sweet Mary." Recker whistled softly. "You're kidding, right?"

Rick sighed and shook his head. "Not at all. And that's not even the half of it. We're here to stop this thing."

Over the next three quarters of an hour, Rick and Dr. Evans detailed their journeys from the start of the event to the present moment, answering Recker's questions along the way. As they went on, Rick noticed a change in Recker's attitude and body language. While he had started off acting aggressively and then softened slightly at the sight of Jane's injuries, he had still been keeping Rick and Dr. Evans at a distance, unsure whether or not they would turn out to have a hidden nefarious agenda of some sort. By the time their stories caught up to the present, though, he was convinced that the two men sitting next to him were being nothing if not truthful.

"So the NSA's got the tools to stop this thing, huh?"

"That is our belief, yes," replied Dr. Evans. "But we won't know until we get there. Which, again, is what we were trying to do when we encountered you."

"Captain," started Rick, "Would you mind telling us what you and your officers are doing out here? With the bulldozers and everything, I mean. You said you're on your way to Mount Weather, but what's going on?"

Recker shifted in his seat, feeling his rear end and upper thighs tingling from staying in one position on the bench for too long. "After everything went to hell in a handbasket, we had a few dozen officers who hadn't either been killed or left to take their family out of the city to safety somewhere else. We linked up with a handful of survivors from the fire departments around the city and started running search and rescue operations, bringing people to the auxiliary police building they shut down on the north side of the city. I guess it was isolated enough that it didn't get hit by this... 'Damocles' thing.

"A few days later we picked up a radio broadcast calling for help from Mount Weather. They were saying they had civilians, military and government officials trapped inside and unable to open the bunker doors." Recker looked over and pointed at the bulldozers. "We got those suckers running and started clearing a path out of the city so we could try and mount a rescue operation. I'm still not sure how we'll get through the bunker once we get there, though."

"I'm really glad I didn't head off to Mount Weather." Rick shook his head. "Sounds like that was a one-way trip to hell for a lot of people."

"No kidding. Hopefully we can pull them out, but it sounds like what you three are doing might actually fix all of this."

"Fix?" Dr. Evans shook his head. "No. Keep from getting worse? Yes. One hopes so, at least."

Recker eyed Dr. Evans and Rick closely before nodding at them. "All right. What can we do to help you? I can't commit any manpower to go with you but I can at least give you supplies and armaments. Those pistols and your one rifle aren't going to offer up much protection if you run into trouble."

"Absolutely," Rick answered enthusiastically. "We'd appreciate any help you can give us. We've got food and water for a couple of days, but there's no telling how long we'll be digging through the rubble to find what we're looking for. And yes, some rifles and ammunition would be amazing."

"How're you planning on accessing these computer systems if—sorry, *when*—you find them, anyway? There's no power in the city."

Dr. Evans scratched at his nose as he replied. "I've been thinking about that. Most of the buildings had backup batteries for running critical systems. My guess is that those systems were shut down by Damocles but there may be some that were shut down without damage. If we can find one of those, then—"

"That sounds way too complicated," Recker said, standing up as he interrupted Dr. Evans. "Wait here. I'll be back in a few minutes."

As the captain walked off to talk to a couple of officers standing near the bulldozers, Rick and Dr. Evans looked over at the shop where Jackson was still standing over Jane. She appeared to be talking to him and looked like she was in good spirits, but neither man wanted to interrupt Jackson while he was still working on her so they decided to stay on the bench and wait for Recker to return.

A few minutes later Recker walked back to them and motioned for them to follow him. "Come on. You'll want to see this."

"Can we check on Jane first?" Dr. Evans asked.

"She's in good hands. As soon as Jackson's done with her, he'll let us know. Come on, this way."

Rick and Dr. Evans followed behind Recker, who headed down the street the way the officers had come from, heading for some unknown objective. After a couple of blocks Recker turned the corner and the three men found themselves in front of a pair of officers who were standing around a couple of Capitol Police squad cars, both of which had their hoods open.

"How's it going?" Recker asked. The men turned to look at him, saw Rick and Dr. Evans and instinctively reached for their weapons when he raised his hand. "Relax; they're fine."

"You sure, sir?" A short, stout officer with a thick mustache and a cap that was halfway on his head eyed Rick and Dr. Evans suspiciously.

"One hundred percent. Now tell me how it's going with the cars."

"They're both running, Captain." The other man, a tall lanky fellow, wiped his hands on a dirty rag. "Engine's still rough on this one but I think they'll both get us where we need to go."

"Good. Get the other one ready to roll out. I want two rifles, two thousand rounds of five-five-six, five hundred rounds of nine mil, two weeks' worth of food, a weeks' worth of water and a couple of purifiers in there within thirty minutes."

"Sir?" The shorter of the two officers looked at him in confusion.

"Also," Recker continued, "Make sure the inverter works properly. These gentlemen need to be able to run a computer so don't forget to check that before you're done."

Both officers stared at Recker unblinking, looking as though they had just heard him speaking to them in Mandarin. "Cap... did you... what's this for?" The tall officer finally replied.

"Your funeral if you don't do what I'm telling you." The response was hard, and the two officers glanced at each other before replying to their leader.

"Yes, sir. We'll have it ready for you."

"Good. Bring it down the street to the 'dozers when it's ready. We'll be there." He looked at Rick and Dr. Evans. "Come on, let's head back."

Rick waited until they were back around the corner before replying to Recker. "Captain, we appreciate the gesture more than you realize, but it's really not necessary. We had a vehicle outside the city, an electric car, but we couldn't bring it in. Maybe if you could help us get—"

"No time for that for either of us. As soon as your friend is patched up we have to get back on the move. And you three will need to keep going, too. We've got a few older squad cars that didn't get burned up that we're working on restoring, so we'll be fine. And we can spare plenty of weapons and ammo for you, too.

"You three do what you need to do. We've cleared several of the main streets so you'll be able to move back and forth with ease. The squad car's got an inverter and a battery big enough to power whatever you throw on it, so you'll be able to run any systems that are left standing. Assuming you can find them, of course."

"Captain," Rick said, stopping and tapping Recker on the shoulder. "Thank you. I don't understand why you're helping us like this, but it's incredible." Rick extended his hand and Recker shook it, looking the man dead in the eyes.

"You're welcome, Rick. If we few who are left don't help each other, what's the point of surviving?"

"Captain?" A voice from behind Recker made him turn and he smiled at the sight of the person walking toward him.

"Jackson! What's the good word?"

Jackson pulled off his disposable gloves with a loud snap and threw them to the ground. He looked at Rick and Dr. Evans as he spoke. "Your friend is extremely lucky. There were metal shards on the ground and the rubble drove her legs onto them, embedding the metal in her calves and thighs.

They just barely missed her major arteries, though, so she'll be fine. We got the metal out and patched her up."

"Can she walk?" Rick asked.

"It'll hurt like hell for a few days, but yes. She can walk. I'd advise against it, though, but I'm no doctor so do whatever you want." He tossed a small bottle of pills at Dr. Evans. "Make sure she takes these twice a day for the next week. Her stomach's going to be a mess but they'll keep the wounds from getting infected."

"Thank you, Doctor."

"Doctor?" Jackson laughed. "I'm no doctor. But you're welcome. She's back at the shop, resting until you all are ready to move out." He looked at Recker. "I assume you got them some transport, Captain?"

Recker nodded. "Squad car with supplies will be here shortly."

"Good. She needs to stay off of her feet as much as possible." Jackson took in a deep breath and let it out slowly, glad to be free of the small shop and back out in the open again. "When do we move out, sir?"

"As soon as their vehicle's ready."

"Good, I don't know how much longer those folks at the bunker can hold out if they've lost all power. The air circulation systems might be down, too."

As Recker and Jackson became absorbed in their conversation, Rick tapped Dr. Evans on the shoulder and the two moved away, heading for the shop where Jane was still located. Once they were a short distance from Recker and Jackson, Dr. Evans whispered to Rick. "I can't believe they're helping us like this."

Rick nodded. "Agreed. I'm not about to argue with it, though. They just seriously upped our chances of success and gave us a shot in the arm where we needed it the most. Now let's go get Jane and plan our next move."

Chapter Eleven

B lacksburg, VA

DIANNE LEANED on the back of her truck, chest heaving as she sucked in air, trying to recover her breath from the long run she had just endured. Her heart was still racing and she glanced behind, checking once again to see whether the men had caught up with her or not. Dianne's relative nimbleness compared to her pursuers had served her well, allowing her to escape amongst the cars and ruined buildings while those behind her were slowed down. She soon lost them completely, though their superior numbers meant that they were undoubtedly spreading out to search for her. As soon as one of them figured out where she was, she would quickly be surrounded and flushed out of the enclosed parking area.

"Come on..." Dianne slung her rifle into the back of the truck, quickly reloaded a fresh mag into her pistol and then slipped off her backpack. She unzipped the top and gently fished through the contents, hoping that all of the jarring movement she had endured hadn't broken any of the vials. The glass was cold and sleek to her touch, and she felt every vial she put into her bag, all intact and still nestled in the protective cushions she had made for them. "Hallelujah," she whispered to herself. "Something *didn't* go wrong for once."

After retrieving her rifle from the back of the truck, she loaded it and her backpack into the rear cab of the vehicle and ran around to the driver's door. She climbed inside, feeling her legs begin to shake as the adrenaline started to wear off. As she gripped the steering wheel, preparing to start the truck, she glanced at her right hand and arm. Most of the blood from the second man she had killed was dry, forming a thin crust of red that stained her skin and jacket sleeve even as bits of it flaked off with every movement.

Dianne stared at the red stain, transfixed by the sight. The first person she had killed—back home—had been from a distance. She had shot him, his body had dropped to the ground and she had watched the life drain from him before digging a shallow grave in the woods and burying him without fanfare or even a marker. At the time, she thought that the experience couldn't be worse. But she hadn't gotten so much as a drop of blood on her back then, nor had she stared into his eyes from inches away, pressing down on him to keep him from making a sound as his life flowed out onto her hand and arm.

A distant, barely audible shout broke Dianne from her thoughts and she glanced around, her eyes wide with fear. The men were closing in on her, and she would have to move out or risk being trapped. With a deep breath Dianne turned the key in the ignition and the truck roared to life, the engine noise echoing loudly inside the parking garage. She hadn't expected the noise to be quite as loud as it was and panic set in as she realized she hadn't quite figured out how she was going to escape from the city.

Dianne scrambled to buckle her seatbelt as she pulled the truck forward, circling around to get out of the parking garage. Before she pulled out onto the street she glanced down at her pistol tucked between the seat and her leg, making sure it was still there so she could use it if necessary. As shouts echoed closer from outside the structure, Dianne gripped the steering wheel and pushed down hard on the accelerator, flying down towards the exit from the structure and out into the unknown.

Rubber squealed on road as the pickup truck emerged from the parking garage, the massive frame groaning and creaking as it slid during Dianne's sharp turn of the wheel. She felt the left side of the truck just barely lift up off the ground before the turn was over and she muttered under her breath, urging the vehicle not to roll. While she couldn't tell where the voices outside the parking garage were coming from, she knew that—based on how crowded the streets were—her only chance to escape would be to follow the path she had used to get into the city and to the garage from before. The vehicles driven by the men had, thankfully, not been parked anywhere in the vicinity, as they used part of her original path to drive to the facility but had parked in various small clear spaces just off of the main road.

The appearance of two men in front of her was not entirely unexpected, but Dianne had to fight the instinct to slow down or turn away to avoid hitting them. Years of driving experience had taught her to avoid running over pedestrians in the middle of the road, but considering that the pair in front of her were raising their weapons at her, she managed to overcome her initial urges and press down on the accelerator instead. One of the men barely managed to jump out of the way, the right-hand side mirror striking him in the back as he escaped. The other wasn't so lucky, and Dianne winced as she heard a muffled scream from beneath the truck as the man was toppled over, his limbs crushed beneath the steel frame and rubber tires.

Gunfire ignited from behind her and Dianne ducked down low as a few rounds struck the back of the truck, though none of them passed through the back window. The other men who had been running toward the parking garage upon hearing her truck were firing at her from several positions around the street and buildings nearby as they tried to stop her from escaping. Like on the hill of the LTAC facility, though, as Dianne got farther away the shots waned, but just when she thought she might be getting into the clear, the sound of engines slowly began to filter through the noise of her truck.

"Not again!" Dianne glanced in the rearview mirror to see a pair of vehicles following behind, trailing the path she had originally carved through the city and was now using to escape. As the pair of vehicles drew closer the gunfire resumed, and though most shots went wild, a few landed home and rattled the vehicle.

"Stop shooting my truck, assholes!" Dianne shouted in frustration as she swerved around a pile of rubble in the street, the back of the truck giving a sharp thwang as it bounced off a chunk of a burned out car sitting nearby. She searched the streets frantically, trying to remember which way would take her out of the city when she spotted the next turn up ahead on her left. Another glance in the rearview mirror confirmed that the pair of vehicles were indeed getting closer, but the gunfire had stopped, and she figured it was because they were running low on ammo. The lack of attacks from the men gave her a sudden idea, though, and she took her foot off of the accelerator, letting the heavy vehicle slow itself down without touching the brakes.

Though the distances to the turn ahead and back to the vehicles behind her were hard to judge, Dianne let the truck continue to coast right up until she got close enough to the turn that she was nervous about whether or not she'd be able to make it. At that point the pair of vehicles behind were close enough that she could see the whites of the eyes of the lead driver. The car in front was only inches away from her bumper and it sounded like they were getting ready to ram the truck.

"Buckle up, buttercup." Dianne held fast to the steering wheel and jammed her foot down on the accelerator. The truck took half a second to respond, but when it did it leapt forward. She spun the wheel at the same time, taking the left-hand turn at speed and causing the tires of the truck to squeal as the frame once again groaned in protest. While Dianne had been anticipating such a turn and had prepared by buckling her seatbelt and bracing herself, the drivers of the cars behind her had almost no warning of the maneuver.

If Dianne hadn't been so focused on not crashing the truck that she could have taken a second to look behind her, she likely would have laughed at the expressions worn by the men in the two vehicles. As Dianne's truck left the road and made a turn onto a cross-street, the lead driver was focused on trying to ram the truck and force it off the road. With that no longer an option and his prey suddenly pulling away, he accelerated more and then, upon seeing the truck turn, tried to turn as well. Without careful attention to his driving, though, the man quickly oversteered and slammed into a pair of charred vehicles at the corner, causing his car to spin around wildly and nearly flip.

Meanwhile, the second car—seeing that the truck and the lead pursuer were accelerating—did the same thing, and when both vehicles started to turn, the driver realized that he was not going to make the curve at speed. He slammed on the brakes, causing the poorly maintained vehicle to vibrate madly and begin to fishtail before it, too, spun out of control and t-boned the first vehicle. A single airbag in the second vehicle—on the passenger's side—deployed at impact, though since none of the men in the vehicles were strapped in to their seats, it mattered little. Bone crunched and blood sprayed as the cars finally came to a halt with a sickening crunch, followed by screams of pain and frustration from the men inside them.

As Dianne increased her speed down the road, she chanced a quick look in the mirror and breathed a heavy sigh of relief. There were more men and vehicles that would be chasing after her soon enough, but even a few minutes of lead time would be enough for her to lose them... or so she hoped.

Chapter Twelve

Washington, D.C.

"YOU TWO SUCK."

Rick and Dr. Evans smiled as they walked up to Jane, who was sitting on a folded blanket on the ground in front of the shop. Her legs were both covered in bandages and a pair of crutches lay next to her, a gift courtesy of Jackson.

"How are you doing, Jane?" Rick sat down next to her, wincing slightly as he looked at her bandaged legs.

"My legs are still attached and I've got a bottle of pain pills to go with these antibiotics." She held up a couple of plastic medicine bottles and shook them, the contents rattling loudly in the street. "So it's not all bad."

"Can you walk?" Dr. Evans crouched in front of her.

"Hurts like the dickens, but yeah, I can keep up with you two." She glanced down at the crutches sitting next to her. "Don't judge me for these, either. I can walk without them, but Jackson yelled at me when I tried so I have to keep them for show."

"Just… do what he says, okay?" Rick put his hand on her shoulder, then gave her a hug. "It's good to see you're okay, though. We were worried about you."

Jane nodded and smiled at him and Dr. Evans. "Yeah, well, you two still suck for getting me stuck like that." The three sat in silence for a moment before she spoke again. "So these guys really are cops, huh?"

"Remnants of the Capitol Police force, yeah," Rick replied. "They're trying to get to Mount Weather to rescue a bunch of people who are trapped in a bunker there."

"Mount Weather?" Jane raised her eyebrows. "Isn't that…"

"Yep."

"Wow. Good thing you chose being thrown in jail for a week instead, huh?"

"In retrospect, yeah."

"Did you ask them about the NSA site?"

Dr. Evans nodded. "We spoke briefly. They don't have any information for us, but they're going to give us a vehicle, a few weapons and some extra food and water to help us out."

"What about the Russian plane? Did they see it?"

"It was a Russian plane?" Recker replied as he walked up to them sitting on the sidewalk, concern written on his face. "What the hell would Russians be doing here?"

"That's what we were wondering. We saw it go down on the western edge of the city when we were driving in, but that's it. Did you happen to see any parachutes?"

Recker shook his head. "All we saw was the aircraft going down. The storm was bad enough that there wasn't much else to see. All the more reason for you all to be exceptionally cautious while you're going about your business. I wish I could send some people with you, but we have to get moving and I need everyone with me on this rescue operation."

Rick stood up and held up his hands. "No need, Captain. We appreciate what you've done for us; we'll be fine out there."

"I certainly hope so. If the eggheads you described at Mount Weather can't figure this out, then it seems like it's all on you three."

"No pressure, eh?" Rick chuckled and shook Recker's hand. "Thanks again, Captain. Stay safe out there, okay?"

"You too." Recker turned away, stopped, and turned back. "One more thing, Rick."

"Yes?"

"We've been pulling survivors out of the city off and on since this mess started. We were hounded at the start by some members of MS-13."

"The gang?"

"The very same. They had a strong presence in D.C. and they're still around. We… eliminated enough of them that they left us alone, but they're still very much present here. You need to watch your backs. If a situation seems sketchy, get out. You do not want to mess with these types of scumbags, especially when they don't have anything holding them back anymore."

Rick nodded in appreciation as he looked at Dr. Evans and Jane. "Thank you for the information. We'll watch our backs."

"Make sure you do." With that, Recker turned and walked towards his men, waving his hand in the air and shouting at them to get ready to go.

━━

AS THE BULLDOZERS started up and the group of Capitol Police began moving out, Rick, Dr. Evans and Jane stood next to the squad car and gave them a final wave. Jane opened the back door and sat down inside the vehicle, sighing in relief as she folded up her crutches and put them on the seat next to her. Rick got into the driver's seat while Dr. Evans sat next to him in the front.

"Everyone ready to go?" Rick asked as he started the engine. With only murmurs of affirmation as replies, he put the car into gear and headed toward the bridge ahead, continuing on the path they had been on only a short time before. The road ahead was clear thanks to the work of the officers and their bulldozers, and Rick had no trouble navigating along the path.

As they crossed the Theodore Roosevelt Bridge, Rick spoke to Dr. Evans. "The State Department's just over the bridge, right?"

"The area their main buildings are located in, yes. I'll guide you to the general location, then we'll have to walk around and explore a bit to try and find the exact place."

"Sounds good," Rick said, turning back to focus on his driving. Once they were across the bridge they were faced with a spaghetti nest of roads going in all different directions. Some of the roads—like the one they were on—were clear, while others were covered in remnants of all types of vehicles and debris from collapsed buildings.

From their elevated position coming off of the bridge, Rick could see that many of the large, older government buildings were still intact, though their brick facades were covered in soot and ash. The age and importance of the larger buildings had meant that they had actually suffered the least amount of damage during the event, though they had not survived unscathed.

Parking near many of the structures was forbidden, and lots or garages some distance away were used by a few employees while many used public transportation. This limited the number of exploding vehicles near the buildings and reduced how many were turned into piles of rubble. Many of them also featured outdated gas and electrical systems that Damocles couldn't access simply because they weren't modernized and connected to the web. With no way to reach inside the older buildings and cause leaks and fires, they stood intact, separated by wide streets, sidewalks and medians from buildings burning nearby.

While many buildings survived unscathed, not all were so lucky. From a distance, the trio could see that the Harry S. Truman building had suffered massive amounts of damage, as had several of the buildings to the east. The

National Academy of Sciences just to the south, however, looked as though it had suffered only minor damage from the intense heat of the Truman building's fires, but was otherwise untouched. Trails of smoke drifted up to the north and east in different places, and the pattern of blackened and intact sections of buildings was patchwork and random.

"There," Dr. Evans pointed to a nondescript tan-colored building in the shape of an "H" just ahead of them as Rick followed the curve of the elevated road off of the bridge back down to ground level. "Navy Hill, where the Old Naval Observatory is. That's where we want to go."

"You mean the buildings right in front of us?" Rick slowed down the car, looking for a way to get into the complex.

"Yes, but we'd have to go all the way around to the main entrance if we went in by car, and those streets might still be blocked off. We could park somewhere around here and use the car to boost over the wall."

Rick looked in the rearview mirror at Jane. "You gonna be up for some walking and climbing?"

"Oh yeah, sounds like a blast," she said, nodding with some small amount of sarcasm. "Or I could just stay with the car while you two go see if it's the right place first."

Rick closed his eyes for a moment, contemplating their options before pressing down on the accelerator again. "Doc, tell me where to go to get around to the main entrance. I don't want to split up or risk hurting her legs any more than they are."

Dr. Evans nodded and pointed ahead. "Just keep following this road around until you get to an intersection. I'll tell you where to go from there."

Chapter Thirteen

O utside Ellisville, VA

LATE AFTERNOON IN THE WINTER, when the snow was melting from a particularly warm day, was a pleasant sight in southern Virginia. The trees, mostly stripped of their leaves, rose up from the earth with spindly arms to touch the sky, scraping against the clouds. Fields of grass whose snow had not been protected by shadow lay bare beneath the sun above, a cool breeze rushing over their stalks as they sat in dormancy, awaiting the arrival of spring.

It took just over two hours for Dianne to make her way back home. Not willing to take the main road and surrounding service roads and fields she had used to get into Blacksburg for fear of being caught by her pursuers, she went the long way instead. At the first opportunity she went off-road, taking care not to gun the engine too hard and leave deep tracks in the soft grass and soil. Once she was a few miles away from the city she turned east, making for the general location of a back road that she had frequented some number of years back when she had carted Mark back and forth for piano lessons. Upon hitting the narrow two-lane road she continued east, heading for the general direction of Ellisville, hoping that if her pursuers had gone that way they would already have left the area.

Dianne checked her watch as she neared Ellisville. While it hadn't felt like ten hours since leaving the house before dawn's first light appeared, the clock didn't lie. With a hard deadline of twelve hours given to her by Tina,

Dianne was both relieved that she would be home early and terrified that Jason might have taken a turn for the worse. Risking life and limb only to arrive home and find that she was too late wouldn't be just difficult—it would be devastating for everyone.

As she approached Ellisville proper, Dianne slowed the truck to a halt and shut off the engine, then opened her door and stood up to poke her head up and out. She stayed there for nearly a full minute, listening intently for any sign that the vehicles from Blacksburg might be in the area. The dense tree cover over much of the area surrounding Ellisville would mask any that were only a moderate distance away, but any in town that were still running would be more than audible. With naught but the sound of wind, rustling trees and the ticking of her truck's engine to be heard she sat back down, closed the door and started the engine. "All right, everyone," she said to herself. "I'm coming home."

THE ROAD through Ellisville from the south was more congested than the one heading out to the west towards Blacksburg, forcing Dianne to divert to side streets and alleys more often than not in her attempt to make her way through to the northern side. Most of the southern portion of the small town consisted of residential neighborhoods, and many of the houses had either completely burned to the ground or looked as though someone with a blowtorch had blackened and charred large chunks of the buildings.

When Dianne finally reached the main portion of Ellisville, she felt a sense of familiarity and relief wash over her. There, just a short distance away, stood the grocery store and the town square with the high school and football field a bit farther out. Despite having gotten virtually no sleep over the last few days, she felt a renewed sense of vigor and purpose as she made the final turn onto the road that would lead out to her house. What awaited her there, she didn't know, but she had given the mission her all, nearly sacrificed everything and had still come out on top. That, if nothing else, was at least worth celebrating.

As asphalt turned to gravel and dirt and the road went from smooth to bumpy and rough, Dianne found herself increasing the speed of the truck. Every foot closer she drew to home served to increase her desire to get there even faster. As she made the final turn onto her driveway and approached the closed gate, Dianne felt a lump in her throat. Finally, after what felt like weeks of being away, she was back home.

After getting past the gate and the barriers in the road, she pulled up in front of the house and sat for a moment, staring at it through eyes blurred with fought-back tears. Mark was the first to bound through the front door as it opened, racing across the porch and drive to the truck and wrapping his arms around his mother in a bear hug as she stepped out of the truck.

"Mom! You made it! We were so worried about you, you were taking so long." He looked down at her arm and recoiled a few paces in shock. "Are you hurt?!"

Dianne pulled him back in for another hug and shook her head. "I can't believe I made it back. It's so good to see you. And no, I'm fine, kiddo. It's not my blood."

"Not your... oh." Mark nodded with understanding.

"Dianne? Dianne!" Tina came bounding out of the house next, her thin and wiry body charging across the driveway in a power walk. "What happened to your arm?"

"I'm fine," Dianne replied with a smile. "Not my blood."

"Holy... all right, nevermind." Tina shook her head. "We can talk about it later. Did you find it? Did you find what we needed?"

Dianne smiled at her friend's frankness and priorities and opened the back door, handing her backpack over to Tina. "It's all in here. Plus all the extras I could carry. That place was a gold mine. I'm doing fine, by the way; how are you?"

"Pleasantries later," Tina replied, grabbing the backpack from Dianne. "Jason's at death's door and Sarah's beside herself with him. You and Mark talk and you can fill me in later." With that, Tina hurried back inside and closed the door. Dianne snorted in amusement and looked at her son, who was shaking his head and smiling as he stared at the front of the house.

"She's in a no-nonsense mood, eh?"

Mark nodded. "No kidding."

"Did she and Sarah take good care of you three? Where's your brother and sister?"

"They're upstairs taking a nap; Mrs. Carson has been keeping us busy while you were gone."

"Uh huh." Dianne smiled, then a concerned look crossed her face and she lowered her voice. "How's Mrs. Statler?"

"She's been with Mr. Statler pretty much the whole time you've been gone. Josie talked her into going to the bathroom and getting a drink of water and a few bites to eat, but that was all anyone could do with her. I don't think she's doing well at all."

"Not surprising, given what she's been going through. Do you think I made it back in time to help Jason, or...." Dianne trailed off and Mark shrugged.

"I don't know. Mrs. Carson's kept us too busy to really think about it, but that's been on purpose. Every time I've seen Mr. Statler he's looked bad, but he's been alive."

"Good. I hope he stays that way." Dianne took a deep breath and sighed, rolling her shoulders as she tried to exhale some of the tension that had built up in her body.

"How about you, mom? What happened with your arm?"

Dianne looked down at her red hand and sleeve and grimaced. "Looks pretty bad, doesn't it? There were a few people at the hospital who weren't very friendly."

"Did you kill someone?" Mark's question was asked with innocence and curiosity, reminding Dianne both of Jacob—his younger brother—and of when Mark had been younger, too. Dianne hesitated in answering, wanting to continue to shield him from the harsh new realities before she remembered that he had watched her gun down the man on their farm.

"I... yes. More than one."

Mark looked at her arm, then into her eyes for a long moment before nodding to her decisively. "Good. That means fewer people to try and steal from and kill us." With that, he turned toward the house. "Come on, mom; I'll get some food ready for you while you change."

Dianne watched her eldest son trotting back to the house, rifle on his shoulder, and realized yet again that he was no longer a child. The first one she gave birth to, nurtured, raised and adored had grown up before her eyes and was now a young man. It hadn't been the first time she had that realization, but after being away so much lately she felt like she was seeing everything with a renewed vision. With another sigh, she took her rifle and pistol from the truck and headed toward the house, smiling slightly at the thought of a shower and change of clothes. Mark stood on the porch, looking back at her as he held open the door.

Just as she was about to step onto the porch, she froze. The sound was faint, barely registering as a whisper amongst the trees. It was there, though, a fell wind that signaled something terrible was drawing closer.

"Mark!" Dianne hissed at him and he came back onto the porch, a look of concern on his face.

"What is it?"

"Make sure everyone's inside—check that your brother and sister are really sleeping. Once you check, I want you to get all of the guns and ammo we've stashed throughout the house. Get everything into the living room and start loading any empty magazines, got it?"

"Mom? What's going—"

"I need you to take care of this for me, okay? Get everything ready."

"Ready for what, mom?"

Dianne turned and listened as the sound of distant, angry engines slowly grew louder and more defined.

"Ready for war."

Chapter Fourteen

W ashington, D.C.

"I THINK WE'RE BEING WATCHED."

"Huh?" Dr. Evans looked at Rick as they turned a corner, winding their way through the street and median as they made for the main entrance of Navy Hill. After being a Navy installation for so long—and the observatory being designated as a National Historic Landmark—the name of the place had stuck even after the State Department took over. Dr. Evans understood that a few of the buildings were used for general offices and administrative spaces, but some had received extensive upgrades on the interiors so that they could house classified projects.

"Watched?" Jane parroted back. "All we've done is cross a bridge! How is it we're being watched by anyone?"

"For one thing, we haven't *just* crossed the bridge. We've been driving around for twenty minutes trying to get to the front of this complex and I could swear I've seen movement in a couple of the buildings, following along with us as we've been going."

"Do you think it could be the Russians?" Dr. Evans asked nervously.

"We don't even know if there are any Russians here," Rick replied. "So no, I don't think so. It's either some survivors or possibly MS-13, like Recker was saying."

"Sorry," Jane said from the back seat, "for those of us who aren't intimately familiar with the street gangs of the country, can you fill me in on who or what MS-13 is?"

"Mara Salvatrucha. They came out of Los Angeles in the '80s and spread to a bunch of different cities. As I recall, the D.C. metro area was one place they had a heavy presence, so in the wake of all of this chaos they probably poured into the city proper to start looting whatever they can."

"How do you know about MS-13, Dr. Evans?" Rick asked.

Dr. Evans pointed out the window. "Turn left here. It's sad, actually. One of the programmers I worked with years ago was killed by MS-13 after his kid got tied up with the gang out in LA. I was good friends with him at the time and followed the trial of the eight people involved in the killing."

"Eight?" Jane's eyed widened. "They don't mess around, do they?"

"Nope," Dr. Evans shook his head. "Recker wasn't exaggerating; we need to be very cautious if they're here."

Rick hesitated. "When I was trying to get out of Los Angeles right after the event I had a brief run-in with a gang. I wonder if they were part of MS-13."

"Could be. Or it could have been just a group of people taking advantage of what happened. You're sure you saw someone watching us?"

Rick nodded. "There was movement in some windows and it wasn't just the sun reflecting off of them. Someone's in the area. I have no idea who it is, but we need to be careful. They're going to know exactly where we're going."

"And that," Dr. Evans said," is right here." He pointed off to the left at a closed metal gate standing at the base of a sloping drive that curved up and around into the observatory grounds. Rick eased the car to a stop and put it in park, then grabbed his rifle from the rack behind his head and jumped out of the car. "You two stay here while I check the gate. Dr. Evans, get behind the wheel, would you? Just in case we need to make a fast getaway."

Dr. Evans nodded and climbed out of his seat, jogged around to the driver's side and climbed in. Once he was settled, Rick slowly walked across the street, turning his head and body as he scanned their surroundings. He gave particular attention to the buildings across the street and next to Naval Hill, eying the windows for any signs of movement. None appeared, though, and he pushed forward across the street, gave one final glance around and turned his attention to the gate.

The wrought iron was thick and heavy, and off to the side where the gate met the wall he could see part of the mechanism that would open and close it on the whim of the guard who once sat in a small shack a few feet inside. Rick pushed lightly on the gate with one hand, felt it jiggle a bit, and slung his rifle over his shoulder. He grabbed it firmly with both hands and pulled to the right, nearly gasping in surprise as it creaked, groaned and began to move. Finding the gate unlocked and openable wasn't what he had expected, but the surprise was a welcome one.

Behind him in the car, Dr. Evans watched the gate roll slowly open with great interest and he put the car into drive and turned the wheel. The car crept slowly over the road and median and once the gate was open wide enough for the vehicle to fit through, Rick stepped to the side and waved for Dr. Evans to pull in.

"Keep going," Rick said through the open passenger window. "Pull it up and around out of sight. I'm going to close this and see if I can lock it up, then I'll be up to join you."

Dr. Evans nodded and pulled through, heading up the slope and around the curve before disappearing out of sight. As soon as the car passed by the gate Rick pulled in the opposite direction and soon had it closed again. After looking around on the ground and gate without finding any signs of a way to lock it, Rick ran over to the guard shack and peeked inside. There were a few buttons on a control panel along with a stool, and a small cardboard box beneath the control panel, but no sign of any way to lock the gate even if power had been flowing to both the controls and the gate itself.

"How on earth did they lock it?" Rick muttered to himself as he walked back to the entrance. He glanced over at where the gate met the wall and headed over to look at the mechanism that was sticking through the wall. He crouched down and opened a cover on the mechanism, then grinned as he saw a switch with the symbol of a lock on it. He pressed the switch upward with no small amount of force, feeling something inside the mechanism moving before it finally released, and there was a soft 'thunk' in response. Rick stood up and went back to the gate and pulled on it, then nodded with satisfaction as the gate refused to move even under his best efforts.

"There," he nodded, wiping his hands on his pants. "Someone could still climb over the walls but that should help keep anyone from just wandering through the front door."

Rick turned and headed up the slope, unslinging his rifle and studying the buildings in the complex for the first time since they had arrived. They were plain and nondescript, looking like they would fit in well in any government or university area, with no outward signs that anything secret or secure was housed in them. He rounded the corner to find Dr. Evans and Jane standing outside the squad car, both of them clutching pistols and looking nervously at a far building in the complex as Rick approached. He grew alarmed as he noticed their demeanor and walked swiftly over to them before whispering.

"What's up with you two?"

"Just not really liking sitting around here in the open waiting for you," Jane replied, shifting her weight uncomfortably between her injured legs.

"Let's get inside, then. Dr. Evans? You want to lead the way?"

"Uh, yes. Just, uh… just give me a moment here." Dr. Evans wiped his brow as he looked at the cluster of buildings around them, trying to figure out which one might have housed the individuals and hardware used in the development of Damocles.

As the three individuals stood together looking at the buildings, Rick turned his head as he heard a faint rumble from somewhere far off in the distance. Motioning for Jane and Dr. Evans to stay put, he ran back to the edge of the building and looked down the sloping path leading to the gate where they had entered. From the top of the hill—and thanks to the fact that the trees in the area had all shed their foliage due to the season—he could see a fair distance in all directions. He scanned off to the west, toward the river and saw nothing, then realized that the sound was coming from the east and swung around to look in that direction.

Coming down the road, weaving back and forth in between the rubble and the wrecked vehicles, were six motorcycles, their engines loud and their mufflers nonexistent. They were the type of vehicles that would rumble loudly at six in the morning on a Saturday as their riders prepared for two days of fun and adventure before heading back to work, all while their neighbors secretly wished that something would happen to the motorcycles so that they'd never be awoken by them again.

Instead of the older, leather-clad and long grey-haired passengers that Rick so often associated with the sound, he instead saw young riders, two to a bike, their heads shaved bald or short and their exposed skin covered with ink. None of the riders wore helmets, though they all had makeshift bandoleers with ammunition on the front and rifles and shotguns on the back. Their style of dress seemed to be as much of a statement as it was a uniform—blue jeans and white or grey wife beaters and unzipped jackets that weren't doing much to combat the cold. They pulled close to the Harry S. Truman building across the street and stopped, then the leader got off of his motorcycle, grabbed his shotgun and looked around. "All right! Looks like those assholes decided to finally move on, so they won't be giving us trouble any more. Spread out and get to searching for supplies! We meet back here in twenty!"

"They must be talking about Recker's men. Damn!" Rick hissed to himself as he pressed up against the wall and slunk into a crouch, watching as the dozen riders spread out, weapons in hand, as half of them went towards the Truman building and the other half began meandering towards the general direction of Navy Hill. While the locked gate would slow them down, it wouldn't stop them, and Rick knew that if they wanted to get into the compound they could do so in a very short amount of time. Outmanned and outgunned, Rick racked his brain, furiously trying to figure out what to do before he, Dr. Evans and Jane were spotted.

Author's Notes

January 26, 2017

With episode 9 of Surviving the Fall out of the way, we're in the swing of the final story arcs for both Dianne and Rick and those surrounding them. Buckle up, because in Episode 10 (titled **The Trade of Kings**), we're going to see all-out warfare break out.

In Dianne's case, the war is going to be quite literal. Seeds planted by herself and those around her as well as by the gang will come to fruition, and the harvest is upon both parties. She and her family and friends have some safety in their isolation and through the preparations they've made, but somehow I doubt that what they've done is going to be enough to stop the man in the red shirt.

In Rick's case, he's about to meet some folks that will prove to be deadly, but there may be some allies in the wings waiting to sweep in and offer some temporary salvation. His war is about to become a race against time as Damocles begins to enact some of the late, endgame programs that—if not stopped—could render his, Dr. Evans and Jane's efforts moot.

One of the comments I received earlier in the series when Rick is at Nellis at Las Vegas and turns down the commander's "offer" to head to Mount Weather was something along the lines that Rick wasn't being patriotic and doing his duty to help his country. I thought that was an interesting comment since my viewpoint and priorities on Rick as a character were somewhat different when I wrote him.

Throughout the series, Rick's always been—at his core—a family man. He loves his wife and children and wants to do anything to see them safe and protected. Being stuck on the other side of the country from his family is merely a small bump in the road in his quest to be with them, and he's the type of person who would figure out a way to get back home to his family even if he was stuck on the moon. I would say that his family commitment is one of his most defining features, and his commitment to his country falls behind that. Sure, he wants to help save the world, but he's not going to sacrifice his family to do it.

I really enjoy having that strong, family drive in Rick, and I think it's important that he stayed true to that commitment throughout the series. So what changed in this last episode? Why, when he's so close to home (Northern Virginia is mere hours away from Blacksburg!), is he choosing to abandon the transportation that could take him home and stay with Dr. Evans and Jane to shut down Damocles? The difference to me is that his frame of reference and his knowledge have shifted and changed. Previously, Rick knew next to nothing about Damocles or the escalating danger it posed, and the best way he knew how to take care of his family was to get back to them as soon as possible. Once he discovered that Damocles wasn't going to stop, and the ensuing carnage would certainly kill him and his family both, his knowledge and frame of reference changed and he realized that stopping Damocles was the best way to take care of his family.

Rick wants to do his best. Like anyone else, he screws up. I try my best not to write perfect characters because, well, everyone has flaws. So does Rick. But he's always, no matter what, going to do his best. And I think, at the end of the day, that his best is going to be just enough to make a difference.

(Oh, and besides, if he had gone to Mount Weather, he would have gotten locked inside with the rest of the people there!)

If you enjoyed this episode of Surviving the Fall or if you *didn't* like some-thing—I'd love to hear about it. You can drop me an email or send me a message or leave a comment on Facebook. You can also sign up for my newsletter where I announce new book releases and other cool stuff a few times a month.

Answering emails and messages from my readers is the highlight of my day and every single time I get an email from someone saying how much they enjoyed reading a story it makes that day so much brighter and better.

Thank you so very much for reading my books. Seriously, thank you from the bottom of my heart. I put an enormous amount of effort into the writing and all of the related processes and there's nothing better than knowing that so many people are enjoying my stories.

All the best,
  Mike

Book 10 - The Trade of Kings

Preface

Last time, on Surviving the Fall....

After arriving in Blacksburg, Dianne had to dodge a pair of pursuers that she suspected were connected to the group at the gas station. Once she reached the Long-Term Acute Care facility in the city she had to leave her truck and go in on foot where she found that an unimaginable massacre had taken place. Her problems quickly compounded with the arrival of a dozen men who hunted her through the facility, though she was able to escape—killing a few of them along the way—and make her way home with the medicine needed to cure Jason's infection. Fearing that she was followed, though, she and the others made ready for a confrontation that she was sure wouldn't take long to occur.

In Washington, Rick, Jane and Dr. Evans were making their way forward into the city, searching for the command and control center for Damocles in an effort to crack open the systems and find a way to shut the weapon down. Before they could cross the river, though, they ran into a group of Capitol Police who were moving south toward Mount Weather. Though initially suspicious of the intentions of Rick's group, the officers provided more than a little bit of assistance before moving on to try and free the group trapped in the bunker. Rick's group continued deeper into the city, heading for the old Naval Observatory, not knowing that a group of MS-13 gang members were nearby, along with four mysterious strangers from far, far away.

And now, Surviving the Fall Episode 10.

Chapter One

The Waters' Homestead
Outside Ellisville, VA

THE FIRST ATTACK came three days later.

After Dianne arrived with the much-needed medication for Jason, she heard the distant sound of vehicles roaring closer and was positive that they would be arriving at her home at any moment. Hours ticked by as she and Mark sat inside near the windows, watching and listening as they tracked the vehicle locations. They had to make do with audio cues only, though, since none of the vehicles were visible through the dense rows of trees surrounding the property. Based on everything they heard, it sounded like the cars had split up and were combing the surrounding area, a fact that did not sit well with Dianne.

For three days she, Mark, Tina and—to some extent, Sarah—planned out what they would do if and when the gang ever arrived at their doorstep. Weapons were cleaned, checked and re-checked, vital supplies were hastily brought into the basement and tunnel from the barns and the driveway, house and outbuildings were further reinforced to hopefully prevent anyone from breaking in. It was the early afternoon of the third day that Dianne, Tina and Mark sat out on the front porch together, all of them armed with pistols and rifles. They spoke in low voices, listening to the sound of the distant vehicles fading in and out of earshot.

"Maybe they're not coming." Tina Carson took a deep slurp from her coffee cup before setting it down on the ground and idly rubbing at the handle of her pistol. "Maybe they're just racing or something."

Dianne looked at Tina with a tired expression and sighed. "You know that's not true. They're searching for us."

"I don't see why it's so hard for them to find us," she replied. "We're right off the side road leading into town."

"There are a lot of side roads. They've been going virtually nonstop for three days, though. At some point they're going to start searching around here."

"You did kind of set them off, mom, what with killing a few of them and rescuing Mrs. Carson and destroying their camp." Mark looked at her and smiled as Dianne rolled her eyes.

"I'm pretty sure that if these guys had gotten Tina here in good light they would have thrown her out of the camp—ow! Hey!" Dianne laughed as Tina punched her in the arm, growling good-naturedly at the comment.

"Watch it, Waters! Some of that stuff you brought back'll give you quite the runs if someone happens to slip it into your coffee."

Dianne chuckled and then sighed, staring down at her empty cup. "I wish I had put coffee on the list. Blacksburg had a lot of buildings still intact and no one seemed to be there."

The door behind them creaked open and they heard the shuffle of feet before another voice replied, sounding as though the person behind it was fighting to talk over an immense amount of pain. "Just you wait till I'm all recovered and we'll head out there and bring back all the coffee we need. Along with everything else."

Dianne turned, stood up and took Jason's right arm, guiding him to a chair out on the porch. On his left was Jacob, with Josie trailing behind. "Jason!" Dianne shook her head at him. "You shouldn't be up and about. Should he?" She looked at Tina, who shrugged her shoulders.

"Eh. Let him get out. He needs the fresh air." Though her words and demeanor were casual, Mark noticed that Tina's eyes were sharply trained on Jason's every move, watching him as he went across the porch and sat down on a nearby chair.

"Fwah. Thanks, you three." He smiled at Jacob, Josie and Dianne.

"How's the pain?" Tina asked, still with an air of slight disinterest. "Feeling any better than it was this morning?"

"It is, yes." Jason nodded. "You've been marvelous."

"Nothing to it," Tina replied as she pointed at Dianne. "She did all the hard work."

"You did a wonderful job, dear." Jason smiled at Dianne and she patted him on the arm as she sat down on the porch next to his chair.

"I'm afraid that I stirred up more trouble than we need in doing it, though."

"What's that all about, now?" Jason tried to turn in his seat but winced and clutched at his wound. "I've been so out of it with all the drug's pumping through me that I feel like I've missed most of what you've all been talking about."

"Mom killed three or more of the gang who followed her into Blacksburg," Mark replied before anyone else could, and his brother and sister stood quietly nearby, enraptured yet again by the summation of their mother's activities. "That plus you and her rescuing Mrs. Carson set them off. Now they're combing the area trying to find us."

"You know that for certain?" Jason raised an eyebrow at Dianne.

"Logical assumption," she shrugged. "We've been hearing engines on and off for three days, driving all over the place. They were chasing me out of Blacksburg and they know we're somewhere east of their gas station compound based on the direction we drove when we got Tina back. It doesn't take a rocket scientist to put all of that together."

"Hm." Jason frowned, furrowed his brow and scratched at his chin. Even that slight movement made him wince. "Then we should be getting ready for an attack, shouldn't we?"

"We are, old man." Tina replied with a slight smile. "While you've been lazing about we've been getting everything ready."

"Well, come on then. Fill an old man in on what you've been doing."

Dianne looked at Tina. "You suggested it, you get to show him what we've been getting up to."

Tina gave an exaggerated groan as she stood to her feet. She walked across the porch and held out a hand to Jason, helping him out of the chair and toward the door. Dianne and Mark got up as well, and together with Jacob and Josie they started following Tina and Jason inside. Before they got to the door, though, Sarah was at it, pulling it open with her face as white as a sheet.

"Sarah?" Dianne looked at her in concern. "What's going on?" Sarah's response was whispered and frantic, full of fear that turned Dianne's blood to ice.

"There's someone out back, down by the lake."

Chapter Two

_____

W ashington, D.C.

"ARE you certain the facility was clear? There were more buildings to check."

Oles Belov, technician and all-around genius, sighed in exasperation as he turned to look at the man speaking to him, deliberately not calling him by any rank or honorific. "Ostap. You and Carl are the guns. Jacob and I are the brains. If we say that the facility was clear, it was clear, understand?"

Spetsnaz officer and expedition leader Ostap Isayev grunted and picked up his pace to catch up with his companion, a fellow Spetsnaz officer by the name of Carl Aliyev. "Do you think they're lying?" He asks the question in a hushed tone so that the pair of technicians won't overhear.

"Why would they lie?" Carl raised an eyebrow at Ostap. "You're far too suspicious. If they said it was clear, then it's clear."

"Command told us that was the most likely location of the control room, though."

Carl shrugged. "Since when has command ever been accurate about anything like that? We have two more locations to check so don't worry about it. Why are you acting so odd anyway, Ostap? You've been jittery since we landed."

Ostap glanced up at the towering buildings around them, adjusting his gloved grip on his AK-47. "I don't like this place one bit. I can't shake the feeling that there's someone here just… watching us."

"Thermals showed that the only people here are those thugs driving around." Carl grinned and slapped his friend on the back. "Are you scared of some American criminals, Ostap?"

"Hey." The voice came from Jacob Yermakov, the second technician. He and Oles had caught up with Ostap and Carl. "Shouldn't we be quiet? What if there are people nearby? The Americans might get a little bit agitated if they hear four Russians with weapons talking loudly in the streets of their capital."

"Hm." Ostap grunted and nodded. "Yes. We should. How much longer to the next facility?"

"A couple hours, probably, if we don't stop."

"Then we will not stop."

———

"MOTORBIKES. THERE, ON THE ROAD."

"The Americans usually call them motorcycles, Ostap."

Commander Ostap turned and glared at the technician. "If I wanted to know the correct terminology then I'd go find someone less annoying than you. Now shut up and let us focus!" The words came out in a hissing stream, and Oles backed up, raising his hands and turning his head away in surrender. Jacob shrugged and rolled his eyes as Oles glanced at him, and together the pair of technicians sat down on the sidewalk a few feet away.

"How many do you count?" Carl had a pair of binoculars up to his eyes, studying the windows of the nearby buildings for any signs of movement. Ostap still had his gaze fixated on a location a block and a half down the street, where a collection of motorcycles were sitting in the middle of the road. Their engines made no sound and no one appeared to be nearby, but Ostap could see that the bodies of the motorcycles were red-hot in the thermal scope, an indication that they had only recently been turned off.

"Seven in the street, but there could be more that we can't see from this position. Anyone in the buildings?"

"*Nyet*. Buildings are clear, but this angle is terrible. We need elevation."

"The second site is just past those bikes, off to the right in those buildings on the hill. That's the priority."

"Can we go around?"

"No." Ostap shook his head. "There's a collapse across the street to the north, and my guess is that most of that group went to the south—no, wait." Ostap pulled out his own pair of binoculars and dropped into a crouch. "I see them. A trio, in the complex where we need to go."

"Only three? Should be easy."

"Indeed. Two men, one woman. One of the men is older, and they all have just basic rifles."

Behind the two Spetsnaz officers, the technicians had their binoculars out and were focusing in on the trio outside the buildings at the facility on the hill. While they tried to locate the three individuals, Ostap and Carl were busy unslinging their rifles and adjusting their scopes. There was no verbal communication between the pair. After years of working independently and together on countless missions requiring absolute silence and stealth, both men were well-versed in performing their duties in complete silence. The technicians, however, were another matter.

"What are they looking at?" Oles spoke to Jacob as they knelt a few feet behind the Spetsnaz officers.

"No idea. They look like they're expecting trouble, though." Jacob adjusted the zoom and focus on his binoculars, trying to get a clearer view of the trio. After a few seconds, he gasped and furiously tapped Oles on the shoulder.

"That older one, with the glasses standing behind the other two; don't you recognize him?"

Oles took a few more seconds to zoom in closer, then he gasped as well. "Dr. Michael Evans?! No… it can't be!"

While the two soldiers had been doing their level best to ignore the furious whispering going on behind them, the muted shouts of the two men were too much for Ostap. He turned and snapped at the pair. "What the hell are you two going on about?"

As Ostap spoke, Oles realized that Carl's rifle was pointed at the three people on the hill. He lunged forward, knocking the rifle to the side, then turned to Ostap. "You can't shoot them! One of them is Dr. Evans!"

"Who is that, and why should I give a damn?" Carl spat at Oles as he retrieved his fallen rifle.

Oles groaned, removing his cap and running his fingers through his greasy hair. "He's a prominent computer scientist; he actually designed the precursor to Damocles!"

Carl was just about to level his sight on the three when Ostap held out a hand to stop him. The lead Spetsnaz officer narrowed his eyes at Oles, studying the technician closely. "Are you certain?"

"Positive!"

"Then who are the other two?"

"I've no idea!" Oles was still nearly shouting, and Jacob had to put a hand on his comrade's shoulder to help calm him down. "But if Dr. Michael Evans is here, then that can only mean that he's searching for a way to stop Damocles, too! I'll bet anything that those two are helping him."

"Why would the U.S. government send a lone scientist with a pair of what look like civilians all by themselves into a place like this to search for a way to shut down their own creation?"

"You're assuming, of course, that the U.S. government didn't intend for all this to happen." Carl inserted himself into the conversation and Jacob rolled his eyes.

"Please. Not even they are stupid enough to… well, perhaps. But they still wouldn't do it."

Ostap sighed heavily and rubbed his eyes. Not even years of training and practice could properly prepare him for such a mission, especially when he was having to play babysitter to a pair of eggheads who seemed fragile enough to crack under the slightest pressure. "What do you want to do about it, then? Walk up and say hello to them, introduce ourselves and offer to help them?"

"Is that an option?" Oles' voice was dead serious, and Ostap gave him a long glare until the technician finally turned away. The four sat there for a moment, each of them lost in their own thoughts, until Carl happened to turn and glance back at the hill. He quickly sat back up on his knees and grabbed his binoculars before tapping wildly at Ostap's knee.

"Look. On the edge of the compound. They've got company."

Ostap peered out toward the compound that he was supposed to be guiding the technicians toward. In addition to the trio inside, there were half a dozen individuals lurking near the close side of the wall. Each of them wore blue jeans and leather jackets and wielded rifles and pistols along with pipes and crowbars. They cut imposing figures and looked as though they were aware of the trio inside the compound. The three individuals— including Dr. Evans—seemed oblivious to the presence of the other people as they were still focused on watching something across the street.

After watching everyone down the road closely for just a few more seconds, Ostap put everything together and realized precisely what was going on. This realization came just a few seconds before the shooting started.

Chapter Three

The Waters' Homestead
Outside Ellisville, VA

DIANNE STOOD on the porch with the rest of the group, frozen by Sarah's words for a few seconds before Mark put his hand on her arm. "Mom?" His touch and the single word spurred her to action, and she began giving hasty instructions to the rest of the group, speaking in a low tone as she glanced around at the woods in front of the house.

"Mark, get upstairs and get ready with the rifle like we talked about. Stay in touch by radio and let me know what you see, okay? Jacob and Josie, I want you two in the basement with Tina, Jason and Sarah."

"Oh like hell I'm going in that basement," Tina replied. The wrinkles on her face deepened as she pulled back her lips into a sneer. "Sarah, you and Jason get down there and watch over the kids. I'm going to take a few of these assholes out myself."

"Easy, Tina; we don't know if whoever's out there is with the gang. But that's still a good idea." Dianne nodded to Sarah in confirmation before Jason, Sarah, Jacob and Josie hurried inside and headed down the stairs, picking up a few weapons and ammunition along the way.

"That's bull and you know it," Tina grumbled at Dianne. "There's no way someone's here without having some sort of nefarious motive."

"I know," replied Dianne. "So let's go out and greet them. Mark? Upstairs, now. Stay hidden and tell me what you see. Tina and I are going to stay around the side of the house until you give me a headcount and description of who's out there."

"Got it, Mom." Mark nodded and bounded through the door, racing upstairs with his rifle in hand. Dianne and Tina stood on the front porch near the edge of the house, scanning the area in front for signs of movement, not wanting to show themselves out back until they knew what to expect. It only took a moment for Mark's voice to come through on the radio.

"Mom?"

"What do you see, Mark?"

"Two guys in blue jeans, one wearing a blue jacket and the other in a black jacket. They're down by the barn where you... where you shot that guy who was trying to break in."

"Are they trying to break in?"

"I'm not sure. They're just kind of... standing around?"

"Are they looking at the house?"

"Not really."

"Okay, good. Keep watching them. Tell me if anything changes." Dianne turned to Tina. "Go around to the other side of the house and keep your eyes open. I'm going to the back to see what these idiots are trying to do."

"Will do." Tina hurried off to the other side of the house. Dianne, meanwhile, took a deep breath and walked around the side she was closest to, keeping her rifle at the ready and continuing to scan the trees as she went. With no signs of movement near the house, Dianne eased around the corner near the porch and raised her rifle to look through the scope at the lake and barns at the other end of the property. It took her a second to locate the two men that Mark had described, but once she did she saw that they were just as he had described.

They stood in front of one of the larger barns, looking around as they pawed through a large duffle bag held by the one in the blue jacket. After a moment the one in the black jacket pulled out a tool that looked like a pair of gardening loppers. The man in the black jacket held the tool near the lock to the shed and Dianne realized that it was actually a pair of bolt-cutters, and that they were trying to cut through.

"Seriously?" Dianne whispered to herself in frustration as she tried to decide what to do. She wasn't about to negotiate with the men—even if they weren't with the gang, she had gone through enough talking to last a lifetime. Neither of the two options she saw open to her made her happy. The first, giving off a warning shot and trying to scare them off, was a bad idea because they might return fire or come back later. The second, to shoot them at a distance and kill them, seemed overly cold-hearted to her. *Cold-hearted?* She thought to herself, *Really? Cold-hearted? I've killed four people so far. I think we're beyond cold-hearted.*

As Dianne sighted in on the two men, getting ready to fire on them before they broke through the lock, a shot rang out from the far side of the house. Before she could pull back from the scope she saw the man in the black jacket drop the bolt-cutters and heard his distant cry of pain. He dropped to one knee while his partner whirled around, trying to trace the direction the shot came from as the sound echoed across the fields and trees.

Dianne started to move back around the house to both get into cover and figure out where the shot came from when a second one rang out, sending the already-kneeling man toppling over to the ground. Blood and gore was painted onto his companion and part of the front of the barn, and Dianne could see through her scope that part of his head and skull had been blown away. A second later, on the radio, Tina's voice came through clear and harsh. "One down, one to go. You gonna do any shooting or what?"

"Tina? What are you—"

"Shoot more and talk less, girl, or else that other one's going to get away and warn his friends!" Dianne kept her sights trained on the fallen man for another moment before moving to look at his companion. The second, uninjured man was stumbling back, a pistol having appeared in his hand. He looked around frantically, trying to place the origin of the gunfire while simultaneously checking to see if his friend was alive or not.

Tina's action rendered Dianne's indecision moot and Dianne sighted in on the man, firing off a pair of shots that both just barely missed him. The slight whizz of the passing projectiles and the soggy *thunk* as they embedded in the wood of the barn behind him sent him into a panic, and he turned tail and ran for the woods. A third shot from Dianne's rifle hit home, though, striking him in the center of his back and barely missing his spine.

The man screamed in pain and dropped his pistol, nearly collapsing to the ground in the process. He willed himself to keep moving though, the image of his dead companion still fresh in his mind. Dianne and Tina both ran around to the back porch and looked at each other. "Stay here," Dianne said, "and keep watch with Mark. I'm going to go take care of him."

"Make it snappy before he gets away." Tina's expression was grim as she looked through her scope at the body of the first man.

Dianne nodded and ran down the hill toward the barns, slowing down once she reached the buildings so that she could check alongside them for enemies before continuing forward. She didn't bother to look at the corpse lying on the ground, knowing that Tina and Mark were watching her from afar and would have alerted her if the man was somehow still alive. Her eyes were wide as she searched around the buildings and edge of the woods at the back side of the property, looking for any sign of the man in the blue jacket.

After several minutes of searching, the only signs she found of the second man were several drops of bright red blood scattered across a pile of leaves behind the farthest barn at the edge of the woods. The dry underbrush out into the woods appeared as though someone had crashed through it, but although Dianne stood still for a few minutes watching and listening, she located no trace of the man in the blue jacket. She was debating heading off into the woods to try and find the man when she heard a quiet voice over her radio.

"Dianne? I'm coming up behind you." The crunch of leaves came a few seconds later as Dianne slowly walked behind the barn, her head on a swivel as she kept a close eye on her surroundings. "There you are. What are you doing back here?"

Dianne, still crouched near the drops of blood, pointed to them. "He's hurt something fierce but he still managed to get away."

"Think we should go after him?"

Dianne shook her head slowly. "As much as I want to… no. He could have gone anywhere. Besides, if there were two of them with weapons, I'm sure there are more, and they're going to be pissed that we just killed one of their friends." Dianne glanced up at Tina. "Any reason why you opened fire without talking to me first?"

Tina snorted, "Didn't realize I needed your permission, but if you really want to know, come back over here." She led Dianne back to the man with the black jacket and rolled the body over. "Kind of hard to see now with his face having a new hole in it and everything, but I recognized him from the gas station. He was one of the ones working there; one of the gang."

Dianne's prior indecision, some of which had lingered even after she and Tina had shot the men, completely evaporated. A chill ran down her back and she squared her shoulders as she stood up and looked at the barn. "Good riddance to him, then. Let's get a couple of shovels and get the body underground before rigor sets in."

"What about the other one?" Tina replied. "If he lives, he's going to tell the others about us."

"Yes," Dianne nodded, "he will. And we'll be ready for them."

Chapter Four

Washington, D.C.

"RICK?" Jane crouched next to Rick at the edge of the building nearest the entrance to the compound. "Where did the rest of that group go?"

"No clue. They were walking this way, then they split up and went in all different directions."

"What I want to know," Dr. Evans said, standing behind Jane and Rick, "is why the ones across the street are just milling around. Do you think they spotted us?"

"Anything's possible," Rick replied. "The real question, though, is what we should do. We're stuck here until they decide to move on."

"*If* they move on." Dr. Evans took half a step out from behind the building, trying to get a better eye on the people across the street, when the snap of shattering brick near his head was immediately followed by the crack of a rifle firing from very, very close range.

Shards of brick from the wall of the building exploded outward and showered the trio, and they all dropped low to the ground and pulled back behind the building. As they moved, though, several more shots rang out, and they heard the nearby shouts and jeers of a group of gang members that had snuck around the compound and were just outside the nearby wall. Those on the ground nearby had no angle to shoot the trio, but as Rick took a quick peek back out across the street, he saw that the ones who had been merely standing around were crouched behind cover, their rifles aimed in the direction of the compound.

"Dammit!" Rick cursed under his breath and pulled back behind the building. "They must have seen us when they pulled up. The few across the street are trying to keep us pinned down, and I bet they're just trying to buy time for the ones close by to get inside."

"How many of them are close by?" Jane started to move to peek out as well, but a cluster of bullets hitting the edge of the wall drove her back.

"I only saw a few of them across the street. I think the bulk of them are right on top of us."

"Should we get inside?" Dr. Evans nervously adjusted his grip on one of the rifles the police had given to them.

"Might not be a bad idea," Rick nodded. "Try to get somewhere defensible and hope they give up and leave. We need to get all the equipment from the car in, though. If they take our supplies or ammo, we're screwed."

"How long do we—" Jane started to ask. The clatter of the metal front gate echoed up the drive, though, answering her question before she could finish it. Rick took a deep breath and peeked out at the entrance again, seeing that three men were struggling to climb over the tall gate and enter the compound. Two of them bore long pipes and the third had a rifle slung over his back, though none of them were athletic enough to actually make it over the gate with any ease or grace. The scene would have been humorous had the men's faces not clearly been covered with the desire to do grievous harm to Rick, Jane and Dr. Evans.

"Let's go." Rick pushed Jane and Dr. Evans toward the car and they quickly loaded up with all of their bags of supplies, ammunition and spare weapons. Looking around the compound, Rick tried to decide which building to enter, but the shouts of joy from the men near the gate told him that they had run out of time and would have to settle for whatever was closest. "This way!" Rick ran for the entrance to the nearest building and, finding it unlocked, stepped inside and used his foot to keep the door open while Jane and Dr. Evans followed behind him. Dr. Evans was running full-tilt while Jane was limping heavily, still struggling with her leg injury but fighting through the pain.

The building looked like a plain—if somewhat dated—government building with faux tile floors, barren walls and rows of doors that led to a variety of rooms. Most of the doors were closed, though a few had clearly been left open during the evacuation that sent both government and civilian workers out of the city. Why the building hadn't been locked was a mystery to Rick, considering how most of the open rooms contained expensive-looking equipment and supplies, but it wasn't a mystery he had time to dwell on. The first of the gang members had finally made it over the gate and would likely be opening it for the rest of their comrades, and Rick knew that his group had only minutes at best to find an elevated, defensible position.

"Look for stairs!" Rick called out to Jane and Dr. Evans, both of whom were ahead of him. The heavy bags weighed him down and he took in deep, gasping breaths of air, fighting against both the load he was carrying and his general state of exhaustion.

"Over here, quick!" Dr. Evans poked his head out from a doorway ahead of Rick. Rounding the corner, Rick saw a wide flight of stairs leading both up and down. Jane was already on the next landing up, moving with purpose despite her injury and everything she was carrying. Rick motioned for Dr. Evans to go after her before releasing the hook on the back of the door that was holding it open. He caught it before it slammed shut and slowly closed it before turning and heading up the stairs after Dr. Evans.

The second floor of the building had all of the doors in the hall opened, and as Rick walked along he could see that the majority of them appeared to be conference rooms or shared work spaces. The layout of the larger rooms reminded him of classrooms in college, and he wondered what they were used for before the State Department took over the complex from the Navy.

"Rick, down here." Jane's whispered voice echoed down the hall and Rick followed it until he reached a large room with several rows of windows looking out into the center of the compound. Dr. Evans and Jane had already dropped most of their supplies on the floor and were getting their rifles out and at the ready. Rick did the same, and the three each took up a post at a separate window in the room and peered out at the scene below.

The three gang members that had been trying to get over the gate had been successful, both at getting over it, as well as opening it for their friends. A cluster of men and a couple of women were standing and walking around the vehicle parked in the middle of the compound. They were talking and shouting at each other, and though it was hard to make out what they were saying through the mix of English and Spanish, it quickly became apparent that they weren't sure what to do with the vehicle.

After a moment of arguing amongst the group, a man and woman rounded the corner of the far building. Each of them wore a large black jacket and jeans, and their tattoos and hairstyles were more elaborate than any of the others. The immediate cessation of the arguments between the gang members at the mere sight of the pair instantly drew Rick's attention, and he focused on them as the man began to speak.

"Where are they?" Rick had to press his ear against the glass to hear the man, and he hoped that the thick curtains around the sides of the windows would provide enough concealment to keep him from being spotted.

"Dunno. Took us forever to get over that gate." The man spoke in English, but with a heavy accent.

"Did you search the buildings?" The man stepped up near the car and looked in through the windows at the empty seats.

"Not yet; we were going to search the car first and—"

The relative calmness that the apparent leader of the gang had been demonstrating evaporated. Faster than Rick's eyes could follow, the man whipped out a small collapsible baton from his back pocket and began flailing about with it, striking at everyone he could reach while he screamed at them in Spanish. Near the end of his rant, as the gang members were still running around the car, trying to escape his wrath, he stood still, breathing heavily as he shouted at them. "Find them! This thing's completely empty! If they had anything on them, they took it with them, so go! GO!"

He waved the baton menacingly and the gang scattered, forming into small groups as they spread out through the compound. The woman who had walked in with the leader strode up next to him and wrapped an arm around him, which he shrugged off before turning his eye to the windows on the buildings in the compound. His eyes moved quickly, scanning them for signs of life and movement, and Rick barely pulled his head down below the windowsill before the man looked in his direction.

"Oye! They're up there! Get after them!" The man's shout was loud and forceful, and even though Rick couldn't see what was going on, his heart sank as he saw the curtain next to him jittering back and forth. He glanced over at Jane and Dr. Evans, both of whom had ducked out of sight far earlier, and shook his head at them. With their position compromised, their day was about to get much, much worse.

Chapter Five

The Waters' Homestead
Outside Ellisville, VA

THE EARLY AFTERNOON turned into the early evening before Dianne and Tina finished burying the body of the man in the black jacket in a shallow grave. They put him next to the body of the first man Dianne had killed, digging as deep as they could through the cold earth filled with rocks and tree roots. After they finished, they put the shovels away and checked on the animals again. The barns smelled awful and the animals were restless from spending so much time indoors, but Dianne topped off their food and water and whispered words of encouragement to them. While they hadn't played an integral part in the survival of her family thus far, she knew that she had to keep them safe through whatever storms might come, as they would be vital for sustaining a long-term supply of food.

The evening shadows were growing long as Dianne and Tina trudged up onto the back porch. Dianne raised her hand to knock on the wooden cover but someone inside was already unlocking it from the inside. Dianne and Tina stood back as it swung open to reveal Sarah looking out at them. She wore a mask of concern on her face, though she appeared in better spirits than she had in days, and for good reason since Jason was still looking better and better.

"You two okay?"

"Yep, we're good." Dianne nodded as she and Tina stepped inside and took off their shoes. "We buried one but the other got away."

"Mark said you nailed him in the back." The reply came not from Sarah, but from Jason, who was sitting up on the couch, looking alert as he worked on disassembling and cleaning a semiautomatic pistol. "I'm surprised he got away."

"Must not have hit any vital organs." Dianne raised an eyebrow at Jason. "Aren't you supposed to be in the basement with Jacob and Josie?"

Jason motioned toward the ceiling with an upward nod of his head. "After things died down out there I had them go up and stay with Mark. Figured it was better than all of us sitting around down there with nothing going on. More eyes and ears keeping watch, you know?"

"Good thought." Dianne shrugged off her coat. "You been keeping an eye on the cameras?"

"I have," Sarah replied, "but there's been nothing on them except you two out there."

Dianne sighed heavily as she pulled a chair from the dining room into the living room and sat down in it. Her back, legs and arms all ached from the work she and Tina had put in, and she wanted nothing more than to crawl into bed and fall asleep. The appearance of the two men had, unfortunately, confirmed some of her worst fears, and taking a breather was out the window until she felt like the situation was resolved.

"I want two people on each watch shift tonight," Dianne finally said. "One splitting their time between windows and the cameras and one dedicated to the windows."

"You expecting something bad to happen, Dianne?" Jason looked up at her.

"Yeah. Yeah, I am." Dianne didn't elaborate, but as a somber mood set in across the room, Dianne couldn't help thinking about the possibilities of what might happen next. If the man in the blue jacket survived—which she suspected he did—then he would undoubtedly have made contact with his friends, and they would be on the way to the farm at that very moment. Dianne desperately wanted to do something to prepare for the probable arrival of the group from the gas station, but they had spent every waking moment of the prior three days preparing and there was nothing left to do but sit, watch and wait.

And wait they did. Minutes ticked by slowly as the shadows outside grew longer and the moon began to trade places with the sun in the sky. The chatter of birdsong gave way to the creak and the whistle and the chirp of insects, along with the occasional hoot of a barn owl in search of a meal on a cold night. Dianne and Jason took the first watch, with Jason sitting near the back door looking through a crack in the wood down at the outbuildings with the tablet balanced on his lap. Dianne, meanwhile, meandered slowly through the rooms upstairs, slipping in and out of each bedroom to peer through the windows. She spent no more than half a minute at most at each window, scanning for signs of movement in the trees before moving on to the next spot. Sarah, Tina and the children all slept restlessly while she patrolled, and she was fairly certain that Mark wasn't asleep at all.

It was just after ten o'clock, right as Dianne was feeling drowsy enough that she was about to wake Mark and have him and Tina take the next shift, when the radio on her hip crackled softly. She plucked it from her belt and spoke quietly into it, glancing at Tina sleeping a few feet away.

"You got something?"

"Get down here *right now*, Dianne." Jason's voice had an indescribable edge to it, and the emphasis he put on the words made Dianne's blood run cold. She bolted from the room and took the stairs three at a time, nearly crashing into the kitchen table as she raced through and into the living room. Jason sat there, staring at the tablet on his lap.

"What is it?!" She whispered at him, still feeling her hairs standing on end.

"Here." He held out the tablet to her and she took it. The view was of the western side of the property, just off of the house. Thanks to the infrared view from the cameras she could see the fuzzy, green shapes of multiple individuals making their way through the trees. They were at least fifteen or twenty in number, spread throughout the trees, and they appeared to be maneuvering into a position where they could surround the house on the western side and to the south, around and beyond the driveway.

Dianne stared at the men for several seconds before looking back up at Jason. "We have to deal with this quickly, before they can get into position to fire on us from multiple directions."

"There's a view from the upstairs windows on their positions, right?"

"Yep. I'm going to get Tina and Sarah up. You need to get in the basement with Jacob and Josie, okay?"

"But I can—"

"Don't argue with me, Jason. You're still having enough mobility problems that I don't want you trying to get up and down the stairs and trying to move around quickly." She stood up and started heading back toward the front of the house. "I'm going to get the kids down to you and then we're going to open fire on these assholes. If something goes wrong, use the tunnel in the basement and get them out into the woods, okay? Get as far away as you possibly can."

"Dianne…" Jason hesitated, considered arguing with her again, then thought better of it. "Fine. I'll head down now. Try to keep me posted if things start getting ugly though, okay?"

Dianne reached down to her two-way radio and pressed a button on the front, then slid a small switch to one side. "There. It's in open mode now. You'll hear everything we say." With that, Dianne was gone, turning the corner to run back to the front of the house, up the stairs and straight to Tina and Sarah's sides. It took just a few seconds to rouse them and the children, and in less than a minute from when Dianne first heard Jason's news,

Jacob and Josie were in the basement, Mark had retrieved weapons for himself and Sarah and the four of them stood at the edges of the upper windows in the house, quietly calling out what they could see.

The scene was largely the same as what Dianne had watched on the tablet from the security cameras, except it was in shades of black and white with a hint of color instead of blurry green. Multiple figures slowly walked all throughout the woods on the west and south side of the house. A pair of them stood in the driveway, gesturing at both each other and the nail-filled boards that lay across the dirt and gravel. The lack of a vehicle puzzled Dianne until she realized that they had likely held off on bringing in anything loud until they were in position.

"We've got the element of surprise." Dianne whispered to Tina as she pointed at the men in the driveway. "I don't think they know that we know they're here."

"Looks like they're about to move the nail boards. Probably to bring in a truck or something." Tina snorted. "I think they need to get a rude awakening."

Dianne smiled coldly. "Yes, they do." She reached for the window latch and lifted it gently, then began turning the crank on the window. The house had been built with crank-style windows in all of the rooms, and she was glad that Rick had kept them well-oiled despite how little they were used. The window opened quietly with the tiniest hint of a *snap* as the stuck-together paint separated. Next to Dianne, Tina opened the adjacent window. Once both of the windows were open, the women took aim at the men in the driveway with their rifles.

"Ready?" Dianne whispered faintly.

"Let's get this party started," Tina replied with growl.

Chapter Six

Washington, D.C.

ON ANY DAY before the event, the sight of four Russians—all dressed in black and two armed to the teeth with a variety of weapons—would have sent Washington into a lockdown. Amid the smoke and smoldering ruins of buildings that weren't fortunate enough to escape from being burned from the inside out, though, the sight made more sense. Marginally, at least.

The two Spetsnaz officers led the charge down the sidewalk, keeping their pace at a fast jog. Even weighted down as they were with their weapons and supplies, they could have easily tripled their speed, but the pair of technicians were the weak link when it came to getting around. Oles and Jacob lagged several paces back, breathing hard and holding their sides as they struggled to keep up with Ostap and Carl.

The route Ostap had chosen took them the long way around to the far north of the compound, crossing through the collapsed buildings that he had earlier dismissed as a possible route. With the three individuals inside the compound now a target for saving rather than killing, Ostap determined that they needed to get around the back side of the compound so that they could catch the group of enemies with a frontal assault and—hopefully—defend Dr. Evans as well as the pair with him.

"I can't believe you're listening to that egghead." Carl spat as he spoke, turning his head slightly to give a nasty glare at the two technicians who were hurrying to keep up with the commandos.

"As much as I'd like to kill everyone and let someone else sort it all out, we have our orders. If this Dr. Evans is who they claim he is, he could be the key to ensuring our success, both here and... later."

"Don't you think it's strange, him being here in the same city at the same time as we are? It feels like too much of a coincidence for me."

"I don't believe in coincidences." Ostap ran his tongue across his teeth. "Which is why we're going to be very, very cautious."

Carl rolled his eyes but said nothing. While he and Ostap held the same rank, the small size and special nature of the mission meant that Ostap had been put in charge. Carl was frustrated by a great many things—Ostap, babysitting the technicians and being in a foreign country—but he was loyal and did as he was instructed no matter what he personally thought or wanted.

After crossing to the north and heading west to arrive at the northern edge of the compound, Ostap and Carl used a pair of ropes and hooks to get over the wall. Well-trained in unorthodox methods of combat and movement, they made the ascension with ease, though the two technicians were left standing on the ground looking up. Carl dropped down into the compound first, while Ostap crouched on top of the wall and whispered down at Oles and Jacob.

"Stay low, keep quiet, and wait till we radio you to come in."

"How're we supposed to get in?" Oles looked up and whispered back, gesturing with futility at the rope.

"Just go around front!" Ostap shook his head in frustration before dropping down next to Carl. "Idiots. I hate babysitting."

"Now, now..." Carl tutted in a mocking tone.

A shout from around the building in front of the two Spetsnaz officers made them both close their mouths as their attitudes shifted from casual interest in their environment to being on high alert. Ostap was the first to charge forward, heading to the back door of the building with Carl in tow. They entered the building quietly and moved toward the front, keeping their footsteps quiet and communicating only through hand signals. Each room in the bottom floor of the rectangular building was cleared swiftly, and they soon found themselves near the front door.

Ostap was just about ready to take a peek out through the window on the front door when there was another shout from outside.

"Oye! They're up there! Get after them!"

Carl, standing just feet away on the other side of the double doors, looked at Ostap and the two men nodded to each other. The call from outside was accompanied by the sound of several individuals running for the building, right toward the door where the two Russians were standing. The people outside were chasing down someone on an upper floor based on what one of them had said, and though that information was limited, it was more than enough for the two hyper-trained, elite soldiers to use.

While Ostap stayed near the door, just inside to the left, Carl pulled back a few more feet, ducking inside the first room on the right that offered him both cover and a clear view of the entrance to the building. Seconds later the front door flew open and two people ran in, one carrying a machete and the other wielding a pistol. Ostap remained still as the pair flew past him, not even bothering to watch where they went as he didn't yet want to give away his position. When the two men were but a few steps away from the room that Carl was in, the Spetsnaz officer popped out of the room with his suppressed pistol in hand. Four rounds spat from the barrel, two for each of the intruders' chests and heads.

No sooner had the bodies of the men collapsed to the floor than another three entered the building, shouting and yelling at each other as they saw the bodies of their comrades lying on the ground. Carl fired several more shots in their direction just as Ostap did the same, their combined close-quarters fire bringing down the three before they could do so much as raise a weapon in retaliation.

Outside, the leader of the gang's eyes widened in surprise and he shouted at his people to fall back. A few huddled behind the vehicle while the others, already in the process of running into the building, stacked up against the walls just outside the door. Bursts of gunfire came from behind the vehicle, slamming into the still-open door and decorative windows around it, and Ostap turned to shield his face from the exploding glass. The walls of the building were more than thick enough to absorb the small arms fire aimed in his direction, but with the incoming fire intensifying it would be difficult for him to do much in return.

Down the hall, Carl stepped out of cover and fired through the open doorway with his rifle, aiming for the general direction of the car parked in the middle of the compound. Ostap moved back down the hall at the same time, using Carl's distraction as an opportunity to get away from the front hall and take cover in the next room down from Carl, on the opposite side of the hall.

Outside, behind the vehicle, the leader of the gang snarled as he watched the two figures draped in black retreat deeper into the building, realizing that his overwhelming numbers had just been sliced nearly in half and that it was about to get much, much harder to take out the entrenched enemy within. As someone who had risen to his position in MS-13 through brutal, inelegant violence instead of tactical genius, though, he was ill-equipped to think of any other way to deal with his enemy than taking them head-on. The loss of five good men angered him greatly, and his outlet for anger was simple: more violence.

Foregoing his previous caution, the leader of the group kicked at the others huddled behind the car, forcing them out as he screamed obscenities at them and the others closer to the building. The gang members were lethargic as they moved toward the building, their initial enthusiasm sapped since five of their group had been slaughtered almost instantly. Fear over their leader won out as he continued to kick and curse at them, and they eventually piled up around the door and flooded inside. The bodies of their fallen lay strewn about, dark red blood pooling on the tile floor, but despite how quickly they had died, there were no gunshots as the rest of the group entered the building. The gang members moved slowly down the hall, gripping their pipes, crowbars, pistols, shotguns and rifles as they chattered amongst themselves, none of them wanting to be in front in case the black figures were still lurking around.

At the opposite end of the hall, near the door leading to the stairwell, Carl and Ostap stood in rooms on either side of the passage, hidden from the view of the men walking toward them. Carl was one room farther up the corridor from Ostap, ensuring that they had a wide field of crossfire open to them. Ostap pressed his shoulder against the doorframe as he manipulated a tiny mirror attached to the end of a thin, retractable piece of metal. The mirror offered just enough of a vantage on the approaching men that he was able to make hand signals to Carl, letting the other Spetsnaz officer know exactly how close the gang was getting.

Fear was palpable amongst the group in the narrow hallway, and it was growing by the second. Each empty darkened room that they passed only served to heighten their fear, making them paranoid and increasing the quiet murmurs between them. Used to violence on wide, open streets where their numbers dropped only by one or two during heavy conflicts, walking past five of their members who had been slaughtered inside a dark, tight building was something they hadn't prepared for. The fear that they had spent years of their lives inflicting upon others had been turned around on them in an instant, and all by two shadows that they had barely seen and heard.

"Move faster, *pendejos!*" The leader of the group pushed and shoved the others in front of him, being careful not to expose himself too much in any direction. "It's just two of them!"

"Plus the three upstairs." The woman who had walked up the drive with him whispered in his ear, and he responded with a sharp glare.

"We still have them outnumbered. They were running scared!" His voice rose in volume slightly and his gaze flicked between the rooms in the hall. His best attempt at bravery was faltering, and the others with him noticed.

The unfortunate soul walking at the front of the group, gripping a sawed-off shotgun in his hands and wearing a blue and black bandana, was one of the youngest and newest recruits. His "13" tattoos on his arms were still fresh, the skin still inflamed in patches and the hair not fully grown back from where it had been shaved during the tattoo sessions that took place just before the event.

His hands shook and his heart thumped hard and fast as the others behind him pressed him forward, making him feel like he was going to pass out. He struggled against the feelings, though, mostly to try and impress the leader of the group and the one who had personally recruited him. Sweat trickled down his face and he wiped at it with his upper arm, trying to stay focused and alert.

His recruitment into MS-13 had required escalating stages of initiations, culminating in the midnight murder of an elderly resident in a neighborhood just outside D.C. He hadn't wanted to kill the old man, but not doing so would have meant punishment, or possibly his own death. He had been nervous then, but still efficient, killing the old man quickly and with minimal noise. While he was young, he was strong and capable, with plenty of muscles and the smarts to use them. In any other situation he could have gone on to greatness in some field or another, but instead he became the newest member of MS-13.

It took less than a second for Marcus Rodriguez's life to be snuffed out.

As he took a step past yet another room and turned to look in, a dark figure appeared from nowhere. One hand grabbed his head and pulled him in while the other came down hard on his shotgun, knocking it to the ground. The hand then produced a shining blade that flashed through the air, cutting through his throat before he could even utter a sound. The figure then kicked Marcus's dying body backward, sending him toppling into two others in the hall who had turned to see what the gurgling noise was, only to find the bloody body of one of their members being shoved toward them.

While the gang members struggled to react to the death—and, indeed, near-beheading—of one of their own, Carl ducked back into the room, retreating into the shadows while giving a single shout in Russian.

"*Idti!*"

At the shout of "go!" Ostap drew his pistol with his right hand, swung around the doorframe and pulled the trigger as fast and fluidly as possible. Seventeen rounds went down the hall, all at chest level, and all striking against flesh and bone. He pulled back behind the doorway, slammed the pistol into its holster while slipping the mirror into his pocket, then retrieved his rifle from his shoulder and flicked the switch to automatic. He swung out again and was just about to squeeze the trigger when a blurred form struck him from the front, sending him off-balance and nearly knocking the rifle loose.

The leader of the gang, having barely escaped from the barrage of gunfire by ducking down behind his cronies, leapt forward and caught Ostap on the shoulder, trying to grab at his rifle. Ostap backpedaled into the room, keenly aware that there were still a few of the gang left alive in the hall, and struggled with his right hand to keep the rifle while pawing for his knife with his left hand. Fingers met the steel handle and he drew the weapon, slicing upward toward his enemy's face.

The combat knife, carefully sharpened and unused since put in its sheath before leaving Russia, was every bit as sharp as the one Carl had used to slice the neck of the young MS-13 member. The leader of the gang, while considerably tougher and more experienced than the new recruit, did not possess anything that could keep the blade from slicing cleanly through cloth and flesh. His skin opened as though the knife was a zipper, cutting a long streak across the front of his chest, up the side of his neck and from the bottom right side of his face up over his left eye.

The sudden, vicious assault drove him back and he screamed, clawing at the wounds while trying to escape from the room. There was no escape from the Russian Spetsnaz officer, though, and Ostap brought his rifle up to his shoulder and tapped the trigger three times, sending a trio of full-auto bursts into the man's stomach, back and upper torso.

As the gang leader charged after Ostap, Carl had been in the midst of circling through a side door in the room he was concealed in, looping around to get behind the group in the hall. He threw open a door and entered the corridor just as he heard the gunfire from his partner and then he joined in, eliminating the last few of the gang members with swift, accurate shots to their centers of mass.

Ostap stepped out into the hall, making visual contact with Carl and nodding to him, then received a nod back. Both men relaxed their stances and lowered their weapons before pulling down the masks that had been covering their mouths and noses. They were both breathing hard from the sudden burst of energy they had expended in the fight, and they checked themselves and each other over for any wounds before Ostap began walking back down the hall toward the front door. He peeked out the front door, verifying that the compound was clear of any of the gang members before pulling out his radio and pressing the button on the side.

"You're clear to head in. Rendezvous at the car in the compound. Out." Ostap hung the radio back on his vest and turned to head back inside the building, only to see Carl standing in the middle of the hallway with his hands above his head. At the far end of the hall, standing near the doorway to the stairwell, were figures shouldering rifles. One of the figures gestured to Ostap with his rifle, shouting as he did so.

"Get your hands up, too! Now!"

Ostap ground his teeth together in frustration, torn between obeying the unknown figure and taking his chances with pulling off three lucky shots in a row without him or Carl dying in the interim.

"Now, dammit!" The figure shouted again and Ostap took a deep breath and shifted his weight, feeling the rifle move slightly on its sling on his shoulder, preparing to make his move.

Chapter Seven

The Waters' Homestead
Outside Ellisville, VA

"THERE'S a rope on the end of the board, right there. Just pick it up and drag it."

"What if she rigged it with something?"

"You're scared of an IED now? What do you think this is, Afghanistan? It's a board of nails, just get it out of the way so he can radio for backup to drive in!"

For the two men standing and arguing in the driveway in front of the Waters' house, their night was going as well as could be expected given the circumstances. They had bellies full of canned food, their clothing was keeping them adequately warm and they still had enough friends and weapons that they believed themselves to be invulnerable against whatever dangers might come their way in the new, apocalyptic world.

The barrage of five point five six millimeter bullets passing through the men's' backs and exiting out through their chests destroyed all illusion of invulnerability in the blink of an eye.

Firing from their elevated position, Dianne and Tina opened up on the men in the driveway at the same time, instantly cutting them down. One fell directly onto the board they were moving while the other tried crawling away, making it only a few feet before succumbing to his pain and wounds. The sudden noise and screams from the two men momentarily confused the men stalking through the woods, and Dianne, Tina, Mark and Sarah all used the confusion to their advantage.

Bright flashes of yellow and white light exploded from the upstairs of the quiet house in the middle of the woods as four rifles sang out. Lead tore through wood, cloth and flesh alike, and in just a few seconds there were six more men lying or crawling on the ground, crying out from the wounds they suffered. The confusion did not last for long though, and as the leader of the group finally realized where the shots were coming from, he ordered his men to fall back and hide amongst the trees. There were a few scattered bursts of gunfire from the house, but as Dianne realized that the men were hiding, she told the other to stop firing and get away from the windows, as she expected a barrage of return fire.

"What's going on?" Tina peeked out through the edge of one of the windows, after waiting in silence for what felt like hours. "Why aren't they opening fire on us?"

"I don't know." Dianne shook her head. "I don't like it though."

"Attention!" The voice came from outside, loud and electronic as it was magnified through a megaphone. Dianne peeked up and glanced out the window to see a man looking out from behind a tree near the driveway. A white and red megaphone was up to his mouth and there was a sharp crackle before he spoke again. "You in the house!"

Tina glanced at Dianne before Dianne replied, shouting out the open window with as much gusto and bravado as she could muster. "What do you want?"

"To talk! Are you that bitch from the gas station?"

Tina stifled a snort at the response, then sat up and quickly fired off a pair of rounds at the tree, one of them managing to cut through the end of the megaphone, which was dropped and then hastily retrieved. Tina sat back down and replied, shouting as she leaned her head back at the window. "Yeah, we're the ones from the gas station! Now, what do you want?"

"To stop shooting for a second and just talk!"

"Talk about what? How you've been kidnapping and killing people? Enslaving them? Abusing them and worse?" Tina sat up again and fired, but the man speaking through the megaphone had anticipated her action and concealed both himself and the megaphone fully behind the tree and the rounds plunked harmlessly into the wood.

"Holy hell, woman, stop the shooting! We could light you up right now if we wanted; you know that right?"

Tina opened her mouth to reply, but Dianne put a hand on her arm and shook her head as she whispered. "Don't antagonize them. Let me do the talking." Tina rolled her eyes but didn't reply. Dianne stood next to the window and peeked out again as she called out in response. "So what is it you want, then? Why are you talking instead of 'lighting us up,' as you put it?"

"It's simple!" The man yelled back as he glanced around the edge of the tree. His features were impossible to make out in the darkness, but Dianne could sense that his casual, almost dismissive attitude was a ploy. Something else was going on, but she wasn't sure what just yet.

"All right, then name it!"

"I want you or whoever it was that came into our camp, burned it to the ground and killed a good number of our men, to walk out the front door of the house. You'll come with us and the rest of your people will live."

"What makes you think I have any idea about what you're talking about?"

Dianne could nearly hear the man's deathly smile in his reply. "Not many folks left in these parts. Someone who can snipe one of my men at a decent distance and wound a second is even rarer. Plus, I recognize that old coot's voice from the camp. You can keep her; just send out your leader and we'll be on our way!"

Tina looked over at Dianne and whispered. "You know it's a trap, right?"

Dianne's eyebrows shot up and she shook her head at Tina. "No kidding; you think so?! What do I look like, stupid?" Tina laughed heartily at the response, then Dianne continued. "No, I don't even think he's serious about wanting someone to come out."

Tina's laugh vanished and a serious expression came over her. "You think he's stalling for something?"

"Mom?"

Dianne turned to look over at Mark on the other side of the bedroom. "What's up?"

"A few of the guys out to the side of the house just ran from the trees they were hiding behind."

"Ran? Ran where?"

"Off into the woods far enough that I can't see them anymore."

"He's right, Dianne." Sarah was the next to speak. "There goes another one."

"Oh hell's bells." Tina groaned. "They're taking off out front, too. Looks like three moving farther around to the side."

"Well?" The voice from out front came again, and Dianne called back.

"Oh yeah, sure. We'll get right on that!" Her words were dripping with sarcasm and she whispered to Tina. "If they're surrounding us then they're probably just going to start firing wildly trying to hit us." She turned to look at Mark and Sarah. "You two, get on the floor and crawl to the hallway, then get downstairs. Don't let them see you, okay? I want Mark at the front peeking through the cracks on the side windows and Sarah looking out through the cracks at the back door. As soon as I open fire, I want you two to shoot anything that moves."

Mark and Sarah nodded, dropped to their hands and knees and began shuffling out of the bedroom and down the hall. Dianne turned back to

Tina once they were gone. "Time for round two. Think they'll give up once we kill a few more of them?"

"Not a chance." Tina shook her head. "It's not just about revenge for saving me or destroying their camp anymore. You wounded their pride and they want retribution for that."

A flare of orange light caught Dianne's eye and she looked out the window into the woods, gasping in horror at the sight. No less than five flames had simultaneously appeared amongst the trees, and they were rapidly bobbing across the ground as the men carrying them charged forward, shouting at the tops of their lungs. Dianne turned back to the window and fired off a few shots at the men, but a burst of fire from the trees drove her back as bullets thudded against the siding of the house. With no way to stop the men, she watched from the edge of the window as the flames soared through the air, arcing toward her home.

Chapter Eight

W ashington, D.C.

"STOP!" The shout came from behind Ostap and he spun around, shrugging the rifle off of his shoulder and preparing to fire on the new threat when he saw the forms of Oles and Jacob behind him. "Don't shoot them!"

"How—how did you get here so fast?" Ostap was nearly at a loss for words, his head still spinning from the fight that had just concluded.

"We were near the front gate when we heard the gunfire, so we came in." Both Oles and Jacob shrugged sheepishly.

"Hey!" Carl shouted from inside the building, and Ostap and the two technicians looked at him. "Can you save the question and answer session for later, maybe? These three look more than a little bit trigger happy!"

In the doorway, Rick glanced at Jane and Dr. Evans, surprised to hear an American colloquialism from someone who was very clearly a foreign agent. He could still see the second man standing outside and there were two more who had appeared, but none of the four looked like they were about to open fire, so he took a nervous step out into the hall. The bodies of the MS-13 members were strewn about the floor, the air heavy with the smell of gunpowder and blood. Rick swallowed hard as he tried not to look at the corpses, addressing the man closest to him instead.

"My name's Rick Waters. Who are you and why are you here?" The question seemed simple and childlike in the face of such overwhelming death and destruction, but it was the only one that made sense to ask.

"I'm—"

"My name," said one of the men outside the building, who stepped inside without raising his hands, "is Oles Belov. We don't mean you and your group any harm."

Rick motioned at the bodies on the floor with his rifle. "Could have fooled me."

Ostap pushed his way past Oles and shot the technician a glare. "Ostap Isayev. We're here on a mission to stop the weaponized computer virus known as Damocles. Our... technicians say that one of your group may have the same intent. Is this true?"

Rick eyed Ostap cautiously, weighing the man's tone and attitude against his demeanor. Ostap's hands were down at his side, and Rick could see his right hand swaying slightly just inches away from a holster on his hip. "You four were in that Russian plane that went down, I take it?"

Carl turned his head to look at Ostap, while Oles stepped forward again and jumped into the conversation before he could be stopped. "Yes! Yes, we were! Did you see it go down?"

"Mhm. West side of the city, while the storm was passing through. We didn't know if there were any survivors." Rick lowered his rifle slightly, though Jane and Dr. Evans kept their weapons pressed against their cheeks and shoulders, fingers hovering near the triggers. Rick looked down at the pile of bodies again and shook his head. "I guess we have you to thank for taking care of these a-holes."

Carl nodded and lowered his hands slightly until his palms were level with his shoulders. Ostap walked forward slowly, stepping over the bodies on the floor until he stood next to Carl. "Mr. Waters—"

"Just call me Rick."

"Rick." Ostap nodded. "Our technicians believe you have someone in your group, a Dr. Michael Evans. Is this true?"

Rick stiffened, raising his rifle back up and adjusting his stance. "What if we do?"

Ostap put his palms in a non-threatening gesture, then turned to Oles. "Do you mind explaining this?"

Oles nodded eagerly and began talking at a high rate of speed. "We took one of the last remaining planes out of our country and came here with the purpose of finding access codes to shut down Damocles. Our engineers determined that it was likely going to continue to escalate its attacks unless it was stopped, and apparently military intelligence decided that this is likely where the command and control center is located."

"That doesn't answer my question." Rick's voice was flat and emotionless.

"Oh! Yes, Dr. Evans! He's... well, he's a genius!" While Oles was technically the senior technician of the two, his childlike wonder was just as strong —if not stronger—than Jacob's, and discussing a figure like Dr. Evans made him beam with delight. "He was the lead developer on the project that ultimately turned into Damocles! The breadth and depth of his knowledge on the subject is such that he would be an absolutely invaluable asset in the shutdown of Damocles. Is... is he really here? Was that truly him that we saw?"

Rick heard movement behind him and shifted to the side, clearing a space for Dr. Evans to step out of the doorway. He lowered the rifle and, as his face became unobscured by the weapon, both Oles and Jacob let off shouts of delight and disbelief. Their enthusiasm and friendliness in the face of so much carnage in the very same room was confusing, but given that two of the new arrivals had just slaughtered the MS-13 gang members, he wasn't about to look a gift horse in the mouth.

Rick lowered his rifle and held out his hand to Carl, whose hands were still raised. "Rick Waters. And you are?"

Carl turned to look at Ostap, who merely shrugged, though Rick noticed that the man's hand was easing away from his holster instead of toward it. Carl took a deep breath and extended his hand, clasping Rick's in a firm handshake. "Carl Aliyev. The other technician here is Jacob Yermakov. Ostap is our mission leader."

Ostap walked slowly up to Carl's side and shook Rick's hand. "Carl. Ostap. I'm guessing, based on your dress, that we have you two gentlemen to thank for saving our asses."

"When Oles and Jacob saw who was with your group, they told us it was vital that we keep you out of harm's way."

"Well, thank you. We appreciate it."

An uncomfortable silence descended in the hall until Jane finally broke it by stepping out of the back room and lowering her weapon. "Quick suggestion—how about we get out of the murder chamber in here and go talk outside, where there isn't a pile of bodies and blood on the floor?"

Chapter Nine

The Waters' Homestead
Outside Ellisville, VA

STREAKS OF FIRE soared through the air as the glass bottles filled to the neck with gasoline tumbled end over end from the woods. The first bottle exploded prematurely as its thrower was not nearly as accurate as he could have been. It hit a tree a few meters in front of him, sending flames in all directions, including onto two men who were hiding nearby.

Two more bottles fell short of the house, shattering on the gravel drive and sending their flames out across stone and dirt, only to die off a short time later. The last two bottles were sent flying straight and true, though, with one landing on the roof and the other smashing against the side. Bright orange flames burst forth just below the upstairs window, and a wave of heat drove Tina and Dianne back as the flaming liquid burst out away from the house, tumbling down the siding. The flames found no purchase, though, and soon extinguished themselves.

The bottle on the roof didn't actually break, and instead rolled back down, gaining enough speed that it tumbled out into the driveway, sending a fresh burst of flames up into the air but damaging nothing in the process.

The entirety of the attack was brief, taking no more than ten seconds from start to finish, but to Dianne it appeared as though everything was happening in slow motion. As she and Tina ducked away from the flames beneath the window, a smattering of gunfire emerged from the woods, tearing holes in the side of the house. Only a few of the rounds penetrated through, but the number of weapons firing and the sound of them hitting the wood was enough to both terrify and enrage Dianne.

"Return fire!" Dianne shouted into her radio and stood in full view of the window, jamming the butt of her rifle against her shoulder. She used the bright flashes of light amongst the darkness of the trees to her advantage, lashing out with three and five round bursts at each flash. Only when the bolt slammed open and the trigger fell with a hollow *click* beneath her finger did she drop back down and scurry over to Tina who was standing on the other side of the room, performing the same actions at another group.

"How many'd you hit?" Dianne shouted at Tina over the gunfire and shouts coming from both outside and inside the house.

"No idea! Someone downstairs hit at least three, though; I saw them drop out there near the edge of the woods!"

"I hit two, maybe three or four." Dianne winced as the glass on the windows where she had been standing shattered under a barrage of bullets. "We need to get out of here; they're focusing their fire upstairs!"

Both women dropped to the floor and crawled out as the gunfire from outside the house intensified. As Dianne followed Tina out into the hall, she glanced back at the bedroom, watching as more holes appeared in the walls, letting moonlight in to illuminate swirling masses of dust and particles of wood, drywall and insulation. The last three days had been filled with thoughts in the back of her mind about what might happen if the gang from the gas station were to find her home. Everything from minor structural damage to all of the buildings being burned to the ground along with the loss of all of their supplies and animals.

No matter what scenarios she came up with, though, they all ended with the same thought. *We will win.* Losing her friends and family was never an option, even in her darkest moments, and even while the bullets passed by and her home was slowly being torn apart, she did not waver in that thought. Fear, swirling deep within her gut, was quickly being replaced by another emotion that was far, far stronger.

Anger.

It was *her* home. It was *her* family. It was *hers*. And she would, without a doubt, ensure that everything stayed that way, come hell or high water.

"Tina?"

The older woman looked back at Dianne, the same fire burning in her eyes that Dianne had in her own. "What is it?"

"It's time to punch some holes in their chests."

Tina's pearly teeth glinted in the moonlight streaming in from a nearby window as she smiled, her expression filled with glee. "You don't have to tell me twice."

WHILE THE THREE days in between Dianne's return from the LTAC and the arrival of the two men attempting to loot one of the barns had been spent quietly watching and waiting, that wasn't the only thing that they had done.

Once Jason had started to make his recovery, he and Dianne had spent several hours talking with Sarah, Tina and Mark about the ways in which the property was protected against possible attacks. While Jason agreed that the property was set up in the most defensive and defensible way possible, he pointed out that they were sorely lacking in offensive capabilities. In case of an attack they could defend the house easily enough or, if necessary, escape through the tunnel out into the woods, but he was incredibly unsatisfied with that given the dangers that were threatening to descend upon them.

On the afternoon of the second day, while everyone else was either outside patrolling, cleaning weapons or was otherwise engaged, Jason had worked with Mark and Jacob in the living room while he was propped up on the couch. A pile of shotgun shells, springs, nails, wooden blocks and other odds and ends were combined with a car battery and lengths of wire, and by the next morning Dianne had woken to the sound of a muffled shotgun blast. After a few minutes of panicked searching for the source, they had gone down into the basement to find Jason slowly walking up the stairs from the tunnel with a grin on his face and the smell of gunpowder heavy in the air.

The remotely triggered traps were crude, prone to accidental discharge and nothing to look at, but they worked. A simple spring mechanism held three nails in tension a short distance from the back of a trio of shotgun shells inside of a small wooden box. The simple press of a button released the nails, which punched into the primer of the shells and set them off. Jason's first test with a single shell had been a success. While there were a few failures as he worked to set up the multi-shell devices, by the end of the nearly days-long tinkering process he was satisfied with the low failure rate of the traps and made his suggestion to Dianne that they rig as many as they could throughout the woods around the house.

Dianne had been hesitant to set traps in the woods, both out of fear for the safety of everyone at the house and because she wasn't sure if that type of thing was where she wanted to go. Staging a rescue and fighting for medication to save the lives of family or friends was one thing, but setting traps in her backyard took everything to the next level. A frank talk from Tina had convinced her, though, and they soon rigged dozens of the devices in the trees, all wired in various groups that could be triggered in tandem. The dead leaves made it easy to conceal the wires and in the thick, over-grown woods, it was difficult to see the small boxes containing the shells during the day. At night, seeing them would be nigh-on impossible.

Jason had initially wanted to place them at chest level, but while Dianne, Tina and Mark were outside working, they decided that rigging the traps at staggered heights would be best for maximum coverage and dispersal. The three shells inside each small box were angled in slightly different directions, and that combined with the lack of a barrel to guide the projectiles meant that the field of fire of the traps was incredibly wide, but only deadly at a short distance. Two buckshot shells and one loaded with birdshot went into each trap, with the idea being that if the traps couldn't necessarily kill someone, they could at least give them a very, very bad day. That, combined with the fact that Jason had thousands of buckshot shells that they had brought over to Dianne's house when he and Sarah moved in, meant that it was the best choice for the traps.

While Jason's experiments and tinkering know-how had proven that the concept would work, the only way to know whether or not they would work on a large scale against an invading force would be to test them in battle.

———

"JASON!" Dianne stood on her toes to peek out through a crack in the boards covering the small windows above the front door. "Trigger the first group; right outside the front of the house!"

A moment's pause followed Dianne's cry, and she wondered if Jason had dropped his radio in the dash to get downstairs. Just as she was about to shout in the radio again, a sound like a thousand firecrackers exploded from the woods out in front of the house. Cries of pain accompanied the sounds, which came in bursts as Jason touched pairs of wires to the terminals on a car battery down in the basement. Each new pair of wires set off another group of traps, and even through the thick front door Dianne could hear what the men in the woods were saying.

"What the hell?! Somebody's shooting!"

"Where are they? Where are they?!"

"Right in front of us! It came from there!"

"My eyes! They got me in my eyes!"

"It has to be coming from the house!"

"No, it's—aagh!"

Another burst of explosions cut off what the man was saying, and Tina leapt past Dianne, bounding back up the stairs to peer out the window. "Nice work, Jason!" She called through the radio for both Jason and Dianne to hear. "They're scattering out front!"

"Did it kill any of them?" Dianne asked.

"Looks like maybe one. Hard to tell in this light, but they're scattering hard!"

"Mark, Sarah; how's it looking out there?"

"Nothing out to the side, mom; I think they pulled back. It looked like they were running out toward the front."

"Back's still quiet," called Sarah.

"Good." Dianne nodded firmly. "Now we make our message loud and clear. Jason, can you see where they are on the cameras?"

"There's a decent-sized group near the road. They're about to be passing right by another cluster of traps."

"Good. Trigger it when they're right next to them. I want as many dead or maimed as possible." In the other room, Mark looked down at his radio with wide eyes. Hearing his mother talking about killing and injuring people wasn't something he was used to, and hearing it described in such coarse, matter-of-fact terms was yet another reminder of how much the world had changed.

Several seconds of silence followed Dianne's command, and she stood still next to the door with her ear pressed up against the wood with her eyes closed, waiting for the sound of more staccato explosions. In the basement, Jason watched the tablet closely, sweat beading down his forehead, onto his face and down his neck despite the cold temperature. Though the images from the outside cameras weren't the best quality, he knew from Dianne's detailed descriptions where the traps were, and he could see the vague movements of the men who were moving down the driveway, helping their injured comrades as they tried to maneuver around the nail boards.

The explosions and screams came quickly and with no warning. Dianne jumped at the sound, startled despite expecting it, and pressed her ear harder against the door. Though she couldn't see anything and could only hear vague outlines of what was being said, the counterattack had been an unparalleled success based on what she could make out. Near-simultaneous calls from Tina upstairs and Jason watching the monitor in the basement confirmed her assumption.

"They're running wild, Dianne!"

"Yes they are!" Tina pumped her fist in excitement. "You got at least three more with the traps!"

Dianne closed her eyes, her shoulders slumping with relief and exhaustion. "Does anyone see any sign of them anymore? Mark? Sarah?"

"Nothing here, mom. Everything looks quiet in the woods and side yard."

"Nothing here either, Dianne. They never went out back, at least as far as I could see."

"Good. I want everyone to stay where you are and keep an eye out. It'll be dawn in a few hours and we can head out then to take stock of the damage to the house and to their numbers." Dianne took a deep breath. She was fighting against sleep deprivation and the quickly-depleting adrenaline in her system and wanted nothing more than to lie down on the floor and close her eyes. There was still much to be done, though, and she suspected that in spite of the losses suffered by the gang, they wouldn't give up quite so easily.

Chapter Ten

W ashington, D.C.

HALF AN HOUR LATER, after moving outside and standing near the car in the middle of the compound, the group of seven were talking like they were old friends. The two Spetsnaz officers gravitated toward Rick, eagerly absorbing details from him about how Damocles had progressed in the United States while providing similar information on its progression in Russia. Jane stood near Rick, Ostap and Carl, watching them talk while Dr. Evans found himself pummeled with questions from Oles and Jacob. The two technicians acted as though they had just met their childhood hero and Dr. Evans wondered if the pair might not end up wetting themselves out of excitement.

"So you all are looking to just… shut this thing down?" Jane directed her inquiry at Ostap during a lull in the conversation between him, Jacob and Rick.

"Indeed," he replied, nodding at her. "We and so many others have suffered greatly from this, as has your country. I will admit that we all thought this to be somewhat of a suicide mission, but providence has decided to smile upon us."

"Rick? Jane?" Dr. Evans and the two technicians strode up to the others. "We need to work with them. They've already checked the northern-most site and it didn't have any signs of the servers we'd need to access. With four more people we can scour the last two sites and find the location quite easily."

"We should start by checking this site out, right?" Jane asked.

"Absolutely," Oles replied, "the buildings here are intact and it won't take long to break through whatever physical security has been erected, if this is actually the location. Did you all have a plan for how to access the servers with this lack of power?"

"What was your plan?" Jane replied before Rick or Dr. Evans could jump in.

Oles craned his arm to tap the top of his backpack. "Solar-powered forensic machines. Hardened against EMPs and completely devoid of integrated networking. The only way they can communicate with the outside world is if we explicitly make a physical connection."

Dr. Evans nodded in surprise and approval. "Excellent! Our vehicle's outfitted with an inverter that'll give enough juice to power a server or three. It sounds like, together, we'll be able to access whatever systems we encounter!" The smile rapidly vanished from his face and he sighed. "Assuming that there's a way to bypass the local encryption that's no doubt been applied to the systems."

Rick patted Dr. Evans' back and smiled at him. "Cheer up; where there's a will, there's a way. Besides, if three Americans and four Russians can't beat this, who can?"

Dr. Evans nodded and Rick turned to Ostap. "So, with this being one of the locations, we should check it out. Do you have any equipment you need to gather before we take off?"

"No. Everything we have, we carry on our backs."

"Well," Rick chuckled, "what are we waiting for? We'll grab our gear from upstairs and then we can get started searching this compound. Hopefully it's here, but if not, we'll just head to the last location."

"Excellent." Ostap nodded, then looked at Carl and the two technicians. "Carl and I will secure the gate and perform a perimeter sweep. Oles and Jacob, you two stay here."

The group split up, with Rick, Jane and Dr. Evans heading back into the building where they did their best to ignore the bodies on the floor as they headed upstairs to retrieve their gear. Oles and Jacob stayed in the parking lot near the police car, talking in low voices about the technical details involved in accessing the systems they anticipated finding.

Ostap and Carl, walking together, headed down the drive to the entrance to the compound where they closed the gate and began securing it in place so that it couldn't be easily opened again from the outside. They spoke quietly as they worked, not wanting either the technicians nor the new trio to hear what they discussed. They lingered for several minutes at the gate as they spoke, occasionally gesturing to the compound or to each other, before nodding and turning to head back up toward the buildings.

Jane, who upon retrieving her gear had moved to the far end of the building, stared out the window at the pair, shaking her head slowly as they sauntered back up the drive, their rifles loosely held in their hands. "I don't like this," she whispered to herself.

"Don't like what?" Jane started at the voice behind her and turned to see Rick standing behind her, watching out the window as well.

Jane turned and shook her head as she started walking out of the room. "It's... nothing."

Rick reached out and took her arm, stopping her and looking her dead in the eyes. "If you think something's wrong—*anything*—I need you to tell me, okay?"

Jane started to speak, stopped, let out a sigh, shook her head and rubbed her eyes, trying to come up with a way to say what she was thinking about without sounding insane. "You... you know how you helped me, back in Vegas?"

Rick snorted in amusement. "It hasn't been *that* long. Of course I remember."

"Why did you help me? What was it about me that made you trust me enough to let your guard down and help me instead of leaving me there?"

Rick furrowed his brow and pursed his lips as he pondered the question. "I suppose... well, you needed help. And you seemed trustworthy enough."

"When we got out of that casino, before the military took us to the base, I had plenty of opportunities to run. I didn't, though. You want to know why?"

Rick shrugged. "I'm not sure I follow all of this, but sure; why?"

"Because I had a good feeling about you. You were kind, helpful, self-sacrificing and you never once made me feel unsafe. You had a goal in mind to reach your wife and children but you never once made me feel like I was going to be jeopardized if I stuck with you. That's the same feeling I had about Dr. Evans, when I met him before you popped up again. Out of everyone I've seen and met since all of this terrible stuff started, you two have been the only ones that haven't given me a bad feeling when I first met you."

"Well, Dr. Evans is a nice guy."

"He is. He's genuine and kind and all of those things I said about you; he's like that too."

"So... you think the Russians aren't?"

"The two technicians? I don't know. I don't get a bad feeling about them."

"But the Spetsnaz. You get a bad feeling about them?"

Jane shook her head, her voice dropping an octave as she answered. "More than that. I get a *terrible* feeling about them. They're playing some kind of game here. I don't think they're out to stop Damocles, not like we are."

"But the technicians—"

"Are just that. They're engineers. They carry pistols and fawn over Dr. Evans like he's a rock star and they're a couple of groupies who can't wait to get him backstage and strip him down."

Rick tried—and failed—to suppress a sharp laugh at the mental image, but the humor drained almost immediately from him upon seeing Jane's face remain stoic and serious. He cleared his throat. "Okay, well, if you have a bad feeling about them then that's good."

"How is that good?! We're going to be working with them!"

"We don't have much of a choice right now. They slaughtered those gang members like they were three-legged puppies. We don't stand anywhere near the same level of chance as they did."

"But we had them at gunpoint. We could do that again, if we had to."

Rick shook his head, growing more serious. "No. We never had them. They weren't there to hurt us. They were protecting us from the gang. But, if you're right about them… maybe Ostap and Carl have different orders from the technicians. Or maybe they're in it together. They clearly want us to help them, though."

"So what do we do?"

Rick squared his shoulders decisively. "We keep our eyes open, our fingers on our triggers and get the drop on them before they can get the drop on us."

"That doesn't sound like a very solid plan."

"Nope." Rick smiled at her. "But it's the best we've got. And, I have to say, we've gotten pretty good at winging it so far, so I think we can do it here, too. Now come on, let's not make them suspicious by taking too long up here."

Jane nodded, took a deep breath and followed Rick out and down the hall to the stairs, trying to put on a brave face in spite of the pit of nauseating fear that was roiling in her gut.

Chapter Eleven

The Waters' Homestead
Outside Ellisville, VA

A SERIES OF CLOUDY, overcast mornings finally gave way to one that was both clear and frigid. The lake shimmered as the bright morning sun, unhindered by even the hint of a cloud, rose swiftly in the sky. A light breeze sent a shiver through the trees, disrupting the hint of warmth offered by the sunlight and reminding everyone that even with the occasional warm day, it was still autumn.

Frost crunched lightly underfoot as three figures slowly made their way through the yard outside the Waters' home. Dressed in thick coats, long pants, boots, hats and thin gloves, they each carried a rifle at the ready. They swept their weapons from side to side in slow, lazy arcs as they scanned the trees and buildings, searching for any signs of life or movement. They didn't speak as they went along, relying upon mouthed instructions and hand signals to guide their steps. The silent search and patrol around the perimeter of the house, outbuildings and edge of the forest surrounding the property took about twenty minutes, and while tensions were high when it started, there was a relaxed atmosphere by the end.

"Looks clear."

"Yep. No sign of anyone."

"Anyone alive, you mean."

Dianne shivered slightly, though not because of the cold. Tina's morbid assessment reminded her that, while the property looked to be clear of any intruders, there were still multiple corpses lying between the trees and across the gravel driveway.

"Yeah, thanks for that reminder." Dianne glanced over at Mark as she replied to Tina, watching as he took a few steps toward one of the bodies. "Mark, don't get too close, okay?"

Mark didn't turn, either ignoring her or too wrapped up in what he was seeing to have heard her.

"Mark!" She shouted at him and he jumped, whirled around and took several quick breaths.

"What, mom?!"

"Don't get too close, okay? We need to do one more sweep before we figure out what to do with them."

"There's seven of them," Mark replied as he stepped back from the corpse and walked back over to Dianne and Tina.

"You been keeping count, eh?" Tina looked at him with a sharp eye.

He nodded. "Yeah… three on the driveway and four more in the woods. They're kind of spread out in the woods, though."

Dianne sighed and looked at Tina. "How about you two go get some shovels from the barn and check on the animals? I'll start checking the bodies for anything we could use and get them rounded up so we can get them under the ground."

Tina nodded and pulled on Mark's sleeve, guiding him away from the bodies in the driveway that he was staring at. Once they were a fair distance away, Dianne sighed and slowly walked over to the three bodies lying in the gravel. She used the tip of her rifle barrel to prod at the body, testing its stiffness both to verify that the man was deceased and to see how hard it was going to be to get him under the ground.

Both his clothing and body were stiff, and his flesh was nearly frozen solid from the frigid overnight temperatures. The gravel around his chest and head was stained red for a couple of feet in every direction, and Dianne realized that he must have bled out on the gravel while his friends ran for their lives. As she looked closer, she saw that there were spatters of blood all across the driveway leading out to the gate, and based on their position most of them couldn't have been made by any of the three who were dead.

Dianne walked slowly across the drive, her eyes darting between scanning the trees for any signs of threats and following the trail of blood. One of the nail boards was askew and several of the nails near one end were slightly bent and there were small patches of black rubber and red stains on them, indicating that someone had put his full weight on the nails during his escape.

"Ouch. That had to smart." Dianne whirled at the voice only to breathe a sigh of relief and chastise the one who had spoken.

"Jason! What are you doing out here? You scared the piss out of me!"

Jason moved slowly, still feeling the effects from his injury and near-death infection, but while his body was lethargic his eyes were bright and quick. "Figured you could use some backup out here." He hesitated, turning back toward the house for a moment. "Plus... there's only so much oatmeal a man can eat before he has to escape."

In spite of their morbid surroundings, Dianne couldn't help but chuckle. "I think Sarah's plan to cure you by force-feeding you her version of it is working."

Jason smiled and laughed, then glanced down at the bodies. He prodded one of them with his rifle just as Dianne had done. "How many've we got to bury?"

"Seven, according to Mark."

Jason watched Dianne intently as she looked down at the barns, thinking about her eldest son. "He'll be okay, Dianne. He's old and mature enough that I think he can handle all of this nastiness."

"No," Dianne shook her head, "it's not him I'm worried about."

"Ah." Jason walked slowly along the driveway, kicking at the blood-stained rocks. "You're thinking about the rest of these punks, eh?"

"There were way more than seven, Jason. There's clear evidence all along here that they were wounded by that last blast, and there were probably several more who were wounded by the first blasts in the woods. They've pulled back for now, but I can't imagine that they won't try coming back again once they've licked their wounds."

"So we get ready for them. The traps worked like a charm so we set more of them out in the woods and all around the perimeter of the house. Once they come knocking, we'll set 'em straight."

All-out warfare had never been in Dianne's blood. As she stood in the driveway of her home, looking at the bodies strewn on the gravel and off in the leaves amongst the trees, she realized that she wasn't half-bad at it.

"How long will it take you to make more traps? Enough to replace all the ones in the woods, add twice as many out there and plant plenty outside the house?"

"The rest of the day, if I'm quick and have help. Jacob and Josie can do a bit, but I'll need more hands than that if you want to be able to set them all up by tomorrow."

Dianne nodded. "That should be fine. My guess is that they won't be back for another couple days at the soonest. They'll be coming back with a vengeance, though, so we need to be ready for them."

Jason slowly strode up next to Dianne and planted a firm hand on her shoulder. "Oh, we'll be ready for them. We'll be ready."

Chapter Twelve

W ashington, D.C.

"GENTLEMEN!" Rick was in the lead as he, Jane and Dr. Evans walked out of the building with packs on their backs and bags in their hands. "Sorry that took so long. We have everything we need and we're ready to assist."

Ostap nodded in the affirmative and turned to Oles. "Our two eggheads were just discussing the three possible locations for this facility where the command and control network is located. They conferred with your Dr. Evans who concluded that this facility is least likely to contain it, but is still necessary to explore."

"Oh yes, we must explore it thoroughly." Dr. Evans nodded. "Since the most likely facility to the north was also empty, we just have two locations left, so the sooner we start, the better."

"Sounds great, Dr. Evans." Rick nodded at him. "Where do we start?"

In addition to the rectangular office-like buildings in the compound and the old observatory, a few smaller buildings sat here and there. Checking each and every one wouldn't take a huge amount of time in the small compound, but every second they spent actually solving problems instead of hunting for them would be a boon.

The two technicians looked at Dr. Evans expectantly after Rick posed his question, appearing like a pair of dogs who were waiting on their master to tell them to go "fetch." He seemed to ignore or not notice them, though, and gave Rick an answer without hesitation.

"These rectangular structures—one of which we were just in—were completely rebuilt from the inside-out after the State Department took over from the Navy. As part of the whole inter-bureau agreement, they decided to make the four basement floors of one of the buildings into a high-security location."

"Which building do we look in, then?"

Dr. Evans pointed at the building opposite the one they had taken refuge in. "It should be in that one. The one we were in didn't have a staircase that descended beyond the ground floor, so it's more than likely not the right place."

"All right, then. How are we going to do this?" Rick looked at Ostap and Carl, studying them carefully as he sensed Jane was doing from beside him.

"If he," Ostap said, nodding toward Dr. Evans, "knows the building layout, then he should lead with Oles and Jacob. I'll remain out here as a lookout and Carl can come with you to help provide protection should you run into trouble."

"Great idea. I'll stay up here as well, though." Rick smiled as he spoke, being overly cautious to keep his words and tone as even as possible. "Two is better than one and after that group came through I'd rather not risk having just one person alone—even one as well-armed as yourself."

For the briefest moment, Rick thought Ostap might argue, but the man merely nodded and gave a slight smile in return. "That would be most appreciated. Thank you."

"Fantastic. Dr. Evans? You take the lead and see if you can sniff out the hidden bunker or offices or whatever it ends up being. If you find it, send a runner back up and we'll head down and join you. Jane, make sure you help Carl with watching everyone's back. Somehow I doubt there's anyone down in these buildings but you never know."

Rick felt bad for dividing the group up without having a chance to talk to Jane or fill Dr. Evans in on what was going on, but in the end things had to be like they were for a reason. Dr. Evans, as competent and clever as he was, wouldn't be able to focus on his job if he knew about Jane's feelings on the Russians. With Jane, though, Rick simply wasn't able to talk to her ahead of time before dividing them all up, but his logic was sound enough that he hoped it made sense to her.

With the Spetsnaz officers offering to split up, Rick wanted to make sure that he stuck with one of them, and with Jane being as sensitive and paranoid as she was about them, it only made sense to have her go with the other. Rick knew he could count on her to keep a close eye on Carl, and he hoped that—if things went south—Dr. Evans would be able to handle himself.

There was always the chance that Jane's feelings about the two Spetsnaz officers were wrong, but despite having known Jane and Dr. Evans for such a short period of time, he was completely comfortable with entrusting his life to them. If one of them had a bad feeling, no matter how crazy it sounded, he was going to listen. The fate of his family—and the world—were at stake.

Chapter Thirteen

The Waters' Homestead
Outside Ellisville, VA

"MOM?"

Dianne's eyelids fluttered and she took in a short, swift breath and let out a slight groan as she woke. The bedroom was dark, she was fully clothed—including her shoes—and lying on top of the covers with a light blanket draped over her. She glanced to her side to find Mark standing next to her bed, pushing on her shoulder with a concerned expression on his face.

It had taken hours to bury the men from the woods and the driveway, and in the end she was fairly certain that anyone still living on the property would have to deal with scavengers come the springtime thaw. The work was miserable, the soil was hard and full of roots and even though the bodies were frozen near-solid she could swear the scent of death was overpowering. After finishing the burials in a shallow mass grave in the woods between the house and the road out in front, Dianne spent far too long in the shower, using up nearly all of the hot water in the heater tank as she tried to wash the dirt and filth off of her—both literal and metaphorical.

Tina and Mark's reactions to the activity had been substantially more muted, though none of the trio spoke much to each other for the rest of the day. Even though normal life had only been gone for a short period of time, Dianne could scarcely remember anything about it. The smell of a fresh-brewed cup of coffee, the warmth of her husband's embrace, the ploddingly slow life of the residents of the town and the security of not knowing what it was like to kill and bury multiple people were all foreign to her. The worst part of it all, she had started to realize, wasn't that she couldn't remember what those things were like. It was that she was growing numb to not knowing what they were like.

"What's up, kiddo?" She rolled over in the bed and swung her feet over the side, feeling sick from having slept for less than an hour. Mark and Tina were on watch while everyone else tried to rest, but as Dianne woke up and recognized the stress in Mark's voice, she grew more and more concerned.

"The cameras have gone dark."

"...what?" Dianne rubbed one eye and yawned, certain that she misheard her son.

"The cameras have gone dark!" His voice was still at a whisper, but the way in which he said it sent chills down her spine.

"What do you mean, gone dark?" She was fully awake, moving into a standing position and grabbing her rifle.

"The only ones that are working are on that side of the house." He pointed to the east.

"Where's the tablet?"

"I've got it here, Dianne." Tina came walking into the room, the concern on her face a mirror of Mark's. She handed the tablet to Dianne and Dianne tapped on the images. Of the several cameras that had been set up on the house, only two of them were working while the rest displayed "No Signal" messages.

"When did this start?" Dianne asked as she fiddled with the settings on the tablet.

"Less than five minutes ago," Tina replied. "We thought it was a glitch at first but we couldn't get it fixed."

"Not good." Dianne shook her head. "Have you spotted anything outside?"

"Nothing." Tina shook her head. "No sight or sound of anyone or anything. Couldn't it just be a problem in the wiring or something?"

"On all these cameras on just these sides of the house? No way." Dianne passed the tablet back to Mark. "Keep an eye on the cameras and radio me the second you see anything. Tina, get everyone else awake. I want everyone getting ready for another attack. Jacob and Josie need to get into the basement with someone."

Tina nodded in confirmation and hurried off to wake the others. Once she was gone, Dianne turned to Mark. "Get to the windows overlooking the driveway. Don't expose yourself, though. The curtains should still be drawn so crawl in and peek through a crack. If they come from any direction, it's probably going to be from that one. If you see that it's clear, give me three clicks on the radio, okay?"

"Where are you going, mom?"

"I need to get outside and get an eye on the dead cameras to see what's going on with them."

"Be careful, mom."

Dianne nodded, patted Mark on the back and slipped down the stairs. She waited at the front door for several seconds before hearing three slow, steady clicks through her radio. With a racing heart and a deep breath she cracked the front door and peered out into the darkness. The house had only a few low lights on inside so her eyes needed no adjustment to the outside, and as she scanned the driveway and woods visible through the door she confirmed Mark's signal.

Here goes nothing. Dianne pulled open the door and stepped onto the porch, raising her rifle and preparing herself for the sudden barrage of gunfire she expected to encounter. When none came, though, she closed the door behind her and walked slowly across the porch, each step ticking softly on the wooden slats.

The night was colder than the last, and she could see frost sparkling in the moonlight, dancing on the few blades of grass and on the edges of the leaves. A faint, light wind blew through the barren branches, causing thin, reedy shadows to wave, each one catching Dianne's peripheral vision and making her flinch as she wondered which would turn out to be a person.

The minutes slowly ticked by with no signs of anyone, though, and Dianne finally worked up the nerve to step off of the porch and out into the drive. She looked upward as she stepped out, craning her neck and straining her eyes to catch a glimpse of one of the security cameras that they had rigged on the upper corner of the house. She walked around for a moment, trying to find the small silver device in the shadows of the eaves when her foot collided with something on the ground. There was a sound of metal scraping against stone and dirt as the object skidded several inches across the gravel and she looked down, resisting the temptation to flick on her flashlight as she didn't want to draw any attention to herself.

Dianne squatted down and plucked the object from the ground, turning it over in her hand as she tried to figure out what it was. While it had the color of steel, it was lightweight, and several cracks passed through its center along with a long, slender object that was jagged and sharp at one end. She flipped the object over once more and saw three black screws hanging off of the side, then suddenly realized what she was staring at.

The security camera had been pulled or shot down from its place high on the edge of the house, and it had suffered greatly in its fall. The silver plastic case was broken and the electronics and lens inside were broken beyond repair. While Dianne recognized the camera itself soon enough, the long shaft passing through the middle of it vexed her until she nearly cut her finger on its sharp, jagged, uneven end.

"An arrow?" Dianne spoke the words out loud, softly, and traced the length of the piece of fiberglass. The head of the arrow was firmly embedded somewhere inside the guts of the camera while the shaft had snapped in half, most likely from the impact, shattering bits of fiberglass and leaving a dangerously sharp end sticking out of the device. Whoever had fired the arrow was clearly a good marksman, as they had managed to both destroy the camera's function and knock it off of the house with what appeared to be a single shot.

Whether it was the lateness of night, the long-term lack of sleep or some other factor, the seriousness and gravity of Dianne's find didn't set in for a few more minutes. When it did, though, she stood up straight, dropped the camera to the ground and bolted for the front door. All semblance of stealth was forgotten as she realized that there were likely eyes in the woods watching her every move. Why they hadn't fired upon her with the same bow they had used to destroy the cameras on the house was anyone's guess, but the last thing she wanted was to suffer from a similar fate.

Dianne's feet were both on the wooden porch and she was reaching for the handle of the front door when a searing, red-hot pain exploded in her lower left leg. Though her brain was sending it signals to keep moving, to keep her up and continue going toward the door, Dianne's leg didn't listen. She felt like she was moving in slow motion as she collapsed to the ground, just barely grabbing onto the handle to keep herself partially upright, wondering why her leg had stopped working and why it hurt so very much.

As Dianne Waters looked down and saw the fiberglass shaft of an arrow protruding through her calf, she realized what had happened. The men they had driven off weren't taking a few days to lick their wounds. They might not have even been driven off in the first place. They had regrouped, formed a new strategy and had managed to successfully sabotage one of the most important parts of the house's defense mechanisms. They had drawn her outside, wounded her and were likely preparing to do something even worse.

The battle for the Waters' homestead had finally come to a head, and it was about to get far, far worse.

Chapter Fourteen

Three days before the mission
Deep in the Republic of Bashkortostan, Russia
Beneath Mount Yamantau

OSTAP ISAYEV IS NOT NORMALLY *a nervous man. A career soldier and veteran of countless wars fought in both the light and the shadow, he is used to interacting with people of all statures in government and civilian life. Extracting information from an adversary in the field, performing a night raid on terrorists who have kidnapped dozens of schoolchildren or performing HALO jumps into the heart of enemy territory have nothing on the current situation.*

As the weaponized computer virus continues to escalate its attacks across the globe, the Russian government is in a state of turmoil. Inside the mountain bunker the President still reigns supreme, but fractures are forming as small groups of military personnel begin whispering about how things should be done. Unlike most parts of the world where one of the biggest issues is a lack of food and water, the slow-burning chaos inside the mountain is focused on things further up on the hierarchy of needs.

"Mr. President?" The office is cold and dark, chilled by the layers of impenetrable rock that surround it and all the rest of the bunker. A small fire crackles off in a corner, one of the luxuries afforded to the man who was once in charge of an entire nation.

"Da." The answer comes from a large chair near the fire. The outline of an outstretched arm appears, and the figure beckons Ostap to draw closer.

"You wanted to see me, sir?"

"Da." There is a long moment of silence following the answer before the man speaks again. "You have been given your mission, correct?"

"Yes, sir. And all of the relevant information surrounding it. We will stop this weapon, Mr. President, or—"

"Nyet. You will not."

"I… sir?"

Another long silence. "You will not stop the weapon. Not completely."

Ostap's initial panic at the President's negative response quickly turns to confusion. He stands near the chair, opening and closing his mouth as he struggles to figure out what to say. The President continues before he can say anything.

"This 'Damocles' is a weapon that we must have in our arsenal, if we want to rebuild in this shattered world. Once you have retrieved the access information for the weapon, you will transmit that information back to us. You will not shut down the weapon yourself. We will access it, analyze it and ensure that it no longer poses a threat to our people." The President turns in his seat and faces Ostap, his thin eyes cold and hard as he studies the figure standing nearby. "Do you understand?"

"Of course, sir. We'll handle it."

"Good." He shifts back to his original position. "Ensure that your partner knows about this requirement. Do not inform the technicians, however. Once they have retrieved and verified the information is legitimate, you are to consider them expendable."

"Yes, sir."

The silence from the President is a notice. Ostap is to leave. He gladly does, exiting the room as quickly as possible. Though he does not understand the intricacies behind the order he has been given, he will obey it without question, no matter who or what stands in his way.

Chapter Fifteen

The Waters' Homestead
Outside Ellisville, VA

"MOM!" Mark shouted as he opened the door, having seen what happened through one of the front windows. Dianne waved him back as she struggled to pull herself through the door, expecting another arrow to come flying in and embed in her back or skull at any second. Mark reached out and pulled her inside, twisting her leg and sending another wave of pain through it as the arrow flexed and bounced. "Mom, what happened?"

"Arrow. Leg. Close the door. They're outside… in the woods." Dianne spoke haltingly as she struggled to remain calm. Her pant leg was slick and heavy with blood and she ground her teeth together as she rolled over, handing her rifle to Mark as she kicked the door shut with her right leg. Mark furiously scrabbled with the latches before turning and sprinting for the kitchen, calling out for Tina in a loud stage whisper.

"Dianne, what the—holy hell, what happened to you?!" Tina ran into the foyer and stared at Dianne lying on the floor for a few seconds before jumping into action. She reached down and helped Dianne up and onto the nearby bench, then knelt down to examine her leg. "How'd you take an arrow through your leg?"

Dianne waved Tina off, shaking her head. "No time. They're outside. They shot out the cameras with arrows as a distraction."

"They shot them out… with arrows?" Tina's eyes grew wide.

"They've got to be trying something; maybe trying to break in, or something else. Where are Jacob and Josie?"

"In the kitchen with Jason. Sarah's watching out the back door, but—" A scream from the other side of the house cut through Tina's words, chilling Dianne to the bone and momentarily making her forget all about her pain. Before she or Dianne could react, though, there was the sound of several gunshots followed by Sarah's panicked shouting.

"They're on the back porch! They're coming in!"

Dianne lunged for her rifle, toppling from the bench in the process, while Tina snatched at the pistol on her waistband and charged back toward the kitchen and living room. "Get them downstairs, hurry!" Tina shouted at Jason, who was already up and out of his seat at the dining room table, getting his rifle ready to fire across the living room at the back door. Sarah, meanwhile, was backpedaling from the door, firing her rifle at it in random spots, trying to stop the men who had suddenly appeared on the porch from advancing any farther.

As Jason started to squeeze the trigger on his rifle to put more blind fire through the back door, Tina swatted at the rifle, forcing it down to the ground as she shouted at him again. "Get them out right now, Jason!" Jason hesitated, glancing at Jacob and Josie who were cowering in their chairs from the nearby gunshots, then relented. He threw his rifle over his shoulder and grabbed at both Jacob and Josie as Tina threw open the door to the basement.

While the basement door was still being thrown open by Tina, the back door to the house suddenly exploded inward, showering the living room with shards of glass and wood. An intense flash of light and an overwhelmingly loud *bang* accompanied the explosion, making it impossible for anyone in the living or dining room to see what was going on.

While Dianne was stuck in the front of the house in severe pain, trying to hobble around through the small side room and through to the living room from the opposite side of the kitchen, she was too late to be of any use. With blood dripping steadily onto the wood floor as she pulled herself forward, she too was blinded by the flash and the ringing in her ears kept her from hearing anything. She thought about blind-firing into the living room, weighing the risk of hitting Sarah with potentially taking out one or more of the intruders, but the risk was too great and the reward was middling. She had no idea how many invaders were about to pour into her house, and didn't even know if she could aim in the general direction of the back door.

Several seconds later, the battle for the Waters' homestead was over. Seven heavily armed men poured through the back door, their muddy, booted feet clomping as they ran through the living and dining room throwing weapons to the ground, kicking the feet out from under the survivors and swiftly securing them with zip-ties.

"Is that all of them?" The voice thundered through the house, coming from a man looking in through the back door. As Dianne's vision slowly returned to her she looked in his direction, realizing with no small amount of horror that he was the same man in the red shirt that she had seen in the gas station compound, the de facto leader of the group.

He was of average height and build and sported a thick beard and a short-cropped haircut that gave him a scruffy but militant appearance. He wore thick tan canvas pants, the same red t-shirt she had seen on him before and an unzipped dark green jacket, also made of canvas. The slight bit of exposed skin she could see harbored thick layers of dirt, grease and grime and both he and his men smelled like they had never showered—even before the apocalypse. Unlike the others, though, he didn't carry a rifle, but he did have an oversized holster strapped to his leg containing a large, silver revolver whose barrel was sticking out through the bottom.

"How many were there supposed to be, Michael?" One of the men turned to the man in the red shirt, who promptly rolled his eyes and sighed.

"Bunch of useless idiots. Stand aside, dammit!" He barged in through the door, pushing his men aside and stared at the group of tied-up prisoners lying on the carpet. Dianne stared up at him through wide, unblinking eyes, finally knowing the name of the leader of the group that had antagonized her, her family and her friends since the event took place.

"No, that's not all of 'em. You got two women and a couple of kids. Wasn't there a man here, too? The one we shot but who got away? And what about that woman they took from us?" Michael turned and looked around, his eyes finally settling on Jason's wife. "You. Where's the other man and woman?"

Dianne shifted her stare to Sarah before glancing around the room, realizing that there were actually three people missing. Mark, Tina and Jason were nowhere to be seen, and the door to the basement was closed tight. She looked back at Sarah and pleaded silently with her eyes, hoping that Sarah would be quick enough to think up something believable.

"My husband's dead." Sarah replied flatly, sneering at the man. "He died after we got him back. Severe infection from the gunshot you bas—"

"Yeah, yeah," Michael waved her off, "save it. What about the woman, the one you all took from the station?"

Sarah shrugged and let her head sag back to the ground as she closed her eyes. "She left. You killed her husband, too. She swore she'd find a way to get revenge for it."

"Ha." Michael snorted out a dry laugh and looked down at Jacob and Josie. Dianne saw his gaze shift toward them and struggled to move, but the pain in her leg from the still-embedded arrow and the fact that her hands were tied behind her back kept her from going anywhere. Michael, however, caught her movement and took a step over to her and crouched down next to her face.

"And you... I think my men know you pretty well. They've described you well enough for me. The ones who've survived, anyway. These your little brats?"

"Stay the *hell* away from them." Dianne's response came out like a viper's venom, unlike the relatively detached reply that Sarah had given. Jacob and Josie were both being surprisingly quiet, but Dianne could see that they were in shock, their eyes wide with fear.

Michael laughed and stood back up, looking around at his men. "Check the house top to bottom. Once it's clear, we head out." He looked back at Dianne and smiled cruelly, exposing rows of pearly white teeth. "Time to replace some of that labor we lost."

Dianne and Sarah shouted at the men as Jacob and Josie were roughly picked up and tossed over shoulders, but their screams of protest were drowned out by the laughter of the triumphant horde. They ransacked the house as they searched for other survivors, taking food, water, medical supplies and any ammunition and weapons that weren't at least casually concealed. Dianne did her best to fight against the men, but her blood loss was continuing to accelerate and she found herself growing too weak to even stand up on her own. Throughout the process, though, and even as she, Sarah, Jacob and Josie were being dragged down the driveway to be thrown into vehicles, Dianne didn't see any sign of Mark, Tina or Jason.

They had, quite astonishingly, vanished.

Chapter Sixteen

I SS, International Space Station

"WELL, THIS IS FUN." Jackie sighs as she squeezes the last bit of paste out of a foil packet. The "meal"—if it can even be called one—is more depressing than anything else, though her survival instincts override her malaise.

"You really want to be out here?" Commander Palmer's voice is tinny as it comes through the short-range radio, and Jackie reaches out to flip a switch on the control console.

"Anything's better than being in here," she replies. "It wouldn't be so bad if we could at least turn on the receiver and see what's going on down there."

"We'll know soon enough, Jackie." Ted's voice comes through, just as tinny as Commander Palmer's. "Hang tight; we'll be done here in fifteen or so."

Jackie sighs and pushes herself off of the nearest wall toward a trash receptacle mounted on the opposite side of the room. She stuffs the empty foil packet inside and pushes herself back toward the control console. As per her standard operating procedures, she checks the gauges and dials and lights and readouts, comparing them to numbers she knows by heart, even on the older systems of the ISS.

After four days spent in the comparatively cramped quarters of the old station, she almost wishes she had stayed onboard the ISS-2, despite the fact that it is only a day or so away from burning up in the atmosphere. The plan to refuel the escape module and use it to get back to Earth went awry after the jury-rigged refueling lines became clogged. Commander Palmer and Ted have been on seven spacewalks to try and repair them, though each potential fix merely reveals yet another problem with the aging station.

The lack of communication from the Earth is Commander Palmer's doing, and though

Jackie respects his decision, she's still not happy about it. His analysis of bits of the transmissions that came through to the ISS-2 are indisputable, though. Someone—or something—disrupted and took control of the ISS-2's systems, sabotaging their natural station-keeping functions and forcing the station to begin a descent.

With the only explanation for the source of the problem being a transmission from earth, Commander Palmer has ordered that they sit tight, repair the module and get off the station—all while maintaining radio silence over long-range frequencies. All receiving equipment has been physically disconnected and only short-range, low power transmissions on specific frequencies are allowed so that Jackie can communicate with the EVA team.

No matter how badly they want to contact someone on the burning, smoldering blue rock below them, neither Jackie nor Ted want the same fate that doomed the ISS-2 to befall the ISS.

"Jackie? You daydreaming again?" Ted's voice is loud in her ear, and Jackie snaps out of her reverie and looks out the window.

"Nope, all good here."

"Ha. You were. Get it together, though; we're coming in."

"Copy. Is it fixed?"

Ted's voice is full of optimism, though it's tempered with experience from the previous six spacewalks. "It's looking good from out here. We won't know until we try to push a bit of fuel through the lines."

"I'll meet you at the airlock." Jackie pushes herself off the wall and moves through the station's tubes and sections to the main airlock. The outer door is already open, and she can see two suited figures making their way inside. Twenty minutes later, after the hatch has sealed, the airlock has pressurized and Ted and Commander Palmer have discarded the bulk of their suits, Jackie looks at Ted with a hopeful expression.

"You ready to try it again?"

"Ready as ever. You two stay at the control station. I'll head downstairs again." The three move to the same positions that they've occupied several times before, each taking a role in monitoring and controlling the complicated flow of fuel from the reserve tanks in the ISS to the escape module still sitting outside. Each time before, the procedure has failed, and they've had to dump the fuel in the line out into space to keep from damaging the web of pipes. Every bit of precious fuel they waste is another bit that could make the difference between getting home and starving to death in a dilapidated space station.

"Ready?" Commander Palmer shouts through the corridors of the ISS, and Ted calls back.

"Green!"

"Starting in five! Four! Three! Two! One! Mark!"

Jackie watches the gauges on a section of the control panel carefully. The needles are moving, indicating the expected pressure buildup as the fuel begins flowing through the valves and tubes, making its way through the maze toward the escape module. Ted doesn't take his eye off of his own gauges as he talks softly to her, keeping quiet so that he can hear any shouts from Commander Palmer.

"Good to go?"

"Still green here. You?"

"Green. We're past the block we just cleared. Still looking green."

"Status!" Commander Palmer shouts again and Ted bellows back.

"Green!"

"Almost there! Increasing flow!" The call comes back, and the pair can hear the excitement in Commander Palmer's voice. Jackie continues to watch the dials without blinking, silently urging them to stay in the green and not to deviate too much in either direction. She is tired. Exhausted, even. The feeling of safety associated with being in space while untold destruction spreads across the globe has grown weary. She wants to see solid ground again.

So she continues to watch the gauges, hoping and praying that this time it will work. That this time they can finally go home.

Chapter Seventeen

T he Waters' Homestead
     Outside Ellisville, VA

"GET THEM OUT RIGHT NOW, JASON!"

Despite the intense commotion in the next room over, Mark was doing his level best to follow his mother's instructions and keep an eye out the window for any intruders. By the time the flashbangs went off, though, Mark was on the move, making his way toward the kitchen and, from there, into the living room beyond. The flashbangs went off just before he crossed the threshold from the dining room into the kitchen, though, and thus he was the only person inside the house to be spared from the worst of the blinding light. In the several second timespan between when he heard Tina's frantic shout and when the men stormed into the house, he was the only one in the group who saw everything that transpired.

Jason's grip on Jacob and Josie was precarious, and between his injury and the intensity of the flashbangs, he only managed to grasp at them before the sound and light blinded him and he fell back, groping at the wall for purchase. He stumbled backwards down the stairs into the basement, narrowly avoiding falling by turning himself around at the last second, and came to rest on his rear end at the very bottom of the staircase.

Meanwhile, as Jason was trying to keep from breaking every bone in his body, Tina was still trying to open the basement door all the way. Jason's motion combined with his flailing grasp knocked her off-balance, though, and she tripped forward down the stairs, but she managed to stop herself just a few steps down.

Even as the ringing in Mark's ears—which was still far less than the rest of the group suffered—was still echoing strongly, he could hear the faint shouts of the men outside the porch as they started a brief countdown to fully breach the door and enter the home. Time seemed to slow for Mark as he ran forward, charging toward his brother and sister only to find himself being pulled to the side just as he was about to reach them. A strong, bony hand and arm grabbed him by the sleeve of his jacket and tugged him hard into the basement stairwell before pulling the basement door shut.

"Let me go!" Mark squirmed in Tina's grasp, trying to get back to his brother and sister and mother, but Tina's grip on him only tightened as she pulled him down the stairs, wrapping her other hand around his mouth to quiet him down.

"You hear that? They're in the house! They're not shooting, though, which means they're going to take prisoners." Tina whirled Mark around and he gulped nervously as he saw her wild-eyed expression. The ferocious, tenacious, unchained and unrestrained Tina Carson was on full display. The thin coating of sanity she had kept up ever since being rescued was gone and in its place was a woman who was smart, determined and would not let anything stand in her way. "If they're being taken prisoner, then we have to escape so that we can mount a rescue."

"But Jac—"

"Mark, if you want to save them, you have to trust me." She turned to Jason, who was standing up and staring at her. "If they wanted them dead, they'd have killed them by now. I'm telling you, our best—no, our *only*—chance is to not let them find us. We have to move, now!" Tina's hissed words didn't make sense to Mark, but he was too numb to think much of them. The ferocity and intenseness displayed by Tina moved him to follow her instructions, and he and Jason fell in line behind her as she ran past the hydroponics and toward the double doors leading down into the tunnel.

Upstairs, the clomping bootsteps began to spread out across the house as the men spread out, searching for anyone else. Tina pulled open one of the thick doors down into the tunnel with a grunt, then grabbed a flashlight sitting nearby on the floor. "Quick," she said, pointing at a handful of guns and cases of ammunition sitting nearby on a table, "grab as much as you can! We're going to need whatever we can take!" Jason and Mark filled their arms and just a few seconds later they dropped down the stairs into the tunnel and Tina pulled the door shut behind them. With handles on both the inside and outside of the double doors, Tina grabbed a nearby piece of lumber and jammed it through the handles, effectively locking the doors and ensuring no one could follow them. She then turned and jogged down the tunnel with Jason and Mark in hot pursuit.

With nothing but a few random weapons, the clothes on their backs, a flashlight and a couple crates of miscellaneous ammunition to their names, Mark had no idea how they could possibly mount a rescue operation for Sarah and his family. His mother, brother and sister had been seized and having who-knew-what done to them. Despite all of the years of subtle training and preparation and the recent lessons learned since the event, Mark was lost without a clue of what to do. How could a wizened woman, an injured man and a young boy hope to do anything against a group like the one that had repeatedly attacked them and won?

Mark closed his eyes, shook his head and continued walking forward. Somehow, they would find a way.

Somehow.

Author's Notes

March 10, 2018

And there we are. Episode 10 is finished, and there are only two more books left in the series (unless something drastic changes, which I don't think it will).

After an intense battle that was initially won, Dianne has finally come face to face with one of her greatest fears. In spite of all she's done to protect her family and friends and ensure that they and her home are kept safe, everything is falling apart. Her children have been taken, she's been wounded, and the only people left uncaptured are Mark, Jason and Tina. The people who've taken Dianne and the others are not nice people.

They're the personification of the type of evil you'd expect to see in a situation like the one presented in this story. People who are waiting in the shadows, keeping their worst natures hidden from society until the time arrives when they can act like their true selves without fear of retribution.

To make matters worse, Rick and his companions have formed a tenuous alliance akin to grabbing a tiger by the tail. So long as they don't actually find a way to access Damocles, they'll be fine. Once that pivotal moment arrives—and arrive it shall—then the tail slips away, the leverage is gone and the tiger turns and bares its claws.

This is going to be an exciting conclusion to this series, and I can't wait to get the last two books written. There's going to be more action, more character development, more intrigue, more surprises and more fun than ever before.

I'm working hard on getting this finished up, as well as finishing up No Sanctuary, working on my two co-authored series (Darkness Rising and The Long Fall) and getting some prep work done for new series that I'll be writing once No Sanctuary and Surviving the Fall are finished. In the year that I've been back in the writing and publishing game I've gone from re-publishing my first series to writing two new series, writing a couple of short stories in two new genres, starting a publishing company and working with two (and soon to be many more) co-authors on even more awesome books. It's only going to get more awesome from here on out.

If you enjoyed this episode of Surviving the Fall or if you *didn't* like something—I'd love to hear about it. You can drop me an email or send me a message or leave a comment on Facebook. You can also sign up for my newsletter where I announce new book releases and other cool stuff a few times a month.

Answering emails and messages from my readers is the highlight of my day and every single time I get an email from someone saying how much they enjoyed reading a story it makes that day so much brighter and better.

Thank you so very much for reading my books. Seriously, thank you from the bottom of my heart. I put an enormous amount of effort into the writing and all of the related processes and there's nothing better than knowing that so many people are enjoying my stories.

All the best,
　　Mike

Book 11 - To Steal a March

Preface

Last time, on Surviving the Fall….

A vicious assault by the group of attackers began at the Waters' homestead. A large group attacked the home at once, but with the help of everyone at the home—along with some cleverly concealed booby traps in the woods—Dianne was able to drive back the attackers. After a brief respite, though, the attack was renewed and the man in the red shirt was able to break into the house where he captured Dianne, Sarah, Jacob and Josie. Mark, Jason and Tina, meanwhile, were able to slip into the basement during the confusion of the invasion where they hid in the tunnel, wondering what they could do next…

Meanwhile, in Washington, an attack by members of MS-13 nearly led to the deaths of Rick, Jane and Dr. Evans. The appearance of four Russians —two Spetsnaz and two technicians—meant the quick end of the gang, though, and after a tense standoff between Rick's group and the Russians, a tenuous alliance was formed out of their shared goal of finding the key to stopping Damocles. While the technicians seemed genuine enough, Jane had her suspicions about the Spetsnaz officers, suspecting that they weren't being completely truthful about their objective…

And now, Surviving the Fall Episode 11.

Chapter One

Washington, D.C.

SITTING atop one of the buildings at the old Naval Observatory with a Russian Spetsnaz officer at his side, Rick slowly let his gaze drift across the city. Rick had lost all sense of time over the last few days. Catching a few minutes of rest at odd moments here and there, long hours of travel and more than a few altercations had made it hard for him to tell the difference between evening and morning, let alone what day of the week it was.

The trees growing in small parks and in medians dividing roads were bare, though their limbs shook in passing breezes. A month ago they would have shook at the passage of cars and trucks zipping through the city as a million people went about their daily business. Aside from the run-in with the group of MS-13 gang members, though, there had been no other signs of movement or life in the city.

Two hours stretched by with a few visits from one of the techs to relay messages about their progress, though none of the news was exactly encouraging. Rick and Ostap had spoken in fits and bursts since climbing onto the roof. Most of the discussion was surface-level, talking in abstract about things in the city, bits and pieces of their lives and what they thought their chances were of stopping Damocles. Though the conversation was mostly superficial, Rick appreciated the opportunity to hear a bit of news from someone outside the country—even if said person might be about to try and kill him.

That still bothered him, as well it should. Jane's warning to him, based solely on her gut feeling, still ate at his gut. Each time he had a hushed conversation with Ostap about some new subject was a new opportunity to feel a bit of kinship and trust in someone trying to shut down Damocles, but it always ended the same way. He would remember Jane's warning, his stomach would tighten and he'd wonder if she was right.

Whether the Spetsnaz were out to stop Damocles or not didn't matter at the moment. They had yet to find the server room where the NSA/CIA collective would have worked on the virus, and the encroaching darkness and lack of progress from the group in the central building left Rick with the feeling they'd be packing up soon. If the Spetsnaz were keeping Rick and his little group alive for as long as they had, there must have been some sort of reason.

Or maybe she's just paranoid and it's rubbing off on me. Rick let his eyes drift sideways until they rested on the back of Ostap. Clad in black, his rifle lying casually across his legs, the Russian looked formidable but not threatening. He and his fellow Spetsnaz officer, Carl, had been cordial enough. But they had also torn through the gang of MS-13 thugs like hot knives through butter.

"Ostap? Rick?" The thickly-accented voice made both men turn to see Oles standing at the door to the roof, nervously looking around.

"What is it, Oles?" Ostap had to force himself to put on a smile and a friendly tone of voice. He had sensed every sideways glance the American had given him and knew that Rick's suspicions about the Russians had been aroused.

Oles stared at Ostap slightly too long, wondering where the officer's friendliness was coming from before glancing at Rick. "I think we found it. The basement of the building is enormous, but we were able to break into every locked room—except this one. The door looks normal, but it has a retinal scanner on it."

"Does the scanner have power from the backup systems?"

Oles nodded. "It does. Jacob and Dr. Evans are already setting up a bypass. It'll take time, but Jane said I should come and tell you both right away."

"Excellent. We'll be right down. Wait for us at the entrance, please." Ostap smiled again and Oles backed down the stairs, slowly, still wondering why Ostap was being so nice.

Rick slowly stood to his feet, exaggerating his movements. He had caught Oles' puzzled expression and seen through Ostap's forced smile. His heart quickened and his stomach flipped as he realized once again that Jane was possibly—no, *probably*—right.

Chapter Two

The Waters' Homestead
Outside Ellisville, VA

A COOL BREEZE wafted through the leafless trees, stirring the bare branches and carrying the sounds of a few still-active insects far and wide. The faint glow of stars shone through from above, but the thickness of the rough branches and thick bark meant that none of the light passed through to the cold, frozen soil beneath. Dead leaves, scraggly brown vines and twigs sat atop the ground, still aside from the occasional flutter when the wind picked up from time to time.

Far from the gunshots and noise occurring up the nearby hill, the insects continued their song through the night, oblivious to the violence being inflicted by and upon those on both sides of the fight. They crawled through the debris on the ground as they sang, though they were soon disturbed—not by what was going on far away, but by a shaking in the ground itself. It wasn't severe, but it was odd, arousing those in slumber and those in motion.

Old wood, treated but still succumbing to the ravages of moisture and time, shifted beneath the detritus and rusted metal hinges creaked and groaned in protest. Leaves and dirt fell to the side as a large wooden door was pushed open from the ground below and a pale face appeared, illuminated by the soft glow of a handheld light. The face peered around the interior of the small shack in which the wooden hatch in the ground was located.

The shack was old and poorly cared for, with a sagging roof, no insulation against the elements and an impressive collection of cobwebs. Its sole purpose was to act as a shelter for the hatch in the ground, keeping the weight of snow and the liquid from heavy downpours from damaging the hatch and the tunnel beneath. A few leaks in the roof hadn't kept the shelter from performing its task, but it was still dank and musty, its denizens perturbed by the disturbance caused by the moving of the hatch.

"All clear." A young voice whispered as the eyes set on the pale face glanced around, then the hatch moved more, slowly opening until it fell backward with a thunk. Mark Waters ascended from the tunnel, a pistol clutched tight in his hands that were shaking ever so slightly.

Tina Carson and Jason Statler were the next to emerge, with Tina helping to pull Jason up while he wheezed softly, winded from their walk down through the tunnel. Jason leaned against the inside wall of the shack while Mark peeked out through the front door, seeing nothing but the darkened shape of trees that appeared to go on in an unending fashion. "Still clear."

"Good." Tina kept her flashlight pointed at the ground as she and Jason dropped the armfuls of weapons and ammunition they had taken with them from the basement. "No noise from the tunnel. Maybe they didn't check the basement or notice the doors if they did."

Mark reached for the door, starting to push it open when Jason grabbed his arm and shook his head. "No, wait. We shouldn't go out now. It's too dangerous."

"Too dangerous?" Mark looked at Tina. "They're probably still back at the house. We should try to get back there and rescue Mom and the rest!"

"No." Jason shook his head firmly. "We can't take on a group like that right now, at night."

"Mark's right." Tina stood next to the young man, putting her arm around his shoulder. "If they haven't left yet then we need to try a counterattack. We can't let them take four of us—especially when two of them are children."

Jason opened his mouth to argue but stopped himself and sighed in resignation. "You're right. I just…"

"We'll be careful, Mr. Statler. I promise."

⸺

THE TRIO STUCK to the tree line as they went along, their pockets bulging with extra ammunition and spare magazines that they had hastily filled in the shed before moving out. They wound around the perimeter of the property as quickly as possible, with Mark in the lead, Tina just behind him and Jason slowly bringing up the rear.

The house was lit from inside on the main floor and moving lights could be seen shining through the cracks in between the boards covering the windows. As they continued moving closer to the house, they heard the sound of car engines, slamming doors and loud shouting and calling. Mark and Tina looked at each other and increased their speed, trying to get around to see the front of the house.

They were, in the end, too late. By the time the pair were in the right position to see around the front of the house the last vehicle—the truck belonging to the Waters—was on its way out. In the back of the truck in front of it, Mark could make out the shape of a pair of figures that were sitting in the bed. Though he couldn't make out who they were, he was certain that it was his mother and Sarah Carson. He very nearly shouted out to them, but Tina's rough hand on his shoulder directed his attention to the house instead.

"They set the place on fire!" She hissed at him as she pointed at the front porch. A flickering orange glow was just barely visible, but it was growing in size and intensity even as they stood and watched.

Mark was the first to take action, moving without thinking as he broke from the trees and sprinted across the yard toward the back porch. Though he couldn't see the entirety of the front of the house to see how bad the fire was, he saw no glow around the back, and knew that time was of the essence. Tina and Jason both called out to him in low voices, trying to beckon him back, but he ignored them, staying low and running as fast as he could.

Once on the back porch he eased through the broken glass and wood that had once formed the back doors. The acid smell of the stun grenade still clung to the air and the floor was covered in dirt, glass and boot prints. He held his breath as he stood just inside the back door, turning his head in all directions as he searched for a sign that anyone was still inside. Seconds ticked by slowly and all he could hear was the sound of his own heartbeat so he stepped forward, pistol clutched in both hands and extended outward. Each step brought with it the crunch and crackle of glass and dirt beneath his feet, and he braced himself for the attack that never came.

As he moved into the kitchen, a new smell invaded his nostrils, along with the same orange glow he had seen before. The kitchen had been ransacked, but he paid little attention as he ran for the cupboard beneath the sink, hoping that of all the things that had been taken, the large red cylinder hadn't been one of them.

He flung the doors open and snatched the fire extinguisher up in one hand as he tucked the pistol into his belt with the other, then ran for the front door. The glow was brighter and he hesitated near the door, wondering if he had chosen the best course of action. Out front, beyond the glass, he could see Tina and Jason moving outside. He swallowed his fear and opened the door, immediately taking a step back as a blast of heat greeted him. Kindling had been stacked and doused with lighter fluid near the base of the door and the flames were already licking up to the top of the porch. He pulled the pin on the fire extinguisher and aimed it at the base of the flames as he squeezed the handle, sending out a jet of white chemical powder.

The fire, while burning hot thanks to the accelerant, had been created in haste as an afterthought by the man in the red shirt. As such, the extinguisher quenched the fire almost instantly, reducing the heat and light within seconds. In less than half a minute, with constant streams of powder, the fire was out. Tina and Jason stood just off the edge of the porch, watching Mark put out the fire, and once it was over Tina ran to him and embraced him.

"You idiot." She wrapped her arms around him, causing him to drop the extinguisher. "Don't do that again! Your mother's going to wring my neck if she finds out what you did."

Mark couldn't help but smile as he hugged her back, then took a step back and looked at the damage caused by the flames. "Sorry, Mrs. Carson. I just couldn't… we can't lose the house. Not along with Mom and Josie and Jacob and Mrs. Statler."

Tina glanced at Jason, who was already looking at the damage. "We won't lose them. Will we, Jason?"

"No." He kept his eyes on the blackened wood, but both Mark and Tina could see the traces of tears forming at the mention of his wife's name. "This is all superficial. You caught the fire before it could do any real damage." He looked at Mark, his eyes glimmering in the reflection of the flashlight. "Nice work, Mark. You saved your home."

"And now," Tina intoned, "we're going to save the rest of our family and friends."

Chapter Three

W ashington, D.C.

AFTER COMBING the above-ground halls of the expansive building, Jane, Carl, Dr. Evans and the two technicians began searching the basement levels. While a simple visual inspection would have been enough for some types of searches, trying to find a system that contained information about Damocles was incredibly slow and methodical. Each room had to be scanned for any materials that referenced Damocles and, if it looked like anything was present, the computer had to be taken up to the squad car where it was connected to the power inverter, turned on and forensically analyzed by one of the techs.

After searching dozens of machines, Jane and Dr. Evans made the call to abandon any more searches of the rooms above ground and focus on the more secure areas in the basement levels. There were three such levels according to the maps located at each floor's stairwell, but Dr. Evans was the first to call that number out as suspicious.

"These stairwells are too wide and thick. Government contractors use this type when they want to dig deep. I guarantee there's at least five, maybe seven floors below ground."

The first two floors of the basement were virtually identical to those aboveground, albeit far darker. Most of the windows on the building were false anyway, but belowground the only illumination besides flashlights were the faint flickers from a few emergency lights whose batteries hadn't completely died.

Insulated from any external sounds, the basement levels were eerily quiet, and the whole search group—even the normally unaffected Carl—found themselves whispering. The shadows in the halls were long and hard, dancing with each sway and flicker of the lights. By the time the group reached the third and, supposedly, final floor of the basement, Dr. Evans could see that his suspicions were correct.

"Anybody notice the stairs?"

The two technicians, eager to please their idol, started stumbling over each other as they tried to speak, though neither of them said much at all. It was Jane who realized what Dr. Evans was talking about, as she stood on the last stair leading down into the third floor.

"This flight of stairs is shorter than the others."

"Exactly right!" Dr. Evans beamed at her. "Notice also that the roof seems shorter. It's because the floor is thicker."

"For insulation and isolation!" The two technicians spoke in unison, then Jacob continued. "So you were right. There's another floor below us."

"More than one. We need to find the entrance, though. It'll be disguised, locked and heavily armored. I don't know how we'll break through."

Oles grinned and tapped the shoulder strap of his backpack. "Leave that to us."

WHILE THE ROOFTOP watch session had been stress-free, Rick could feel tensions rising as he and Ostap slowly descended the stairs to see what the search team had uncovered. He couldn't pinpoint the source of the tension, but when he glanced over at the Russian officer he could see that Ostap's body movements had become more rigid and deliberate, eschewing the casualness from before. Something was going on. He didn't know what, but Jane's words once again rang in his ears.

"Rick!" Jane's voice carried down the dark hallway as he and Ostap came to the bottom of the stairs. She jogged down toward him and put her hands on her hips as she addressed the two men. "We found the door leading down into the lower levels. Ostap, I have to say, your techs are some talented guys. The equipment they're using to break the electronic lock is—"

"Not supposed to be seen by those who aren't authorized to do so." Ostap interjected, his voice cold and hard. Realizing at the last second what he sounded like, he forced himself to relax and put on a smile. "Still. At the end of the world, what's a bit of covert tech between friends? Come on, let's go see the progress they've made."

As Ostap led the way down the hall, Jane hung back and leaned in close to Rick, whispering to him as they walked. "What's with him?"

"I don't know. He's been acting odd."

"You think I'm right about him?"

"Maybe. I hope not. What about Carl and those technicians?"

"The technicians look like they want to marry Dr. Evans; pretty sure they're harmless. Carl's been fine. Helpful, quiet, nothing but professional. Maybe he's not in on it with Ostap."

"Don't count on it." Rick shook his head. "Keep your pistol close by and don't hesitate to use it."

"Gentlemen," Ostap announced as he walked up to the two technicians, "please report on your progress. And spare no details."

Oles and Jacob glanced at each other before Jacob cleared his throat. "There's emergency power still running through the security systems on the door. We're wired in and the decryption software's running. We're close to finishing on it."

"Rick!" Dr. Evans looked up at the arrival of the last two members of the group, beckoning him over. "You have to see this!"

Rick walked over to the normal-looking door with a metal touchpad mounted to the wall. The touchpad had been cracked open and a cable ran from it down to a small laptop on the floor. Oles sat back down in front of the computer and Rick knelt down to peer over the technician's shoulder.

"I didn't realize you all were this advanced. Are you brute forcing the system?"

"No, actually, we… uh…" Oles glanced at Ostap, who nodded. "We're exploiting a weakness inherent to this particular type of security system."

One of Rick's eyebrows shot up. "A zero-day?"

"More or less."

"Pretty interesting how you guys manage to have your hands on something like that for a NSA/CIA system."

"Like your government," Ostap interjected, "ours engages in espionage as well."

"Relax, Ostap. I'm not judging. I'm actually glad for it. Without you guys we'd be stuck trying to figure out how to break through the door."

"Wouldn't be possible." Dr. Evans shook his head firmly. "We'd need a bulldozer to break it down."

"Fortunately, Dr. Evans," Jacob exclaimed with a grin, "that won't be necessary." He stood up, made a wide flourish at the door and pressed a button on his computer. "We're in."

Chapter Four

I SS, International Space Station

"WE DON'T NEED that much food."

"What if we land in an isolated area? If we're off by a degree or two on the return trajectory, we could be stuck somewhere remote for an extended period of time."

"Fine." Commander Palmer sighs and nods as he examines his clipboard. "We'll store it in the exterior compartment, aft side."

"Commander?" Ted floats into the room, a collection of small silver pouches in his hands. "Got all the emergency blankets I could find."

"Good. We'll keep those inside the main compartment. Can you take over this and work with Jackie to finish up? I need to start the landing calculations." Commander Palmer gently tossed the clipboard through the compartment and Ted snatched it out of the air.

"Sure thing. We going for water or land?"

"I'm not sure. Water's preferable but we won't have anyone there to pick us up. I don't really want to be floating in the ocean for the rest of my life."

"You and me both." Jackie replied. "Why not go for land? We've got the basic training for it."

"A million things could go wrong. But the biggest reason is that." Commander Palmer gestured out the window at the Earth below. Areas that were supposed to be covered in lush foliage were obscured by smoke, tainting the atmosphere with black clouds of soot. "No way in hell are we going to land in Russia, and if we go somewhere in the USA it's going to be *like throwing a dart at the wall. We might land in an open field or we might veer off course and land in the middle of a fire or smash through a skyscraper."*

"So water's our best option." Ted scratched his chin, hooking his feet into the small loops on the wall to keep from floating away from the window. "I guess I'd rather be floating for a while than risk rolling and breaking bones or landing in the middle of a fire."

"If we end up in the middle of the ocean then we won't be floating for a while. There won't be any ship traffic down there, and if we can't call anyone on the radio then…"

"I know, Jackie." Commander Palmer runs his fingers through his hair as he stares at the landscape through the window, trying to determine their best course of action. "What if we landed off the coast of Florida, though? Just a mile or two out?"

"That kind of precision's going to be difficult with all the cargo we'll have on board." Ted glances down at the clipboard. "Plus this is an emergency maneuver. It's not exactly supposed to be precise."

"What if we adjust during the parachute phase with the maneuvering thrusters?" Both Ted and Commander Palmer turn to look at Jackie.

"Come again?" Commander Palmer blinks a few times, not sure if he heard her correctly.

"We have full fuel for those and we'll barely use them in setting up our deorbit trajectory. The main engine will be what we use mostly. Why can't we use the maneuvering thrusters to guide us closer to land once the parachutes deploy?"

Commander Palmer glances at Ted, who has an odd look on his face as he slowly nods. "That… could be possible. If you can set up a burn that gets us close to the coastline, the thrusters will give us a few dozen miles more of leeway."

"That," Palmer replies, "is still an incredibly small bullseye. And once we land in the water, what are we supposed to do to get to shore? Swim a couple of miles with the module in tow?"

"Build some makeshift paddles, stand on the sides and row in?" Jackie shrugs. "What've we got to lose?"

The mention of paddles triggers an old memory in Palmer, of when he and his grandfather used to go fishing. The memory is old and vague and worn out, but one specific detail surges to the forefront of his mind. He looks up at Ted. "Change of plans. Jackie, you're taking care of the loading plans solo. Ted, come with me. I've got a new job for you while I'm working out the deorbit calculations."

"New job?" Ted glances at Jackie has he passes her the clipboard. "What do you mean?"

"Oh, you'll see."

Chapter Five

The Waters' Homestead
Outside Ellisville, VA

"THIS IS HOPELESS!" Mark kicked at pieces of one of the broken kitchen chairs in frustration, then sat down in one of the two unbroken ones with a sigh. The last few hours of darkness had been spent combing the house for supplies, but what they found had been less than encouraging. Most of the obvious supplies—food stashed away in cupboards, for instance—had been taken by the intruders. They hadn't been subtle or gentle in their smash and grab, choosing to rip doors off of hinges and put their boots through anything breakable as they searched the house from top to bottom. The end result was a home that had been ripped apart, its innards torn to shreds in an effort to take anything that looked useful or valuable.

"It's not hopeless, Mark." Tina forced a smile. Behind her, Jason shuffled in from the dining room with a small box of medical supplies.

"They missed this under the table. I assume it's from when you all were treating me."

Tina rifled through the box before nodding and sighing. "Yeah. Not a whole lot in here but it's worth keeping just in case."

"How's the basement look?"

"The plants are all overturned and half the equipment was crushed. I didn't look at it too closely but I think it's salvageable. It looks like they completely missed the tunnel, though. The doors weren't even scratched."

Jason shook his head. "How on earth did they manage to do that?"

"Guys…" Mark spoke again, bothered by Jason and Tina's calm conversation. "Why are you acting like nothing happened? We only found a couple weeks' worth of food and water, and we only have a pair of rifles, a bow and a few pistols. How are we going to rescue Mom and the others with just this?"

Tina knelt down next to Mark and wrapped her arm around him. His breaths were fast and his heart was racing and she sensed that he was growing close to having a breakdown. "Mark. Listen to me." Her voice was soft and soothing, and Mark put his arms around her, feeling tears pouring unbidden from his eyes. "Your mom, brother, sister and Mrs. Statler are going to be just fine. If these guys wanted any of them dead they would have done it when they broke in. That means they're going to be fine, you hear me?"

"How are they going to be fine?" Mark's voice cracked. "You don't know that."

"Because they're strong. And because we're going to find them."

"But how?" Mark pulled away and wiped his eyes and nose with his grimy shirt sleeve, smearing dirt across his face. "They took our truck."

"We've all got two legs," replied Jason, "so we'll use them. And with what we did to their little operation at the gas station, I wouldn't be surprised if they set up shop somewhere else so maybe we won't have to go quite as far."

"Jason," Tina stood next to him, whispering to try and keep Mark from hearing, "are you sure you can handle walking long distances?"

"Just don't ask me to climb any mountains or go up a bunch of stairs. I'll be fine." Jason patted at his wound. "My legs are fine, but I just get out of breath easily. I'm good to go, though."

"Then let's go." Mark stood up suddenly, wiping the last remnants of his tears away. "It's already been a few hours and we need to go after them while the trail's still hot."

Jason chuckled and patted Mark on the shoulder, nodding in agreement. "You're right. We should go."

"How are you so calm about this, Mr. Statler? I mean, they have my family and your wife. Why are you so calm about it?"

Jason's smile slowly faded away and his expression grew serious. "Because I have to be, Mark. Because I have to be."

━━

THE GATE across the driveway squeaked loudly as Mark tried to shut it, only to find that the chain that had once held it in place was severed into three separate pieces. He draped the longest piece around the gate and the post and wrapped it around itself, trying to keep it closed. Out in front, Tina and Jason continued toward the main road, both of them with packs on their backs and rifles held tightly in their hands.

Dawn was breaking off to the east, but the shadows of the trees on the driveway and the country road beyond were still long, precipitating the need to use a flashlight to avoid tripping on any loose stones or sticks in the road. Mark quickly took the lead, walking impatiently ahead as he scanned the ground with the light, calling out any obstacles along the way. They took a right out of the gate, heading toward town based on nothing more than intuition. There were deep gouges in the road from the melting snow and vehicular travel, but it wasn't clear which way the exiting vehicles had gone when they left. Mark thought he had seen them heading toward town, but there wasn't a confirmation of whether or not they were on the right track until they got a hundred feet or so from the end of the driveway.

"Mr. Statler?" Mark abruptly stopped in the road and slipped his pistol into a holster on his belt before kneeling down, aiming the flashlight just a few inches above the ground.

"What's up, Mark?" Jason tried desperately to avoid sounding like he was out of breath so that Tina wouldn't start worrying about him.

"Is this what I think it is?" There was a tremor in Mark's voice as he leaned down to touch the spot in the road, fearful of what confirming the physical nature of what he was seeing could mean.

Chapter Six

W ashington, D.C.

WHEN THE DOOR to the stairwell leading down into the hidden fourth floor of the building's basement opened, Rick was prepared for just about anything, including a surprise attack from the Russians, someone emerging from behind the door or anything in between. He was not, however, prepared for the smell.

A pungent odor rushed out of the room, washing over the group like a wave at a beach. It enveloped them, covering them from head to toe with the distinct smell of death. One body would have smelled bad enough, but the intensity of the stench was so nauseating from the outset that Rick instinctively knew that something horrible had happened in the basement.

Suspicions about the Russians forgotten, he took a step forward, rifle pulled tight to his shoulder. Ostap followed him in lockstep, matching his every movement as he whispered. "Carl, cover our rear."

"Da." The other officer nodded and moved behind Rick and Ostap, following them down two flights of stairs and onto the fourth floor.

The smell only grew stronger with each step down, and Rick had to pull his shirt up over his face to try and drown it out with the smell of his own sweat. It did little to help, though, and he flinched with each breath, making his inhalations as fast as possible and his exhalations as long as possible. Another door stood at the bottom of the stairs, this one with the same type of locking mechanism as the one up top.

Ostap called for Jacob and Oles who hurried down the stairs, both of them trying to keep from retching. They quickly connected their equipment to the door and, knowing what was required to open the one up top, had the new door unlocked in a matter of seconds. Ostap waved the technicians back and pulled the door open, motioning for Carl to proceed forward. If the smell in the stairwell was bad, opening the door turned it from bad to unbearable. Rick's eyes watered and he felt his stomach churning uncontrollably before he vomited, first from the smell, then from the sight.

No less than six bodies lay on the floor just inside the room. All of them had been leaning up against the sealed door and they fell into the stairwell. They hadn't been sitting in the sealed environment for nearly long enough to desiccate, and as such when they hit the ground it was with a sickening splat. Rancid flesh split open, coating the inside of their clothing with gore and increasing the smell even more.

"Holy..." Rick tried to speak but vomited again. Ostap took a few steps back, his face twisted up as he tried to keep from following Rick's example. Carl, Jacob and Oles all backed halfway up the stairs, and all of the Russians scrambled with their gear, pulling out filtration masks and slipping them over their faces.

"Here, quick!" Ostap's words were faint through his mask as he held out a spare one for Rick. Rick accepted it, wiped his mouth on his sleeve and slipped the mask on. The relief was overwhelming as the smell from the bodies was nearly completely removed by the multi-layer filters in the mask. He took a moment to breathe slow and long, steadying himself before turning back to face the scene of tragedy that lay before them.

"What... what happened here?" Jacob whispered through his mask.

"Looks like the place was sealed up, from the inside." Ostap stepped back up to the door and knelt down next to the bodies. "They couldn't get out for some reason."

"Security, probably. Or Damocles. Either way, they were trapped and couldn't get out."

"What's going on down there?" Jane's voice echoed down the stairwell. "That smell is getting *really* strong!"

"You have any more of those masks?" Rick looked at Ostap, who nodded and pointed at Carl.

"Collect the spares from the technicians. Take them up, explain what is happening, and escort them both down."

Carl nodded and got to work while Ostap turned back and stepped up next to Rick. "See anything useful on the bodies?"

"Military IDs on two of them and some paperwork referencing project Damocles." Rick grimaced as he turned over a pair of suspiciously damp wallets before dropping them and rubbing his hands on his pants. "I think we're in the right place."

AFTER CARL, Ostap and Rick moved the corpses aside, the group ventured beyond the second security door and into a floor of the building that was remarkably similar to the ones above. Unlike those above, however, it had a more sterile, clean feel due to the transparent walls and doors that comprised the majority of the workspaces. Rows of computers, server racks, test benches, desks and conference tables were visible as the seven walked down the hall, their weapons relaxed and their flashlights swinging in every direction.

Despite the clean, almost medical look of the place, death was not far and the bodies near the entrance weren't the only ones present. One of the walls in a conference room was covered in rust-colored splatter and two bodies were on the floor next to each other in what looked like a double suicide. In another office a man was curled up on the floor, having died of starvation, dehydration or a combination of the two. The people who had been trapped were mostly young, except for those dressed in military uniforms, of which there were more than a few. Age, rank, position of authority and status before Damocles was unleashed had no sway against death's scythe.

"We should check some of these systems." Rick murmured almost too quietly to hear through his mask. "See if we can find out where to start hunting for the data we need."

Rick's voice broke the seal covering the silence in the room, and Jane immediately spoke next. "How did this happen? So many people just... dead."

"Assuming this is the place where we'll find the information we need," Dr. Evans said, "then it was likely Damocles that sealed it off."

"To prevent anyone here with knowledge on how to stop it from getting out." Oles let out a whistle, an impressive feat given that he was wearing a mask.

"Yes, well. We're here now." Ostap turned and clapped his hands together. "And we're going to stop it. Oles, Jacob. I want you two to start checking through each room. Look for any notes or paperwork that might describe what we need. If you find a system that you want to check, carry it up to the car and run a diagnostic." The two technicians nodded and turned to start work on their task.

"I'll go with them," Dr. Evans turned and headed after Jacob and Oles, "I know more about what they're looking for than they do."

"Excellent." Ostap's eyes crinkled under the weight of his overexagger-ated smile. With Dr. Evans and the technicians gone, the only people left standing in the hall were Rick, Jane, Ostap and Carl. The two Russians stood next to each other, staring in silence at Rick and Jane until Jane cleared her throat.

"We should help search as well, shouldn't we? Lots of rooms here to go through."

"Of course." Ostap smiled again. "Carl and I will start looking for another stairwell down, in case there are more floors to search, while you two help on this floor. Sound good?"

Rick was glad for the mask and that it hid the twitch at the corner of his mouth. Ostap's voice was too cheery and he was smiling far too much. The Russian was planning something, but he didn't know what.

"Of course." Jane smiled back, perfectly mimicking Ostap's previous statement. "Come on, Rick. Let's get to work."

Chapter Seven

O utside Ellisville, VA

"SHUT UP!"

Dianne arched her back, moving in front of her daughter. A man with a large beard, wielding one of the shotguns they had stolen from inside the house, stood at the back of the truck bed. His face was coated with dirt and grime, and his teeth looked like they hadn't been brushed in years. Spittle flew from his mouth as he shouted at Josie, who simply started to cry even louder.

"Josie, come on now." Dianne wrapped her bound hands around her daughter and pulled her in close, muffling her cries. The motion seemed to pacify the man, who turned and stalked away to help his comrades continue to ransack the house. Jacob and Sarah sat close to each other just behind Dianne, with Sarah's arms around Jacob, as they tried not to watch what was going on.

It didn't take long for the ransacking to conclude, at which point the men who had been standing around the three vehicles were joined by those in the house, including the leader who Dianne still referred to as the man in the red shirt.

"Load up!" He leered at Dianne as he walked by, rapping his gloved hand against the back of the truck and grinning wider as Josie and Jacob both shook with fear at the sound. "We're heading out to put these four to work!"

Dianne's leg ached as she shifted to block Josie's view of the man, the arrow still lodged deep and causing her tremendous pain. "Screw you." She spat at the man and he laughed, then moved up to jump in the back of the next vehicle up.

"Move out!" He gave the order and the vehicles started up and began heading down the driveway. Behind, at the house, the beginnings of a fire were visible on the front porch, and Dianne felt her heart leap into her throat.

"They're going to burn down the house." She spoke softly, wishing she could do something. Both women's ankles and wrists were bound, but their arms were in front and not behind, so they each clung to one of the children as the truck bounced, the driver going too fast for the poor condition of the driveway. The flames and the house itself both vanished behind the trees as the truck continued forward, and she tried to push the thought from her mind.

"Dianne, what do we do?" Sarah looked over the edge of the truck as though she was contemplating jumping out, but a rap on the window from inside the cab drew her attention. The window slid open and a pistol emerged, pointed at her face.

"You sit your ass down and shut up. Got it?" The voice was rough like gravel and Sarah immediately abandoned the idea, turning around and hugging Jacob even tighter.

"I don't know, Sarah." Dianne whispered, hoping that she wouldn't be heard over the sound of the engines.

There were cardboard boxes at the back of the truck filled with food and water that the men had taken from the house, and through the open window of the back of the cab she could hear the driver and two passengers laughing and joking about how they were finally going to get a break thanks to the "new workers" they picked up.

"You think Jason and Mark and Tina survived? That they made it to... you know." Sarah scooted closer to Dianne, lowering her voice even more.

"They must have. There were no gunshots when they were trashing the house. I think they must have gotten down there and gone out."

"They'll come after us, you know."

"I... I don't know." Dianne struggled with the desire to have the trio try and mount a rescue. Weighing the life of her eldest son against her two younger children and mixing in three loyal friends was an impossible calcula-tion. It was also a calculation that was entirely out of her hands, a fact that she was reminded of when the truck pulled sharply to the right, throwing them together on the left side.

All four grunted as Sarah and Jacob slid up against Dianne and Josie, and the sound of metal rattling against metal came like a torrent of water rushing over a riverbed. Dianne glanced down and saw a small mountain of discarded brass sliding and tumbling across the width of the truck bed. She leaned forward and plucked one of the discarded 5.56 shells from the floor of the truck, then glanced over at Sarah with a questioning look.

Sarah nodded at her and Dianne stared at the casing, trying to decide what to do when her daughter whimpered and spoke quietly. "Mom? Where are we going?"

Dianne's decision was made before the question was answered. With a flick of her bound wrists she flipped the casing over the side of the truck, keeping her movement at a minimum to avoid drawing the attention of the vehicle driving behind them. She leaned forward and grabbed another casing while Sarah did the same, then they took turns flipping the casings off opposite sides, hoping that they weren't being ground into the dirt and gravel by the tires of the truck.

Mark, Tina and Jason wouldn't rest before attempting a rescue. A trail of breadcrumbs would mean putting her son in danger, but Jacob, Josie and Sarah needed help as well, and Tina's tenacity and Jason's all-around skills meant there was a fighting chance they could pull off a rescue. And, if not… she pushed the thought from her mind. There was no sense in worrying about it when nothing could be done.

Not yet, she thought. *Not yet.*

―

"IT'S A CASING." Jason rolled the piece of dirty brass in between his thumb and forefinger. "Five five six." He looked from the round to the road, then around at the trees as he slowly turned. "Now why on earth would this be out here in the road?"

Tina stood next to Jason, looking at the shell in his hand while Mark continued down the road, scanning the ground with his flashlight. It didn't take long for him to bend over and pluck another casing from the ground, though it was smaller than the first. "I found another one!"

"Nine mil. What the…" Jason shook his head in confusion and looked at Mark. "Were you all doing any shooting out here before Sarah and I showed up?"

"On the road? No, never." Mark shook his head vigorously. "We never even left the property except to gather supplies."

"Huh." Jason cupped both casings in his hand, rattling them around as he thought through what they could mean.

"Do you think they…" Tina started, then stopped as she glanced at Mark. "We didn't hear any gunshots as they were driving off, so these can't be from them."

"But maybe they are." Jason slipped the casings into his pocket and motioned at Mark. "Spread out; see if you can find any more."

"How do you figure they're from that group?" Tina asked as she stepped away from Jason and Mark and began staring at the ground as she walked slowly along.

"They're not buried in the dirt so they're fresh. If anyone had been shooting recently then we would have heard. And Mark says they never shot on the road. So it has to be from the attackers. Look, see? Another one."

"And one over here." Tina scooped up another casing.

"It's a trail." Mark's face lit up and he turned to look at Tina and Jason. "It's a trail! Mom must have left us a trail!"

"Her and Sarah both from the looks of it." Jason pointed at another casing on the ground, not bothering to pick it up. "They're coming in pairs now." He looked down the road ahead of them, watching as the dirt and gravel faded off into nothingness as it approached town. "So they did go this way."

"And we can follow them now. No matter where they go." Elation was wrapped around every syllable that Mark spoke, and Tina and Jason couldn't help but grin as well. They all sped up, stopping only to kick dirt around to confirm the finding of each new casing, hurrying to follow the trail that would, they hoped, lead them to their family and friends.

Chapter Eight

W ashington, D.C.

"YOU'RE CRAZY." Dr. Evans shook his head vigorously, his arms crossed over his chest and his face a mask of defiance and disbelief. "They've been nothing but helpful."

"The techs, yes. The Spetsnaz? No."

Jane nodded in agreement with Rick and put her hand on Dr. Evans' arm. "I know this is hard, but I'm telling you those two are up to something. Both of us have noticed."

"I didn't believe her at first either," Rick continued. "But after spending a while with Ostap, I can guarantee you that they're just waiting for the perfect opportunity to screw us over."

"He's right." The voice came from behind Rick and Jane. It was barely a whisper and they both whirled around to find Oles standing there, staring at them. "They are planning something."

"Oles?" Dr. Evans' eyes crinkled in concern. "What are you talking about?"

"Ostap and Carl are special forces. Before we flew out here, they were speaking with top government officials. Anytime we've tried to speak with them about the specifics of stopping Damocles they've told us to not worry about it. Jacob and I have been concerned that... that they will consider him and I expendable."

"See?" Jane turned to look at Dr. Evans. "I told you something was up."

"Are you sure about this, Oles? Why didn't you say something before?"

"Because we weren't sure about it." Oles sighed nervously, his breath hissing through his mask. "After hearing what you all said, though, I think our suspicions are confirmed."

"Do you trust us, Oles? You and Jacob?" Rick watched the technician's eyes for any hint of a lie, though he found none as Oles replied.

"Yes. You are trying to stop this. To save everyone. They... I do not think they have the same goal in mind."

"Now what would make you say that?" The new voice was different from the others, echoing loudly in everyone's ears and carrying the telltale hiss and static that indicated it was coming through a radio. Rick, Jane, Dr. Evans and Oles all looked around the room, searching for the source of the voice.

"Who's there?" Jane shouted, pulling out her pistol at the same time as Rick readied his rifle.

"It's funny, you know," the voice continued. "I was certain you knew. Carl was not. Listening in on you was impossible until fortune smiled upon us."

"The masks." Oles hissed, pointing to the bulky piece of equipment covering his whole face and wrapping around to cover his ears and part of his head.

"Transmitters in them." Rick felt his stomach churn again, though it wasn't from the smell.

"Very good." The voice was different, not coming through the small speakers in the masks but from somewhere nearby. "Drop your weapons. All of you."

The group turned to see Carl and Ostap standing at the end of the hall. Ostap's rifle was leveled at the group while Carl had Jacob in a headlock with a pistol pointed at the technician's head. Jacob clawed at Carl's arm but the officer's hold was tight and unbreakable.

"Oles, did you know about the transmitters?" Rick gave the technician a sideways glance, but the surprise in Oles' eyes gave him a confirmation of the answer from Ostap.

"No, neither of these bumbling idiots knew. Which also gave us insight into something curious about Jacob, t—" He looked at Jane, who had started moving to try and get into a position where she could fire on him. "Make another move and Jacob joins the former inhabitants from this bunker." Carl tightened his grip on Jacob's neck and Jane clenched her fists, resisting the urge to try and help the man.

"Now," Ostap continued, "I want your weapons on the ground. Slowly."

Rick's face twisted in anger as he unslung his rifle. "Why're you doing this, Ostap?"

"To save my people."

"We're trying to save *everyone*! I thought you wanted to do that, too!"

"He was undoubtedly told to get the codes to disable Damocles, but they will probably only use them to save our country." Oles shook his head as he spoke, then addressed Ostap. "Don't you realize what's going to happen if this continues to spread through the world? It won't matter if our country is saved. It's on the verge of moving from infrastructure collapse to complete destruction!"

"I'll be happy to give the keys to the program to everyone in the world," Ostap smiled. "For a price."

If the questions and confusion and wondering had all been puzzle pieces flying around Rick's head, Ostap's statement was what put them all together, forming a complete picture that Rick felt foolish for not seeing sooner. "You're not going to use the access codes to order Damocles to stand down on Russian soil, are you?"

"Of course he is." Oles scoffed. "And he's going to kill all of us in the process."

"You're only half correct," Ostap sneered. "Now come on. Kick the weapons across the floor, then send the old man and Oles over. Damocles awaits a bearer and I intend to be the one who wields it."

Chapter Nine

E llisville, VA

THE TRIP out to the gas station was long at the slow pace the group of vehicles was traveling. Dianne was expecting to be spending a long period of time in the back of the truck bouncing around but was distracting herself by tossing over shell casings several times per minute. She had wondered, at first, whether or not they would run out but every bump and turn brought forth more. They rolled and tumbled end over end out from behind boxes, from underneath a hole-filled tarp and from within holes in the sides of the truck bed.

"How have they not seen what we're doing?" Dianne murmured to Sarah as she watched the driver of the vehicle—*her* vehicle—behind them.

"Just be thankful it's still dark, okay? And pray that we get wherever we're going before the sun goes up or even that blind sack of crap'll notice the brass flipping in the air."

"You think we're going to the gas station?"

"Where else would we be going? The way you all described it makes it sound like the perfect base of operations for them." Sarah snorted and gave a slight chuckle. "Guess I'll get to see it for myself."

An abrupt bump came next, then the noise of the road vanished, replaced with the smooth hissing and gentle popping of asphalt. The brass tinged softly as it hit the ground, bouncing and rolling around in the dark, but the sound was impossible to hear over the roar of the engines. The speed of the vehicles picked up momentarily, but Dianne was surprised when she slid over toward Sarah as the truck took a sharp left-hand turn.

"Where—wait." Dianne craned her head around, trying to catch a glimpse of something recognizable in the lights of the truck. "We're heading into town."

"Yeah, so?" Sarah pulled Jacob closer as the truck swerved to avoid an obstacle in the road.

"This isn't the way to the gas station." Another casing went over the side, followed by two more in quick succession. "They're taking us somewhere else."

"Where?!" Sarah's voice rose in volume and the man inside the truck rapped on the glass and shouted something unintelligible.

"I don't know." Dianne whispered, still trying to look around to see where they were going even as she blindly felt for empty casings. She felt Josie's small hands in hers, pressing brass into Dianne's fingers. She kissed her daughter as tears welled at the corners of her eyes and then tossed the casings over the side. "I don't know. Just keep tossing, okay?"

They wound around the outer edge of the city, traveling no more than twenty or so miles an hour. The journey lasted several more minutes, and by the time the vehicles began to slow to a stop, Sarah had to lean over and punch Dianne in the arm to get her to stop tossing brass onto the ground.

"Dianne!" Sarah hissed at her and Dianne shook her head in confusion. She had been lost in her own thoughts, speculating and wondering about what would happen next. She looked around as the truck's brakes whined and the engine coughed and sputtered before finally dying.

The closest homes and stores were a good half mile away, past scattered trees and wide-open fields. Old, rusted-out fences outlined three squares in the nearby fields and the once-trimmed grass was completely overgrown. Vines pulled and tugged at the bleachers near the fences, working with the never ending cycles of sun and rain to splinter the wood and wrap around the metal frames. A dilapidated one-story wooden building stood off from the fields, the lettering above the front door too faded to read in the darkness, though there was a glimmer of light through the cracks in the boards covering the windows.

"We're out at the edge of town. Isn't this where the old baseball fields used to be?" Dianne leaned in close to Sarah and whispered to her.

"Yeah, before they moved to the new ones closer in. You think they took over the old community center?"

"Why yes. Yes we did." The voice came from near the front of the truck and both women turned in their seats to see the origin. The man in the red shirt was leaning up against the front of the vehicle, one hand resting on a holster on his hip while the other fished a cigarette out of his front pocket. "After you... *idiots* trashed our base we had to construct a new one." He pulled the cigarette out, stuck it in his mouth and lit it. "Of course, we barely got started so there's plenty of work left for you two. And your little ones."

The men who had been riding in the truck walked around to the back and opened the bed, then began pulling boxes of supplies out. "Who are you?" Dianne asked, unable to keep a look of pure hatred off of her face. Her tone matched her expression, but the man in the red shirt chuckled as he exhaled a plume of smoke, amused by her anger.

"Kenneth Nealson." He crossed one leg in front of the other and extended his arms in a mock curtsy. "Parolee and your new boss." His smile turned cruel as the last of the boxes were pulled from the back of the truck. "Get 'em out, get 'em chained and put 'em with the rest." His voice raised as he spoke, and Dianne and Sarah turned to look on the other side of the truck, realizing that he was speaking to more than just them.

"The rules around here have changed since you destroyed our little gas and trading operation." Four other people were standing out near the truck, bound together by ankle chains as they moved the boxes from the ground into the nearby building. They looked at Dianne, Sarah and the two children with sympathetic expressions as Kenneth continued. "Now there's just one rule: you work or you die."

▭

THE INITIAL ENERGY felt by Jason, Tina and Mark as they discovered the trail of brass breadcrumbs only took a few hours to wane. Jason was the primary reason why they had to slow down, though it wasn't entirely his decision. Tina was more than slightly concerned about his injury and forced him to slow down to a moderate walking pace as they trudged along the paved road.

Discarded brass was still appearing on the ground at short intervals and the change of road type and full appearance of the sun meant that it was much easier to spot. They didn't bother picking up any of the brass and Mark had even emptied his pockets of the few pieces he had collected before, tired of the sharp edges digging through and poking him in the leg.

The weather turned pleasant within an hour of sunrise and they had unzipped their jackets, grateful for another brief respite from the bitter cold that had intermittently plagued the region. Comfortable warmth soon turned to sweat, though, forcing them to slow down even further as they struggled to mix comfort with security and the desire to find their missing family and friends as soon as possible.

It wasn't until just after noon that they reached the edge of town and, at that point, Tina veered suddenly off of the road to sit down on the front porch of a nearby home. Jason and Mark, too tired to argue, joined her and the three sat in silence as they dug through their packs and divvied up some of the few supplies they had scrounged from the house. Deep, panting breaths soon turned slower and more regular as they gulped water and tore into packaged energy bars and it wasn't long before Tina spoke.

"How much farther do you think they went?"

The question wasn't directed at anyone in particular, but Mark was the first to respond. "I kind of figured they would go back to the gas station. You all talked about their setup there."

"Like I said," Jason cleared his throat and took another sip of water, "we did a number on that place. We're heading in the wrong direction to be headed there so they must have picked somewhere else."

"Yeah, but where?" Mark finished his bottle of water and put it down on the porch. "The trail of casings have us going around the edge of town but who knows how far it'll go?" The volume and pitch of Mark's voice was steadily rising until Tina clamped a hand down on his shoulder, holding him firmly in place.

"Mark. Take a breath." He looked over at her and she continued. "I know you're scared. I know you don't want to admit that you're scared. That's okay. You don't have to. I'm scared too, though. So's Jason. So's Sarah, your mom, Jacob and Josie. They're all scared more than we are. But we're going to find them, okay?" Tina's voice was soothing, chasing away the fear and trepidation in Mark's mind with reassurance and a sense of confidence.

"Best get back to it." Jason took a long breath, sighed deeply and slowly stood to his feet. Mark and Tina followed, and the three headed back to the road, picking up on the trail of casings and continuing on.

As the trio settled into their walking pattern—Jason on the left side of the street, Mark in the middle and Tina on the right—they expected to be continuing on for quite a while. When Mark stopped in his tracks not ten minutes after they had left the porch, both Tina and Jason were confused.

"Mark?" Tina looked at him, then looked in the direction he was staring. Down the road, on the right, were a series of wide fields. A couple of farms with small houses and barns sat off in the middle of them, and beyond them —just barely visible to her—was the old community center and baseball fields.

"Someone's down there."

Jason raised his rifle and peered down the scope as he knelt down to steady his aim. "Where?"

"That building down there, off to the right a bit."

"He's talking about the community center—the abandoned one."

"Mm. I don't—wait. Holy Toledo, you weren't kidding." Jason shook his head. "What I wouldn't give to have your eyes. I can barely make anything out even with this optic."

Tina knelt down as well and squinted as she looked through her 4x optic. There were a collection of vehicles parked in a ring out in front of the building and the shapes of more than a few people moving around outside the brown building. Details beyond that were impossible to make out, but it was obvious to all of them what they were seeing.

"That's got to be where Mom is. Isn't it?" Mark looked over at Jason, then at Tina, who finally replied after a long second.

"Let's go find out, shall we?"

Chapter Ten

Washington, D.C.

RICK SAT on the floor next to Jane in a glass-enclosed conference room, their hands bound in front of them with zip-ties. Outside, in the hall, Carl stood on watch, his flashlight pointed at the pair to make sure they couldn't go anywhere. Even if Rick and Jane had wanted to try and fight back, though, the removal of their filtration masks had made doing so nearly impossible. The smell was still as unbearable as when they first cracked the place open and both of them had vomited the full contents of their stomachs. Every movement was both nauseating and, thanks to their dehydration, painful as well.

Rick turned his head from the light and closed his eyes, taking a slow breath through his mouth to try and ward off any further nausea. "How long's it been?"

"Why would I know? It feels like days."

"Weeks."

"You think they let Dr. Evans and the techs keep their masks?"

"I don't see how they could work down here without them." There was a long pause before Rick spoke again. "I wonder why they haven't just killed us already."

"You've worked with stuff like this before, like Dr. Evans. They probably want to make sure they don't have a use for you first."

"What about you?"

"Oh, gee, thanks." Jane snorted and quickly regretted the swift intake of air that followed. "Way to make me feel useless."

"No, that's… no, sorry. Not what I meant."

"I'm jerking your chain. I know exactly what you meant. I don't know, though. Maybe they think I know more than I do."

Rick's eyes fluttered open at the statement. His mind started to race, connecting more dots and wondering if maybe—just maybe—there might be a way for them to get an advantage over the Russians after all.

"How much have you and Dr. Evans discussed Damocles? On a technical level?" Rick asked, still keeping his head to the side and moving his lips as little as possible.

"He's talked a lot about it, in great detail. I've tuned a lot of it out, though."

"Do you think you could bluff your way through some of it? Repeat a few things he said?"

Jane's face crinkled in confusion. "Why would I do that?"

"If we stay here, in this room, they're going to kill us eventually. If one or both of us can get mobile, though, maybe we can take advantage of a slipup. Grab a gun, free Dr. Evans or the techs… something. Anything's better than sitting here waiting for death."

There was silence for a long moment before Jane's whisper came through, barely audible even in the silent room. "I can't."

"Why not?"

"I'm… that's not me. I can't do that kind of thing."

"Yes you can."

"No, I—"

"Remember Vegas? And then, after you got hurt coming into the city? You've been incredibly strong. And you can do this."

"Why can't you?"

"They already know I know about the system, but they know my knowledge is limited. You can play yourself off as his assistant. Start a scene about him needing medication or something, then talk about Damocles to sell it. Just make it seem real. They'll take you to him, I'm sure of it."

"What do I do then?"

"You wait for the opportune moment and seize it. Seize it and don't let go of it."

Jane took in a long, slow breath and grimaced. "This smell is awful."

"No kidding." Another long silence. "You ready?"

"Nope."

Chapter Eleven

E llisville, VA

"...DAMNED BRIARS."

"Language, Jason!"

"Tina, the boy's watched people die. Pretty sure he's not going to be harmed by—"

"Guys! Seriously! Do you *want* them to hear us?"

Tina and Jason stared at Mark, who was looking at them both with wide eyes from which metaphorical daggers were being fired. Tina elbowed Jason in the side and continued walking forward through the woods, clinging to trees and branches as she went along to keep her footing on the steep slope.

With everything on the opposite side of the road being open land with nary a single object to mask their approach, Mark, Jason and Tina had been forced up the slope on the left side of the road which was thickly wooded and overgrown despite losing its foliage to the winter season. The trees and brush were thick and never traversed, which made the walking slow, painful and cumbersome. The only good part about their path was that they could walk along without fear of being spotted by anyone.

As they came to a small clearing in the woods, Tina stopped to catch her breath and waited for Mark and Jason to catch up. They both came stumbling out through the trees, both of them tripping and almost falling over the same exposed root that Tina had deftly avoided. She ignored their mumbled groans and pointed down the hill, across and up the road just a little bit farther.

"We're nearly across from the community center. And, as a bonus, the hill's starting to flatten out. Should make for a lot easier and less noisy approach."

Mark bobbed his head in all directions, trying to find an unobstructed view through the dense branches and brown vines. "How are we supposed to see them from here? It's too thick."

Jason slowly dropped down to one knee, then sank back into a sitting position. "We'll have to move forward, closer to the edge of the trees."

"Then what?" Tina leaned against a nearby trunk for support. "It's wide open all around the building, including the front."

"We'll have to wait for an opportunity to present itself." Jason took another sip of water and began checking the straps on his pack.

"Or we can just spread out and open fire on them." Mark looked through the trees at the obscured building. "Surely with the element of surprise we could—"

"No. We're three poorly-armed people against a large group that's heavily armed." Jason shook his head. "No, we have to be smart about this. We do have to be ready to jump on any opportunity that comes along, though."

"Agreed." Tina nodded and picked up her backpack. "Looks like the ditch is deep enough we can hide in it without being seen."

"Once we're down there," Jason slowly pushed himself back into a standing position, "we need to stay still and quiet. Whispers only, no moving around unless absolutely necessary. If they spot us, then we'll open fire and move in opposite directions down the ditch to maximize the effectiveness of our firepower by spreading out."

"Well?" Mark shuffled his feet anxiously. "Let's go, already!"

SET back a few hundred feet from the road, the old community center and baseball fields were far enough away that no one inside the compound noticed three figures sliding through the trees and rolling into the ditch. The guards out in front of the community center were too busy talking with each other to pay attention so they wouldn't have noticed regardless.

There were a total of three men out in front of the building standing around the cluster of vehicles parked there, with others scattered around the sides and interior of the structure. A generator sitting beneath an awning out behind the center coughed and sputtered as one of the men tried to get it working. In between the building and the baseball fields stood another cluster of men, each paying close attention to the prisoners that were shackled to each other.

Thick chains bound the feet of Dianne, Sarah, Jacob and Josie, keeping them together so that they couldn't easily run off. A padlock and a long chain connected their shackles to those of the three other people who had been taken prisoner. Dianne's group had only been at the center for a few hours, but it was already clear that things were being handled much differently than they had at the gas station.

In addition to being bound with shackles and tied together, no one was allowed to speak to each other. Dianne had to resort to hand gestures with Jacob and Josie, trying her best to shield them from the wrath of the guards by giving them stern looks and shaking her head when they started to speak. The labor was almost more intense than she had seen when overlooking the gas station compound. The group of three prisoners—whose names Dianne didn't even know—had been tasked with digging soil from one of the fields and transporting it over to Dianne's group by wheelbarrow.

Dianne, Sarah, Jacob and Josie were given twine and large burlap sacks which they filled with soil, tied off and stacked along marked sections around the center to form a protective barrier. The work was slow and ponderous, made worse by being bound to each other, but the guards were relentless. Since the moment Kenneth Nealson gave them their task they had been forced to work with only a few moments of rest here and there. Water, thankfully, had been plentiful and both Dianne and Sarah made sure Jacob and Josie were drinking plenty and staying warm as they piled dirt into the bags.

The hopelessness of the situation combined with the dramatic turn of events was not lost on Dianne, nor was her injury. The arrow had been removed and her wound was bandaged by one of the men in the compound, but it was neither pretty, gentle or what she would consider high quality. Each time she had to stand and help haul full bags over to their designated places she nearly cried from the pain as the wound continued to bleed, soaking through the bandage and spreading a red stain across her jeans.

From their position in the ditch, Mark, Jason and Tina were unable to see anything that was going on behind the center. They watched the front carefully, though, counting different men as they wandered back and forth, trying to build up an estimate of the number of enemies they would face while trying to rescue their loved ones. It was, in the end, good that they weren't able to see the labor that Dianne, Sarah, Jacob and Josie were being forced to perform for the day. When the line of bags continued around one side of the building and Mark caught a glimpse of his dirt-covered brother and sister and his limping mother, Jason's quick reaction time was the only thing that kept Mark from leaping out of the ditch and charging across the road.

"Mark!" Jason pressed his mouth against Mark's ear, hissing as he whispered as quietly as possible. "Stay still!"

"But—"

"I know!" Jason wrapped an arm around Mark and squeezed him tight, hearing Mark's breaths quicken as tears began to well up in his eyes. "I know. But if we rush in there right now, we're going to die. And that won't help them at all, will it?"

Mark shook his head and Jason eased up on his grip, still keeping his arm around him, trying to comfort him. "The good news, though, is that we know they're safe." Jason continued whispering. "I need to talk with Tina and see if we can come up with a plan. You gonna stay put if I let you go?"

Mark nodded and Jason patted him on the back, then slowly scooched over close to Tina. He leaned in and whispered to her, keeping his head low and near hers so that they could quietly speak without their voices carrying over the road.

"He spotted them."

"How many?"

"All four."

"Surprised you managed to keep him from jumping and running."

"He's going to soon if we don't come up with a plan."

Tina glanced back over the edge of the ditch, shaking her head. "I don't know, Jason. We can't handle that many of them. They clearly didn't bring everyone to their assault on the house. What's the count up to?"

"Twelve." Mark whispered softly, crawling over and joining in on the quiet conversation. "Maybe a few more or less, but we've been keeping track of them based on their clothes and stuff so I think that's right."

"At least twelve. We can't handle that." Tina sighed. "No way can we handle that."

"Then we find a different way." Jason pulled off his wool cap and ran a finger through his hair. "Nightfall's going to be our best bet. I say we try and get a bit of rest before then. Once the sun goes down we can reevaluate and try to figure something out."

"Will they even survive till the night?" Mark's words hung in the air, unanswered, fostering a sense of dread and trepidation. Dianne, Jacob and Josie had all looked the worse for wear and Sarah appeared to be with them. The details of what was going on were impossible to know from their location huddled in a damp ditch across the road, but as the sun began crawling back down toward the horizon, they hoped the answers would come soon.

Whether the answers were good or not was anyone's guess.

Chapter Twelve

W ashington, D.C.

"SIT DOWN!" Carl snarled as he approached the glass wall of the conference room, rifle raised at Jane. With her hands bound at the wrists the most she could do was raise them to chest level as she walked forward, shouting and pleading at the top of her lungs.

"Please! You have to take me to him! He needs his medication! Dr. Evans could die unless he gets it!"

Carl hesitated, then shook his head. "No, he doesn't take any."

"I've been his assistant for the last three years. I think I'd know if he takes heart medication! If he doesn't get his shot once a day he could have a stroke or a heart attack!"

"Good girl." Rick whispered to himself as he sat on the floor, watching the drama unfold in front of him.

"Please, just take me to him." She took another step forward. "It's in his bag. I'll give him his shot then you can bring me back here, all right? Unless you want him dead before you're able to decrypt the master unlock codes?" Jane had racked her brain to remember something of what Dr. Evans spoke of about Damocles, and the master unlock codes were the first thing to spring to mind.

The phrase, while vague, was enough to make Carl lower his rifle ever so slightly. He watched her carefully, looking for a sign that she was lying, but her nausea and subsequent sweating masked her subterfuge. After a long look at Jane, Carl touched the side of his mask and spoke softly, waited for a reply, responded and had a dialogue that went on for a good thirty seconds before Jane advanced again, shouting at him.

"Please, Dr. Evans needs his shot!"

"Where is it?"

"In his bag!"

"Describe it."

"Small needle, around three inches long, and several vials with a green label. You have to prime the syringe, first though, by—"

"There's nothing of the sort in his bag."

Jane rolled her eyes in an exaggerated manner. "It's in a pouch in a side pocket—look, just take me there. I'll give him the shot, then you can bring me back."

Carl watched her as he spoke softly again. Another thirty seconds passed in which Rick grew increasingly nervous until the Russian finally relented. "We're going down one floor. You," Carl pointed at Rick, "will not move. If you do, she dies."

Rick shrugged and nodded, then Carl raised his rifle again as he approached the glass door. "Step back!" He barked the order at Jane and she complied, still keeping her hands up at chest level. Carl reached for the door to the conference room, removed the chain around the handle and a support column next to it, pulled it open, then kept it in place with his boot. He motioned at Jane with his free hand, keeping the rifle loose so that he could swing it either in her direction or in Rick's if either of them tried anything.

Jane's heart pounded as she walked toward Carl, and time seemed to slow as she thought over Rick's words to her about waiting for the "opportune moment." She still wasn't sure when that moment would arrive, but when he said it she assumed it wouldn't be until she reached the room where Dr. Evans was being held.

Fortune, as the saying goes, though, favors the bold.

As Jane passed over the threshold out of the conference room, she saw Carl turn and focus his attention on Rick. Seizing upon the Russian's split second of distraction, she lunged at him, slamming into his frame with her entire weight, which wasn't even three-quarters of what he weighed. The surprise of the attack overwhelmed him, though, and he tumbled to the ground inside the conference room, the rifle spilling out of his hands and scattering across the floor.

Rick was on the Russian like a panther, springing from his spot on the floor while Jane clawed at Carl's face. Bile rose in Rick's throat with the sudden movement but he pushed past it, running around the conference table and delivering a kick to the side of Carl's head that landed with a satisfying—albeit gruesome—crunch of both mask and bone. Carl's cursing and flailing movements ceased in an instant as his neck twisted to the side, snapping his spine at the base of his skull.

"Here, quick!" Rick grabbed a knife out of the Russian's vest with both hands and held it out for Jane. She ran the zip-tie around her wrists over the blade, snapping the plastic in a few seconds. She then took the knife, did the same for Rick and then tossed the weapon aside in favor of Carl's rifle. Rick, meanwhile, rolled the Russian over and opened his backpack, pulling out the two masks that he had confiscated from Rick and Jane. He turned them over and examined the interiors of the devices before using Carl's knife to dig out a small plastic plate in the center of each mask. A small bundle of wires and electronics came out with the plate, and Rick tossed them to the side before handing one of the masks to Jane.

All feelings of nausea, exhaustion and dehydration vanished as they put on the masks, breathing in filtered air free of almost all traces of rancid, rotten flesh. Rick and Jane knelt next to Carl, each on one side of the dead Russian, until Jane pushed herself up with the help of the rifle and held out her hand to help Rick to his feet.

"Nice work." He nodded at her as he caught his breath. "Now we need to take out Ostap and save Dr. Evans."

"Do you think they heard anything?"

Rick shook his head. "I don't know. We need to get moving quickly, though, just in case Carl's mask was transmitting out and Ostap heard something."

"Agreed. Grab his pistol, I'll check the hall and make sure the coast is clear."

Rick nodded and leaned down to pluck Carl's pistol off his hip. At the same time, Jane turned around and headed back across the threshold of the conference room. She pivoted to the right, taking a look down the hall where the stairs leading down into the next area were located, and let out a muffled shriek. Her cry was barely registered by Rick, though, over the explosive sound of gunfire rattling in the confined space. Several shots rang out and he raised his head, first seeing Jane slowly toppling over, then seeing the blood already beginning to stain her shirt and pants.

Time felt like it was slowing again as he looked to his right, seeing a glimpse of a masked figure moving down the hall, rifle in hand as he continued to put rounds into Jane's limp body, each shot sounding like cannon fire in the enclosed space. Emergency lights, Carl's flashlight and a headlamp on the advancing figure all flickered and bounced around, though none of it mattered one whit to Rick. He wondered, ever so briefly, if the glass of the conference room walls was bulletproof as he raised Carl's pistol, lined up the sights on the figure and squeezed the trigger.

Glass exploded as the rounds passed through, thrown ever so slightly off course by the angle at which they penetrated the barrier, but not enough to keep them from hitting their target. So laser-focused was Ostap on gunning down Jane that he didn't notice he was being shot until the third round penetrated into his side, passing through his kidney and tearing apart his bowels in the process. Pain shot through his body and he felt himself falling as he ran, losing control over his hands and arms and skidding to a stop with a wheezing, gasping breath.

Rick dropped the pistol and ran into the hall before dropping to his knees next to Jane. Blood poured from her wounds, her skin already turning pale, as she opened her eyes at his touch. Her lips moved behind the mask but no words came out, and Rick tore it off to see thick rivulets of blood running down the sides of her face to join that which had already pooled beneath her body. He looked her over, trying to figure out which wound to tend to first when her eyes fluttered open and she tried to speak again.

"Thank you... thank you for everything." The words were barely a whisper, and Rick shook his head at her.

"You're not dying! No!" Tears stung Rick's eyes beneath his mask as he spoke to her, trying to convince himself of what he was saying more than he was trying to convince her. "Ostap's dead and I'll go get Dr. Evans; he can help you. We can find the Capitol police again, too! They fixed you up last time; they can do it again!"

Jane's body heaved and a splatter of blood came from her mouth in a choking, gasping cough before she whispered again. Her eyes widened and she reached for Rick, grabbing at his hand and digging her nails into his skin as she whispered again.

"I'm scared, Rick."

"I know. It'll be okay, though. I promise. It'll be okay!" Rick pulled off his mask and looked her over again. Wounds littered her chest, and two had passed through her right leg. From the paleness of her skin and the amount of blood beneath her, it looked like one of the bullets had torn through an artery.

Her grip on his hand tightened again and she took in one final, ragged, determined breath. Her grip on his hand loosened and he lowered her arm to her side before rocking back onto his heels. The overwhelming smell of the bunker meant nothing as tears poured down his cheeks, though wiping them away did nothing. It took less than a minute for the tears to turn to rage, though, as Rick heard a pained grunt from off to the side, pulling his attention away.

He rose and took a few steps over to Ostap, who was crawling along the ground, trying to get to his rifle. Rick kicked the weapon to the side and pushed Ostap over on his back, unable to repress a sneer at the sound of the Russian crying out in pain. He knelt down, tore Ostap's mask off and flung it away before taking out Ostap's knife from his vest and holding it at the man's throat.

"Why. Would. You. Kill her."

For a long moment Ostap lay still, his eyes closed, his breaths coming in slow, shuddering waves. When he opened his eyes, a cruel smile played across his lips and he whispered to Rick as blood trickled from the corner of his mouth.

"If you spent more time worrying about what's really important, you might ask yourself a very simple question."

"Which is?" Rick's voice shook with rage and grief, and he grabbed Ostap by the collar.

The smile turned into a grin as Ostap, too, took one final breath.

"Don't you want to know where your precious Dr. Evans is at?"

Chapter Thirteen

E llisville, VA

MARK HAD BEEN a heavy sleeper for many years, much to the annoyance of both his parents. His ability to fall asleep within minutes in virtually any position or situation was convenient for him, but it often took multiple tries to wake him in the morning, a fact that irked his mother nearly each and every day. Ever since the event, though, Mark's sleeping habits had changed. No longer was he able to fall asleep wherever and whenever he wanted and the slightest noise woke him, often causing his heart to start pounding as his mind jumped to assigning the sound to some terrible calamity.

After being on his feet for so long, though, the damp ground at the deepest part of the ditch seemed like a feather mattress and he had barely put up any sort of a fight or argument when Tina told him and Jason to get some rest. He was asleep within seconds of putting his head down and he quickly fell into a dreamless slumber. The hood of his jacket was pulled up and over his head and eyes to help block out the fading sun, and Jason laid down a few feet away in a similar position. Tina, meanwhile, stayed leaning up against the slope of the ditch, alternating her gaze between the magnified optic on Jason's rifle and off of it to take in a wider view of the movement across the road.

Hours ticked in painful slowness, the mental note-taking and constant watching of the center doing nothing to alleviate the sheer boredom of the task. Occasionally, when a cluster of the men would gather together, Tina felt the urge to shoulder the rifle and try to take several of them out at once, but common sense quickly overtook her and she resumed her watch.

It wasn't until the late afternoon that the bleak situation took a sharp turn toward the unexpected. A car with a pair inside of it pulled up in front of the center and the driver and passenger went inside, carrying a few bags between them. Later, as a group of men gathered out in front of the community center, near the vehicles parked there, they began to move a large covered trailer into position behind one of the trucks. After connecting it to the truck they began working on the back door of the trailer—which was apparently broken and wouldn't shut correctly—though they didn't make much progress. As they worked, the volume of their shouts and cursing at the trailer and at each other increased, and Tina began to hear bits and pieces of their conversation. After listening for a few minutes, she finally caught a phrase that made her eyes grow wide. She turned and slid down the slope of the ditch to Jason and Mark, putting her hands on their chests and shaking them.

"Wake up!" She whispered to both of them, one after the other, then threw herself against the slope again and looked at the center. Sounds of hammering and more cursing came from the back of the trailer, and she soon saw one of the men toss a tool through the air before throwing up his hands in frustration. Mark and Jason joined her a moment later, and they both looked at her with bleary eyes.

"What's going on over there?" Jason spoke softly, just barely loud enough for her to hear.

"They're going back to the house." Tina didn't take her eyes off of the men as she spoke.

"They—wait, what?" Mark and Jason both blinked rapidly, trying to figure out if they had really heard what they thought they heard. Tina nodded again and put a finger to her lips as she leaned in close.

"They sent out another truck early this morning, after they got back with Dianne and the rest. It's going on a supply run for food and fuel but they don't expect it back for another couple days. For the last half hour, though, they've been shouting at each other, trying to get the box trailer repaired. The rear door's broken and the hitch is giving them quite a time but they're going to leave soon. They want to get back to the house and get supplies from the barns; anything that didn't burn up in the fire they started. They figure all that plus the supply run from this morning will get them all set up."

"Which means they'll be ransacking the house since we put that fire out... and then they'll figure out that we're still alive. We have to get on that trailer." Jason rubbed a dirty thumb and forefinger against the bridge of his nose as though the action could somehow drive away the headache that was already gathering there.

"On... the trailer?" It was Tina's turn to stare slack-jawed in Jason's direction. "How do you figure we'll do that? Magic?!" Her voice was dangerously close to breaching the level of a whisper and Jason had to motion for her to quiet down.

"No. We make some kind of a distraction as they're pulling out. Get them to look away from the back for a minute. Then we climb on board, ride it to the house and surprise them when they open it up."

"How is that going to help us?" Mark's eyes were wide, partially from fear and partially from the excitement and anticipation of finally *doing* something.

"Good question." Tina stared at Jason expectantly.

"If we get aboard and ambush them at the house, we'll gain a vehicle and weapons. Plus we'll be able to reduce their numbers and get the element of surprise. If we're fast, they won't be able to report back to red shirt and we can mount a rescue operation."

Before Tina could respond, Jason slid back down the slope of the ditch and began rummaging through his bag. At the same time, she saw the door to the front of the community center open and a man flanked by a few others came out, bellowing at the group trying to get the trailer hooked up. His voice was clear and carried far, making it easy to understand what he was saying even from across the road.

"Rip out the solar panels and tear open the barns! Take anything that the fire didn't consume. I want you back before sunrise, understand? We have to…" the voice grew quieter as he stepped inside the trailer, but Tina, Jason and Mark had heard enough.

"Here." Jason slithered back up the slope, cradling a small cardboard box in his hands. He opened the flaps to reveal a pair of shotgun shells connected to wires, a simple switch and a pair of springs, all of which was mounted to a small block of wood. "When I was making the traps before, I made this as a prototype. It's got a ten second timer on it. You set the timer, throw it and the shells go off ten seconds later. It's not likely to do much harm to anyone but it'll make one heck of a noise."

Tina took the small box and looked at it. "We toss this as they're pulling out, get them distracted by it, then make a run for the trailer?" She shook her head. "What'll we do when they find it? They're going to know some-one's around."

"So?" Jason grinned, his mood bolstered by the formation of their plan. "By the time they figure out what's going on, we'll be nice and hidden beneath their noses. They'll search the area, find nothing, assume that the scraps of this thing were contained within the supplies they brought back from the house and that it must have fallen off. They're bound to remember the traps, so they'll put two and two together and then keep going. They have no reason to search inside the trailer which is where we'll be."

"This is insane." Tina rubbed her eyes and took a long, slow breath. "But," she sighed, "what choice do we have?"

"Wait till they leave then storm the center?" Mark replied. "What if they immediately start searching around after they hear the device go off? They'll find us before we get anywhere near the trailer."

"See?" Tina jerked her thumb over at Mark. "He's got a point, Jason. This little strategy is dependent on a lot of variables."

An exasperated expression crossed Jason's face. "What do you want to do, then? Assault the fortress? Get shot before we get halfway across the road? We'd need some sort of insane distraction to pull that off. Something a lot bigger than a couple of shells going off. We can do that if you want, but I don't think it'll go well."

"No. No it won't. But I know what will."

"What's that?"

Tina looked over at Mark, then at Jason. Her worry, frustration, exhaustion and fear had all melted away, replaced instead by a cool demeanor that showed that she knew exactly what she needed to do. She took off her backpack and jacket as she spoke and began rubbing dirt and grass across her clothing and skin. "Neither of you are going to like this, but it's the best solution. We're going to do a combination of the plans. I'm going to be the distraction. They won't shoot me if I come in unarmed, looking like I barely survived a fire. They'll take me in, put me with the others and I'll be able to get Dianne and the rest ready to help once you two carry out the other part of the plan."

"What?" Jason shook his head emphatically, trying to reach for Tina, but she slipped away, moving a few feet further down the ditch.

"You two are going to get in that trailer. I'll make sure you have ample time to do it. Get inside, wait for them to get to the house, then take them out. Every last one of them. Once you do, wait a few hours and head back. I'll make sure everyone's ready to do anything we can to take advantage of whatever chaos you can bring with you."

"Tina, there's no way that we're going to go along with something as idiotic as that!" Jason's eyes were wide and he hissed at her, but she kept slithering back through the ditch, staying out of his reach.

She smiled at him before looking at Mark who was slowly nodding his head in understanding and agreement. "You don't have a choice, Jason. And Mark? Make sure he gets on that trailer, okay?"

"I will." Mark nodded.

"Tina!" Jason whispered again, but she was already gone, half crawling and half slipping through the ditch, covering herself with dirt and debris as she went along.

"Damn fool! She's gonna get herself killed!" Jason shook his head and leaned back, slipping down the slope as he watched her go. A moment later she was a hundred feet away, still keeping out of sight, when the sound of an engine roaring to life brought both him and Mark up to the top of the ditch to see what was going on.

Across the road the truck and trailer began moving, making a wide turn in front of the community center. Five men sat inside the truck as it went along, the trailer bumping and squeaking behind it, barely held to the truck with a collection of chains and a half-broken hitch. Down the ditch, farther than either Mark or Jason would have thought it possible to crawl in such a short length of time, Tina was nearing a shallow portion. She peeked up and over at the truck and watched it closely. Revealing herself too early would mean that the trailer would be in the wrong position for Jason and Mark to hop aboard but waiting too long could mean an immediate search of the surrounding area which would also keep them from slipping into the trailer.

Truth be told, Tina had no idea why she was risking life and limb with a plan that could easily end up with her being shot and Mark and Jason being discovered. They didn't have many options, though, and if—by some miracle —they took her captive and Mark and Jason were able to get on board without being seen, they might have a shot at rescuing the captives.

Might. The word ran through Tina's mind repeatedly as she watched the truck bump along the gravel drive of the community center, slowly pull onto the road and begin to straighten out. *Well. Here's hoping 'might' works out.*

Chapter Fourteen

E llisville, VA

"I CAN'T BELIEVE she's doing it." Mark whispered to Jason as they both crouched low in the ditch watching Tina.

"She's insane."

"She's just trying to help."

"And she's gonna get herself shot doing it."

Mark and Jason stared as Tina shuffled down the road, limping in an exaggerated manner toward the truck. She kept her head low as the truck pulled to a stop and four of the five men inside jumped out, weapons drawn, and began shouting at her. She stopped in the middle of the road and looked at them before slowly raising her arms and starting a backward shuffle.

"Hey! Stop right there!" The group advanced, keeping their weapons trained on her as they ignored what was going on around them.

"We've got to go now, before anyone comes out of the community center!" Jason whispered to Mark who nodded and pulled himself up to the top of the ditch.

"Ready when you are."

"Go!"

The pair scurried across the road, keeping as low as possible as they took a direct path for the rear end of the trailer. Ahead of the truck Tina tracked them for a split second before she diverted her attention back to the men, ready to try and continue distracting them. "Please, you have to help me!" She groaned at them, intentionally making as much noise as possible.

"Keep your hands up!" The men circled around Tina and the driver of the truck honked the horn several times, causing the others around the community center to start moving toward the road.

"Now! Get inside!" Jason pulled on Mark's shoulder and they slipped around the back of the trailer. The doors were held together with a tightly-wound bungee cord which Jason quickly slipped off of the handles. He opened one door and Mark went inside, then Jason went inside and looped the cord around the open door handle before pulling the door closed. He tied the cord off on a metal securing ring on the floor before turning back to Mark and motioning toward the front of the trailer.

"Inside more, quick. In case they search this thing." He whispered inside the stuffy air of the trailer, his nose wrinkling as they stirred up swirls of dust with each shuffling footstep. The trailer was dark, the only source of light coming from an opaque plastic window mounted on the ceiling and a few cracks in the back doors. A few cardboard boxes were stacked up on one side and old scraps of wood littered the floor, remnants of some long-forgotten home improvement project. The smell of old manure clung to the floor and walls and Mark couldn't help but pull his shirt up over his mouth and nose.

"Smells like they hauled horses in here."

"Or just their crap." Jason glanced at Mark. "Poop. Sorry."

Mark smirked and raised an eyebrow. "I can handle the word 'crap.'"

"Good. Here, behind these boxes." Jason pushed the stack of boxes around and crouched down, hiding himself from view of the doors at the back of the trailer. "Get down and stay down. Sounds like things are heating up out there."

The pair pressed their ears up against the side of the trailer as Tina's shouting cut through, followed by the angry shouts and conversations of several nearby men. It was impossible to make out exactly what everyone was saying, but Tina was clearly very much alive and was acting the part of someone who was very upset to be taken prisoner. The men, meanwhile, were busy binding her hands while simultaneously wondering where she came from. Jason wondered with every new exclamation whether or not they would start searching the area and, if so, if they would search in the trailer. There was no reason for them to do so, but the fear persisted for several long, agonizing minutes until things began to change.

"She's getting quieter." Mark spoke softly.

"They're taking her inside or out back, I'll bet."

"Maybe that means we're going to be moving soon."

The telltale clicks of doors opening and the soft thunks of them closing again signaled that the men from the truck were climbing back inside. The pitch of the engine changed abruptly and the trailer lurched as the truck pulled forward, sending Mark and Jason tumbling into the boxes.

"Does—does that mean it worked?" Mark pushed himself up into a crouch, keeping his center of gravity low to help counteract the swaying motion of the trailer.

"It got us on the trailer, so yeah. I just hope they aren't going to hurt her too badly."

———

"WHERE ARE THE OTHERS?!"

Tina kept her eyes closed as Nealson struck her with an open-palmed slap across the face. She was old but never frail, and though each blow stung worse than the one before, she kept to the same line she had been using ever since she was dragged inside the community center and thrown into a chair.

"They burned to death. Like I keep telling you."

Nealson turned and grabbed her by her jacket collar, pulling her roughly to her feet. His eyes were wide, his breath was rancid with the scent of stale coffee and his hair and beard were unkempt. "I know there were more people there with you! A man, maybe more children! Another woman, perhaps? *Where are they!?*"

Tina stiffened as he hit her again, then she shook her head and opened her eyes. It wasn't hard to force a few tears out; the pain in her face ensured that. Getting her tone and her look just right was the difficult part. Her arms were free, the temporary binding having been cut away after he threw her into the chair. With the way he was holding her all she wanted to do was rip and claw at his face, tearing at his eyes and throat and making him suffer like he had made her husband and so many others suffer.

Doing so would jeopardize everything, though. Her life, Dianne's life, Sarah's life, the kids' lives and more. So, instead of taking revenge, she unlocked the bottled-up pain from her husband's death and used it. She breathed it in, letting it envelope her entire body and drive her every emotion.

"They're dead." She let loose a few ragged breaths before looking Nealson in the eye. "If you want to kill me, too, then just do it. It's not like I have anything to live for anymore."

"Why did you come here?"

"Was just trying to find shelter. How would I know you'd be here?"

Nealson growled at her before dropping her back into the chair. "Take her out back, with the others." Two of the other men who had been standing nearby grabbed Tina from the chair and pulled her along in between them. Nealson watched her go, calling out just before she was taken out through the back door to the building.

"Nice to have you back again! Try not to leave us so soon this time, okay?"

⊏⊐

THE TRAILER JOSTLED AND SHOOK, nearly throwing Jason and Mark off balance. They reached out and grabbed at the side of the structure for support as the road noise increased along with the bounciness of their ride.

"We must be close; road just turned to gravel." More bumps accompanied a drastic sway of the trailer, confirming Jason's words.

"So just a few more minutes till we get to the house. How are we going to do this when we get there?"

Jason put his hand on Mark's shoulder, steeling himself for the uncomfortable conversion that he had been trying to avoid. "I think you should hang back, Mark. Hang back and let me do this."

"Hang... back? To do what, try and flank them somehow?" Mark glanced around the trailer. "There aren't any other exits from this thing. I'm not sure how—"

"No. Just to hang back. Out of danger."

"I don't understand." A confused frown passed over his face. "Are you saying you don't want my help?"

"I want it, yes. But... your mother... she would—"

"My mother, my brother and my sister are chained together back at that place." Mark's voice remained relatively quiet, but his tone and facial expression changed completely. "They're chained together with your wife, Mrs. Statler. The men in the truck in front of us want to do... terrible things to them all. And to other people. My mother would want me to do the right thing." Mark hesitated as he stared through Jason, remembering back to when he watched his mother shoot the man who had been trying to break into their property. He snapped back to reality and shrugged Jason's hand off of his shoulder.

"Even when the right thing is hard," Mark finished with a defiant and definite tone, "we still have to do it. That's why it's the right thing."

Jason's internal struggle was complicated by the unexpected burst of maturity from Mark, and he didn't know what to say. They knelt, quietly, as the trailer bumped and rocked along until the situation itself forced Jason to accept the inevitable. A slowing of the truck and trailer, then a motion to the left indicated that they were making the turn to the house.

"Fine. Just stay behind me and do what I tell you. Okay?"

Mark nodded and Jason slipped quietly to the back of the trailer. Taking a piece of old lumber from the floor, Jason quietly slipped it into the grooves running alongside both of the back doors, near the bottom. He then took the bungee cord and wrapped it around the wood before tying it off, creating a crude—but effective—bar for the doors.

"That's your plan?" Mark whispered to Jason, befuddlement thick in his voice. "To keep them out of the trailer?"

Jason walked back up to Jason and knelt back down. "If you have to shoot fish in a barrel, you want them in the smallest, most compact barrel you can possibly get."

Mark's eyes lit up and a devious smirk spread across his lips. "So you want to gather them all at the back of the trailer before we let them know we're here."

"Exactly." Jason nodded before shrugging off his pack and his rifle. He dug through his backpack before pulling out the shotgun shell trap he had proposed using as a distraction earlier. "Once they're gathered, I'll loosen the board and set this thing up. Once the doors open and this thing goes off, we go out there guns blazing."

Mark gulped hard and looked at the pistol in his hand. "I'll do my best."

Jason put on his best smile and gave Mark a quick squeeze. "I know you will. Now get some more boxes stacked up to hide us behind while I get my rifle squared away."

While Mark did as Jason requested, Jason gathered his meager assortment of spare magazines and triple-checked that his rifle was loaded with the safety off and one in the chamber. He had never been in war, nor had he ever been in a shootout until after the event. That didn't matter, though. His wife's life was in his hands and one of his friends' children was sitting next to him trying to mentally prepare himself for what was to come.

The right thing was hard. But that didn't matter. It still had to be done, no matter what.

Chapter Fifteen

The Waters' Homestead
        Outside Ellisville, VA

WHILE MARK and Jason couldn't see the expressions on the faces of the men in the truck, if they had they might have enjoyed a hearty chuckle in spite of the gravity of the situation. Confusion reigned supreme as the five all leaned forward in their seats, staring at the home standing directly where they expected a pile of ash and blackened debris. All of them started talking at once as they climbed out of the truck, their weapons loose in their hands as they spoke to and over each other, all of them trying to decipher what they were seeing.

Inside the trailer Mark and Jason kept their ears to the wall, listening to the muffled shouting and arguing as they tried to figure out when the group would start making their way toward the trailer. The voices slowly grew louder and easier to discern as the men walked back from examining the scorched patch at the front of the house.

"...sense why it didn't catch. There was plenty of accelerant."

"Maybe someone pissed it out. Who cares? We've got a house to ransack now. They had some nice looking plants in the basement; maybe we can get something fresh out of the place, eh?"

"*I* care. And so will Nealson." The sound and reverberation of someone being pushed roughly against the trailer nearly caused Mark and Jason to fall over. "We need to call him and let him know about this. It could mean that someone survived the fire!"

"Nealson's already beyond pissed. Did you see him with that one from the road?"

"You realize that was the one that they came and pulled out from the station base, right?"

"Well yeah, but everyone else is dead. So who cares?"

Another thud. "I told you that *I* do!"

A different voice, one that hadn't been understandable, interrupted the argument. "Hey, check it out. They've got a ton of chickens down there and some other stuff, too. Barns are full of food for 'em, too. We're gonna have to make several trips to get everything!"

"No. Nealson wants this done fast." It was the voice of the one who seemed like he was in charge. "We'll prioritize on what we need the most, then come back for the rest later." Another thud. "And *you*—get the trailer open, then call Nealson on the radio!"

Jason nudged Mark. "That's our cue. Get ready." He spoke into Mark's ear, his voice barely above a whisper just like it had been when they spent the day in the ditch.

The sound of under-the-breath grumbling accompanied slow, plodding footsteps as the chastised member of the group walked around to the back of the trailer. Jason held his breath, half-expecting his jury-rigged lock on the back of the trailer to fall apart upon being looked at.

"What the hell?" The confused exclamation was accompanied by a rattle of the trailer doors. Another, stronger rattle followed, then came a shout. "Hey, what'd you do to this thing?"

"Do? I did what he said and got it fixed."

"What'd you fix it with? Glue? Stupid thing won't open!"

The second voice drew closer and the doors continued to rattle and shake as the two men worked to try and open them. "What the… this isn't what I did."

"Yeah, sure. Stop making excuses already."

"No, I swear! I didn't put the cord inside the trailer. How could I have done that?"

"Because you're stupid, that's how. Just go get the others; we need to pry this thing open and undo your screwup."

More mumbling and grumbling followed as the chastised man walked off and shouted at the other three. The rattling and thumping on the back of the trailer ceased for a moment and Jason seized his opportunity. He quickly moved to the back of the trailer and removed the board that had been keeping the doors shut, then unwound the bungee cord and reconnected it to the metal loop on the floor. The change would keep the doors shut, but would make it easy for the men to open them by simply cutting the cord.

Jason moved back behind the boxes with Mark once again and picked up the shotgun shell device and fiddled with the trigger, changing the timer from a ten-second delay to a three-second delay. "As soon as the doors open," he whispered, "I'll arm it and throw. As soon as it goes off, I'll start shooting first. You follow up behind me and watch my back and sides. Got it?"

Mark nodded and Jason took a deep breath, bracing himself for the inevitable. Seconds turned into minutes, both ticking by in slow agony as he and Mark waited for the men to return. When they finally heard the voice of the first man, it was filled with annoyance.

"Took you all long enough!"

"He said to get supplies, so we got supplies. And do we really all need to be here to help you figure out how to open a door?"

"Why don't you try it, tough guy, and see how easy it is for you?"

More rattling came from the doors, then the sound of a metallic click, then the bungee cord snapped as it was severed from the outside with a quick slice from a sharpened blade. The broken door began to swing open on its own accord, revealing a group of four men standing around just outside. The one who had first tried to open the trailer threw his hands up and began cursing loudly while the others laughed. They all turned toward the trailer and one reached for the second door, pulled it open and was greeted by a smack in the head by a small, hard object.

"What the—"

The object hit the ground and the words barely came out of the man's mouth when a loud, ear-piecing *bang* echoed from the end of the trailer. A scream accompanied the tail end of the small explosion and the man whom Jason had hit square on the forehead with the small shotgun shell bomb collapsed, grabbing for his calves as though he could somehow pull out the pellets and their associated pain.

The next several seconds played out in slow motion from Jason's perspective, but for the other three men standing behind the one closest to the back of the trailer, it was all over before they realized what was happening. Momentarily disoriented by the makeshift explosive device, they never saw Jason stand up from behind the pile of cardboard boxes and take aim at them. He walked forward as he fired, putting four rounds into the center of mass of his first target.

After the injured man was downed Jason moved onto the next three in line, finger squeezing the trigger smoothly as he kept the rifle pressed tight against his shoulder. A firm hand on the grip kept the recoil in check and each piece of hot brass that bounced off the floor, walls and ceiling of the trailer meant another round had connected with its intended target.

By the time Jason reached the back of the trailer, all four men standing outside were on the ground, gasping and choking from debilitating pain or lying still as blood drained from already-fatal chest and head wounds. Jason felt a presence next to him and glanced over to see Mark standing nearby.

The boy's eyes were cold and his expression hardened as he looked over the group of bodies.

"Where's the fifth one?" Mark whispered to Jason.

"No idea. Stay behind me. We need to find him before he gets the drop on us." Jason took a step out of the trailer and swung to the left, checking on the right side of the truck and trailer. The area was empty and he waved for Mark to follow behind. "C'mon. We'll use the truck as cover while we—"

Jason's instruction was interrupted by the sharp report of a rifle spitting rounds from somewhere near the edge of the house. Mark yelped and scrambled as the incoming fire thudded against the back end of the trailer, tripping over himself and nearly dropping his pistol as he clawed to get around to the opposite side. Jason reached out and pulled Mark in and panic seized his heart as he saw a streak of blood across Mark's face.

"Are you hit?!" The words stuck in his throat as he forced them out, ignoring all pretense of stealth.

"No, no I'm good. Bashed my head on the door handle when he started firing." Mark reached up and wiped his arm across his forehead. He grimaced at the blood and wiped it on his pants. "Mom's going to be mad about the blood stains."

"She'll manage. Now stay low while I deal with this joker, okay?" Rounds continued to hit the trailer, slower than they were originally, but still steadily enough to make Jason and Mark both not want to take a peek out. Jason swallowed his fear and moved up along the side of the box trailer to the back of the truck where he ducked down and continued around to the front of the vehicle. From there he crouched down and peeked underneath the truck, looking for the source of the shots. The source, unfortunately, found him first.

Two shots hit the ground just beneath the truck, the second one mere inches from Jason's face. He couldn't help but let out a pained shout as he shot back up and started hurrying around to the right side of the truck where he could put the wheel in between him and the shooter. He was almost there when he looked down the length of the trailer to see Mark turn around the end of the trailer and fire seven slow, clean and steady shots from his pistol. Each shot was slow and methodical, and by the time he reached the fourth there was a howl of pain from near the house.

Three more rounds followed after the fourth before Mark turned back around behind the trailer and stood still, his eyes wide and his breathing heavy. "Mark!" Jason called to him. "You okay?"

"Yeah. He's not, though."

━━

JASON DIDN'T REALIZE JUST how amped up he had been on adrenaline until he nearly collapsed while walking from the edge of the house back to the truck. Mark had been with him, though, and kept him steady until he could sit down in the back of the trailer. The sun was low in the sky and the shadows were long. The air felt chilled and Mark zipped up his jacket and shoved his hands into his pockets as he scooted closer to Jason.

The older man wrapped an arm around Mark and spoke softly. "You did good here today. Your mom and dad would be proud."

"What are we going to do about her and the rest?"

"Well," Jason said slowly, a thin smile spreading across his face, "if I know your mother, Tina and my Sarah at all, they're already cooking up something. Tina's bound to have let them know what we did, so they'll hopefully be ready for us when we go in guns blazing."

"Is that what we'll do?"

"More than that." Jason scratched his chin and patted Mark on the arm. "Come on. Let's head down to the barns and take a look around. I think I might have an idea of what we can do."

Chapter Sixteen

Ellisville, VA

"THEY DID *WHAT?*" Dianne didn't dare look over at Tina as she scooped another cup full of dirt and sand into the nearest sack. Over the course of the day she had figured out what speaking volume allowed her to communicate with the children and Sarah while simultaneously not attracting the attention of the guards.

"They got on the trailer back to the house. They're going to stop the guys with the trailer then come back here for us. We need to be ready for them."

"How could you let Mark do that?!" Dianne risked a quick glare, but Tina didn't look up. Her face was red and swollen and she had bruises already starting to appear on her arms. While Dianne was angered by what Tina told her, she had to admit that the older woman was handling the current situation well.

"You'd rather him be here? Or still hiding in that ditch, trying to find a way to get across an open road and rescue you? Jason's with him." Tina glanced at Sarah. "They'll both be fine. I'm sure of it."

"She's right, Dianne." Sarah's whisper was barely audible. "It's not a good choice, but it's the best one they had. And now we know that they're alive."

"But for how long?" Dianne finished tying off the sack and pushed it aside before wiping a filthy sleeve across her brow. The sky was dark overhead but a loud generator kept a series of halogen lights running, though they flickered in time with the fluctuations of the generator. The back door to the community center creaked open and Nealson stepped out, his left hand holding a cigarette and his right hand resting on the handle of a revolver tucked into a leather holster.

"Midnight!" He crowed, a satisfied smile on his face. "Time for food and sleep!"

"Food?" Tina raised an eyebrow.

"Don't get excited." Dianne looked away from Nealson, unable to stand the sight of him. "They gave us so-called lunch. Josie threw up from it."

"So glad to see the little family's growing bigger!" Nealson walked across the grass, flicking his cigarette to the side before coming to a halt before Dianne, Tina and the two children. The other four prisoners were huddled together across the yard, watching Nealson's every move.

"Let the kids go, you monster." Sarah spoke softly; loud enough for him to hear, but with a growling, menacing undertone.

"Go where? Out to fend for themselves in the wild? Nah." He pulled another cigarette from his shirt pocket, squatted down and lit it. "What I can do, though, is promise you some edible food, extra clean water and a soft spot for your heads." He looked at Sarah while taking a long, slow drag. "If you tell me where the others from the house got to."

"They died. I told you that already." Tina straightened her back, trying to draw attention to herself.

"And yet I don't believe you. Funny how that works." Nealson sniffed and stuck the cigarette in the edge of his mouth, then stood up and nodded at a pair of men standing nearby. "Take 'em all inside. We'll continue this conversation in the morning."

Dianne's group along with the other four slowly stood, stretching their legs as they shuffled toward the building. Josie began to weep uncontrollably and Dianne put a hand on her daughter's shoulder, her entire body seizing up in anger over not being able to protect her children. Jacob was doing slightly better but Dianne could tell that he was confused more than anything else and dearly wished that he could go back home.

Because the two groups weren't bound to each other but had instead been separated to perform two distinct tasks, Dianne, her two children, Sarah and Tina were a fair distance closer to the community center and under greater supervision than the four strangers whose names were still unknown. With Sarah in the lead, the two children behind her, then Dianne and finally Tina pulling up the rear, the group shambled toward the center, all of them wondering what was going to come from their first night as prisoners.

Tina glanced up and off to the left, her gaze drawn by the sight of something in the corner of her eye. In the distance, toward Ellisville, emerged a twinkling pair of yellow headlights accompanied by the low rumble of an engine. Nealson, who was still standing near the back of the community center, walked to the corner of the building upon hearing the sound.

"You," he shouted, turning and pointing to all but two of the men standing near the door, "out front now. Truck's getting back and I want the supplies off the trailer and inside!"

One of the men grumbled as he walked by, shaking his head in frustration. "What's the point of having these people do work for us if we have to do stuff like this?"

Tolerating no dissent or disagreements, Nealson stepped forward and grabbed the man by the arm, swinging him around into a headlock. Dianne's group slowed their pace as they watched Nealson growl at the man, hissing in his ear too quietly to be heard. The effect was instant, though, as all traces of fight went out of the man and he submitted to Nealson, holding his hands in the air and pleading for his life.

The thought of attempting an escape flashed through Dianne's mind, but she threw the idea out as soon as it appeared, knowing full well that they wouldn't have a snowball's chance of making it very far with the chains on their legs. Adding to that the fact that Nealson was armed and had a group of minions on the other side of the building meant that fleeing was not a good idea. When someone is trapped in a bad situation, though, sometimes a bad idea feels like the only option available.

So it went with the group of four, the ones who Dianne's group hadn't even gotten a chance to speak with. Three men and one woman, all looking like they were in their thirties or older, turned in unison and began shuffling away toward the baseball fields as soon as Nealson turned away. Nealson's preoccupation with the man he was chastising continued as he let the man go and shoved him to the ground.

Beyond the baseball fields was a grove of trees and a few buildings, but they were far enough away that any rational mind would have immediately known that it would be impossible to make it. Healthy individuals who hadn't been pushed to the breaking point for an extended period of time and who weren't literally shackled to one another might have stood a slim chance. The group of four, however, didn't make it beyond the bleachers.

Nealson turned and saw the four figures vanishing out from beneath the bright halos cast by the halogen lights. He opened his mouth to shout at them but stopped himself, shaking his head and sighing instead. In one smooth motion he drew his handgun, took aim at the man at the back of the group and fired three rounds. The man cried out in pain and fell to the ground, the force of his fall pulling the chain taut and dragging the women down as well. Nealson turned and looked at Dianne as he walked toward the group, shrugging and sighing.

"Some people, right?"

WHILE NEALSON WAS busy herding Dianne's group into the community center and killing one of the members of the other group of prisoners, two individuals sitting in a truck a quarter mile away were trying to deal with their nerves. Jason sat behind the wheel, driving the truck at just a few miles an hour while Mark sat next to him holding a rifle scope up to his eye. The slow speed had many purposes, including ensuring that the gang at the center knew that the truck was coming as well as giving Mark ample time to get the lay of the land. The biggest reason for driving slowly, though, was to ensure that the fragile contraption in the back of the trailer wasn't set off prematurely.

"Six out front. Wait. No. Eight of them now."

"Eight? How many do they have left?!"

"That looks like all of them, maybe. Wait... no I see one more inside. Now two. One of the ones inside is the leader."

"Red shirt himself, eh?" Jason's eyes narrowed. "I hope he's one of the ones standing at the back when they open it up."

"Are you sure it's going to work? We didn't get a chance to test it out."

"Oh it'll work, all right. Just remember what you're supposed to do, okay?"

"I'll handle it." Mark visibly stiffened as he focused back on the scope.

"I know you will." A short, uncomfortable pause followed. "Still see six out front?"

"Yeah. There's more movement inside, but I can't tell who it is. Maybe mom?"

"Possibly. I don't see anyone outside. Check out back."

Mark turned his head slightly before shaking it. "Nothing."

"Probably brought them inside for the night. That's a good thing."

"What if they make them unload the trailer?"

"I'll make sure that doesn't happen."

Mark looked like he might say something else but sat quietly instead, staring through the scope with one eye as they crept closer to the community center.

⌐⌐

INSIDE THE BUILDING, Dianne closed her eyes as three more gunshots rang out, a long moment of silence hanging in the air between each of them. She, Sarah, Tina and the two children sat in a corner along with a gallon of water and a few bars of granola which the guard inside had given to them.

"Why would he do that?" Tina whispered to Dianne. "He's killing free labor."

"As an example to us. If we try to escape, he kills us all."

Tina snorted and narrowed her eyes. "That truck coming in hasn't arrived yet. It's got to be Jason and Mark."

"If it's them," Sarah looked between Dianne and Tina, "then Jason's going to have a surprise in store. Just watch and see."

⸏

"TH' hell took you so long!?"

Jason squirmed under the scarf wrapped around his face. It smelled like body odor, stale beer and cigarettes. Between it, the hat and the thick jacket he had taken from one of the men he and Mark had killed, though, he looked like he belonged in the truck. At least at a distance. Or so he hoped.

He shrugged and threw up his hands for a second as he pulled the truck off the main road and into the parking area in front of the community center. The sandbag barricade had yet to be extended all the way around, leaving him more than enough room to slowly maneuver the trailer into an optimal position.

The man who had shouted at him threw up his arms in return and took a few steps back, shaking his head while the other five looked on. In spite of the noise of the truck and the covering over his face, Jason kept his voice low and tried not to move his lips as he spoke.

"Six out front, like you said. No sign of your mom or any of the others. They must be inside right now. You ready?"

In the back of the truck, Mark gulped hard, squiggling around as though the motion could somehow cause the seat to absorb his prone form and render him entirely invisible to the hostiles outside. In his left hand he tightened his grip on the pair of bolt-cutters, the metal warm from being held against his body. In his right hand he felt the rough surface of plastic and metal bonded together into a small, sleek and deadly shape.

"Ready." He whispered back, not feeling ready at all.

"As soon as you hear the booms, you move. Don't hesitate for a second, you hear me? All of our lives count on it."

Mark nodded for his own sake, grunted in affirmation and swallowed hard again. The plan was foolhardy, dangerous and had a high chance of going sideways. If even one part of their hastily constructed plan happened to be altered or encounter some unexpected obstacle then the whole thing could easily collapse around them. With the lives of their friends and family at stake, though, there wasn't another choice.

"Careful opening the back!" Jason rolled down the driver's side window and bellowed out as the six men neared the end of the trailer. "Pretty sure some things shifted!"

"Where's the rest of the boys?" One of the six shouted back.

"In the trailer, keepin' the valuables from getting broken!"

"Why the… whatever, just park it already."

Jason rolled his window back up and unlatched his seatbelt as he brought the slow-moving truck to a halt and put it in park. He stared out the side window as the six gathered around the back of the trailer, hoping that they wouldn't tell him to get out and help.

"Hey!" Jason swung his head around to see a figure stalking out of the front of the community center. It was the same one he had seen at the gas station, then again at the house. The man in the red shirt. "What's going on out here? Where's everyone else?"

Jason felt his chest tighten as he rolled down the side window. "In the trailer!"

Nealson cocked his head, a confused expression on his face. "Why'd they get in there?"

"Solar panels and whatnot. We broke one just getting 'em in and didn't want to break more."

"You *broke* one?!" He turned and began yelling at the six men milling around at the back of the trailer. "Get it open! Now! I want to see what damage these idiots did!"

Time seemed to slow for Jason as he watched the man in the red shirt walk around to the back of the trailer. He saw one of the six men step up to the rear of the trailer, holding his arm out to open the back doors, and smiled as he rolled up the side window.

Chapter Seventeen

Ellisville, VA

FORTY-EIGHT. That was the number of metal tubes, mechanisms and shotgun shells that Jason and Mark were able to rig during the three hours they spent at the house. The tubes were mounted with zip ties to a metal shelf that they had managed to force into the back of the trailer and were arranged in an even pattern to ensure for maximum lethality and dispersal. The tubes in the very center of the shelf were angled straight while those near the edges were angled to the sides by a few degrees. Jason had hoped that the setup would lead to at least a couple of injuries or deaths if a few of the shells fired without a hitch, but never imagined what might happen if all of the tubes successfully fired on a large group.

The back of the trailer amplified the sound of the four dozen shotgun shells, making them sound more like a cannon. The timer that was tripped when the back doors were opened was too short resulting in several of the shots hitting one of the trailer doors, but that did nothing to curb the lethality of the contraption. In an instant the scene at the back of the trailer went from quiet annoyance to complete carnage.

Three of the group fell to the ground, dead before they hit the dirt thanks to slugs tearing through their hearts and heads. The other three screamed in pain, one losing a leg to a nasty grouping of slugs as the metal tubes bucked loose from the shelf and another losing both eyes to a spray of buckshot.

As soon as the shots went off, Mark and Jason both dove out of the truck, though they went in opposite directions. Mark headed straight for the community center, cutting through a couple of other vehicles parked out front. Jason ran around the back of the truck, rifle in hand as he raced for the back of the trailer. It took him less than a second to see that the six men behind the trailer had been incapacitated or killed and he looked up from their bodies to see the man in the red shirt standing unscathed.

Jason raised his rifle and fired, but Nealson was faster. He dove for a space in between a nearby two-door sedan and another small box trailer, Jason's shots just barely missing him. He crawled through the dirt for a few feet before picking himself up and dashing around to the back of the sedan where he drew his revolver as he tried to catch his breath and figure out what had just happened.

As Nealson was crawling through the dirt, the door to the community center was thrown open by Mark, who was still carrying a pair of bolt-cutters in one hand and a pistol in the other. "Get in, take down the hostile and then free everyone" had been the instructions given to him by Jason. At the time, when they were coming up with the outlandish plan, it had sounded so simple. Get in, kill anyone who was trying to hurt his family, then free his family.

Mark glanced around the room, struggling to make sense of the place. Stacks of crates and boxes were scattered around, illumination came from both generator-powered sources and from what looked like propane lanterns, making the whole place a mishmash of dark shadows and painfully bright lights. Two voices cried out one after the other as Mark walked through the door.

"Mark! Behind you!" The first voice was familiar, squeezing Mark's heart with warmth and love even though the voice itself was full of panic.

"What the..." The second was low and rough, like gravel across a wash-board. Mark swiveled from his instinctive turn to his mom's voice, pivoting on his heels to face the man's voice on his left. He raised the pistol as he turned, aimed it at the center of the blurry mass in front of him and pulled the trigger. Sound and light bit at his ears and eyes, though it was nothing compared to the fury echoing outside. Mark squeezed again, three more times, until the mass that had been moving in his direction stopped and fell to the floor with a groan and a garbled cry for help. He stared at the body, the pistol wavering slightly in his grip as he kept it trained on the man's still-warm corpse.

"Mark!" The first voice came again, breaking him out of his trance. He turned and saw his mother, sister and brother staring at him. Tina was the first to speak, though, hissing at him as she gestured wildly.

"Get over here, boy! Give me those bolt cutters!"

Mark obliged, putting the man behind him out of his mind. He raced for his family, dropping the cutters in front of Tina before wrapping his arms around Dianne. Tears flowed freely as he held her tight and he began to sob. Jacob and Josie embraced him and Dianne as well, crying not because they were frightened but because he was crying.

"Are you okay?!" Dianne whispered in his ear, feeling him top to bottom as she continued holding him tight to her chest.

"I'm fine," he wheezed, taking a step back and wiping his nose on his sleeve. "Mr. Statler's outside, though. We need to help him."

The sharp snap of metal attracted Dianne's attention, and she looked down to see Sarah pulling the shackles off of her and her children's legs. "Then let's get going, shall we?"

After a brief argument over who should wield Mark's pistol, Tina threw her hands in the air and hurried over to the man who was still lying motionless on the ground by the front door to the community center. She rolled him over with a grunt, taking a step back to avoid the rapidly enlarging puddle of blood, then plucked his rifle off the ground and dug two spare blood-covered magazines from his vest pockets. "Now," she intoned as she popped out the mag, checked it, then slammed it back home, "*I'm* leading the way out. Got it?" Another burst of gunfire from out front prevented any further arguments and she slipped up to the front door, putting her head against the wood to try and figure out what was going on.

⸺

OUTSIDE, in the two and a half minutes it took for Mark to get in, reunite with his family and for everyone to be freed by Tina and Sarah, Jason kept still behind the trailer. Occasionally he peeked out and caught a glimpse of movement behind the sedan which he fired upon, but each time his fire was met with the sound of metal and glass being torn apart instead of flesh and bone.

"Just give up!" He called out, not realizing how out of breath he was until he had to speak. "Your men are dead!"

From behind the sedan, Nealson curled his lip in anger. He didn't bother responding, not wanting to give away the fact that he was slowly making his way to the back of the vehicle where, if he was lucky, he'd be able to move around to the side and get a view on whoever it was that had so thoroughly managed to kill six of his accomplices.

With the gunfire from Jason making so much noise, Nealson hadn't noticed the pistol going off inside the community center so the sound of the front door creaking open made his heart jump with excitement. He had forgotten about Reggie, whom he had left inside to guard the remaining prisoners. He rotated around, getting ready to both instruct and chastise Reggie about not coming out sooner when he saw a small, thin form instead of the large and imposing one he had expected.

It took Nealson a few seconds to register that the person was standing in the doorway was the old woman whose husband his men had killed and who had escaped from the gas station. As soon as he realized who she was, though, he knew that things inside must have gone poorly for Reggie. If the old woman was free, that meant the others were likely free as well. Which meant that—until the other scavenging group returned—he was alone and sorely outnumbered. He needed a distraction, something that would enable him to escape before one of the prisoners or the new arrival managed to get the upper hand.

The flash of metal in the woman's hand sealed Nealson's decision and her fate. He raised his revolver, taking careful aim at her chest, and fired a single shot. The barrel belched fire, sending the hollow-point .357 round across the short distance in the blink of an eye. Expanding and tumbling as it encountered resistance, the round tore through skin, muscle, flesh and organs as it veered off course, rolling to the side and finally stopping as it lodged into bone.

Tina shrieked as she collapsed to the ground. While the others rushed to her aid, Mark scooped up her rifle and joined Jason in firing upon Nealson, but the distraction offered to him lasted just long enough for him to jump into the sedan, start it up and peel out of the parking area in front of the community center. The vehicle lurched as it thumped over the bags of sand and dirt on the perimeter, gunfire trailing after it as Tina continued to cry out in pain.

Chapter Eighteen

M ount Yamantau

"DOCTOR YERMAKOV here to see you, sir."

"Send him in."

The voice matches the darkened lighting of the room, carrying a distinct tone of malice even in the simplest of expressions. A young man enters, a wool cap wrung between his hands, and he immediately begins speaking.

"Mr. President, I don't know what this is about but I can assure you that I did—"

"Dr. Yermakov." The voice cuts through the man's rambling. "Please. Have a seat."

"Yes, sir." It takes the man a moment to make his way through the room before hesitantly lowering himself into the cushioned chair across from a man he never imagined he would meet.

"You have received information about this mission, yes?"

"Yes, sir."

"Good. What I am about to tell you is supplemental to what you have already learned. It is to remain between you and I, and no one else. Not your co-workers, your friends, your family or even God himself is to know this information."

"Yes... sir."

There's a brief silence accompanied by the steadily brightening glow of the end of a cigar, the appearance of a cloud of smoke and the dimming of the same glow.

"Your protection on this mission have been instructed to carry out a secondary, covert operation. However, given the nature of the mission and the isolation involved, I have reason to believe that some things may not go as planned. If, at any point in time, you

should sense that your protection has decided to abandon their loyalty to their country, I am ordering you to treat them as hostile entities. You will dispatch them and carry on the mission on your own."

"Sir? What... I don't understand what you're saying."

A few papers are shuffled and the President passes over an envelope with Cyrillic lettering stamped on the front. Dr. Yermakov opens the envelope and reads the contents, his eyes growing wider with each paragraph. When he reaches the end he looks back over at the man across from him, unsure of what to say.

"Do you understand now?"

"Yes... yes, sir. I believe so. But... I'm not a special operative. Not like them. If they were to betray us, how would I overcome that?"

A thin smile passes over the other man's lips. "I believe strongly in... motivation. Anything can be accomplished with the proper motivation."

"Sir?"

Another long pause, another draw on the cigar and another cloud of smoke fills the air.

"You have a beautiful wife and son, Dr. Yermakov. They are here, in the base, yes?"

Dr. Yermakov nods slowly, not understanding what the President is saying. "Yes, sir... they are."

"They are doing well? Well fed, well taken care of?"

"Of course, sir. We all are. I'm exceptionally grateful that you allowed our families to join us he—"

"I'm very, very glad that they are doing well. With so many people in a place like this, it's astounding how things sometimes go wrong." Another long draw on the cigar. "But I'm very glad that your family is doing well."

Dr. Yermakov feels his heart twist, his stomach clench and all of the moisture in his mouth evaporate as he realizes what he is being told. "I..." he squeaks, clears his throat as his whole body trembles, nods and tries again. "I am glad too, sir. And yes. I... I'll watch for anything."

"Good." Another smile passes over the President's lips. "I'm glad to hear that. I'm certain things will go well, but just in case they don't, make sure you retrieve the codes and get them back here, no matter the cost."

"Of course, sir. I will."

"Good. Now, I want you to report down to the armory. You and Dr. Belov will be going through a crash-course in survival and weapons training before the mission, just in case you do happen to end up in a situation where your protection become... indisposed."

"Yes, sir. I'll do that right now."

The President nods as Dr. Yermakov rises from his chair and hurries toward the door, trying to escape from the oppressive weight of the room as fast as his legs can carry him. He is stopped just before he reaches the door, though, as the man still seated in his chair speaks again.

"Oh, and Jacob?"

"Yes, sir?"

"Do not fail me. Remember what's at stake."

"Yes, sir. I won't."

Author's Notes

May 31, 2018

With this, the penultimate episode of Surviving the Fall, there is but one last book to write before the adventures in this series are over.

When I wrote book 11, I started with Dianne's perspective and wrote that entire portion first before moving on to Rick's side. I used to flip back and forth between writing one perspective and then another, but over the last few books I've started needing to focus on one at a time in order to make sure I'm getting everything in that needs to be taken care of. And, as I'm sure you noticed, there is a *lot* going on. Death(s) and betrayal(s) seem to be spreading, and it's going to get worse before it gets better.

So what's up with Jacob? When I first wrote the outline for this book, I didn't intend to have Jacob betray everyone, but as I got about midway through writing the scenes for Rick's group, I realized that I needed a counter for Ostap and Carl. Their betrayal was obvious from the start, first to the reader thanks to the flashbacks and then to Jane and Rick as they watched the behavior of the Russians.

Having that progress without some sort of wild card to come in at the end and muck things up wasn't working so well. Hence the revelation that Jacob, someone who would normally be completely on Rick's side, was coerced into acting as an insurance policy on the mission, to try and ensure that even if the normally loyal Spetsnaz were to turn their back on their country, Jacob's devotion to his family would ensure that they were brought in line.

Book 12 will be the last book in this series, and all of the loose ends will be tied up. It's safe to assume that some type of victory will be had. After all, what kind of a book ends on an unhappy note? Whether the victory will be pyrrhic or not, though... well. That'll have to wait until the final book.

If you enjoyed this episode of Surviving the Fall or if you *didn't* like something—I'd love to hear about it. You can drop me an email or send me a message or leave a comment on Facebook. You can also sign up for my newsletter where I announce new book releases and other cool stuff a few times a month.

Answering emails and messages from my readers is the highlight of my day and every single time I get an email from someone saying how much they enjoyed reading a story it makes that day so much brighter and better.

Thank you so very much for reading my books. Seriously, thank you from the bottom of my heart. I put an enormous amount of effort into the writing and all of the related processes and there's nothing better than knowing that so many people are enjoying my stories.

All the best,
Mike

Book 12 – A New Dawn

Preface

Last time, on Surviving the Fall....

The final battle lines have been struck, for both Rick and Dianne. As Jane lays dying in a secret bunker in Washington, D.C., Rick has to face down two Spetsnaz officers in an effort to salvage his and Dr. Evans' plans to stop Damocles. In Virginia, meanwhile, Dianne has been reunited with her children and friends, but the joy is short-lived as Nealson shoots Tina to help make good on his escape. As he seeks revenge for the blow Dianne's group struck to his gang, Rick must fight against the clock—and an unexpected enemy—to stop Damocles before it can destroy everything he holds dear.

And now, the final chapter in Surviving the Fall.

Chapter One

Washington, D.C.

DYING ALONE, in the basement of a secretive bunker in a foreign country far from home had never been on Ostap Isayev's bucket list. As the finality of darkness overtook his senses and he let the pain ferry him away, he sensed the figure standing over him move back. He couldn't remember who the figure was, why he was there or anything at all, really. Nothing except the swirling void mattered as the last breath of life passed out from between his lips.

Scooping up the mask he had ripped from Ostap's face only a moment prior, Rick slipped it on and tightened the straps. The smell of the bunker had come rushing back at him after hearing Ostap's final words. *Don't you want to know where your precious Dr. Evans is at?*

Jane's death was a fresh wound, but the words spoken by Ostap pointed to an even darker possibility. If Dr. Evans was dead, as the Spetsnaz officer seemed to imply, Rick wasn't sure what the next step in putting a halt to Damocles could be. He cast a glance over to Jane's blood-soaked body, hoping for a brief second that she might start moving again. She was still gone, though, and as Rick picked up Ostap's rifle, he took hold of the pain and anger that was building within him and held firm to it. It, like the rifle in his hands, was a weapon, and a potent one at that.

With a final look at Jane, Rick turned and trotted down the hall, heading in the direction that Ostap had come from a few moments prior. The base-

ment levels of the building that had housed the staff responsible for Damocles went on at least one more floor down, and it was from there that Ostap
had come. As Rick got to the end of the hall and saw a doorway leading to
another staircase to his left, he suddenly questioned what he was doing.
Ostap and Carl—the two Spetsnaz officers and the most direct threats to
him, Jane and Dr. Evans, were gone. The only Russians left alive in the
building were the technicians, and unless Rick had missed something big
with one of them…

Don't you want to know where your precious Dr. Evans is at?

Ostap's last words echoed through Rick's mind as he slowly walked down
the stairs, holding the rifle loosely in both hands. The door at the bottom of
the stairwell was ajar, held in place by an office chair that someone had
jammed in between the door and the wall. Rick pushed the chair out of the
way as he eased the door open, then swung the chair back into place with his
left foot.

The sound of his own breathing was loud in Rick's ears as he peered
down the hall with his rifle light, looking for Dr. Evans, the technicians and
any potential threats. Unlike the floors above that were now dark since no
one was on them, the very bottom floor had a glow at the far end that did
not come from Rick. As he moved toward the glow he passed more offices,
glass-walled conference rooms and an increasing number of server racks
stacked high in the corner of each room.

The room with the glow was large, with glass walls like the others, but
instead of being devoted mostly to space for individuals to work, it had obviously been designated as the server room for the project. A single, small table
and pair of chairs sat at the far back wall while the rest of the room was
filled from floor to ceiling with rows of dark racks of servers. Cables from the
servers twisted and wound their way into the low ceiling where a mesh cage
kept the wires contained and out of the way.

A pair of lanterns and a couple of flashlights were balanced on the table
and the edges of a couple of server racks, all of them angled to offer the
most illumination of the table and chairs at the back of the room. A pair of
figures sat in the chairs, Dr. Evans and Oles, their backs facing the hall where
Rick stood. He watched them as they pointed at an obscured screen in front
of them, Oles tapping away on a keyboard while Dr. Evans gestured and
spoke in a voice that Rick couldn't hear from out in the hall.

After watching the pair for a moment, Rick stepped through the broken
door into the room, his shoes crunching broken glass. Dr. Evans stiffened in
his seat but didn't turn around, though Oles managed a half turn of his
head before straightening back up.

"Dr. Evans?" Rick felt his stomach tighten, the feeling of impending
doom growing, though he still didn't know why.

"Drop the gun, Rick." Rick froze, the voice full of nervousness and trepidation coming from behind him. His fingers played across the trigger guard

of the rifle as he tried to pinpoint exactly where the voice came from. "Don't do it. Just drop the gun. Now!" The last word was spoken harshly, with a bark.

"What the hell are you doing, Jacob?" Rick slowly lowered the rifle to the ground with his right hand, dropping it the last few inches and wincing as it clattered against the glass on the floor.

"Raise your hands and walk forward. Slowly." Jacob sounded even more nervous after being called out. Rick sighed and did as he was told, stepping across the last of the glass and toward the desk where Dr. Evans and Oles were seated. Dr. Evans stole a look back at Rick, his eyes wide and full of fear.

"What's going on?" Rick whispered to Dr. Evans, but a sharp jab on his back made him close his mouth.

"Keep quiet. No questions. Get the chair from over there, to your right. Sit down, face the wall next to the others and stay still." Jacob's voice was audibly shaking and he nearly stuttered a few times. Weighing his options, Rick chose to turn instead of obeying the instructions, though he kept his hands in the air. As he turned, he saw Jacob standing between a pair of server racks, a pistol grasped so tightly in his shaking hands that his knuckles had turned white.

"Jacob." Rick shook his head. "What are you doing?"

"Don't make me shoot you, Rick." Jacob swallowed hard. "I don't want to, but I will! I swear!"

A grunt of pain came from the other side of the room and Rick turned to see Dr. Evans slumped over, hand on his shoulder. "Did you shoot Dr. Evans, Jacob?"

"He wouldn't listen to me! I told him to listen but he wouldn't. He's fine, though!"

"No he's not, you idiot!" Oles turned in his seat, his face covered in worry and stress. "He's losing a lot of blood!"

"Shut up!" Jacob screamed at Oles, waving the pistol around with one hand. Rick winced at the action, nearly ducking down, but stood firm.

"Jacob, just tell me what's going on. I can help you, I promise."

"No you can't. Only the decryption codes will help me right now."

"The codes?" Rick's eyes narrowed and confusion clouded his expression. He swiveled his head to look over at Oles and Dr. Evans. "Can one of you three *please* tell me what's going on down here? There's a pair of dead Spetsnaz upstairs, Jane's dead too and it looks like Dr. Evans is going to bleed out!"

"Jane is… dead?" Jacob's eyes widened and his weapon-laden arms dropped slightly. Rick nearly made a move on him, but Jacob noticed Rick's tensing muscles and pulled the weapon back up. His hands were still shaking, even more so than before, that he inadvertently squeezed the trigger in the process. Even though Rick's ears were still ringing from the gunfire mere moments ago, the shot still sounded deafeningly loud in the confines of the small room. He winced, expecting to feel a lance of searing pain pass through his chest.

Instead, there was a scream from behind as Oles dropped from his chair and rolled on the ground, clutching his arm in pain. *"Ublyudok*! Why?!"

Rick swiveled his head back around to see Jacob's arms drop yet again, a look of shock crossing his face as he realized that he had inadvertently shot his friend. Taking advantage of the distraction, Rick wasted no more time. He charged at Jacob, colliding with him in a full-body tackle that brought both men to the floor and sent Jacob's pistol skittering off into the darkness.

Chapter Two

Outside Ellisville, VA

"*TINA!*" The scream was shrill, hoarse and raw, filled with agony and desperation, with an unspoken plea for the word to somehow affect reality and change what had already transpired. The gunshots from Mark and Jason's rifles were distant thumps as Dianne knelt down, scooping Tina's body into her arms and pulling the older woman back into the community center.

Tina had been shot for no more than a few seconds, but her form already seemed incredibly small and frail to Dianne as she lay Tina down on a pallet inside the door. Tina's groans and cries of pain continued even as Dianne began tearing at her shirt, pulling it off and away to get a clear picture of where the shot had landed.

"You'll be okay, Tina! I promise!" She turned to Sarah, who had followed her inside. "We need bandages and compresses; something to stop this bleeding!"

"I'll check their supplies." Sarah fought the panic in her voice as she stood and ran to a pile of boxes and duffle bags stacked on a wall inside the center.

"Tina, stay with me, okay?" Dianne finally cleared away Tina's jacket and shirt, revealing a mess of blood that was steadily pouring from a large wound in the upper right quadrant of her chest. "Sweet mercy," Dianne whispered, her hands frozen over the wound as her eyes danced back and forth.

"It's bad." Tina whispered through the pain, groaning out the words. "Isn't it?"

"Don't talk, okay? Just stay awake."

"Gauze, and lots of it!" Sarah fell to her knees, dumping a large pile of individually-wrapped packets of gauze rolls onto the ground.

"Lung." Tina gasped, her eyes rolling back from the pain. "Hole. Chest. Have to… seal it. Fast. Got to get… air out…cavity…"

"What's she talking about?" Sarah furiously unwrapped the gauze and passed it to Dianne, who used it to clean the blood from around the wound before pressing layers of it down in an attempt to stop the flow of blood.

"No!" Tina gasped again, putting her hand on Dianne's arm. Her grip was furiously strong and her nails dug into Dianne's flesh. "Seal it. Quickly. Air getting in." Dianne glanced down to Tina's chest, seeing bubbles in the blood as Tina gasped again, and felt a wave of recognition wash over her. Her first responder class had been so long ago, but one of the few things that had stuck in her brain was bubbles in the blood—a sure sign of a sucking chest wound.

"I need tape!" Dianne looked at Sarah.

"What kind?"

"Something big, just tape that'll hold tight to form a seal."

Sarah nodded and got up, hurrying off to try and pull yet another rabbit out of a hat. Dianne began removing the bandages from around the wound and placed her hand directly over the hole in Tina's chest as she spoke. "You'll have to walk me through this, hon. I need to seal off the wound to keep air from going in, though, right?"

Tina nodded, a slight smile passing across her increasingly pale face. "I think the bullet… went into… collarbone or shoulder. Hurts… like the dickens." Another breath, though this time with Dianne's hand forming a seal over the wound, there were no bubbles.

"So, I need to seal this up. Then what?"

"Not much to do. Hope it clots. Pray… it went around the lung." Each word and breath was accompanied by a pained expression, and it was all Dianne could do to not wrap her arms around Tina and hug her as tight as possible.

"All I could find is this," Sarah knelt back down, holding out a roll of duct tape with a shrug and an apologetic expression.

"This can't be sanitary." Dianne looked at the roll for a moment before nodding. "All right, fine. Get me some bandages, then tear off strips of tape about a foot and a half long. We'll cover the wound with bandages, then seal it off with tape to keep it airtight." She looked down at Tina. "Will that work?"

Tina's eyes were closed but she nodded and licked her lips before replying in a whisper. "Yeah. Should. Once it's on… wait a while… then you need to use a needle… suck out the air."

"Needle to the chest to suck out the air." Dianne gulped hard and closed her eyes. "Oh boy."

Chapter Three

W ashington, D.C.

WHEN RICK TACKLED JACOB, he had thought in the back of his mind that subduing the technician would be relatively straightforward compared to battling against the pair of Spetsnaz. His assumption that Jacob would be naturally weak and ineffectual in a physical struggle was not borne out by reality, though, as the technician refused to be taken out without a fight.

Jacob rolled his body and pushed Rick off before pushing and pulling himself forward deeper into the darkness between the server racks, feeling with his hand on the ground for the pistol. Rick clambered after him, grabbed hold of Jacob's pant leg and pulled sharply, sending the technician's head slamming forward against the ground with a sharp crack and a cry of pain. Jacob, in turn, kicked with both his feet, causing Rick to see stars as the heel of one boot collided with his head. He refused to let go of Jacob's leg, though, and instead pulled harder, dragging the lighter man back toward him and away from the firearm that Jacob was so desperate to locate.

With a quick heave, Rick pushed himself off the floor and landed back on top of Jacob, though this time he was more prepared. Taking Jacob's face in both hands he slammed the technician's head back against the floor, first once, then twice, each time cringing at the sound of cracking bone and the muffled cries of pain beneath his hands. He nearly stopped attacking Jacob both times, but the image of Jane's body and the knowledge that both Dr. Evans and Oles had been shot spurred him on.

"Rick!" The voice was distant and hazy, and Rick didn't register it until he felt a hand on his shoulder. "Rick!!"

Rick turned, grabbing for the hand to try and fight off his attacker, but found himself staring into the pained eyes of Dr. Evans instead. "Leave him be, Rick! You got him!"

Rick looked back down, realizing that Jacob had stopped fighting back more than a few blows earlier. He released the technician's head and it dropped to the floor with a sickening thud, then he stood up and slowly backed away from Jacob's body.

"I—I didn't mean—"

"Yes you did. And it's a damned good thing you did it, too." Dr. Evans groaned as he put his hand on Rick's shoulder again. "He would have killed us all. Oles! You okay over there?"

"Hurts like hell but he just barely nicked me."

"Nice acting there." Dr. Evans snorted approvingly. "You did good on distracting Jacob."

"I was hoping Rick would take advantage." Oles smiled as he approached Rick, then his smile turned sour as he looked at his former friend. "I just wish it hadn't come to all this."

"I hate to be the odd man out," Rick said with frustration, "but would you two *please* explain to me what's going on?!"

Dr. Evans nodded. "Let's sit down, though. I don't need this to start bleeding again."

"You need medical attention, Dr. Evans." Oles took him by the arm and helped ease him into a seat.

"Later. Once we've finished this." He cast a glance over at Jacob's body, then looked up at Rick. "Is Jane truly... gone?"

Rick felt his stomach twist into knots and nodded solemnly. "She is. Gunned down by Ostap as he was running upstairs. She never had a chance."

Resilient all the way up to and through watching Jacob being killed by Rick's hand, the usually indefatigably resilient attitude of Dr. Evans broke. His forced smile faded, his shoulders slumped and the light went out of his eyes. His wound, still untended, was forgotten as he felt his soul empty out into the dark room.

Rick felt a chill run up his spine as he carefully watched Dr. Evans, seeing more of a lack of a reaction than anything else. Both he and Oles sensed the change that came over the man, and they glanced at each other before Rick approached Dr. Evans and sat down nearby.

"I'm... sorry, doc. I know she meant a lot to you."

Dr. Evans looked up at Rick, his eyes clouded with tears. "She spoke to me like a person. Not a resource, or a tool, or something to be used." He took a deep breath and let it out in a long, slow sigh. "She was the first one to talk to me like that in... ages. Before that it was all government suits and other socially low-functioners like myself. Do this, do that, solve this, figure out that. Not her. First thing she asked me when she arrived at Cheyenne was where was I from and if I was feeling okay."

"She was a good person. There's no doubt about that." Rick glanced over at Oles. "Dr. Evans, we *will* remember her. But right now I need to know what's been going on down here. What happened with Jacob and Ostap? Were you able to find the codes to Damocles?"

Dr. Evans closed his eyes, sending double trails of wetness down his cheeks. He leaned back in his chair, taking in yet another long breath before releasing it in a slow sigh. "Oles?" Dr. Evans spoke softly. "You fill him in."

Chapter Four

Outside Ellisville, VA

TO DIANNE AND SARAH, as they worked feverishly to save their friend's life, it felt like hours had passed since Tina had been shot. For Mark and Jason, though, it had only been a couple of minutes since Nealson fired a round into Tina's chest and taken off in his car. The pair had rained hellfire down upon the vehicle, but Nealson's erratic driving and the pair's amped up adrenaline meant the man was able to make good on his escape.

With the car fading into the distance, Mark and Jason turned to one another, suddenly remembering what had happened to Tina. They bolted for the entrance to the community center, skidding to a halt just inside the door as they looked down and saw Dianne and Sarah kneeling over Tina's still form.

"Holy... Mom! Is she okay?"

"Jason!" Dianne ignored her son and barked at Sarah's husband. "Where's Nealson? Did you kill him?"

"We couldn't get him, Dianne," Jason shook his head. "He got away."

"You sure he's gone?" Dianne didn't look away from Tina as she placed another strip of duct tape across the older woman's chest.

"Very."

"Good. We need to get Tina in the truck and get her home, to where we've got more than gauze and duct tape to work with." She looked over at Mark. "I want you and Sarah to go through everything in this room. Get any supplies that look useful and throw them in the back of the truck. Jason, get it parked outside. We'll have to slide her into the back seat."

"Dianne, are you—"

"Just *do it*, Jason!" Dianne's eyes burned white-hot and her lips curled, her voice taking on a new pitch as she shouted at him. "We don't have time to discuss this!"

With a quick glance at Sarah and an exchange of nods, Jason ran outside, heading for Dianne's truck that the group from the community center had stolen previously. Mark held out a hand, helping Sarah to her feet and they began hurrying through the room, calling out the names of things they found to Dianne who responded with a simple "yes" or "no" to indicate whether the items should be brought along.

Outside, the sound of the truck's engine grew loud as Jason pulled it up in front of the community center, parked, then jumped out and threw open the doors to the rear section of the cab. Mark and Sarah began carrying supplies out while Jason ran over to Dianne's side and dropped to one knee.

"How is she?"

"Bad. I've got the hole closed up but she's lost a lot of blood and I have no idea what kind of internal damage there is."

"You did... good." Tina grabbed Dianne's arm again, her grip feeling weaker than before but still stronger than it had a right to be. "Could use something... for the pain."

"We'll be home in a jiffy." Dianne looked up at Jason. "Can you get her in the car by yourself?"

Jason nodded and leaned down, scooping Tina up in a smooth motion. She groaned at the movement but didn't cry out, and Jason carried her to the car and slipped her onto the back seat.

"Josie, Jacob!" The two younger children who had been huddled together in a corner of the community center's main room hurried over next to their mother, looking wide-eyed and shell-shocked. "Get in the car; sit with Mrs. Carson and make sure she doesn't fall off the seat, okay? She's hurt pretty badly and we're taking her back home."

"Is she going to be okay?"

"What happened to her?"

"Are those bad men coming back?" Josie and Jacob both exploded with questions, but Dianne threw up her blood-soaked hands and shook her head.

"Do what I said, *now*. Questions later, after we get home. Got it?"

They both nodded and ran for the truck, hopping in and sitting on either side of Tina with Jason's help. Dianne looked around the room for a few seconds to see if she noticed anything that Mark and Sarah might have missed. When things looked clear she ran for the door and began shouting more instructions.

"Sarah, in the front! Jason, you're driving. Mark, in the back with me. Let's go already, we need to get home now!"

Chapter Five

L ow Earth Orbit

"READY TO CUT BURN?"

"Ready!"

"Three... two... one... now!"

The small module, shuddering under the force of the engine propelling it forward, suddenly grows still and quiet. The vibrations that rocked the three passengers all but vanish and an unnatural silence overtakes the craft.

"How long until reentry?" Jackie speaks to Commander Palmer without turning her head. Not by choice, but because the small craft is crammed to the gills with supplies and she's physically unable to do so.

"Sixteen minutes." He stretches out a hand and flips a trio of switches. "Ted, how's our course?"

"We're smack dab in the green. Couldn't be better."

"If that isn't a miracle then I don't know what is." Commander Palmer gives a bemused snort. "Everybody take five to relax, then we'll start the checklist for reentry. Not that it'll do much good given how overweight and unbalanced we are."

There is silence in the small capsule as it hurtles through the upper reaches of earth's atmosphere, falling in a steadily decreasing arc in a direction that the crew hopes will get them home. White clouds and blue ocean that pass by underneath are marred by black smoke as they pass across populated areas, the fires from Damocles still burning across much of the planet.

"What's going on down there?" Jackie whispers so softly that only Ted, sitting to her

right, hears her. He shakes his head quietly, wondering the same thing. From so high above their home, the feeling of utter insignificance is normally overwhelming. Dubbed the over-view effect, the three have become accustomed to the cognitive shift and range of emotions that come with seeing the Earth from the heavens. To see it burn, though, and be unable to lift a finger to help or even know why it is burning is enough to break down the mental walls constructed by even the toughest, most experienced astronauts.

"All right." Commander Palmer's voice is rougher than normal, and he clears his throat before continuing. "I don't know what's going on down there, but we're going to go find out."

Chapter Six

W ashington, D.C.

"JACOB BETRAYED US ALL."

"No kidding. I sort of figured that out when he had the gun on us. Why did he do it, though?"

"When we first came down here, Ostap started acting… how do you say it? Funny? Off?"

"Squirrely?"

"Exactly." Oles nodded. "He was squirrel. I tried to talk to Jacob, but he was different too. All he did was watch Ostap carefully, like he expected something to happen. I tried to warn Dr. Evans, but Ostap played his hand too quickly. Once we verified that these were the correct systems, Ostap shot Dr. Evans through the shoulder. He was about to shoot me when Jacob shot him—well, *at* him. Sent him running away, surprised that someone was shooting back, I guess."

"Wait, so Ostap shot first? Why?"

"Dirty ruskie was working for the Russians."

Rick looked confused. "Of course he was."

"No, no," Dr. Evans shook his head. "Not like that. Him and Carl and Jacob were all sent here with one goal—get the codes and give them to the Russians. Then the Russians would have the keys to the castle. They could take control over Damocles and be in total control of everything."

"But, somewhere along the line, Ostap and Carl must have gotten greedy." Oles continued. "And Jacob was the mole that was sent to take care of them if they deviated from their orders."

Rick shook his head and let out a whistle. "Wow. How'd you figure that out?"

"Even with a gun on us Jacob couldn't keep his fat mouth shut." At that point Oles turned and hocked a loogie at Jacob's body. "He told us that his family was in danger if he didn't take the codes back. Said he'd kill us both if we didn't help him get the codes."

"And that's where you came in." Dr. Evans snorted. "Literally. Unfortunately, that was also the point where we were going to have to give him the bad news."

"Which is?"

Oles turned and gestured at the servers sitting out on the desk on the table. "There's a bullet hole right through the system we needed to access."

Rick looked at where Oles was pointing, and even in the dim light he could see the shattered plastic and bent metal where a round had entered the front of a rackmount server that was sitting on the desk. "Did it hit the drives?"

"Unfortunately." Dr. Evans nodded.

"How'd you all even get these systems up and running?" Rick looked around at the dim emergency lighting.

"There's about a dozen backup power units in the corner, each one good for a few minutes of power to a monitor and one of these systems. It was janky, but it worked."

"Well then," Rick took a step forward and examined the machine, "since this system's dead now, what's the backup plan?"

"One of these other machines could have the codes, but it'll take time to examine them. Time we don't have."

"Come again?" Rick had been distracted by the damaged server and looked up at Oles. "Time we don't have how?"

Oles and Dr. Evans exchanged a glance, then Dr. Evans began to explain. "I've suspected that Damocles would reach its final stages of attacks soon. That's always been in its programming. Escalation until it either receives a kill command, alternate commands or until it reaches its final stages."

"It can't possibly do much more harm than it's already done."

"There's plenty left it can do." Dr. Evans swallowed hard. "It's designed to infect every system of the target. Civilian and military. *Every* system."

"He's talking about missiles," Oles interjected. "Nuclear missiles."

"I guess that would be the final stage, wouldn't it? What are we supposed to do to stop it if the system with the codes is dead?"

Oles and Dr. Evans exchanged another glance. "Oh, no," Oles said, "you misunderstand. We have the codes. They were the first things we pulled."

"What?!" Rick shouted, louder than he had intended. "Then what's the problem?"

"This system that was damaged was a clean system with authorization on the internal network to get into the outside world. This was supposed to be how we would broadcast the shutdown codes that Damocles would then self-propagate out. Without it… I don't know how we'll get the signal out."

"How much time do we have before Damocles starts blowing more stuff up?"

Dr. Evans shook his head. "It's impossible to know for certain. Hours, though. Maybe six or eight."

"Good. That's enough time." Rick turned and started walking for the exit.

"For what?"

Rick stopped and looked back at the pair. "To bury our dead."

Chapter Seven

O utside Ellisville, VA

"*BITCH!*"

A pile of boxes toppled over, spilling their contents across the wood floor in response to Nealson's swing of his leg. A few cans of food managed to roll their way across the entirety of the room, only coming to a rest when they hit the thin piles of bedding that had been put down for those whom Nealson and his group had captured. The room was empty, save for himself, though there were signs that the woman and her group had ransacked the place before departing.

Nealson gingerly removed his right hand from his left shoulder, grinding his teeth together as a fresh wave of pain went down his arm and across his chest. The pair that had been firing at him during his frantic escape had gotten off at least two full mags, and though several had plinked off the back of his car, only one had actually hit him.

After spending a few hours on the other side of Ellisville with his hand clamped to the through-and-through wound, he decided to risk heading back to the community center. He would need food, water, bandages and more if he wanted to stay alive for more than a few days. Unfortunately, Mark and Sarah's searching for supplies left him lacking when it came to most of what he immediately needed.

"Looks like she bled out good." Nealson kicked at a pile of bloody bandages near the front door as he walked around the room, smirking with satisfaction. He had never been one to show mercy to anyone, no matter what their age, but he had taken a large amount of pleasure in shooting Tina in particular. Remembering how much trouble she had been back at the gas station and then again at the farm during the attack made him hope that she was still alive, suffering horribly as she slowly died.

Digging through the boxes with one hand, Nealson finally found what he was looking for. He pulled one of the whisky bottles out and unscrewed the top before tilting it back and drinking deep. The burning in his throat and stomach soon turned to warmth that spread through his whole body, lessening the pain in his shoulder and dulling some of the effects of the cold weather.

With a bit of liquid courage resting in his belly, Nealson once again turned his attention to his wound. The bullet had passed through cleanly, tearing apart muscle and ligament but missing bone entirely. The blood flow had mostly stopped, too, and he gently prodded the wound to see if he could feel any fragments of the bullet at either side. A fresh dribble of blood and another wave of pain made him pull back sharply and he sighed, turning his attention back to the boxes.

"She couldn't have used up *all* the bandages." Nealson mumbled to himself while digging through the boxes, growing more impatient until he finally found a sealed package of gauze. He tore it open with his teeth and divided it across both sides of the wound before taking the remnants of a roll of duct tape from the floor and taping it down to keep it in place. A long, thin towel was quickly fashioned into a makeshift sling and within half an hour of arriving back at the community center he was sitting on a stool, eating cold canned corn with the edge of a knife blade while wondering what to do next.

"Boss?" A voice called from outside, and Nealson froze up for half a second before recognizing the voice and relaxing.

"Get in here." He answered back before taking another bite. A moment later a pair of faces peeked through the front door.

"Boss? What... what happened here?" The pair entered the community center, eyes wide at the sight of the bloody pile of bandages, the general state of disarray and at Nealson sitting with his arm in a sling.

"*She* happened. Her and that family of hers."

"Where's everyone else?"

"Dead. All of 'em."

One of the pair shook his head. "We saw a couple bodies out front but didn't think... how'd you stay alive, boss?"

"Luck and skill." Nealson took a last bite before tossing the can to the floor. He wiped the knife clean on his pant leg before standing up and slipping it back into his pocket. "Where's the truck?"

"Down the road. Things looked off so the boys stayed with it while we came up to take a look."

"Good thinking. Signal them; tell 'em to get up here." One of the pair nodded and ran out the front of the building while Nealson addressed the other. "What'd you bring back?"

"Couple bags of meds—the good stuff—more ammo, a few guns, a couple water purifiers and a bunch of boxes of food. Mostly canned stuff. Oh, and seeds. Enough to start growing some food…" he paused. "I guess we'll need to find some new labor to work on that, huh?"

"Nah." Nealson shook his head. "We don't need new ones. There's still a few perfectly good ones. They just up and ran off is all." The sound of a truck engine came from down the road, and the other man walked back through the door.

"They're coming up, boss."

"Good. As soon as they're here I want something to deal with the pain from this, then I want a full stock of our weapons and ammo."

"Boss," the first man replied, "you want to go after them again?"

"Of course. Why wouldn't I?" Nealson nearly growled at the pair.

"Because they nearly killed you, and took out everyone else. Maybe we should just leave them alone."

The pain all but vanished as Nealson felt the rage rising up in his gut. Even in his weakened and wounded state he was still a force to be reckoned with, and he demonstrated that for the man who was talked to him. Two steps forward were followed by a powerful right hook, catching the man in the jaw and sending him spinning around as he toppled to the floor. Nealson towered over the man while the other one slowly backed up, silently wishing he could somehow melt into a wall and disappear.

"*What did you say to me?!*" Nealson bellowed at the man on the floor. "I don't just leave someone alone! They killed my men, they *shot me* and you want me to just *leave them alone?!*"

The man on the floor clutched his jaw, slurring his words as he tried to speak. "Bossh, I di'n't mean…"

"You didn't *think*! That's what you didn't do! I don't back down, so neither do any of you!" Nealson kicked the man savagely in the stomach, making him cry out in pain.

"Boss, what're you—" The rest of the group from the truck walked into the community center to see Nealson standing over the man on the floor. He looked up at them with fire in his eyes.

"Get everything ready for an assault! And the next one to argue with me gets a bullet in between the eyes!"

Chapter Eight

S omewhere off the Eastern Seaboard

"I'LL NEVER GET USED to this." Commander Palmer's unusually candid confession surprises both Ted and Jackie.

"Get used to what?" Ted wonders.

"The silence. Especially after all that noise."

"The waiting's what I hate," Jackie joined in, "especially with a broken altimeter."

"Only another minute or two till splashdown. Just remember your training and we'll get out of this just fine."

Trapped inside the small module with no view of the outside except through a small, obstructed porthole, the three astronauts try their best to imagine what is going on outside. A cluster of red and white parachutes pull taut lines fastened to the module, keeping it stable as it drifts along on a breeze that carries it over the open ocean. The weather is clear aside from the smoke and soot that clog the air across the planet, caused by the seemingly infinite number of fires that still burn out of control.

When the module touches down, it does so with a bang and a splash, leaning over so far to one side due to its momentum that the trio think it might not stand upright again. When it does, though, it rocks back and forth, each time with less force until the creaking, groaning and sound of water against the hull finally dies down.

"Straps off, check for leaks." Commander Palmer speaks with a loud, confident voice. He, Jackie and Ted each unbuckle their harnesses and begin shuffling in their seats, looking around to see if any water has managed to find its way into the module. The seams held firm, though, and there's no sound or sight of any water.

"Clear."

"Clear."

"Confirmed," Commander Palmer nods. *"Clear. Ted, blow the hatch and get topside. Jackie, what's the battery look like?"*

"Better than we thought. We've got more than enough juice, assuming we're close to shore."

"Excellent. Ted, see if you can spot land once you're up there." Commander Palmer leans forward and looks at Jackie. *"Once he's up, you and I will get the motor assembled in here then we'll pass it up and go out to attach it to the hull."*

Jackie and Ted both nod and set about their work, moving with a renewed purpose. Their bodies feel weak and ineffectual after so long spent in space, and gravity pulls hard against them, straining their muscles and bones. Normally, upon returning from space, they would be greeted by a recovery and rescue team, but they are completely alone and must rely on themselves if they wish to survive.

Ted groans as he twists the handle on the module hatch, and Commander Palmer looks up at him. *"Easy, Ted. Don't break anything."*

The handle finally spins free and Ted huffs as he pushes the door open. The smell of the ocean instantly permeates through the module, bringing with it the scent of a warm breeze, fresh air and just a hint of smoke. Jackie wrinkles her nose as she tosses her helmet to the side, then slowly stands up and turns to locate the equipment that she and Commander Palmer worked on assembling.

"Anything in sight up there, Ted?" Commander Palmer looks up through the hatch as he speaks to Ted who is sitting on the edge of the hatch opening.

"You... you could say that, yeah." Ted's voice is shaking and cracked, and Commander Palmer and Jackie share a quizzical look before Commander Palmer speaks again.

"How close are we to land?"

"Couple miles, probably less."

"Excellent. Did the floats deploy automatically?"

"One did. I'll go pull the manual release on the other two now."

"Good. We'll pass the motor up once you finish."

There's no reply from Ted, who stays seated on the edge of the hatch for a few more seconds before finally starting to move. The hiss of air and the soft bumps of inflating floats bumping up against the outside of the module echo through the quiet chamber, then Ted's face appears at the top of the hatch. *"We're good now. Floats look like they're undamaged."*

Commander Palmer nods and begins taking parts from Jackie and passing them through the hatch up to Ted. The process is slow, partly because Ted seems incredibly distracted, constantly looking around as he takes the pieces of the motor up through the hatch and places them on top of one of the floats. When the entire process is finished, Commander Palmer helps Jackie climb up through the hatch before passing a cable to her and then following her up the ladder.

As Commander Palmer's head emerges from the hatch, he gasps involuntarily at the sight, joining Ted and Jackie as they stare transfixed at the horizon. The coast of Virginia

Beach is less than two miles to the west, and in the afternoon light the fires, smoke and destruction are clearly visible. Along the entire coastline there doesn't appear to be a single intact building, and the normally green backdrop is brown not just because of the season, but because of the fires that already burned out.

Chosen over a Florida landing due to its proximity to Norfolk and Washington, D.C., the choice of Virginia Beach as the target landing site is unusual and Commander Palmer begins to wonder whether it was the right one or not. He pushes himself out of the module and holds on to the side, next to Jackie and Ted. They stare at the carnage-strewn horizon for a few moments before Commander Palmer finally speaks.

"Let's get this set up and start making for land. We've got a ways to go and the light won't last forever."

Chapter Nine

The Waters' Homestead
  Outside Ellisville, VA

"CLEAR THE TABLE, QUICKLY!"

"I've got her, just make a space. Make a space!"

"Tina? Just relax and stay with us, okay? You'll be fine! Mark, I need a syringe with a needle!"

"What kind, mom?"

"Doesn't matter; I have to try to suck out some of the air from her wound."

"Suck out… the air?"

"Just get a syringe and needle! And someone get a light over here; Jacob, you do that. Get some lanterns or something!"

"Dianne, I'm taking a quick look around the outbuildings to make sure there aren't any surprises here."

"Good thinking, Jason. We'll hold it down here. Sarah, you got a hold on her arm? I need to cut off her shirt."

Jason took a few steps back, watching in the dimly lit interior of the house as his wife and friend worked on a body lying on the table. Tina was still alive, but the bumpy ride back home hadn't done her any favors and her chest wound was leaking bubble-filled blood from around the edges of the duct tape that had been hastily applied.

Hoping that Tina would make it, Jason stalked out of the dining room and into the kitchen before making a quick tour through the entire house.

He checked in each and every nook and cranny that was large enough to conceal a person, just on the off chance that one of the gang had hung around and was waiting in ambush. With the house checked and cleared, Jason made his way outside, casting a wary eye at the burned section of the porch.

Out at the edge of the woods, just beyond the driveway, he could make out the forms of the men he and Mark had slain. In too much of a hurry to do anything with the corpses before, they had stripped them of their weapons and thrown them beyond the driveway. They were all still there, just as they had been previously, and Jason nodded grimly and whispered to himself as he added up the bodies. "Guess no one showed up to try and help you fellas."

The rest of the property was as quiet as the front yard, aside from the animals which were both hungry and tired of being cooped up for so long. Jason slung his rifle on his shoulder and distributed feed to them in the barns, wrinkling his nose at the smell and at the prospect of likely having to help clean out the messes they had been making.

With the outbuildings checked and cleared and the edge of the property looking clear, too, Jason made his way to the small shed in the woods and pulled open the trapdoor leading down into the tunnel. Rifle and flashlight in hand, he made his way down the tunnel until he reached the barred doors that led up into the basement. It took a few moments of grunting and levering, but he eventually freed the doors and swung them open to emerge into the basement of the house.

"Mr. Statler!" Mark cried out from the base of the stairs before stepping out, a pistol gripped between two nervously shaking hands. "I didn't know you were coming back in through the tunnel. I thought you were one of them breaking back in or something."

"Good instincts," Jason smiled, "but no, I was just finishing up checking outside. Everything's clear for the moment. How's Tina?"

"Mom said she's alive, which is all we can hope for right now."

"Morbid, but I can't say I disagree."

"Do you think they'll come back? The gang, I mean."

"I don't see how. Their leader's the only one who was alive there, and I doubt if he'd be foolish enough to try attacking us by himself." Jason paused. "I hope not, at least."

"If he does, we'll be ready for him." Mark slipped the pistol into a holster on his belt and Jason smiled, wrapping his arms around the boy.

"You're doggone right we will."

Chapter Ten

Washington, D.C.

THE DRAMA AND HORROR–BOTH old and fresh—that had ensued in the basement of the building made all the more stark the differences between the subterranean labyrinth and the cool, clear air of the outside world. The emergence of the three survivors into a sharp breeze and the whisking away of the scent of death that had permeated their clothing was not appreciated, though. Neither was the silence and peace that still reigned over the area after the previous battle that had been fought. The only thoughts on the minds of Rick, Oles and Dr. Evans as they stepped forth back into the natural sunlight were contemplations of their mortality and remembrances of their friend.

The grounds of the old naval observatory were mostly paved with asphalt roads and parking areas, but there were a few places with grass and potted plants that looked like they were well-maintained, once upon a time. It was there, in one of those small patches of grass and soil, that Rick, Dr. Evans and Oles stood over a mound of freshly-dug earth. Moments passed in silence before Oles finally broke it, speaking nervously as he looked at the others.

"Should we say something?"

"We've already said everything we need to." Rick sighed as he leaned on a shovel they had found in a small shed in a corner of the grounds. "She was a friend to us and a genuinely good person. For her to die here is unjust and unfair… but so's everything that's going on. She didn't have to help us, but she did." Rick slammed the point of the shovel into the ground and looked at Oles and Dr. Evans with moist, steely eyes. "So let's finish this."

"For her," added Dr. Evans, meeting Rick's gaze.

"For her," Oles finished.

Rick worked his jaw for a few seconds as he took one final look at the gravesite, then turned and headed back for the police car. He, Dr. Evans and Oles each took a mask off of the hood of the car, grabbed the rest of their gear and headed down into the building from whence they had come. Though the rush of adrenaline and the sheer panic during the struggle with the Russians had left Rick temporarily unaffected by the rancid smell in the building, he, Oles and Dr. Evans had all felt violently ill during their trip back up.

Passing through the halls and down the stairs, Rick stayed in the lead until they reached the bottom server room where he stood back and let Oles and Dr. Evans sit in their seats. Both were still nursing their wounds, but a quick bandaging of each other while Rick had been digging was all they had been able to afford due to their short timetable.

"So you have the codes." Rick looked at the pair. "What do we need to do to broadcast them out? Swap out this server with another one and use the dedicated line?"

"No," Dr. Evans shook his head, "when we were in the system we saw that it had specific authorization to work over their internal network. If there is another authorized system, we have no way of determining what it is."

"Hm." Rick turned and looked at the darkened servers—purposefully ignoring the shape of Jacob's body still lying on the floor—as he pondered their situation. "Are all of these systems clean? Or have they been compromised by Damocles?"

Dr. Evans used his feet to push his wheeled chair over to another desk, then pointed at a box mounted to the wall. "This whole room is sealed off from the outside world, and the only way to allow a connection through is by manually joining the cables together with this box. One and only one system can connect to it at a time. So no, I don't see how any of these could have been compromised by Damocles."

"Good. Where are the access keys for Damocles?"

Oles produced a small thumb drive from his pocket. "Dr. Evans and I made two copies before the system went down. I have one, and he has the other."

"Oles, give me your drive. You and Dr. Evans make sure you don't lose the other one. The pair of you get upstairs, get to the car and get the inverter hooked up and ready for me."

"What've you figured out, Rick?" Dr. Evans narrowed one eye at him, as if he could read Rick's mind. A sly smile passed across Rick's face and he looked back at the servers.

"Hopefully saving our asses. Now hurry up."

OUTSIDE, Oles and Dr. Evans worked together, each favoring their injured arm. The inverter was retrieved from the trunk of the police car, a power strip was retrieved from a nearby building and they even managed to get a small folding table and chair set up, too. They were just about to go looking for Rick when he staggered out of the front of the building, his head concealed by the server and monitor that he was carefully balancing in his arms. He turned to the side to check where he was going, saw the table near the car and beelined for it, huffing and puffing in his mask.

Thud!

The table groaned and creaked under the impact, but held firm. Rick ripped off his mask and threw it to the side before collapsing into the chair. Sweat poured down his face and neck, and he unzipped his jacket and unbuttoned the top of his shirt, pulling on it to help circulate cold air across his skin. Dr. Evans handed him a bottle of water and Rick took a few sips after his breathing slowed, then he zipped his jacket back up and looked at Oles and Dr. Evans. "It's been a long time since I had to haul one of these things anywhere. I forgot just how doggone heavy they are."

"Rick, I hate to say this," Dr. Evans began poking at the equipment Rick had retrieved, "but what good is a server, monitor and all this cabling and such going to do?"

Rick smiled at the question, leaned back in his chair and pointed at the top of the building across from them. The glare from the sun was bright, but they could still make out the edge of the flat roof and the antennas mounted on top. "When I sat up there with Ostap, I noticed that they've got a lot of communications equipment up there. Not surprising, right? Well, one of the devices they've got up there is an LKN Series VI short-range broadcaster and receiver. State of the art, dead simple to use and can transmit and receive radio to satellite and basically anything in between."

"Don't you need specialized equipment to connect with something like that?"

"That's the brilliant part. We worked with the prototypes of these for some of the work my company did in the autonomous car field. They accept half a dozen types of connections and the interface is a simple command line you can get to through almost any OS. They can draw power from the host system and anything you tell them to do is run through their internal system so there's no specialized software required."

"Wouldn't something like that have been infiltrated by Damocles?" Dr. Evans shielded his eyes as he looked up.

Rick stood and grabbed a thick bundle of cabling that he had wrapped around the base of the monitor. "Only one way to find out, eh?"

Chapter Eleven

 few miles off the Virginia Coast

"HOW MUCH BATTERY'S LEFT?"

"At least four more hours before we deplete the main cell. The two backups might give us a couple more hours, tops."

"Good. We'll make land by then for sure." Commander Palmer nods in satisfaction as he climbs back down the side of the module and goes to check on Ted. Seated on one of the floats, next to the jury-rigged outboard motor, he clings to both the float and the motor like his life depends on it.

Thought of in a spur-of-the-moment inspiration before leaving the space station, the idea for the motor was born out of pure necessity. Landing in the water would, as Commander Palmer put it, leave them stranded for *"who-knows-how-the-hell-long"* unless they had a way to get back to shore. Makeshift paddles would work, but pushing the module filled with life-sustaining supplies to the shore with paddles had not been on anyone's wish list. So, before setting off for Earth, they stripped down spare parts from the inside of the station, pulling apart any and everything that looked like it might be useful in constructing a makeshift motor.

"Plastic still holding tight?" Commander Palmer kneels down on the float across from Ted, looking at the motor in the water.

"Seems to be. Haven't had anything short out yet."

"Excellent. At the rate we're going we'll be there in a few hours."

"What'll we do once we reach shore?" Ted looks up at Commander Palmer.

"We'll secure the module and supplies and look for someone who can tell us what's going on."

"Are we going to land at Virginia Beach?" Jackie emerges from the module.

"If the current and wind is in our favor, I think we should try to push around through to Norfolk in the module. It's going to be a hike from the beach over to the Naval base otherwise. I don't want to get stranded out in the water, though, so it all depends. We'll play it by ear."

Ted shivers involuntarily and Commander Palmer looks over at Jackie. "Any luck finding the emergency blankets?"

"Not yet. I think they must have gotten stored in the outer lockers."

"All right. With the temperatures like they are I don't want anyone out here for more than thirty minutes at a time, starting now through dawn. Ted, get back into the module and warm up. I'll take the next thirty minutes, then it'll be Jackie's turn. Bundle up in your suits and amongst the supplies as best as possible; I'll shout if I need anything."

━━

"HEAVE!" Soft sand shifts underfoot and taut lines dig into shoulders as Commander Palmer shouts. He, Ted and Jackie all groan as they strain against the weight of the module, working with the rushing of the waves to pull it farther onto shore. The module shifts several more inches, falling slightly to the side then collapsing down into the white sand as the wave retreats. The three astronauts stand against their lines, panting and gasping while they wait for another wave to come rushing in.

"Once more! Heave!" Again they pull, dragging the module a few more inches before the wave retreats. Instead of ordering another pull or resting, though, Commander Palmer takes up the slack of his line and runs forward along the beach. "Come on, let's tie off!"

Ted and Jackie jog behind him, their boots churning up sprays of sand as they pull their lines, each of them headed for a separate bollard that stand at the edge of the beach. Put in place to stop vehicles from roving off of the road and onto the sand, the bollards are strong enough to stop a tractor-trailer hitting them head-on at sixty miles an hour—more than adequate to keep the module from drifting back into the ocean.

Once the module is secured, the trio collapses onto the sand, panting too heavily to talk about what they just accomplished. It had taken a full five hours to get the module to shore and another two of coordinated pulling to get it far enough up that they could tie the lines off. With the module—and their supplies inside—finally secured, though, they can rest.

Sleep comes fast for the trio, and it isn't until the early afternoon that they wake. Jackie is the first to sit up, checking to make sure the module is still there and smiling when she sees the gleaming silver, white and black contoured shapes of it resting in the sand. Aches and pains from both the labor of dragging the module through the sand and the effects of gravity make her groan as she stands to her feet, and she is soon joined by Ted and Commander Palmer. They make their way to the module and begin going through their supplies while constructing a strategy for their next steps.

"We should head for Norfolk as soon as possible," Commander Palmer says. "We can leave most of the supplies here and take enough for a day or so's worth of travel time."

"Shouldn't we hide some supplies away from the module?" Jackie looks at Commander Palmer. "This thing's a pretty big, obvious target for anyone around here."

"Are we really assuming that this is some kind of an apocalyptic scenario here?" Ted joins in the discussion as he pops out of the module, throwing a bag of dried food out into the sand.

"We all know it is, Ted." Commander Palmer looks back toward land and the burned buildings beyond the sand. "Denial won't do any good. Facing the situation head-on and rolling with whatever punches come our way will, though."

"It'd be nice if we had some way to defend ourselves." Jackie shook her head. "Us walking around with sacks of food and water are going to draw attention if there's anyone left around here."

Commander Palmer looks up at Ted. "Did you find it yet?"

"Yep, just dug out that compartment."

"Good. Bring it down, then close the hatch up tight. We've got enough food and water out now to make it to Norfolk and back, if necessary."

A black case lands in the sand next to Jackie and she picks it up, handing it to Commander Palmer. "What's this, then?"

"Something to deal with anyone who might be unfriendly. Courtesy of the Russian portion of the ISS. Ted grabbed them before we left." Commander Palmer opens the black case to reveal two Makarov 9mm semi-automatic pistols, along with four extra magazines.

Ted drops down into the sand outside the module and glances in the case, then looks at Jackie. "Russians always carry firearms of some sort in their survival kits. I didn't think they would leave any on the ISS but Commander Palmer was right."

The commander picks up one of the pistols, ejects the magazine, racks the slide, inserts the magazine and racks it once more. He then hands it to Ted before looking at Jackie. "You want the other one, or you want me to take it?"

"You go right ahead. I never did very well in the mandatory firearm training sessions."

Commander Palmer smirks and nods as he takes the pistol and spare magazines. "Neither did I, but that's okay. With any luck we won't need to use them."

"I think we've just about used up our fair share of luck just getting back to dry land in one piece, don't you?" Ted shoulders his bag and looks toward the ocean. "But who knows? Maybe it'll keep holding out."

Chapter Twelve

W ashington, D.C.

"HEADS UP!" Rick leaned over the edge of the roof and let the coil of cable drop while keeping a tight grip on one end. It hit the ground with a gentle smack before Oles scooped it up and hurried over to the police car. Rick watched as Dr. Evans and Oles connected the cable to the system sitting atop the hood of the police car. Once Dr. Evans raised his good arm with a thumbs-up gesture, Rick took the end of the cable he was still holding and turned his attention to the array of antennas mounted next to him.

From atop the roof he could once again see a large portion of the city laid out below, but unlike the previous time he had been up on top of the building he had not a second to spare. After securing the cable to a nearby support pole with a length of rope he clambered around amongst the antennas, looking for the best way to connect the cable to the multi-spectrum transmitter.

Around the size of a shoebox, the LKN Series VI had a protective panel on the side that Rick removed to expose a small touchscreen control panel next to several data ports. Rick removed the three cables already plugged into the device and attached the new cable before leaning back over the edge of the roof.

"Good to go!" Rick shouted down at Oles and Dr. Evans. They both waved at him and Dr. Evans slid behind the driver's seat of the car and started up the engine. Oles then connected the power strip to the power inverter and turned on the server and monitor. Rick turned back and watched the transmitter's control panel, and after a few seconds his patience was rewarded. The screen flickered to life, displaying the LKN company logo and Rick pressed down on two of the buttons next to the screen. A moment later a debug boot screen appeared and Rick rubbed his hands together to try and get rid of some of the chill.

"We're in business," he whispered to himself as he read over the information displayed on the screen. It had been a few years since he had put his hands on an LKN transmitter, but the interface was a lightweight Unix/Linux variant, something he was intimately familiar with. Before proceeding to a full bootup of the transmitter, Rick tapped out a few commands and popped open another access panel on the other side of the device. He manually pulled out three connectors and checked the panel again, satisfied to see a message saying "Receiver Offline. Check Connections."

With the receiver's wiring pulled, the device was physically incapable of receiving incoming transmissions, including those from any potentially infected systems. Rick tapped out a few more commands and the device continued its normal bootup sequence. When the device finally finished turning on, Rick began tapping through menus, examining each one for signs that Damocles had infected the system. While early infections were nearly impossible to detect, Damocles had moved far beyond the stage of being subtle, and infections were pronounced and obvious.

"Rick!" A shout drifted up and he leaned over the side to see Dr. Evans with a hand cupped around the side of his mouth. "How's it look?"

Rick glanced back at the screen and raised a thumb in the air at Dr. Evans before returning to the transmitter. He powered it off, replaced the pulled connections and powered it back on into debug mode. With the device fully operational again, Rick stood up and waved to Dr. Evans and Oles. "I'm coming down!"

A few moments later, the trio stood clustered around the monitor sitting atop the police car. With Oles and Dr. Evans injured, Rick had taken the lead on the keyboard, though he was merely entering in commands that were being given to him by the other two. Twenty minutes into a session digging deep into the transmitter's core system files, though, Rick had finally had enough.

"All right, that's it," Rick snapped as he exited from the low-level files. Oles and Dr. Evans glanced at each other before Oles spoke.

"What do you mean? We need to check all the files, to ensure that it's not—"

"It's not. Okay? It's not infected. I checked it, we've been in the system for a while now and nothing's popped up. If Damocles had a tendril in here it would have infected the server and we'd know for sure."

"We can't be sure, Rick, unti—"

"Doc." Rick turned and glared at Dr. Evans with a stare that unquestion-ably communicated what he was feeling. "We've got more pressing concerns, like finding out exactly how much time's left before Damocles starts its final stage and starting the distribution of the shutdown commands. How about we get those all keyed in and hey, even if Damocles is on the system it'll read the shutdown command and it'll be gone anyway."

Dr. Evans raised a finger to argue, but what Rick said suddenly clicked with him and he and Oles exchanged a sheepish look. "I... uh... yes. That would work, I suppose."

"We didn't think of that," mumbled Oles.

"Well, that's why I'm here." Rick ground his teeth together as he forced a smile and pulled out the thumb drive he had taken earlier. "Now walk me through how to get these commands written up."

"Of course." Dr. Evans began to instruct Rick in what to do, and a few minutes into the process Rick stopped and looked at the pair with a quizzical expression.

"You're having me enter all this into a text file."

"...yes?" Dr. Evans appeared confused, as though the question was completely alien to him.

Rick rubbed his eyes, trying to keep from saying anything that might be taken the wrong way. "Dr. Evans... can you explain how this will work? Don't we have to use a specific piece of software to interface with Damocles and issue commands to it?"

"What? No, of course not. The commands can be embedded into any type of file, so long as the authentication key properly surrounds them. Damocles will read the key and commands and act accordingly."

"That... okay, that's surprisingly smart," Rick nodded slowly as he thought about what Dr. Evans was describing. "It ensures that you can always communicate with Damocles no matter what system it's on or where it is. I assume it'll read the authentication key in multiple formats?"

"Of course."

"Huh." Rick raised his eyebrows approvingly. "Well, all right. That's pretty clever." He continued working away, taking instructions from Dr. Evans and Oles. The command's formatting was complex, but the results would be simple enough. Once read and digested by Damocles, it ordered the program to first broadcast the commands to every other instance of Damocles that it could connect to. The second instruction was for Damocles to stand down from any and all system attacks and then delete itself from the device it was on. This self-replicating chain would act precisely like Damocles did when it spread outward, except the spread this time would be a cure, not the disease.

When he finished, he saved the command file to both the system and to the thumb drive before popping the drive out and slipping it into his pocket. He was about to ask the other two what the next step was when the sound of scraping footsteps off to the side followed by the harsh staccato crack of gunshots caught everyone off-guard. Rick turned to look at the building where Jane had lost her life and saw, bloodied and staggering, an impossible sight. Jacob stumbled out of the entrance, his pistol in hand as he howled in pain and rage.

"Stop what you're doing and give me the codes!"

Chapter Thirteen

The Waters' Homestead
Outside Ellisville, VA

"HOW IS SHE?" Jason stood next to Sarah, his arm wrapped around her shoulder and her head on his chest as he looked at Dianne. Dianne glanced behind her at Tina, who was lying on the couch looking smaller and frailer than ever.

"Alive, still."

"Any idea how serious the wound is?"

Dianne shrugged. "My emergency response class was a long time ago. If Tina hadn't pointed out that I needed to seal the wound to keep air out, I wouldn't have even remembered." Dianne pulled her jacket to the side and pushed two fingers up against the soft part below her right clavicle. "She got hit right about here. She's not coughing up blood and her breathing's improved a bit so I don't *think* that her lung got punctured, but I really have no clue. Any guessing I'd be doing in the course of trying to repair the damage might do more harm than good. We'll take shifts watching her tonight and keeping guard. We need to be monitoring her temperature and making sure she's breathing and not bleeding out."

"We just have to wait and see what happens," Sarah looked up at Jason before wrapping her arm around him. He winced slightly and she pulled back, an apologetic look on her face. "Sorry, hon. Sort of forgot about your wound in all of this."

"How are you doing, Jason?" Dianne focused on him, studying him closely.

"Hanging in there, like us all."

"You look like crap. I'll take first watch. Mark can take second, then you, then Sarah."

At any other point in time, Jason would have vigorously argued with Dianne, insisting that he could stay up the whole night keeping guard and watching over Tina. His body, older than he wanted to admit, wasn't having any of it. "Fine," he sighed. "Two hours each. We're all so sleep-deprived that we need to keep these shifts short."

Dianne smiled and nodded at him. "Get some rest, you two. I'll wake up Mark in a couple hours and he'll wake you."

After Jason and Sarah slowly made their way upstairs, Dianne was left in the dark, quiet living room. Tina's gentle wheezing was the only sound that was audible and, for a moment, Dianne seriously contemplated how cozy and comfortable her chair was. Before the urge could overtake her, though, she stood up and shook it off.

Rifle in hand, Dianne walked over close to Tina and pulled back the blanket to check the bandages on Tina's shoulder. "Stay with us," Dianne whispered. "We need you. Now more than ever."

<hr />

OUT BEYOND THE WATERS' homestead, past where the dirt road turned to gravel and then to asphalt, beyond the turn at the edge of town leading past the forest, fields and the long ditch, more whispering was happening. As the five men loaded their gear into a pair of trucks, they did more than a small amount of quiet talking amongst themselves while stealing quick glances at the silhouette that was still stomping around inside the community center.

"We should just leave. He's clearly lost it."

"If he hears us, you know what he'll do to us, right?"

"There's five of us and one of him. Why are we even listening to him?"

"He did manage to set up a pretty good thing for us. Maybe he can do it again."

"He's just out for revenge. I don't blame him; he's supported us and we should support him back. That bitch's luck has got to run out at some point. That's two of theirs that've been shot, now, thanks to him. Now's the perfect time to get them."

"You remember what happened the last time we tried that? They kicked our asses!"

"Sh! Quiet, here he comes!"

Nealson walked out of the community center standing tall in spite of his injury, his eyes ablaze and his expression hardened. Though he hadn't heard any of what his five remaining men were saying while he was inside, he could sense by their body language that they weren't happy with the situation. Fear had already been put into their hearts. Now it was time for something else.

"All right men," Nealson smiled broadly, "gather 'round!" They glanced at each other as they shuffled toward him, murmuring questions to themselves under their breath.

"Now," he continued, "I know you all are tired of all of this. You think this is a fool's errand. You think that we're just going to end up losing again if we charge in there." The five said nothing, but looked at each other with expressions that showed that they agreed with everything he said. "That's fine. I don't need you to believe me. I just need you to believe *in* me.

"Remember when I found each and every one of you?" Nealson began addressing each man in turn. "You two in the prison in Blacksburg? Trapped by that old man you were trying to rob? Stranded in a firestorm? I took each of you in and helped you, just like the rest." Nealson made a half-turn and swept his arm across the sight of the bodies still lying in front of the center. "Just like your fallen brothers. Now it's time for revenge. Two of them are hurt, and the rest are exhausted. They'll be weak and hurting and unable to defend themselves come morning. And that's when we'll go in, kill the *bitch!*" He spat out the word with fury uncontained. "Then we'll chain up the rest and rebuild again!"

Throughout Nealson's short speech, he could see that he was getting the attention of the men. Their attention grew until the end, when they finally went from silently listening to nodding their agreement. Once he saw that they were back on his side, he addressed them individually again, taking each one by the arm and looking them dead in the eyes.

"Are you with me?" He asked of each, and each nodded and replied.

"Yes."

"Good," he said after the fifth had spoken, "get in the trucks. We're going to finish this."

Chapter Fourteen

W ashington, D.C.

OUTSIDE, in the middle of the tightly-packed buildings on the grounds of the old naval observatory, the shots from Jacob's pistol sounded as though they were coming from every direction. Rick was the first to move in response to the gunfire, pulling Oles and Dr. Evans down to the ground as he ducked behind the hood of the car. A spray of plastic was accompanied by the sound of arcing electricity as the monitor fell down on top of Rick's head, a large hole punched clean through the center. Three more shots rang out and Rick heard the server bounce around as shots ricocheted off of the metal backing and one punched through, hitting the drives and causing a loud scrape of metal as the platters ground to a halt.

"*Give me the codes!*" Jacob screamed again as he slowly shuffled toward the car. Rick ducked down low and watched Jacob's feet as he approached, trying to estimate which direction the Russian was going to take when circling around. With his rifle sitting on the roof of the car, grabbing it would be a large risk, and one that would likely result in him taking a bullet or two in the process.

"Jacob, please! You don't have to do this!" Rick glanced over and saw Oles sitting next to him, leaned over and shouting at his former friend. "You can stop this right now!"

"No I can't!" Jacob yelled back, continuing his slow walk toward the car.

"Jacob, listen to me, please!" Oles was nearly in tears as he continued pleading with Jacob. "The endgame is near. This is about to get a whole lot worse for everyone in the world. You can help us stop it, though!"

Jacob stopped, a few feet from the side of the car's trunk. Rick took a quick peek up through the windows and saw the Russian standing there, his body swaying back and forth. Dried blood matted his hair and flaked off of his neck as he rubbed a hand across it, and Rick briefly felt bad for him. How he had managed to live through the brutal beating Rick had given him was nothing short of impressive.

"I'm sorry, Oles. If I could stop, I would. My... my family, though..." Jacob choked up, and Rick could see tears starting to run down his face. "They have my family, you know. He does. He took me in, told me that if the Spetsnaz failed or turned, it would be my job to bring the codes back. If I don't... they die." A long, deep breath and the shakiness went out of Jacob's voice. "I can't let that happen."

"Neither can I." Rick peeked out again, seeing that Jacob was focused on the rear of the car, and made his move. He turned and stood up just far enough to reach for the rifle on the top of the car. Metal scraped on metal as he grabbed it, and he pulled it down and got back into cover just as Jacob turned and fired. A spray of safety glass blew over the three men, but Rick didn't hesitate. He scuttled around Dr. Evans, moving to the front of the car where he got on his knees, slammed his arms down on the hood and shouldered the rifle in a single, smooth motion.

One more shot, louder than the others, rang out. It bounced off the walls of the buildings at the observatory, traveled down the empty streets and petered out as it disappeared off into the sky. Jacob's form wavered for a moment before he collapsed, smacking his head on the trunk of the car before falling into a heap. The distant returning echoes of the bullet were the only sounds in the observatory grounds for a long moment until Oles finally cried out.

"Damn it, Jacob!" He stood and walked over to his former friend's corpse, crossing himself and continuing on in a string of Russian that neither Rick nor Dr. Evans could understand. While the words were unintelligible to them, the emotion was clear. Anger, raw and primal, mixed with regret and profound sadness tinged them, permeating into Rick and Dr. Evans and making them both feel what Oles felt.

Dr. Evans slowly approached Oles and put his good arm around him. "I'm sorry. I know you two were friends. It sounds like... like this might not have been entirely under his control."

Oles shook his head vigorously. "No. He still bears responsibility. It doesn't matter what they threatened him with... but it was his family." He shook his head, unsure what to think.

"Whatever there is to figure out, we'll figure out later," Rick replied as he stood up and looked at the damage done to the computer systems that had been sitting atop the car. "For right now, we need to decide what to do about all of... *this.*" The damage that Rick had heard being done to the server was as bad as it had sounded in the midst of the firefight. Shards of hard drive platters were embedded on the interior plastic of the case, rendering them inoperable.

"We can get another system," Oles replied.

"Do we even need one?" Rick asked, looking at the pair. "The commands are written. You said Damocles will read it off of anything that it infects, right?" He turned and gazed at the nearby rooftop. "The LKN will accept this type of data source. We might not have power, though, with the abuse this system went through."

"Maybe we do need a system then, just to power the LKN."

"Hmm." Rick scratched his chin. "Let's pull the dead drives and see if we can get this thing powered on."

Dr. Evans pulled the plug from the back of the server and they quickly went to work disassembling the device. A few minutes in, as a stiff breeze was kicking up, Rick cocked his head to the side. "You two hear that?"

Noises signaling danger had been a constant theme since the start of the event, and the mere mention of an odd sound set Dr. Evans and Oles on edge. It was a muffled warble, coming from somewhere close by yet sounding too faint to easily pinpoint the source. The longer they listened, the more confused they grew until Dr. Evans drew in a sharp gasp of air.

"Warning alarm. It's from the bunker."

"Alarm in the bunker?"

Dr. Evans was already on the move, heading for the very door that Jacob had emerged from. He moved relatively quickly in spite of his injury, and he paused at the entrance to the building after pulling open the door, a look of panic crossing his face.

"What is it?" Oles' face began to match Dr. Evans'.

"It's an advanced launch warning." He glanced at Rick, seeing the look of confusion. "Certain launch conditions include broadcasts to high-priority stations. The birthplace of Damocles would qualify, without a doubt."

"How could that possibly be happening?" Rick shook his head.

"Damocles would have left emergency communications alone, so that enemies under attack would have a final chance to surrender."

"Does that mean..." Rick started.

"Yes. Damocles has entered the final stages."

"How long do we have?"

"Minutes. At most."

Rick looked down at the thumb drive in his hand, then up at the roof. "Time to find out if this works." He broke into a run, ignoring Oles and Dr. Evans as they started throwing theories and speculations back and forth and dashed forward to the building that housed the transmitter on top. Shouting over his shoulder, he cried out to the pair as he vanished inside. "Get the power on to that system! The transmitter won't work without it!"

Chapter Fifteen

Washington, D.C.

RICK'S HEARTBEAT pounded in his ears as he ran down the hall, the thumb drive containing the text file clutched tight in his hand. He had questions for Dr. Evans about the early warning system, the commands on the drive and so much more but none of it mattered. If Dr. Evans said that a launch was imminent, then it was imminent.

In the back of Rick's mind, pushed there when he started his run for fear that thinking about it would overwhelm him to the point of incapacitating him, sat his family. Dianne, Mark, Jacob and Josie. His four shining stars, lost to him for so long and now just a relative stone's throw away. Choosing to go after stopping Damocles over returning to them had been a difficult decision, but thinking about it all not mattering if the launch were successful was too much to bear.

So he ran. Leaping over the still-slick bloodstains in the hall from the gunfight that now seemed a distant memory. Slamming his shoulder into the wall as he rounded the corner on a landing. Taking the stairs two, three even four at a time. By the time he burst out onto the roof his already-exhausted body felt like it was going to give up, but his mental fortitude carried him through. It was just about the only thing keeping him standing, but it was enough. For the moment, at least.

From atop the roof Rick was far enough away from the entrance to the opposite building that he couldn't hear the faint alarms going off, but the panicked body language of Dr. Evans and Oles below told him that the noise was still ongoing. Rick dropped to his knees at the LKN transmitter and popped open the cover, revealing a blank screen. A moment of panic clutched at him, but a cry of joy from down below accompanied a flash on the screen as the device powered up.

"Is it working?!" The shout came from Oles, and Rick stuck his head over the side of the roof and shouted back.

"Yes! It just came on!"

"Well hurry up! This thing isn't sounding good... I don't know how long before it dies again!"

Seconds ticked by slower than Rick could have ever dreamed they could as the transmitter's lightweight operating system powered up. The splash screen appeared, then disappeared, and then he was staring at the menu.

Alone on the rooftop, Rick fumbled with the thumb drive in his hand before he pushed it into one of the transmitter's data ports. A small symbol of a rotating hourglass appeared in a corner of the transmitter's screen for what felt like forever before it turned into a green checkmark, signaling that the drive had been successfully inserted, detected and recognized as a valid device.

Rick's fingers trembled as he pushed the buttons next to the screen, trying to hurry through the menus to get to what he was looking for. Finally, in a sub-menu, there was the option that he recalled from when he had worked with one of the transmitters in the past.

Activate standalone search?

Rick pushed the button next to the option, then confirmed with a second button press. Normally the transmitter would need to be controlled by an external device in order to send and receive signals, but one of the debug options allowed the transmitter to be placed in an "open" mode where it would constantly broadcast a test signal and open itself up for connections from outside sources. While outside connections would have to be properly authenticated in order to connect to the transmitter, Rick knew full well that Damocles had that capability.

With a final press of a button the option was confirmed yet again and small gears inside the transmitter whirred to life. Higher up on its pole a small antenna unfurled, and even higher the small satellite dish began to rotate back and forth, searching for something to connect to.

"Rick?" Dr. Evans and Oles appeared at the door to the roof, both of them panting from the exertion of running up the stairs.

"What are you two doing here? You need to stay by the server, make sure the power doesn't go out!"

"It's as good as it'll get," Dr. Evans nodded at his companion, "Oles here is better with hardware than he'd like you to know. It's stable for the moment."

"Is it… working?" Oles pointed at the slowly-rotating dish atop the transmitter's tower.

Rick glanced back at the screen and shook his head. "It's sending out a signal and waiting for a connection at the same time. I have no idea if it's actually working, though. It'll be—wait." The screen flickered so quickly that Rick thought he might have blinked his eyes too slowly and imagined the distortion.

"Wait what?"

"Nothing… thought I saw—wait, there it is again!" The second time he definitely, without a doubt, saw the screen flicker. Dr. Evans and Oles walked over and crouched down behind Rick, all three of them staring at the transmitter's screen.

"What did you see?"

"The screen flickered, once or twice. But maybe it's a power surge from the server." Rick studied the screen top to bottom before shrugging. "Guess I can run a diagnostic while it's searching." He pushed one of the buttons next to the screen, but nothing happened. A brief rush of panic seized him before it was replaced with elation. "This… this isn't working! It's not working!"

"Damocles is in the system." Dr. Evans spoke with a broadening smile.

"Sure seems that way." Rick tapped his fingers across the buttons in a futile effort to get a response from the transmitter, but none was forthcoming. "But now what? Shouldn't it have read the commands and disabled itself?"

"Just wait," Dr. Evans patted Rick on the shoulder, "its first priority is infection. Once it's secure in the system then it'll move on to scanning all the data. After that it'll sabotage the system in a way that makes the most sense based on its instruction sets before it tries to use the system to replicate itself. I'm betting it's either still ensuring that it has full control over everything bef—ha! See!"

Dr. Evans jabbed his finger at the screen as it flickered again, then turned off. It snapped back to life a second later, white text scrolling fast across a black background. The text was gibberish to the human eye, though, a mix of binary and seemingly random ASCII characters and Rick raised an eyebrow. "Is this a good thing?"

"It's performing a deep scan of the system. All it has to do is hit the thumb drive and it'll disable itself."

"The operating system on these is pretty small. Couple of gigs at most. Shouldn't take Damocles more than a few seconds to scan everything, right?"

"I wouldn't think so," Dr. Evans nodded.

Rick sat, staring at the screen for over a full minute before looking over at Dr. Evans again. "You sure those commands were right?"

Oles and Dr. Evans exchanged another glance. "They were precise; we're sure of it." Oles replied.

"Indeed."

"So why's it not working?"

The trio stared at the screen, the jumble of characters still flying across, each of them consumed with their own private doubts and worries. Oles, over whether he had somehow inadvertently messed things up. Dr. Evans, over whether every single line was given and typed in correctly. Rick, over his family, and wishing that—if the end was going to come—then all he wanted, more than anything else in the world, was to be there holding tight to them until the fire and flames ripped them apart.

Beep.

The sound was soft, created by the tiniest of integrated speakers inside the transmitter and designed primarily to help technicians working on repairs and to give audio feedback on buttons being pressed. Rick opened his eyes and stared at the screen, bright and regular again, no longer the wave of symbols but instead containing a line of text that was the sweetest and most satisfying thing he could have ever imagined reading.

Broadcast in progress. Please stand by.

Chapter Sixteen

The Waters' Homestead
        Outside Ellisville, VA

"OVER THERE! BEHIND THE TRUCKS!" Frantic shouting is followed by the swift fire of shots, followed up by return fire.

"I see him!"

"I need him suppressed or else I can't get an angle on the other one!"

"*Augh!*" A scream accompanied by the shattering of glass.

"How bad is it?!"

Jason slid down the wall next to the window he had been shooting from and held a hand to his upper arm. "Just grazed me; I'm fine!"

Rapid, unending fire continued to pour into the upper windows of the house as Mark crawled across the floor to examine Jason's wound for himself. Delays in the fire only occurred when individual assailants needed to stop and reload, and even then there were still at least three or four who were firing nonstop.

The attack had come the next morning, just a couple hours after Tina had awoken. She was still pale and weak, but her breathing had improved and she was able to instruct Dianne in the proper medications to give and how to redress the wound without risking more air leaking into her chest cavity. Jason had just finished up a long-overdue and extremely welcome hot shower when the roar of engines made him abandon his towel as he leapt around, pulling clothes on over his still-dripping form.

The pair of trucks that roared down the driveway ignored the gate and the boards with nails entirely, the lead truck ramming through the gate and both trucks popping all of their tires as they screamed across the traps. Nealson had no plans to make an escape—he would either triumph or he would not be leaving. It was as simple as that.

"Stop playing around and shoot them!" Dianne roared up the stairs at Mark and Jason as she charged through a hall, sprays of shrapnel and bullets whizzing past her. She slid to a stop near the kitchen window and looked over at Sarah, who was cradling Tina in her arms as she tried to move the injured woman and the two younger children to the basement door. "Hurry! Get them downstairs quickly!"

"I'm trying!"

Dianne put her head back against the wall and closed her eyes as the storm of fire continued to rain down on the house. They had been expecting an attack from Nealson—it was foolish not to expect one—but one so ferocious? That was the surprise. The last time, when he had taken all of them except Tina, Jason and Mark, their attack had been coordinated and calculated. This felt completely different, like all Nealson wanted was to use brute force to try and bring the entire place down around them.

The fire directed at the kitchen area stopped and Dianne used the opportunity to poke the barrel of her rifle through a gap in the splintered boards and fire back. The fire was mostly blind, though before she emptied the entire magazine she heard a cry of pain and withdrew, satisfied with at least wounding one of the attackers.

Wounding one of the six would only go so far. They were spread out, had apparently brought enough ammunition to keep up a continuous stream of fire for an extended period of time and had the advantage over those in the house. As Dianne ejected her spent mag and felt in her pockets for a fresh one, the memory of being dragged off by Nealson's men flashed across her mind. It was immediately followed by the remembrance of Jason, Mark and Tina not being taken because they had managed to slip away into the basement and escape through the tunnel.

The tunnel. She looked over at the kitchen, where the door to the basement was closing and then looked upward and shouted at the top of her lungs. "Mark! Jason! I have to run an errand!"

▭

"AN ERRAND?" Mark's eyes widened as he looked over at Jason. "What's she talking about?"

"No idea," Jason shook his head before taking a few more shots at a target moving through the woods. "Your mom's a smart woman, though and it sounds like she's got a plan up her sleeve."

Mark stood up from where he had been hiding behind a dresser and pulled back the bolt on his rifle. He inched along the wall before holding the gun out at arm's length and firing blindly out into the drive. The recoil from the rifle was strong, but he managed to keep a grip on it as he tried to find a target without taking shots himself. Two of the rounds smacked on metal and glass instead of the gravel drive, and though he couldn't see it, he had driven back two of Nealson's men who had been gearing up to make a run for the front door of the house.

"Whatever she's doing, I hope it works." Mark squeezed back into his spot behind the dresser and flinched as more rounds came through the window. He fumbled with the magazine on his rifle as he tried to keep a calm, stoic face, but Jason could see quite clearly that the teen was terrified beyond belief. Terrified for his family, for himself, for what had happened and what could happen in the near or far future if they managed to survive that long.

"Chin up, lad." Jason smiled at Mark from across the room. "We'll get through this."

"MOVE, MOVE!" Dianne practically flew down into the basement, breaking every rule she had set for the children when it came to how to travel safely on staircases. Tina, though still in pain and unable to move for fear of hurting herself, watched Dianne with eyes that were still sharp and focused.

"Dianne." Her voice was soft, but still possessed strength.

"Hm?" Dianne didn't look back at Tina, too focused on unlocking and removing the chains around the tunnel doors.

"Be safe out there."

Dianne pulled open the doors and took a few steps down before turning and nodding at Tina. "I will. Sarah, get them into the tunnel and then lock it behind you, okay? Don't come out till it's all clear." With a final, loving look at Jacob and Josie, Dianne descended the rest of the stairs and took off at a run down the tunnel.

Chapter Seventeen

M ount Weathers
Outside Washington, D.C.

"IT'S NO GOOD, CAPTAIN." The uniformed officer was breathing heavy as she took off her jacket and wrapped it around her waist. Beads of sweat ran down her head and neck, though the cold weather and sharp breeze were helping to alleviate her discomfort.

"Hammers give out again?"

"No, they just won't budge anything. Whoever designed these doors wasn't kidding around."

Captain Lance Recker took a bite out of a stale energy bar and chewed slowly as he sat on the hood of a squad car. He and a couple dozen other officers were scattered around the entrance to the Mount Weathers bunker, which they had been trying to break into for nearly two days. The heavy equipment they brought from the city—the equipment that he had been sure would make short work of the bunker doors—had been thwarted by the thick, impenetrable steel.

A few of the officers stood around near the doors, pointing at the seams and mechanisms as if they could divine some way of opening the place up. Recker had seen enough to know that there was no way they would be getting through, not unless whatever had sealed the place up released its hold.

"Without power, how long do you figure they've got in there before the air goes bad and they all start suffocating?"

"Dunno, Captain. Can't be more than another day or so at the most. There's nothing we can do for them. All the vents we've been able to find are closed up and we can't get those open, either. I hate to say it, but it's possible that everyone inside is already... gone."

Recker finished off his energy bar and slowly stood, picking up a medium-sized stone from the ground in front of the car. "We went through all this work to rescue them, brought in all the heavy equipment we could find and that's it? We get nothing?" He chucked the stone in a high arc over the heads of the other officers, then turned away before it bounced off the bunker door with a low, metallic rumble.

Recker was about to get another energy bar from the back of the car when he stopped, realizing that the rumble from the stone's impact wasn't stopping—it was growing louder. He turned with the rest of the men and women there with him, watching as the mechanisms for the door began to move as they slowly moved the locks out of position.

"What the..." Recker stared at the door, taking a few slow steps toward it along with the rest of the officers. When the locks finally finished moving, a siren began to sound and Recker's eyes opened wide.

"Get those cars back! Get the backhoes and bulldozer out of the way!" The officers scrambled to move under Recker's order as the doors to the bunker began to slowly swing open a moment later. Figures began emerging out from between the double doors, waving their arms and stumbling as they tried to shield their vision from the intense sunlight after so long underground. Recker ran forward and caught a woman wearing a sweat-stained skirt and blouse as she tripped and nearly fell, easing her to the ground as she screwed her eyes shut.

"Medics, spread out! Help these people now!" He looked down and spoke softly to the woman as she gripped his arm. "Ma'am, it'll be okay."

"It was... it was horrible. The batteries gave out a few days ago. We've been in the dark since then."

"What happened? Were you able to get the locks open from the inside?"

"No... a few minutes ago they just opened. We heard them from downstairs and crawled up." A panicked look crossed the woman's face. "There are dead down there... so many."

Recker patted the woman on the arm and motioned for a nearby officer. "Move her to the staging area. And get a search team in there with lights; she says there are dead in the lower levels."

As the woman was taken away and Recker stepped back to watch his people work, the officer who had been talking with him before the doors opened jogged up to him. "Captain, I can't believe so many survived. Sounds like they were in the final hours before the air gave out, though. We're lucky that the doors opened when they did."

Recker snorted. "Luck had nothing to do with it."

"You know what caused it, sir?"

Recker looked out in the direction of Washington, thinking back to the strange run-in he had a few days prior with two men and a young woman who were on their way into the city. "I've got a hunch," he replied, scratching his chin as he stared off in thought. Finally, after a moment of silence, he abruptly turned to the officer. "What's our total force strength stand at?"

"Including our officers here now and the few that went out with the civvies in search of supplies this morning, about fifty in total."

"Good. Find me eleven of the best officers we've got; they're coming with me on a little mission. You'll be in charge here till I return."

"Sir?" The woman blanched. "What about this attack? The whole virus and everything?"

Recker smiled and looked back out in the direction of Washington. "It's over. He stopped it and saved these people. And now we're going to go find him and his crew and return the favor."

Chapter Eighteen

The Waters' Homestead
Outside Ellisville, VA

"I JUST DON'T UNDERSTAND why we're trying to kill them. We need labor!"

Nealson's eyes were practically glowing as he spat back at the man crouched next to him behind one of the trucks in the driveway. "Are you questioning me?!"

"N-no, I just—"

"You'd better 'just' keep them pinned down!" He looked around the truck and house, searching in the woods for a sign of the pair that he had sent out in a flanking maneuver. Without radios at hand, they would have to rely on visual communications to let him know that they were in position. A moment later, amongst the trees at the edge of the property, he saw the two emerge from the deep of the woods where they had traveled to avoid detection.

The pair stopped and turned toward Nealson, waving at him. He waved back and began signaling for them to move in on the back of the house when the color drained from his face and a look of pure rage passed over him. He began waving frantically, trying to get them to pay attention and look behind them, but he was far, far too late.

▭

"HELLO, BOYS." The seething whisper from between clenched teeth reached out and enveloped the pair like a serpent. Before they could turn and ready their rifles, a pair of shots rang out and they dropped to the ground, blood pouring from the holes in the backs of each of their heads.

Dianne stepped over the men without a second thought, hurrying into the woods where they had come from as she heard Nealson screaming in rage from behind the truck in the front drive. At any other point she would have felt guilt over taking life, no matter how horrid it might have been. Killing the two men elicited no emotions except satisfaction over eliminating yet another threat to her family and getting one step closer to ending the leader of the continual stream of threats.

Nealson fired at the figure as it vanished into the woods, hitting nothing but air and trees in the process. While he hadn't gotten a good look at the person who gunned down two of his remaining men, he knew without a shadow of a doubt that it was her. The same devil who had been plaguing him practically since the event started. He had done well after the event, first killing two of his neighbors and plundering their homes before heading south and connecting with old prison mates from years gone past. That had swiftly turned into setting up shop along a highway where he could sell fuel and other goods to the locals, though more than a few of his customers had turned into slave labor.

He had been doing well. Until *she* showed up in camp, killing and stealing and turning the place on its head. In another situation, at another point in time, he might have been impressed and tried to convince her to join him. But she wasn't that type of person, so she had to die. Unfortunately, she kept slipping from his grasp. Not this time, though.

"Stay here," Nealson growled to the man next to him, "I'm going after her."

"Are you…" the man started to question Nealson but thought better of it, instead just nodding and turning around to unload another magazine into the side of the house.

Nealson took off through the woods, heading parallel to the driveway in an effort to intercept the woman before she could sneak up and surprise him. Wearing camouflage pants and a jacket with a dark shirt on underneath, Nealson slowed down and dropped to his knees once he got far enough into the woods to be invisible to those inside the house. His wound made it impossible for him to crawl along like he wanted so he settled for sitting down with his back against a tree and pistol in his hand, waiting for the woman to come wandering through the trees.

He didn't have to wait for long.

Dianne walked quickly through the woods, heading for the driveway and a clear view on the side of the truck where she had spotted two men—one of them the leader of the group—hiding while they continued to shoot up her home. Nealson held his breath as she came close, his outfit concealing him neatly amongst the dead foliage. When she came within a few feet of him he lunged forward, ignoring the burning pain in his shoulder and arm. Dianne felt something grab onto her leg and for an instant thought she tripped on a branch. The loud growl as she fell to the ground and the feeling of someone jumping on top of her dispelled that thought, doubly so once she looked up and found herself staring into Nealson's face.

His bloodshot eyes stared down at her as she recoiled, turning her head from his rancid breath and body odor, and he sneered at her, keeping his pistol pressed firmly against the side of her head with his good hand and arm. "Got you now, *bitch*." He spat as he spoke, and though Dianne was terrified by him, she couldn't help but make a face of disgust.

"You really need to brush your teeth."

Without thinking, Nealson used his injured arm to strike her across the face, which caused him to grind his teeth together in pain. Dianne choked back a laugh, suddenly incredibly amused by the situation.

"Guess my son managed to wing you, eh? I bet that hurts."

The pistol dug deep into her temple, sending waves of pain through her head. "Bet this'll hurt more. Got any last words?"

A branch snapped behind Nealson and Dianne's eyes flicked to the source, widening as her mouth fell open. "…you?"

A single shot rang out through the woods and Nealson's eyes rolled back in his head before he could turn to see what Dianne had spotted. His limbs went limp along with the rest of his body and he sagged forward, rolling off of Dianne as she pushed him to the side.

She scrambled backwards through the leaves and dead underbrush, shaking her head and muttering, "no, no, no," the whole time. After a few feet of backwards crawling she hit a tree that she pressed her back against, still shaking her head, unable to accept that the face she had seen in her dreams for what felt like eternity was finally real. It was still a dream; it had to still be a dream. For it to be reality would be asking far, far too much.

But her dreams had never spoken to her. At least not until now.

"Hey babe," the figure was caked in dirt and sweat and spoke with a crooked grin and tear-filled eyes. "Miss me?"

Chapter Nineteen

The Waters' Homestead
Outside Ellisville, VA

RICK'S HAND was rougher and older-looking than Dianne remembered. She stared at it as he held it out to her, standing over her wearing a pair of blue jeans and a thick jacket with a Capitol Police symbol emblazoned on the chest and shoulder. She took his hand slowly, feeling its warmth envelop her own as Rick pulled her to his feet. They stood there, standing and looking at each other for a long moment before she punched him hard in the shoulder, then grabbed him in a tighter hug than she had ever given in his life.

"Ow! What was that for?"

"For taking so long!"

Rick chuckled and wrapped his arms around her, enveloping her in an embrace that she had dreamt of nearly every night since the event. This time, though, there was no waking up in a dark room with a cold space next to her while feeling frantically for her pistol in case there happened to be someone in the house. There was only Rick, her husband and love who had somehow found his way back home. They stood there, together in the woods near the drive, until the sound of an engine and the snapping of more branches around them alerted Dianne. She let go of Rick and started diving for her rifle when he caught her and held her fast.

"Whoa! Easy there; these guys are with me."

Dianne hesitated, still not completely convinced that she wasn't having some sort of ultra-realistic dream. From the woods around her walked several more men wearing jackets like Rick's and carrying rifles. One of the closer men looked at the body next to Rick and Dianne before glancing at Rick.

"She okay?"

Rick nodded. "Thanks, Captain."

A squawk came from Captain Lance Recker's shoulder and he pressed a button on his radio. After a moment he turned back to the pair. "Ma'am," Captain Recker looked at Dianne and nodded, "we've got two bodies in the woods on the east side and three more we just captured on the west side. There anyone in the house?"

Dianne's heart flew into her throat and she gasped. "The kids! Jason, Sarah and—do you have a medic? We have multiple injuries inside!"

Recker glanced at Rick. "Lead us to them, ma'am."

"Mom?!" A shout went out from the front door and Dianne turned to see Mark poking his head out, with Jason right behind him. "See," he looked at Jason, "I told you I saw cops!" He burst out the door, his rifle slung over his back, and headed towards Dianne. When he was nearly there he stopped short, eyes wide at the sight of who was standing next to her.

"...dad?"

Seeing Dianne had filled Rick's heart with joy, but hearing his son's cracked voice whispering to him nearly broke his heart. Rick held open his arms and Mark ran forward, embracing his father and mother together, scarcely able to believe that the moment he had been hoping would come had finally arrived. Still standing at the door, Jason watched the commotion around the house with a slack jaw for a few moments before shaking off his surprise as two of the Capitol Police approached him, asking where the injured inside the house were located.

As Jason led the officers into the house, Mark finally let go of Rick and took a look around at the uniformed men and women who were traipsing through the yard and woods. Going from a frantic gun battle to being surrounded by—presumably, anyway—a veritable pack of allies was overwhelming, and the only thing he could think to ask was the obvious question.

"Dad... who are all these people?"

"Some friends I made while I was getting home."

"Friends?" Captain Recker stepped forward again. "Fans, more like it." He looked at Dianne. "Your husband's a hero, ma'am. It wouldn't be an exaggeration to say he saved the world."

Rick shrugged and smiled. "It was a team effort."

"How... why..." Dianne was just as confused and overwhelmed as Mark, and as she tried to wrap her head around the sudden change in scenery, she too had an obvious question. "Why are they all here? And what does he mean, you saved the world?"

Rick pulled Mark and Dianne in close, wrapping his arms around them, not wanting to ever let them out of his sight again. "That... is a very, very long story."

Chapter Twenty

N orfolk, Virginia

GUNFIRE ECHOES down the dark street, following the footsteps of three individuals as they run without looking back. They move in erratic paths, weaving in and out between burned-out cars while trying to stay together.

"This way!" Ted hisses, trying to ensure that his voice is heard only by his two companions. He points to a sign with an arrow leading off to the right, down a wide avenue that was once filled with traffic and lit by overhead streetlights. Jackie and Commander Palmer follow, glancing at the sign as they run by.

Norfolk Visitor's Entrance – 0.3 Miles

More gunfire cracks through the dark sky, joined by the sound of desperate voices calling out after the astronauts. "They're heading for the base! Grab 'em fast!"

In spite of their exhaustion, their weakened bones and the loads each is carrying on their backs, the trio does not falter in their movement. Ted leads the way as they weave down the avenue, his eyes roving between the burned vehicles on the road and the darkened windows and doorways of buildings on either side. Jackie follows him, focusing all of her attention on staying on the move and not falling too far behind. Commander Palmer, in the rear, keeps his head on a swivel as he constantly checks for signs of their pursuers.

The mention of their luck seemed to have turned the tide, as they discovered a few hours into their journey to Norfolk. The destruction of portions of the area near the beach soon waned as they headed inland, and intact homes and businesses grew more common. With this, though, came a rise in signs that there were still people living in the area, subsisting off of whatever they could scrounge or steal.

The group chasing the trio, while not nourished or in shape to the degree that the astronauts are, are nevertheless persistent. The packs on the astronaut's backs are tantalizing promises of food and other supplies that are so desperately needed. Backed into a corner, the astronauts fought just long enough to get away—killing two attackers and wounding a third. Doing so did not stop the attackers from their pursuit. On the contrary, it only brought more down upon them.

"The gates are ahead!" Ted gasps as he calls out to the pair behind him.

"Any signs of activity?"

"I don't… wait! They've got lights on in there!"

Commander Palmer pauses from his scan of the area behind and looks ahead at the entrance to Norfolk. While most of the visible portion of the base are dark, one of the buildings a short distance from the entrance is, indeed, lit. The sight of artificial lighting fills all three of the astronauts with hope and energy and they increase their speed, furthering the gap between them and their pursuers.

"Halt!" The shout comes from ahead, at the entrance to the base as several individuals appear, their figures barely visible behind the bright flashlights that all click on simultaneously. While Ted and Jackie slow down, Commander Palmer charges ahead, slipping his pistol into his pocket and raising his hands.

"We need help!" Commander Palmer cries out. "We're under attack and need refuge!"

"I said halt!" The voice bellows back. Commander Palmer motions at Ted and Jackie to follow him and he slows to a stop a few dozen feet from the entrance to the base, his arms still raised over his head. "Now turn around! This is a restricted zone!"

"We're not civilians! I am Commander Palmer; we're astronauts just returned from the International Space Station in an escape module yesterday. We splashed down off the coast and we've come here for assistance!" He knows how ludicrous the claim is even as he says it, but he hopes that the uniforms he, Ted and Jackie are wearing will help offset the apparent insanity.

"You… you're what?" There is hesitation in the next reply, and with each passing second the trio wonders if their pursuers will finally catch up to them.

"We splashed down in an escape module just off the coast. It's tied up on the beach a few hours back in that direction." Commander Palmer turns and points. "We were on the space station when everything went to hell." He takes a step forward, keeping his hands high. "Please, at least just tell us what's going on!"

There is a long moment of silence punctuated by the faint noise of radio chatter. The voice on the other side of the gate speaks too quietly for the astronauts to hear. When he finishes, he steps forward and waves to someone closer to the gate. A motor engages and the gate begins to rise, more lights go on and several uniformed MPs on the other side of the gate emerge from the shadows. Their weapons are lowered as they approach the astronauts, and the figure that spoke to Commander Palmer speaks again.

"Base wants to have a word with you, Commander Palmer. You and your associates. Come on in before the locals decide to put a bullet through your back. Quick now." The trio hurry through the gates, the MPs watching down the darkened road for any potential attackers.

"What on earth's been going on here?" Commander Palmer looks around at the MPs as he, Jackie and Ted walk along.

"Armageddon, Commander Palmer." The MP looks him up and down. "Can't believe you actually got back in one piece. We were tracking your module on a scope yesterday when you hit the atmosphere. We figured it was another satellite, though I'm glad to see we were wrong."

"We're glad we made it back too, Lieutenant…?"

"Samuels."

"Lieutenant Samuels," Ted interjects, "what did you mean by 'Armageddon?'"

"End of the world. Apocalypse. Call it what you will."

"What's causing it?"

"Caused, you mean."

"You mean it's over?"

"Sort of. They stopped the cause but the effects… those'll be around for who-knows-how-long."

"What caused it?" Jackie asks, an eyebrow raised.

"That… is a long story. The Admiral will be able to fill you in more on the details, and he'd like to get some details from you on the global outlook of things."

"Global outlook?" Commander Palmer asks.

"We've got almost zero eyes anywhere in the world. Communications only started coming back up a few hours ago, but even those are rudimentary at best. Knowing what things look like across the world, even as late as a few days ago, would be exceedingly helpful strategically."

"Of course." Commander Palmer glances at Ted and Jackie. "Anything we can do to help."

Lieutenant Samuels stops in front of the door to the illuminated building and motions at the astronauts. "Excellent. If you'll step inside, the Admiral would like to speak with you." The three move toward the door, but Lieutenant Samuels puts out his hand to shake each of theirs in turn before they can go inside. "And welcome back. All of you."

Epilogue

Two billion.

It took three years to get an accurate count of the total number of people who died across the world. By the time the exact figures were decided upon by the various countries working to find, identify and count the dead, the survivors had lost their interest in the exact number. So two billion—slightly under the actual total—was what went into the record books.

Most of the deaths in the industrialized portions of the world came from lack of access to food, water and medical supplies. Loss of power killed a large swath of the sick and elderly, and transportation interruptions had a ripple effect that was felt as far out as remote villages that had only a tertiary reliance upon modern infrastructure.

Recovery was slow, and because Damocles had affected all countries to some extent, a sense of togetherness and camaraderie developed even between fierce rivals. Initial outrage toward the United States for developing Damocles eventually waned thanks to the fact that Damocles had merely disabled—not destroyed—many key infrastructure points across the globe. That a rogue agent was responsible for leaking Damocles to the world and causing its accidental activation added to the voices calling for reason over revenge. (A substantial amount of relief aid from the United States didn't hurt, either.)

For the Waters, life never fully returned to how it had been before the event. Though Tina and Jason recovered from their injuries, they and Sarah elected to stay at the Waters' homestead, converting one of the barns on the property into a home where they stayed, not feeling comfortable with being very far from Dianne and the kids.

Oles and Dr. Evans were whisked away as soon as the federal govern-ment got back on its feet, and while Rick still heard from them in occasional letters and emails, their work on helping to create a defense against another such disaster in the future was clouded in secrecy. Though Rick was never able to find Jane's family, a letter from Dr. Evans some six months later included a photograph of a small gravestone that had been placed on the grounds of the old naval observatory, marking where Jane had been laid to rest.

Over the months following the event, Dianne saw the effects of it on her children. Night terrors were frequent for Jacob and Josie and it took years for them to be able to sleep through the night without waking up screaming or drenched in sweat. Mark's resilience throughout the ordeal continued to shine, and his parents leaned on him constantly as they worked to pick up the pieces of their lives after the event and continue soldiering on.

The small farm on the Waters' property was quickly expanded once a portion of the woods around their home was cleared, and though they had to stay vigilant against people seeking to steal from them, they were able to continue to provide food for themselves quite handily. As Blacksburg, like the rest of the world, began to rebuild, Rick eventually took a part-time job serving as a consultant to the state government. He was called upon multiple times by the federal government both to help assist Dr. Evans and Oles and to receive a number of awards, but he always declined, saying that he was never again going to travel more than a few hours walking distance from his family.

Each night, as the sun set and the light shone between the trees off to the side of the property, Rick would sit out on the back porch and watch the orange glow turn to black. His thoughts always came back to those he had met—and lost—along his journey, and how unbelievably blessed he had been to make it through alive when so many others did not. After the sun went down, Dianne would join him on the porch and they would sit together in silence, holding hands as they watched the stars come out against the rich inky blackness, each of them grateful that they still had their family and each other.

Author's Notes

AUGUST 7, 2018

And there we have it; the end of Surviving the Fall.

Writing the last chapter took a long time, both because of the number of projects I'm working on and because I wanted to make sure it was done right. There were a *lot* of loose ends to tie up, but if the reaction from the Beta Readers is any indication, I think I got most all of them tied up decently enough.

The whole goal with Surviving the Fall – and with any story I write – is to tell a fun, engaging story. Part of that was ensuring that the ending was appropriate both for your expectations and to the world as told in the book. In a "SHTF" scenario, people are going to die left and right. Loved ones will be killed and there won't be anything a lot of people will be able to do about it.

But writing just about the bad stuff doesn't tell the whole picture. It doesn't look at the tenacity and ferocity that some will have to cling to life and family and do everything they possibly can to survive. Rick and Dianne went to hell and back more than once all for the love of their family. That fictional example is a representation of what I'd try my hardest – and I'm sure you would, too – if something bad were to happen, and while there were bitter moments along the way, writing the reunion of Rick and Dianne was tear-inducing and I'm really glad it ended that way.

This has been, all around, an absolutely amazing story to write. One of my favorite parts has been getting to hear what readers like yourself have said about each book and the characters within throughout the last year. Thank you so much for reading along, and I hope you'll keep reading – there are lots more stories to come. :)

If you enjoyed this episode of Surviving the Fall or if you *didn't* like something—I'd love to hear about it. You can drop me an email or send me a message or leave a comment on Facebook. You can also sign up for my newsletter where I announce new book releases and other cool stuff a few times a month.

Answering emails and messages from my readers is the highlight of my day and every single time I get an email from someone saying how much they enjoyed reading a story it makes that day so much brighter and better.

Thank you so very much for reading my books. Seriously, thank you from the bottom of my heart. I put an enormous amount of effort into the writing and all of the related processes and there's nothing better than knowing that so many people are enjoying my stories.

All the best,
    Mike

Made in the USA
Columbia, SC
29 June 2024

37744480R00446